THE DEATH OF THE HEART

Elizabeth Bowen was born in Dublin in 1899, the only child of an Irish lawyer and landowner. She was educated at Downe House School in Kent. Her book *Bowen's Court* (1942) is the history of her family and their house in County Cork, and *Seven Winters* (1943) contains reminiscences of her Dublin childhood. In 1923 she married Alan Cameron, who held an appointment with the BBC and who died in 1952. She travelled a good deal, dividing most of her time between London and Bowen's Court, which she inherited.

She is considered by many to be one of the most distinguished novelists of the twentieth century. She saw the object of a novel as 'the non-poetic statement of a poetic truth' and said that 'no statement of it can be final'. Her first book, a collection of short stories, *Encounters*, appeared in 1923, followed by another, *Ann Lee's*, in 1926. *The Hotel* (1927) was her first novel, and was followed by *The Last September* (1929), *Joining Charles* (1929), another book of short stories, *Friends and Relations* (1931), *To the North* (1932), *The Cat Jumps* (short stories, 1934), *The House in Paris* (1935), *The Death of the Heart* (1938), *Look at All Those Roses* (short stories, 1941), *The Demon Lover* (short stories, 1945), *The Heat of the Day* (1949), *Collected Impressions* (essays, 1950), *The Shelbourne* (1951), *A World of Love* (1955), *A Time in Rome* (1960), *After-thought* (essays, 1962), *The Little Girls* (1964), *A Day in the Dark* (1965) and her last book, *Eva Trout* (1969).

She was awarded the CBE in 1948, and received the honorary degree of Doctor of Letters from Trinity College, Dublin, in 1949 and from Oxford University in 1956. In the same year she was appointed Lacy Martin Donnelly Fellow at Bryn Mawr College in the United States. In 1965 she was made a Companion of Literature by the Royal Society of Literature. Elizabeth Bowen died in 1973.

THE
DEATH OF THE HEART

Elizabeth Bowen

PENGUIN BOOKS

PENGUIN BOOKS

Published by the Penguin Group
Penguin Books Ltd, 27 Wrights Lane, London W8 5TZ, England
Penguin Books USA Inc., 375 Hudson Street, New York, New York 10014, USA
Penguin Books Australia Ltd, Ringwood, Victoria, Australia
Penguin Books Canada Ltd, 10 Alcorn Avenue, Toronto, Ontario, Canada M4V 3B2
Penguin Books (NZ) Ltd, 182–190 Wairau Road, Auckland 10, New Zealand

Penguin Books Ltd, Registered Offices: Harmondsworth, Middlesex, England

First published in Great Britain by Jonathan Cape 1938
First published in the United States of America by
Alfred A. Knopf, Inc., 1939
Published in Penguin Books 1962
15 17 19 20 18 16

Published in the United States by
arrangement with Alfred A. Knopf, Inc.

Printed in England by Clays Ltd, St Ives plc

Contents

Part One

THE WORLD

I

THAT morning's ice, no more than a brittle film, had cracked and was now floating in segments. These tapped together or, parting, left channels of dark water, down which swans in slow indignation swam. The islands stood in frozen woody brown dusk: it was now between three and four in the afternoon. A sort of breath from the clay, from the city outside the park, condensing, made the air unclear; through this, the trees round the lake soared frigidly up. Bronze cold of January bound the sky and the landscape; the sky was shut to the sun – but the swans, the rims of the ice, the pallid withdrawn Regency terraces had an unnatural burnish, as though cold were light. There is something momentous about the height of winter. Steps rang on the bridges, and along the black walks. This weather had set in; it would freeze harder tonight.

On a footbridge between an island and the mainland a man and woman stood talking, leaning on the rail. In the intense cold, which made everyone hurry, they had chosen to make this long summerlike pause. Their oblivious stillness made them look like lovers – actually, their elbows were some inches apart; they were riveted not to each other but to what she said. Their thick coats made their figures sexless and stiff as chessmen: they were well-to-do, inside bulwarks of fur and cloth their bodies generated a steady warmth; they could only see the cold – or, if they felt it, they only felt it at their extremities. Now and then he stamped on the bridge, or she brought her muff up to her face. Ice pushed down the channel under the bridge, so that while they talked their reflections were constantly broken up.

He said: 'You were mad ever to touch the thing.'

'All the same, I feel sure you would have, St Quentin.'

'No, I doubt that. I never do want to know, really, what anyone thinks.'

'If I'd had the slightest idea —'

'However, you did.'

'And I've seldom been more upset.'

'Poor Anna! ... How did you find it, though?'

'Oh, I wasn't looking for it,' said Anna quickly. 'I should far rather not know that the thing existed, and till then, you see, I'd had no idea that it did. Her white dress came back with one of mine from the cleaners; I unpacked mine because I wanted to put it on, then, as Matchett was out that day, I took hers up to hang it up in her room. Portia was out at lessons, of course. Her room looked, as I've learnt to expect, shocking: she has all sorts of arrangements Matchett will never touch. You know what some servants are – how they ride one down, and at the same time make all sorts of allowance for temperament in children or animals.'

'You would call her a child?'

'In ways, she's more like an animal. I made that room so pretty before she came. I had no idea how blindly she was going to live. Now I hardly ever go in there; it's simply discouraging.'

St Quentin said rather vaguely: 'How annoying for you!' He had screwed round his head inside the folds of his scarf, to consider Anna with abstract attentiveness. For she had this little way of travestying herself and her self-pities, till the view she took of herself, when she was with him, seemed to concert exactly with the view he took of her sex. She wrote herself down like this, obligingly, to suit him, with a touch of friendly insolence. He saw in this over-acting a kind of bluffing, which made him like Anna, whom he liked much more. Her smoothness of contour, her placid derisive smile, her way of drawing her chin in when she did smile, often made him think of a sardonic bland white duck. But there seemed no doubt at this moment that, beyond acting, she was really put out: her chin was tucked inside her big fur collar, and under the fur cap she wore peaked forward her forehead was wrinkled up. She was looking down unhappily at her muff, with her fine blonde lashes

cast on her cheek; now and then a hand came out of her muff and she dabbed at the tip of her nose with a handkerchief. She could feel St Quentin looking, but took no notice: she detected the touch of malice in his pity for women.

'All I did,' she went on, 'when I had hung her dress up, was to take one look round, rather feeling I ought. As usual, my heart sank; I really did feel it was time I took a line. But she and I are on such curious terms – when I ever do take a line, she never knows what it is. She is so unnaturally callous about *objects* – she treats any hat, for instance, like an old envelope. Nothing that's hers ever seems, if you know what I mean, to belong to her: which makes it meaningless to give her any present, unless it's something to eat, and she doesn't always like that. It may be because they always lived in hotels. Well, one thing I had thought she'd like was a little *escritoire* thing that came from Thomas's mother's – her father may well have used it. I'd had that put in her room. It has drawers that lock and quite a big flap to write on. The flap locks too: I hoped that would make her see that I quite meant her to have a life of her own. You know, though it may seem rash, we even give her a latchkey. But she seems to have lost the keys – nothing was locked, and there was no sign of them.'

'How annoying!' said St Quentin again.

'It was indeed. Because if only – However ... Well, that wretched little *escritoire* caught my eye. She had crammed it, but really, stuffed it, as though it were a bin. She seems to like hoarding paper; she gets almost no letters, but she'd been keeping all sorts of things Thomas and I throw away – begging letters, for instance, or quack talks about health. As Matchett would say, it gave me rather a turn.'

'When you opened the desk?'

'Well, it looked so awful, you see. The flap would not shut – papers gushed out all round it and even stuck through the hinge. Which made me shake with anger – I really can't tell you why. So I scooped the papers all out and dropped them into the armchair – I intended to leave them there, then tell her she must be tidy. Under the papers were some exercise books with notes she had taken at her lessons, and under the exercise books this

9

diary, which, as I say, I read. One of those wretchèd black books one buys for about a shilling with *moiré* outsides ... After *that*, of course I had to put everything back the way it was.'

'Exactly as it had been?'

'Exactly, I'm quite certain. One may never reproduce the same muddle exactly, but she would never know.'

There was a pause, and St Quentin looked at a seagull. Then he said: 'How inconvenient it all is!'

Inside her muff, Anna drove her hands together; raising her eyes she looked angrily down the lake. 'She's made nothing but trouble since before she was born.'

'You mean, it's a pity she ever was?'

'Well, naturally, I feel that at the moment. Though I would rather, of course, that you didn't say so – she is Thomas's sister after all.'

'But don't you think perhaps you exaggerate? The agitation of seeing something quite unexpected often makes one think it worse than it is.'

'That diary could not be worse than it is. That is to say, it couldn't be worse for me. At the time, it only made me superficially angry – but I've had time since then to think it over in. And I haven't quite finished yet – I keep remembering more things.'

'Was it very ... unkind?'

'No, not meant to be that. No, she'd like to help us, I'm sure.'

'Then, mawkish, you mean?'

'I mean, more, completely distorted and distorting. As I read I thought, either this girl or I are mad. And I don't think I am, do you?'

'Surely not. But why should you be so upset if it simply shows what is the matter with her? Was it affected?'

'Deeply hysterical.'

'You've got to allow for style, though. Nothing arrives on paper as it started, and so much arrives that never started at all. To write is always to rave a little – even if one did once know what one meant, which at her age seems unlikely. There are ways and ways of trumping a thing up: one gets more dis-

criminating, not necessarily more honest. *I* should know, after all.'

'I am sure you do, St Quentin. But this was not a bit like your beautiful books. In fact it was not like *writing* at all.' She paused and added: 'She was so odd about me.'

St Quentin, looking frustrated, started feeling about for his handkerchief. He blew his nose and went on, with iron determination: 'Style is the thing that's always a bit phony, and at the same time you cannot write without style. Look how much goes to addressing an envelope – for, after all, it's a matter of set-out. And a diary, after all, is written to please oneself – therefore it's bound to be enormously written up. The obligation to write it is all in one's own eye, and look how one is when it's almost always written – upstairs, late, overwrought, alone ... All the same, Anna, it must have interested you.'

'It opened at my name.'

'So you read straight on from there?'

'No, it opened at the last entry; I read that, then went back and started from the beginning. The latest entry was about dinner the evening before.'

'Let's see: had you a party?'

'No, no: much worse than that. It had been simply her and me and Thomas. She must have bolted upstairs and written everything down. Naturally, when I'd read that I went back to the beginning, to see what had got her into that state of mind. I still don't see why she wrote the thing at all.'

'Perhaps', said St Quentin mildly, 'she's interested in experience for its own sake.'

'How could she be, yet? At her age, look how little she's got. Experience isn't interesting till it begins to repeat itself – in fact, till it does that, it hardly *is* experience.'

'Tell me, do you remember the first sentence of all?'

'Indeed I do,' Anna said. ' "*So I am with them, in London*".'

'With a comma after the "them"? ... The comma is good; that's style ... I should like to have seen it, I must say.'

'Still, I'm glad you didn't, St Quentin. It might make you not come to our house again. Or, if you did still come, it might make you not talk.'

'I see,' said St Quentin shortly. Drumming with stiff, gloved fingers on the bridge rail, he frowned down at a swan till it vanished under the bridge. His eyes, like the swan's, were set rather near in. He broke out: 'Fancy her watching me! What a little monster she must be. And she looks so aloof. Does she think I try to be clever?'

'She said more about your being always polite. She does not seem to think you are a snake in the grass, though she sees a good deal of grass for a snake to be in. There does not seem to be a single thing that she misses, and there's certainly not a thing that she does not misconstruct. In fact, you would wonder, really – How you do stamp, St Quentin! Are your feet so cold? You make the bridge shake.'

St Quentin, abstracted and forbidding, suggested: 'We might walk on.'

'I suppose we ought to go in,' Anna admitted, sighing. 'Though you see, *now*, why I'd rather not be at home?'

St Quentin, stepping out smartly, showed one of his quick distastes for more of the lake scene. The cold was beginning to nip their features, and to strike up through the soles of their feet. Anna looked back at the bridge regretfully: she had not yet done saying what she began there. Leaving the lake behind them, they made for the trees just inside the park fence. The circle of traffic tightens at this hour round Regent's Park; cars hummed past without a break; it was just before lighting-up time – quite soon the All Out whistles would sound. At the far side of the road, dusk set the Regency buildings back at a false distance: against the sky they were colourless silhouettes, insipidly ornate, brittle, and cold. The blackness of windows not yet lit or curtained made the houses look hollow inside ... St Quentin and Anna kept inside the park railings, making towards the corner where she lived. Interrupted in what she had been saying, she swung disconsolately her black muff, walking not quite in step with him.

St Quentin always walked rather too fast – sometimes as though he did not like where he was, sometimes as though resolved to out-distance any attraction of the hour or scene. His erect, rather forbidding carriage made him look old-fashioned,

even military – but this was misleading. He was tall, wore his dark, rather furry hair *en brosse*, and had a small Gallic moustache. He entered rooms with the air of a man who, because his name is well known, may find himself involved in some situation from which his nature revolts – for writers find themselves constantly face to face with persons who expect to make free with them, and St Quentin, apart from the slackish kindness he used with Anna and one or two other friends, detested intimacy, which, so far, had brought him nothing but pain. From this dread of exposure came his tendencies to hurry on, to be insultingly facile, to misunderstand perversely. Even Anna never knew when St Quentin might feel he was being presumed upon – but he and she were on the whole on such easy terms that she had given up caring. St Quentin liked her husband, Thomas Quayne, too, and frequented the Quaynes like a ghost who had once understood what married good feeling was. In so far as the Quaynes were a family, St Quentin was the family friend. Today, unnerved by having said too much, breathless from the desire to say more, Anna wished that St Quentin did not walk so fast. Her best chance to speak had been in keeping him still.

'How very unlike Thomas!' St Quentin said suddenly.

'What is?'

'She must be, I mean.'

'Very. But look what different mothers they had. And poor Mr Quayne, quite likely, never counted for much.'

St Quentin repeated: ' "So I am with them, in London". *That's* what is so impossible,' he said.

'Her being with us?'

'Could it not have been helped?'

'Not when she had been left to us in a will – or in a dying request, which is not legal, and so worse. Dying put poor Mr Quayne in a strong position for the first time in his life – or, at least, for the first time since Irene. Thomas felt very strongly about his father's letter, and even I felt bound to behave well.'

'I do doubt, all the same, whether those accesses of proper feeling ever do much good. You were bound to regret this one. Did you really imagine the girl would enjoy herself?'

'If Mr Quayne had had anything besides Portia to leave us,

the situation might not have been so tricky. But anything that he died with went, of course, to Irene, then, after *her* death, to Portia – a few hundreds a year. With only that will to make, he could not make any conditions: he simply implored us to have his daughter in what seemed (when he was dead like that, when we got the letter) the most quavering voice. It was Thomas's *mother*, you know, who had most of the money – I don't think poor Mr Quayne had ever made much – and when Thomas's mother died *her* money came straight to us. Thomas's mother, as no doubt you remember, died four or five years ago. I think, in some curious way, that it was her death, in the distance, that finished poor Mr Quayne, though I daresay life with Irene helped. He and Irene and Portia, all more and more piano, trailed up and down the cold parts of the Riviera, till he caught a chill and died in a nursing home. A few days before he died, he dictated that letter to us about Portia to Irene, but Irene, detesting us – and I must say with some reason – put it away in her glove-box till she died herself. Of course, he had only meant it to come into effect in case of anything happening to Irene: he didn't mean us to take the kitten from the cat. But he had foreseen, I suppose, that Irene would be too incompetent to go on living for long, and of course he turned out to be right. After Irene's death, in Switzerland, her sister found the letter and posted it on to us.'

'What a number of deaths in Thomas's family!'

'Irene's, of course, was a frank relief – till we got the letter and realized what it would mean. My heavens, what an awful woman she was!'

'It embarrassed Thomas, having a stepmother?'

'Irene, you know, was not what anybody would want at all. We tried to overlook that for Thomas's father's sake. He felt so much in the wrong, poor old man, that one had to be more than naturally nice to him. Not that we saw him much: I don't think he felt it right to see very much of Thomas – because he so wanted to. He said something one day when we all had lunch at Folkestone about not casting a shadow over our lives. If we had made him feel that it didn't matter, we should have sunk in his estimation, I'm sure. When we met – which I must con-

fess was only two or three times – he did not behave at all like Thomas's father, but like an off-the-map, seedy old family friend who doubts if he has done right in showing up. To punish himself by not seeing us became second nature with him: I don't think he *wanted* to meet us, by the end. We came to think, in his own way he must be happy. We had no idea, till we got that letter of his, that he'd been breaking his heart, all those years abroad, about what Portia was missing – or, what he thought she was missing. He had felt, he said in the letter, that, because of being his daughter (and from becoming his daughter in the way that she had) Portia had grown up exiled not only from her own country but from *normal, cheerful* family life. So he asked us to give her a taste of that for a year.' Anna paused, and looked at St Quentin sideways. 'He idealized us rather, you see,' she said.

'Would a year do much – however normal you were?'

'No doubt he hoped in his heart that we'd keep her on – or else, perhaps, that she'd marry from our house. If neither should happen, she is to go on to some aunt, Irene's sister, abroad ... He only *spoke* of a year, and Thomas and I, so far, have not liked to look beyond that. There are years and years – some can be wonderfully long.'

'You are finding this one is?'

'Well, it seems so since yesterday. But of course I could never say so to Thomas – Yes, yes, I know: that *is* my front door, down there. But must we really go in just yet?'

'As you feel, of course. But you'll have to some time. At present, it's five to four: shall we cross by that other bridge and walk once more round the lake? – Though you know, Anna, it's getting distinctly colder – After that, perhaps we might have our tea? Does your objection to tea (which I do frightfully want) mean that we're unlikely to be alone?'

'She just might go to tea with Lilian.'

'Lilian?'

'Oh, Lilian's her friend. But she hardly ever does,' said Anna, despondent.

'But look here, Anna, really – you must not let this get the better of you.'

'That's all very well, but you didn't see all she said. Also you know, you do always seem to think there must be some obvious way for other people to live. In this case there is really not, I'm afraid.'

Beside the criss-cross diagonal iron bridge, three poplars stood up like frozen brooms. St Quentin stopped on the bridge to tighten his scarf and shake himself down deeper into his overcoat – he threw a homesick glance up at Anna's drawing-room window: inside, he saw firelight making cheerful play. 'It all certainly does seem very complex,' he said, and with fatalistic briskness went on crossing the bridge. Ahead lay the knolls, the empty cold clay silence of inner Regent's Park beneath a darkening sky. St Quentin, not in an elemental mood, did not happily turn his back on a drawing-room as agreeable as Anna's.

'Not even complex,' said Anna. 'Stupid from the beginning. It was one of those muddles without a scrap of dignity. Mr Quayne stayed quite devoted to his first wife – Thomas's mother – and showed not the slightest wish to leave her whatever happened. Irene or no Irene, the first Mrs Quayne always had him in the palm of her hand. She was one of those implacably nice women whose niceness you can't get past, and whose understanding gets into every crack of your temperament. While he was with her he always felt simply fine – he had to. When he retired from business they went to live in Dorset, in a charming place she had bought for him to retire to. It was after some years of life in Dorset that poor Mr Quayne started skidding about. He and she had married so young – though Thomas, for some reason, was not born for quite a number of years – that he had had almost no time to be silly in. Also, I think, she must have hypnotized him into being a good deal steadier than he felt. At the same time she was a woman who thought all men are great boys at heart, and she took every care to keep him one. But this turned out to have its disadvantages. In the photographs taken just before the crisis, he looks a full-blooded idealistic old buffer. He looks impressive, silly, intensely moral, and as though he would like to denounce himself. She would never let him denounce himself, and this was rather like taking somebody's toys away. He used to say her belief in him meant everything, but

probably it frustrated him a good deal. It *was* rather slighting, wasn't it?'

'Yes,' said St Quentin. 'Possibly.'

'Have I told you all this before?'

'Not as a story. Of course, I've inferred some things from what you've said.'

'As a story it really is rather long, and in a way it makes me rather depressed ... Well, what happened, happened when Mr Quayne was about fifty-seven, and Thomas at Oxford in his second year. They'd already been living in Dorset for some time, and Mr Quayne seemed to be settled for the rest of his life. He played golf, tennis, bridge, ran the Boy Scouts, and sat on several committees. In addition to that he had paved most of the garden, and when he'd done that she let him divert a stream. Much of his own company put him into a panic, so he was always dangling round after her. People in Dorset said it was good to see them together, because they were just like lovers. She had never cared very much for London, which was why she'd put pressure on him to retire young – I don't think the business had amounted to much, but it was the one thing he'd had that was apart from her. But once she got him to Dorset, she was so nice that she was constantly packing him off to London – that is to say, about every two months – to stay at his club for a few days, see old friends, or watch cricket or something. He felt pretty flat in London and always shot home again, which was very gratifying for her. Till one time, when for a reason that did not appear till later, he sent her a wire to say, might he stay on in London for a few days more? What had happened was that he had just met Irene, at a dinner party at Wimbledon. She was a scrap of a widow, ever so plucky, just back from China, with damp little hands, a husky voice, and defective tear-ducts that gave her eyes always rather a swimmy look. She had a prostrated way of looking up at you, and that fluffy, bird's-nesty hair that hairpins get lost in. At that time, she must have been about twenty-nine. She knew almost nobody, but because she was so plucky, someone had got her a job in a flower shop. She lived in a flatlet in Notting Hill Gate, and was a *protégée* of his Wimbledon friend's wife's. Mr Quayne

was put beside her at dinner. At the end of the party Mr Quayne, all in a daze already, saw her back in a taxi to Notting Hill Gate, and was asked in for some Horlicks. No one knows what happened – still less, of course, why it did. But from that evening on, Thomas's father lost his head completely. He didn't go back to Dorset for ten days, and by the end of that time – as it came out later – he and Irene had already been very wicked. I often think of those dawns in Notting Hill Gate, with Irene leaking tears and looking for hairpins, and Mr Quayne sitting up denouncing himself. His wife was much too nice to have pretty ways, but I daresay Irene had plenty – if that is how you like them. I've no doubt she made the most fussy capitulations; she would make him feel she had never fallen before – and I should think it's likely she never had. She would not be everyone's money. You may be sure that she let Mr Quayne know that her little life was from now on entirely in his hands. By the end of those ten days he cannot have known, himself, whether he was a big brute or St George.

'At all events, he arrived back in Dorset at once pensive and bouncing. He started in digging a lily pond but at the end of a fortnight said something about a tailor, and went dashing off back to London again. This went on, apparently, all through that summer – he and Irene had met in May. When Thomas got back in June he noticed at once, he remembers, that his home was not what it was, but his mother never said anything. Thomas went abroad with a friend; when he got back in September his father was black depressed – it stood out a mile. He didn't once go to London while Thomas was home, but the little person had started writing him letters.

'Just before poor Thomas went back to Oxford, the bomb went off. Mr Quayne woke Thomas's mother up at two in the morning and told her the whole thing. What had happened I'm quite sure you can guess – Irene had started Portia. She had done nothing more about this, beyond letting him know; she had gone on sitting in Notting Hill Gate, wondering what was going to happen next. Mrs Quayne was quite as splendid as ever: she stopped Mr Quayne crying, then went straight down to the kitchen and made tea. Thomas, who slept on the same

landing, woke to feel something abnormal – he opened his door, found the landing lights on then saw his mother go past with a tray of tea, in her dressing-gown, looking, he says, just like a hospital nurse. She gave Thomas a smile and did not say anything: it occurred to him that his father might be sick, but not that he had been committing adultery. Mr Quayne, apparently, made a night of it: he stood knocking his knuckles on the end of the big bed, repeating: "She is such a staunch little thing!" Then he routed out Irene's letters and three photographs of her, and passed Mrs Quayne the lot. When she had done with the letters and been nice about the photos, she told him that now he would have to marry Irene. When he took that in, and realized that it meant the sack, he burst into tears again.

'From the first, he did not like the idea at all. To get anywhere near the root of the matter, one has got to see just how dumb Mr Quayne was. He had not got a mind that joins one thing and another up. He had got knit up with Irene in a sort of a dream wood, but the last thing he wanted was to stay in that wood for ever. In his waking life he liked to be plain and solid; to be plain and solid was to be married to Mrs Quayne. I don't suppose he knew, in his own feeling, where sentimentality stopped and want began – and who *could* tell, with an old buffer like that? In any event, he had not foreseen ever having to put his shirt on either. He loved his home like a child. That night, he sat on the edge of the big bed, wrapped up in the eiderdown, and cried till he had no breath left to denounce himself. But Mrs Quayne was, of course, implacable: in fact by next day she had got quite ecstatic. She might have been saving up for this moment for years – in fact, I daresay she had been, without knowing. Mr Quayne's last hope was that if he curled up and went to sleep now, in the morning he might find that nothing had really happened. So at last he curled up and went to sleep. She probably didn't – Does this bore you, St Quentin?'

'Anything but, Anna; in fact, it curdles my blood.'

'Mrs Quayne came down to breakfast worn but shining, and Mr Quayne making every effort to please. Thomas, of course, saw that something awful had happened, and his one idea was

to stave everything off. After breakfast, his mother said that he was a man now, walked him round the garden and told him the whole story in the most idealistic way. Thomas saw his father watching them round the smoking-room curtain. She made Thomas agree that he and she must do everything possible to help his father, Irene, and the poor little coming child. The idea of the baby embarrassed Thomas intensely on his father's behalf. Words still fail him for how discreditably ridiculous the whole thing appeared. But he was sorry about his father having to go, and asked Mrs Quayne if this *was* really necessary: she said it was. She had got the whole thing sorted out in the night, even down to the train he was to catch. She seemed to be quite taken with her idea of Irene: Irene's letters had gone down better with her than with Mr Quayne, who did not like things in writing. In fact, I'm afraid Mrs Quayne always liked Irene a good deal better than, later, she liked me. Mr Quayne's faint hope that the whole thing might be dropped, or that his wife might find some way to make it all right, must have been dispelled as he watched them walk round the garden. *He* was not allowed a say for one single minute – to begin with, he strongly disapproved of divorce.

'During the two days before his departure (during which he stayed in the smoking-room and had his meals sent in to him on a tray) Mrs Quayne's idealism spread round the house like flu. It very strongly affected poor Mr Quayne. All the kick having gone from the affair with Irene, he fell *morally* in love with his wife all over again. She had got him that way when he was twenty-two, and she got him again like that at fifty-seven. He blubbered and told Thomas that his mother was a living saint. At the end of the two days, Mrs Quayne had him packed for and sent him up to Irene by the afternoon train. Thomas was told off to drive him to the station: all the way, and while they waited on the platform, Mr Quayne said not a word. Just before the train started, he leaned out and beckoned as though he had something to say. But all he said was: "Bad luck to watch a train out." After that he bumped back into his seat. Thomas did watch the train out, and he said its blank end looked quite wretchedly futureless.

'Mrs Quayne went up to London the following day, and put the divorce proceedings on foot at once. It is even said that she called and had a kind word with Irene. She sailed back to Dorset all heroic reserve, kept the house on, and stayed there through it all. Mr Quayne, who detested being abroad, went straight to the south of France, which seemed to him the right place, and months later Irene joined him, just in time for the wedding. Portia was then born, in Mentone. Well, they stayed round about there, and almost never came home. Thomas was sent by his mother to visit them three or four times, but I think they all found it terribly lowering. Mr Quayne and Irene and Portia always had the back rooms in hotels, or dark flats in villas with no view. Mr Quayne never got used to the chill at sunset. Thomas saw he would die of this, and he did. A few years before he did die, he and Irene came back for a four months' visit to Bournemouth – I suppose Bournemouth because he knew no one there. Thomas and I went to see them two or three times, but as they had left Portia behind in France, I never met *her* till she came to live with us here.'

'Live? I thought she was only staying.'

'Whatever it's called, it comes to the same thing.'

'But why was she called Portia?'

Anna, surprised, said: 'I don't think we ever asked.'

Mr Quayne's love life had taken them round the lake. Already, the All Out whistles were blowing: an inch of park gate was kept open for them alone, and a keeper waited by it with such impatience that St Quentin broke into a stately trot. Cars slid lights all round the Outer Circle; lamps blurred the frosty mist from here to the Quaynes' door. Anna swung her muff more light-heartedly; she was less unwilling to go in to tea now.

2

THE front door of 2 Windsor Terrace brushed heavily over the mat and clicked shut. The breath of raw air that had come in with Portia perished on the steady warmth of the hall. Warmth stood up the shaft of staircase, behind the twin white arches. She slid books from under her elbow on to the console table, dropped her latchkey back into her pocket, and went to the radiator, tugging off her gloves. She just saw her reflection cross the mirror, but the hall was a well of dusk – not a light on yet, either upstairs or down. Everywhere, she heard an unliving echo: she entered one of those pauses in the life of a house that before tea time seem to go on and on. This was a house without any life above-stairs, a house to which nobody had returned yet, which, through the big windows, darkness and silence had naturally stolen in on and begun to inhabit. Reassured, she stood warming her hands.

Down there in the basement a door opened: there was an intent pause, then steps began to come up. They were cautious – the steps of a servant pleasing herself. Whitish, Matchett's long face and tablet of apron soared steadily up the dark of an arch. She said: 'Ah, so you're in?'

'This minute.'

'I heard you all right. You were very quick with that door. Likely you left that key outside in the lock again?'

'No, it's here, truly.' Portia scooped the key from her pocket.

'You didn't ought to carry that key in your pocket. Not loose like that – and with your money too. One of these days you'll go losing the lot. She gave you a bag, didn't she?'

'I feel such a goat with a bag. I feel so silly.'

Matchett said sharply: 'All girls your age carry bags.'

Vexed ambition for Portia made Matchett click her teeth; her belt creaked as she gave an irate sigh. The dusk seemed to baulk her; they could barely see each other – her hand went up decidedly to the switch between the arches. Immediately, Anna's cut-glass lamp sprang alight over their heads, dropping its com-

plex shadow on the white stone floor. Portia, her hat pushed back from her forehead, stood askance under the light; she and Matchett blinked; there followed one of those pauses in which animals, face to face, appear to communicate.

Matchett stayed with her hand propped on the pillar. She had an austere, ironical, straight face, flesh padded smoothly over the strong structure of bone. Her strong, springy, lustreless hair was centre parted and drawn severely back; she wore no cap. Habitually, she walked with her eyes down, and her vein-marbled eyelids were unconciliating. Her mouth, at this moment stubbornly inexpressive, still had a crease at each end from her last unwilling smile. Her expression, her attitude were held-in and watchful. The monklike impassivity of her features made her big bust curious, out of place; it seemed some sort of structure for the bib of her apron to be fastened up to with gold pins. To her unconscious sense of inner drama, only her hands gave play: one hand seemed to support the fragile Regency pillar, the other was spread fanwise, like a hand in a portrait, over her aproned hip. While she thought, or rather, calculated, her eyes would move slowly under her dropped lids.

It was five to four. The cook, whose night out it was, lay in her afternoon bath: in front of the pantry mirror the parlourmaid, Phyllis, was trying on a new cap. These two girls in their twenties had been engaged by Anna, and formed, as it were, Anna's party below stairs. Matchett, on the other hand, had been not a matter of choice: she had been years in service in Dorset with Thomas Quayne's mother, and after Mrs Quayne's death had come on to 2 Windsor Terrace with the furniture that had always been her charge. A charwoman, Mrs Wayes, now came in to clean and polish, ostensibly leaving Matchett freer to maid Anna and Portia and valet Thomas. But Mrs Wayes's area was, in fact, jealously limited by Matchett – accordingly, Matchett kept longer hours than anyone in the house. She slept alone, next the box-room: across the same top landing the cook and Phyllis shared an airy attic with a view of Park Road.

By day, she exacted an equal privacy. The front of the basement had been divided into Phyllis's pantry and a slit of a sitting-room, which, by an arrangement Anna did not question,

Matchett occupied in her spare time. Boiling her own kettles on her gas ring, she joined the kitchen party only for dinner: if the basement door happened to be left open, you could hear the fun break out when she had withdrawn again. Her superior status was further underlined by the fact of her not wearing a cap: the two girls took orders from Anna, Matchett suggestions only. The two young servants did not resent Matchett – she might be repressive, but kept herself to herself – they had learnt that no situation is ever perfect, and Anna was as a mistress amiable, even lax. No one knew where Matchett went on her afternoons off: she was a countrywoman, with few friends here. She never showed fatigue, except fatigue of the eyes: in her sitting-room, she would sometimes take off the glasses she wore for reading or sewing, and sit with one hand shading her forehead stiffly, like someone looking into the distance – but with her eyes shut. Also, as though wishing to remain conscious of nothing, she would at the same time often unbutton the tight shoe-straps that cut into the arches of her feet. But mostly she sat bolt upright, sewing, under the pulled-down electric light.

On the middle floors of the house, where she worked and the Quaynes lived, her step on the parquet or on the staircase was at the same time ominous and discreet.

It was five to four, not quite tea time yet. Portia, turning away inconsequently and seriously, faced round once more to the radiator and spread her fingers a few inches above it, so that the hot vibration travelled up between. Her hands were still mottled from the outdoor cold; her fingers had bloodless tips. Matchett looked on in silence, then said: 'That's the way to give yourself chilblains. Those want rubbing – here, give me!' She came over, took Portia's hands and chafed them, her big bones grinding on Portia's painfully. 'Quiet,' she said. 'Don't keep pulling away like that. I never saw a girl so tender to cold.'

Portia stopped wincing and said: 'Where's Anna?'

'That Mr Miller called, and they went out.'

'Then can I have tea with you?'

'She left word they'd be in at half past four.'

'O-oh,' said Portia. 'That's no good, then. Do you think she'll *ever* be out?'

Matchett, impassively not replying, stooped to pick up one of Portia's woolly gloves. 'Mind and take these up,' she said. 'And those books too. Mrs Thomas spoke about those exercise books. Nothing does down here that isn't here for the look.'

'Has anything else been wrong?'

'She's been on about your bedroom.'

'Oh golly! Has she been in there?'

'Yes, she seemed quite put out,' said Matchett monotonously. 'She said to me this morning, did I not find dusting difficult with all that mess about? Your bears' party, she meant, and one and another thing. "Difficult, madam?" I said. "If I made difficulties, I should not be where I am." Then I asked if she had any complaint. She was putting her hat on – up in her room, it was. "Oh dear no," she said, "I was thinking of you, Matchett. If Miss Portia would put some of those things away –" I made no remark, so she asked for her gloves. She went half out of the door, then she gave me a sort of look. "Those arrangements are Miss Portia's hobbies, madam," I said. She said: "Oh, of course," and went out of the house. No more was said at the time. It isn't that she's so tidy, but she thinks how things look.'

Matchett's voice was flat and dispassionate: when she had done she folded her lips exactly. Letting her hair fall forward to hide her face from Matchett, Portia stooped over the table, getting her books together. Books under her arm, she stood waiting to go up.

'All I mean is', went on Matchett, 'don't give her more to pick on. Not for a day or two, till it passes off.'

'But what was she doing in my room?'

'I suppose she just took the fancy. It's her house, like it or not.'

'But she always says it's my room ... Has she touched things?'

'How would I know? What if she did? You didn't ought to have secrets, at your age.'

'I noticed some toothpowder had come off the top of one of my bears' cakes, but I thought that was the draught. I suppose I ought to have known. Birds know if you have been at their eggs: they desert.'

'And, pray, where would you desert to? – You'd better go on

up, if you don't want her and Mr Miller right in on top of you. They'll be in early, likely, with this cold.'

Portia, sighing, started up to her room. The solid stone staircase was so deep in carpet that her feet made no sound. Sometimes her elbow, sometimes her school-girlish overcoat, unbuttoned, brushed on the white wall. When she got to the first landing, she leaned down. 'Will Mr St Quentin Miller be having tea?'

'Why not?'

'He talks so much.'

'Well, then, he won't eat you. Don't you be so silly.'

Portia went on up, up the next flight. When the bedroom door had been heard shutting, Matchett returned to the basement. Phyllis was darting about in her saucy new cap, getting ready the tray for drawing-room tea.

When Anna, with St Quentin on her heels, came into the drawing-room it appeared to be empty – then by the light of one distant lamp and the fire they perceived Portia, sitting on a stool. Her dark dress almost blotted her out against a dark lacquer screen – but now she rose up politely, to shake hands with St Quentin. 'So here you are,' said Anna. 'When did you get back?'

'Just now. I've been washing.'

St Quentin said: 'How dirty lessons must be!'

Anna went on, with keyed-up vivacity: 'Had a nice day?'

'We've been doing constitutional history, musical appreciation, and French.'

'Goodness!' said Anna, glancing at the tea-tray set inexorably with three cups. She switched on all the other lamps, dropped her muff in a chair, came out of her fur coat, and peeled off the two *tricots* she had worn under it. Then she looked round with these garments hanging over her arm. Portia said: 'Shall I put those away for you?'

'If you would be angelic – look, take my cap as well.'

'How obliging ...' St Quentin said, while Portia was out of earshot. But Anna, propping her elbow on the mantelpiece, looked at him with implacable melancholy. In the pretty air-

tight room with its drawn aquamarine curtains, scrolled sofa, and half-circle of yellow chairs, silk-shaded lamps cast light into the mirrors and on to Samarkand rugs. There was a smell of freesias and sandalwood: it was nice to be in from the cold park. 'Well,' St Quentin said, 'we shall all be glad of our tea.' Loudly sighing with gratification, he arranged himself in an armchair – crossed his legs, tipped up his chin, looked down his nose at the fire. By sitting like this, he exaggerated the tension they had found in the room, outside which he consciously placed himself. Everything so nearly was so pleasant – Anna rapped on the marble with her finger-nails.

He said: 'My dear Anna, this is only one of what will be many teas.'

Portia came back again; she said: 'I put your things on your bed: was that right?' For tea, she returned to her stool by the fire; here she sat with her plate on her knees, her cup and saucer on the parquet beside her – when she drank she stooped half way to meet her cup. Sideways on to the hearth she commanded an equal view of Anna on the sofa, pouring out tea and smoking, of St Quentin constantly wiping buttered toast from his fingers on to his handkerchief. Her look, steady, level, and unassuming, missed nothing the other two did. Once the telephone rang: Anna crossly reached round the end of the sofa to answer it.

'Yes, it is,' she replied. 'But I'm not here at tea time; I never am; I told you. I thought this was when you were so busy? Surely you ought to be? ... Yes, of course I have ... Must you really? ... Well six, then, or half past.'

'A quarter past,' put in St Quentin, 'I'm going at six.'

'A quarter past,' Anna said, and hung up with no change of face. She sat back again on the sofa. 'Such affectation. ...'

'Oh, no?' said St Quentin. They just glanced at each other.

'St Quentin, your handkerchief's terribly buttery.'

'Your excellent toast. ...'

'You wave it about so much – Portia, do you really like a stool without any back?'

'I like this particular stool – I walked all the way home, Anna.'

27

Anna did not reply; she had forgotten to listen. St Quentin said: 'Did you really? We just walked in the park. The lake's frozen,' he added, cutting himself some cake.

'Well, it can't be *quite*: I saw swans swimming about.'

'You are quite right: it's not frozen completely. Anna, what *is* the matter?'

'I'm sorry, I was just thinking. I hate my lax character. I hate it when people take advantage of it.'

'I'm afraid we can't do much about your character now. It must have set – I know mine has. Portia's so lucky; hers is still being formed.'

Portia fixed St Quentin with her blank dark eyes. An alarming vague little smile, already not quite childish, altered her face, then died. She went on saying nothing – St Quentin rather sharply recrossed his legs. Anna bit off a yawn and said: 'She may become anything ... Portia, what hundreds of bears you've got on your mantelpiece. Do they come from Switzerland?'

'Yes, I'm afraid they collect dust.'

'I didn't notice the dust; I just thought what hundreds there were. All hand-carved, I suppose, by the Swiss peasants ... I went in there to hang up your white dress.'

'If you'd rather, Anna, I could put them away.'

'Oh no, why? They seemed to be having tea.'

The Quaynes had a room-to-room telephone, which, instead of ringing, let out a piercing buzz. It buzzed now, and Anna put out a hand, saying: 'That must be Thomas.' She unhooked. 'Hullo? ... Yes, St Quentin is, at the moment. Very well, darling, soon.' She hung up the receiver. 'Thomas is back,' she said.

'You might have told him that I am just going. Does he want anything special?'

'Just to say he is in.' Anna folded her arms, leaned her head back, looked at the ceiling. Then: 'Portia,' she said, 'why don't you go down to Thomas in the study?'

Portia lit up. 'Did he say for me to?' she said.

'He may not know you are in. He'd be ever so pleased, I'm sure ... Tell him I'm well and will come down as soon as St Quentin goes.'

'And give Thomas my love.'

Getting up from the stool carefully, Portia returned her cup and plate to the tray. Then, holding herself so erect that she quivered, taking long soft steps on the balls of her feet, and at the same time with an orphaned unostentation, she started making towards the door. She moved crabwise, as though the others were royalty, never quite turning her back on them – and they, waiting for her to be quite gone, watched. She wore a dark wool dress, in Anna's excellent taste, buttoned from throat to hem and belted with heavy leather. The belt slid down her thin hips, and she nervously gripped at it, pulling it up. Short sleeves showed her very thin arms and big delicate elbow joints. Her body was all concave and jerkily fluid lines; it moved with sensitive looseness, loosely threaded together: each movement had a touch of exaggeration, as though some secret power kept springing out. At the same time she looked cautious, aware of the world in which she had to live. She was sixteen, losing her childish majesty. The pointed attention of St Quentin and Anna reached her like a quick tide, or an attack: the ordeal of getting out of the drawing-room tightened her mouth up and made her fingers curl – her wrists were pressed to her thighs. She got to the door, threw it ceremonially open, then turned with one hand on it, proudly ready to show she could speak again. But at once, Anna poured out another cup of cold tea, St Quentin flattened a wrinkle out of the rug with his heel. She heard their silence till she had shut the door.

When the door shut, St Quentin said: 'Well, we might do better than that. *You* did not do well, Anna – raving about those bears.'

'You know what made me.'

'And how silly you were on the telephone.'

Anna put down her cup and giggled. 'Well, it is something', she said, 'to be written up. It's something that she should find us so interesting. If you come to think of it, we are pretty boring, St Quentin.'

'No, I don't think I'm boring.'

'No, I don't either. I mean, I don't think I am. But she does, if you know what I mean, rather bring us up to a mark. She

insists on our being something or other – what, I'm not quite sure.'

'A couple of cads – What a high forehead she's got.'

'All the better to think about you with, my dear.'

'All the same I wonder where she got that distinction. From what you say, her mother was quite a mess.'

'Oh, the Quaynes have it: one sees it in Thomas, really,' Anna said – then, palpably losing interest, curled up at her end of the sofa. Raising her arms, she shook her sleeves back and admired her own wrists. On one she wore a small soundless diamond watch. St Quentin, not noticing being not noticed, went on: 'High foreheads suggest violence to me ... Was that Eddie, just now?'

'On the telephone? Yes. Why?'

'We know Eddie is silly, but why must you talk to him in such a silly way? Even if Portia *were* here. "I'm not here; I never am here." *Tcha!*' said St Quentin. 'Not that it's my affair.'

'No,' Anna said. 'I suppose it isn't, is it?' She would have said more, had not the door opened and Phyllis sailed in to take away the tea. St Quentin looked at his handkerchief, frowned at the butter on it, and put it away again. They did not pretend to talk. When tea had gone, Anna said: 'I really ought to go down and talk to Thomas. Why don't you come too?'

'No, if he'd felt like me,' said St Quentin, without resentment, 'he'd have come up here. I shall go very soon.'

'Oh, I wanted to ask you – how is your book going?'

'Very nicely indeed, thank you very much,' said he promptly, extremely repressively. He added with some return of interest: 'What happens when you go down? Do you turn Portia out?'

'Out of her brother's study? How ever could I?'

Thomas Quayne had been standing near the electric fire, holding a tumbler, frowning, trying to shake the day off, when his half-sister came round the study door. Her face – hair back in a snood from the high temples, wide-apart unfocusing dark eyes – seemed to swim towards him over the reading lamp. To come in here at all was an act of intimacy, for this was Thomas's own room. He never studied down here, except in so far as his re-

laxation was studied, but the room had been called the study to suggest importance and quiet. It had matt grey walls, Picasso-blue curtains, armchairs and a sofa covered in striped ticking, tables for books, book-shelves, and a desk as large as a dinner-table. Having heard a step that was not Anna's, Thomas ground his feet pettishly into the goat's-hair rug.

'Oh, hullo, Portia,' he said. 'How are you?'

'Anna said you might like me to come down.'

'What's Anna doing?'

'Mr Miller is there. They're not doing anything special, I don't think.'

Shaking what was left of the drink round in his glass, Thomas said: 'I seem to be back early.'

'Are you tired?'

'No. No, I just got home.'

Portia stood with her hand on the back of an armchair; she ran one finger along a dark red stripe, then a grey stripe, looking down at the finger attentively. Then, as Thomas said nothing more, she came round the chair and sat down – drew up her knees, nursed her elbows, and stared forward into the red concavity of the electric fire. At the other end of the hearth-rug Thomas sat down also, and remained also staring, but staring at nothing, with a concentration of boredom and lassitude. Anyone other than Anna being near him, anyone other than Anna expecting something gave Thomas, at this time of the evening, a sense of pressure he could hardly endure. He liked best, at this time of the evening, to allow his face to drop into blank lines. Someone there made him feel bound to give some account of himself, to put on some expression or other. Actually, between six and seven o'clock he thought or felt very little.

'It's freezing,' he unwillingly said at last. 'It bites your face off, out there.'

'Yes, it nearly bit mine off – and my hands too. I walked all the way home.'

'Do you know if Anna went out?'

'I think she walked in the park.'

'Mad,' said Thomas, with an intimate pleasure. He brought out his cigarette case and looked into it flatly: it was empty.

'Would you mind', he said, 'passing that cigarette box – No, just there by your elbow – What did you do today?'

'Would you like me to fill your case?'

'Oh, thank you so much: thanks – What did you say you'd been doing?'

'Constitutional history, musical appreciation, French.'

'Liking it? I mean, how are you getting on?'

'I do think history is sad.'

'More, shady,' said Thomas. 'Bunk, misfires, and graft from the very start. I can't think why we make such a fuss now: we've got no reason to expect anything better.'

'But at one time, weren't people braver?'

'Tougher, and they didn't go round in rings. And also there was a future then. You can't get up any pace when you feel you're right at the edge.'

Portia looked blank, then said: 'I know some French. I know more French than some of the other girls.'

'Oh well, that is always something,' said Thomas. His voice trailed off – slumped in his chair, across the fire from Portia, he sat slowly turning his head with an uneasy baited look, like an animal being offered something it does not like. Thomas had very dark hair, always brushed very flat, and decidedly drawn eyebrows, like his father's and Portia's. Like his father's, his expression was obstinate, but with a hint of deep indecision behind. His head and forehead were rather grandly constructed, but at thirty-six his amiable, mobile face hung already loosish over the bony frame. His mouth and eyes expressed something, but not the whole, of him; they seemed to be cut off from the central part of himself. He had the cloudy, at some moments imperious look of someone conscious of fulfilling his destiny imperfectly; he looked not unlike one of the lesser Emperors. Now, one hand balanced his tumbler on the arm of his chair, the other hung to the floor, as though rather vaguely groping for something lost. There was clearly, at this moment, nothing that Thomas was at all moved to say. The vibration of London was heard through the shuttered and muffled window as though one were half deaf; lamplight bound the room in rather unreal circles; the fire threw its hard glow on the rug. The house held such tense, posi-

tive quiet that he and she might have been all alone in it. Portia raised her head, as though listening to this.

She said: 'A house *is* quiet, after a hotel. In a way, I am not used to it yet. In hotels, you keep hearing other people, and in flats you had to be quiet for fear they should hear you. Perhaps that is not so in flats with a big rent, but in our flats we had to be very quiet, or else the landlord jumped out.'

'I didn't think the French minded.'

'When we took flats, they were in people's villas. Mother liked that, in case something should happen. But lately, we lived in hotels.'

'Pretty awful,' said Thomas, making an effort.

'It might be if you *had* ever lived in a house. But mother and I got fond of it, in some ways. We used to make up stories about the people at dinner, and it was fun to watch people come and go. Sometimes, we got to know some of the other people.'

Thomas absently said: 'I expect you quite miss all that.'

At that, she looked away in such overcome silence that he beat a tattoo on the floor with his hanging-down hand. He said: 'I realize much more than that, of course. It was rotten about your mother – things like that shouldn't happen.'

She said with quite surprising control: 'It's nice being here with you, though, Thomas.'

'I wish we could give you a better time. We could if you were grown-up.'

'But by that time perhaps I –'

She stopped, for Thomas was frowning into his empty tumbler, wondering whether to get another drink. Deferring the question, he turned to look doubtfully at the books stacked beside him at elbow-level, at the reviews and magazines balancing on their top. He rejected these after a glance, put his glass down and reached the *Evening Standard* from the edge of his desk. 'Do you mind', he said, 'if I just have a look at this?' He frowned at one or two headlines, stopped, put down the paper, went across to his desk, and defiantly jabbed a button of the house telephone.

'I say,' he said into the receiver, 'is St Quentin living here? ... Well, as soon as he does, then ... No, don't do that ... Yes, I

33

suppose I am, rather.' He hung up the receiver and looked at Portia. 'I suppose I *am* back rather early,' he said.

But she only looked through him, and Thomas felt the force of not being seen ... What she did see was the *pension* on the crag in Switzerland, that had been wrapped in rain the whole afternoon. Swiss summer rain is dark, and makes a tent for the mind. At the foot of the precipice, beyond the paling, the lake made black wounds in the white mist. Precarious high-upness had been an element in their life up there, which had been the end of their life together. That night they came back from Lucerne on the late steamer, they had looked up, seen the village lights at star-level through the rain, and felt that that was their dear home. They went up, arm-in-arm in the dark, up the steep zigzag, pressing each others' elbows, hearing the night rain sough down through the pines: they were not frightened at all. They always stayed in places before the season, when the funicular was not working yet. All the other people in that *pension* had been German or Swiss: it was a wooden building with fretwork balconies. Their room, though it was a back room facing into the pinewoods, had a balcony; they would run away from the salon and spend the long wet afternoons there. They would lie down covered with coats, leaving the window open, smelling the wet woodwork, hearing the gutters run. Turn abouts, they would read aloud to each other the Tauchnitz novels they had bought in Lucerne. Things for tea, the little stove, and a bottle of violet methylated spirits stood on the wobbly commode between their beds, and at four o'clock Portia would make tea. They ate, in alternate mouthfuls, block chocolate and *brioches*. Postcards they liked, and Irene's and Portia's sketches were pinned to the pine walls; stockings they had just washed would be exposed to dry on the radiator, although the heating was off. Sometimes they heard a cow bell in the thick distance, or people talking German in the room next door. Between five and six the rain quite often stopped, wet light crept down the trunks of the pines. Then they rolled off their beds, put their shoes on, and walked down the village street to the viewpoint over the lake. Through torn mist they would watch the six o'clock steamer chuff round the cliff and pull in at the pier. Or

they would attempt to read the names on the big still shut hotels on the heights opposite. They looked at the high chalets stuck on brackets of grass – they often used to wish they had field-glasses, but Mr Quayne's field-glasses had been sent home to Thomas. On the way home they met the cows being driven down through the village–kind cows, damp, stumbling, plagued by their own bells. Or the Angelus coming muffled across the plateau would make Irene sigh, for once she had loved church. To the little Catholic church they had sometimes guiltily been, afraid of doing the wrong thing, feeling they stole grace. When they left that high-up village, when they left for ever, the big hotels were just being thrown open, the funicular would begin in another day. They drove down in a fly, down the familiar zigzag, Irene moaning and clutching Portia's hand. Portia could not weep at leaving the village, because her mother was in such pain. But she used to think of it while she waited at the Lucerne clinic, where Irene had the operation and died: she died at six in the evening, which had always been their happiest hour.

A whir from Thomas's clock – it was just going to strike six. Six, but not six in June. At this hour, the plateau must be in snow, and but for the snow dark, with lights behind shutters, perhaps a light in the church. Thomas sits so fallen-in, waiting for Anna, that his clock makes the only sound in his room. But our street must be completely silent with snow, and there must be snow on our balcony.

'The lake was frozen this morning,' she said to him.

'Yes, so I saw.'

'But it broke up this afternoon; there were swans on it ... I suppose it will freeze again.'

St Quentin could be heard saying good-bye to Anna, outside in the hall. Thomas quickly picked up the *Evening Standard* and played at reading it. Portia pressed the palms of her hands to her eyes, got quickly up, and went to turn over books at a far table, so that she could keep her back to the room. The table toppled with books that had no place: Anna wanted this room to look cheerfully casual, Thomas made it formlessly untidy. When St Quentin had slammed the hall door on his own last remark, Anna came smiling into the study. Thomas seemed to

wait while he counted three, then he looked at her over the *Evening Standard*.

'Well, darling,' said Anna, 'poor St Quentin has gone.'

'I hope you didn't turn him out?'

'Oh no,' said Anna vaguely, 'he just shot out in his usual way.' She found Thomas's glass on the floor, and said: 'Have you and Portia been having a drink?'

'No, that's only mine.'

'How I wish you'd put them on the table.' She raised her voice: 'Oh, Portia, I hate to worry, but if they have given you any homework, don't you think you ought to do it now? We might all go to a movie later on.'

'I've got an essay to write.'

'My dear, you sound very snuffly. Did you catch cold to-day?'

Portia turned, at the table, and faced Anna – who stopped, though with something further on the tip of her tongue. Lips drawn in, clutching her belt, Portia, with stricken determination, walked straight past Anna out at the study door. Anna went to the door to make sure it was shut, then exclaimed: 'Thomas, you've been making her cry.'

'Oh, was she? I think she's missing her mother.'

'Goodness!' said Anna, stricken. 'But what started her off? Why is she missing her mother *now*?'

'You say I have no idea what people feel – how can I know when they are going to?'

'In some way, you must have unsettled her.'

Thomas, who had been looking hard at Anna, said: 'If it comes to that, you unsettle me.'

'No, but listen,' said Anna, catching hold of his hand but holding it at a distance away from her, 'is she really missing Irene? Because, if so, how awful. It's like having someone very ill in the house. Oh yes, I can easily pity her. I wish I could manage to like her better.'

'Or love her, even.'

'My dear Thomas, that's not a thing one can *mean* to do. Besides, would you really like me to love her? To get wrapped up in her, to wait for her to come in? No, you'd only like me

to seem to love her. But I'm not good at seeming – I was horrid
to her at tea. But I had my reasons, I must say.'

'You don't have to remind me that you don't like this.'

'After all, she's in some way yours, and I married you, didn't
I? Most people have something in their family. For God's sake
don't get worked up.'

'Did I hear you say we'd got to go to a movie?'

'Yes, you did.'

'Why – now, Anna, why? We haven't stayed still for weeks.'

Anna, touching her pearls with an undecided hand, said:
'We can't all just sit around.'

'I don't see why not.'

'We can't all *three* sit around. It gets me down. You don't
seem to know what it's like.'

'But she goes to bed at ten.'

'Well, it never *is* ten, as you know. I cannot stand being
watched. She watches us.'

'I cannot see why she should.'

'I partly see. Anyhow, she makes us not alone.'

'We could be tonight,' said Thomas. 'I mean after ten.' With
an attempt at calmness, he once more put his hand out – but
she, one mass of nervosity, stepped clear. She posted herself at
the far side of the fire, in her close-fitting black dress, with her
folded arms locked, wrapped up in tense thought. For those
minutes of silence, Thomas fixed on her his considering eyes.
Then he got up, took her by one elbow, and angrily kissed her.
'I'm never with you,' he said.

'Well, look how we live.'

'The way we live is hopeless.'

Anna said, much more kindly: 'Darling, don't be neurotic. I
have had such a day.'

He left her and looked round for his glass again. Meanwhile,
he said to himself in a quoting voice: 'We are minor in everything but our passions.'

'Wherever did you read that?'

'Nowhere: I woke up and heard myself saying it, one night.'

'How pompous you were in the night. I'm so glad I was
asleep.'

3

THOMAS QUAYNE had married Anna eight years ago. She used to visit friends near his mother's house in Dorset, so they had met down there. She was then an accomplished, on the whole idle girl, with various gifts, who tried a little of everything and had even made money. She posed as being more indolent than she felt, for fear of finding herself less able than she could wish. For a short time, she had practised as an interior decorator, but this only in a very small way – she had feared to commit herself, in case she could not succeed. She had been wise, for she had not really succeeded, even in that small way. She did not get many clients, and almost at once drew in, chagrined by the rebuff. She drew satirical drawings, played the piano sometimes, had read, though she no longer did, and talked a good deal. She did not play outdoor games, for she did nothing she did not happen to do casually and well. When she and Thomas first met, she was reticent and unhappy: she had not only failed in a half chosen profession but failed in a love affair. The love affair, which had been of several years' duration, had, when Thomas and she met, just come to a silent and – one might guess from her manner – an ignominious end. She was twenty-six when she married Thomas, and had been living with her father at Richmond, in an uphill house with an extensive view.

Thomas liked from the first her smiling, offhand melancholy, her good head, her good nature, an energy he detected under her indolence. Though ash blonde she had, in some way, the personality more of a dark woman. She was, in fact, the first blonde woman who had attracted Thomas: for one thing, he had always detested pinkness, but Anna had an opaque magnolia skin. Her well-built not very slender body moved with deliberation, well in her control. He was affected by the smoothness and unity of her manner, which just was not hard. Her clothes, as part of her style, also pleased and affected him.

Before they met, his few loves had been married women, and the suspicion, later the certainty, that Anna had already had a

lover only made her seem kinder, less far from himself. He did not do well with young girls; he was put off by their candid expectancy. He dreaded (to be exact, he dreaded at that time) to be loved with any great gush of the heart. There was some nerve in his feeling he did not want touched: he protected it without knowing where it was. Already, when he met Anna, he had been thinking of marriage; his means would by now allow it; he did not like the stresses of an affair. Back in London from Dorset, he and Anna met often, alone or at the houses of mutual friends: they dropped into an idiom of sentimental teasing or of intimate sharpness with one another. When they agreed to marry, Thomas was happy enough, and Anna perfectly willing. Then they married: Thomas discovered himself the prey of a passion for her, inside marriage, that nothing in their language could be allowed to express, that nothing could satisfy.

Using capital transferred to him by his mother, Thomas had bought himself into, and now controlled with his partner, an advertising agency, Quayne and Merrett. The business did very well. Anything opportunist or flashy about the venture (of which old Mrs Quayne had not liked the idea, at first) was discounted by Thomas's solid, sub-imperial presence at his official desk. He got back the confidence of his father's associates – this business with no past soon took on, for the old men, an almost dusty prestige. Flair might be suspect, but they saluted ability: Thomas was a chip of better quality than the old block had been. Quayne and Merrett held their ground, then got more ground; Thomas showed weight, his partner, Merrett, acumen. The vivacious young men they needed were recruited by Merrett. From the business, and from interest on the residue of his mother's capital, Thomas derived, at present, an income of about two thousand five hundred a year. Anna, upon the death of her father, had succeeded to five hundred a year.

The Quaynes had expected to have two or three children: in the early years of their marriage Anna had two miscarriages. These exposures to false hopes, then to her friends' pity, had turned her back on herself: she did not want children now. She pursued what had been her interests before marriage in a leisurely, rather defended way. As for Thomas, the longer he

lived, the less he cared for the world. He turned his face away from it, in on Anna. Now he was thirty-six, he could think of nothing with which he could have wished to endow a child.

When his father died, and then finally when Irene died, Thomas had felt himself disembarrassed. His mother had made a point of keeping Mr Quayne's photographs where they had always been, all over the Dorset house, as though the old gentleman were no more than away on some rather silly holiday. She spoke constantly, naturally, of 'Your father'. When *she* died, he discontinued his visits to the couple abroad, telling himself (and no doubt rightly) that these visits were not less embarrassing to Mr Quayne and Irene than they were to him. In those sunless hotel rooms, those chilly flats, his father's disintegration, his laugh so anxious or sheepish, his uneasiness with Irene in Thomas's presence, had filled Thomas with an obscure shame – on behalf of his father, himself, and society. From the grotesqueries of that marriage he had felt a revulsion. Portia, with her suggestion – during those visits – of sacred lurking, had stared at him like a kitten that expects to be drowned. Unavowed relief at the snuffing-out of two ignominious people, who had caused so much chagrin, who seemed to have lived with so little pleasure, had gone far to make Thomas accord with his father's wish. It was fair, it was only proper (he said when the letter came) that Portia should come to London. With obsessed firmness, he had stood out against Anna's objections. 'For one year,' he said. '*He* only said for a year.'

So they had done what was proper. Matchett, when she was told, said: 'We could hardly do less, madam. Mrs Quayne would have felt it was only right.'

Matchett had helped Anna get ready Portia's room – a room with a high barred window, that could have been the nursery. Standing up to look out of the window, you saw the park, with its map of lawns and walks, the narrow part of the lake, the diagonal iron bridge. From the bed – Anna tried for a moment with her head on the pillow – you saw, as though in the country, nothing but tops of trees. Anna had, at this moment before they met, the closest feeling for Portia she ever had. Later, she stood on a chair to re-set the cuckoo clock that had been hers as a

child. She had new sprigged curtains made, but did not re-paper the room – Portia would only be in it for a year. Stuff from the two cupboards (which had made useful store-places) was moved to the box-room; and Matchett, who was as strong as a nigger, carried the little desk from another floor. Anna, fitting a pleated shade on the bed lamp, could not help remarking: 'This would please Mrs Quayne.'

Matchett let this pass with no comment of any kind: she was kneeling, tacking a valance round the bed. She never took up a remark made into the air – thus barring herself against those offhand, meaning approaches from which other people hope so much. She gave, in return for hire, her discretion and her unstinted energy, but made none of those small concessions to whim or self-admiration that servants are unadmittedly paid to make. There were moments when this correctness, behind her apron, cut both ways: she only was not hostile from allowing herself no feeling at all. Having done the valance she got up and, with a creak of her poplin dress at the armpits, reached up and hung a wreathed Dresden mirror Anna had got from somewhere on a nail above a stain on the wall. This was not where Anna meant the mirror to hang – when Matchett's back was turned she unostentatiously moved it. But Matchett's having for once exceeded her duties put Anna less in the wrong. When the room was ready, it looked (as she told St Quentin) very pretty indeed: it ought to be dear to Portia after endless hotels. There was something homely, even, about the faded paper – and also they added, at the last minute, a white rug by the bed, for the girl's bare feet. If Anna had fought against Portia's coming, she knew how to give her defeat style . . . Portia arrived as black as a little crow, in heavy Swiss mourning chosen by her aunt – back from the East in time to take charge of things. Anna explained at once that mourning not only did not bring the dead back but did nobody good. She got a cheque from Thomas, took Portia shopping round London and bought her frocks, hats, coats, blue, grey, red, jaunty, and trim. Matchett, unpacking these when they came home, said: 'You have put her in colours, madam?'

'She need not look like an orphan: it's bad for her.'

Matchett only folded her lips.

'Well, what, Matchett?' Anna said touchily.

'Young people like to wear what is usual.'

Anna had been askance. The forecast shadow of Portia, even, had started altering things – that incident of the mirror had marked an unheard-of tendency in Matchett, to put in her own oar. She said, more defensively than she intended to: 'I've got her a dead white evening dress, and a black velvet one.'

'Oh, then Miss Portia is to dine downstairs?'

'Surely. She's got to learn to. Besides, where else could she eat?'

Matchett's ideas must date from the family house, where the young ladies, with bows on flowing horsetails of hair, supped upstairs with their governess, making toast, telling stories, telling each other's fortunes with apple peel. In the home of today there is no place for the miss: she has got to sink or swim. But Matchett, upstairs and down with her solid impassive tread, did not recognize that some tracts no longer exist. She seemed, instead, to detect some lack of life in the house, some organic failure in its propriety. Lack in the Quaynes' life of family custom seemed not only to disorientate Matchett but to rouse her contempt – family custom, partly kind, partly cruel, that has long been rationalized away. In this airy vivacious house, all mirrors and polish, there was no place where shadows lodged, no point where feeling could thicken. The rooms were set for strangers' intimacy, or else for exhausted solitary retreat.

The Marx Brothers, that evening at the Empire, had no success with Portia. The screen threw its tricky light on her unrelaxed profile: she sat almost appalled. Anna took her eyes from the screen to complain once or twice to Thomas: 'She doesn't think this is funny.' Thomas, who had been giving unwilling snorts, relapsed into gloom, and said: 'Well, they are a lowering lot.' Anna leaned across him: 'You liked Sandy Macpherson, didn't you, Portia? – Thomas, do kick her and ask if she liked Sandy Macpherson?' The organist still loudly and firmly playing had gone down with his organ, through floodlit mimosa, into a bottomless pit, from which *Parlez-Moi d'Amour*

kept on faintly coming up till someone down there shut a lid on him. Portia had no right to say that people were less brave now ... Now the Marx Brothers were over, the three Quaynes dived for their belongings and filed silently out – they missed the News in order to miss the Rush.

Anna and Portia, glum for opposing reasons, waited in the foyer while Thomas went for a taxi. For those minutes, in the mirror-refracted glare, they looked like workers with tomorrow ahead. Then someone looked hard at Anna, looked back, looked again, registered indecision, raised his hat, and returned, extending a large anxious delighted hand. 'Miss *Fellowes*!'

'Major Brutt! How extraordinary this is!'

'To think of my running into *you*. It's extraordinary!'

'Especially as I am not even Miss Fellowes, now – I mean, I am Mrs Quayne.'

'Do excuse me –'

'How could you possibly know? ... I'm so glad we've met again.'

'It must be nine years plus. What a great evening we had – you and Pidgeon and I –' He stopped quickly: a look of doubt came into his eyes.

Portia stood by, meanwhile. 'You must meet my sister-in-law,' said Anna at once: 'Major Brutt – Miss Quayne.' She went on, not with quite so much assurance: 'I hope you enjoyed the Marx Brothers?'

'Well, to tell you the truth – I knew this place in the old days; I'd never heard of these chaps, but I thought I would drop in. I can't say I –'

'Oh, you find them lowering, too?'

'I daresay they're up to date, but they're not what I call funny.'

'Yes,' Anna said, 'they are up to date for a bit.' Major Brutt's eyes travelled from Anna's smiling and talking mouth, via the camellia fastened under her chin, to the upturned brim of Portia's hat – where it stayed. 'I hope', he said to Portia, '*you* have enjoyed yourself.'

Anna said: 'No, I don't think she did, much – Oh, look, my husband has got a taxi. Do come back with us: we must all

43

have a drink ... Oh, Thomas, this is Major Brutt' ... As they walked out two-and-two to the taxi, Anna said to Thomas out of the side of her mouth: 'Friend of Pidgeon's – we once had an evening with him.'

'*Did* we? I don't – When?'

'Not you and I, silly: I and Pidgeon. Years ago. But one really must have a drink.'

'Naturally,' said Thomas. Putting on no expression, he steered her by one elbow through the crowd at the door – for whenever you come out, you never avoid the Rush. In the taxi, infected by Major Brutt, Thomas sat bolt upright, looking hard at everything through the window in a military way. Whereas, Major Brutt, beside him, kept glancing most timidly at the ladies' faces flowering on fur collars in the dark of the cab. He remarked once or twice: 'I must say, this is an amazing coincidence.' Portia sat twisted sideways, so that her knees should not annoy Thomas. Oh, the charm of this accident, this meeting in a sumptuous place – this was one of those polished encounters she and Irene spied on when they had peeped into a Palace Hotel. As the taxi crawled into Windsor Terrace, she exclaimed, all lit up: 'Oh, thank you for taking me!'

Thomas only said: 'Pity you didn't like it.'

'Oh, but I did like being there.'

Major Brutt said firmly: 'Those four chaps were a blot – This where we stop? Good.'

'Yes, we stop here,' Anna said, resignedly getting out.

The afternoon mist had frozen away to nothing: their house, footlit by terrace lamps, ran its pilasters up into glassy black night air. Portia shivered all down and put up her hands to her collar; Major Brutt's smart clatter struck a ring from the pavement; he slapped his coat, saying: 'Freezing like billy-o.'

'We can slide tomorrow,' said Thomas. 'That will be jolly.' He scooped out a handful of silver, stared at it, paid the taxi, and felt round for his key. As though he heard himself challenged, or heard an echo, he looked sharply over his shoulder down the terrace – empty, stagy, E-shaped, with frigid pillars cut out on black shadow; a façade with no back. 'We're wonderfully quiet up here,' he told Major Brutt.

'Really more like the country.'

'For God's sake, let us in!' Anna exclaimed – Major Brutt looked at her with solicitude.

It was admirably hot and bright in the study – all the same, indoors the thing became too far-fetched. Major Brutt looked about unassumingly, as though he would like to say 'What a nice place you've got here,' but was not sure if he knew them well enough. Anna switched lamps on and off with a strung-up air, while Thomas, having said: 'Scotch, Irish, or brandy?' filled up the glasses on the tray. Anna could not speak – she thought of her closed years: seeing Robert Pidgeon, now, as a big fly in the amber of this decent man's memory. Her own memory was all blurs and seams. She started dreading the voice in which she could only say: 'Do you hear anything of him? How much do you see him, these days?' Or else, 'Where is he now, do you know?' Magnetism to that long-ago evening – on which Robert and she must have been perfect lovers – had made her bring back this man, this born third, to her home. Now Thomas, by removing himself to a different plane, made her feel she had done a thoroughly awkward thing. The pause was too long: it smote her to see Major Brutt look, uncertain, into his whisky, clearly feeling ought he not, then, to drink this? Ought he not to be here?

Otherwise, he could wish for nothing better. The Quaynes had both seen how happy he was to come. He was the man from back somewhere, out of touch with London, dying to go on somewhere after a show. He would be glad to go on almost anywhere. But London, these nights, has a provincial meanness bright lights only expose. After dark, she is like a governess gone to the bad, in a Woolworth tiara, tarted up all wrong. But a glamour she may have had lives on in exiles' imaginations. Major Brutt was the sort of man who, like a ghost with no beat, hesitates round the West End about midnight – not wanting to buy a girl, not wanting to drink alone, not wanting to go back to Kensington, hoping something may happen. It grows less likely to happen – sooner or later he must be getting back. If he misses the last tube, he will have to run to a taxi; the taxi lightens his pocket and torments him, smelling of someone else's

woman's scent. Like an empty room with no blinds his imagination gapes on the scene, and reflects what was never there. If this *is* to be all, he may as well catch the last tube. He may touch the hotel porter for a drink in the lounge – lights half out, empty, with all the old women gone to bed. There is vice now, but you cannot be simply naughty.

'Well, here's luck,' Major Brutt said, pulling himself together, raising his glass boldly. He looked round at their three interesting faces. Portia replied with her glass of mild-and-soda: he bowed to her, she bowed to him, and they drank. 'You live here, too?' he said.

'I'm staying here for a year.'

'That's a nice long visit. Can your people spare you?'

'Yes,' Portia said. 'They – I –'

Anna looked at Thomas as much as to say, check this, but Thomas was looking for the cigars. She saw Portia, kneeling down by the fire, look up at Major Brutt with a perfectly open face – her hands were tucked up the elbows of her short-sleeved dress. The picture upset Anna, who thought how much innocence she herself had corrupted in other people – yes, even in Robert: in him perhaps most of all. Meetings that ended with their most annihilating and bitter quarrels had begun with Robert unguarded, eager – like that. Watching Portia she thought, is she a snake, or a rabbit? At all events, she thought, hardening, she has her own fun.

'Thanks very much, no: no, I never smoke them,' Major Brutt said, when Thomas at last found the cigars, Having lit his own, Thomas looked at the box suspiciously. 'These *are* going,' he said. 'I told you they were.'

'Then why don't you lock them up? It's Mrs Wayes, I expect; she has got a man friend and she's ever so good to him.'

'Has she been taking your cigarettes?'

'No, not lately: Matchett once caught her at it. Besides, she is far too busy reading my letters.'

'Why on earth not sack her?'

'Matchett says she is thorough. And thorough chars don't grow on every bush.'

Portia excitedly said: 'How funny bushes would look!'

'Ha-ha,' said Major Brutt. 'Did you ever hear the one about the shoe-tree?'

Anna swung her feet up on the sofa, a little back from the others, and looked removed and tired – she kept touching her hair back. Thomas squinted through his glass of drink at the light: now and then his face went lockjawed with a suppressed yawn. Major Brutt, having drunk two-thirds of his whisky, in his quiet way started dominating the scene. Portia's first animation was in the room somewhere, bobbing up near the ceiling like an escaped balloon. Thomas suddenly said: 'You knew Robert Pidgeon, I hear?'

'I should say so! An exceptional chap.'

'I never knew him, alas.'

'Oh, is he dead?' said Portia.

'*Dead?*' Major Brutt said. 'Oh, Lord, no – at least, I should think that is most unlikely. He had nine lives. I was with him most of the War.'

'No, I'm sure he wouldn't be dead,' Anna agreed. 'But do you know where he is?'

'I last had actual news of him in Colombo, last April – missed him there by about a week, which was bad. We are neither of us much of a hand at letters, but we keep in touch, on the whole, in the most astonishing way. Of course, Pidgeon is full of brain: the man could do anything. At the same time, he is one of those clever fellows who can get on with almost anyone. He is not a chap, of course, that I should ever have met if it hadn't been for the War. We both took it on the Somme, and I got to know him best after that, when we were on leave together.'

'Was he badly wounded?' said Portia.

'In the shoulder,' said Anna, seeing the pitted scar.

'Now Pidgeon was what you could call versatile. He could play the piano better than a professional – with more go, if you know what I mean. In France, he once smoked a plate and did a portrait of me on it – exactly like me, too; it really was. And then, of course, he wrote a whole lot of stuff. But there was absolutely no sort of side about him. I've never seen a man with so little side.'

'Yes,' Anna said, 'and what I always remember is that he could balance an orange on the rim of a plate.'

'Did he do that often?' said Portia.

'Very often indeed.'

Major Brutt, who had been given another drink, looked straight at Anna. 'You haven't seen him lately?'

'No, not very lately. No.'

Major Brutt quickly said: 'He was always a rare bird. You seldom hear of him twice in the same place. And I've been rolling round myself a good bit, since I left the Army, trying one thing and another.'

'That must have been interesting.'

'Yes, it is and it's not. It's a bit uncertain. I commuted my pension, then didn't do too well out in Malay. I'm back here for a bit, now, having a look round. I don't know, of course, that a great deal will come of it.'

'Oh, I don't see why not.'

Major Brutt, a good deal encouraged, said: 'Well, I've got two or three irons in the fire. Which means I shall have to stick around for a bit.'

Anna failed to reply, so it was Thomas who said: 'Yes, I'm sure you're right to do that.'

'I'll be seeing Pidgeon sometime, I dare say. One never knows where he may or may not turn up. And I often run into people – well, look at tonight.'

'Well, do give him my love.'

'He'll be glad to hear how you are.'

'Tell him I'm very well.'

'Yes, tell him that,' Thomas said. 'That is, when you do see him again.'

'If you always live in hotels,' said Portia to Major Brutt, 'you get used to people always coming and going. They look as though they'd be always there, and then the next moment you've no idea where they've gone, and they've gone for ever. It's funny, all the same.'

Anna looked at her watch. 'Portia,' she said, 'I don't want to spoil the party, but it's half past twelve.'

Portia, when Anna looked straight at her, immediately looked

away. This was, as a matter of fact, the first moment since they came in that there had been any question of looking straight at each other. But during the conversation about Pidgeon, Anna had felt those dark eyes with a determined innocence steal back again and again to her face. Anna, on the sofa in a Récamier attitude, had acted, among all she had had to act, a hardy imperviousness to this. Had the agitation she felt throughout her body sent out an aura with a quivering edge, Portia's eyes might be said to explore this line of quiver, round and along Anna's reclining form. Anna felt bound up with her fear, with her secret, by that enwrapping look of Portia's: she felt mummified. So she raised her voice when she said what time it was.

Portia had learnt one dare never look for long. She had those eyes that seem to be welcome nowhere, that learn shyness from the alarm they precipitate. Such eyes are always turning away or being humbly lowered – they dare come to rest nowhere but on a point in space; their homeless intentness makes them appear fanatical. They may move, they may affront, but they cannot communicate. You most often meet or, rather, avoid meeting such eyes in a child's face – what becomes of the child later you do not know.

At the same time, Portia had been enjoying what could be called a high time with Major Brutt. It is heady – when you are so young that there is no talk yet of the convention of love – to be singled out: you feel you enjoy human status. Major Brutt had met her eyes kindly, without a qualm. He remained standing: his two great feet were planted like rocks by her as she knelt on the rug, and from up there he kept bellowing down. When Anna looked at her watch, Portia's heart sank – she referred to the clock, but found this was too true. 'Half past *twelve*,' she said. 'Golly!'

When she had said good night and gone, dropping a glove, Major Brutt said: 'That little kid must be great fun for you.'

4

MOST mornings, Lilian waited for Portia in the old cemetery off Paddington Street: they liked to take this short cut on the way to lessons. The cemetery, overlooked by windows, has been out of touch with death for some time: it is at once a retreat and a thoroughfare not yet too well known. One or two weeping willows and tombs like stone pavilions give it a prettily solemn character, but the gravestones are all ranged round the walls like chairs before a dance, and half way across the lawn a circular shelter looks like a bandstand. Paths run from gate to gate, and shrubs inside the paling seclude the place from the street – it is not sad, just cosily melancholic. Lilian enjoyed the melancholy; Portia felt that what was here was her secret every time she turned in at the gate. So they often went this way on their way to lessons.

They had to go to Cavendish Square. Miss Paullie, at her imposing address, organized classes for girls – delicate girls, girls who did not do well at school, girls putting in time before they went abroad, girls who were not to go abroad at all. She had room for about a dozen pupils like this. In the mornings, professors visited her house; in the afternoon there were expeditions to galleries, exhibitions, museums, concerts, or classical *matinées*. A girl, by special arrangement, could even take lunch at Miss Paullie's house – this was the least of many special arrangements: her secretary lived on the telephone. All her arrangements, which were enterprising, worked out very well – accordingly Miss Paullie's fees were high. Though Thomas had rather jibbed at the expense, Anna convinced him of Miss Paullie's excellent value – she solved the problem of Portia during the day; what Portia learned might give her something to talk about, and there was always a chance she might make friends. So far, she had made only this one friend, Lilian, who lived not far away, in Nottingham Place.

Anna did not think Lilian very desirable, but this could not be helped. Lilian wore her hair forward over her shoulders in

two long loose braids, like the Lily Maid. She wore a removed and mysterious expression; her rather big pretty developed figure already caught the eye of men in the street. She had had to be taken away from her boarding school because of falling in love with the cello mistress, which had made her quite unable to eat. Portia thought the world of the things Lilian could do – she was said, for instance, to dance and skate very well, and had one time fenced. Otherwise, Lilian claimed to have few pleasures: she was at home as seldom as possible, and when at home was always washing her hair. She walked about with the rather fated expression you see in photographs of girls who have subsequently been murdered, but nothing had so far happened to her ... This morning, when she saw Portia coming, she signalled dreamily with a scarlet glove.

Portia came up with a rush. 'Oh dear, I'm afraid I have made us late. Come on, Lilian, we shall have to fly.'

'I don't want to run: I am not very well today.'

'Then we'd better take a 153.'

'If there is one,' said Lilian. (These buses are very rare.) 'Have I got blue rings under my eyes?'

'No. What did you do yesterday evening?'

'Oh, I had an awful evening. Did you?'

'No,' said Portia, rather apologetic. 'Because we went to the Empire. And imagine, quite by chance we met a man who knew someone Anna used once to know. Major Brutt, his name was – not the person she knew, the man.'

'Was your sister-in-law upset?'

'She was surprised, because he did not even know she was married.'

'I am often upset when I meet a person again.'

'Have you seen a person make an orange balance on the rim of a plate?'

'Oh, anyone could: you just need a steady hand.'

'All the people Anna always knows are clever.'

'Oh, you've brought your handbag with you today?'

'Matchett said I was such a silly not to.'

'You carry it in rather a queer way, if you don't mind my saying. I suppose you will get more used to it.'

'If I got too used, I might forget I had it, then I might forget and leave it somewhere. Show me, though, Lilian, how you carry yours.'

They had come out into Marylebone High Street, where they stood for a minute, patiently stamping, on chance of there being a 153 bus. The morning was colder than yesterday morning; there was a black frost that drove in. But they did not comment upon the weather, which seemed to them part of their private fate – brought on them by the act of waking up, like grown-up people's varying tempers, or the state, from day to day, of their own insides. A 153 did come lurching round the corner, but showed every sign of ignoring them, till Lilian, like a young offended goddess, stepped into its path, holding up a scarlet glove. When they were inside the bus, and had settled themselves, Lilian said reproachfully to Portia: 'You do look pleased today.'

She said, in some confusion: 'I do like things to happen.'

Miss Paullie's father was a successful doctor; her classes were held in a first-floor annexe, built for a billiard-room, at the back of his large house. In order that they might not incommode the patients, the pupils came and went by a basement door. Passers-by were surprised to see the trim little creatures, some of whom hopped out of limousines, disappear down the basement like so many cats. Once down there, they rang Miss Paullie's special bell, and were admitted to a fibre-carpeted passage. At the top of a flight of crooked staircase they hung their hats and coats in the annexe cloakroom, and queued up for the mirror, which was very small. Buff-and-blue tiles, marble, gilt embossed wallpaper, and a Turkey carpet were the note of the annexe. The cloakroom, which had a stained-glass window, smelt of fog and Vinolia, the billiard- (or school-) room of carpet, radiators, and fog – this room had no windows: a big domed skylight told the state of the weather, went leaden with fog, crepitated when it was raining, or dropped a great square glare on to the table when the sun shone. At the end of the afternoon, in winter, a blue-black glazed blind was run across from a roller to cover the skylight, when the electric lights had been turned on. Ventilation was not the room's strong point – which

may have been why Portia drooped like a plant the moment she got in. She was not a success here, for she failed to concentrate, or even to seem to concentrate like the other girls. She could not keep her thoughts at face-and-table level; they would go soaring up through the glass dome. One professor would stop, glare, and drum the edge of the table; another would say: 'Miss Quayne, please, *please*. Are we here to look at the sky?' For sometimes her inattention reached the point of bad manners, or, which was worse, began to distract the others.

She was unused to learning, she had not learnt that one must learn: she seemed to have no place in which to house the most interesting fact. Anxious not to attract attention, not to annoy the professors, she *had* learned, however, after some weeks here, how to rivet, even to hypnotize the most angry professor by an unmoving regard – of his lips while he spoke, of the air over his head ... This morning's lecture on economics she received with an air of steady amazement. She brought her bag in to lessons, and sat with it on her knee. At the end of the hour, the professor said good morning; the girls divided – some were to be taken round somebody's private gallery. The rest prepared to study; some got their fine pens out to draw maps; they hitched their heels up on the rungs of their chairs, looking glad they had not had to go out. Some distance away from the big table, Miss Paullie sat going through essays, in a gothic chair, at a table of her own. Because the day was dark, a swan-necked reading lamp bent light on to what Miss Paullie read. She kept turning pages, the girls fidgeted cautiously, now and then a gurgle came from a hot pipe – the tissue of small sounds that they called silence filled the room to the dome. Lilian stopped now and then to examine her mapping nib, or to brood over her delicate state. Portia pressed her diaphragm to the edge of the table, and kept feeling at her bag against her stomach. Everybody's attention to what they were doing hardened – optimistically, Portia now felt safe.

She leant back, looked round, bent forward, and, as softly as possible, clicked open her bag. She took out a blue letter: this she spread on her knee below the table and started to read for the second time.

53

Dear Portia: What you did the other night was so sweet, I feel I must write and tell you how it cheered me up. I hope you won't mind – you won't, you will understand: I feel we are friends already. I was sad, going away, for various reasons, but one was that I thought you must have gone to bed by then, and that I should not see you again. So I cannot tell you what a surprise it was finding you there in the hall, holding my hat. I saw then that you must have been seeing how depressed I was, and that you wanted, you darling, to cheer me up. I cannot tell you what your suddenly being there like that in the hall, and giving me my hat as I went away, meant. I know I didn't behave well, up there in the drawing-room, and I'm afraid I behaved even worse after you went away, but that was not altogether my fault. You know how I love Anna, as I'm sure you do too, but when she starts to say to me 'Really, Eddie', I feel like a wild animal, and behave accordingly. I am much too influenced by people's manner towards me – especially Anna's, I suppose. Directly people attack me, I think they are right, and hate myself, and then I hate them – the more I like them this is so. So I went downstairs for my hat that night (Monday night, wasn't it?) feeling perfectly black. When you appeared in the hall and so sweetly gave me my hat, everything calmed down. Not only your being there, but the thought (is this presumptuous of me?) that perhaps you had actually been waiting, made me feel quite in heaven. I could not say so then, I thought you might not like it, but I cannot help writing to say so now.

Also, I once heard you say, in the natural way you say things, that you did not very often get letters, so I thought perhaps you might like to get this. You and I are two rather alone people – with you that is just chance, with me, I expect, it is partly my bad nature. I am so difficult, you are so good and sweet. I feel particularly alone tonight (I am in my flat, which I do not like very much) because I tried just now to telephone to Anna about something and she was rather short, so I did not try any more. I expect she gets bored with me, or finds me too difficult. Oh Portia, I do wish you and I could be friends. Perhaps we could sometimes go for walks in the park? I sit here and think how nice it would be if –

'*Portia!*' said Miss Paullie.

Portia leaped as though she had been struck.

'My dear child, don't sit hunched like that. Don't work under the table. Put your work *on* the table. What have you got there? Don't keep things on your knee.'

As Portia still did nothing, Miss Paullie pushed her own small table from in front of her chair, got up, and came swiftly round to where Portia sat. All the girls stared.

Miss Paullie said: 'Surely that is not a letter? This is not the place or the time to read your letters, is it? I think you must notice that the other girls don't do that. And, wherever one is, one never does read a letter under the table: have you never been told? What else is that you have on your knee? Your bag? Why did you not leave your bag in the cloakroom? Nobody will take it here, you know. Now, put your letter away in your bag again, and leave them both in the cloakroom. To carry your bag about with you indoors is a hotel habit, you know.'

Miss Paullie may not have known what she was saying, but one or two of the girls, including Lilian, smiled. Portia got up, looking unsteady, went to the cloakroom, and lodged her bag on a ledge under her coat – a ledge along which, as she saw now, all the other girls' bags had been put. But Eddie's letter, after a desperate moment, she slipped up inside her woollen directoire knickers. It stayed just inside the elastic band, under one knee.

Back in the billiard-room, the girls' brush-glossed heads were bent steadily over their books again. These silent sessions in Miss Paullie's presence were, in point of fact (and well most of them knew it), lessons in the deportment of staying still, of feeling yourself watched without turning a hair. Only Portia could have imagined for a moment that Miss Paullie's eye was off what any girl did. A little raised in her gothic chair, like a bishop, Miss Paullie's own rigid stillness quelled every young body, its nervous itches, its cooped-up pleasures in being itself, its awareness of the young body next door. Even Lilian, prone to finger her own plaits or to look at the voluptuous white insides of her arms, sat, during those hours with Miss Paullie, as though Lilian did not exist. Portia, still burning under her pale

skin, pulled her book on the theory of architecture towards her and stared at a plate of a Palladian façade.

But a sense of Portia's not being quite what was what had seeped, meanwhile, into the billiard-room. She almost felt something sniffing at the hem of her dress. For the most fatal thing about what Miss Paullie had said had been her manner of saying it – as though she did not say half of what she felt, as though she were mortified on Portia's behalf, in front of these better girls. No one had ever read a letter under this table; no one had even heard of such a thing being done. Miss Paullie was very particular what class of girl she took. *Sins* cut boldly up through every class in society, but mere misdemeanours show a certain level in life. So now, not only diligence, or caution, kept the girls' smooth heads bent, and made them not glance again at Irene's child. Irene herself – knowing that nine out of ten things you do direct from the heart are the wrong thing, and that she was not capable of doing anything better – would not have dared to cross the threshold of this room. For a moment, Portia felt herself stand with her mother in the doorway, looking at all this in here with a wild askance shrinking eye. The gilt-scrolled paper, the dome, the bishop's chair, the girls' smooth heads must have been fixed here always, where they safely belonged – while she and Irene, shady, had been skidding about in an out-of-season nowhere of railway stations and rocks, filing off wet third-class decks of lake steamers, choking over the bones of *loups de mer*, giggling into eiderdowns that smelled of the person-before-last. Untaught, they had walked arm-in-arm along city pavements, and at nights had pulled their beds closer together or slept in the same bed – overcoming, as far as might be, the separation of birth. Seldom had they faced up to society – when they did, Irene did the wrong thing, then cried. How sweet, how sweetly exalted by her wrong act was Irene, when, stopping crying, she blew her nose and asked for a cup of tea ... Portia, relaxing a very little, moved on her chair: at once she felt Eddie's letter crackle under her knee. What would Eddie think of all this?

Miss Paullie, who had thought well of Anna, was sorry about Portia, and sorry for Anna. She was sorry Portia should have

made no friend here but the more than doubtful Lilian, but she quite saw why this was, and it really could not be helped. She regretted that Mrs Quayne had not seen her way to go on sending someone to fetch Portia, as she had done for the first weeks. She had a strong feeling that Portia and Lilian loitered in the streets on the way home. Miss Paullie knew one must not be old-fashioned, but it gave better tone if the girls were fetched.

Any girls who stayed to lunch at Miss Paullie's lunched in a morning-room in the annexe basement: down here the light was almost always on. The proper dining-room of the house was a waiting-room, with sideboards like catafalques: where Dr Paullie himself lunched no one asked or knew.

The lunch given the girls was sufficient, simple, and far from excellent – Lilian, sent to lunch here because of the servant shortage, always messed about at it with her fork. Miss Paullie, at the head of the table, encouraged the girls to talk to her about art. This Wednesday, this Wednesday of the letter, Portia seated herself as far away from Miss Paullie as she possibly could, whereupon Lilian seized the place next to Portia's with unusual zest.

'It really was awful for you,' Lilian said, 'I didn't know where to look. Why didn't you tell me you'd had a letter? I did think you were looking very mysterious. Why didn't you read it when you had your breakfast? Or is it the kind of letter one reads again and again? Excuse my asking, but who is it from?'

'It's from a friend of Anna's. Because I got him his hat.'

'Had he lost his hat?'

'No. I heard him coming downstairs, and his hat was there, so I gave it to him.'

'That doesn't seem a thing to write a letter about. Is he not a nice man, or is he very polite? What on earth were you doing in the hall?'

'I was in Thomas's study.'

'Well, that comes to the same thing. It comes to the same thing with the door open. You had been listening for him, I suppose?'

'I just was down there. You see, Anna was in the drawing-room.'

'You are extraordinary. What does he do?'

'He is in Thomas's office.'

'Could you really feel all that for a man? I'm never sure that I could.'

'He's quite different from St Quentin. Even Major Brutt is not at all like him.'

'Well, I do think you ought to be more careful, really. After all, you and I are only sixteen. Do you want red-currant jelly with this awful mutton? I do. Do get it away from that pig.'

Portia slipped the dish of red-currant jelly away from Lucia Ames – who would soon be a débutante. 'I hope you are feeling better, Lilian?' she said.

'Well, I am, but I get a nervous craving for things.'

When the afternoon classes were over – at four o'clock today – Lilian invited Portia back to tea. 'I don't know,' said Portia. 'You see, Anna is out.'

'Well, my mother is out which is far better.'

'Matchett did say that I could have tea with her.'

'My goodness,' Lilian said, 'but couldn't you do that any day? And we don't often have my whole house to ourselves. We can take the gramophone up to the bathroom while I wash my hair; I've got three Stravinsky records. And you can show me your letter.'

Portia gulped, and looked wildly into a point in space. 'No, I can't do that, because I have torn it up.'

'No, you can't have done that,' said Lilian firmly, 'because I should have seen you. Unless you did when you were in the lavatory, and you didn't stay in there long enough. You do hurt my feelings: *I* don't want to intrude. But whatever Miss Paullie says, don't you leave your bag about.'

'It isn't in my bag,' said Portia unwarily.

So Portia went home to tea with Lilian and, in spite of a qualm, enjoyed herself very much. They ate crumpets on the rug in front of the drawing-room fire. Their cheeks scorched, but a draught crept under the door. Lilian, heaping coals of fire, brought down, untied from a ribbon, three letters the cello mistress had written to her during the holidays. She also told Portia how, one day at school when she had a headache, Miss

Heber had rubbed with magnetic fingers Lilian's temples and the nape of her neck. 'When I have a headache I always think of her still.'

'If you've got a headache today, then ought you to wash your hair?'

'I ought not to, but I want it nice for tomorrow.'

'Tomorrow. What are you doing then?'

'Confidentially, Portia, I don't know what may happen.'

Lilian had all those mysterious tomorrows: yesterdays made her sigh, but were never accounted for. She belonged to a junior branch of emotional society, in which there is always a crisis due. Preoccupation with life was not, clearly, peculiar to Lilian: Portia could see it going on everywhere. She had watched life, since she came to London, with a sort of despair – motivated and busy always, always progressing: even people pausing on bridges seemed to pause with a purpose; no bird seemed to pursue a quite aimless flight. The spring of the works seemed unfound only by her: she could not doubt people knew what they were doing – everywhere she met alert cognisant eyes. She could not believe there was not a plan of the whole set-up in every head but her own. Accordingly, so anxious was her research that every look, every movement, every object had a quite political seriousness for her: nothing was not weighed down by significance. In her home life (her new home life) with its puzzles, she saw dissimulation always on guard; she asked herself humbly for what reason people said what they did not mean, and did not say what they meant? She felt most certain to find the clue when she felt the frenzy behind the clever remark.

Outdoors, the pattern was less involuted, very much simplified. She enjoyed being in the streets – unguarded smiles from strangers, the permitted frown of someone walking alone, lovers' looks, as though they had solved something, and the unsolitary air with which the old or the wretched seemed to carry sorrow made her feel that people at least knew each other, if they did not yet know her, if she did not yet know them. The closeness she felt to Eddie, since this morning (that closeness one most often feels in a dream) was a closeness to life she had only felt,

THE DEATH OF THE HEART

so far, when she got a smile from a stranger across a bus. It seemed to her that while people were very happy, individual persons were surely damned. So, she shrank from that specious mystery the individual throws about himself, from Anna's smiles, from Lilian's tomorrows, from the shut-in room, the turned-in heart.

Portia turned over records and re-wound the gramophone on the shut seat, and Stravinsky filled the bathroom while Lilian shampooed her hair. Lilian turbaned herself in a bath towel, and Portia carried the gramophone back to the fire again. Before Lilian's cascade of hair, turned inside out and scented in the heat, was quite dry, it had struck seven; Portia said she would have to be going home.

'Oh, they won't bother. You rang up Matchett, didn't you?'

'You said I could, but somehow I never did.'

As Portia let herself into Windsor Terrace, she heard Anna's voice in the study, explaining something to Thomas. There came a pause while they listened to her step, then the voices went on. She stole over that white stone floor, with the chill always off, and made for the basement staircase. 'Matchett?' she called down, in a tense low voice. The door at the foot of the stairs was open: Matchett came out of the little room by the pantry and stood looking up at Portia, shading her eyes. She said: 'Oh, it's you!'

'I hope you didn't wonder.'

'I had your tea for you.'

'Lilian made me go back with her.'

'Well, that was nice for you,' said Matchett didactically. 'You haven't had your tea there for some time.'

'But part of the time I was miserable. I might have been having tea with you.'

' "Miserable"!' Matchett echoed, with her hardest inflection. 'That Lilian is someone your own age. However, you did ought to have telephoned. She's that one with the head of hair?'

'Yes. She was washing it.'

'I like to see a head of hair, these days.'

'But what I wanted was, to make toast with you.'

'Well, you can't do everything, can you?'

'Are they out for dinner? Could you talk to me while I have my supper, Matchett?'

'I shall have to see.'

Portia turned and went up. A little later, she heard Anna's bath running, and smelled bath essence coming upstairs. After Portia had shut her door, she heard the reluctant step of Thomas turn, across the landing, into his dressing-room: he had got to put on a white tie.

5

EDDIE's present position, in Quayne and Merrett's, made his frequentation of Anna less possible. She saw this clearly - when Thomas, more or less at her instance, got Merrett to agree to take Eddie on, she had put it to Eddie, as nicely as possible, that in future they would be seeing less of each other. For one thing – and leave it at that, why not? – Eddie would be quite busy: the firm expected work. However, this did not dispose of him. He felt grateful (at first) to Thomas, but not to Anna. No doubt she was kind, and no doubt he needed a job – badly needed a job: he had been on his beam ends – but in popping him like this into Quayne and Merrett's, was she using the firm as an *oubliette*? Suspiciousness made him send her frequent bunches of flowers, and post her, during his first few weeks at work, a series of little letters that seemed blameless, but at the same time parodied what he ought to feel. He wrote that this new start had made a new man of him, that no one would ever know how down he had been, that no one would ever know how he now felt, etc.

For some years, a number of people had known how Eddie felt. Before Anna had ever met him (he had been a friend of a cousin of hers, at Oxford) she had been told about his cosmic black moods, which were the things he was principally noted for. Her cousin knew no one else who went on like that, and did not believe that anyone else did, either. Denis, her cousin,

and Eddie belonged about that time to a circle in which it was important to be unique. Everyone seemed to get a kick out of their relations with Eddie; he was like a bright little cracker that, pulled hard enough, goes off with a loud bang. He had been the brilliant child of an obscure home, and came up to Oxford ready to have his head turned. There he was taken up, played up, played about with, taken down, let down, finally sent down for one idiotic act. His appearance was charming: he had a proletarian, animal, quick grace. His manner, after a year of trying to get the pitch, had become bold, vivid, and intimate. He became a quite frank *arriviste* – at the same time, the one thing no one, so far, knew about Eddie was quite how he *felt* about selling himself. His apparent rushes of Russian frankness proved, when you came to look back at them later, to have been more carefully edited than you had known at the time. All Anna's cousin's friends, who found Eddie as clever as a monkey, regarded his furies, his denunciations (sometimes) of the whole pack of them as Eddie's most striking turn – at the same time, something abstract and lasting about the residue of his anger had been known, once or twice, to command respect.

When he left Oxford, he had a good many buddies, few responsible friends: he had grown apart from his family who, obscure and living in an obscure province, were not, anyhow, in a position to do anything for him. He came to London and got a job on a paper; in his spare time he worked off his sense of insult in a satirical novel which, when published, did him no good at all. Its readers, who were not many, were divided into those who saw no point in the book whatever, and those who did see the point, were profoundly offended, and made up their minds to take it out of Eddie. What security he had rested so much on favour that he could not really afford to annoy anyone: he had shown himself, not for the first time, as one of those natures in which underground passion is, at a crisis, stronger than policy. Some weeks after the appearance of the novel, Eddie found himself unstuck from his position on the paper, whose editor, though an apparently dim man, was related to someone Eddie had put in his book. Eddie's disillusionment, his indignation knew almost no bounds: he disappeared,

saying something about enlisting. Just when people were beginning to notice, partly with relief, partly with disappointment, that he was not there, he reappeared, very cheerful, every sign of resentment polished away, staying indefinitely with a couple called the Monkshoods, in Bayswater.

Where he had got the Monkshoods nobody knew: they were said to have all been up Cader Idris together. They were a very nice couple, middle-aged, serious, childless, idealistic, and full of belief in youth. They were well off, and seemed disposed to make Eddie their son – with Mrs Monkshood, possibly, there was just a touch of something more than this. During the Monkshood period, Eddie helped his patrons with some research, went to useful parties, did a little reviewing, and wrote some pamphlets, which were printed by a girl who had a press in a loft. Arts and crafts had succeeded *Sturm und Drang*. It was at this time, when he looked like being less of a trouble, that Eddie was first brought to Anna's house by Denis: he found his way there again with kitten-like trustfulness. All seemed to be going almost too well when a friend whose girl Eddie had taken – or had, rather, picked up and put down again – got the Monkshood's ear and began to make bad blood. Eddie – unconscious, though perhaps a little affected by some threat of dissolution in the air – galloped towards his doom: he brought the girl back to his room in the Monkshoods' flat: the flat was too small for this, and the Monkshoods, already uneasy, heard more than they liked. Seeing no way to get rid of Eddie, they gave up their flat and went to live abroad. This made a deep wound in Eddie – he had been good to the Monkshoods, filial, attentive, cheerful. Quite at a loss to understand their very cruel behaviour, he began to see in his patrons perverse cravings he must all the time have flouted unconsciously. There appeared, now, to be no one he might trust.

Anna declared to whoever was interested that the Monkshoods had treated Eddie badly: she had shared his impression that they proposed to adopt him. Up to now, he had been a pleasure at Windsor Terrace, not in any way a charge on the nerves. The morning Denis had told her, not without pleasure, the bad news, Anna sent Eddie an impulsive message. He came

round and stood in her drawing-room: she had been prepared to find him looking the toy of fate. His manner was, in fact, not much more than muted, and rather abstract – it showed, at the same time, a touch of savage reticence. She found he did not know, and did not apparently care, where he would eat next, or where he would sleep tonight. His young debauched face – with the high forehead, springy bronze hair, energetic eyebrows, and rather too mobile mouth – looked strikingly innocent. While he and Anna talked he did not sit down but stood at a distance, as though he felt disaster set him apart. He said he expected that he would go away.

'But away where?'

'Oh, somewhere,' said Eddie, dropping his eyes. He added, in a matter-of-fact voice: 'I suppose there really is something against me, Anna.'

'Nonsense,' she said fondly. 'What about your people? Why not go home for a bit?'

'No, I couldn't do that. You see, they're quite proud of me.'

'Yes,' she said (and thought of that simple home), 'I should think they were ever so proud of you.'

Eddie looked at her with just a touch of contempt.

She went on – making a little emphatic gesture. 'But, I mean, you know, you will have to live. Don't you want to get some sort of work?'

'That's quite an idea,' said Eddie, with a little start – of which the irony was quite lost on Anna. 'But look here,' he went on, 'I do hate *you* to worry. I really shouldn't have come here.'

'But I asked you to.'

'Yes, I know. You were so sweet.'

'I'm so worried about all this; I feel the Monkshoods are monsters. But perhaps it wouldn't have worked, in the long run. I mean, your position is so much freer, now. You can make your own way – after all, you are very clever.'

'So they all say,' said Eddie, grinning at her.

'Well, we'll just have to think. We've got to be realistic.'

'You're so right,' said Eddie, glancing into a mirror.

'And listen: do keep your head, do be more conciliating.

Don't go off at the deep end and have one of your moods – you really haven't got time. I've heard all about those.'

'My moods?' said Eddie, raising his eyebrows. He seemed not just taken aback, but truly surprised. Did he not know he had them? Perhaps they were really fits.

For the rest of that day, Anna had felt deeply concerned: she could not get Eddie out of her mind. Then at about six o'clock, Denis rang up to report that Eddie had just moved into his, Denis's, flat, and was in excellent spirits. He had just had a series of articles commissioned: they were the sort of articles he could do on his head. On the strength of this, he had borrowed two pounds from Denis and gone off in a taxi to the Piccadilly tube station left luggage office to bail out his things; he had promised, also, to bring back with him several bottles of drink.

Anna, considerably put out, said: 'But there's not room for two of you in that flat.'

'Oh, that will be all right, because I'm going to Turkey.'

'What on earth do you want to go to Turkey for?' said Anna, still more crossly.

'Oh, various reasons. Eddie can stay on here while I'm away. I think he'll be all right; he seems to have sloughed that girl off.'

'What girl?'

'Oh, that girl, you know, that he had at the Monkshoods's. He didn't like her a bit; she was a dull little tart.'

'I do think all you college boys are vulgar and dull.'

'Well, Anna darling, do see that Eddie isn't lonely. Eddie's such a dear, isn't he?' said Denis. 'He's what I always call so volatile.' He hung up before Anna could reply.

After two days, in which Anna's annoyance subsided, Denis really did go to Turkey, and Eddie sounded lonely in the flat. Anna, feeling he ought to be someone's responsibility, made him more or less free of Windsor Terrace. She hoped very much to keep him out of mischief. At first, these visits worked very well: Anna had never cared to be the romantic woman, but now Eddie became her first troubadour. He lent himself, gladly and quickly, or appeared to lend himself, to Anna's illusions

about living. He did more: by his poetic appreciation he created a small world of art round her. The vanities of which she was too conscious, the honesties to which she compelled herself, even the secrets she had never told him existed inside a crystal they both looked at – not only existed but were beautified. On Anna, he had the inverse of the effect that Portia's diary was to produce later. He appeared to marvel at Anna – and probably did. If he went into black thoughts, he came out again, for her only, with a quick sweet smile. He showed with her, at its best, his farouche grace; the almost unwilling sweetness he had for her used to make her like hearing people, other people, call Eddie cold or recalcitrant ... This phase of sublime flattery, flattery kept delicate by their ironic smiles, lasted about six weeks. Then Eddie made a false move – he attempted to kiss Anna.

He not only attempted to kiss her, but made the still worse blunder of showing he thought this was what she would really like. When she was very angry (because he gave that impression) Eddie, feeling once more betrayed, misled, and insulted, lost his grip on the situation at once. Having lost his grip, he then lost his head. Though he did not love Anna, he had honestly tried to repay some of her niceness in a way he thought she could but like. It had been his experience that everyone did. If, in fact, in these last years he had found himself rather ruthlessly knocked about, it was because people *had* wanted only that: their differing interests in him, however diverse, seemed in the end to lead to that one point. Another thing that had led him to kiss Anna, or try to, was that he took an underlying practical view of life, and had no time for relations that came to nothing or for indefinitely polite play. When Anna made this fuss, he thought her a silly woman. He did not know about Pidgeon, or how badly she had come out of all that – if, in fact, she *had* ever come out of it. He suspected her of making all this fuss for some rather shady reason of her own.

They were both nonplussed, chagrined, but unhappily neither of them was prepared to cut their losses. Up to now, their alliance had been founded on hopes of pleasure: from now on they set out to annoy each other, and could not help playing each other up. Eddie began to dart devouring looks in com-

pany, to steal uneasy touches when they were alone. Anna would have been less annoyed by all this had she felt herself completely unmoved by Eddie; as it was, aware of the lack of the slightest passion behind it, she was offended by the pantomime. She countered his acting up with insulting pieces of irony. Her one thought was, to put him back in his place – a place she had never quite clearly defined. The more she tried to do this, the worse Eddie behaved.

There were times when Anna almost hated Eddie, for she was conscious of the vacuum inside him. As for him, he found her one mass of pretence, and detested the feeling she showed for power. Through all this, they did still again and again discover reaches of real feeling in one another. Anna did ask herself what they were both doing, but Eddie apparently never did. Could she be injuring genius? Once, in a fit of penitence, she rang up Denis's flat and heard Eddie in tears. The extreme pity she felt brought her, for some reason, to snapping point: she went straight downstairs and complained to Thomas that Eddie tired her more than she could bear.

This was a moment Thomas had seen coming, and he had awaited it philosophically. He had looked on at other declines and falls. He did not at that time dislike Eddie, whose efforts to please him pleased by their very transparency. He had watched, not without pleasure, Eddie annoy St Quentin and others of their friends. He had also read Eddie's novel with a good deal of pleasure, and more sympathy than Anna had brought to it: Eddie was still free to say a good deal about life that he, Thomas, was too deeply involved to say. So Thomas had read the novel with an appeased smile, almost with a sense of complicity. He passed on the book to Merrett, who, liking its savage glitter, pigeon-holed Eddie for possible future use. This was well, for the time came when Anna announced to Thomas that what Eddie needed was straight, regular work, that need not quite waste his wits – in fact, could they not use Eddie in Quayne and Merrett's? The moment happening to be propitious, Eddie was sent for for an interview.

The day Anna heard that Quayne and Merrett were prepared to give Eddie three months' trial, she rang Eddie up and asked

him to come round. Their relation from now on, promised to be ideal: she was his patroness.

That morning Eddie was wearing a sober tie, and already seemed to belong to another world. His manner was civil, and extremely remote. He said how kind they had been at Quayne and Merrett's, and what fun it would no doubt be to write funny advertisements. 'How can I thank you?' he said.

'Why should you? I wanted to help.'

Eddie met her smile with an equally pious look.

She went on: 'I have been worried about you: that's what may have made me seem unsympathetic. I felt sure you needed a more regular life. Thomas thinks I am bad for you,' she added, rather unwisely.

'I don't think that's possible, darling,' said Eddie blithely. Then he bit off that manner. 'You've both been so good,' he said. 'I do hope I haven't been difficult? When I'm worried I seem to get everything on my nerves. And all the jobs I've been after turned me down flat. I really did begin to think there was something against me – which was stupid, of course.'

'But *have* you been looking for jobs?'

'What did you think I'd been doing, all this time? I didn't tell you about it, partly because it depressed me, partly because I thought you'd think it was sordid. All my friends seem to be rather out with me at the moment, so I didn't like to go round to them for backing. And of course, I owe a good deal of money – apart from everything else, I owe thirty-five shillings to Denis's charwoman.'

'Denis should not have left you with an expensive charwoman,' Anna angrily said. 'He never thinks. But surely you've had *some* money?'

'Well, I had till I spent it.'

'What have you been eating?'

'Oh, one thing and another. I must say, I was grateful for your very nice lunches and dinners. I do hope I wasn't snappy at meals? But being anxious gives me indigestion. I'm not like St Quentin and Denis and all those other people that you see – I'm afraid I haven't got very much detachment, darling, and getting nothing to do made me feel in disgrace.'

'You might have known we would help you. How silly you were!'

'Yes, I thought you probably might,' said Eddie, with perfect candour. 'But in a sort of way I rather hated to ask, and while you had it on me, it made it more difficult. However, look how lucky I am now!'

Anna collected herself. 'I'm so glad to know', she said, 'that what has been the matter was simply money. I was afraid, you know, it was really you and me.'

'Unfortunately', said Eddie, 'it was a good deal more.'

'I should rather call it a good deal less. To be right or wrong with people is the important thing.'

'I expect it would be if you had got money. However, Anna, you've got beautiful thoughts. It must have done me good to know you. But I'm not really interesting, darling: I'm all stomach.'

'Well, I'm so pleased that everything is all right,' Anna said with a slightly remote smile. She got up from the sofa and went to lean on the mantelpiece, where she tinkled a lustre. She could stay so still, and she so greatly disliked other people to fidget, that to fidget herself was almost an act of passion – and Eddie, aware of this, stared round in surprise. 'All the same,' she said, 'leaving aside money – which I do see is very, very important – what *has* been making you quite so impossible?'

'Well, darling, for one thing I wanted to make you happy, and for another I thought you might get bored if we kept on and on and nothing ever happened. You see, people have sometimes got bored with me. And while everything round me was such a nightmare, I wanted something with you that wasn't such an effort, something to stop me from going quite mad.' Anna tinkled the lustre harder. 'Have no more nightmares,' she said.

'Oh no, darling: Quayne and Merrett's will be like a lovely dream.'

Anna frowned. Eddie turned away and stood looking out of the window at the park. Shoulders squared, hands thrust in his pockets, he took the pose of a chap making a new start. Her

aquamarine curtains, looped high up over his head with cords and tassels, fell in stately folds each side of him to the floor, theatrically framing his back view. He saw the world at its most sheltered and gay: it was, then, the spring of the year before; the chestnuts opposite her window were in bud; through the branches glittered the lake, with swans and one running dark pink sail; the whole scene was varnished with spring light. Eddie brought one hand out of his pocket and pinched a heavy *moiré* fold of the curtain by which he stood. This half-conscious act was hostile: Anna heard the *moiré* creak between his finger and thumb.

She did not for a moment doubt that in his own mind Eddie was travestying the scene. Yes, and he showed her he felt he was bought goods, with 'Quayne and Merrett' pasted across his back. She said in a light little voice: 'I'm glad you're pleased about this.'

'Five pounds a week, just for being good and clever! How could I not be pleased!'

'I'm afraid they may want just a little more than that. You really will work, I hope?'

'To do you credit?'

Then, because she did not reply, there was a pause. Eddie swung round at her with his most persuasive, most meaningless smile. 'Do come and look at the lake! I don't suppose I shall ever look at it with you in the morning again: I shall be much too busy.' To show how immaterial this was, Anna good-temperedly came to join him. They stood side by side in the window and she folded her arms. But Eddie, with the affectionate nonchalance of someone whose nearness does not matter, put a hand on her elbow. 'How much I owe you!'

'I never know what you mean.'

Eddie's eyes ran over her doubtful face – the light seemed to concentrate in their brilliant shallows; his pupils showed their pin-points of vacuum. 'Marvellous,' he said, 'to have a firm in your pocket.'

'When did you first think I might fix this up for you?'

'Of course it occurred to me. But the idea of advertising was so repellent, and to tell you the truth, Anna, I'm so vain, I kept

hoping I might get something better. You're not angry, are you, darling? You shouldn't judge people by how they have to behave.'

'Your friends say you always fall on your feet.'

The remark was another thing that he would never forgive her. After a stonelike minute he said: 'If I have to know people who ruin me, I mean to get something out of it.'

'I don't understand. Ruin you? Who does?'

'You do, and your whole lot. You make a monkey of me, and God knows what else worse. I'm ashamed to go back home.'

'I don't think we can have done you much harm, Eddie. You must still be quite rugged, while you can be so rude.'

'Oh, I can be rude all right.'

'Then what is upsetting you?'

'Oh, I don't know, Anna,' he said, in a burst of childishness. 'We seem to be on an absurd track. Please forgive me – I always stay too long. I came round to thank you for my lovely job; I came here intending to be so normal – Oh, look, there's a gull sitting on a deck chair!'

'Yes, it must be spring,' she said automatically. 'They've put the deck chairs out.' She opened her case and lighted a cigarette with a rather uncertain hand. Sun shone on the white gull on the green deck chair; a striped sail blew after the pink sail down the lake; smiling people walking and children running between the harp-shaped lawns composed a pattern of play. The carillon played a tune, then the clock struck.

'Is this the last time I shall call you darling, darling?'

It possibly was, she said. This gave her the chance to put it to him, as nicely as possible, that in future they would be seeing less of each other. 'But I know,' he insisted. 'That is what I was saying. That's exactly why I have come to say good-bye.'

'Only good-bye in a way. You exaggerate everything.'

'Well, good-bye in a way.'

'This won't really make any difference.'

'I quite understand, darling. But it will have to appear to.'

It turned out to have been hardly good-bye at all. But it was,

as Anna said to herself, the start of a third, and their most harmonious, phase. That evening, half a dozen camellias came, and three days later, when he had started work, a letter – the first of a series on the imposing office notepaper. In his open writing, so childish as to be sinister, he wrote how nice they all were in the office. In fact, his resentment against her kind act lasted for some weeks. The letter in which he said that this new start had made quite a man of him Anna tore up: she left the scraps in the grate. She asked Thomas how Eddie was really getting on, and Thomas said he was still showing off rather, but that there seemed no reason why he should not shape up.

Eddie came round to report six evenings later, bearing three sprays of flowering cherry in a blue paper sheath. After that, perspicacity, money to spend, or new friends elsewhere made him not repeat the visit for some time. He settled down to a routine of weekly tulips, cosy telephone calls, equivocally nice letters, and after the tulips, roses. Thomas, questioned further, reported that Eddie was doing well, though not so well as Eddie himself thought. When Denis came back from Turkey and wanted his flat, Anna wrote and said the flowers must stop: Eddie would have to begin to pay rent now. The flowers stopped, but Eddie, as though he felt communication imperilled, started coming round more often again. Office or no office, he was once more a familiar feature of Windsor Terrace when Portia arrived to join the family.

6

IT was half past ten at night. Matchett, opening Portia's door an inch, breathed cautiously through the crack: a line of light from the landing ran across the darkness into the room. Portia, without stirring on her pillow, whispered: 'I'm awake.' The entire top of the house was, in fact, empty: Thomas and Anna had gone to the theatre, but Matchett never let their going or

coming temper her manner in any way. She was equally cautious if they were out or in. But only when they were not out did she not come up to say good night.

If, after ten o'clock, Matchett sank her voice and spoke still more shortly, this seemed to be in awe of approaching sleep. She awaited the silent tide coming in. About now, she served the idea of sleep with a series of little ceremonials – laying out night clothes, levelling fallen pillows, hospitably opening up the beds. Kneeling to turn on bedroom fires, stooping to slip bottles between sheets, she seemed to abase herself to the overcoming night. The impassive solemnity of her preparations made a sort of an altar of each bed: in big houses in which things are done properly, there is always the religious element. The diurnal cycle is observed with more feeling when there are servants to do the work.

Portia instinctively spoke low after dark: she was accustomed to thin walls. She watched the door shut, saw the bend of light cut off, and heard Matchett crossing the floor with voluminous quietness. As always, Matchett went to the window and drew the curtains open – a false faint day began again, tawny as though London were burning. Now and then cars curved past. The silence of a shut park does not sound like country silence: it is tense and confined. In the intricate half dark-ness inside Portia's room the furniture could be seen, and Matchett's apron – phosphorescent, close up as she sat down on the bed.

'I thought you were never coming.'

'I had mending to see to. Mr Thomas burnt the top of a sheet.'

'But does he smoke in bed?'

'He did last week, while she was away. His ash-tray was full of stumps.'

'Do you think he would always like to, but doesn't because she's there?'

'He smokes when he doesn't sleep. He's like his father; he doesn't like to be left.'

'I didn't think anyone left father. Mother never did – used *she* to, ever? I mean, did Mrs Quayne? – Oh Matchett, listen:

if she was alive now – I mean, if Thomas's mother was – what would I call her? There wouldn't be any name.'

'Well, what matter? She's gone: you don't have to speak to her.'

'Yes, she's dead. Do you think she is the reason Thomas and I are so unlike?'

'No, Mr Thomas always favoured his father more than he did her. You unlike Mr Thomas? How much liker are you wanting to be?'

'I don't know – Listen, Matchett, *was* Mrs Quayne sorry? I mean, did she mind being alone?'

'Alone? She kept Mr Thomas.'

'She'd made such a sacrifice.'

'Sacrificers', said Matchett, 'are not the ones to pity. The ones to pity are those that they sacrifice. Oh, the sacrificers, they get it both ways. A person knows themselves what they're able to do without. Yes. Mrs Quayne would give the clothes off her back, but in the long run she would never lose a thing. The day we heard you'd been born out there in France, she went on like a lady who'd got her first grandchild. She came after me to the linen room to tell me. "The sweet little thing," she said. "Oh, Matchett!" she said, "he always wanted a girl!" Then she went down in the hall to telephone Mr Thomas. "Oh Thomas, good news," I heard her say.'

Fascinated as ever by the topic, Portia turned over on to her side, drawing up her knees so that she lay in a bend round Matchett's sitting rump. The bed creaked as Matchett, bolt upright, shifted her weight. Sliding a hand under her pillow, Portia stared up through the dark and asked: 'What was that day like?'

'Where we were? Oh, it was quite a bright day, spring-like for February. That garden was very sheltered; it was the sunny side of that hill. I saw her go down the lawn without her hat, and across the stream Mr Quayne made: she started picking herself snowdrops down there the other side of the stream.'

'How could he *make* a stream?'

'Well, there was a brook, but not where Mrs Quayne wanted,

74

so he dug a new ditch and got it to flow in. He was at it all that summer before he went – how he did sweat: I could have wrung his clothes out.'

'But that day I was born – what did *you* say, Matchett?'

'When she said you were born? I said, "To think of that, madam", or something to that effect. I've no doubt she expected to hear more. But I felt it, the way I felt it quite went to my throat, and I couldn't say more than that. Besides, why should I? – not to her, I mean. Of course, we had all known you were to be coming: the others were all eyes to see how Mrs Quayne took it, and you may be sure she knew they were all eyes. I went back to putting away the linen, and what I said to myself was "The poor little soul!" She saw that, and she never forgave me for it – though that was more than she knew herself.'

'Why did you think me poor?'

'At that time I had my reasons. Well, she kept picking snowdrops, and now and then she'd keep stopping and looking up. She felt the Almighty watching, I daresay. None of that garden was out of sight of the windows – you could always see Mr Quayne, while he was working, just as if he had been a little boy. Then she came back in and she did the snowdrops, in a Chinese bowl she set store by – oh, she did set store by that bowl, till one of the girls broke it. (She came to me with the bits of it in her hand, smiling away she was. "Another little bit of life gone, Matchett," she said. But she never spoke a cross word to the girl – oh no, she liked herself far too well.) Then, that afternoon, Mr Thomas came back by a train from Oxford: he felt he ought to see, I daresay, how his mother really *was* taking it. I made up his room for him, and he stayed that night. He went about looking quite taken aback, with three snowdrops she gave him stuck in his buttonhole. He stopped and looked at me once, by the swing door, as though he felt he ought to say something. "Well, Matchett," he said to me, rather loud, "so I've got a sister." "Yes, indeed, sir," I said.'

'Was that all Thomas said?'

'I daresay the house felt funny that day for a young fellow like him, quite as though there had been a birth there. It did

to us all, really. Then later on, Mrs Quayne sat down and played the piano to Mr Thomas.'

'*Did* they look at all pleased?'

'How should I know? They kept on at the piano till it was time for dinner.'

'Matchett, if Thomas does like a piano, why haven't they got a piano here?'

'He sold the piano when she died. Oh, she was fair to me, the fifteen years I was with her. You couldn't have had a better employer, as far as the work went: the one thing that put her out was if you made her feel she wasn't considerate. She liked me to feel that she thought the world of me. "I leave everything in safe charge with you, Matchett," she'd say to me on the doorstep, times when she went away. I thought of that as I saw her coffin go out. No, she'd never lift her voice and she always had a kind word. But I couldn't care for her: she had no nature. I've often felt her give me a funny look. She liked what I did, but she never liked how I did it. I couldn't count how often I've heard her say to her friends, "Treat servants nicely, take an interest in them, and they'll do anything for you." That was the way she saw it. Well, I liked the work in that house, I liked that work from the first: what she couldn't forgive me was that I liked the work for its own sake. When I had been the morning polishing in my drawing-room, or getting my marbles nice with a brush and soft soap, she would come to me and she'd say, "Oh, it does all look nice! I am so pleased, I am really." Oh, she meant well, in her own way. But with work it's not what you show, it's what you put into it. You'd never get right work from a girl who worked to please you: she'd only work to show. But *she* would never see that. Now, when Mr Quayne would come on me working in his smoking-room, or working in any place that he wanted to be, though he was so sweet-tempered, he'd give me a black look as though to say "You get out!" He'd know well I was against him, working in his smoking-room where he wanted to be. If he found a thing left different he used to bellow, because my having my way had put him out. But then, Mr Quayne was all nature. He left you to go your own way, except when it started to put him out.

But she couldn't allow a thing that she hadn't her part or share in. All those snowdrops and that piano playing – to make out she'd had her share in your being born.

'The day she died, though I wasn't up in her room, I could feel her watching how I'd take it. "Well," I said to myself, "it's no good – *I* can't play the piano." Oh, I did feel upset, with death in the house and all that change coming. But that was the most I felt. I didn't feel a thing here.' With a dry unflinching movement, Matchett pressed a cuffed hand under her bust.

She sat sideways on to the bed, her knees towards Portia's pillow, her dark skirts flowing into the dark round, only her apron showing. Her top part loomed against the tawny square of sky in uncertain silhouette; her face, eroded by darkness like a statue's face by the weather, shone out now and then when a car fanned light on it. Up to now, she had sat erect, partly judicial, partly as though her body were a vaseful of memory that must not be spilt; but now, as though to shift the weight of the past, she put a hand on the bed, the far side of Portia's body, and leant heavily on it so that she made an arch.

Through this living arch, the foot of the bed in fluctuations of half-darkness was seen. Musky warmth from her armpit came to the pillow, and a creak from the stays under her belt as she breathed in the strain of this leaning attitude. She felt as near, now, as anyone can be without touching one. At the same time, as though to re-create distance, her voice pitched itself further away.

'Oh, I felt bad,' she said, 'because I couldn't forgive her. Not about Mr Quayne – I could never forgive her that. When the nurse sent down word Mrs Quayne was going, cook said maybe we should go up. She said, having sent word they'd expect us to do something. (Cook meant, *she'd* expect us to do something.) So Cook and I went up and stood on the landing: the others were too nervous; they stayed below. Cook was a Catholic, so started saying her prayers. Mr and Mrs Thomas were there in the room with her. We knew it was over when Mrs Thomas came out, quite white, and said to me, "Oh Matchett." But Mr Thomas went by without a word. I had had his whisky put out in the dining-room and quite soon I heard them both in there.

Mr and Mrs Thomas were different to Mrs Quayne: they had their own ways of passing a thing off.'

'But Matchett, she meant to do good.'

'No, she meant to do right.'

Tentatively sighing and turning over, Portia put on Matchett's knee, in the dark, fingers that by being urgently living tried to plead for the dead. But the very feel of the apron, of the starch over that solid warm big knee, told her that Matchett was still inexorable.

'You know what she did,. but how can you know what she felt? Fancy being left with somebody gone. Perhaps what was right was all she had left to do. To have to stay alone might be worse than dying.'

'She stayed there where she wanted, go who might. No, he had done her wrong, and she had to do herself right. Oh, she was like iron. Worse than dying? For your father, going away was that. He loved his home like a child. Go? – He was sent. He liked his place in the world; he liked using his hands. That stream wasn't the only thing he'd made. For a gentleman like him, abroad was no proper place. I don't know how she dared look at that garden after what she had done.'

'But if I had to be born?'

'He was sent away, as cook or I might have been – but oh no, we suited her too well. She stood by while Mr Thomas put him into the car and drove him off as if he had been a child. What a thing to make Mr Thomas do to his own father! And then look at the way your father and mother lived, with no place in the world and nobody to respect them. He had been respected wherever he was. Who put him down to that?'

'But mother explained to me that she and father had once done what was cruel to Mrs Quayne.'

'And what did she do to them! Look how they lived, without a stick of their own. You were not born to know better, but he did.'

'But he liked keeping moving on. It was mother wanted a house, but father never would.'

'You don't break a person's nature for nothing.'

Portia said in a panic: 'But we were happy, Matchett. We

had each other; he had mother and me – Oh, don't be so angry: you make me feel it was my fault for having had to be born.'

'And who had the right to quarrel with you for that? If you had to be, then you had to be. I thought that day you were born, as I went on with my linen. Well, that's one more thing happened: no doubt it is for a purpose.'

'That's what they all feel; that's why they're all always watching. They would forgive me if I were something special. But I don't know what I was meant to be.'

'Now then,' said Matchett sharply, 'don't *you* get upset.'

Portia had unconsciously pushed, while she spoke, at the knee under Matchett's apron, as though she were trying to push away a wall. Nothing, in fact, moved. Letting her hand fall back on to her face in the dark, she gave an instinctive shiver that shook the bed. She ground the back of her hand into her mouth – the abandoned movement was cautious, checked by awe at some monstrous approach. She began to weep, shedding tears humbly, without protest, without at all full feeling, like a child actress mesmerized for a part. She might have been miming sorrow – in fact, this immediate, this obedient prostration of her whole being was meant to hold off the worst, the full of grief, that might sweep her away. Now, by crossing her arms tightly across her chest, as though to weight herself down with them, she seemed to cling at least to her safe bed. Any intimations of Fate, like a step heard on the stairs, makes some natures want to crouch in the safe dark. Her tears were like a flag lowered at once: she felt herself to be undefendable.

The movement of her shoulders on the pillow could be heard; her shiver came through the bed to Matchett's body. Matchett's eyes pried down at her through the dark; inexorably listening to Portia's unhappy breaths she seemed to wait until her pity was glutted. Then – 'Why goodness,' she said softly. 'Why do *you* want to start breaking your heart? If that wasn't finished, I wouldn't go on about it. No doubt I'm wrong, but you do keep on at me, asking. You didn't ought to ask if you're going to work up so. Now you put it out of your head, like a good girl, and go right off to sleep.' She shifted her weight from her hand, groped over Portia, found her wet wrists, uncrossed

them. 'Goodness,' she said, 'whatever good does *that* do?' All the same, the question was partly rhetorical: Matchett felt that something had been appeased. Having smoothed the top of the sheet, she arranged Portia's hands on it like a pair of ornaments: she stayed leaning low enough to keep guard on them. She made a long sibilant sound, somewhere right up in space, like swans flying across a high sky. Then this stopped and she suggested: 'Like me to turn your pillow?'

'No,' said Portia unexpectedly quickly, then added: 'But don't go.'

'You like it turned for you, don't you? However –'

'Ought we both to forget?'

'Oh, you'll forget when you've got more to remember. All the same, you'd better not to have asked.'

'I just asked about the day I was born.'

'Well, the one thing leads to the other. It all has to come back.'

'Except for you and me, nobody cares.'

'No, there's no past in this house.'

'Then what makes them so jumpy?'

'They'd rather no past – not have the past, that is to say. No wonder they don't rightly know what they're doing. Those without memories don't know what is what.'

'Is that why you tell me this?'

'I'd likely do better not to. I never was one to talk, and I'm not one to break a habit. What I see I see, but I keep myself to myself. I have my work to get on with. For all that, you can't but notice, and I'm not a forgetter. It all goes to make something, I daresay. But there's no end to what's been said, and I'll be a party to nothing. I was born with my mouth shut: those with their mouths open do nothing but start trouble and catch flies. What I am asked, I'll answer – that's always been sufficient.'

'Does no one but me ask you?'

'They know better,' said Matchett. Satisfied that the fold of Portia's upper sheet wanted no more attention, she drew back and once more propped herself on her hand. 'What's not said keeps,' she went on. 'And when it's been keeping some time

it gets what not many would dare to hear. Oh, it wasn't quite welcome to Mr Thomas when I first came to this house after his mother dying, though he did speak civil and pass it off so well. "Why, Matchett," he said, "this feels like home again." Mrs Thomas took it quite easy; it was the work she wanted and she knew I was a worker. The things that came to them here from Mrs Quayne's were accustomed to the best care; Mrs Thomas knew they must have it. Oh, it is lovely furniture, and Mr and Mrs Thomas see the value of it. Valuables were the one thing Mrs Quayne and Mrs Thomas saw eye to eye about. You can see ten foot into my polish, and Mrs Thomas likes the look of a thing.'

'But what made you come here?'

'It seemed to me proper. I hadn't the heart, either, to let that furniture go: I wouldn't have known myself. It was that that kept me at Mrs Quayne's. I was sorry to leave those marbles I'd got so nice, but those had to stop and I put them out of my mind.'

'The furniture would have missed you?'

'Furniture's knowing all right. Not much gets past the things in a room, I daresay, and chairs and tables don't go to the grave so soon. Every time I take the soft cloth to that stuff in the drawing-room, I could say, "Well, you know a bit more." My goodness, when I got here and saw all Mrs Quayne's stuff where Mrs Thomas had put it – if I'd have been a silly, I should have said it gave me quite a look. Well, it didn't speak, and I didn't. If Mr and Mrs Thomas are what you say, nervous, no doubt they are nervous of what's not said. I would not be the one to blame them: they live the best way they can. Unnatural living runs in a family, and the furniture knows it, you be sure. Good furniture knows what's what. It knows it's made for a purpose, and it respects itself – when I say *you're* made for a purpose you start off crying. Oh, furniture like we've got is too much for some that would rather not have the past. If I just had to look at it and have it looking at me, I'd go jumpy, I daresay. But when it's your work it can't do anything to you. Why, that furniture – I've been at it years and years with the soft cloth: I know it like my own face ... Oh yes, I notice them all right.

But I'm not the one to speak: I've got no time. When they made a place for it, they made a place for me, and they soon saw nothing would come of *that*.'

'When I came, though, it was worse.'

'It was proper,' said Matchett quickly. 'The first mortal thing he had ever asked since he went –'

'Yes, this was the house my father talked about. He used to tell me how nice it was. Though he never came here, he did walk past it once. He told me it had a blue door and stood at a corner, and I expect he imagined the inside. "That's the part of London to live in," he used to say. "Those houses are leased direct from the King, and they have an outlook fit for Buckingham Palace." Once, in Nice, he bought a book about birds and showed me pictures of the water birds on this lake. He said he had watched them. He told me about the scarlet flowerbeds – I used to imagine them right down to the lake, not with that path between. He said this was the one gentleman's park left, and that Thomas would be wrong to live anywhere else. He used to tell me, and to tell people we met, how well Thomas got on in business, and how pretty Anna was – stylish, he used to call her – and how much they entertained, and what gay parties they had. He used to say, a young man getting on in the world is quite right to cut a bit of a dash. Whenever we spent a day in any smart place, he always used to notice the ladies' clothes, and say to me, "Now that would look well on Anna." Yes, he was ever so proud of Thomas and her. It always made him happy to talk about them. When I was little and stupid, I used to say, "Why can't we see them soon?" and he used to say, "Some day." He promised that some day I should be with them – and now, of course, I am.'

Matchett said triumphantly: 'Ah, he got his way – in the end.'

'I liked them for making father proud. But when I was with mother, I had to forget them – you see, they were a sort of trouble to her. She thought Anna laughed at how we lived.'

'Oh, Mrs Thomas didn't trouble to laugh. She'd let live and let die – so long as she wasn't trespassed upon. And she wasn't trespassed upon.'

'She had to have me here.'

'She had this room empty, waiting,' said Matchett sharply. '*She* never filled it, for all she is so clever. And she knows how to make a diversion of anything – dolling this room up with clocks and desks and frills. (Not but what it's pretty, and you like it, I should hope.) No, she's got her taste, and she dearly likes to use it. Past that she'll never go.'

'You mean, she'll never be fond of me?'

'So that's what you want?' Matchett said, so jealously pouncing that Portia drew back in her bed.

'She had a right, of course, to be where I am this minute,' Matchett went on in a cold, dispassionate voice. 'I've no call to be dawdling up here, not with all that sewing.' Her weight stiffened on the bed; drawing herself up straight she folded her arms sternly, as though locking love for ever from her breast. Portia saw her outline against the window and knew this was not pique but arrogant rectitude – which sent her voice into distance two tones away. 'I have my duties,' she said, 'and you should look for your fond-ofs where it is more proper. I'd be glad you should get them. Oh, I was glad somehow, that day she came and said you had been born. I might have done better to wish you out of it.'

'Don't be angry – oh, don't be! You're quite enough, Matchett!'

'Now don't you work yourself up again!'

'But don't, don't keep going off –' began Portia, desperate. Stopping, she put both arms out, with a rustle of sheet falling away. Matchett, reluctantly softening, inch by inch, unlocked her arms, leaned across the bed again, leaned right down – in the mysterious darkness over the pillow their faces approached, their eyes met but could not see. Something steadily stood between them: they never kissed – so that now there followed a pause at once pressing and null. Matchett, after the moment, released herself and drew a judicial breath. 'Well, I'm hasty, I daresay.' But Portia's hand, with its charge of nervous emotion, still crept on the firm broad neck, the strong spine. Matchett's embrace had made felt a sort of measured resistance, as though she were determined to will, not simply to suffer, the power of

the dividing wall. Darkness hid any change her face might allow itself. She said finally: 'I'll turn your pillow now.'

Portia at once stiffened. 'No,, don't. I like it this way – No, don't.'

'Why ever not?'

'Because I like it this way.'

But Matchett's hand pushed underneath the pillow, to turn it. Under there, going wooden, her hand stopped. 'What's this you've got under here? *Now*, what have you got?'

'That's only just a letter.'

'What have you got it here for?'

'I must just have put it there.'

'Or maybe it walked,' said Matchett. 'And who's been writing *you* letters, may I ask?'

As gently as possible, Portia tried saying nothing. She let Matchett turn the pillow, then settled with her cheek on the new, cool side. For nearly a minute, propitiatingly, she acted someone grateful going to sleep. Then, with infinite stealth, she felt round under the pillow – to find the letter gone. 'Oh, *please*, Matchett!' she cried.

'The proper place for your letters is in your desk. What else did Mrs Thomas give you a desk for?'

'I like having a letter here when it's just come.'

'That's no place for letters at your age – it's not nice. You didn't ought to be getting letters like that.'

'It's not a letter like that.'

'And who wrote it, may I ask?' said Matchett, her voice rising.

'Only that friend of Anna's – only Eddie.'

'Ah! So he did?'

'Only because I got him his hat.'

'Wasn't he civil?'

'Yes,' Portia said firmly. 'He knows I like getting letters. I haven't had any letters for three weeks.'

'Oh, he does, does he – he knows you like getting letters?'

'Well, Matchett, I do.'

'So he saw fit to thank you kindly for getting his hat? It's the first manners he's shown here, popping in and out like a weasel.

Manners? He's no class. Another time, you leave Phyllis get him his hat, else let him get it himself – he's here often enough to know where it should be ... Yes, you mind what I'm saying: I know what I say.'

Matchett's voice, so laden and unemphatic, clicked along like a slow tape, with a stop at the last word. Portia lay in a sort of coffin of silence, one hand under the pillow where the letter had been. Outside the room there sounded a vacuum of momentarily arrested London traffic: she turned her eyes to the window and looked at the glass-dark sky with its red sheen. Matchett's hand in the cuff darted out like an angry bird, knocked once against the pleated shade of the bed lamp, then got the light switched on. Immediately, Portia shut her eyes, set her mouth, and lay stiff on the pillow, as though so much light dug into a deep wound. She felt it must be very late, past midnight: that point where the river of night flows underneath time, that point at which occurs the mysterious birth of tomorrow. The very sudden, anaesthetic white light, striped by the pleats of the shade, created a sense of sick-room emergency. As though she lay in a sick-room, her spirit retreated to a seclusion of its own.

Matchett sat with the captured letter in the trough of her lap. Meanwhile, her spatulate fingers bent and injured, with unknowing sensuous cruelty, like a child's, the corners of the blue envelope. She pinched at the letter inside's fullness, but did not take it out. 'You'd be wrong to trust him,' she said.

Safe for the minute, sealed down under her eyelids, Portia lay and saw herself with Eddie. She saw a continent in the late sunset, in rolls and ridges of shadow like the sea. Light that was dark yellow lay on trees, and penetrated their dark hearts. Like a struck glass, the continent rang with silence. The country, with its slow tense dusk-drowned ripple, rose to their feet where they sat: she and Eddie sat in the door of a hut. She felt the hut, with its content of dark, behind them. The unearthly level light streamed in their faces; she saw it touch his cheekbones, the tips of his eyelashes, while he turned her way his eyeballs blind with gold. She saw his hands hanging down between his knees, and her hands hanging down peacefully beside him as they sat together on the step of the hut. She felt the touch of

calmness and similarity: he and she were one without any touch but this. What was in the hut behind she did not know: this light was eternal; they would be here for ever.

Then she heard Matchett open the envelope. Her eyes sprang open; she cried: 'Don't touch that!'

'I'd not have thought this of you.'

'My father would understand.'

Matchett shook. 'You don't care what you say.'

'You're not fair, Matchett. You don't know.'

'I know that Eddie's never not up to something. And he makes free. *You* don't know.'

'I do know when I'm happy. I know that.'

7

MAJOR BRUTT found it simple to pay the call: everything seemed to point to his doing that. To begin with, he found that an excellent bus, a 74, took him from Cromwell Road the whole way to Regent's Park. He was not a man to ring up; he simply rang a door bell. To telephone first would have seemed to him self-important, but he knew how to enter a house unassumingly. He had lived in parts of the world where you drop in: there seemed to him nothing complex about that. His impression of Windsor Terrace had been a warm and bright one; he looked forward today to seeing the drawing-room floor. Almost unremitting solitude in his hotel had, since his last visit, made 2 Windsor Terrace the clearing-house for his dreams: these reverted to kind Anna and to that dear little kid with fervent, tender, quite sexless desire. A romantic man often feels more uplifted with two women than with one: his love seems to hit the ideal mark somewhere between two different faces. Today, he came to recover that visionary place, round which all the rest of London was a desert. That last night, the Quaynes, seeing him out, had smiled and said heartily: 'Come again.' He took

it that people meant what they said – so here he was, coming again. Thomas's having added 'Ring up first' had made no impression on him whatever. They had given him *carte blanche*, so here he was, dropping in. He judged that Saturday should be a good day.

This Saturday afternoon Thomas, home from the office, sat at his study table, drawing cats on the blotter, waiting for Anna to come back from a lunch. He was disappointed with her for lunching out on a Saturday and for staying so late. When he heard the bell ring he looked up forbiddingly (though there was just a chance Anna might have forgotten her key), listened, frowned, put whiskers on to a cat, then looked up again. If it had been her, she would ring two or three times. The ring, however, did not repeat itself – though it lingered on uneasily in the air. Saturday made it unlikely that this could be a parcel. Telegrams were almost always telephoned through. That it could be a caller did not, at his worst moment, enter Thomas's head. Callers were unheard of at Windsor Terrace. They had been eliminated; they simply did not occur. The Quaynes' home life was as much their private life as though their marriage had been illicit. Their privacy was surrounded by an electric fence – friends who did not first telephone did not come.

This being so, even Phyllis, with all her aplomb, her ever-consciousness of a pretty cap, had forgotten how to cope with a plain call. She well knew the cut of 'expected' people, people who all but admitted themselves, who marched in past her without the interrogatory pause. Some smiled at her, some did not – but well did she know the look of someone who knew the house. And, except for a lunch party or a dinner, nobody ever came who did not.

So, directly she opened the door and saw Major Brutt, she knew it was in her power to oppress. She raised her eyebrows and simply looked at him. For him, that promising door had opened on something on which he had not reckoned. He knew, of course, that people have parlourmaids – but that last time the hall had been so full of light, of good-bye smiles, of heaps of women's fur coats. He faltered slightly at once: Phyllis saw the drop in his masculine confidence. Her contempt for humility

made her put him down as an ex-officer travelling in vacuum cleaners, or those stockings that are too shiny to wear.

So it was with snappy triumph that she was able to say Mrs Quayne was not at home. Modifying his expectant manner, he then asked for Mr Quayne – which made Phyllis quite sure that this person must be wanting something. She was quite right: he was – he had come all this way to see a holy family.

'Mr Quayne? I couldn't say,' Phyllis replied pursily. She let her eye run down him and added, 'sir'. She said: 'I could inquire if you like to wait.' She looked again – he did not carry a bag, so she let him in to a certain point in the hall. Too sharp to give Thomas away by looking into the study, she started downstairs to ring through on the room-to-room telephone. As she unhooked the receiver at the foot of the basement stairs, intending to say, 'Please, sir, I think there is someone –' she heard Thomas burst open his door, come out, and make some remark. Now Mrs Quayne would not have allowed that.

In the seconds before Thomas came to his door, Major Brutt may have realized this was a better house to be brought back to in triumph than to make one's way into under one's own steam. While he looked up the draughtless stairs behind the white arches, some aspirations faded out of his mind. He glanced at the console table, but did not like to put down his hat yet: he stood sturdily, doubtfully. Then a step just inside that known door made him re-animate like a dog: his moustache broadened a little, ready for a smile.

'Oh, *you*: splendid!' said Thomas – he held his hand out, flat open, with galvanized heartiness. 'I thought I heard some-one's voice. Look here, I'm so sorry you –'

'Look here, I do hope I'm not –'

'Oh, good God, no! I was simply waiting for Anna. She's out at some sort of lunch – you know how long those things take.'

Major Brutt had no idea – it had seemed to him rather more near tea time. He said: 'They must be great places for talk,' as Thomas, incompletely resigned, got him into the study, with rather too much fuss. The room now held fumy heavy afternoon dusk – Thomas had been asleep in here for an hour before un-

screwing his pen, opening the blotter, and sitting down with some of his papers out. 'Everyone talks,' said Thomas. 'I can't think, can you, how they keep it up.' He looked at his cats with nostalgia, shut the blotter, swept some papers in a drawer, and shut the drawer with a click. That was that, he seemed to say, I *was* busy, but never mind. Meanwhile, Major Brutt pulled his trousers up at the knees and lowered himself into an arm-chair.

Thomas, trying to concentrate, said: 'Brandy?'

'Thanks, no: not just now.'

Thomas took this with just a touch of rancour – it made the position less easy than ever. Major Brutt was clearly counting on tea, and the Quaynes would be likely to cut tea out; Anna, with whom large lunches did not agree, would be likely to come home claustrophobic and cross. She and Thomas had planned to walk once right round the park, after that, at perhaps about five, to go to a French film. At the cinema they felt loverlike; they often returned in a taxi arm-in-arm. Thomas had a notion that, for Major Brutt, the little kid Portia might do just as well – in fact, she might really be his object. But, annoyingly, Portia was not to be found either. Saturday was her free day, when she might have been expected to be about. But having come for her lunch, Thomas was told, she had gone out immediately – nobody knew where. Matchett was said to say that she might not be in for tea. Thomas found he had formed, with regard to Portia, just enough habit of mind to be cross that she was not about on Saturday afternoon.

This accumulating worry made Thomas ask himself what on earth had made him go to the door when he might have stayed playing possum. Had the sense of siege in here oppressed him, or had he, in fact, felt lonelier than he thought? The *worry* of sitting facing this patient man! Then he gave Major Brutt a quick, undecided, mean look. One had clearly got the idea this Brutt was out of a job: had he not said something about irons in the fire? That meant he was after something. That was why he had come. *Now*, no doubt, he had something soft in Quayne and Merrett's in view – he would not be the first old buffer who had.

Then, Thomas had a crisis of self-repugnance. Twitching his head away, with a shamefaced movement, from that block of integrity in the armchair, he saw how business had built him, Thomas, into a false position, a state of fortification odious, when he noticed it, to himself. He could only look out through slits at grotesque slits of faces, slits of the view. His vision became, from habit, narrow and falsified. Seeing anything move, even an animal, he thought: What is this meant to lead to? Or a gesture would set him off: Oh, so *that's* what he's after ... Oh, then what *does* he want? Society was self-interest given a pretty gloss. You felt the relentless pressure behind small-talk. Friendships were dotted with null pauses, when one eye in calculation sought the clock. Love seemed the one reprieve from the watchfulness: it annihilated this uneasy knowledge. He could love with regard to nothing else. Therefore he loved without any of that discretion known to more natural natures – which is why astute men are so often betrayed.

Whatever he's after, or not after, he thought, we certainly can't use him. Quayne and Merrett's only wanted flair, and one sort of distilled nervosity. They could use any number of Eddies, but not one Brutt. He felt Brutt ought to try for some sort of area travel in something or other – perhaps, however, he was trying for that already. All he seemed to have to put on the market was (query) experience, that stolid alertness, that pebble-grey direct look that Thomas was finding morally hypnotic. There was, of course, his courage – something now with no context, no function, no outlet, fumbled over, rejected, likely to fetch nothing. Makes of men date, like makes of cars; Major Brutt was a 1914–18 model: there was now no market for that make. In fact, only his steadfast persistence in living made it a pity that he could not be scrapped ... No, we cannot use him. Thomas once more twitched his head. Major Brutt's being (frankly) a discard put the final blot on a world Thomas did not like.

Major Brutt, offered Thomas's cigarette case with rather hostile abruptness, hesitated, then decided to smoke. This ought to steady him. (That he wanted steadying, Thomas had no idea.) The fact, the fact of Thomas, Thomas as Anna's hus-

band, was a lasting shock. Major Brutt remembered Anna as
Pidgeon's lover only. The picture of that great evening together
– Anna, himself, Pidgeon – was framed in his mind, and could
not be taken down – it was the dear possession of someone with
few possessions, carried from place to place. When he had come
on Anna in the Empire foyer, it could be no one but Pidgeon
that she was waiting for: his heart had gone up because he
would soon see Pidgeon. Then Thomas had come through the
foyer, spoken about the taxi, put his hand under Anna's elbow
with a possessing smile. That was the shock (though she had
first said she was married), and it was a shock still. That one
great evening – hers, Pidgeon's, his own – had made one continuous thread through his own uncertain days. He would recall
it at times when he felt low. Anna's marriage to Pidgeon had
been one great thing he had to look forward to. When Pidgeon
kept saying nothing, and still said nothing, Major Brutt only
thought they were waiting a long time. There is no fidelity like
the fidelity of the vicarious lover who has once seen a kiss. By
being married to Thomas, for having been married to Thomas
for eight London years, Anna annihilated a great part of Major
Brutt. He thought, from her unhappily calm smile in the Empire foyer, that she must see what she had done to him; he
had taken some of her kindness for penitence. When later, back
in her home, she with her woman's good manners had led him
to talk of Pidgeon, their sole mutual friend, she had laid waste
still more. He had not known how to bear it when she spoke of
Pidgeon and the plate and the orange. Only Portia's presence
made him bear it at all.

But a man must live. Not for nothing do we invest so much
of ourselves in other people's lives – or even in momentary pictures of people we do not know. It cuts both ways: the happy
group inside the lighted window, the figure in long grass in the
orchard seen from the train stay and support us in our dark
hours. Illusions are art, for the feeling person, and it is by art
that we live, if we do. It is the emotion to which we remain
faithful, after all: we are taught to recover it in some other
place. Major Brutt, brought that first night to Windsor Terrace
at the height of his inner anguish on Pidgeon's account, already

began to attach himself to that warm room. For hospitality, and that little girl on the rug, he began to abandon Pidgeon already. Even he had a ruthlessness in his sentiments – and he had been living alone in a Cromwell Road hotel. The glow on the rug, Anna on the sofa with her pretty feet up, Thomas nosing so kindly round for cigars, Portia nursing her elbows as though they had been a couple of loved cats – here was the focus of the necessary dream. All the same it was Thomas he, still, could not quite away with. He hoped, by taking Thomas's cigarette, by being a little further in debt to him, to feel more naturally to him, as man to man.

He looked on Thomas as someone who held the prize. But in this darkening light of Saturday afternoon, loneliness lay on his study like a cloud. The tumbled papers, the ash, the empty coffee-cup made Pidgeon's successor look untriumphant, as though he had never held any prize. Even the fire only grinned, like a fire in an advertisement. Major Brutt, whose thought could puzzle out nothing, had, in regard to people, a sort of sense of the weather. He was aware of the tension behind Thomas's manners, of the uneasy and driven turnings of his head. Without nerves, Major Brutt had those apprehensions that will make an animal suddenly leave, or refuse to enter, a room. Was Pidgeon in here with them, overtowering Thomas, while Thomas did the honours to Pidgeon's friend? He had decided to smoke, so he pulled at his cigarette, reflecting the fire in his fixed, pebble-grey eyes. He saw that he ought to go soon – but not yet.

Thomas, meanwhile, gave a finished representation of a man happily settling into a deep chair. He gave, inadvertently, one overstated yawn, then had to say, to excuse this: 'It's too bad, Anna's not in.'

'Oh well, of course, I chanced that. Just dropping in.'

'It's too bad Portia's not in. I've no idea where she's gone.'

'I daresay she goes about quite a bit?'

'No, not really. Not yet. She's a bit young.'

'There's something sweet about her, if I may say so,' said Major Brutt, lighting up.

'Yes, there is, rather ... She's my sister, you know.'

'That's awfully nice.'

'Or rather, my half-sister.'

'Comes to much the same thing.'

'Does it?' said Thomas. 'Yes, I suppose it does. In a way, it feels a bit funny though. For one thing, she and I are a half generation out. However, it seems to work out all right. We thought we might try it here for a year or so, see how she liked things with us, and so on. She's an orphan, you see – which is pretty tough on her. We had never seen as much as we'd have liked to of her, because my father liked living abroad. We rather felt she might find us a bit of a proposition. Having just lost her mother, and not being grown up yet, so not able to go about with Anna, we thought she might find London a bit ... well – However, it seems to work out all right. We found some quite good classes for her to go to, so she's been making friends with girls of her own age. ...'

Overcome by the dullness of what he had been saying, Thomas trailed off and slumped further back in his chair. But Major Brutt, having listened with close attention, evidently expected more to come. 'Nice to have a kid like that to keep one cheerful,' he said. 'How old did you say she was?'

'Sixteen.'

'She must be great company for – for Mrs Quayne.'

'For Anna? Oh yes. Funny you and Anna running into each other. She's slack about keeping up with her old friends, and at the same time she certainly misses them.'

'It was nice of her to remember my name, I thought. You see, we'd only met once.'

'Oh yes, with Robert Pidgeon. Sorry I never met him. But he seems to move round, and I'm rooted here.' Casting at Major Brutt one last uneasy flash of suspicion, Thomas added: 'I've got this business, you know.'

'Is that so?' said Major Brutt politely. He knocked off his ash into the heavy glass tray. 'Excellent, if you like living in town.'

'You'd rather get out somewhere?'

'Yes, I must say I would. But that all depends, at the moment, on what happens to come along. I've got a good many –'

'Irons in the fire? I'm sure you are absolutely right.'

'Yes, if one thing doesn't turn up, it's all the more likely that another will ... The only trouble is, I've got a bit out of touch.'

'Oh yes?'

'Yes, I've stuck out there abroad too long, it rather seems. I'd rather like, now, to be in touch for a bit; I'd rather like to stay for a bit in this country.'

'But in touch with what?' said Thomas. 'What do you think there is, then?'

Some obscure hesitation, some momentary doubt made Major Brutt frown, then look across at Thomas in a more personal manner than he had looked yet. But his look was less clear – the miasma thickening in the study had put a film over him. 'Well,' he said, 'there must be something going on. You know – in a general way, I mean. You know, something you all –'

'We all? We who?'

'Well, you, for instance,' Major Brutt said. 'There must be something – that's why I feel out of touch. I know there must be something all you people get together about.'

'There may be,' said Thomas, 'but I don't think there is. As a matter of fact, I don't think we get together. We none of us seem to feel very well, and I don't think we want each other to know it. I suppose there is nothing so disintegrating as competitiveness and funk, and that's what we all feel. The ironical thing is that everyone else gets their knives into us bourgeoisie on the assumption we're having a good time. At least, I suppose that's the assumption. They seem to have no idea that we don't much care for ourselves. We weren't nearly so much hated when we gave them more to hate. But it took guts to be even the fools our fathers were. We're just a lousy pack of little Christopher Robins. Oh, we've got to live, but I doubt if we see the necessity. The most we can hope is to go on getting away with it till the others get it away from us.'

'I say, don't you take a rather black view of things?'

'What you mean is, I ought to take more exercise? Or Eno's, or something? No, look here, my only point was that I really can't feel you are missing very much. I don't think much goes on – However, Anna might know – Cigarette?'

'No thanks: not at the moment.'

'What's that?' said Thomas sharply.

Major Brutt, sympathetic, also turned his head. They heard a key in the hall door.

'Anna,' Thomas said, with a show of indifference.

'Look here, I feel I probably ought –'

'Nonsense. She'll be delighted.'

'But she's got people with her.' There certainly were voices, low voices, in the hall.

Repeating 'No, stay, do stay,' with enormous concentration, Thomas heaved himself up and went to the study door. He opened the door sharply, as though to quell a riot. Then he exclaimed with extreme flatness: 'Oh ... Hullo, Portia ... oh, *hullo*; good afternoon.'

'Good afternoon,' returned Eddie, with the matey deference he now kept for Thomas out of office hours.

'I say, don't let us disturb you: we're just going out again.' Expertly reaching round Portia, he closed Thomas's hall door behind Thomas's sister. His nonchalance showed the good state of his nerves – for since when had old Thomas taken to popping out? Portia said nothing: close beside Eddie she stood smiling inordinately. To Thomas, these two appeared to be dreadful twins – they held up their heads with the same rather fragile pride; they included him in the same confiding smile. Clearly, they had hoped to creep in unheard – their over-responsiveness to Thomas only showed what a blow Thomas had been. They both glowed from having walked very fast.

Thomas showed what a blow they were by looking heavily past them. He explained: 'I thought you were Anna.'

Eddie said nicely: 'I'm so sorry we're not.'

'Isn't she in?' said Portia mechanically.

'But I'll tell you who *is* here,' said Thomas. 'Major Brutt. Portia, you'd better show up, just for a minute.'

'We – we were just going out.'

'Well, a minute won't hurt you, will it?'

The most stubbornly or darkly drawn-in man has moments when he likes to impose himself, to emerge and be a bully. The diversion of a raindrop from its course down the pane, the

frustration of a pet animal's will in some small way all at once become imperative, if the nature is to fulfil itself. Thomas took pleasure in thrusting Portia into the study, away from Eddie, to talk to Major Brutt. A hand on her shoulder-blade, he pushed her ahead of him with colourless, unadmitted cruelty. Eddie, dogged, determined to be as much *de trop* as he could, followed along behind.

Major Brutt, during the colloquy in the hall, had sat with his knees parted, turning his wrists vaguely, making his cuff-links wink. What he may have heard he shook off, like a dog shaking its ears. The little kid was propelled round the door at him: Thomas then made a pause, then introduced Eddie. Portia and Eddie lined up shoulder to shoulder, smiling at Major Brutt with a captive deference. In their eyes he saw the complicity of a suspended joy.

'I've come crashing round here,' Major Brutt said to Portia. 'Disturbing your brother a good bit, I'm afraid. But your sister-in-law had very kindly said –'

'Oh, I'm sure she did really mean it,' said Portia.

'At all events,' he went on, going on smiling with agonized heartiness, 'she's been well out of it. I gather she's out at lunch. But I've been keeping your brother from forty winks.'

'Not at all,' said Thomas. 'It's been frightfully nice.' He sat down again in his own chair so firmly that Portia and Eddie had either to sit down somewhere also, or else, by going on standing (as they continued to do), to make their semi-absence, their wish to be elsewhere, marked. They stood a foot apart but virtually hand in hand. Portia looked past Eddie liquidly, into nowhere, as though she did not exist because she might not look at him. Eddie began to smoke, but smoked very consciously. This announcement of their attachment – in a way that showed complete indifference to the company – struck on Thomas coldly: one more domestic fatigue. He also wondered how Eddie had the nerve ... To Major Brutt, kinder to love than Thomas, this seemed a holy anomaly.

'And where have you been?' said Thomas – who had, after all, every right to ask.

'Oh, we've been to the Zoo.'

'Wasn't it very cold there?'

They looked at each other, not seeming to know. 'It's all draughts and stinks,' Eddie said. 'But we did think it was pretty, didn't we, Portia?'

Thomas marvelling, thought: He really *has* got a nerve. What happens when Anna comes in?

8

'WHO was that old bird?'

'Major Brutt. He was a friend of someone Anna knew.'

'Who that she knew?'

'His name was Pidgeon.'

Eddie tittered at this, then said: 'Is he dead?'

'Oh no. Major Brutt says he thinks he is very well.'

'I've never heard of Pidgeon,' said Eddie, frowning.

Without guile, she said: 'But do you know all her friends?'

'I said we'd run into someone, you little silly. I told you we would, if we went back.'

'But you did ask me to fetch it –'

'I suppose I did – I must say I think Brutt's a rather nasty old thing. He leers.'

'Oh no, Eddie – he *doesn't*.'

'No, I suppose he doesn't,' said Eddie, looking depressed. 'I suppose he's really much nicer than I am.'

Turning and anxiously eyeing Eddie's forehead, Portia said: 'Today he looked rather sad.'

'You bet he did,' said Eddie. 'He wanted an innings. He may be a great deal nicer than I am, darling, but I do feel I ought to tell you that that sort of person makes me perfectly sick. And look how he'd rattled Thomas – poor old Thomas was all over the place. No, Brutt is a brute. Do you realize, Portia darling, that it is because of there being people like him that there are people like me? How on earth did he get into the house?'

'He said Anna'd asked him to come again.'

'What a cynic Anna is!'

'I do think, Eddie, you are exaggerating.'

'I've got no sense of proportion, thank God. That man palpably loathed me.' Eddie stopped and blew out his lower lip. 'Oh dear,' said Portia, 'I quite wish we hadn't met him.'

'Well, I told you we would if we went back. You know that house is a perfect web.'

'But you said you wanted my diary.'

They were having tea, or rather their tea was ordered, at Madame Tussaud's. Portia, who had not been here before, had been disappointed to find all the waitresses real: there were no deceptions of any kind – all the waxworks were in some other part. He and she sat side by side at a long table intended for a party of four or six. Her diary, fetched from Windsor Terrace, lay still untouched between their elbows, with a strong india-rubber band round it. She said: 'How do you mean that Anna is a cynic?'

'She has depraved reasons for doing the nicest things. However, that doesn't matter to me.'

'If it really doesn't, why does it upset you?'

'After all, darling, she is a human soul. And her character did upset me, at one time. I'm several degrees worse since I started to know her. I wish I had met you sooner.'

'Worse how? Do you think you are wicked?'

Eddie, leaning a little back from the table, looked all round the restaurant, at the lights, at the other tables, at the mirrors, considering the question seriously, as though she had asked him whether he felt ill. Then he returned his eyes closely to Portia's face, and said with an almost radiant smile: 'Yes.'

'In what way?'

But a waitress came with a tray and put down the teapot, the hot-water jug, a dish of crumpets, a plate of fancy cakes. By the time she had done, the moment had gone by. Eddie raised a lid and stared at the crumpets. 'Why on earth', he said, 'didn't she bring salt?'

'Wave to her and ask her – Shall I really pour out? ... But, Eddie, I can't see you are wicked. Wicked in what way?'

'Well, what do you hate about me?'

'I don't think I –'

'Try the other way round – what do you like least?'

She thought for a moment, then said: 'The way you keep making faces for no particular reason.'

'I do that when I wish I had no face. I can't bear people getting a line on me.'

'But it attracts attention. Naturally people notice.'

'All the same, it throws them on the wrong-track. My goodness, they think, he's going to have a nerve-storm; he may be really going to have a fit. That excites them, and they start to play up themselves. So then that gives me time to collect myself, till quite soon I feel like ice.'

'I see – but –'

'No, you see the fact is, darling, people do rattle me – You do see?'

'Yes, I do.'

'It's vitally important that you should. In a way, I believe I behave worse with other people, Anna for instance, when you're there, because I always feel you will know why, and to feel that rather gins me up. You must never make me feel you don't understand.'

'What would happen if I did make you feel I didn't?'

Eddie said: 'I should stay unreal for ever.' He rolled her gloves up into a tight ball, and squeezed them in the palm of one hand. Then he looked in horror past the brim of her hat. She turned her head to see what he saw, and they both saw themselves in a mirror.

'I feel I shall always understand what you feel. Does it matter if I don't sometimes understand what you *say*?'

'Not in the least, darling,' said Eddie briskly. 'You see, there is really nothing intellectual between us. In fact, I don't know why I talk to you at all. In many ways I should so much rather not.'

'But we have to do something.'

'I feel it is a waste of you. You puzzle so much, with your dear little goofy face. Is it simply you've never met anybody like me?'

99

'But you said there wasn't anybody like you.'

'But there are lots of people who imitate what I really am. I suppose you haven't met any of them, either – Look, darling, do pour out; the tea's getting cold.'

'I hope I shall do it well,' said Portia, grasping the metal tea-pot handle in her handkerchief.

'Oh Portia, has no one really taken you out to tea before?'

'Not by myself.'

'Nor to any other meal? You do make me feel happy!' He watched her slowly filling his cup with a gingerly, wobbling stream of tea. 'For one thing, I feel I can stay still. You're the only person I know I need do nothing *about*. All the other people I know make me feel I have got to sing for my supper. And I feel that you and I are the same: we are both rather wicked or rather innocent. You looked pleased when I said Anna was depraved.'

'Oh, you didn't; you said she was a cynic.'

'When I think of the money I've wasted sending Anna flowers!'

'Were they very expensive?'

'Well, they were for me. It just shows what a fool I've learnt to be. I haven't been out of debt now for three years, and I've got not a soul to back me – No, it's all right darling, I can pay for this tea – To lose my head is a thing I literally can't afford. You must hear of the way I keep on living on people? But what it *has* come to is: I've been bought up. They all think I want what they've got and I haven't, so they think if they get me that is a fair deal.'

'I suppose it is, in a way.'

'Oh, you don't understand, darling – Would you think I was vain if I said I was good-looking?'

'No. I think you are very good-looking, too.'

'Well, I am, you see, and I've got all this charm, and I can excite people. They don't really notice my brain – they are always insulting me. Everyone hates my brain, because I don't sell that. That's the underground reason why everyone hates me. I sometimes hate it myself. I wouldn't be with these pigs if I hadn't first been so clever. Last time I went home, do you

know, Portia, my younger brother laughed at my soft hands.'

Portia had not for some time looked straight at Eddie, for fear her too close attention might make him stop. She had cut her crumpet up into little pieces; she nibbled abstractedly, dipping each piece in salt. When the first crumpet was eaten she paused, wiped her fingers on the paper napkin, then took a long drink of tea. Drinking, she looked at Eddie over her cup. She put down her cup and said: 'Life is always so complicated.'

'It's not merely life – It's me.'

'I expect it is you *and* people.'

'I expect you are right, you sweet beautiful angel. I have only had to do with people who liked me, and no one nice ever does.'

She looked at him with big eyes.

'Except you, of course – Look, if you ever stop you never will let me see you *have* stopped, will you?'

Portia glanced to see if Eddie's cup were empty. Then she cast her look down at her diary – keeping her eyes fixed on the black cover, she said: 'You said I was beautiful.'

'Did I? Turn round and let me look.'

She turned an at once proud and shrinking face. But he giggled: 'Darling, you've got salt stuck all over the butter on your chin, like real snow on one of those Christmas cards. Let me wipe it off – stay still.'

'But I had been going to eat another crumpet.'

'Oh, in that case it would be rather a waste – No, it's no good; I'd hate you to give me serious thoughts.'

'How often do you have them?'

'Often – I swear I do.'

'How old are you, Eddie?'

'Twenty-three.'

'Goodness,' she said gravely, taking another crumpet.

While she ate, Eddie studied her gleamingly. He said: 'You've got a goofy but an inspired face. Understanding just washes over it. Why am I ever with anybody but you? Whenever I talk to other people, they jeer in their minds and think I am being dramatic. Well, I am dramatic – why not? *I* am dramatic. The

whole of Shakespeare is about me. All the others, of course, feel that too, which is why they are all dead nuts on Shakespeare. But because I show it when they haven't got the nerve to, they all jump on me. Blast their silly faces –'

While she ate, she kept her eyes on his forehead, at present tense with high feeling, but ventured to say nothing. Her meticulous observation of him made her like somebody at a play in a foreign language of which they know not one word – the action has to be followed as closely as one can. Just a shade unnerved by her look he broke off and said: 'Do I ever bore you, darling?'

'No – I was just thinking that, except for Lilian, this is the first conversation with anybody I've had. Since I came to London, I mean. It's much more the sort of conversation I have in my head.'

'It's a lot more cheerful than the conversations in *my* head. In those, reproaches are being showered on me. I don't get on at all well with myself – But I thought you said you talked to Matchett at nights?'

'Yes – but she's not in London, she's in the house. And lately, she's been more cold with me.'

Eddie's face darkened at once. 'Because of me, I suppose?'

Portia hesitated. 'She never much likes my friends.'

Annoyed by her fencing, he said: 'You haven't got any friends.'

'There's Lilian.'

He scowled this aside. 'No, the trouble with *her* is, she's a jealous old cow. And a snob, like all servants. You've been too nice to her.'

'She was so nice to my father.'

'I'm sorry, darling – But listen: for God's sake never talk about me. Never to anyone.'

'How could I, Eddie? I never possibly would.'

'I could kill people when I think what they would think.'

'Oh Eddie, mind – you've splashed tea on my diary! Matchett only knows you because she came on your letter.'

'You *must not* leave those about!'

'I didn't: she found it where it was put.'

'Where?'

'Under my pillow.'

'Darling!' said Eddie, melting for half a moment.

'I was there all the time, and she didn't do more than hold it. All she knows is, I've had a letter from you.'

'But she knows where it was.'

'I'm sure she would never tell. She likes knowing things they don't, about me.'

'I daresay you're right: she's got a mouth like a trap. And I've seen her looking at Anna. She'll keep this to use in her own way. Oh, do beware of old women – you've no notion how they batten on things. Lock everything up; hide everything! Don't bat an eyelid, ever.'

'As if this was a plot?'

'We are a plot. Keep plotting the whole time.'

She looked anxious and said: 'But then, shall you and I have any time left?'

'Left for what, do you mean?'

'I mean, for ourselves.'

He swept this aside and said: 'Plot – It's a revolution: it's our life. The whole pack are against us. So hide, hide everything.'

'Why?'

'You've no idea what people are like.'

Her mind went back. 'Major Brutt noticed, I think.'

'Idealistic old wart-hog! And Thomas caught us – I told you we should never have gone in.'

'But you did say you wanted my diary.'

'Well, we were mad. You only wait till Anna has had a word with Brutt. Shall I show you the talk I and Anna will have then?' Eddie posed himself, leaning sideways on one elbow with Anna's rather heavy nonchalant grace. He drew his fingers idly across his forehead, putting back an imaginary wave of hair. Seeming to let the words drop with a charming reluctance, he began: ' "Now Eddie, you mustn't be cross with me. This bores me just as much as it bores you. But I feel –" '

Portia cast an anxious look round the tea-room. 'Oh, ought you to imitate Anna here. . .?'

'I may not feel in the mood to do it again. As a rule, the thought of Anna makes me much too angry. I should like you to hear the things she would say to me if she got this un-paralleled opening ... She would say, to remember you're quite a child. She would imply she wondered what I could see in you, and imply that of course I must be up to *something*, and that she only just wondered what it was. She would say that of course I could count on her not to say a word to you about what I am really like. She would say that of course she quite realized that she and Thomas were dull compared to me, because I was a genius, too superior to do any work that she did not come and offer me on a plate. She would say, of course, people who pay their bills *are* dull, Then she would say she quite saw it must be a strain on me, having to live up to my reputation, and that she saw I must have what stimulus I could get. Last of all, she would say, "And, of course, she *is* Thomas's sister." '

'Well, I don't see the point of any of that.'

'No, you wouldn't, darling. But I would. Anna'd be on the sofa; I should sit screwed round on one of her bloody little yellow chairs. When I tried to get up she would say: "You do make me so tired." She'd smoke. Like this' – Eddie opened his cigarette case, raked the contents over languidly with his finger-tips, his head on one side, as though playing the harp, selected one cigarette, looked at it cryptically, fastidiously lit it, and once more shook back an imaginary lock of hair. 'She would say,' he said, ' "You'd probably better go now – Portia's probably waiting down in the hall." '

'Oh Eddie – would she ever say that?'

'She'd say anything. The thing about Anna is, she loves making a tart of another person. She'd never dare be a proper tart herself.'

Portia looked puzzled. 'But I'm certain you like her.'

'Yes, I do in a way. That is why she annoys me so.'

'You once said she'd been very kind.'

'Indeed she has – that's her way of getting under my skin. Darling, didn't you think me being Anna was funny?'

'No, not really. I didn't think you enjoyed it.'

'Well, it was: it was very funny,' said Eddie defiantly.

Then he made several faces, pulling his features all ways, as though to flake off from them the last figments of Anna. The impersonation had (as Portia noticed) had fury behind it: each hypothetical arrow to him from Anna had been winged by a demoniac smile. Now he pulled his cup towards him and abruptly drank up some cold tea. He looked so threatening, Portia thought for a moment he might be going to spit the tea out – as though he were no more than rinsing his mouth with it. But he did swallow the tea, and after that smiled, though in a rather fagged-out way, like an actor coming off after a big scene. At the same time, he looked relieved, as though he had shot a weight off, and pious, as though a duty had been discharged. He seemed now to exist in a guiltless vacuum. At last he turned her way and sat filling his eyes with Portia, as though it were good to be home again.

After a pause he said: 'Yes, I really do quite like Anna. But we have got to have a villain of some sort.'

But Portia had a slower reaction time. During the villain's speech, while she ate crumpet, her brows had met in a rather uncertain line. While not really surprised, she had seemed to be hypnotized by this view of Anna. She was disturbed, and at the same time exhilarated, like a young tree tugged all ways in a vortex of wind. The force of Eddie's behaviour whirled her free of a hundred puzzling humiliations, of her hundred failures to take the ordinary cue. She could meet the demands he made with the natural genius of the friend and lover. The impetus under which he seemed to move made life fall, round him and her, into a new poetic order at once. Any kind of policy in the region of feeling would have been fatal in any lover of his – you had to yield to the wind. Portia's unpreparedness, her lack of policy – which had made Windsor Terrace, for her, the court of an incomprehensible law – with Eddie stood her in good stead. She had no point to stick to, nothing to unlearn. She had been born docile. The momentarily anxious glances she cast him had only zeal behind them, no crucial perplexity. By making herself so much his open piano that she felt her lips smile by reflex, as though they were his lips, she felt herself learn and gain him: this was Eddie. What he said, how

he looked was becoming inevitable. From the first, he had not been unfamiliar to her. It might be said that, for the first time since Irene's death, she felt herself in the presence of someone ordinary.

Innocence so constantly finds itself in a false position that inwardly innocent people learn to be disingenuous. Finding no language in which to speak in their own terms they resign themselves to being translated imperfectly. They exist alone; when they try to enter into relations they compromise falsifyingly – through anxiety, through desire to impart and to feel warmth. The system of our affections is too corrupt for them. They are bound to blunder, then to be told they cheat. In love, the sweetness and violence they have to offer involves a thousand betrayals for the less innocent. Incurable strangers to the world, they never cease to exact a heroic happiness. Their singleness, their ruthlessness, their one continuous wish makes them bound to be cruel, and to suffer cruelty. The innocent are so few that two of them seldom meet – when they do meet, their victims lie strewn all round.

Portia and Eddie, side by side at the table, her diary between them under one of her hands, turned on each other eyes in which two relentless looks held apart for a moment, then became one. To generate that one look, their eyes seemed for the first time to be using their full power. The look held a sort of superb mutual greeting rather than any softness of love. You would have said that two accomplices had for the first time spoken aloud to each other of their part in the same crime, or that two children had just discovered their common royal birth. On the subject of love, there was nothing to say: they seemed to have no projects and no desires. Their talk today had been round an understood pact: at this moment, they saluted its significance.

Portia's life, up to now, had been all subtle gentle compliance, but she had been compliant without pity. Now she saw with pity, but without reproaching herself, all the sacrificed people – Major Brutt, Lilian, Matchett, even Anna – that she had stepped over to meet Eddie. And she knew that there would be more of this, for sacrifice is not in a single act. Windsor

Terrace would not do well at her hands, and in this there was no question of justice: no outside people deserve the bad deal they got from love. Even Anna had shown her a sort of immoral kindness, and, however much Matchett's love had been Matchett's unburdening, it had *been* love: one must desert that too.

For Eddie, Portia's love seemed to refute the accusations that had been brought against him for years, and the accusations he had brought against himself. He had not yet told her of half the indignation he felt. Older than she was, he had for longer suffered the guilty plausibility of the world. He had felt, not so much that he was in the right as that he was inevitable. He had gone wrong through dealing with other people in terms that he found later were not their own. However kind seemed the bosom he chose to lean his head on, he had found himself subject to preposterous rulings even there – and this had soon made the bosom vile for him. With love, a sort of maiden virtue of spirit stood outside his calamitous love affairs – the automatic quick touches he gave people (endearments, smiles to match smiles, the meaning-unmeaning use of his eyes) were his offensive-defensive, in defence of something they must not touch. His pretty ways had almost lost correspondence with appetite; his body was losing its naïvety. His real naïvety stayed in the withheld part of him, and hoped for honour and peace. Though he felt cut apart from his father and mother, in one sense he had never left home. He hated Anna, in so far as he did hate Anna, because he saw in her eyes a perpetual 'What next?' Himself, he saw no Next, but a continuous Now.

He looked down at Portia's hand and said: 'What a fat diary!'

Lifting her hand, she uncovered the black-backed book. 'It's more than half full', she said, 'already.'

'When that's done, you're going to start another?'

'Oh yes, I think so: things are always happening.'

'But suppose you stopped minding whether they did?'

'There would always be lunch and lessons and dinner. There have been days that were simply that already, but in that case I always leave a blank page.'

'Do you think they were worth a whole blank page?'

'Oh yes, because they were days, after all.'

Eddie picked the diary up and weighed it between his hands. 'And this is your thoughts, too?' he said.

'Some. But you make me wonder if I might stop thinking.'

'No, I like you to think. If you stopped, I should feel as though my watch had stopped in the night ... Which of your thoughts are these?'

'My more particular ones.'

'Darling, I love you to want me to take it home ... But supposing I went and left it in a bus?'

'It's got my name and address, inside: it would probably come back. But perhaps, though, you could put it in your pocket?' They squeezed the note-book into his overcoat pocket. 'As a matter of fact,' she said, 'now there is you, I may not want my diary so much.'

'But we shan't often meet.'

'I could keep what I think for you.'

'No, write it down, then show me. I like thoughts when they were thought.'

'But, in a way, that would not be quite the same thing. I mean, it would alter my diary. Up to now, it's been written just for itself. If I'm to keep on writing the same way, I shall have to imagine you do not exist.'

'*I* don't make you different.'

'You make me not alone. Being that was part of my diary. When I first came to London, I was the only person in the world.'

'Look – what will you write in while I've got this book? Shall we go to Smith's and buy you another?'

'Smith's near here is shut on Saturday afternoon. I don't think, anyhow, I shall write about today.'

'No, don't; you're perfectly right. I don't want you to *write* about you and me. In fact you must never write about me at all. Will you promise me you will never do that?'

'Why not?'

'I just don't like the idea. No, just write about what happens.'

Write about lessons, and those sickening talks I'm certain you have with Lilian, and what there is for meals, and what the rest of them say. But *swear* you won't write down what you feel.'

'You don't know yet if I do.'

'I hate writing; I hate art – there's always something else there. I won't have you choosing words about me. If you ever start that, your diary will become a horrible trap, and I shan't feel safe with you any more. I like you to think, in a sort of way; I like to think of you going, like a watch. But between you and me there must never be any thoughts. And I detest after-thoughts. In fact, I'm just as glad to be taking this book right away from you, even for a few days. Now, I suppose, you don't understand what I'm saying?'

'No, but it doesn't really matter.'

'The chap *you* ought to talk to is Major Brutt ... Oh, heavens!'

'Why?'

'It's six. I ought to be somewhere else. I must go – Here, angel, take your gloves ... *Now*, what's the matter?'

'You won't forget it's in your overcoat pocket?'

9

THE DIARY

Monday

THIS diary has come back from Eddie by post. He did not write any letter as he did not have time. The parcel had the office label outside. I shall have to write hard now, as I will have missed nine days.

The white rug from by my bed has gone away to be cleaned where I upset the varnish for my bears. Matchett has put a red one that pricks my feet.

Today we did Umbrian Art History, Book Keeping, and German Composition.

Tuesday

Eddie has not said about the diary yet. Lilian was bilious in lessons and had to go out, she says when she has feelings it makes her bilious. Today when I got home Anna was out, so I could have tea down with Matchett. She was busy mending Anna's purple chiffon dress so did not ask me anything at all. When Anna came in she sent for me to come up and said she meant to take me to a concert this evening as she had a spare ticket. She looked put out.

Today we did English Essay, First Aid, and a Lecture on Racine. I must dress for the concert now.

Wednesday

Eddie has not said about the diary yet. This morning Lilian and I were late for the first class, her mother is putting her on a diet. Last night when I was in the taxi with Anna she said she hoped I had enjoyed Eddie's and my walk. I said yes, and she said, Eddie says he did. So I looked out of the window. She said she had a headache, and I said then didn't the concert make it worse, and she said yes, naturally it did. It was a disappointment having to take me.

Today we did Hygiene and French Composition about Racine, and were taken to look at pictures of Umbrian Art at the National Gallery.

Tonight Thomas and Anna are going out to dinner. I do wonder if Matchett will say good night. I do wish my white rug would come back.

Thursday

Today I have got a letter from Eddie, he still does not say about this diary. He says he had lunch with Anna and that she was nice. He says he did think of ringing me up, but did not. He does not say why. He says he feels he is starting a new life.

I do wonder who it was who did not go to that concert with Anna after all.

He says we must meet soon.

Today we did essays on our favourite Umbrian Art, and had to say what its characteristics were. We did Heine and were given our German Compositions back. We had a Lecture on Events of the Week.

Friday

I have written to Eddie but not about this diary.

I wrote to Eddie at half past four, when I got in, then went out again to buy a stamp to post it. Matchett did not hear the door either time, or at least she did not come up. Having tea with Anna were two new people who did not know if they ought to talk to me. Anna did not make any special impression on them, and they did not make any special impression on her. I did not stay there when I had had my tea.

It felt funny to come in twice, because once I am in I am generally in. When I came in after buying the stamp I felt still odder than I generally do, and the house was still more like always than usual. It always gets more so in the afternoon. When Thomas comes in he looks as though he was smelling something he thought he might not be let eat. This house makes a smell of feeling. Since I have known Eddie I ask myself what this smell is more.

Today we got our Essays on Racine back, and some of the girls discussed what they had put. We did Metternich and were taken out to a Lecture on the Appreciation of Bach.

Tomorrow will be another Saturday.

Saturday

I got a letter from Eddie, saying about Sunday. He said to ring him up if I could not go, but as I can I need not ring up. Before lunch Thomas and Anna drove away in the car, they are going off for the week-end. Anna said I could ask Lilian to tea, and Thomas gave me five shillings to go to the pictures with, he said he did hope I should be all right. Lilian cannot, so I am by the study fire. I like a day when there is some sort of tomorrow.

Sunday

I shall just put 'Sunday', Eddie prefers that.

Monday

Today we began Siennese Art, and did Book Keeping, and read a German play. Anna is having quite a big dinner party, she says I should not really enjoy myself.

Anyhow I should not mind, after yesterday.

Tuesday

Today I have had a sort of conversation with Thomas. When he came in he rang to ask if Anna was there, so I said no and said should I come down and he was not sure but said yes. He was leaning on his desk reading the evening paper, and when I came in he said it was warmer wasn't it? He said in fact he felt stuffy. As he had not seen me last night, because of the dinner party, he asked had I had a nice week-end? He said he hoped I had not been at all lonely, so I said oh no. He asked if I thought Eddie was nice. I said oh yes, and he said, he was round here yesterday, wasn't he? I said oh yes and said we had sat down here in the study, and that I did hope Thomas did not mind people sitting down here in his study. He said oh no, oh no in a sort of far-off voice. He said he supposed I and Eddie were rather friends, and I said yes we were. Then he went back to reading the evening paper as if there was something new in it.

He did half want me to go, and I did half want to go too, but I did not. This was the first time Thomas had asked me something he did seem to want to know. I was pleased to hear the name of Eddie and sat on the arm of the armchair. When he wanted a cigarette himself he started to offer me one by mistake. I could not help laughing. He said, I forgot, then said, no, don't start being grown-up. He said, you know mistakes run in our family. He said when my father started getting to know my mother, while my father still lived in Dorset with Mrs Quayne, my father started to smoke a lot more. He said my father got so ashamed of smoking so much that he started to save his cigarette stumps up in an envelope, then buried them in the garden. Because it was summer with no fires to burn them in, and he didn't want Matchett to count the stumps. I said, how

did Thomas know, and he gave a sort of laugh and said, I once caught him at it. He said, my father did not like being caught, but to Thomas it only seemed a joke.

Thomas said he did not know what had put this into his head and after that he gave me a sort of look when he did not think I was looking. All Thomas's looks, except ones at Anna, are at people not looking. But he did not mind when he found I was looking. After all he and I have our father. Though he and Anna have got that thing together, there is not the same thing inside him and Anna, like that same thing inside him and me. He said in a sort of quick way that was near me, I hope Eddie is polite? I said, what did he mean? And he said, well, I don't know Eddie, does he try it on? He said, no you probably don't know what I mean, I said no, and he said in that case it was all right, he supposed. I said, we talked, and Thomas looked at the rug, as though he knew where we had sat, and said, oh did you, I see.

Then Thomas sort of rumpled the rug up with his heel, as if he did not like people to have sat there. That lamp makes Thomas's face all bags and lines, as if he was alone in his room. He said oh well, we shall see how you make out. He took a book up and said it was a mistake to love any person, I said it is all right if you are married, isn't it? And he said quickly, oh of course, *that* is all right. I heard a taxi stopping like one of Anna's, so I said I must go and I went up. I felt so like Thomas I had been quite glad to hear the taxi stop.

Wednesday

Today we did Hygiene and French Elocution, and were taken to the National Gallery to look at pictures of Siennese Art. On the way to the National Gallery, Lilian said, what ever was on my mind? I said nothing, but she said that I was not attending. After the National Gallery she asked me to come to Peter Jones's with her to help her choose a semi-evening dress. Lilian's mother lets her choose her clothes so as to let her form her taste. But Lilian has got taste. I said I must telephone to Matchett, and Lilian said that the day might come when it would be awkward for me having to do that. Lilian chose a

beautiful blue dress that just goes on her figure and cost four guineas.

When I got back I heard Anna in the study. I have not seen Thomas since yesterday.

Thursday

I got a letter from Eddie to ask if anyone had asked about Sunday. He says he drew a picture for me, but he forgot to put that in. He says next week-end he has got to be away.

My white rug has come back, it is fluffier than it was, it is fluffy like the underneath of a cat. I hope I shall not upset something on it again.

Today we did Essays on Siennese Art, we were asked to say what characteristics it had got that Umbrian Art has not got. We had a Lecture on Events of the Week, and a lady to teach us to read out.

Lilian's mother says her blue dress is too clinging, but Lilian does not agree that it is.

Tonight there is quite a fog.

Friday

When I woke my window was like a brown stone, and I could hardly see the rest of the room. The whole house was just like that, it was not like night but like air being ill. While I was having breakfast, I could just see people holding our railings tight. Thomas has his breakfast after I have mine, but today he came and said, this must be your first fog. Then Anna sent down to say, would I rather not go to Miss Paullie's, but I said, oh no, I would rather go. She sent down another message to say Matchett had better go with me, then. Thomas said, she's quite right, you'll never see the traffic, you'll just have to push it back with your hand. And of course Matchett's hand is stronger than mine.

The walk there was just like an adventure. Outside the park gate there were fires burning, Matchett said they were flares. She made me wrap my mouth up and not speak, or I should swallow the fog. Half way there we took a taxi, and Matchett sat straight up as if she was driving the taxi herself. She still

made me not speak. When we got to Miss Paullie's, half the girls had not got there at all. We had the lights on all day, and it felt more like a holiday. At the end of it there was not so much fog left, but all the same Matchett came to fetch me home.

We were to have had a lecture on the Appreciation of Mozart, but because of the fog we had a Debate on Consistency being the Hobgoblin of Small Minds. We also wrote essays on Metternich's policy.

Tonight Anna and Thomas stayed at home for dinner. She said that whenever there was a fog she always felt it was something that she had done, but she did not seem to mean this seriously. Thomas said he supposed most people felt the same and Anna said she was certain they did not. Then we sat in the drawing-room, and they wished I was not there.

Tomorrow is Saturday, but nothing will happen.

Saturday

I was quite right in saying nothing would happen, even the fog had gone, though it has left a brown stain. Thomas and Anna went away for the week-end, but this time by a train. I sat in the drawing-room and started *Great Expectations*. Matchett was busy with Anna's clothes. I went down to her for tea, she said, well, *you're* quite a ghost. But really it is this house that is like that. Phyllis invited me in to hear the kitchen gramophone. They can only play that when Anna is away.

Until I went out with Eddie I did not feel like this, unless I felt like this without knowing.

Sunday

This time this day last week.

This morning I went for a walk in the park. It was rather empty. Dogs kept running round till they got lost and people whistled, and everything smelt of clay. I looked at the places we liked best, but they were not the same. Some Sundays are very sad. In the afternoon Matchett took me on a bus to afternoon service at St Paul's Cathedral. They sang 'Abide With Me'. On the way home Matchett said, did I know Thomas and Anna were going away in April? She said, they're set on going abroad.

This was a surprise. She said, the way I was always one to notice, she wondered I hadn't picked anything up. She said, no doubt you'll be told in their good time. I said, shall I stay here? And she said, you can't do that, I'll be spring cleaning the house. I said, well I do wonder, but she just shut her mouth. The streets outside the bus looked much darker, because of all the shops being shut.

I wish someone liked me so much that they would come to the door when I was out and leave surprises for me on the hall table, to find when I came in.

When we got back from St Paul's, Matchett went in at the basement, but she made me go in at the front door with my key.

After supper, I sat on our rug in front of Thomas's fire. I thought some of the things that Eddie had told me on this rug.

His father is a builder.

When he was a child he knew pieces of the Bible straight off by heart.

He is quite afraid of the dark.

His two favourite foods are cheese straws and jellied *consommé*.

He would not really like to be very rich.

He says that when you love someone all your saved-up wishes start coming out.

He does not like being laughed at, so he pretends he wants people to laugh at him.

He has thirty-six ties.

Written down these look like the characteristics of things we have to write down at lessons. I do wonder if it would ever strike Eddie to leave a surprise for me on the table when I was out.

Monday

Eddie wrote to me while he was away. He says he is with people he does not like at all. He asks me to ring him up at the office and say what evening Anna will be out, but I do not know how to find out.

Today we did more about Siennese Art, Book Keeping, and

German Composition. Lilian was not waiting in the churchyard, in fact she got to lessons late. She has been upset by an actor, and asked me to tea with her tomorrow. When I got back Anna was quite pleased and told me about her week-end away as if I was St Quentin. Perhaps she is pleased about going to go abroad. She cannot tell me this till she thinks what to do with me.

Tuesday

Oh, it is just like an answer to a prayer, Major Brutt has sent me a jigsaw puzzle. I found it on the table when I came in. He says he would like to imagine me doing it.

Today we did English Essay and First Aid, and were taken to see *Le Cid* at a girls' school. Then I went to tea with Lilian for her to tell me about the actor. She was introduced to him somewhere, then wrote to him to say that she did admire his art, because she does admire it very much. The actor did not answer till she wrote the third time, then he invited Lilian to tea. She wore her blue dress with a coatee over it. There were other people at tea, but he asked her to stay on, and then he behaved in an awful way. She says he was passionate. Lilian was upset, and she says when she got home she wrote him two letters explaining the way she felt. But he did not answer either of the letters, and Lilian thinks now she must have hurt his feelings. This is making her quite bilious again.

No table in my room looks large enough to hold the whole of my jigsaw. I wonder if Matchett would mind if I did it on the floor.

Wednesday

Matchett is sending Anna's white velvet dress to the express cleaners, because Anna has to wear it tomorrow night. I said here, and Matchett said, no, out. So I ought to tell Eddie, I said I would.

Today we did Hygiene and French Elocution and were taken to look at historical dresses at the London Museum, which made a change. We also looked at a model of London burning, and

Miss Paullie said we must all do all that we could to prevent a future war.

I have telephoned to Eddie.

Thursday

Eddie says our lies are not our fault. So I am supposed to be going out with Lilian. They say that will be all right so long as I'm in by ten. I shall have to get to Lilian's house on the way back, because they might send Matchett to fetch me there. But where Eddie lives is quite somewhere else. What shall I do if I have not enough money?

Friday

Yesterday was all quite all right.

Saturday

This morning Anna took me out shopping. This afternoon, Thomas took me to the Zoo. She let me choose what we would have for lunch. Have they been saying things to each other, or have they got to tell me they are going away?

Sunday

They took me with them to lunch with people who live in Kent. So most of the day I have sat in the car and thought, except when we got out to have lunch. Anna and Thomas sat in front of the car, every now and then he said, how is she getting on? So Anna would turn round and have a look.

Since we got back, I have been getting on with my puzzle.

Last Thursday evening, when I first got to Eddie's, it was not like where I imagined he lived. He does not like his room and I'm sure it knows. He showed me all his books and said he was so glad I was not fond of reading at all. We had very nice cold foods off cardboard dishes, Eddie had thought of macaroons for me, and we then made coffee on his gas ring. He asked if I could cook, and I said my mother did when she lived in Notting Hill Gate. There were forks but he could only find one knife, fortunately the ham was in ready-made slices. He said he had never had a person to supper before, when he is alone he goes

to a restaurant, and with people he goes to restaurants too. I said that must be lovely, and he said no it wasn't. I said, has no one been here before, then, and he said, oh, yes, I have people, to tea. I said who, and he said oh, ladies, you know. Then he did an imitation of a lady coming to tea with him. He pretended to throw his hat off on the divan and pat his hair up in front of the glass. Then he walked round the room, looking at things and sort of swaying himself. Then he did a lady curling up in his chair and smiling at him in a mysterious way. Then he showed me all sorts of things he does himself, like picking up the lady's fox fur and making a cat of it. I said, what else do you do, and he said, as little as I can get away with, darling. I said, why ever did he ask them to tea, and he said it was cheaper than giving them lunch out, but more tiring in the long run.

Then he picked the imaginary hat off the divan and pretended to jump hard on it with both feet. He said that I was such a weight off his mind. Then he gave me the last macaroon to finish, and put his head on my lap and pretended to go to sleep, but he said, don't drop crumbs in my eyes. When he woke up, he said that if he was a lady's fox fur and I was him, I would certainly stroke his head. While I did, he made himself look as if he had glass eyes, like a fur.

He said, what a pity we are too young to marry. Then he laughed and said, didn't that sound funny? I said, I don't see why Eddie, and he said, no, it doesn't sound funny, it sounds sweet. Then he shut his eyes again. At twenty minutes to ten I moved his head and said I must get a taxi.

I promised him I would not write down that. But Sundays make one have to think of the past.

Major Brutt will be disappointed if I don't get on with that puzzle more than I do.

Monday

When I got back from Miss Paullie's this afternoon I found Anna in my room doing my puzzle. She said she was sorry but she could not stop, so she and I went on doing the puzzle. She said where did I get the table it's on from, and I said it was a

table Matchett had got from somewhere. She said, oh. She had got one whole corner done, a bit of sky with an aeroplane in it. She smiled away to herself and looked about for more pieces, and said well, how are all your beaux? She said she had better ask Major Brutt to dinner, and, then we could make him do the plainer part of the sky. Then she said, who else shall we ask, Eddie? She said, you say, it is your party you know. We went on with the puzzle till past the time for Anna to get dressed.

Today we started Tuscan Art, and did Book Keeping and German Grammar.

Tuesday

When I went down to breakfast past Anna's door it was a crack open, she was talking to Thomas. She was saying, well it's your something-or-other not mine. Thomas often sits on their bed while she drinks her morning coffee. Then she said, she's Irene's own child, you know.

Lilian has still heard nothing more from the actor.

Today we did First Aid and discussed our English Essays, and were taken to a lecture on Corneille.

Wednesday

I had a letter from Eddie, he does not say what he did at the week-end. He says not to say to Anna about those imitations, because once or twice she has been to tea there herself. What does he think I tell Anna? He does sometimes puzzle me.

Today it rained a great deal. We did Hygiene, and had a discussion on Corneille, and were taken to the National Gallery.

This afternoon, Anna took me to a grand afternoon party with gold chairs, but there were several girls of my age there. I wore my black velvet. Some lady came up and said to Anna, I hear you're just going abroad, too. Anna said, oh, I don't know, then gave me a sort of look.

Thursday

Today we had a lecture on Events of the Week, and a special lecture on Savonarola, and Elocution (in German).

Thomas and I were alone for dinner tonight, as Anna was

having dinner with somebody. He asked if I minded if we did not go out to anything, as he said he had had rather a day. He did not seem to want to talk about anything special. At the end of dinner he said I'm afraid this is rather dull, but it is family life. I said that when we lived in the South of France we often did not talk. He said, oh, talking of the South of France, I forget if I told you we are going to Capri. I said that would be very nice. He coughed and said, I mean Anna and I are going. He went quickly on to say, we have been wondering what would be the nicest plan for you. I said I thought London was very nice.

Friday

Last night, when I had just finished putting away this diary, Matchett came up to say good night. She clapped her hands at me for not being in bed yet. Then I told her I *had* been told that they were going abroad. She said, oh, you have? and sat down on my bed. She said, she's been on at him to tell you. I said, well they can't help it, I'm not their fault. She said no, but if they did right by you you wouldn't be always out after that Eddie. I said, well after all, they are married, and I'm not married to either of them. She said, it's one marriage and then another that's done harm all along. I said to Matchett that at any rate I'd got her. Then she leaned right on my bed and said, that's all very well, but are you a good girl? I said I didn't know what she meant, and she said no, that is just the trouble. She said, if Mr Thomas had been half of the man his father was, I'd have – I said, what, Matchett? And she said, never you mind.

She got up, stroking her apron, with her mouth tight shut. She said, he's a little actor, he is. She said, he had a right to leave you alone. Her good nights are never the same now.

Tomorrow will be Saturday.

Saturday

This morning Anna came with a quite ordinary smile and said, Eddie's wanting you on the telephone. It was quite a time since I'd heard the telephone ring, so Anna must have been having a talk first. He said, what about another walk in the

park? He said, it's all right, I know, they are going out to Richmond. He said to meet on the bridge at three.

Matchett took no notice when we met on the stairs.

We did meet on the bridge at three.

Sunday

This morning they got up late, so I got on with my puzzle. When they were up they said they would do whatever I liked. I could not think what, so one of them said Epping. So we drove there to a place called The Robin Hood and had sausages for our lunch. Then Thomas and I went for a walk in the forest, Anna stayed in the car and read a detective story. The forest is full of blackish air like London, the trees do not look the same in it. He told me they had arranged for me to stay at the seaside at the time when Anna and he would be in Capri. I said oh, yes, that that would be fun. Thomas gave me a sort of look and said yes he thought it would.

When we got back to the car Thomas said, I've been talking plans with Portia. Anna said, oh, have you, I'm so glad. She was so interested in her detective story, she went on with it all the way home.

I told them how much I had enjoyed my day.

Anna said, it will be spring before we know where we are.

Part Two

THE FLESH

I

EARLY in March the crocuses crept alight, then blazed yellow and purple in the park. The whistle was blown later: it was possible to walk there after tea. In fact, it is about five o'clock in an evening that the first hour of spring strikes – autumn arrives in the early morning, but spring at the close of a winter day. The air, about to darken, quickens and is run through with mysterious white light; the curtain of darkness is suspended, as though for some unprecedented event. There is perhaps no sunset, the trees are not yet budding – but the senses receive an intimation, an intimation so fine, yet striking in so directly, that this appears a movement in one's own spirit. This exalts whatever feeling is in the heart.

No moment in human experience approaches in its intensity this experience of the solitary earth's. The later phases of spring, when her foot is in at the door, are met with a conventional gaiety. But her first unavowed presence is disconcerting; silences fall in company – the wish to be either alone or with a lover is avowed by some look or some spontaneous movement – the window being thrown open, the glance away up the street. In cities the traffic lightens and quickens; even buildings take such feeling of depth that the streets might be rides cut through a wood. What is happening is only acknowledged between strangers, by looks, or between lovers. Unwritten poetry twists the hearts of people in their thirties. To the person out walking that first evening of spring, nothing appears inanimate, nothing not sentient: darkening chimneys, viaducts, villas, glass-and-steel factories, chain stores seem to strike as deep as natural rocks, seem not only to exist but to dream. Atoms

of light quiver between the branches of stretching-up black trees. It is in this unearthly first hour of spring twilight that earth's almost agonized livingness is most felt. This hour is so dreadful to some people that they hurry indoors and turn on the lights – they are pursued by the scent of violets sold on the kerb.

On that early March evening, Anna and Portia both, though not together, happened to be walking in Regent's Park. This was Portia's first spring in England: very young people are true but not resounding instruments. Their senses are tuned to the earth, like the senses of animals; they feel, but without conflict or pain. Portia was not like Anna, already half way through a woman's checked, puzzled life, a life to which the intelligence only gives a further distorted pattern. With Anna, feeling was by now unwilling, but she had more resonance. Memory enlarged and enlarged inside her an echoing, not often visited cave. Anna could remember being a child more easily and with more pleasure than she could remember being Portia's age: with her middle teens a cloudy phase had begun. She did not know half she remembered till a sensation touched her; she forgot to look back till these first evenings of spring.

At different moments, they both crossed different bridges over the lake, and saw swans folded, dark white ciphers on the white water, in an immortal dream. They both viewed the Cytherean twisting reaches at the ends of the lake, both looked up and saw pigeons cluttering the transparent trees. They saw crocuses staining the dusk purple or yellow, flames with no power. They heard silence, then horns, cries, an oar on the lake, silence striking again, the thrush fluting so beautifully. Anna kept pausing, then walking quickly past the couples against the railings: walking alone in her elegant black she drew glances; she went to watch the dogs coursing in the empty heart of the park. But Portia almost ran, with her joy in her own charge, like a child bowling a hoop.

You must be north of a line to feel the seasons so keenly. On the Riviera, Portia's notions of spring had been the mimosa, and then Irene unpacking from storage trunks her crushed cotton frocks. Spring had brought with it no new particular

pleasures – for little girls in England spring means the Easter
holidays: bicycle rides in blazers, ginger nuts in the pockets,
blue violets in bleached grass, paper-chases, secrets, and mixed
hockey. But Portia, thanks first to Irene, now to Anna, still knew
nothing of this. She had come straight to London ... One
Saturday, she and Lilian were allowed to take a bus into the
country: they walked about in a wood near the bus stop. Then
it thundered and they wanted to go home.

The day before Thomas and Anna were to start for Capri,
Portia was to go to a Mrs Heccomb, living at Seale-on-Sea. Here
Mrs Heccomb's late husband, a retired doctor, had been the
secretary of the golf club. Mrs Heccomb, before her rather late
marriage, had been a Miss Yardes, once Anna's governess. She
had stayed on with Anna and her father at Richmond, keeping
house and supporting the two of them gently, till Anna was
nineteen. She had not been teaching Anna for several years
before that: she had done no more than escort her to and from
day school, see that she practised the piano, and make her feel
her position as a motherless girl. But she had been quite a feature of Anna's home – that house uphill with a fine view of the
river, an oval drawing-room, a terraced garden with almond
trees. Anna used to call her Poor Miss Taylor: she had been as
much pleased as surprised when Miss Yardes had followed Miss
Taylor's pattern and, at the end of her annual holiday, announced her engagement to a widower. Anna and Miss Yardes
had just at that time reached an uncomfortable phase of semi-
confidence – for one thing, Robert Pidgeon had just appeared,
and Miss Yardes was being too conscious of him. Though this
loss had made a sad tear in daily habit, it had been on the whole
a relief to see Miss Yardes go. Anna took on the housekeeping;
the bills went up but meals became more amusing. Anna's
father footed the bills without a quiver, and touched her by
saying how much nicer this was. It turned out he had only kept
Miss Yardes on all this time because he fancied a girl should
have a woman about. During Miss Yardes's reign, Anna's father
had felt free to form the habit of being self-protectively unob-
servant: this he did not discontinue after Miss Yardes had gone.

He continued, therefore, hardly to notice Robert or any of the less important young men.

Robert had celebrated Miss Yardes's wedding by bringing out to Richmond a package of fireworks; he and Anna went down the garden together and let the fireworks off on the wedding night. On their way back to the house, he kissed Anna for the first time. After that, he had gone abroad for two years, and she began to go about by herself. His subsequent irresponsible behaviour had been, she since understood, just as much her fault as his. This began after he came back from abroad. Late at nights, in fact in the small hours, they would rush in his car up Richmond Hill, to the house in which Anna's father slept soundly, where the thermos of milk no longer waited, where Miss Yardes no longer kept her door ajar. In the drawing-room, the embers of the fire would be coaxed alight again by the knowing Robert, then the Chinese cushion slipped under Anna's head ... They did not marry because they refused to trust each other.

On her marriage, then, Mrs Heccomb *née* Miss Yardes had gone to live at Seale, on the Kentish coast, about seventy miles from London. Here her husband had bought a strip of reclaimed beach, just inland from the esplanade. On this he built a house facing the Channel, with balconies, a sun porch, and Venetian shutters to batten against storms. For in winter storms flung shingle on to the lawns, and even, if the windows were left open, on to the carpets and pianos of these exposed houses along the esplanade. This house of his Dr Heccomb considered a good investment — and so it proved: in July, August, September he, his second wife, and the children of his first marriage moved out of Seale and took rooms at a farm inland, while the house was let for six guineas a week. During these summer exiles, Dr Heccomb drove himself daily to the Seale golf club in a small car. He was popular; all the members knew him well; he came in on every celebration there was. It was on the return from one of these parties that Dr Heccomb, driving home too gaily into the sunset, drove himself head-on into a charabanc. After this shocking affair, the hat went round at the golf club for Mrs Heccomb; and the widow received eighty-five pounds in token

of sympathy. This did not seem worth investing, so she spent it on mourning for herself and the children, a secretarial training for Daphne Heccomb, and a fine cross for Dr Heccomb in Seale churchyard.

During her years at Richmond she not only had not had to worry about money but had formed rather luxurious ideas. As a widow after several years of marriage she was contented but incompetent. Her well-wishers were more worried about her than she was herself. She had not, it is true, been left with nothing, but she did not seem to know how little she had. Anna's father had insisted on adding a small pension, and on his death had left an annuity. Anna sent Mrs Heccomb clothes she no longer wore, as well as various perquisites. Mrs Heccomb rather enjoyed eking out her income: she gave piano lessons in Seale and Southstone, painted table mats, lamp shades, and other objects, and occasionally took paying guests — but her house's exposed position in bad weather, the roar of the sea on the shingle, and the ruthless manners of the two Heccomb children almost always drove these guests away after a short time.

The Heccomb children helped her by growing up and becoming self-supporting. Daphne worked in a library at Seale, Dickie in a bank at Southstone, four miles away. They continued to live at home, and could contribute their share to the house. Dr Heccomb's friends at the club or their mother's relations had found these positions for them, for Mrs Heccomb had not exerted herself. Inevitably, she had had rather grander ideas: she would have liked Dickie to go into the Army; she had tried to model Daphne on the lines of Anna. When she first took them on — and she had been married, as she may have realized, very largely in order *to* take them on — the young Heccombs had been rough little things, not at all the type of children she would have stayed with had she been their governess. And they grew up rough, in spite of all she had done. The fact was, though one did not refer to this, that her husband's first wife had not been quite-quite. But her affectionate nature resigned her to these young people, who continued to stay on because they were comfy with her, because all their friends lived around, because

they had no desire to see the rest of the world. They tired soon of the sport of baiting her paying guests, so, when they could each contribute fifteen shillings a week, asked that the paying guests might be given up. This made a quieter home.

Daphne and Dickie Heccomb, when they were not working, were to be found with the rest of their gay set at rinks, in cafés, cinemas, and dance halls. On account of their popularity and high spirits, other people were glad to pay for them. Seaside society, even out of season, is ideal for young people, who grow up in it gay, contented, and tough. Seale, though itself quiet, is linked by very frequent buses to Southstone, which boasts, with reason, almost every resource.

Mrs Heccomb herself had a number of friends at Seale. The sea front is rather commercial and not very select: most of her friends lived in those pretty balconied villas or substantial gabled houses up on the hill. In fact, she had found her level. She did a few good works and attended the choral society. Had she not been so worried about her step-children growing up common, hers would have been a very serene life. She was glad to have achieved marriage, not sorry that it was over.

At Charing Cross, Matchett put Portia into the train, then narrowly watched the porter put in the suitcases. When the train began to draw out, she waved several times after it, in a mystic semaphore, her fabric-gloved hand. She had given Portia a bottle of boiled sweets, though with instructions not to make herself ill. Her manner, during the drive in the taxi, had threatened the afternoon like a cloud that covers the sky but is almost certain never to break. Her eyelids looked rigid – tear-bound, you would have said. By giving such a faultless impersonation of a trusted housemaid seeing a young lady into a train, she had made Portia feel that, because of Eddie, the door between them had been shut for ever. While she bought the sweets at the kiosk, her face went harder than ever, in case this action be misunderstood. She said: 'Mr Thomas would wish it. Those are thirst-quenchers, those lime drops are. You don't know when you'll get your tea.'

Portia could not but be glad when the train steamed out. She

put a sweet in both cheeks and began to look at her book. She had not travelled all by herself before, and for some time dared not look at anyone else in the carriage for fear of not doing so unconcernedly.

As the train drew in Lymly, the junction for Seale, Mrs Heccomb waved two or three times – first at the engine, as though signalling it to stop, then in order that Portia should not overlook her. This was unlikely, for hers was the only figure on the platform stretching its dead length. This unfrequented junction, far from the village, at the mouth of a cutting, exists alone among woods. Ground ivy mats its lozenge-shaped flowerbeds, and a damp woody silence haunts it – except when boat trains, momentary apparitions, go rocking roaring through. Mrs Heccomb wore a fur coat that had been Anna's, that cut her a little across the back. She wore the collar turned up, because a draught always blows down a main line. Methodically, she began to search down the train, beginning with the first carriage after the engine. On seeing Portia alight from the far end she broke into a smooth trot, without any break in deportment. When she came up to Portia she looked at her small round hat, took a guess at her mental age, and kissed her. 'We won't try and talk', she said, 'till we're quite settled.' A porter took the luggage across the platform to another, waiting, train, very short, with only three coaches. Not for some minutes after they *were* settled did this train puff off down the single line through the woods.

Mrs Heccomb, sitting opposite Portia, balanced on her knee a coloured wicker shopping-basket, empty. She had a plump abstracted rather wondering face, and fluffy grey hair piled up under her hat. Portia noted scars in her fur coat where buttons had been cut off and moved out. 'So isn't this nice,' she said. 'You've come, just as Anna said. Now tell me, how is my dear Anna?'

'She told me to be sure and give you her love.'

'Fancy thinking of that, when she's just going abroad! She takes things so calmly. Are they all packed up?'

'Matchett's still got to finish.'

'And then she'll spring-clean the house,' said Mrs Heccomb,

viewing this vision of order. 'What a treasure Matchett is. How smoothly things can run.' Seeing Portia looking out at the woods, she said:

'And perhaps you'll quite enjoy a little time in the country?'

'I am sure I shall.'

'Where we live, I'm afraid, is not really the country, it is the sea. However –'

'I like the sea, too.'

'The sea in England, or rather the sea round England, will be quite new to you, won't it?' said Mrs Heccomb.

Portia saw Mrs Heccomb did not expect an answer, and guessed that Anna had told her the whole story – where they had lived, and why they never came home. Anna would not have gone on seeing Mrs Heccomb if this had meant her having to be discreet. Anna was truly fond of Mrs Heccomb, but there would have been nothing to say, when they were not at matinées, had Anna not made stories out of her passing worries and got sympathy for them. About three times a year, Anna sent Mrs Heccomb the price of a day ticket to London, then very warmly devoted the day to her. This was always a great success – it was never known, however, whether Mrs Heccomb's worries came up too. Did she talk to Anna about her step-children? 'I'm afraid they are pretty awful,' Anna had said.

'Do you skate?' Mrs Heccomb said suddenly.

'I'm afraid I don't know how to.'

Mrs Heccomb relieved, said: 'Perhaps that is just as well. You need not go to the rink. Are you fond of reading?'

'Sometimes.'

'You are quite right,' said Mrs Heccomb, 'there is plenty of time to read when you are older, like I am. At one time, Anna read too much. Fortunately she loved gaiety, too: she always had so many invitations. In fact, she still enjoys herself like a young girl. How old are you, Portia, if I may ask?'

'Sixteen.'

'That makes such a difference,' said Mrs Heccomb. 'I mean, it's not as though you were eighteen.'

'I do quite enjoy myself, even now.'

'Oh yes, I'm sure you do,' said Mrs Heccomb. 'I do hope

you'll enjoy the sea while you are with us. And there are some interesting places, ruins, for instance, round. Yes, I do hope . . .'

'I'm sure I shall enjoy myself very much.'

'At the same time,' said Mrs Heccomb, flushing under her hair, 'I don't want you to feel a *visitor* here. I want you to feel completely at home, just as you do with Anna. You must come to me about any little trouble, just as you would to her. Of course, I hope there may be no little troubles. But you must ask me for anything that you want.'

Portia chiefly wanted her tea: lime drops do leave you thirsty, and she still tasted the tunnels in her mouth. She feared they must still be far from the coast – then the train ran clear of the woods along a high curved ridge. Salt air blew in at the carriage window: down there, across flat land, she saw the sea. Seale station ran at them with no warning; the engine crawled up to buffers: this was a terminus. The door through from the book-ing-hall framed sky, for this was an uphill station, built high on a ramp. While Mrs Heccomb had her chat with the porter, Portia stood at the head of the flight of steps. She felt elated here, thinking: 'I shall be happy.' The view of sea, town, and plain, all glassy-grey March light, seemed to be tilted up to meet her eyes like a mirror. 'That is my house,' said Mrs Hec-comb, pointing to the horizon. 'We're still rather far away, but this is the taxi. He always comes.'

Mrs Heccomb smiled at the taxi and she and Portia got in.

The taxi drove down a long curve into Seale, past white gates of villas with mysterious gardens in which an occasional thrush sang. 'That would be our way really,' said Mrs Heccomb, nod-ding left when they reached the foot of the hill. 'But today we must go the other, because I have to shop. I do not often have a taxi to shop from, and it is quite a temptation, I must say. Dear Anna begged me to have the taxi *up* to the station, but I said no, that the walk would be good for me. But I said I might take the taxi the rather longer way home, in order to do my shopping.'

The taxi, which felt narrow, closed everything in on them, and Portia now saw only shop windows – the High Street shop windows. But what shops! – though all were very small they all looked lively, expectant, tempting, crowded, gay. She saw num-

bers of cake shops, antique shops, gift shops, flower shops, fancy chemists, and fancy stationers. Mrs Heccomb, holding her basket ready, wore a keyed-up but entirely happy air.

The shopping basket was soon full, so one began to pile parcels on the taxi seats. Every time she came back to the taxi, Mrs Heccomb said to Portia: 'I do hope you are not wanting your tea?' By the Town Hall clock it was now twenty past five. A man carried out to them a roll of matting, which he propped upright opposite Portia's feet. 'I am so glad to have this,' said Mrs Heccomb. 'I ordered it last week, but it was not in till to-day ... Now I must just go to the end' – by the end she meant the post office, which was at the end of the High Street – 'and send Anna that telegram.'

'Oh?'

'To say you've arrived safely.'

'I'm sure she won't be worried.'

Mrs Heccomb looked distressed. 'But you have never been away from her before. One would not like her to go abroad with anything on her mind.' Her back view vanished through the post-office door. When she came out, she found that she had forgotten something right down the other end of the town. 'After all,' she said, 'that will bring us back where we started. So we can go back the shorter way, after all.'

Portia saw that all this must be in her honour. It made her sad to think how Matchett would despise Mrs Heccomb's diving and ducking ways, like a nesting water-fowl's. Matchett would ask why all this had not been seen to before. But Irene would have been happy with Mrs Heccomb, and would have entered into her hopes and fears. The taxi crossed a canal bridge, heading towards the sea across perfectly flat fields that cut off the sea-front from the town. The sea-line appeared between high battered rows of houses, with red bungalows dotted in the gaps. These were all raised above the inland level, along a dike that kept the sea in its place.

The taxi turned and crawled along the back of the dike; Mrs Heccomb brisked up and began to muster her parcels. From here, the chipped stucco backs of the terraces looked higher than anything seen in London. The unkempt lawns and tamarisks at

their foot, the lonely whoosh of the sea away behind them made them more mysterious and forbidding. Gaunt rusted pipes ran down between their windows, most of which were blank with white cotton blinds. These fields on their north side were more grey than the sea. That terror of buildings falling that one loses in London returned to Portia. 'Who lives there?' she said, nodding up nervously.

'No one, dear; those are only lodging houses.'

Mrs Heccomb tapped on the glass, and the taxi, which already intended stopping, stopped dead with a satirical jerk. They got out; Portia carried the parcels Mrs Heccomb could not manage; the taximan followed with the suitcases. They all three scrabbled up a steep shingly incline and found themselves alongside the butt end of a terrace. Mrs Heccomb showed Portia the esplanade. The sea heaved; an oblique wind lifted her hat. Shingle rolled up in red waves to the brim of the asphalt; there was an energetic and briny smell. Two steamers moved slowly along the horizon, but there was not a soul on the esplanade. 'I do hope you will like it,' said Mrs Heccomb. 'I do hope you can manage those parcels: can you? There is no *road* to our gate – you see, we're right on the sea.'

Waikiki, Mrs Heccomb's house, was about one minute more down the esplanade. Numbers of windows at different levels looked out of the picturesque red roof – one window had blown open; a faded curtain was wildly blowing out. Below this, what with the sun porch, the glass entrance door, and a wide bow window, the house had an almost transparent front. Constructed largely of glass and blistered white paint, Waikiki faced the sea boldly, as though daring the elements to dash it to bits.

Portia saw firelight in the inside dusk. Mrs Heccomb rapped three times on the glass door – there was a bell, but it hung out of its socket on a long twisted umbilical wire – and a small maid, fixing her large cuffs, could be seen advancing across the living-room. She let them in with rather a hoity-toity air. 'I have *got* my latchkey,' said Mrs Heccomb, 'but I think this is practice for you, Doris ... I always latch this door when I'm out,' she, added to Portia. 'The seaside is not the country, you see ... Now, Doris, this is the young lady from London. Do you re-

member how to take her things to her room? And this is the matting that the man is just bringing. Do you remember where I told you to put it?'

While Mrs Heccomb thanked and paid off the driver, Portia looked politely round the living-room, with eyes that were now and again lowered so as not to seem to make free with what they saw. Though dusk already fell on the esplanade, the room held a light reflection from the sea. She located the smell of spring with a trough of blue hyacinths, just come into flower. Almost all one side of the room was made up of french windows, which gave on to the sun porch but were at present shut. The sun porch, into which she hastily looked, held some basket chairs and an empty aquarium. At one end of the room, an extravagant fire fluttered on brown glazed tiles; the wireless cabinet was the most glossy of all. Opposite the windows a glass-fronted book-case, full but with a remarkably locked look, chiefly served to reflect the marine view. A dark blue chenille curtain, faded in lighter streaks, muffled an arch that might lead to the stairs. In other parts of the room, Portia's humble glances discovered such objects as a scarlet portable gramophone, a tray with a painting outfit, a half-painted lamp shade, a mountain of maga-zines. Two armchairs and a settee, with crumpled bottoms, made a square round the fire, and there was a gate-legged table, already set for tea. It was set for tea, but the cake plates were still empty – Mrs Heccomb was tipping cakes out of paper bags.

Outside, the sea went on with its independent sighing, but still seemed an annexe of the living-room. Portia, laying her gloves on an armchair, got the feeling that there was room for everyone here. She learned later that Daphne called this the lounge.

'Would you like to go up, dear?'

'Not specially, thank you.'

'Not even to your room?'

'I don't really mind.'

Mrs Heccomb, for some reason, looked relieved. When Doris brought in tea she said in a low voice: 'Now, Doris, the mat-ting. . . .'

Mrs Heccomb took off her hat for tea, and Portia saw that her

hair, like part of an artichoke, seemed to have an up-growing tendency: it was pinned down firmly to the top of her head jn a flat bun. This, for some reason, added to Mrs Heccomb's expression of surprise. At the same time, her personality was most reassuring. She talked so freely to Portia, telling her so much that Portia, used to the tactics of Windsor Terrace, wondered whether this really were wise. And what would be left to say by the end of the first week? She had yet to learn how often intimacies between women go backwards, beginning with revelations and ending up in small talk without loss of esteem. Mrs Heccomb told stories of Anna's youth at Richmond, which she invested with a pathetic prettiness. Then she said how sad it would always be about those two little babies Anna had almost had. Portia ate doughnuts, shortbread, and Dundee cake and gazed past Mrs Heccomb at the vanishing sea. She thought how gay this room, with its lights on, must look from the esplanade, thought how dark it was out there, and came to envy herself.

But then Mrs Heccomb got up and drew the curtains. 'You never know,' she said. 'It does not quite do.' (She referred to being looked in at.) Then she gave Portia another cup of tea and told her how much she must miss her mother. But she said how very lucky she was to have Thomas and Anna. For years and years, as Miss Yardes, she had had to be tactful and optimistic, trying to make young people see things the right way. This may have exaggerated her feeling manner. Now independence gave her a slight authority: when she said a thing *was* so, it became so forthwith. She looked at the mahogany clock that ticked loudly over the fire and said how nice it was that Daphne would soon be home. This Portia could not, of course, dispute. But she said: 'I think I will go up and brush my hair, then.'

While she was up in her room combing her hair back, hearing the tissue paper in her suitcase rustle, watching draughts bulge the new matting strip, she heard the bang that meant Daphne was in. Waikiki, she was to learn, was a sounding box: you knew where everyone was, what everyone did – except when the noise they made was drowned by a loud wind. She heard Daphne loudly asking something, then Mrs Heccomb must have put up a warning hand, for the rest of Daphne's question got

bitten off. Portia thought, I do hope Daphne won't mind me ...
In her room, the electric light, from its porcelain shade, poured
down with a frankness unknown at Windsor Terrace. The light
swayed slightly in that seaside draught, and Portia felt a new
life had begun. Downstairs, Daphne switched the wireless on
full blast, then started bawling across it at Mrs Heccomb: 'I
say, when *is* Dickie going to mend that bell?'

2

WHEN Portia ventured to come down, she found Daphne pot-
tering round the tea table, biting pieces out of a macaroon, while
Mrs Heccomb, busy painting the lamp shade, shouted above the
music that she would spoil her supper. Mrs Heccomb's shouting
had acquired, after years of evenings with Daphne and the
music, the mild equability of her speaking voice: she could
shout without strain. There was, in fact, an air of unconscious
deportment about everything that she carried through, and as
she worked at the lamp shade, peering close at the detail then
leaning back to get the general effect, she looked like someone
painting a lamp shade in a play.

As Portia came round the curtain Daphne did not look at her,
but with unnerving politeness switched the wireless off. It
snapped off at the height of a roar, and Mrs Heccomb looked up.
Daphne popped the last piece of macaroon into her mouth,
wiped her fingers correctly on a *crêpe de Chine* handkerchief,
and shook hands, though still without saying anything. She
gave the impression that she would not speak till she had
thought of something striking to say. She was a fine upstanding
girl, rather tall; her close-fitting dark blue knitted dress showed
off her large limbs. She wore her hair in a mop, but the mop was
in an iron pattern of curls, burnished with brilliantine. She had
a high colour, and used tangerine lipstick. Pending having
something to say to Portia, she said over her shoulder to Mrs
Heccomb: 'None of them will be coming in tonight.'

'Oh, thank you, Daphne.'

'Oh, don't thank *me*.'

'Daphne has so many friends,' Mrs Heccomb explained to Portia. 'But she says that none of them will be coming in to-night.'

Daphne gave the rest of the cakes a rather scornful once-over, then bumped into an armchair. Portia, as unostentatiously as possible, edged round the room to stand beside Mrs Heccomb, who worked with her tray of painting materials drawn up under a special lamp. Though all this was alarming, she did not feel so alarmed as she did at Windsor Terrace, where St Quentin and all those other friends of Anna's always tacitly watched. On the lamp shade she saw delphiniums and marble cupids being painted in against a salmon-pink sky. 'Oh, *how* pretty!' she said.

'It will look better varnished. I think the idea is pretty. This is an order, for a wedding present, but later I hope to do one for Anna, as a surprise – Daphne dear, I'm sure Portia wouldn't mind the music.'

Daphne groaned, but got up and restarted the wireless. Then she kicked off her court shoes and lighted a cigarette. 'You know,' she said, 'I feel spring in my bones today.'

'I know, dear; isn't it nice?'

'Not in my bones.' Daphne looked with a certain interest at Portia. 'Well,' she said, 'so they didn't take *you* abroad.'

'They couldn't, you see, dear,' said Mrs Heccomb quickly. 'They are going to stay with people who have a villa. And also, Portia comes from abroad.'

'Oh! And what do *you* think of our English policemen, then?'

'I don't think I –'

'Daphne, don't always joke, dear. Be a good girl and tell Doris to clear tea.'

Daphne put her head back and bellowed, *'Doris!'* and Doris gave her a look as she nimbled in with the tray. Portia realized later that the tomb-like hush of Smoot's library, where she had to sit all day, dealing out hated books, was not only antipathetic but even dangerous to Daphne. So, once home, she kept fit by making a loud noise. Daphne never simply touched objects, she slapped down her hand on them; she made up her mouth with

the gesture of someone cutting their throat. Even when the wireless was not on full blast, Daphne often shouted as though it were. So, when Daphne's homecoming step was heard on the esplanade, Mrs Heccomb had learned to draw a shutter over her nerves. So much of her own working life had been spent in intercepting noise that might annoy others, in saying 'Quietly, please, dear,' to young people, that she may even have got a sort of holiday pleasure from letting Daphne rip. The degree of blare and glare she permitted Daphne may even have been Mrs Heccomb's own tribute to the life force it had for so long been her business to check. So much did she identify noise with Daphne's presence that if the wireless stopped or there were a pause in the shouting, Mrs Heccomb would get up from her painting and either close a window or poke the fire – any lack felt by any one of her senses always made her imagine she felt cold. She had given up hoping Daphne might grow like Anna. But it was firmly fixed in her mind now that she would not wish Portia to return to London and Anna having picked up any of Daphne's ways.

When tea had been cleared, and the lace cloth folded by Doris and put away in the bookcase drawer, Mrs Heccomb uncorked a bottle of varnish and with a tense air applied the first coat. This done, she returned to the world and said: 'Doris seems to be coming on quite well.'

'She ought to,' said Daphne. 'She's got a boy.'

'Already? Oh dear! *Has* she?'

'Yes, they were on the top of the bus I was on. He's got a spot on his neck. First I looked at the spot, then I looked at the boy, then who should I see but Doris grinning away beside him.'

'I do hope he's a nice boy. . . .'

'Well, I tell you, he's got a spot on his neck . . . No, but I say, really, Mumsie, I do wish you'd fly out at Dickie about that bell. It looks awful, hanging out at the root like that, besides not ringing. Why don't we have an electric, anyway?'

'Your father always thought they went out of order, dear.'

'Well, you ought to fly out at Dickie, you ought really. What did he say he'd mend that bell for if he wasn't going to mend it? No one asked him to say he would mend that bell.'

'It was very good of him, dear. I might remind him at supper.'

'He won't be in for supper. He's got a date. He said.'

'Oh yes, so he did. What am I thinking about?'

'Don't ask me,' said Daphne kindly. 'However, don't you worry: I'll eat the old sausage. What is it, by the way?'

'Egg pie. I thought that would be light.'

'*Light?*' said Daphne appalled.

'For Portia after the journey. If you want more, dear, we can open the galantine.'

'Oh well,' said Daphne resignedly.

Portia sat at one end of the sofa, looking through a copy of *Woman and Beauty*. Mrs Heccomb was so much occupied with the lamp shade, Daphne by simply sitting and glooming there, that she wished she could have brought Major Brutt's puzzle – she could have been getting on with that. But you cannot pack a jigsaw that is three-quarters done. As it was, sitting under an alabaster pendant that poured a choked orange light on her head, she felt stupefied by this entirely new world. The thump of the broadcast band with the sea's vibration below it, the smell of varnish, hyacinths, Turkey carpet, drawn out by the heat of the roaring fire came at her overpoweringly. She was not yet adjusted to all this. How far she had travelled – not only in space.

Wondering if this could ever make her suffer, she thought of Windsor Terrace. *I am not there.* She began to go round, in little circles, things that at least her senses had loved – her bed, with the lamp turned on on winter mornings, the rug in Thomas's study, the chest carved with angels out there on the landing, the waxen oilcloth down there in Matchett's room. Only in a house where one has learnt to be lonely does one have this solicitude for *things*. One's relation to them, the daily seeing or touching, begins to become love, and to lay one open to pain. Looking back at a repetition of empty days, one sees that monuments have sprung up. Habit is not mere subjugation, it is a tender tie: when one remembers habit it seems to have been happiness. So, she and Irene had almost always felt sad when they looked round a hotel room before going away from it for always. They could not but feel that they had betrayed something. In unfamiliar places, they unconsciously looked for fami-

liarity. It is not our exalted feelings, it is our sentiments that build the necessary home. The need to attach themselves makes wandering people strike roots in a day: whenever we unconsciously feel, we live.

Upstairs in Waikiki, the bedroom ceilings sloped because of the roof. Mrs Heccomb, saying good night to Portia, had screwed a steel-framed window six inches open, the curtain flopped in the light of a lamp on the esplanade. Portia put her hand up once or twice to touch the slope of ceiling over her bed. Mrs Heccomb had said she hoped she would not be lonely. 'I sleep just next door: you need only tap on the wall. We are all very near together in this house. Do you like hearing the sea?'

'It sounds very near.'

'It's high tide. But it won't come any nearer.'

'Won't it?'

'No, I promise, dear, that it won't. You're not afraid of the sea?'

'Oh, no.'

'And you've got a picture of Anna,' Mrs Heccomb had added, with a beatific nod at the mantelpiece. That had already been looked at – a pastel drawing of Anna, Anna aged about twelve, holding a kitten, her long soft hair tied up in two satin bows. The tender incompetence of the drawing had given the face, so narrow between the hair, a spiritual look. The kitten's face was a wedge of dark on the breast. 'So you won't be lonely,' said Mrs Heccomb, and, having so happily concluded, had turned out the light and gone.... The curtain started fretting the window sill; the sea filled the darkness with its approaching sighing, a little hoarse with shingle. High tide? The sea had come as near as it could.

Portia dreamed she was sharing a book with a little girl. The tips of Anna's long fair hair brushed on the page: they sat up high in a window, waiting till something happened. The worst of all would be if the bell rang, and their best hope was to read to a certain point in the book. But Portia found she no longer knew how to read – she did not dare tell Anna, who kept turning pages over. She knew they must both read – so the fall of

Anna's hair filled her with despair, pity, for what would have to come. The forest (there was a forest under the window) was being varnished all over: it left no way of escape. Then the terrible end, the rushing-in, the roaring and gurgling started – Portia started up from where they were with a cry –

'– *Hush, hush*, dear! Here I am. Nothing has happened. Only Daphne running her bath out.'

'I don't know where I –'

'You're here, dear.'

'Oh!'

'Did you have a dream? Would you like me to stay a little?'

'Oh no, thank you.'

'Then sleep with no dreams, like a good girl. Remember, you can always rap on the wall.'

Mrs Heccomb slipped out, closing the door by inches. Then, out there on the landing, she and Daphne started a whispering-match. Their whispers sounded like whispers down the clinic corridor, or sounds in the forest still left from the dream. 'Goodness,' said Daphne, 'isn't she highly strung?' Then Daphne's feet, in mules, clip-clopped off across the landing: the last of the bath ran out; a door shut.

Perhaps it was Portia's sense, that by having started awake she had not been a good girl, that now kept her in the haunted outer court of the dream. She had not been kind to Anna; she had never been kind. She had lived in that house with her with an opposed heart ... That kitten, for instance – had it died? Anna never spoke of it. Had Anna felt small at day school? When had they cut her hair off? In the electric light, that hair in the portrait had been mimosa yellow. Did Anna also, sometimes, not know what to do next? Because she knew what to do next, because she knew what to laugh at, what to say, did it always follow that she knew where to turn? Inside everyone, is there an anxious person who stands to hesitate in an empty room? Starting up from her pillow Portia thought: And she's gone. She may never come back.

Mrs Heccomb must have stayed up to keep Dickie quiet. His no-nonsense step had grown loud on the esplanade. Through the floor, Mrs Heccomb was to be heard hush-hushing as Dickie

crashed open the glass door. Then he rolled an armchair round and kicked the fire: it sounded like a giant loose in the lounge. There was then the muted clatter of a tray being brought: perhaps they were opening the galantine. Mrs Heccomb may have said something about the bell, for Dickie was to be heard replying: 'What is the good of telling me that now?. . .' Portia knew she must meet him in the morning. She had heard he was twenty-three: the same age as Eddie.

When she came down next morning, at eight o'clock, Dickie was in the act of polishing off his breakfast. There was one particular bus to Southstone he must catch. When she came in he half got up, wiping egg from his chin: when they had shaken hands and both muttered something he bumped back again and went on drinking his coffee, not saying anything more. Dickie was not so enormous as he had sounded, though he was fine and stocky: he had a high colour, a tight-fitting skin, stag-like eyes with a look of striking frankness, a large chin, and hair that though sternly larded would never stay down. Dickie, indeed, looked uncompromisingly vigorous. This working morning, he wore a dark suit and hard collar in a manner that made it clear these things were not really his type. The plunging manner in which he bathed and dressed had been, before this, heard all over the house: he had left behind in the bathroom the clean, rather babyish smell of shaving soap. At Windsor Terrace, with its many floors and extended plumbing, the intimate life of Thomas was not noticeable. But here Dickie made himself felt as a powerful organism. With a look past Portia that said that nothing should alter his habits, he now rose, withdrew from the breakfast table, and locked himself in somewhere behind the chenille curtain. About five minutes later he emerged with his hat and a satisfied, civic air, nodded the same good-bye to Portia and Mrs Heccomb (who passed in and out of the lounge with fresh instalments of breakfast as more people came down) and plunged out through the glass door to dispose of the day's work. Mrs Heccomb, looking out through the sun porch to watch Dickie off down the esplanade, said: 'He is like clockwork', with a contented sigh.

Daphne's library was in Seale High Street, only about ten minutes from Waikiki down the tree-planted walk that links the esplanade to the town. She did not have to be on duty till a quarter past nine, and therefore seldom came down to breakfast before her brother had gone, for she slept voraciously. When Daphne was to be heard coming out of the bathroom, Mrs Heccomb used to signal to Doris: the egg or kipper for Daphne would then be dropped in the pan. Breakfast here was a sort of a running service, which did credit to Mrs Heccomb's organization – possibly her forces rather spent themselves on it, for she looked fatalistic for the rest of the day. Daphne always brought down her comb with her and, while waiting for the egg or kipper, would straddle before the overmantel mirror, doing what was right by her many curls. She did not put on lipstick till after breakfast because of the egg, not to speak of the marmalade. Mrs Heccomb, while Daphne saw to' her hair, would anxiously keep the coffee and milk hot under the paisley cosy that embraced both jugs. Her own breakfast consisted of rusks in hot milk, which was, as she said to Portia, rather more Continental. Portia sat on through Dickie's exit and Daphne's entrance, eating the breakfast that had come her way, elbows in as closely as possible, hoping not to catch anyone's eye.

But as Daphne took her place she said: 'So sorry my bath gave you a jump.'

'Oh, that was my fault.'

'Perhaps you had eaten something?'

'She was just tired, dear,' Mrs Heccomb said.

'I daresay you're not used to the pipes. I daresay your sister-in-law has Buckingham Palace plumbing?'

'I don't know what . . .'

'That is one of Daphne's jokes, dear.'

Daphne pursued: 'I daresay *she's* got a green china bath? Or else one of those sunk ones with a concealed light?'

'No, Daphne dear: Anna never likes things at all extreme.'

But Daphne only snorted and said: 'I daresay *she* has a bath that she floats in just like a lily.'

At the same time, making a plunge at the marmalade, Daphne sucked her cheeks in at once sternly and hardily, with the air of

someone who could say a good deal more. It was clear that her manner to Portia could not be less aggressive till she had stopped associating her with Anna. Anyone who came to Waikiki straight from Anna's seemed to Daphne likely to come it over them all. She had encountered Anna only three times – on which occasions Daphne patiently, ruthlessly, had collected everything about Anna that one could not like. She was not, as far as that went, a jealous girl, and she had a grudging regard for the upper class – had she been more in London, she would have been in the front ranks of those womanly crowds who besiege crimson druggets under awnings up steps. She would have been one of those on-looking girls who poke their large unenvious faces across the flying tip of the notable bride's veil, or who without resentment sniff other people's gardenias outside the Opera. Contented, wry, decent girls like Daphne are the bad old order's principal stay. She delighted to honour what she was perfectly happy not to have. At the same time, and underlying this, there could have been a touch of the *tricoteuse* about Daphne, once fully worked up, and this all came out in her constantly angry feeling against Anna.

She did not (rightly) consider Anna properly upper class. All the same, she felt Anna's power in operation; she considered Anna got more than she ought. She thought Anna gave herself airs. She also resented dimly (for she could never word it) Anna's having made Mumsie her parasite. Had Anna had a title this might have been less bitter. She overlooked, rightly and rather grandly, the fact that had it not been for Anna's father, the Heccombs could not have opened so much galantine.

Some people are moulded by their admirations, others by their hostilities. In so far as anything had influenced Daphne's evolution, it had been the wish to behave and speak on all occasions as Anna would not. At this moment, the very idea of Anna made her snap at her toast with a most peculiar expression, catching dribbles of marmalade on her lower lip.

The Waikiki marmalade was highly jellied, sweet, and brilliantly orange; the table was brightly set with cobalt-and-white breakfast china, whose pattern derived from the Chinese. Rush mats as thick as muffins made hot plates wobble on the syn-

thetic oak. Sunlight of a pure seaside quality flooded the breakfast table, and Portia, looking out through the sun porch,
thought how pleasant this was. The Heccombs ate as well as
lived in the lounge, for they mistrusted, rightly, the anthracite
stove in the should-be dining-room. So they only used the dining-room in summer, or for parties at which they had enough
people to generate a sterling natural heat. . . . Gulls dipped over
the lawn in a series of white flashes; Mrs Heccomb watched
Daphne having a mood about Anna with an eye of regret. 'But
one does not put lilies in baths,' she said at last.

'You might do, if you wanted to keep them fresh.'

'Then I should have thought you'd put them in a wash basin,
dear.'

'How should I know?' said Daphne. '*I* don't get lilies, do I?'
She thrust her cup forward for more coffee, and, with an air of
turning to happier subjects, said: '*Did* you fly out at Dickie
about that bell?'

'He didn't seem to think . . .'

'Oh, he didn't, did he?' said Daphne. 'That's just Dickie all
over, if you know what I mean. Why not let you get the man
from Spalding's in the first place? Well, you had better get the
man from Spalding's. I want that bell done by tomorrow night.'

'Why specially, dear?'

'Some people are coming in.'

'But don't they almost always give a rap on the glass?'

Daphne looked hangdog (her variation of coyness). Her eyes
seemed to run together like the eyes of a shark. She said: 'Mr
Bursely talked about dropping in.'

'Mr Who?' Mrs Heccomb said timidly.

'Bursely, Mumsie. B, U, R, S, E, L, Y.'

'I don't think I have ever –'

'No,' Daphne yelled patiently. 'That is just the point. He
hasn't been here before. You don't want him to see that bell.
He's from the School of Musketry.'

'Oh, in the Army?' said Mrs Heccomb, brightening. (Portia
knew so little about the Army, she immediately heard spurs,
even a sabre, clank down the esplanade.) 'Where did you meet
him, dear?'

'At a hop,' said Daphne briefly.

'Then some of you might like to dance tomorrow night, I expect?'

'Well, we might put the carpet back. We can't all just stick around. — Do you dance?' she said, eyeing Portia.

'Well, I have danced with some other girls in hotels ...'

'Well, men won't bite you.' Turning to Mrs Heccomb, Daphne said: 'Get Dickie to get Cecil ... Goodness, I *must* rush!'

She rushed, and soon was gone down the esplanade. Daphne used nothing stronger than 'goodness' or 'dash': all the vigour one wanted was supplied by her manner. In this she was unlike Anna, who at moments of tension let out oaths and obscenities with a helpless, delicate air. Where Anna, for instance, would call a person a bitch, Daphne would call the person an old cat. Daphne's person was sexy, her conversation irreproachably chaste. She would downface any remark by saying, 'You *are* awful', or simply using her eyes ... When she had quite gone, Portia felt deflated, Mrs Heccomb looked dazed. For Portia, Daphne and Dickie seemed a crisis that surely must be unique: she could not believe that they happened every day.

'Remind me to go to Spalding's,' said Mrs Heccomb.

At this moment the sun was behind a film, but the sea shone and the lounge was full of its light. Mrs Heccomb, to air the place after breakfast, folded back a window on to the sun porch, then opened a window in the porch itself. A smell of seaweed stiffening and salting, of rolls of shingle drying after the sea, and gulls' cries came into Waikiki lounge. One's first day by the sea, one's being feels salt, strong, resilient, and hollow — like a seaweed pod not giving under the heel. Portia went and stood in the sun porch, looking out through its lattice at the esplanade. Then she boldly let herself out by the glass door. A knee-high wall with a very high and correct gate cut the Heccomb's lawn off from the public way. Before stepping over the wall (which seemed, in view of the gate's existence, a possible act of disrespect) Portia glanced back at the Waikiki windows. But no one watched her; no one seemed to object. She walked across to the lip of the esplanade.

Seale sea front takes the imperceptible curve of a shallow, very wide bay. Towards the east horizon, the coast rises – or rather, inland hills approach the sea: an imposing bluff is crowned by the most major of Southstone's major hotels. That gilt dome, the flying flags receive at about sunset their full glory, and distantly glitter, a plutocratic heaven, for humbler trippers on the Seale esplanade. On sunless clear mornings, the silhouette of the Splendide seems to be drawn on the sky in blue-grey ink ... On from Seale towards Southstone, the forcible concrete sea wall, with tarmac top, stretches empty for two miles. The fields the sea wall protects drop away from it, unpeopled and salty, on the inland side. The abstract loneliness of the dike ends where the Seale–Southstone road comes out to run by the sea.

West of Seale, you see nothing more than the marsh. The dead flat line of the coast is drawn out into a needle-fine promontory. The dimming gleaming curve is broken only by the martello towers, each smaller, each more nearly melted by light. The silence is broken only by musketry practice on the ranges. Looking west of Seale, you see the world void, the world suspended, forgotten, like a past phase of thought. Light's shining, shifting slants and veils and own interposing shadows make a world of their own ... Along this stretch of the coast, the shingle has given place to water-flat sands: the most furious seas only slide in flatly to meet the martello towers.

Standing midway between these two distances, hands knotted behind her back, Portia looked out to sea: the skyline was drawn taut across the long shallow bow of the bay. Three steamers' smoke hung in curls on the clear air – the polished sea looked like steel: amazing to think that a propeller could cut it. The edge of foam on the beach was tremulous, lacy, but the horizon looked like a blade.

A little later this morning, that blade would have cut off Thomas and Anna. They would drop behind the horizon, leaving behind them, for only a minute longer, a little curl of smoke. By the time they landed at Calais, their lives would have become hypothetical. To look at the sea the day someone is crossing is to accept the finality of the defined line. For the senses bound

our feeling world: there is an abrupt break where their power stops – when the door closes, the train disappears round the curve, the plane's droning becomes inaudible, the ship enters the mist or drops over the line of sea. The heart may think it knows better: the senses know that absence blots people out. We have really no absent friends. The friend becomes a traitor by breaking, however unwillingly or sadly, out of our own zone: a hard judgement is passed on him, for all the pleas of the heart. Willing absence (however unwilling) is the negation of love. To remember can be at times no more than a cold duty, for we remember only in the limited way that is bearable. We observe small rites, but we defend ourselves against that terrible memory that is stronger than will. We defend ourselves from the rooms, the scenes, the objects that make for hallucination, that make the senses start up and fasten upon a ghost. We desert those who desert us; we cannot afford to suffer; we must live how we can.

Happily, the senses are not easy to trick – or, at least, to trick often. They fix, and fix us with them, on what is possessable. They are ruthless in their living infidelity. Portia was learning to live without Irene, not because she denied or had forgotten that once unfailing closeness between mother and child, but because she no longer felt her mother's cheek on her own (that Eddie's finger-tip, tracing the crease of a smile, had more idly but far more lately touched), or smelled the sachet-smell from Irene's dresses, or woke in those hired north rooms where they used to wake.

With regard to Eddie himself, at present, the hard law of present-or-absent was suspended. In the first great phase of love, which with very young people lasts a long time, the beloved is not outside one, so neither comes nor goes. In this dumb, exalted, and exalting confusion, what actually happens plays very little part. In fact the spirit stays so tuned up that the beloved's real presence could be too much, unbearable: one wants to say to him: 'Go, that you may be here.' The most fully lived hours, at this time, are those of memory or of anticipation, when the heart expands to the full without any check. Portia now referred to Eddie everything that could happen: she saw him in everything that she saw. His being in London, her being here,

no more than contracted seventy miles of England into their private intense zone. Also, they could write letters.

But the absence, the utter dissolution, in space of Thomas and Anna should have been against nature: they were her Everyday. That Portia was not more sorry, that she would not miss them, faced her this morning like the steel expanse of the sea. Thomas and Anna, by opening their door to her (by having been by blood obliged to open their door) became Irene's successors in all natural things. He, she, Portia, three Quaynes, had lived, packed close in one house through the winter cold, accepting, not merely choosing each other. They had all three worked at their parts of the same necessary pattern. They had passed on the same stairs, grasped the same door handles, listened to the strokes of the same clocks. Behind the doors at Windsor Terrace, they had heard each other's voices, like the continuous murmur inside the whorls of a shell. She had breathed smoke from their lungs in every room she went into, and seen their names on letters each time she went through the hall. When she went out, she was asked how her brother and sister were. To the outside world, she smelled of Thomas and Anna.

But something that should have been going on had not gone on: something had not happened. They had sat round a painted, not a burning, fire, at which you tried in vain to warm your hands ... She tried to make a picture of Thomas and Anna leaning over the rail of the ship, both looking the same way. The picture was just real enough, for the moment, to make her want to expunge from their faces a certain betraying look. For they looked like refugees, not people travelling for pleasure. Thomas – who had said he always wore a cap on a ship – wore the cap pulled down, while Anna held her fur collar plaintively to her chin. Their nearness – for they stood with their elbows touching – was part of their driven look: they were one in flight. But already their faces were far less substantial than the faces of Daphne and Dickie Heccomb ... Then Portia remembered they would not be aboard yet: in fact, they would hardly have left London. And the moment they *were* aboard, Anna would lie down: she was a bad sailor; she never looked at the sea.

3

2 Windsor Terrace,
N.W.I.

DEAR Miss Portia: You will be sorry to hear that Phyllis has interfered with your puzzle, which I had put newspaper over like you said. She had orders not to, but overlooked that. Owing to me being busy packing Mrs Thomas, Phyllis was sent to see to your room, she did not know what was under the newspaper so gave the table a nudge. She upset some sky and part of the officers, but I have put the pieces in a box by your bed. She was upset when I told her you set store by it. I think it well to tell you, lest you should be disappointed when you get back. Phyllis will not be let go in your room again, where she has no business really.

Mr and Mrs Thomas were got off in good time for their train to Italy, and today I am getting the curtains to the cleaners. I was glad to know from Mrs Heccomb's telegram that you reached Seale. I have no doubt Mr and Mrs Thomas were glad also. I hope you are taking care of that wind along the front, which is very treacherous at this time of year. Mrs Heccomb spoke of the cold there last time she was up, she seemed pleased to get Mrs Thomas's former nutria coat. You did ought to wear a cardigan between your coat and your jumper, I packed you two but likely you will forget.

I hear Major Brutt called this afternoon and was disappointed to find the family gone. It seems he mistook the day, owing to what he thought Mrs Thomas had said. He asked for you and was told you were at the sea. You would not know the house with the curtains gone, not what you have been used to. Also Mr Thomas's books are out to be electric cleaned, preparatory to washing the shelves down. Your friend Mr Eddie came to the door after a muffler he says he left, and particularly remarked on the smell of soap. He also took from the drawing-room some French book he says he loaned to Mrs Thomas. I had to unsheet the drawing-room for him to find this, the room having been covered ready for the sweep.

I trust that you will do well at the seaside. I once visited Seale along with my married sister who lives at Dover. It is said to be a nice residential place. No doubt the time will fly till you come back. I must now close. Yours respectfully,

R. MATCHETT

P.S. Should you wish anything sent, no doubt you would write. A picture postcard would be sufficient.

Q. and M. S',
Friday

Darling Portia: Thanks for your letter written before starting. It is awful to realize you are away, in fact I hoped I might not, but I do. I rashly went round to Windsor Terrace to get back that red scarf, and it was as if you had all died of the plague and Matchett was disinfecting it after you. The house reeked of awful soap. Matchett had got all Thomas's books in a heap, and seemed to be dancing on them. She gave me a singularly dirty look. I felt your corpses must be laid out in the drawing-room, which was all sheets. That old crocodile took me up under protest and stood snapping her jaws while I dug out *Les Plaisirs et les jours*, which I'm anxious to get back before Anna loses it. It felt odd, while I was in the drawing-room, to know I wouldn't hear you scuttering on the stairs. Everything really had a charnel echo and I said to myself, 'She died young'.

I say, darling, how much do you think Matchett knows about you and me? It was a foul bleak day and I could have cried.

Now remember how awful I often feel and write me long letters. If you write too much about Dickie I shall come down and shoot him, I am a jealous man. Is he as awful as Anna says, and is Daphne? I really do want you to tell me everything, you are horrid to say that I don't read your letters. Shall I come down one week-end, even not to shoot Dickie? It might be frightfully funny if I did. I suppose they could have me to stay, don't you? But of course that all depends how things pan out; at present I am having an awful time.

This office is going to bits without Thomas, which would be gratifying for Thomas to know. I can't tell you how awful they all are. I always did know all these people were crooks. They

intrigue in really a poisonous way, and nothing is getting done. However, that gives me more time to write to you. You see I'm not using the office paper: I look after Thomas's interests while he's gone.

Oh, darling Portia, it's awful not to see you. Please do feel awful too. I saw a pair of Indian silver baby's bangles in Holborn. I think I'll send them to you for your silly wrists.

Do you remember Saturday?

I think it is just like them, packing you off like that to the seaside when everything could be so nice now. Anna locks you up like jam. I hope it will sleet and freeze all the time she is in that vulgar Italian villa. I really should laugh if I went to Seale. Do you hear the sea when you are in bed?

I must stop. I do feel homeless and sad. I have got to go out now for drinks with some people, but that isn't at all the same thing. Wouldn't it be nice if you were poking our fire and expecting me home at any minute?

Good-bye, Good night, you darling. Think of me last thing.

EDDIE

The Karachi Hotel,
Cromwell Road,
s.w.

Dear Miss Portia: I was sorry to miss you all when I called at 2 Windsor Terrace. I had hoped to wish your brother and sister-in-law luck on their trip, and hoped to reply personally to that very sweet little message you sent me through Mrs Quayne, reporting your progress made with a certain puzzle. I also meant to have asked if you would care to have another puzzle, as that must be nearly done. To do the same puzzle twice would be pretty poor fun. If you would allow me to send you another puzzle, you could always send on the first to a sick friend. I am told they are popular in nursing homes, but as I enjoy excellent health I have never checked up on this. That kind of puzzle was not much in vogue during the War.

The weather has turned quite nasty, you are 'well out of London' as the saying goes. Your brother's hospitable house

was, when I called, dismantled for spring cleaning. What a dire business that is! I hope you have struck some pleasant part of the coast? I expect you may find it pretty blowy down there. I have been kept pretty busy these last days with interviews in connexion with an appointment. From what I hear, things look quite like shaping up.

Some good friends of mine in this hotel, whose acquaintance I made here, have just moved on, and I find they leave quite a gap. One is often lucky in striking congenial people in these hotels. But of course people rather come and go.

Well, if you feel like trying your skill with yet another puzzle, will you be so good as to send me a little line? Just possibly you might care to have the puzzle to do at the seaside, where the elements do not always treat one as they should. If I were to know your address, I could have the puzzle posted direct to you. Meanwhile, your excellent parlourmaid will no doubt forward this. Very sincerely yours,   ERIC E. J. BRUTT

Portia had never had such a morning's post as this: it seemed to be one advantage of having left London. These three letters came on Saturday morning; she re-read them at a green-tiled table at the Corona Café, waiting for Mrs Heccomb. By this, her second morning, she was already into the Waikiki routine. Mrs Heccomb always shopped from ten-thirty to midday, with a break for coffee at the Corona Café. If she was not 'in town' by ten-thirty, she fretted. With her hive-shaped basket under her elbow, Portia in her wake, she punted happily, slowly up and down the High Street, crossing at random, quite often going back on her tracks. Women who shop by telephone do not know what the pleasures of buying are. Rich women live at such a distance from life that very often they never see their money – the Queen, they say, for instance, never carries a purse. But Mrs Heccomb's unstitched morocco purse, with the tarnished silver corners, was always in evidence. She paid cash almost everywhere, partly because she had found that something happens to bills, making them always larger than you think, partly because her roving disposition made her hate to be tied to one set of shops. She liked to be *known* in as many shops as possible,

to receive a personal smile when she came in. And she had by this time managed things so well that she was known in every Seale shop of standing. Where she had not actually bought things, she had repeatedly priced them. She did admit herself tied to one butcher, one dairy because they *sent*: Mrs Heccomb did not care for carrying meat, and the milk supply for a household must be automatic. Even to these two shops she was not wholly faithful: she had been known to pick up a kidney here and there, some new shade of butter, a crock of cream.

To Portia, who had never seen a purse open so often (when you live in hotels there is almost nothing to buy) Mrs Heccomb's expenditure seemed princely – though there was often change out of a florin. When Mrs Heccomb had too many pennies, she would build them up, at the next counter she came to, into pillars of twelve or six, and push them across cautiously. Where she paid in coppers only, she felt she had got a bargain: money goes further when you do not break into silver, and any provident person baulks at changing a note. Everything was bought in small quantities, exactly as it was wanted day by day. Today, for instance, she made the following purchases:

> One cake of Vinolia for the bathroom,
> Half a dozen Relief nibs,
> One pot of salmon and shrimp paste (small size),
> One pan scrubber of crumpled metal gauze,
> One bottle of Bisurated Magnesia tablets (small size),
> One bottle of gravy browning,
> One skein of 'natural' wool (for Dickie's vests),
> One electric light bulb,
> One lettuce,
> One length of striped canvas to reseat a deck chair,
> One set of whalebones to repair corsets,
> Two pair of lambs' kidneys,
> Half a dozen small screws,
> A copy of the *Church Times*.

She also made, from a list of Daphne's, and out of a special ten shilling note, a separate set of purchases for the party to-night. Portia bought a compendium – lightly ruled violet paper,

purple lined envelopes – and nine pennyworth of three-halfpenny stamps. Infected by the sea air with extravagance, she also bought a jade green box to keep a toothbrush in, and a length of red ribbon for a snood for tonight.

Now Mrs Heccomb had gone to the house agent's for her annual consultation about the summer let. Probably no other householder in Seale began to discuss the summer let so early. The fact was that Daphne and Dickie objected each year more strongly to turning out of Waikiki for the three best months. But their father had built the house for summer letting, and his widow adhered to this with a touch of piety. In July, August, September she took her painting things with her and moved on a round of visits to relatives: meanwhile, Daphne and Dickie were put out to board with friends. In view of the objections they always raised, she liked to get the let clinched well in advance, then to let them know of it as a *fait accompli*. But she was made sad, when she went to the house agent's, by the sense of conspiring against Daphne and Dickie.

So she did not take Portia with her to witness this dark act, but sent her to the Corona to book a table. The Corona was very full at this hour; the fashionable part was upstairs, looking down on the High Street. Only outsiders drank their coffee downstairs. And how bright it was up here, with the smell of hot roasting coffee, the whicker of wicker chairs. A stove threw out roaring heat: sun streamed through the windows, curdling the smoke of a few bold cigarettes. Ladies waiting for ladies looked through back numbers of the *Tatler* and *Sketch*. Dogs on leads wound themselves round the table legs. Paper tulips in vases, biscuits in coloured paper on the tile-topped tables struck bright notes. The waitresses knew everyone. It was so much gayer than London – also, there was abandonment about this morning feast: to be abandoned you must be respectable.

Several times Portia had looked up from her letters to watch one more lady's hat come up past the banisters. But for a long time no hat was Mrs Heccomb's. When Mrs Heccomb did finally come, she shot out of nowhere like a Jack-in-the-box. The three envelopes were still all over the table. Mrs Heccomb threw them a glance whose keenness was automatic, though the keenness

was quickly veiled by tact. Not for nothing had she been for years a duenna. Eddie's writing was, to the simple eye, disarming, but Major Brutt's was unflinchingly masculine. Matchett's letter could be put down at once as a letter that was likely to be from Matchett. Mrs Heccomb had not yet seen these handwritings: it was Daphne who galloped out to meet the morning post.

'Well, dear, I'm glad you have not been lonely. Mr Bunstable kept me. Now I shall order coffee. Look, eat a chocolate biscuit while we wait.'

Still slightly flustered by her own arrival, Mrs Heccomb balanced her basket on an empty chair and signalled to a waitress. She looked pink. On top of this she wore, like an extra hat, a distinct air of caution and indecision. 'It is so nice to get letters,' she said.

'Oh yes. This morning I had three.'

'I expect, travelling so much, you and your mother made many nice friends?'

'No, you see we travelled rather *too* much.'

'And now you have made friends with Anna's friends, I expect?'

'Some of them. Not all.'

Mrs Heccomb looked less anxious by several degrees. 'Anna', she said, 'is a wonderful judge of people. Even as a young girl she was always particular, and now such distinguished people come to her house, don't they? One would always be right in liking anyone Anna liked. She has a wonderful way of gathering people round her: it's so nice for you, dear, to have come to a happy house like that. I am sure it must be a great pleasure to her to see you get on so nicely with the people she knows. She would be so wonderfully sympathetic. I expect you love to show her the letters you get, don't you?'

'I only get many letters when I am at the sea.'

Momentarily, Mrs Heccomb looked nonplussed. Then her shoulder was given a sharp tap by a lady leaning across from one of the other tables. A playful, reproachful conversation ensued between them. Portia, herself considerably puzzled, poured cream on to her coffee out of a doll's jug. Soon she was

made known to Mrs Heccomb's lady, and stood up politely to shake hands. She stuck the letters back in the pocket of her tweed coat.

When they had left the café and were in the High Street, Mrs Heccomb, pausing outside Smoots', showed with a rather rueful upward gesture where Daphne worked. Portia pictured Daphne behind that window like a furious Lady of Shalott. 'Is she fond of reading?' she said.

'Well, no, but that's not so much what they want. They want a girl who *is* someone, if you know what I mean. A girl who – well, I don't quite know how to express it – a girl who did not come from a nice home would not do at all, *here*. You know, choosing books is such a personal thing; Seale is a small place and the people are so nice. Personality counts for so much here. The Corona Café is run by ladies, you know.'

'Oh.'

'And of course everyone knows Daphne. It is wonderful how she has settled down to the work. I'm afraid her father would not have thought it ideal. But one cannot always foresee the future, can one?'

'No.'

'Almost everyone changes their books there. You must go and see her one morning: she would be delighted. Oh dear, look; it's twelve! We shall have to hurry home.'

They dashed back to the sea down the asphalt walk, then waited about an hour in the lounge at Waikiki while Doris dealt with lunch. Mrs Heccomb turned her lamp shade round and round and said the varnish on it was drying. After lunch she said she'd be quiet just for a minute, then took a nap on the sofa with her back to the sea.

Portia looked several times at Mrs Heccomb napping, then took her shoes off and crept up to explore the bedroom floor of Waikiki, to see which Eddie's room could be. Mrs Heccomb's room, in which she dared not linger, contained a large double bed with a hollow in the middle, and a number of young girls' photographs. Daphne's room smelled of Coty powder (Chypre), an army of evening shoes was drawn up under the bureau, and a Dismal Desmond dog sat on the bed. Snapshots of confident

people of both sexes were stuck round the mirror. Dickie's room looked north towards the town, and had that physical smell north rooms so soon acquire. It contained boot jacks, boxing gloves, a stack of copies of *Esquire*, three small silver trophies on ebony stands gleaming underneath framed groups. Doris's room was so palpably Doris's that Portia quickly shut the door again. But she did also discover another room – it was wedge-shaped, like the end of a piece of cheese. Its dormer window looked north. In here were stacks of old cardboard boxes and a dressmaker's bust of quite royal arrogance: the walls were hung with photographs of such tropics as Dr Heccomb had visited. Here also, promisingly, were a stretcher bed, a square of mirror, and a bamboo table. Portia took one more look round, then crept downstairs again. By the time Mrs Heccomb woke, she was half way through a letter.

She was writing: 'There is a room, and I think you would like everything. There are two directions for us to walk in. I will not broach about this till tomorrow, which will be Sunday –'

Mrs Heccomb woke with a little snatch at her hair, as though she heard something in it. 'Busy, dear?' she said. 'We shall have to go out in about an hour. We are going out to tea up the hill – there are two daughters, though both a little older than you.' She tucked in her blouse at the back of her belt again, and for some time moved contentedly round the lounge, altering the position of one or two objects, as though she had had some new idea while asleep. A draught creeping through the sun porch rattled the curtain rings: Waikiki gave one of its shiplike creaks, and waves began to thump with greater force on the beach.

As Mrs Heccomb and Portia, both in chamois gloves, walked sedately up the hill out to tea, the daffodil buds in gardens knocked to and fro. Seale gave one of its spring afternoon dramas of wind and sun, and clouds bowled over the marsh that one saw from here. Down there, the curve of the bay crepitated in changing silver light.

'I expect you often go out to tea with Anna?'

'Well, Anna doesn't often go out to tea.'

On the way home, Mrs Heccomb took Portia to Evensong, which was intoned in the Lady Chapel. Then they went round to the vestry for some surplices, which Mrs Heccomb took home to mend. She could not aspire to do the altar flowers, as she could not afford beautiful flowers, so this was her labour of love for the church. 'The little boys are very rough,' she said, 'the gathers nearly always go at the neck.' It took some time to go through the surplices, and longer still to pin them up in brown paper – Mrs Heccomb, with other ladies with access to the vestry, kept a hoard of brown paper, for their own uses, behind a semi-sacred cupboard of pitched pine. The Vicar did not know of the existence of this. Whenever Mrs Heccomb opened a parcel, she saved the paper to take up to the church, so there was never brown paper at Waikiki ... When they did get back to Waikiki with the surplices, Daphne was punting chairs about the lounge.

Daphne's hair had been re-set, and looked like gilded iron. The door through to the dining-room stood open, so that the heat of the lounge fire might take some of the chill off the dining-room: the breath that came out from there was rather cold, certainly. They all went in there to have a look round, and Daphne blew the dust off a centre-piece of Cape gooseberries with an exasperatedly calm air.

'The bell rings beautifully now, dear.'

'Yes, the bell's all right, but when I tried ringing it Doris shot out and had a sort of fit.'

'Perhaps it's still rather loud.'

'But what I mean is, she must learn not to do that. She can't find the potted meat, either.'

'Oh, I'm so sorry, dear; it's hanging up in my basket.'

'Well, really, Mumsie ... As it is, you see, she hasn't even started the sandwiches. I suppose you've been at that church?' said Daphne, pouncing.

'Well, we just –'

'Well, I do think church might keep. It's Saturday, after all.'

Supper was cold that night, and was eaten early in order to give Doris plenty of time to clear. So they were to dress afterwards. Dickie was rather cold about this evening party, as he

had wished to watch an ice hockey match. He had spent his Saturday afternoon in Southstone playing ordinary hockey in the mud. 'I don't see why they want to come,' he said.

'Well after all, Clara's coming.'

'What does she want to come for? This is the first I've heard of it.'

'Well I really must say – I *must* say, really! You asked her yourself, Dickie: you did! You said why not drop in Saturday, and of course she jumped at it. I daresay she's cutting some other date.'

'Well, I don't know what dates all your friends have, but I know I never asked Clara. *Would* I ask Clara when the Montreal Eagles are here?'

'Which eagles, dear?' said Mrs Heccomb.

'They're at the Icedrome tonight – as Daphne has known for weeks.'

'Well, I don't care where your beastly old eagles are. All I know is that you did ask Clara. And you needn't go on as if *I* knew what dates Clara had. I should have thought that was your business, not mine.'

'Oh, would you really?' said Dickie, giving his sister a brassy stare. 'And what grounds, may I ask, have you for saying that?'

'Well, she's only round when you're here,' said Daphne, weakening slightly.

'Where the girl may choose to be is her own business, I take it.'

'Then don't you go making out she's a friend of mine.'

'Oh, all right, all right, all right, you didn't ask her, I did. *I* didn't want to see the Montreal Eagles, oh *no*. Must Cecil come?'

'I just slipped in and asked him,' said Mrs Heccomb. 'I thought you two might forget, and he would have been so hurt.'

Dickie said: 'I don't see why we have got to have Cecil.'

'I do,' said Daphne. 'Mumsie and I thought he would do for Portia.'

'Oh, Daphne, that was your idea, you know.'

For the first time, Dickie looked full at Portia with his commanding stag's eyes. 'You will find Cecil a bit cissie,' he said.

'Oh, Dickie, he's not.'

'Oh, I like Cecil all right, but I can't stand those cissie pullovers.'

'Well, you wear pullovers.'

'I don't wear cissie pullovers.'

'Oh, by the way, Dickie, you ought to see Doris bounce when
she hears that bell.'

'Oh, so it rings now, does it?'

'No thanks to you, either.'

'Dickie's so busy, dear – Look, we ought to go up and dress
now. And Doris is in there wanting to clear.'

'Then for goodness' sake why doesn't she? Make her open
the windows – we don't want the whole place smelling of veal
and ham.'

The three ladies went upstairs, Mrs Heccomb taking her last
cup of coffee with her. Dickie, after an interval for reflection,
could be heard going up to change his appearance, too. Now, all
over the bedroom floor of Waikiki, chests of drawers were
banged open, taps were run. A black night wind was up, and
Waikiki breasted it steadily, straining like a liner: every fix-
ture rattled. This all went to heighten a pre-party tensity of
the nerves. Portia wormed her way into her black velvet,
which, from hanging only behind a curtain, had taken on a
briny dampness inside: the velvet clung to her skin above her
chemise top. She combed back her hair and put on the red
snood – so tight that it drew the ends of her eyebrows up. With
eyes too much dilated to see, she looked past herself in the
mirror.

She was first downstairs and, squatting on the tiled kerb in
front of the fire, heard the chimney roar. With arms raised from
the elbows, like an Egyptian, she turned and toasted her body,
feeling the clammy velvet slowly unstick from between her
shoulder blades.

This was to be her first party. Tonight, the ceiling rose
higher, the lounge extended tense and mysterious. Columns of
translucent tawny shadow stood between the orange shades of
the lamps. The gramophone stood open, a record on it, the arm
with the needle bent back like an arm ready to strike. Doris not

seeing Portia, Doris elate and ghostly in a large winged cap passed through the lounge with trays. Out there at sea they might take this house for another lighted ship – and soon this magnetic room would be drawing people down the dark esplanade. Portia saw her partners with no faces: whoever she danced with, it would always be Eddie.

Dickie came down in a dark blue pin-striped suit, and asked if she'd like to help him roll the carpet back. They had got as far as rolling back the settee when a sort of bat-like fumbling was heard at the glass door, and Dickie stopped with a grunt to let in Cecil.

'I say,' Cecil said, 'I'm afraid I've come rather early.'

'Well, you have rather in one way. However, give a hand with the carpet. As usual, everything has been left to me – Oh, by the way, this is Mr Cecil Bowers, Miss Portia Quayne ... By the way, Cecil,' said Dickie, rather more sternly, 'the bell does ring now.'

'Oh? Sorry. It didn't use to.'

'Well, make a note that it does.'

'Dickie, who's *that*?' Daphne wailed over the banisters.

'Only Cecil. He's rolling up the carpet.'

When Cecil had finished rolling up the carpet he straightened his tie and went off to wash his hands. Portia found no special fault with his appearance, though it was certainly not as manly as Dickie's. When he came back, he was beginning to say to her: 'I understand that you have just come from London,' when Daphne appeared and made him carry a tray.

'Now, Cecil,' she said, 'there's no time to stand there chatting.' Her manner made it quite clear that if Cecil *were* for Portia, he would come on to her as one of Daphne's discards. Daphne wore a *crêpe de Chine* dress, cut clinging into the thighs and draped lusciously elsewhere: on it poppies, roses, nasturtiums flowered away, only slightly blurred by the folds. In her high-heeled emerald shoes, she stepped higher than ever. When the bell rang, seeming to tweak at the whole house, and Dickie went to let some more people in, Daphne sent Cecil and Portia into the dining-room to stick the flags on the sandwiches and to count the glasses for cider-cup.

They could only find what was inside the sandwiches by turning up the corners to have a look. Even so, they could not be sure which kind of fish paste was which: Cecil, having made sure they were alone in the room, tasted a crumb of each with his finger-tip. 'Not quite in order,' he said, 'but *que voulez vous?*'

'No one will know,' said Portia, standing behind him.

The complicity set up between her and Cecil made them sit down on two chairs, when they had planted the flags, and look at each other with interest. There was a hum in the lounge, and no one was missing them. 'These do's of Daphne's and Dickie's are very jolly,' said Cecil.

'Do they often have them?'

'Quite frequently. They are always on Saturdays. They always seem to go with rather a swing. But I daresay this may seem quiet after London?'

'It doesn't really. Do you often go to London?'

'Well, I do – when I don't slip over to France.'

'Oh, do you slip over to France?'

'Yes, I must say I often do. You may think me mad, too: everyone here does. Everyone here behaves as though France did not exist. "What is that you see over there?" I sometimes say to them, when it's a clear day. They say, "Oh, that's France." But it makes no impression on them. I often go to Boulogne on a day trip.'

'All by yourself?'

'Well, I have been by myself, and also I often go with a really wonderfully sporting aunt of mine. And once or twice I have been with another fellow.'

'And what do you do?'

'Oh, I principally walk about. In spite of being so easy to get at, Boulogne is really wonderfully French, you know. I doubt if Paris itself could be much Frencher. No, I haven't yet been to Paris: what I always feel is, supposing it rather disappointed me ... "Oh, hullo," all those others always say to me, when I haven't shown up at the Pav or the Icedrome or the Palais, "you've been abroad again!" What conclusions they come to I've no idea,' said Cecil consciously, looking down his nose. 'I

don't know if you've noticed,' he went on, 'but so few people care if they don't enlarge their ideas. But I always like to enlarge mine.'

'Oh, so do I.' She looked timidly at Cecil, then said: 'Lately, my ideas have enlarged a lot.'

'I thought they must have,' said Cecil. 'You gave me just that impression. That is why I am talking like this to you.'

'Some of my ideas get enlarged almost before I have them.'

'Yes, that was just what I felt. Usually, I am a bit reserved ... Do you get on well with Dickie?'

'Well, when you came he and I were just going to roll the carpet up.'

'I hope I was not tactless.'

'Oh no.'

'Dickie's extremely popular,' Cecil said with a mixture of gloom and pride. 'I should say he was a born leader of men. I expect you find Daphne awfully fascinating?'

'Well, she is out most of the day.'

'Daphne', said Cecil, a shade reproachfully, 'is one of the most popular girls I have ever met. I don't suppose one will get near her the whole evening.'

'Oh dear! Couldn't you try?'

'To tell you the truth,' said Cecil, 'I am not doing so badly where I am.'

At this interesting point Mrs Heccomb, in a claret lace dress that could not have come from Anna, looked anxiously into the dining-room. 'Oh, here you are, dear,' she said. 'I was wondering. Good evening, Cecil, I'm so glad you could come. I think they are thinking of dancing quite soon now.'

Portia and Cecil rose and trailed to the door. In the lounge, an uncertain silence told them that the party's first impetus had lapsed. About a dozen people leaned round the walls, sat rather stonily on the settee-back, or crouched on the roll of carpet. They were all looking passively at Daphne, willing though not keen to fall in with her next plan. Mrs Heccomb may have been right when she said they were thinking of dancing – if they *were* thinking, no doubt it was about that. Daphne gave them one

164

or two hostile looks – this was what she called sticking about. She turned, and with Mr Bursely beside her, stickily fingering records, began to hover over the gramophone.

But there was a deadlock here, for she would not start the gramophone till they had got up, and they would not get up till she had started the gramophone. Dickie stood by the mantelpiece with Clara, clearly feeling that he had done enough. His manner rather said: 'Now if we had gone to the Eagles, this would not have happened.' Clara was a smallish girl with crimped platinum hair, a long nose, a short neck, and the subservient expression of a good white mouse. Round her neck she wore a frill of white organdie roses, which made her head look as though it were on a tray. Her manner of looking up made Dickie look still more virile. Any conversation they did seem to be having seemed to be due to Clara's tenacity.

Portia's appearing in the doorway with Cecil released some inside spring in Daphne immediately. No doubt she thought of Anna – stung to life, she let off the gramophone, banged the needle down, and foxtrotted on to the parquet with Mr Bursely. Four or five other couples then rose and faced each other to dance. Portia wondered if Cecil would ask her – so far, they had been on such purely mental terms. While she wondered, Dickie stepped from Clara's side, impressively crossed the room, and stood over Portia, impassive. 'Shall we?' he said.

She began to experience the sensation of being firmly trotted backwards and forwards, and at each corner slowly spun like a top. Looking up, she saw Dickie wear the expression many people wear when they drive a car. Dickie controlled her by the pressure of a thumb under her shoulder blade; he supported her wrist between his other thumb and a forefinger – when another couple approached he would double her arm up, like someone shutting a penknife in a hurry. Crucified on his chest against his breathing, she felt her feet brush the floor like any marionette's. Increasingly less anxious, she kept her look fixed on the cleft of his chin. She did not flatter herself: this *démarche* of Dickie's could have only one object – by chagrining Clara to annoy Daphne. Across Mr Bursely's shoulder, Daphne threw Dickie a furious, popping look. For Clara was both grateful and

well-to-do, and Daphne, by an unspoken arrangement, got her percentage on any fun Clara had.

But Dickie, though inscrutable, was kind: half way through the second record, he said: 'You seem to be getting on quite well.' Too pleased, she left behind one toe, and Dickie immediately trod on it. 'Sorry!' 'Oh, *I'm* sorry!' She had reason to be, so Dickie accepted this. Taking her more in hand, he splayed the whole of one palm against her ribs and continued to make her foxtrot. When the record was over, he took her in state to the fire, where poor Clara had stood. Shrinking but elated queen of the room she looked down it, saw Mrs Heccomb knitting, saw Mr Bursely's hand over the *crêpe de Chine* bow just above Daphne's bottom as they talked in the sun porch with their backs to the room, saw Cecil despondently being civil elsewhere, Clara's head sadly aslant on her white ruff. She hoped no one was bearing her any malice.

'You don't smoke, do you?' Dickie said rather threateningly.

'I'm not really sure how to.'

Dickie, having slowly lighted a cigarette of his own, said: 'I should not let that worry you. Most girls smoke too much.'

'Well, I may never begin.'

'And another thing you had much better not begin is putting stuff on your nails. That sort of thing makes the majority of men sick. One cannot see why girls do it.'

'Perhaps they don't know.'

'Well, I always tell a girl. If one is to know a girl, it is much better to tell her what one thinks. Another thing I don't like is messed-up mouths. When I give a girl tea, I always look at her cup. Then, if she leaves any red muck on the rim, I say, "Hullo, I didn't know that cup had a pink pattern." Then the girl seems quite taken aback.'

'But suppose the cup had really got a pink pattern?'

'In that case, I should say something else. Girls make a mistake in trying to be attractive in ways that simply lose them a man's respect. No man would want to give his children a mother with that sort of stuff all over her face. No wonder the population is going down.'

'My sister-in-law says men are too particular.'

'I cannot see that it is particular to have ideals. I should only care to marry a girl who seemed natural and likely to make a good home. And I think you would find that the majority of fellows, if you asked them, would feel the same. Will you have some lemonade?'

'No, thank you; not yet.'

'Well, if you'll excuse me, I think I must fix myself up for this next dance. You and I might have the sixth from now. I will look for you by the gramophone.'

Portia was going to sit beside Mrs Heccomb when Cecil came up and asked for the next dance. 'You were swept away before I could speak,' he said – but all the same, he looked at her with respect. Cecil's method of dancing was more persuasive, and Portia found she did not get on so well. She took a look at Clara's mouselike hand splayed rather imploringly on a partner's shoulder (Dickie was waltzing with a fine girl in orange) and saw Clara wore no varnish on her nails. Dickie's partner did. After that, she kept twisting round to look at every girl's hands, and this made her collide and bump with Cecil. After three rounds he suggested another talk: clearly he liked her more on the mental plane. They sat down on the settee, in a draught from the sun porch, and Portia began to reproach herself for feeling that Cecil's manner lacked authority. Cecil stopped talking to give a glare. 'Here comes that fellow Bursely from the School of Musketry. He seems to think he can behave all anyhow here. I don't think Dickie really thinks much of him. We must let him see that we are deep in talk.'

But though she obediently fixed her eyes on Cecil, Mr Bursely bumped on to the settee on her other side. 'Am I butting in?' he said, but not anxiously.

'You should know,' muttered Cecil.

Mr Bursely said brightly: 'Didn't catch what you said.'

'I said, I am going to look for a cigarette.'

'Now, what's eating him?' said Mr Bursely. 'As a matter of fact,' he went on, 'you and I *were* introduced, but I don't think you heard: you were looking the other way. I asked Daphne who you were the moment you buzzed in, but she didn't seem to be too keen we should meet. Then I asked the old lady to put

us in touch, but she couldn't make herself heard above the up-roar. Quite a little gathering, what?'

'Yes, quite.'

'You having a good time?'

'Yes, *very*, thank you.'

'You look it,' said Mr Bursely. 'The eyes starry and so on. Look here, like to slip out to the so-called bar? Soft drinks only: no licence. Some little bird told me that was the drill here, so I had one or two in the mess before pushing round.' This was more or less evident. Portia said she would rather stay where they were. 'Oh, right-o,' said Mr Bursely: sliding down on the sofa he stuck his feet in their tan shoes a good way out. 'You a stranger in these parts?'

'I only came on Thursday.'

'Getting to know the natives?'

'Yes.'

'I'm not doing badly, either. But of course we mostly cut into Southstone.'

'Who is we?'

'We licentious soldiery. Listen: how young are you?'

'Sixteen.'

'Gosh – I thought you were about ten. Anyone ever told you you're a sweet little kid?'

Portia thought of Eddie. 'Not exactly,' she said.

'Well, I'm telling you now. Your Uncle Peter's telling you. Always remember what Uncle Peter said. Honestly when you first keeked round that door, I wanted to cry and tell you about my wicked life. And I bet you take a lot of chaps that way?'

Not happily, Portia put a finger inside her tight snood. Mr Bursely slewed right round on the sofa, with one arm right along the back. His clean-skinned face, clotted up with emotion, approached Portia's – unwilling, she looked at, not into, his eyes, which were urgent blue poached eggs. Her unnerved look seemed to no more than float on his regardlessness of it.

'Just tell me', said Mr Bursely, 'that you'd be a bit sorry if I was dead.'

'Oh yes. But why should you be?'

'Well, one never knows.'

'No – I suppose not.'

'You *are* a sweet little kid –'

'– Portia,' said Mrs Heccomb, 'this is Mr Parker, a great friend of Dickie's. Mr Parker would like to dance with you.' Portia looked up to find a sort of a rescue party, headed by Mrs Heccomb, standing over the settee. She got up rather limply, and Mr Parker, with an understanding smile, at once danced her away. Bobbing, just out of time, below Mr Parker's shoulder, she looked round to see Daphne, with set and ominous face, take her place on the settee next to Mr Bursely.

4

In church, during the sermon, Portia asked herself for the first time why what Mr Bursely had said had set up such disconcerting echoes, why she had run away from it in her mind. There was something she did not want to look straight at – was this why, since the party yesterday night, she had not once thought of Eddie? It is frightening to find that the beloved may be unwittingly caricatured by someone who does not know him at all. The devil must have been in Mr Bursely when he asked, and asked with such confidence, if she had not been told she was a sweet little kid. The shock was that she could not, now, remember Eddie's having in effect called her anything else. Stooping down, as she sat beside Mrs Heccomb, to examine the stitching on her brown mocha gloves – which in imitation of Mrs Heccomb she kept on while she sat, wrists crossed on her knee – she wondered whether a feeling could spring straight from the heart, be imperative, without being original. (But if love were original, if it were the unique device of two unique spirits, its importance would not be granted; it could not make a great common law felt. The strongest compulsions we feel throughout life are no more than compulsions to repeat a pattern: the pattern is not of our own device.)

Had Mr Bursely had, behind that opaque face, behind that

expression moulded by insobriety, the impulse that had made Eddie write her that first note? Overlaid, for the rest of the party, by the noise and excitement, was dread that the grace she had with Eddie might reduce to that single maudlin cry. This dread had haunted her tardy sleep, and sucked at her when she woke like the waves sucking the shingle in the terribly quiet morning air.

Everything became threatened.

There are moments when it becomes frightening to realize that you are not, in fact, alone in the world – or at least, alone in the world with one other person. The telephone ringing when you are in a day-dream becomes a cruel attacking voice. That general tender kindness towards the world, especially kindness of a young person, comes from a pitying sense of the world's unreality. The happy passive nature, locked up with itself like a mirror in an airy room, reflects what goes on but demands not to be approached. A pact with life, a pact of immunity, appears to exist – But this pact is not respected for ever – a street accident, an overheard quarrel, a certain note in a voice, a face coming too close, a tree being blown down, someone's unjust fate – the peace tears right across. Life militates against the seclusion we seek. In the chaos that suddenly thrusts in, nothing remains unreal, except possibly love. Then, love only remains as a widened susceptibility: it is felt at the price of feeling all human dangers and pains. The lover becomes the sentient figurehead of the whole human ship, thrust forward by the weight of the race behind him through pitiless elements. Pity the selfishness of lovers: it is brief, a forlorn hope; it is impossible.

Frantic smiles at parties, overtures that have desperation behind them, miasmic reaches of talk with the lost bore, short cuts to approach through staring, squeezing, or kissing – all indicate that one cannot live alone. Not only is there no question of solitude, but in the long run we may not chose our company. The attempt at Windsor Terrace to combat this may have been what made that house so queasy and cold. That mistaken approach to life – of which at intervals they were all conscious, from Thomas Quayne down to the cook – produced

the tensions and hitches of an unpromising love affair. Each person at Windsor Terrace lived impaled upon a private obsession, however slight. The telephone, the door bell, the postman's knock were threatening intimations, though still far off. Crossing that springy door mat, the outside person suffered a sea change. In fact, something edited life in the Quayne's house – the action of some sort of brake or deterrent was evident in the behaviour of such people as Eddie. At the same time, no one seemed clear quite *what* was being discarded, or whether anything vital was being let slip away. If Matchett were feared, if she seemed to threaten the house, it was because she seemed most likely to put her thumb on the thing.

The uneditedness of life here at Waikiki made for behaviour that was pushing and frank. Nothing set itself up here but the naïvest propriety – that made Daphne shout but not swear, that kept Dickie so stern and modest, that had kept even Mr Bursely's hand, at yesterday evening's party, some inches above the bow on Daphne's behind. Propriety is no serious check to nature – in fact, nature banks itself up behind it – thus, eyes constantly bulged and skins changed colour with immediate unsubtle impulses. Coming from Windsor Terrace, Portia found at Waikiki the upright rudeness of the primitive state – than which nothing is more rigidly ruled. The tremble felt through the house when a door banged or someone came hurriedly downstairs, the noises made by the plumbing, Mrs Heccomb's prodigality with half-crowns and shillings, the many sensory hints that Doris was human and did not function in a void of her own – all these made Waikiki the fount of spontaneous living. Life here seemed to be at its highest voltage, and Portia stood to marvel at Daphne and Dickie as she might have marvelled at dynamos. At nights, she thought of all that force contained in those single beds in the other rooms.

In terms of this free living, she now saw, or resaw, not only the people she met at Waikiki, but everyone she had known. The few large figures she saw here represented society with an alarming fairness, an adequacy that she could not deny. In them, she was forced to see every motive and passion – for motives and passions are alarmingly few. Any likeness between Mr Bursely

and Eddie her love did still hope to reject. All the same, something asked her, or forced her to ask herself, whether, last night on the settee, it had not been Eddie that emerged from the bush?

Portia felt her sixpence for the collection between the palm of her right hand and the palm of her glove. The slight tickling, and the milled pressure of the new coin's edge, when she closed her hand, recalled her to where she was – in Seale church, in a congregation of stalwart elderly men and of women in brown, grey, navy, or violet, with collars of inexpensive fur. The sun, slanting moltenly in at the south windows, laid a dusty nimbus over the furs, and printed cheeks with the colours of stained glass. Turning her head a little, she perceived people with whom she had been to tea. Above the confident congregation the church rose to its kind inscrutable height. Tilting her chin up, she studied the east window and its glittering tale: she had joined the sermon late and just got the gist of it – though it was after Easter, one must not be more callous than one had been in Lent.

Fanned on down the aisle by blasts from the organ, the choir disappeared in the vestry under the tower. Mrs Heccomb, as the procession passed, cast some appraising looks at the surplices. Brasso and the devotion of her fellow ladies had given a blond shine to the processional cross. As the last chords sounded, discreet smiles were exchanged across the aisle, and the congregation jumbled happily out. Mrs Heccomb was a great porch talker, and it was therefore in quite a knot of friends that she and Portia at last started downhill. Daphne and Dickie were not great church-goers: the Sunday after a party they always voted against it. Back at Waikiki the lounge, restored to order, was full of sun; Daphne and Dickie read the Sunday papers in a very strong smell of roasting meat. They had not been down at twenty minutes past ten, when Mrs Heccomb and Portia had started for church. Outside, gulls skimmed in the rather cold air, and Mrs Heccomb quickly shut the glass door.

'Hullo,' said Dickie to Portia. 'And how are *you* this morning?'

'Very well, thank you.'

'Well, at least it is over,' said Dickie, returning to the *Sunday Pictorial*.

Daphne was still wearing her red mules. 'Oh goodness,' she said. 'Cecil is so wet! Coming early like that, then sticking round like that. I don't know how he has the nerve, really ... Oh, and I ought to tell you: Clara's left her pearl bag.'

Mrs Heccomb, rearranging one or two objects, said: 'How wonderfully you have tidied everything up.'

'All but the bookcase,' Dickie said pointedly.

'What do you mean about the bookcase, dear?'

'We shall need a glazier to tidy up *that* bookcase. Daphne's soldier friend put his elbow through it – as you might notice, Mumsie, if you cared to look. There seems to be no suggestion that he should foot the bill.'

'Oh, I don't think we could quite ask him, dear ... It seemed to be a very successful party.'

Daphne, from behind the *Sunday Express*, said: 'It was all right.' She raised her voice. 'Though some people cut their own friends, then are stuffy to other people's. Mr Bursely was shoved against the bookcase by Wallace Parker shoving in that rude way. I'm only thankful he didn't hurt himself. I didn't like him to see us so rough house.'

'If you ask me,' said Dickie, 'I don't suppose he noticed. He'd have stayed stuck in the bookcase if Charlie Hoster hadn't pulled him out. He arrived here pretty lit, and I'm told he nipped down the front and had two or three quick ones at the Imperial Arms. I wonder what he'll smash next time he comes blowing in. I cannot say that that is a fellow I like. But apparently I do not know what is what.'

'Well, Clara liked him all right. That is how she forgot her bag. She stopped on to give him a lift home in her car.'

'So you pointed out. Well, if that bag is Clara's, I don't like it: it seems to me to be covered with ants' eggs.'

'Well, why don't you tell her so?'

'I no doubt shall. I shall no doubt tell her this afternoon. Clara and I are going to play golf.'

'Oh you *are* a mean, Dickie! You never said! Evelyn's expecting us all to badminton.'

'Well, she will simply have to expect me, I'm afraid. Clara's picking me up at half past two. We may buzz back here for tea, or we may go back to her place — By the way, Mumsie, can Doris be sharp with dinner?'

'She's just going to lay, dear. May I move your paper? Daphne, what are you doing after lunch?'

'Well, a lot of us thought we might go for a short walk. Then we're all going round to Evelyn's to badminton. Do you mean you'd like me to take Portia along?'

'That might be nice, dear. You'd like that, wouldn't you, Portia? In that case I may just take a little rest. Last night was so successful that we were rather late.'

The walking party – Daphne, Portia, Evelyn (the fine girl who had worn orange last night), Cecil (who did not seem to have been asked), and two other young men called Charlie and Wallace – deployed slowly along the top of the sea wall in the direction of Southstone. The young men wore plus-fours, pullovers, felt hats precisely dinted in at the top, and ribbed stockings that made their calves look massive. Daphne and Evelyn wore berets, scarves with dogs' heads, and natty check overcoats. Evelyn had brought her dog with her.

The road on top of the wall was as deserted as ever: at the foot of the wall the sea, this afternoon mackerel blue, swelled sleekly between the breakwaters. Here and there a gull on a far-out post would be floated off by the swell, looking rather silly. There was a breakwater smell – a smell of sea-pickled planks, of slimy green boards being sucked by the tides. The immense spring sky arched from the inland woods to the marine horizon. The wall made a high causeway on which the walkers walked between sea and land: here you smelled not only the sea but a land breath – from the market gardens, the woods in clefts of the chalk hills, the gorse budding in its spiny darkness up there on the links where Dickie and Clara were. The crests of two airy tides, the sea's and the land's, breaking against each other above the asphalt, made a nervous elation, so that you spun, inwardly, in the blue-whiteness of the quiet and thrilling day.

Daphne's party walked in a Sundayish dogged manner, using

without sensation their deep lungs. They knew every inch of the sea wall; they looked ahead to Southstone, where the dome of the Splendide was bright gold. The sense of exposure this airy bareness gave them made them, with one another, at once sidelong and bold. On the whole, they walked abreast, but as far apart as they could; at times they converged so close that they jogged elbows; if they split up into twos, the twos called across to each other – this was daylight: there was no *tête-à-tête*. At the end of a mile and a half they reached the old lifeboat station, where without a word they all wheeled round to return. The girls fell into a three; the three young men kept pace exactly behind them. They faced west.

With the first touch of evening, the first dazzle, a vague poeticness invaded them. Yawnfuls of ozone stopped the desultory talk. Evelyn took Daphne's arm; Cecil veered out alone to the edge of the esplanade and began to kick a lonely pebble along. A lovely brigantine appeared on the Channel, pink with light.

Portia drew a breath, then suddenly said to Daphne: 'A friend of mine – could he ever come and stay here?'

Brought out with a bang like this, it sounded quite all right.

Daphne veered thoughtfully round, hands in her pockets, chin deep in the folds of her doggy scarf, and Evelyn peered across Daphne, holding on to her arm. '*What* say?' Daphne said. 'A boy friend, do you mean?'

Evelyn said: 'That's what she's been in such a study about.'

'Could he how much?' said Daphne.

'Ever come and stay here?'

'Come and stay here when?'

'For a week-end.'

'Well, if you *have* a boy friend. I don't see why not. Do you see why not, Evelyn?'

'I should have thought it depended.'

'Yes, it depends, naturally. Have you really got a friend, though?'

'Just fancy, her,' added Evelyn. 'Still, *I* don't see why not.'

Daphne said swiftly: 'Friend of your sister-in-law?'

'Oh yes. She, he, they –'

'He'll be a bit ritzy for us, then, won't he? However,' said Daphne looking at Portia derisively, but with a touch of respect, 'if he's really as keen as all that it won't hurt him to lump it. Well, you certainly don't lose any time, do you? Of course, you'll have to square it with Mumsie, of course ... Go *on*: don't be such a little silly. She won't think anything of it; she's used to boys.'

But boys were not Eddie. Portia paused, then said: 'I thought I would ask you, then I thought you might ask her.'

'What's your friend in?' put in Evelyn. 'The Diplomatic?'

'*Who's* in the Diplomatic?' said Charlie, coming alongside.

'Portia's friend who's coming.'

'Well, he is not really: he's in my brother's office.'

'Well, after all,' said Evelyn, adjusting to this. She was the receptionist in Southstone's biggest beauty parlour: her face, whatever Dickie might think of it, continued to bloom in luscious and artificial apricot tones. Her father was Mr Bunstable, the important house agent who not only negotiated the Waikiki summer let but had clients throughout the county. Evelyn was thus not only a social light but had a stable position – consequently, she could not be hoped to enter into Daphne's feeling against the Quaynes. Business people were business people. She said kindly: 'Then it's been nice for him, picking up with you.'

'Your sister-in-law', said Daphne with some relish, 'would probably have a fit.'

Evelyn said: 'I don't see why.'

'Say, Cecil,' cried Daphne, whisking round sharply at him, 'must you keep on kicking that old stone?'

'So sorry: I was thinking something out.'

'Well, if you want to think, why come for a walk? Anyone might think this was a funeral – I say, Wallace, I say do listen, Charlie: Portia doesn't think much of any of you boys! She's having her own friend down.'

'Local talent', said Wallace, 'not represented. Well, these ladies from London – what can you expect?'

'Yes, you'd think', said Daphne, 'it should be enough for anyone, watching Cecil kicking that old stone.'

'Oh, it isn't that,' said Portia, looking at them anxiously. 'It's not that, really, I mean.'

'Well, I don't see why she shouldn't,' said Evelyn, closing the matter. She went to the head of some steps to whistle to her dog, which had got down on to the beach and was rolling in something horrid.

The others waited for Evelyn. The act of stopping sent a slight shock through the party, like the shock felt through a train that has pulled up. They were really more like a goods than a passenger train – content as a row of trucks, they stood solidly facing the way they would soon walk. Over still distant Seale, crowned by the church, smoke dissolved in the immature spring sun. The veil etherealized hillside villas with their gardens of trees; behind the balconies and the gables the hill took a tinge of hyacinth blue and looked like the outpost of a region of fantasy. Portia, glancing along the others' faces, was satisfied that Eddie had been forgotten. They did more than not think of Eddie, they thought of nothing.

She had learned to be less alarmed by Daphne's set since she had learned to plumb their abeyances. People are made alarming by one's dread of their unremitting, purposeful continuity. But in Seale, continuity dwelt in action only – interrupt what anybody was doing, and you interrupted what notions they had had. When these young people stopped doing what they were doing, they stopped all through, like clocks. Thus nothing, completely nothing filled this halt on their way to Sunday tea. Conceivably, astral smells of tea-cakes with hot currants, of chocolate biscuits, and warmed leather chairs vibrated towards them from Evelyn's home. They had walked; they would soon be back; they must have done themselves good.

Evelyn's dog came up the steps with a foul smear on its back, was scolded and wagged its rump in a merrily servile way. The dog was ordered to heel, where it did not stay, and the party, still with no word spoken, dropped forward into steady motion again.

At Evelyn's, Portia had time to think about next Sunday (or the Sunday after, was it to be?) for no one said much and she did not play badminton. The Bunstables' large villa had been

built in the early twenties in the Old Normandy manner – inside and out it was dark and nubbly with oak. It was a complex of nooks, inside which leaded windows of thick greenish glass diluted the spring sky. The stairs were manorial, the living-rooms sumptuously quaint. Brass or copper disks distorted your face everywhere; there were faience tiles. This Norman influence had blown so obliquely across the Channel that few Seale people knew it as not British, though of some merrier period. The dining-room was so impressively dark that the antiqued lights soon had to be switched on. Evelyn's manner to her mother was disdainful but kindly: her father was out. Cecil, on showing a wish to sit by Portia, was sent to sit next the tea-pot, to talk to Mrs Bunstable. He almost at once dropped a quarter of buttered tea-cake on to one thigh of his plus-fours, and spent most of tea time trying to look *dégagé*, while, with a tea serviette dipped in hot water, he secretly failed to get the butter off.

Tea over, they moved to the glass-roofed badminton court: here the rubber shoes of the whole party hung by their laces from a row of hooks. While the rest put their shoes on, Portia climbed on a high stool close to the radiator. To hitch her heels on an upper rung of the stool made her feel like a bird. She began to imagine Eddie, next Sunday, taking part in all this. Or, when it came to the moment, would they find they would rather stay by the sea – not on the sea wall but out there near the martello towers, watching waves rush up the flat sands in the dusk? No, not for too long – for she and Eddie must on no account miss the Sunday fun. He and she had not yet been together into society. Even his name said on the sea front had made Daphne's friends show several shades more regard for her – though since then they had forgotten why – she felt more kindly embraced by these people already. Supposing she had a wish to be put across, who could do this for her better than Eddie could? How much ice he would cut; how proud she would be of him. The wish to lead out one's lover must be a tribal feeling; the wish to be seen as loved is part of one's self-respect. And, they would be in each other's secret; she would see him just not winking across the room. Alone, one has a rather incomplete outlook –

one is not sure what is funny, what is not. One solid pleasure of
love is to check up together on what has happened. Since they
were together last, she did not think she had laughed – she had
smiled, of course, but chiefly to please people. No, it would be
wrong to stay down by the sea.

Cecil, left out of the first set, edged round the court, and
came to stand by Portia: he propped one foot on the lower rung
of the stool and sent through it the vibration of a sigh. She put
her thoughts away quickly. Away in the lounge, at the far end
of the passage, Evelyn's mother switched the Luxemburg music
on: this fitted the game – the pouncing, slithering players, the
ping of the shots – into a sprightly rhythm, that pleased Portia
but further depressed Cecil. 'I don't care for spring, somehow,'
he said. 'It makes me feel a bit seedy.'

'You don't look seedy, Cecil.'

'I do with all this butter,' said Cecil, plucking unhappily at
his plus-fours. He went on: 'What were you thinking about?'

'I'm not thinking any more.'

'But you were, weren't you? I saw you. If I were a more oncoming sort of fellow I should offer you a penny, and so on.'

'I was wondering what next Sunday would be like.'

'Much the same, I expect. At this time of year, one begins
to want a change.'

'But this is a change for me.'

'Of course it's nice to think it's a change for someone. It will
be a change for your friend too, I expect. Funny, when I first
saw you at Daphne's party, you didn't look as though you had
a friend in the world. That was what drew me to you, I daresay.
I seem to have got you wrong, though. Are you really an
orphan?'

'Yes, I am,' said Portia a shade shortly. 'Are you?'

'No, not at present, but I suppose it's a thing one is bound
to be. The thought of the future rather preys on my mind. I am
quite enough of a lone wolf as it is. I get on well with girls up
to a certain point, but then they seem to find me too enigmatic.
I don't find it easy to let myself go. I don't think most girls appreciate friendship; all they want is to be given a rush.'

'I like friendship very much.'

'Ah,' said Cecil, and looked at her gloomily. 'But if you will excuse my saying so, that may be because you are so young that no fellow has started to rush you yet. Once that starts, it seems to go straight to a girl's head. But you have still got a rather timid manner. Yesterday I felt quite sorry for you.'

She did not know how to reply. Cecil bent down and once more studied his plus-fours. 'Of course,' he said, 'these can go to the cleaners, but that all costs money, you see, and I had been hoping to run over to France.'

'Perhaps your mother could get it off with petrol. Butter is always got off my clothes that way.'

'Oh, is it?' said Cecil. 'I say,' he added, 'I had been rather wondering if you would care to run into Southstone one evening, on the five-thirty bus, and meet me after the office. We could then come in on the second half of the concert at the East Cliff Pavilion, and might get a spot of food there; it is a nice rather cosmopolitan place. If you would really care –'

'Oh, yes, I should simply love it!'

'Then we might call it a date. We'll fix the date itself later.'

'Oh, that is kind of you. Thank you.'

'Not at all,' said Cecil.

The game was over: Charlie and Daphne had just beaten Wallace and Evelyn. Evelyn came across and pulled Cecil on to the court, saying he must now play instead of her. '*Sure* you wouldn't care to try?' she said to Portia nicely. 'Oh well, I see how you feel. I tell you what, you ought to come round one week-day and have a knock up with Clara. *She* wants practice, you know. Then you could play next time ... My goodness,' exclaimed Evelyn, 'we do want some air in here! The ventilation is awful!'

Kindly pulling Portia along by one elbow, she went to the end of the court and threw open a door. The garden, after the glare of the court lights, was in very dark blue dusk; the door opening made an alarmed bird break out of a thicket. The town lights blinked through bare moving branches: down there they heard the crepitating sea. Evelyn and Portia, standing in the doorway, filled their lungs with the dark sweet salt spring air.

5

DARLING Portia: What a marvellous idea! Of course I should love to come, but shall I be able to get away? But if they expect me I really must have a try. No, I don't mind if I sleep in their lumber room. I suppose I shall hear Dickie snore through the wall. We are still making fine hay with Thomas out of the office, and if Mr Rattisbone doesn't have one of his phases I do think that I should be able to nip off. Another thing is, though, that I seem to have filled up my next three week-ends. Next week-end, I think, on the whole, should be the easiest for me to get out of – if I make enemies, you must stand by me. If I do come, I will come on that morning train you said. I shall be able to let you know on Friday. I'm so sorry to leave it as late as that.

I do hope all your dashing friends will like me. I shall be so shy. Well, I must stop, you sweet: I've had three late nights and I do feel like death. Directly you go away I start to go to the bad, which shows how important you are to me. But I simply have to be out. You know how I hate my room.

I had just a line from Anna. She sounds quite pleased with everything. Well, I'll let you know. I *do* hope I can come. All my best love.   EDDIE

This rather tormenting letter came on Wednesday morning – by which time Mrs Heccomb was already busy beautifying the lumber room. She had fallen in quite serenely with the idea of this visit, for Eddie had, somehow, been represented to her as an old family friend of Anna's and Thomas's, coming down to see how Portia was getting on. This seemed to her most fitting. What she could not get herself happily reconciled to was, that any friend of the Quaynes should sleep in her lumber room. But Daphne and Dickie refused to make any offer, and they kept a close eye on her every evening to see that she did not move out of her own room. The more briskly Daphne asserted that the lumber room would not kill Eddie, the more Mrs Heccomb's forehead wrinkled up with concern. She could only buy more

matting, and move in her Sheraton looking-glass. She also moved in her *prie-dieu* to act as a bedside table, and improvised a red paper frill for the light. She borrowed an eiderdown from Cecil's mother. Portia watched these preparations with growing misgivings; they made her dread more and more that Eddie might not come. She felt a great threatening hill of possible disappointment rising daily over the household's head – for even Daphne was not indifferent, and Dickie had taken note that they must expect a guest. In vain, she implored Mrs Heccomb to remember that Eddie's plans for the week-end hung on a thread.

She was also alarmed when she found what a stalwart preconception of Eddie Mrs Heccomb had – she clearly saw him as a Major Brutt. Daphne knew otherwise: at any mention of Eddie a piglike knowing look would come into Daphne's eyes. Daphne's own affairs were not going too well, for Mr Bursely, in spite of the good beginning, had not been seen since Saturday – Daphne now took a low view of Wallace and Charlie with their civilian ways.

Major Brutt's second puzzle had come on Wedesday morning, by the same post as Eddie's letter, and Portia worked at the puzzle at a table in the sun porch, with a diligence that helped to steady her nerves. It soon promised to represent a magnificent air display. The week was very sunny – her eyes dazzled as she fitted piece into piece, and a gull's shadow flashing over the puzzle would make her suddenly look up. The planes massing against an ultramarine sky began each to take a different symbolic form, and as she assembled the spectators she came to look for a threat or promise in each upturned face. One evening Dickie offered to help her: the table was moved in to under a lamp, and Dickie completed an ambulance she had dreaded to tackle.

She got a postcard from Anna, a short letter from Thomas, a long letter from Lilian, whose sorrows seemed far away.

She went into town every morning with Mrs Heccomb. Mrs Heccomb pressed her to drop in on Daphne at Smoot's. The first call was alarming – in the upstairs library heating drew out a gluey smell from the books; Daphne's nostrils wore a permanent crinkle. In all senses, literature was in bad odour here. The sun

slanted its stuffy motes straight on to Daphne's cross curled
head; in the dusk at the back of the library Daphne's colleague
crouched at a table, reading. Contempt for reading as an occupation was implicit in the way Daphne knitted, stopped knitting
to buff her nails, and knitted again, impatiently hiking by the
long strand towards her her ball of coral wool. The twitch of
the coral ball did not disturb the apathy of the library cat – this
furious mouser had been introduced when mice began to get
at the *belles lettres*, but he only worked by night. No subscribers
were in the library when Portia came in, and Daphne, already
leaning back from her desk, looked up with a quite equable
scowl.

'Oh, hullo!' she said. 'What do *you* want?'

'Mrs Heccomb thought you might like me to drop in.'

'Oh, by all means do,' said Daphne. Moving her tongue across
from one cheek to the other, she went on knitting. Portia, one
finger on Daphne's desk, looked round and said : 'What a large
number of books.'

'And that isn't all, either. However, do sit down.'

'I do wonder who reads them.'

'Oh, that's quite simple,' said Daphne. 'You'd soon see. Does
your sister-in-law read?'

'She says she would like to if she had more time.'

'It's extraordinary how much time people do have. I mean, it
really does make you think. I daresay she has a guaranteed
subscription? People with those give an awful lot of fuss – they
come popping back for a book before one has ordered it. I suppose they feel they are getting their money's worth. What I
always say is . . .'

Miss Scott, from the back of the room, gave a warning cough,
which meant subscribers were coming in. Two ladies approached
the table, said, 'Good morning' placatingly and returned their
books. Daphne rolled up her knitting and gave them a look.

'Such a lovely morning. . . .'

'Yes,' said Daphne repressively

'And how is your mother?'

'Oh, she's getting along.'

The lady who had not spoken was already dithering round

183

a table of new novels. Her friend threw the novels rather a longing look, then turned strongmindedly to the cabinet of *belles lettres*. Raising her nose so as to bring her pince-nez to the correct angle, she took out a succession of books, scanned their title pages, looked through all the pictures, and almost always replaced them with a frustrated sigh. Did she not know that Daphne hated people to stick around messing the books about? 'I suppose there *is* something here I should really like?' she said. 'It's so hard to tell from the outsides.'

'Miss Scott,' said Daphne plaintively, 'can't you help Mrs Adams?'

Mrs Adams, mortified, said: 'I *ought* to make out a list.'

'Well, people do find it helps.'

Mrs Adams did not half like being turned over to Miss Scott, who gave her a collection of well-known essays she was ashamed to refuse. She looked wistfully at her friend, who came back with a gay-looking novel and a happy face. 'You really oughtn't to miss these; they were beautifully written,' said Miss Scott, giving poor Mrs Adams a shrewish look – in her subservient way, she was learning to be as great a bully as Daphne.

Daphne flicked the subscribers' cards out of the box and sat with pencil poised, preparing to make disdainful marks on them. It was clear that Daphne added, and knew that she added, *cachet* to Smoot's by her air of barely condoning the traffic that went on there. Her palpable wish never to read placed at a disadvantage those who had become dependent on this habit, and it was a disadvantage they seemed to enjoy. Miss Scott, though so much more useful, cut no ice: she (unlike Daphne) was not a lady, and she not only read but was paid to read, which was worse. Also, she had not Daphne's dashing appearance: most of the Seale subscribers were elderly, and age and even the mildest form of intellect both tend to make people physical snobs. There may be libraries in which Daphne would not have done so well. But for this clientele of discarded people her bloom and her nonchalance served, somehow, to place her above literature. These were readers who could expect no more from life, and just dared to look in books to see how much they had missed. The old are often masochists, and their slackening hearts

twitched at her bold cold smile. Perhaps there was an inter-change of cruelty, for Smoot's subscribers had, after all, the power to keep this fine girl chained. A bald patch in the carpet under her desk would have showed, had they cared to look, with what restless fury she dug in her heels. On a sunny day they would tell her it seemed hard she should not be out of doors, then they doddered off with their books in the salty sun down the street.

Portia's respect for Daphne went up with every moment as she watched her flick at the cards in the filing box. Looking up round the shelves she found the authors arranged in quite faultless alphabetical order, and this in itself seemed the work of a master mind. Also, though Daphne loathed print she had rather a feeling for dressy bindings: the books in her keeping had a well-groomed air ... When Mrs Adams had taken her friend away, Miss Scott returned to her reading with a peculiar smile, while Daphne rose and paced once or twice to the win-dow, with both hands moulding her skirt over her hips. Then she bumped back with a snort and went on with her knitting.

'Heard anything more from your boy friend?'

'Not yet. ...'

'Oh well. No doubt he'll come.'

Late that same Thursday, by arrangement, Portia took the bus into Southstone to meet Cecil. Mrs Heccomb's entire con-fidence in Cecil deprived the expedition of any glamour. Portia, arriving a little too early, waited outside the block of buildings from which Cecil at last emerged, blowing his nose. They walked through draughty streets of private hotels to the East Cliff Pavilion. This vast glassy building, several floors deep, had been clamped skilfully to the face of the cliff, and was entered from the top like a catacomb. Tiers of glazed balconies overhung the sea, which had diluted into a mauvish haze by the time the concert finished. Portia had not a good ear, but she went up in Cecil's estimation by spotting a tune from *Madame Butterfly*. In fact, the orchestra played a good deal of music to which she and Irene had illicitly listened, skulking outside palace hotels abroad. At half past six, attendants drew the curtains over the now extinct view. When the concert was over, Cecil and Portia

quitted their plush *fauteuils* for a glass-topped table, at which they ate poached eggs on haddock and banana splits. Though exceedingly brilliantly lit, the hall with its lines of tables was almost empty, and lofty silence filled it. No doubt it would be gay at some other time. Portia listened with an unfixed eye to Cecil's thoughtful conversation: by this time tomorrow, she would know if Eddie were coming or not. They caught the quarter to nine bus back to Seale, and at the gate of Waikiki, saying good night, Cecil gave her hand a platonic squeeze.

The time between Eddie's Friday morning letter and his arrival seemed to contract to nothing. In so far as time did exist, it held some dismay. The suspense of the week, though unnerving, had had its own tune or pattern: now she knew he was coming the tune stopped. For people who live on expectations, to face up to their realization is something of an ordeal. Expectations are the most perilous form of dream, and when dreams do realize themselves it is in the waking world: the difference is subtly but often painfully felt. What she *should* have begun to enjoy, from Friday morning, was anticipation – but she found anticipation no longer that pure pleasure it once was. Even a year ago, the promised pleasure could not come soon enough: it was agony to consume intervening time. *Now*, she found she could wish Saturday were not on her so soon – she unconsciously held it off with one hand. This lack of avidity and composure, this need to recover both in a vigil of proper length, showed her already less of a child, and she was shocked by this loss or change in her nature, as she might have been by a change in her own body.

On Saturday morning, she was awake for a minute before she dared open her eyes. Then she saw her curtains white with Saturday's light – relentlessly, the too great day was poured out, on the sea, on her window sill. Then she thought there might be a second letter from Eddie, to say he was not coming after all. But there was no letter.

Later, the day became not dark but muted; haze bound the line of the coast; the sun did not quite shine. There had been no more talk, when it had come to the point, of Eddie's catching

the morning train: he would come by the train by which Portia had come. Mrs Heccomb wanted to order the taxi to meet him, but Portia felt Eddie would be overpowered by this, besides not being glad to pay for the taxi – so it was arranged that the carrier should bring down his bag. Portia walked up the station hill to meet him. She heard the train whistle away back in the woods; then it whistled again, then slowly came round the curve. When Eddie had got out they walked to the parapet and looked over at the view. Then they started downhill together. This was not like the afternoon when she had arrived herself, for a week more of spring had already sweetened the air.

Eddie had been surprised by the view from the parapet: he had had no idea Seale was so far from the sea.

'Oh yes, it is quite a way,' she said happily.

'But I thought it was once a port.'

'It was, but the sea ran back.'

'Did it really, darling: just fancy!' Catching at Portia's wrist, Eddie swung it twice in a gay methodical way, as, with the god-like step of people walking downhill, they went down the station incline. All at once he dropped her wrist and began to feel in his pockets. 'Oh God,' he said, 'I forgot to post that letter.'

'Oh – an important letter?'

'It had to get there tonight. It was to someone I put off by telegram.'

'I really do thank you for coming, Eddie!'

Eddie smiled in a brilliant but rather automatic and worried way. 'I invented all sorts of things. It *had* to get there tonight. You don't know how touchy people are.'

'Couldn't we post it now?'

'The postmark ... However, everyone hates me already. Anyway, London seems beautifully far away. Where's the next post box, darling?'

At the idea of this desperate simplification, Eddie's face cleared. He no longer frowned at the letter but, crossing the road, plunged it cheerfully into the corner letter box. Portia, watching him from across the road, had a moment in which to realize he would be back beside her; in fact, they were together again. Eddie came back and said: 'Oh, you've tied your hair-

ribbon in a bow at the top. And you are still wearing your woolly gloves.' Taking her hand in his, he scrunched the fingers inside her glove together. 'Sweet,' he said. 'Like a nest of little weak mice.'

They lagged along, all down the turning road. Eddie read aloud the names on the white gates of all the villas – these gates were streaked with green drips from trees; the houses behind them looked out through evergreens. The sea was, for the moment, out of view: a powerful inland silence, tinted grey by the hour, filled the station road. Seale was out of sight behind the line of the hill: its smoke went up behind garden conifers. Later, they heard a stream in a sort of gulch. All this combined to make Eddie exclaim: 'Darling, I do call this an unreal place!'

'Wait till we get back to tea.'

'But where on earth is Waikiki?'

'Oh, Eddie, I told you – it's by the sea.'

'Is Mrs Heccomb really very excited?'

'Yes, very excited – though I must say, it does not take much to excite her. But even Dickie said this morning at breakfast that he supposed he would bump into you tonight.'

'And Daphne – is she excited?'

'I'm sure she really is. But she's afraid you're ritzy. You must show her you're not.'

'I'm so glad I came,' said Eddie, quickening his step.

At Waikiki, Mrs Heccomb's deportment was not, for the first minute, equal to the occasion. She looked twice at Eddie and said: 'Oh ...' Then she rallied and said how pleased to see him she was. Holding her hand out, she nervously circumscribed the tea table, still fixing her eyes on the silhouette of Eddie as though trying to focus an apparition. When they all sat down to tea, her own back was to the light and she had Eddie in less deceptive view. Each time he spoke, her eyes went to his forehead, to the point where his hair sprang back in its fine spirited waves. In pauses that could but occur in the talk, Portia could almost hear Mrs Heccomb's ideas, like chairs before a party, being rolled about and rapidly rearranged. The tea was bountiful, but so completely distracted was Mrs Heccomb that Portia had to circulate the cakes. It occurred to her to wonder who would pay for

them, and whether she had done wrong, on account of Eddie, in tempting Waikiki to this extra expense.

She wondered, even, whether Mrs Heccomb might not pause to wonder. Having lived in hotels where one's bills wait weekly at the foot of the stairs, and no 'extra' is ever overlooked, she had had it borne in on her that wherever anyone is they are costing somebody something, and that the cost must be met. She understood that by living at Windsor Terrace, eating what she ate, sleeping between sheets that had to be washed, by even so much as breathing the warmed air, she became a charge on Thomas and Anna. *Their* keeping on paying up, whatever they felt, had to be glossed over by family feeling – and she had learned to have, with regard to them, that callousness one has towards relatives. Now she could only hope they were paying largely enough for her own board at Waikiki to meet the cost of the cake Eddie might eat. But uncertainty made her limit her own tea.

Eddie had the advantage, throughout tea, of not being familiar with Mrs Heccomb. All he thought was that she was exceedingly shy. He therefore set out to be frank, easy, and simple, which were three things he could seem to be on his head. He could not be expected to know that his appearance, and that the something around him that might be called his aura, struck into her heart its first misgiving for years – a misgiving not about Portia but about Anna. He could not know that he started up in her mind a misgiving she had repressed about Anna and Pidgeon – a misgiving her own marriage had made her gladly forget. A conviction (dating from her last year at Richmond) that no man with *bounce* could be up to any good set up an unhappy twitch in one fold of her left cheek. Apprehensions that someone might be common were the worst she had had to combat since she ruled at Waikiki. No doubt it must be in order, this young man being Portia's friend, since Portia said that he was a friend of Anna's. But what was he doing *being* a friend of Anna's? ... Portia, watching the cheek twitch, wondered what could be up.

Eddie felt he was doing wonderfully well. He liked Mrs Heccomb, and was anxious to please. Not a scrap of policy underlay

his manner. Perfectly guilelessly, he understood Mrs Heccomb to be just a little dazzled by him. Indeed, he looked well here – from the moment of coming in, he had dropped into a happy relationship with the things in the room: the blue chenille curtain to the left of his head, the dresser he tilted his chair against, the finished lamp shade that he had seen and praised. He seemed so natural here, so much in the heart of things, that Portia wondered how the Waikiki lounge could have fully existed before he came. There in the sun porch stayed the unfinished puzzle, into which, before he came, she had fitted her hopes and fears. After tea, she took a retrospective look at the puzzle, as though it were a thing left from another age. Eddie stood gaily talking, gaily balancing on the fire kerb. He attracted a look from Doris as she slithered in to clear away the tea.

'It's nice to get back to a proper fire,' he said. 'I have only gas in my flat.'

Mrs Heccomb took the cloth from Doris to fold: it had a crochet border eight inches deep. 'I suppose you have central heating in Mr Quayne's office?'

'Oh yes,' Eddie said. 'It is all completely slap up.'

'Yes, I have heard it is very fine.'

'Anna, of course, has the loveliest log fire in *her* drawing-room. You go and see her quite often, I expect?'

'Yes, I go to Windsor Terrace when I am in London,' said Mrs Heccomb, though still not forthcomingly. 'They are extremely hospitable,' she said – discounting a right to the house as any one person's privilege. She turned on the light over her painting table, sat down, and began to go through her brushes. Portia, watching dusk close round the porch, said: 'I think perhaps I might show Eddie the sea.'

'Oh, you won't see much of the sea, dear, *now*, I'm afraid.'

'Still, we might just look.'

So they went out. Portia went down the path pulling on her overcoat, but Eddie only wound his scarf round his neck. The tide was creeping in; the horizon was just visible in the dark grey air. The shallow curve of the bay held a shingly murmur that was just not silence and imperceptibly ended where silence was. There was no wind, just a sensation round one's collar and

at the roots of one's hair. Eddie and Portia stood on the esplanade, watching the sky and water slowly blot themselves out. Eddie stood aloofly, like someone who after hours allows himself to be freely alone again. There was never much connexion between his affability and his spirit – which now, in a sombre way, came out to stand at its own door. Only Portia had this forbidding intimacy with him – she was the only person to whom he need not pretend that she had not ceased existing when, for him, she had ceased to exist. The tender or bold play of half-love with grown-up people becomes very exacting: it tired Eddie. It was only Portia that he could pack off – like that, at the turn of a moment – with tired simplicity. She did, therefore, enjoy one kind of privilege: he allowed her at least to stay in body beside him when he was virtually not there, gone. No presence could be less insistent than hers. He treated her like an element (air, for instance) or a condition (darkness): these touch one with their equality and lightness where one could endure no human touch. He could look right through her, without a flicker of seeing, without being made shamefully conscious of the vacuum there must be in his eyes.

Portia, waiting for Eddie as she had often waited, turned her fists round slowly in her pockets, regretting that he should have been called away just now. The autumnal moment, such as occurs in all seasons, the darkening sea with its little commas of foam offered no limits to the loneliness she could feel, even when she was feeling quite resigned. All at once, a light from mid Channel darted over the sea, picking out its troughs and its polished waves. The lighthouse had begun its all-night flashing. The tip of this finger of light was drawn across Eddie's face – and a minute later, the lamps sprang alight all down the esplanade. She saw, when she turned round, tamarisk shadows cast on lodging-house walls.

'What a blaze!' said Eddie, starting alight also. 'Now this really *is* like the seaside. Have they got a pier?'

'Well, no. But there's one at Southstone.'

'Come down on the beach.'

As they scrunched along, Eddie said: 'Then you've been happy here?'

'You see, it's more like what I was accustomed to. At Anna's, I never know what is going to happen next – and here, though I may not know, I do not mind so much. In a way, at Anna's nothing does happen – though of course I might not know if it did. But here I do see how everyone feels.'

'I wonder if I like that?' said Eddie. 'I suspect how people feel, and that seems to me bad enough. I wonder if the truth would be worse or better. The truth of course I mean, about other people. I know only too well how *I* feel.'

'So do I.'

'Know how I feel?'

'Yes, Eddie.'

'You make me feel rather guilty.'

'Why?'

'Well, you haven't the slightest notion how I behave *sometimes*, and it isn't till I behave that I know quite how I feel. You see, my life depends entirely on what happens.'

'Then you don't know how you may be going to feel?'

'No, I've no idea, darling. It's perfectly unforeseeable. That is the worst of it. I'm a person you ought to be frightened of.'

'But you are the only person who doesn't frighten me.'

'Wait a moment – damn. I've got a stone in my shoe.'

'I have, too, as a matter of fact.'

'Why didn't you say so, silly? Why suffer away?'

They sat down on a roll of beach and each took a shoe off. The light from the lighthouse swept round to where they sat and Portia said: 'I say, you've got a hole in your sock.'

'Yes. That lighthouse is like the eye of God.'

'But are you frightening, do you really think?'

'You ask such snubbing questions. You mean I make a fuss. I suppose, that I'm I at all is just a romantic fallacy. It may be vulgar to feel that I'm anyone, but at least I'm sure that I'm not anyone else. Of course we have all got certain things in common, but a good deal that we have in common is dreadful. When I so much hate so much I see in myself, how do you expect me to tolerate other people? Shall we move on, darling? I love sitting here like this, but these pebbles hurt my behind.'

'Yes, they hurt mine rather, as a matter of fact.'

'I do hate it when you are a dear little soul – It's sweet to be here with you, but I don't feel really happy.'

'Have you not had a nice week in London, then?'

'Oh, well – Thomas gives me five pounds a week.'

'Good gracious.'

'Yes, that is what brains cost by the pound ... I nearly got another stone in my shoe: I think we'd better get back to the promenade. Who lives all along there?'

'Those are just lodging houses. Three of them are to let.'

They climbed back on to the esplanade, faced round and started back to Waikiki. 'All the same,' said Portia, 'don't you think Mrs Heccomb is very nice?'

On a gust of at once excellent spirits Eddie swept in upon Daphne and Dickie, who with the wireless on were standing about the hearth. They looked at him doubtfully. He exchanged a manly handshake with Dickie, and with Daphne a bold look. Then Mrs Heccomb came downstairs, and Daphne at once adopted her policy of addressing striking remarks only to her. Above the wireless going full blast, Mrs Heccomb and Daphne agreed that supper ought to be early, as some of the party wished to go to a movie.

Daphne bawled: 'And Clara's going to meet us there.'

Dickie did not react.

'I say, Clara's coming along to meet us.'

Dickie looked up coldly from the *Evening Standard* to say: 'This is the first I have heard of that.'

'Well, don't be so silly. Clara'll probably pay.'

Dickie grunted and stooped down to scratch his ankle as though an itch *were* a really urgent matter. For a minute Daphne's eyes, dull with consideration, seemed to be drawn right into her face. Then she said to Portia: 'You and your friend coming?' and shot her most nonchalant look into the mantelpiece mirror behind Eddie's ear. '*Shall* we, Eddie?' said Portia, kneeling up on the sofa. At once Eddie dropped into her eyes the profoundest of those quick glances of his. A peaceful malicious smile illuminated his features as he continued not to

look Daphne's way. 'If we really are invited,' he yelled back above the music, 'it would be quite divine.'

'Do you really want us, Daphne?'

'Oh, it's all the same to *me*. I mean, *just* as you like.'

So directly after supper they set out. They stopped at Wallace's house to pick up Wallace, then marched, five abreast, down the asphalt walk to the town. It was dark under the trees and the lights twinkled ahead. A breath mounted from the canal as they trooped over the footbridge with a clatter: through an evergreen grove the Grotto Cinema glittered its constellation of gold, red, blue. Clara, with her most sacrificial expression, waited by a palm in the foyer, wearing a mink coat. There was polite confusion at the box-office window, where Dickie, Wallace and, less convincingly, Eddie all made gestures of preparing to stand treat. Then Clara bobbed up from under Dickie's elbow and paid for them all, as they had expected her to do. They filed down the dark aisle to seat themselves in this order – Clara, Dickie, Portia, Eddie, Daphne, Wallace. A comic was on the screen.

During most of the programme, Dickie was more oncoming with Portia than he was with Clara – that is to say, he put one elbow on Portia's arm of his *fauteuil*, but did not put the other on Clara's arm. He breathed heavily. Clara, during a brief hitch in the comic, said she hoped Dickie had had nice hockey. When poor Clara dropped her bead bag, money and all, she was left to recover it. Portia sat with eyes fixed on the screen – once or twice, as Eddie changed his position, she felt his knee touch hers. When this made her glance his way, she saw light from the comic flickering on his eyeballs. He sat with his shoulders forward, in some sort of close complicity with himself. Beyond Eddie, Daphne's profile was tilted up correctly, and beyond Daphne comatose Wallace yawned.

Then the news ran through, then the big drama began. This keyed them all up, even the boys. Something distracted Portia's mind from the screen – a cautiousness the far side of Eddie's knee. She held her breath – and failed to hear Eddie breathe. Why did not Eddie breathe? Whatever could be the matter? She felt some tense extra presence, here in their row of six.

Wanting to know, she turned to look full at Eddie – who at once countered her look with a bold blank smile glittering from the screen. The smile was diverted to her from someone else. On her side, one of his hands, a cigarette between the two longest fingers, hung down slack: she only saw one hand. Hitching herself up on her seat, she looked at the screen, beseechingly, vowing not to wonder, never to look away.

The screen became threatening with figures, which seemed to make a storm: she heard Clara let out a polite gasp. Proof against whatever more was to happen, Dickie heaved till he got his cigarette case out. Not ceasing to give the screen impervious attention, he selected a cigarette, closed his lips on it, and re-settled his jaw. Then he started to make his lighter kick. When he had used the flame, he kindly looked down the row to see if anyone wanted a light too.

The jumping light from Dickie's lighter showed the canyon below their row of knees. It caught the chromium clasp of Daphne's handbag, and Wallace's wrist-watch at the end of the row. It rounded the taut blond silk of Daphne's calf and glittered on some tinfoil dropped on the floor. Those who wanted to smoke were smoking: no one wanted a light. But Dickie, still with the flame jumping, still held the lighter out in a watching pause – a pause so marked that Portia, as though Dickie had sharply pushed her head round, looked to see where he looked. The light, with malicious accuracy, ran round a rim of cuff, a steel bangle, and made a thumb-nail flash. Not deep enough in the cleft between their *fauteuils* Eddie and Daphne were, with emphasis, holding hands. Eddie's fingers kept up a kneading movement: her thumb alertly twitched at the joint.

6

THE empty lodging-house rustled with sea noises, as though years of echoes of waves and sea sucking shingle lived in its chimneys, its half-open cupboards. The stairs creaked as Portia

and Eddie went up, and the banisters, pulled loose in their sockets, shook under their hands. Warped by sea damp, the doors were all stuck ajar, and ends of torn wallpaper could be heard fluttering in draughts in the rooms. The front-room ceilings glared with sea reflections; the back windows stared north over salt fields. Mr Bunstable's junior partner Mr Sheldon had inadvertently left the key of this house at Waikiki the other night, when he had come in to cards. The key bore the label 5 Winslow Terrace: Dickie had found it, Eddie had had it from Dickie, and now Eddie and Portia let themselves in. There is nothing like exploring an empty house.

It was Sunday morning, just before eleven: the church bells from uphill came through the shut windows into the rooms. But Mrs Heccomb had gone to church alone. Dickie had gone off to see a man about something; Daphne had stayed reading the *Sunday Pictorial* in a *chaise longue* in the sun porch – though there was no sun. She had set her hair a new way, in a bang over her forehead, and she had not so much as batted an eyelid as Eddie, steering Portia by one elbow, walked away from Waikiki down the esplanade.

The front top bedrooms here were like convent cells, with outside shutters hooked back. Their walls were mouldy blue like a dead sky, and looking at the criss-cross cracks in the ceiling one thought of holiday people waking up. A stale charred smell came from the grates – Waikiki seemed miles away. These rooms, many flights up, were a dead end: the emptiness, the feeling of dissolution came upstairs behind one, blocking the way down. Portia felt she had climbed to the very top of a tree pursued by something that could follow. She remembered the threatening height of this house at the back, and how it had frightened her that first afternoon when she was in the taxi with Mrs Heccomb. Today when they turned the key and pushed open the stuck door boldly, they had heard papers rustle in the hall. But it was not only here that she dreaded to be with Eddie.

He lighted a cigarette and leaned on the mantelpiece. He seemed to measure the small room with his eye, swinging the key from his finger on its loop of string. Portia went to the

window, and looked out. 'All these windows here have got double glass,' she said.

'A fat lot of good that would do if the house blew down.'

'Do you think it might really? ... The bells have stopped.'

'Yes, you ought to be in church.'

'I went last Sunday – but it doesn't really matter.'

'Then why go last Sunday, you little crook?'

Portia did not reply.

'I say, darling, you are funny this morning. Why are you being so funny with me?'

'Am I?'

'You know you are: don't be so silly. Why?'

Her back turned, she mutely pulled at the window clasp. But Eddie whistled twice, so that she had to face him. By now, he had twirled the string round his finger so tight that the flesh, with its varnish of nicotine, stood out in ridges between. His eyes held behind their brightness a warning tense look, as though the end of the world were coming. Instinctively putting up one hand to her cheek, she looked at his teeth showing between his lips. He said: 'Well!'

'Why did you hold Daphne's hand?'

'When do you mean?'

'At the cinema.'

'Oh, that. Because, you see, I have to get off with people.'

'Why?'

'Because I cannot get on with them, and that makes me so mad. Yes, I noticed you gave me rather a funny look.'

'You mean, that time you smiled at me? Were you holding her hand then?'

Eddie thought. 'Yes, I would have been, I expect. Were you worried? I thought you cut off rather early to bed. But I thought you always knew I was like that. I like touching, you know.'

'But I have never been there.'

'No, I suppose you haven't.' He looked down and unwound the string from his finger. 'No, you haven't, have you?' he said much more affably.

'Was that what you meant on the beach when you said you never knew how you might behave?'

'And you shot back and wrote it down, I suppose? I thought I had told you not to write down anything about me?'

'No, Eddie, it's not in my diary. You only said it yesterday, after tea.'

'Anyhow, what you mean is not what I'd call behaving – it's not even as important as that. It didn't mean anything new.'

'But it did to me.'

'Well, I can't help that,' he said, smiling reasonably. 'I can't help the way you are.'

'I knew something was happening before Dickie moved his lighter. I knew from the way you smiled.'

'For such a little girl, you know, you're neurotic.'

'I'm not such a little girl. You once spoke of marrying me.'

'Only because you *were* such a little girl.'

'That it didn't matter?'

'No, and I also thought you were the one person who didn't take other people's completely distorted views. But now you're like any girl at the seaside, always watching and judging, trying to piece me together into something that isn't there. You make me –'

'Yes, but why *did* you hold Daphne's hand?'

'I just felt matey.'

'But ... I mean ... You knew me better.'

Eddie's metallic mood broke up, or completely changed. He went across the room to the wall cupboard that he had fixed his eyes on, and carefully latched it. Then he looked round the room as though he had stayed here, and were about to remove his last belongings. He picked up his dead match and dropped it into the grate. Then he said vaguely: 'Come on; let's go down.'

'But did you hear what I said?'

'Of course I did. You're always so sweet, darling.'

Going downstairs brought them one floor nearer the mild sound of the sea. Eddie stepped into the drawing-room for another look round. The margin of floor round where there had been a carpet was stained with reddish varnish, and in the wood-work over the bow window was a hook from which a bird-cage must have hung.

Through the window the sea light shone on Eddie's face as he turned quickly and said, in his lightest and gentlest way: 'I can't tell you how bad I feel. It was only my bit of fun. I honestly didn't think you'd bother to notice, darling – or, that if you did, you'd ever think twice of it. You and I know each other, and you know how silly I am. But if it really upset you, of course it was awful of me. You really mustn't be hurt, or I shall wish I was dead. This is just one more of the ways I keep on and on making trouble. I know I oughtn't to say so, when I've just said I was sorry, but really, darling, it was such a small thing. I mean, you ask old Daphne. It's simply the way most people have to get on.'

'No, I couldn't ask Daphne.'

'Then take it from me.'

'But, Eddie, they thought you were my friend. I was so proud because they all thought that.'

'But, darling, if I hadn't wanted to see you would I have come all this way and broken all those dates? *You* know I love you: don't be so silly. All I wanted was to be with you at the seaside, and here we are, and we're having a lovely time. Why spoil it for a thing that means simply nothing?'

'But it does mean something – it means something else.'

'You are the only person I'm ever serious with. I'm never serious with all these other people: that's why I simply do what they seem to want me to do ... You do know I'm serious with you, don't you, Portia?' he said, coming up and staring into her eyes. In his own eyes, shutters flicked back, exposing for half a second, right back in the dark, the Eddie in there.

Never till now, never since this half-second, had Portia been the first to look away. She looked at the ghostly outline of some cabinet on the paper with its bleaching maroon leaves. 'But you said', she said, 'up there' (she nodded at the ceiling) 'that you need not mean what you say because I am a little girl.'

'When I talk through my hat, of course I'm not serious.'

'You should not have talked about marriage through your hat.'

'But darling, I do think you must be mad. Why should you want to marry anybody?'

'Were you talking through your hat on the beach when you said I ought to be afraid of you?'

'How you do remember!'

'It was yesterday evening.'

'Perhaps yesterday evening *I was* feeling like that.'

'But don't *you* remember?'

'Look here, darling, you must really not exasperate me. How can I keep on feeling something I once felt when there are so many things one can feel? People who say they always feel as they did simply fake themselves up. I may be a crook but I'm not a fake – that is an entirely different thing.'

'But I don't see how you can say you are serious if there's no one thing you keep feeling the whole time.'

'Well, then I'm not,' said Eddie, stamping his cigarette out and laughing, though in an exasperated way. 'You will really simply have to get used to me. I must say I thought you were. You had really better not think I'm serious, if the slightest thing is going to make you so upset. What I do remember telling you last evening is that you don't know the half of what I do. I do do what you would absolutely hate. Yes, I see now I was wrong – I did think once that I could tell you, even let you discover, *anything* I had done, and you wouldn't turn a hair. Because I had hoped there would be one person like that, I must have let myself make an absurd, quite impossible image of you ... No, I see now, the fact is, dear darling Portia, you and I have drifted into a thoroughly sickly, not to say mawkish, state. Which is worlds worse for me than a spot of necking with Daphne. And now it comes to this – you start driving me up trees and barking at the bottom like everyone else. Well, come on, let's go down. We've had enough of this house. We'd better lock up and give the key back to Dickie.'

He moved decisively to the drawing-room door.

'Oh stop, Eddie: wait! Has this spoilt everything for you? I would rather be dead than a disappointment to you. *Please* ... You are my whole reason to be alive. I promise, please, I promise! I mean, I promise not to hate anything. It is only that I have to get used to things, and I have not got used to quite everything, yet. I'm only stupid when I don't understand.'

'But you never will. I can see that.'

'But I'm perfectly willing not to. I'll be not stupid without understanding. *Please* –'

She pulled at his near arm wildly with both hands, making no distinction between the sleeve and the flesh. Not wildly but with the resolution of sorrow, her eyes went round his face. He said: 'Look here, shut up: you make me feel such a bully.' Freeing his arm, he caught both her hands in his in a bothered but perfectly kindly way, as though they had been a pair of demented kittens. 'Such a *noise* to make,' he said. 'Can't you let a person lose an illusion without screaming the house down, you little silly, you?'

'But I don't want you to.'

'Very well, then. I haven't.'

'Promise, Eddie. You swear? I don't mean just because it's about me, but you told me you had so few – illusions, I mean. You do promise? You're not just keeping me quiet?'

'No, no – I mean, yes. I promise. What I said was all in my eye. That's the worst of talk. Now shall we get out of here? I should not mind a drink, if they have got such a thing.'

The echoes of their voices followed them down: once more the stairs creaked; once more the banisters wobbled. In the hall, a slit of daylight came through the letter box. They kicked through drifts of circulars, musty catalogues. Their last view of the hall, with its chocolate walls that light from a front room only sneaked along, was one of ungraciousness, of servility. Would people ever come to this house again? And yet it faced the sun, reflected the sea, and had been the scene of happy holidays.

They ran into Dickie at the gate of Waikiki, and Eddie handed him back the key. 'Thanks very much,' Eddie said, 'it's a nice piece of property. Portia and I have been over it carefully. We rather thought of starting a boarding house.'

'Oh, did you?' said Dickie, with a certain *méfiance*. He headed the two guests up the garden path, then clicked the gate behind them. Daphne could still be seen extended in the sun porch, with the Sunday paper over her knee.

'Here we all are,' Eddie said, but Daphne did not react. They grouped round her *chaise longue*, and Eddie with a rather masterful movement flicked the *Sunday Pictorial* from her person and began to read it himself. He read it with overdone attention, whistling to himself at each item of news. Just after twelve struck, he began to look rather anxiously round the Waikiki lounge, in which he saw no signs (for there were none) of sherry or gin and lime. He at last suggested they should go out and look for a drink, but Daphne asked: 'Where?' adding: 'This is not London, you know.'

Dickie said: 'And Portia does not drink.'

'Oh, well, she can come along.'

'We cannot take a girl into a bar.'

'I don't see why not, at the seaside.'

'It may be that to you, but it's rather more to us, I am afraid.'

'Oh naturally, naturally – well, er, Dickie, shall you and I roll along?'

'Well, I don't mind if I –'

Daphne yawned and said: 'Yes, you two boys go along. I mean, don't just stick around.' So the two boys went along.

'What a thirst your friend always has,' said Daphne looking after them. 'He wanted me to cut off with him somewhere last night, after the movies, but of course I told him everywhere would be shut. How do you think those two boys get along?'

'Who?' said Portia, going back to her puzzle.

'Him and Dickie?'

'Oh . . . I don't think I'd thought.'

'Dickie thinks he chatters rather too much, but of course Dickie would think that. Is what's-his-name, I mean Eddie, a popular boy?'

'I don't know who you mean with.'

'Do girls fall for him much?'

'I don't know many girls.'

'But your sister-in-law likes him, didn't you say? Not that *she's* a girl, of course. I must say, that gives one a funny idea of her. I mean to say, he's awfully fresh. I suppose that's the way he always goes on?'

'What way?'

'The way he goes on here.'

Portia walked round her puzzle and stared at it upside down. Pushing a piece with her finger, she mumbled vaguely: ' I suppose he always goes on about the same.'

'You don't seem to know much about him, do you? I thought you said he and you were such friends.'

Portia said something unintelligible.

'Well, look here, don't you trust that boy too far. I don't know, I'm sure, if I ought to say anything, but you're such a kid and it does seem rather a shame. You shouldn't let yourself be so potty about him, really. I don't mean to say there's any harm in the boy, but he's the sort of boy who must have his bit of fun. I don't want to be mean on him, but honestly – Well, you take it from me – Of course he's no end flattered, having you stuck on him, anybody would be; you're such a nice little thing. And a boy in a way likes to have a girl round after him – look at Dickie and Clara. I wouldn't see any harm in your going round with an idealistic sort of a boy like Cecil, but honestly Eddie's not idealistic at all. I don't mean to say he'd try anything on with you; he wouldn't want to: he'd see you were just a kid. But if you get so potty about him without seeing what he's like, you'll get an awful knock. You take it from me. What I mean to say is, you ought to see he's simply playing you up – coming down here like that, and everything. He's the sort of boy who can't help playing a person up; he'd play a kitten up if we had a kitten here. You've no idea, really.'

'Do you mean about him holding your hand? He does that because he feels matey, he says.'

Daphne's reaction time was not quick: it took her about two seconds to go rigid all over on the *chaise longue*. Then her eyes ran together, her features thickened: there was a pause in which slowly diluted Portia's appalling remark. In that pause, the civilization of Waikiki seemed to rock on its base. When Daphne spoke again her voice had a rasping note, as though the moral sound box had cracked.

'Now look here,' she said, 'I simply dropped you a word because I felt in a sort of way sorry for you. But there's no reason for you to be vulgar. I must say, I was really surprised when you

said you had got a boy friend. What I thought was, he must be rather a sap. But as you were so keen to have him, I was all for his coming, and, as you know, I fixed Mumsie about that. I don't wish to blow my own trumpet, I never have, but one thing I will say is that I'm not a cat, and I'd never put in my oar with a girl friend's boy friend. But the moment you brought that boy here, I could see in a moment anybody could have him. It's written all over him. He can't even pass the salt without using his eyes. Even so, I must say I thought it was a bit funny when —'

'When he held your hand? Yes, I did just at first. But I thought perhaps you didn't.'

'Now Portia, you look here — if you can't talk like a lady, you just take that puzzle away and finish it somewhere else. Blocking up the whole place with the thing! I had no idea at all you were so *common*, and nor had Mumsie the least idea, I'm sure, or she wouldn't have ever obliged your sister-in-law by having you to stop here, convenient or not. This all simply goes to show the way you're brought up at home, and I am really surprised at them, I must say. You just take that awful puzzle up to your room and finish it there, if you're really so anxious to. You get on my nerves, always picking about with it. And this is *our* sun porch, if I may say so.'

'I will if you like. But I'm not doing my puzzle.'

'Well, don't just fidget about: it drives anyone crazy.' Daphne's voice and her colour had kept steadily rising: now she cleared her throat. There was a further pause, with that remarkable tension that precedes the hum when a kettle comes to the boil. 'The matter with you is', she went on, gathering energy, 'you've had your head thoroughly turned here. Being taken notice of. Cecil sorry because you are an orphan, and Dickie fussing you up to get a rise out of Clara. I've been letting you go about with our set because I thought it would be a bit of experience for you, when you're always so mousy and shy. I took poor Mumsie's word that you were a nice little thing. But as I say, this does only go to show. I'm sure I have no idea how your sister-in-law and all her set behave, but I'm afraid down here we are rather particular.'

'But if it seemed so very funny to you, why were you patting Eddie's hand with your thumb?'

'People creeping and spying', said Daphne, utterly tense, 'and then talking vulgarly are two things that I simply cannot stick. It may be funny of me, no doubt it is, but I just never could and I never can. Angry with you. I should never lower myself. It's not my fault that you've got the mind of a baby – and an awful baby, if you'll excuse my saying so. If you don't know how to behave –'

'I don't know why to behave ... Then Eddie told me this morning that people have to get off when they can't get on.'

'Oh! So you've had quite a talk!'

'Well, I asked him, you see.'

'The fact is you are a jealous little cat.'

'I'm not any more *now*, Daphne, really.'

'Still, you felt you could do with a bit of that – Oh yes, *I* saw you, shoving up against him.'

'That was the only side I had any room. Dickie was right on the other arm of my chair.'

'You leave my brother out of it!' Daphne screamed. 'My goodness, who do you think *you* are?'

Portia, her hand behind her, murmured something uncertain. '*Pardon? What* did you say?'

'I said, I didn't know ... But I don't see, Daphne, why you're so shocked with Eddie. If what you and he were doing was *not* fun, why should I be jealous? And if you hadn't liked it, you could always have struggled.'

Daphne gave up. 'You're completely bats,' she said. 'You'd better go and lie down. You don't even understand a single thing. Standing about there, not looking like anything. You know, really, if you'll excuse my saying so, a person might almost take you for a natural. Have you got *no* ideas?'

'I've no idea,' said Portia in a dazed way. 'For instance, my relations who are still alive have no idea why I was born. I mean, why my father and mother –'

Daphne bulged. She said: 'You'd really *better* shut up.'

'All right. Would you like me to go upstairs? I'm very sorry, Daphne,' said Portia – from the far side of the puzzle, her down-

cast eyes meanwhile travelling from Daphne's toe-caps, up the plump firm calves stretched out on the *chaise longue* to the hem of the 'snug' wool dress – 'very sorry to have annoyed you, when you have always been so nice to me. I wouldn't have said about you and Eddie, only I thought that was what you were talking about. Also, Eddie did say that if I didn't understand about people feeling matey, I'd much better ask you.'

'Well, of all the *nerve*! The thing is, you and your friend are both equally bats.'

'Please don't tell him you think so. He is so happy here.'

'I've no doubt he is – Well, you'd better run on up. Here's Doris just coming to lay.'

'Would you rather I stayed upstairs for some time?'

'No, stupid, what about dinner? But do try and not look as though you'd swallowed a mouse.'

Portia pushed round the chenille curtain and went up. Standing looking out of her bedroom window, she mechanically ran a comb through her hair. She felt something in the joints of her knees, which shook. The Sunday smell of the joint Doris was basting crept underneath the crack of her door. She watched Mrs Heccomb, with umbrella and prayer book, come happily down the esplanade with a friend – a lunch-hour breeze must have come up, for something fluttered the wisps of their grey hair; and at the same time the hems of her short curtains twitched on the window sill. The two ladies stopped at Waikiki gate to talk with emphasis. Then the friend went on; Mrs Heccomb waved her red morocco prayer book at the window, as she came up the path, jubilantly, even triumphantly as though she brought back with her an extra stock of grace. While Portia stood at the window there were still no signs of Eddie and Dickie, but later she heard their voices on the esplanade.

The set of temple bells had not yet been struck for dinner, so Portia sat down near her chest of drawers and looked hard at the pastel-portrait of Anna. She did not know what she looked for in the pastel – confirmation that the most unlikely people suffer, or that everybody who suffers is the same age?

But that little suffering Anna – so much out of drawing that she looked like a cripple between her cascades of hair – that

urgent soul astray in the bad portrait, only came alive by electric light. Even by day, though, the unlike likeness disturbs one more than it should: *what* is it unlike? Or is it unlike at all – is it the face discovered? The portrait, however feeble, transfixes something passive that stays behind the knowing and living look. No drawing from life just fails: it establishes something more; it admits the unadmitted. All Mrs Heccomb had brought to her loving task, besides pastels, had been feeling. She was, to put it politely, a negative artist. But such artists seem to receive a sort of cloudy guidance. Any face, house, landscape seen in a picture, however bad, remains subtly but strongly modified in so-called real life – and the worse the picture, the stronger this is. Mrs Heccomb's experiment in pastels had altered Anna for ever. By daylight, the thing was a human map, scored over with strawy marks of the chalks. But when electric light struck those shadeless triangles – hair, the face, the kitten, those looking eyes – the thing took on a misguided authority. As this face had entered Portia's first dreams here, it continued to enter her waking mind. She saw the kitten hugged to the breast in a contraction of unknowing sorrow.

What help she did not find in the picture she found in its oak frame and the mantelpiece underneath. After inside upheavals, it is important to fix on imperturbable *things*. Their imperturbableness, their air that nothing has happened renews our guarantee. Pictures would not be hung plumb over the centres of fireplaces or wallpapers pasted on with such precision that their seams make no break in the pattern if life were really not possible to adjudicate for. These things are what we mean when we speak of civilization: they remind us how exceedingly seldom the unseemly or unforeseeable rears its head. In this sense, the destruction of buildings and furniture is more palpably dreadful to the spirit than the destruction of human life. Appalling as the talk with Daphne had been, it had not been so finally fatal, when you looked back at it, as an earthquake or a dropped bomb. Had the gas stove blown up when Portia lit it, blowing this nice room into smithereens, it would have been worse than Portia's being called spying and common. Though what she had said had apparently been dreadful, it had done less harm than a

bombardment from the sea. Only outside disaster is irreparable. At least, there would be dinner at any minute; at least she could wash her hands in Vinolia soap.

Before the last chime of the temple bells, Mrs Heccomb had raised the cover and was carving the joint. She did not know that the boys had been to a pub; she understood that they had been for a turn. When Portia slipped into her place between Daphne and Dickie, she was at once requested to pass the broccoli. Upon Waikiki Sunday dinner, the curtain always went up with a rush: they ate as though taking part in an eating marathon. Eddie seemed to be concentrating on Dickie – evidently the drinks had gone off well. Now and then he threw Daphne a jolly look. As he passed up his plate for a second helping of mutton, he said to Portia, '*You* look very clean.'

'Portia always looks clean,' said Mrs Heccomb proudly.

'She looks *so* clean. She must just have been washing. She's still no lady; she uses soap on her face.'

Dickie said: 'No girl's face is the worse for soap.'

'They all think so. They clean with grease out of pots.'

'No doubt. But the question is, *do* they clean?'

'Oh, have you got enlarged pores on your mind? Those are one of the worries I leave behind in the office. They are one of our greatest assets; in fact I have just been doing a piece about them. I began: "Why do so many Englishmen kiss with their eyes shut?" but somebody else made me take that out.'

'I must say, I don't wonder.'

'Still, I'm told Englishmen do. Of course I take that on hearsay: I've got no way to check up.'

There were signs, all round the table, of Eddie's having once more gone too far, and Portia wished he would take more care. However, by the time the plum tart came in, the talk had begun to take a happier turn. They examined night starvation, imperfectly white washing, obesity, self-distrust, and lustreless hair. Eddie had the good taste not to bring up his two great professional topics – halitosis and flabby busts. Doris had found the nine-pennyworth of cream too stiff to turn out of the carton, so brought it in as it was, which made Mrs Heccomb flush. Daphne said: 'Goodness, it's like butter,' and Eddie spooned a chunk of

it out for her. By this time, she looked at him with a piglike but not unfriendly eye. When they had had cream crackers and gorgonzola they rose to settle heavily on the settee. Eddie said: 'Another gambit of ours is fullness after meals.'

Evelyn Bunstable was said to be dropping in, to give Portia's boy friend the once over. However, at about a quarter to three, just when Daphne had asked if they all meant to stick about, something better and far more important happened: Mr Bursely reappeared. Dickie heard him first, looked out of the window, and said: 'Why, who *have* we here.' Mrs Heccomb, coming back from the stairs on her way up to lie down, went quite a long way out into the sun porch, then said: 'It's that Mr Bursely, I think.'

Wearing a hat like Ronald Colman's, Mr Bursely came up the path with the rather knock-kneed walk of extreme social consciousness, and Eddie, who had heard all about him, said: 'You can't beat the military swagger.' Daphne squinted hard at her knitting; Eddie leant over Portia and pinched her gaily in the nape of her neck. He whispered: 'Darling, how excited I am!' Mr Bursely was let into the lounge. 'I'm afraid I've given you rather a miss,' he said. 'But it's been a thickish week, and I got all dated up.' Having hitched his trousers up at the knee, he plumped down on the settee beside Eddie. Portia looked from one to the other face.

Mr Bursely said to Portia: 'How's the child of the house?'

'Very well, thank you.'

Mr Bursely gave her a sort of look, then discreetly passed Daphne his next remark. 'I left my car just along. I thought you and I might go for a slight blow.'

'Oh, I'm fixed up *now*, I'm afraid.'

'Well, unfix yourself, why don't you? Come on, be a good girl, or I shall think you're ever so sick with me. Too bad I can't take you all, but you know what small cars are. I call mine the Beetle; she buzzes along. She –'

'– Actually,' said Dickie, 'I'm playing golf.'

'Clara didn't say so.'

'Because I'm playing with Evelyn.'

'Well, look here, why don't we all forgather somewhere in

Southstone? What about the E.C.P. Why not all forgather there?'

'Oh, all right.'

'Right-o. Well, make it sixish. Bring the whole gang along.'

'Portia and I', Eddie said, 'will just go for a walk.'

'Well, bring young Portia along to the E.C.P.'

'Someone ought to tell Clara. . . .'

'Right-o, then sixish,' Mr Bursely said.

7

THEY walked inland, uphill, to the woods behind the station – the ridge of the woods she had seen from the top of the sea wall. That Sunday, when she had been looking forward to Eddie, woods had played no part in the landscape she saw in her heart.

But here they were this Sunday, getting into the woods over a wattle fence, between gaps in the vigilant notices that said *Private*. Thickets of hazel gauzed over the distances inside; boles of trees rose rounded out of the thickets into the spring air. Light, washing the stretching branches, sifted into the thickets, making a small green flame of every early leaf. Unfluting in the armpit warmth of the valley, leaves were still timid, humid: in the uphill woods spring still only touched the boughs in a green mist that ran into the sky. Scales from buds got caught on Portia's hair. Small primroses, still buttoned into the earth, looked up from ruches of veiny leaves – and in sun-blond spaces at the foot of the oaks, dog violets burned their blue on air no one had breathed. The woods' secretive vitality filled the crease of the valley and lapped through the trees up the bold hill.

There were tunnels but no paths: doubling under the hazels they every few minutes stood up to stretch. '*Shall* we be prosecuted, do you think?'

'Boards are only put up to make woods disagreeable.'

Portia, unlacing twigs in front of her face, said: 'I only imagined us walking by the sea.'

'I've had *quite* enough seaside – one way and another.'

'But you are enjoying it, Eddie, I do hope?'

'Your hair's full of flies – don't touch; they look very sweet.'

Eddie stopped, sat, then lay down in a space at the foot of an oak. Slowly flapping one unhinged arm from the elbow, he knocked the place beside him with the back of his hand till she sat down too. Then, making a double chin, he slowly began to shred up leaves with his thumb-nails, now and then stopping to glance up at the sky – as though someone there had said something he ought to have heard. Portia, her hands clasped round her knees, stared straight down a tunnel of hazel twigs. After some time he said: 'What an awful house that was! Or rather, what awful things we said.'

'In that empty house?'

'Of course. How glad we were to get back to Waikiki. I'm frightened there, but it feels to me rather fine. The mutton bled, did you see? – No, I mean that house this morning. Did I hurt you, darling? Whatever I said, I swear I didn't mean. What did I say?'

'You said you hadn't meant some other things you had said.'

'Well, nor did I, I expect – Or were they things you set store by?'

'And you said there were things you didn't like about us,' said Portia, keeping her face away.

'That's not true, across my heart. I think we are perfect, darling. But I'd much rather you *knew* when I didn't mean what I said, then we shouldn't have to go back and put that right.'

'But what can I go by?'

'Yourself.'

'But Daphne thinks I am bats. She told me not to be potty, before lunch.'

'Don't sit right *up*: I can't look at you properly.'

Portia lay down and turned her cheek on the grass till her eyes obediently met his at a level. His light, curious look glanced into hers – then she dropped one hand across her eyes and lay

rigid, crisping her fingers up. 'She says I'm potty about you. She says I haven't got any ideas.'

'Bitch,' Eddie said. 'They all try and pervert you, but no one but me could really do it, darling. I suppose one day you will have ideas of your own, but I really do dread your having any. Being just as you are now makes you the only person I love. But I can see that makes me a cheat. Never *be* potty about me: I can't do anything for you. Or, at least, I won't: I don't want you to change. We don't want to eat each other.'

'Oh no, Eddie – But what do you mean?'

'Well, like Anna and Thomas. And it can be much worse.'

'What do you mean?' she said apprehensively, raising her hand an inch over her eyes.

'What happens the whole time. And that's what they call love.'

'You say you never love anyone.'

'How would I be such a fool? I see through all that hanky-panky. But you always make me happy – except you didn't this morning. You must never show any sign of change.'

'Yes, that's all very well, but I feel everyone waiting; everyone gets impatient; I cannot stay as I am. They will all expect something in a year or two more. At present people like Matchett and Mrs Heccomb are kind to me, and Major Brutt goes on sending me puzzles, but that can't keep on happening – suppose they're not always there? I can see there is something about me Daphne despises. And I was frightened by what you said this morning – is there something unnatural about us? Do you feel safe with me because I am bats? What did Daphne mean about ideas I hadn't got?'

'Her own, I should think. But –'

'But what ideas do you never want me to have?'

'Oh, those are still worse.'

'You fill me with such despair,' she said, lying without moving.

Eddie reached across and idly pulled her hand away from her eyes. Keeping her hand down in the grass between them, he gently bent open her fingers one by one, then felt over her palm with his finger-tip, as though he found something in Braille on

it. Portia looked at the sky through the branches over their heads, then sighed impalpably, shutting her eyes again. Eddie said: 'You don't know how much I love you.'

'Then, you threaten you won't – that you won't if I grow up. Suppose I was twenty-six?'

'A dreary old thing like that?'

'Oh don't laugh: you make me despair more.'

'I have to laugh – I don't like the things you say. Don't you know how dreadful the things you say are?'

'I don't understand,' she said, very much frightened. 'Why?'

'You accuse me of being a vicious person,' said Eddie, lying racked by her on the grass.

'Oh, I do *not*!'

'I should have known this would happen. It always does happen; it's happening now.'

Terrified by his voice and face of iron, Portia cried, '*Oh no!*' Annihilating the space of grass between them she flung an arm across him, her weight on his body, and despairingly kissed his cheek, his mouth, his chin. 'You are perfect,' she said, sobbing. 'You are my perfect Eddie. Open your eyes. I can't bear you to look like that!'

Eddie opened his eyes, from which her own shadow completely cut the light from the sky. At the same time frantic and impervious, his eyes looked terribly up at her. To stop her looking at him he pulled her head down, so that their two faces blotted each other out, and returned on her mouth what seemed so much her own kiss that she even tasted the salt of her own tears. Then he began to push her away gently. 'Go away,' he said, 'for God's sake go away and be quiet.'

'Then don't think. I can't bear it when you do that.'

Rolling away from her, Eddie huntedly got to his feet and began to go round the thicket: she heard the tips of the hazels whipping against his coat. He paused at the mouth of every tunnel, as though each were a shut door, to stand grinding his heels into the soundless moss. Portia, lying in her form in the grass, looked at the crushed place where he had lain by her – then, turning her head the other way, detected two or three violets, which, reaching out, she picked. She held them over

her head and looked at the light through them. Watching her from his distance, spying upon the movement, he said: 'Why do you pick those? To comfort yourself?'

'I don't know. . . .'

'One cannot leave things alone.'

She could do nothing but look up at the violets, which now shook in her raised hand. In every pause of Eddie's movements a sea-like rustling could be heard all through the woody distance, a tidal movement under the earth. 'Wretched violets,' said Eddie. 'Why pick them for nothing? You'd better put them in my buttonhole.' He came and knelt impatiently down beside her; she knelt up, fumbling with the stalks of the flowers, her face a little below his. She drew the stalks through till the violets looked at her from against the tweed of his coat. She looked no higher till he caught both her wrists.

'I don't know how you feel,' he said, 'I daren't ask myself; I've never wanted to know. *Don't* look at me like that! And don't tremble like that – it's more than I can bear. Something awful will happen. I cannot feel what you feel: I'm shut up in myself. All I know is, you've been so sweet. It's no use holding on to me, I shall only drown you. Portia, you don't know what you are doing.'

'I do know.'

'Darling, I don't want you; I've got no place for you; I only want what you give. I don't want the whole of anyone. I haven't wanted to hurt you: I haven't wanted to touch you in any way. When I try and show you the truth I fill you with such despair. Life is so much more impossible than you think. Don't you see we're all full of horrible power, working against each other however much we may love? You agonize me by being so agonized. Oh cry out loud, if you must: cry, cry – don't just let those terrible meek tears roll down your face like that. What you want is the whole of me – isn't it, *isn't it?* – and the whole of me isn't there for anybody. In that full sense you want me I don't exist. What's started this terrible trouble in you, that you can't be happy with the truth of me that you had – however small it was, whatever might be beyond it? Ever since that evening when you gave me my hat, I've been as true to you as I've

got it in me to be. Don't force me to where untruth starts. You say nothing would make you hate me. But once make me hate myself and you'd make me hate you.'

'But you do hate yourself. I wanted to comfort you.'

'But you have. Ever since you gave me my hat.'

'Why may we not kiss?'

'It's so desolating.'

'But you and me –' she began. She stopped, then pressing her face into his coat, under the violets, twisting her wrists in his unsure grip, she said some inaudible things, and at last moaned: 'I can't bear it when you talk.' When she got her wrists free, she once more locked her arms round him, she started rocking her body with such passionless violence that, as they both knelt, he rocked in her arms. 'You stay alone in yourself, you stay alone in yourself!'

Eddie, white as a stone, said: *'You must let go of me.'*

Sitting back on her heels, Portia instinctively looked up at the oak, to see whether it were still vertical. She pressed together her hands, which, torn roughly from Eddie, had been chafed in the palms by the rough tweed of his coat. Her last tears blistered her face; beginning to lose momentum they stuck in smarting patches: she felt in her coat pockets and said: 'I have got no handkerchief.'

Eddie drew from his own pocket a yard of silk handkerchief: while he still held one corner she blew her nose on another, then diligently blotted her tears up. Like a solicitous ghost whose touch cannot be felt, Eddie, with his two forefingers, tucked her damp hair back further behind her ears. Then he gave her one sad kiss, relevant to their two eternities, not to a word that had been said now. But her fear of having assailed, injured, betrayed him was so strong that she drew back from the kiss. Her knees received from the earth a sort of chilly trembling; the walls of the thicket, shot with those light leaves, flickered beyond her eyes like woods passed in a train.

When they settled back on the grass, with about a yard between them, Eddie pulled out his twenty packet of Players. The cigarettes looked battered. 'Look what you've done, too!' he said. But he lit one: threads of smoke began to swim from

his nostrils; the match he blew out sputtered cold in the moss. When he had finished the cigarette he made a grave in the moss and buried the stump alive – but before this, several healing minutes had passed. 'Well, darling,' he said, in his natural light intonation, 'you must have had Anna tell you Eddie is so neurotic.'

'*Is* that a thing she says?'

'You ought to know: you've been with her half a year.'

'I don't always listen.'

'You ought to: sometimes she's so right ... Look, let's see ourselves in the distance, then we shall think, how happy they are! We're young; this is spring; this is a wood. In some sort of way or other we love each other, and our lives are before us – God pity us! Do you hear the birds?'

'I don't hear very many.'

'No, there are not very many. But you must hear them – play the game my way. What do you smell?'

'Burnt moss, and all the rest of the woods.'

'And what burnt the moss?'

'Oh, Eddie ... your cigarette.'

'Yes, my cigarette I smoked in the woods beside you – you darling girl. No no, you mustn't sigh. Look at us sitting under this old oak. Please strike me a match: I am going to smoke again, but you mustn't, you are still too young to. I have ideals, like Dickie. We don't take you into bars, and we love you to give us pious morbid thoughts. These violets ought to be in your hair – oh, Primavera, Primavera, why do they make you wear the beastly reefer coat? Give me your hand –'

'– No.'

'Then look at your own hand. You and I are enough to break anyone's heart – how can we not break our own? We are as drowned in this wood as though we were in the sea. So of course we are happy: how can we not be happy? Remember this when I've caught my train tonight.'

'*Tonight?* Oh, but I thought –'

'I've got to be in the office on time tomorrow. So what a good thing we are happy now.'

'But –'

'There's not any but.'

'Mrs Heccomb will be so disappointed.'

'Yes, I can't sleep in her lovely box-room again. We shan't wake tomorrow under the same roof.'

'I can't believe that you will have come and gone.'

'Check up with Daphne: she will tell you for certain.'

'Oh, please, Eddie, don't –'

'Why must I not? We must keep up something, you know.'

'Don't say we're happy with that awful smile.'

'I never mean how I'm smiling.'

'Can we walk somewhere else?'

Following uphill dog paths, parting hazels, crossing thickets upright, they reached the ridge of the woods. From here, they could see out. The sun, striking down the slope of trees, glittered over the film of green-white buds: a gummy smell was drawn out in the warm afternoon haze. To the south, the chalk-blue sea, to the north, the bare smooth down: they saw, too, the gleam of the railway line. In spirit, the two of them rose to the top of life like bubbles. Eddie drew her arm through his; Portia leaned her head on his shoulder and stood in the sun by him with her eyes shut.

On the top of the bus, riding into Southstone, Eddie pulled shreds of moss and a few iridescent bud scales from Portia's hair. He ran a comb through his hair, then passed her the comb. His collar was crumpled; their shoes were muddy; they were both of them hatless; Portia wore no gloves. For the Pavilion they would not be smart enough. But as the Southstone bus rolled along the sea front, they both felt very gay; they enjoyed this ride in the large light lurching glass box. Eddie chain-smoked; Portia put down the window near her and leaned out with her elbow over the top. Sea air blew on her forehead; she borrowed his comb again. As the bus changed gear at the foot of Southstone hill they looked at a clock and saw it was only five – but that gave them time for tea before the others should come.

'I tried to ask Daphne what made one feel matey.'

'Well, you *were* a fish: whatever made you do that?'

'Do you know, I once thought, at a party, that Mr Bursely was rather like you?'

'Bursely? – Oh yes, the chappie. Well I really *must* say . . . I wonder where he and Daphne buzzed to, don't you?'

'They might even go to Dover.'

They were still sitting over their tea at the Pavilion when Dickie, Evelyn, Clara, and Cecil filed in. Evelyn wore a canary-coloured two piece, Clara a teddy-bear coat tied in a bow at her chin. Dickie and Cecil were pin-striped all over – evidently everybody had changed. By this time, the Pavilion hung like an unlit lantern in the pinkish air; the orchestra was playing something from *Samson and Delilah*. Evelyn took her first look at Eddie, and asked if he liked hiking. Cecil, showing incuriosity, looked rather low. Clara kept her eyes on Dickie and said nothing: now and then she looked anxiously into her suède bag. As this was believed to be Mr Bursely's party, nothing could start until he came. Dickie folded open a glass and chromium door and said the girls might like to look at the view.

From the balcony they looked down at the Lower Road, at the tops of the pines and the roof of the skating rink. Eddie leaned so far out over the railing that Portia feared he might be going to show them (as he had shown her) how far he could spit. All that happened, however, was that the violets fell through space from his buttonhole. 'Now you've lost your flowers,' said Evelyn brightly.

'Suppose I'd felt giddy?' Eddie said, with a look.

'Oh, would you be such a sap?'

'Your marvellous yellow coat might make me come over queer.'

'I never,' said Evelyn, not knowing how to take this. 'I say, Dickie, your friend's got a bad head. Don't you think we all ought to go in?'

Dickie looked at his watch, still more sternly than he had looked at it in the time before. 'I can't understand,' he said. 'I told Bursely I would have you girls along here by six. I took it that that was understood – it is now between twenty and twenty-five past. I hope he's not having trouble.'

'Oh well, that's up to Daphne, isn't it?' said Evelyn, saucy,

putting stuff on her mouth. Dickie paused till she put away the lipstick, then said coldly: 'I mean, with the car.'

'Oh, it's quite an easy car: I've driven it, so has Clara. I daresay Daphne's driving this afternoon. Look at Clara shivering. Do you feel cold, dear?'

'Slightly.'

Indoors, among the mirrors and pillars, they found Mr Bursely and Daphne, cosy over a drink. Reproaches and rather snooty laughs were exchanged, then Mr Bursely, summoning the waiter, did what was right by everyone. Clara and Portia were given orangeade, with hygienic straws twisted up in paper; Daphne had another bronx, Evelyn a side-car. The men drank whisky – with the exception of Eddie, who asked for a double gin with a dash of angostura: this he insisted in dashing in himself, and so much fuss had seldom been made before. Daphne looked flushed and pleased. She had taken her hat off: while she talked she re-set her curls with one hand or the other, or glanced down confidentially at the dagger in her green velvet choker scarf. Mr Bursely and she – sitting side by side, saying not much – looked extremely conscious of one another.

Sucking quietly, leaning back from the party, isolated at the end of her long straw, Portia looked on. Now and then her eyes went to the clock – in three hours, Eddie would be gone. She watched him getting excited, saying the next were on him. She watched his hand go to his pocket – would he have enough money? He showed Evelyn what was in his pocket-book; he rolled back his cuff to show the hairs on his wrist. He asked Mr Bursely whether he was tattooed. He picked up the straw that Clara had done sucking, and tickled her neck with it as she burrowed into her bag. 'Oh, I say, Clara,' he said, 'you have never spoken to me.' She looked at him like an askance mouse. He dashed too much angostura into his second gin, then had to send for another gin to drown it. Propping an elbow on Cecil's shoulder, he said how much he wished they could go to France together. He printed his name with Evelyn's lipstick on the piece of paper off Clara's straw. 'Don't forget me,' he said. 'I'm certain you will forget me. Look, I'm putting my telephone number too.'

Dickie said: 'We are making rather a row.'

But Mr Bursely was also out of control. He and Eddie had made one of those genuine contacts that are only possible after drinks. With watery, dream-like admiration they kept catching each other's eye. There was no doubt, Eddie worked Mr Bursely up – first Mr Bursely gave an imitation of Donald Duck, then, making a snatch at Daphne's green celluloid comb, he endeavoured to second the orchestra on it. When the music stopped, he tried a tune of his own. He said: 'I'm a shepherd tootling to my sheep.' 'Sheep yourself,' said Daphne, upsetting her third bronx. 'Give me that back! Stop monkeying with my comb!' 'Look here,' Dickie said, 'you can't make that row here.' 'There's no can't about it,' said Mr Bursely, 'we are.'

Portia heard a rush behind her; the curtains were being drawn; swathes of yellow silk rushed across the dark mauve dusk. Cecil went on with his whisky and said nothing. 'Look here,' said Dickie to Mr Bursely and Eddie, 'if you two don't shut up, I am taking the girls home.'

'No, no, don't do that: we can't do without women.'

Dickie said: 'Better shut up, or you'll find yourself chucked out. This is not the Casino de Paris ... I shall take the girls home, then.'

'Right you are, Mussolini. Or let me.'

'Not all the girls, you can't,' said Mr Bursely, shutting one eye and looking through Daphne's comb.

'Can't I?' giggled Eddie, whacking Cecil's shoulder. 'You just ask Cecil: he knows France.'

'I must say, said Evelyn sedately, 'I do think you boys are awful.'

'Well, you tell Cecil. Cecil's all in a dream.'

'Cecil's a gentleman wherever he is,' said Daphne, tenderly fingering Cecil's glass. 'Cecil's a really nice boy, if you know what I mean. I've known Cecil since we were both kids. Haven't we known each other since we were kids, Cecil? ... I *asked* you to stop monkeying with my comb. That's *my* comb you've got. Give that comb back here!'

'No, I'm tootling on it: I'm tootling to my sheep.'

Dickie uncrossed his legs and leant back from the table. 'Cecil,' he said, 'we had better get the girls home.'

Cecil carefully smiled, then put his hand to his forehead. Then he rose and left the table abruptly. He was seen to steer his way between several other tables and vanish with the flash of a swing door. Clara said: 'Now there are only seven of us.'

'What a gap he leaves,' said Eddie. 'He was our only thinker. I dread feeling; I know Clara dreads feeling; I see that in her face. You do dread feeling, don't you, Clara? Oh God, look at the time. How am I to catch a train when I don't know where a train is? I say, Daphne, where do I find a train?'

'The sooner the better.'

'I didn't ask when, I know when, I said where? Oh dear, you *are* a hard girl – I say, Evelyn, will you drive me to London? Let us rush through the night.'

But Evelyn, buttoning her yellow coat, only said: 'Well, Dickie, I'm off. I don't know what father would say – No thanks, Mr – er – *I* don't want your telephone number.'

'Oh God,' Eddie said, 'then you are casting me off?'

Then he turned full on Portia, across the table, his frantic swimming eyes. He said loudly: 'Darling, what shall I do? I am behaving so badly. What *shall* I do?' Then he dropped his eyes, giggled, and struck a match and burnt the long spill with his name on it in lipstick. 'There I go,' he said: the ash dropped on the table and Eddie blew some about and ground the rest with his thumb. 'I'd go,' he said, 'but I don't know where there's a train.'

'We'll ask,' Portia said. She got up and stood waiting.

'Well, good-bye, everybody, I've got to get back to London. Good-bye, good-bye: thanks ever so much.'

But: 'It's no use your saying good-bye,' said Dickie contemptuously. 'You must get back to Waikiki to get your things – if you can remember where *that* is? You also said that your train was at ten o'clock; it is now five minutes past eight. It is therefore no use your saying good-bye here. *Hi, look here*, you all: are you all going? Someone must wait for Cecil.'

Eddie went white and said: 'Well, you organize Cecil, blast

you: let Portia organize me. That's the way we get drunks home.'

The three other girls, at these words, scurried ahead like rabbits. Portia turned away to the yellow curtains: she got two apart and wrenched open the glass doors. A gash of dark air fell into the room; several people shivered and looked round. She stepped on to the balcony hanging over the black sea, lit by the windows' muffled yellow light. In a minute, Eddie came after her: he looked round the dark and said: 'Where are you? Are you still here?'

'Here I am.'

'That's right: don't go over the edge.'

Eddie leaned on the frame of another window, folded his arms, and broke out into sobbing: against the windows she saw his shoulders shake. Someone sobbing like that must not be gone near.

8

THE DIARY

Monday

THIS morning Mrs Heccomb did not say anything, as though yesterday had been all my dream. I have gone on with the puzzle, it has been knocked, so part that I did is undone and I could not begin again where I left off. Perhaps it *is* in the way in the sun porch? Daphne did not say anything more either. It is raining, but more dark than it rains.

Tuesday

When I woke, it rained as much as it could, it has stopped now and the esplanade looks shiny. Mrs Heccomb and I went into Toyne's this morning, to buy clips to stop things blowing away, and coming out of Toyne's she looked as though she was going to say something but she did not, perhaps she was not

going to. On wet days the street smells much more of salt. This afternoon we went to tea with some people to talk about the church fête and they said what a pity I should not be there. It will be in June, by June I wonder what will have happened?

Wednesday

It is queer to be in a place when someone has gone. It is not two other places, the place that they were there in, and the place that was there before they came. I can't get used to this third place or to staying behind.

Mrs Heccomb has a new piano pupil in Southstone, and took me in there when she went to give the lesson. I waited for her on a seat on the cliff. I saw the flags on the East Cliff Pavilion, but did not go near that.

Thursday

Daphne says Cecil is hurt with me. And she says Eddie burnt a hole in the eiderdown Cecil's mother lent for his bed, which has made an awkward position with Cecil's mother. Daphne says it cannot be helped but she does think I ought to know.

Friday

I got a letter from Eddie, so did Mrs Heccomb, he says to her he will always have memories of here. She showed me the letter and said wasn't it nice, but still did not say any more about Eddie. She looked once as if she was going to but she did not, perhaps she was not really going to.

Cecil came this evening and said he had had an internal chill. I do not think he is really hurt with me.

Saturday

Last week this was the day Eddie was coming.

Dickie is kindly taking me into Southstone to watch that ice hockey, Clara is coming too and we shall go in her car. Daphne

and Evelyn are going to dance at the Splendide with Mr Bursely and a man he will bring. Cecil says he has still rather a chill.

Sunday

I went to church with Mrs Heccomb this morning, it was raining hard on the church roof. You can hardly see inland because of all the rain. It must be wet in those woods and everywhere. Today I am going to tea with Cecil's mother.

Monday

I got a letter from Major Brutt thanking me for my letter thanking him for the puzzle. He wonders when we will all be back.

I think they have all forgotten everything that has happened.

Clara has been so kind, she asked me to come with her to Evelyn's house to practise badminton, and we did, but did not get on very well. After that I went back to tea with Clara. Her father is rich, he is in tea. Her house is hot inside and has big game rugs, and on the landings there are flowers with their pots put inside big brass pots. Clara took me up to her bedroom with her, she has Dickie's photograph by her bed, with Yours Dickie written by him on it. She said it was often dull for me and her, because of all the others always working all day, and Clara sometimes thinks she will take something up. She gave me a chiffon handkerchief she has never used, and two necklaces off her own tray. I shall show these at once to Dickie to show how kind Clara is.

Tuesday

I had a letter from Eddie, he says he is well and he asks how they all are. And I have had a letter from Thomas, with a postscript by Anna on one page. Anna said it did make her laugh to think of Eddie at Waikiki. I did not say he'd been here, perhaps Mrs Heccomb did. She says not to write if I'm having such a good time, as they will be back soon and will hear all news then.

Wednesday

Mrs Heccomb suddenly said she was upset about me. I was glad when Cecil took me for a walk on the beach.

Thursday

Mrs Heccomb said she did hope she hadn't said too much, she said she had had a quite sleepless night. I said oh no, she hadn't, because of Cecil. I said I hoped I had not done anything, she said oh no it was not that, only she did wonder. I said wonder what, and she said she did wonder what she ought to have done. I said done when, and she said that was just it, she was not sure when she should have done it, she meant, if she *had* done anything. She said she did hope I knew she was so fond of me and I said I was so glad.

Friday

There are still places I cannot walk past, though we only walked here those two days. When I walk I look for places we did not go. Today I stood on a canal bridge, another canal bridge that we never stood on. I watched two swans, they sailed under the bridge. They say the swans are nesting, but these two kept their heads turned away from each other. Today it is not raining but quite dark, black is all through the air though the green looks such bright green. All the days that go by only make me seem to be getting further and further away from the day I last saw Eddie, not nearer and nearer the day I shall see him again.

Saturday

A fortnight since Eddie came. My last Saturday here.

Dickie came back at three from the Hockey Lunch. He says they have been winding up for the year. I was in the sun porch doing my puzzle, and he asked why I looked like that when he came in. I said it was my last Saturday here. So he asked if I'd like to walk round while he played golf. So when Clara came in her car to call for him they put me into the back part of the car and we drove up to the links. Clara tries with her golf be-

cause of Dickie, but Dickie plays a sort of game by himself. You see the woods from the links, right across a valley, but it is lovely up there, there is so much gorse. At the end Dickie said we would have tea, so we went and had tea in the club house. It is handsome in there, there is a huge fire and we had tea right in the bow-window. I did enjoy myself. I think my being there made Clara feel rather more like Dickie's wife, she insisted on getting some more jam. At the end of our tea, Clara got her bag out, but Dickie said, Here, I say, and he paid for the tea. It is only in front of Daphne he is unkind to Clara.

We had been so long that Clara said good gracious, she had to hurry, a judge was coming to dinner at her home. So Dickie said she had better buzz straight back, so she did, and he and I walked home. He said, was I sorry I was going away? I said I was (I am) and he turned round and gave a look at the top of my head and said, so were they all. He said I had become quite one of them. That made me ask, did he like Eddie too. He said, of course he's an amusing chap. I said I was so glad he thought Eddie was funny. He said, he is something of a Lothario, isn't he? I said Eddie was not really, and he said, well, he loses his head a bit, if you know what I mean. I said I did not quite, and he said, well to my mind it is largely a matter of character. He said he judged people by their characters. I said *was* that always a quite good way of judging, as people's characters get so different at times, as it depends so much what happens to them. He said no, I was wrong, that what happened to people depended on their characters. I know Dickie sounds right, but I don't feel he is. By that time we were out on the esplanade and there was a sunset right into our eyes. I said didn't the sea look like glass, and he said yes he supposed it did. I said I did like Clara, and he said oh she's all right but she loses her head. I said then did he mean Clara was like Eddie, and he said he did not. Then we got to Waikiki.

Sunday

My last Sunday. It's very very fine, hot. The leaves are out on the chestnuts, though not big leaves, and the other trees have a quite frilly look. After church Mrs Heccomb and I were asked

into someone's garden to have a look at the hyacinths. They are just like all sorts of coloured china. In the garden Mrs Heccomb said to the lady, Next Sunday, alas, we shall not have Portia with us. I thought, next Sunday, I might even see Eddie and yet I still thought, oh I do want to stay here. Now the summer is coming they will do all sorts of things I have not seen them doing yet. In London I do not know what anybody is doing, there are no things I can watch people do. Though things have hurt me since I was left behind here, I would rather stay with the things here than go back to where I do not know what will happen.

On the way back from the hyacinth garden, Mrs Heccomb said what a great pity it was that I had not been for a row on the canal. She says that is where they row in summer. I said, but don't they row in the sea, and she said no, that is so public, the canal is shadier. She said how would it be if she asked Cecil to row her and me there this afternoon. So we went round by Cecil's house, he was out but his mother said she would certainly ask him to row us.

So this afternoon we did. Cecil rowed, and he showed me how to steer, and Mrs Heccomb held up a parasol. It was mauve silk, and once or twice when I was not steering I caught weed in my hands. The weed is strong, and it also caught on the oars. So none of us said much while Cecil was rowing, Mrs Heccomb thought and I looked down in the water or up at the trees. The sun shone almost loudly. A swan came along and Mrs Heccomb said it would be nesting and might likely be cross, so she folded up her parasol to hit at it, and Cecil said, I had better ship my oars. But the swan did not take any notice of us. Later we passed its nest, with the other one sitting there.

All the others were playing tennis somewhere. When I first got here, Mrs Heccomb was wearing her fur coat. Now though it is all pale green it is summer. Things change very fast at this time of year, something happens every day. All winter nothing happened at all.

Tonight Mrs Heccomb is singing in an oratorio. Daphne and Dickie and Clara and Evelyn and Wallace and Charlie and Cecil are all downstairs playing rummy because she is out. But

Mrs Heccomb made me go to bed early, because I caught a headache on the canal.

Monday

Mrs Heccomb is tired after the oratorio, and Daphne and Dickie do not like fine Mondays. Now I shall go out and lie on the beach.

Tuesday

I have not yet had the letter Eddie said he would write, but that must be because I am coming back. This is a new place this week, this is a place in summer. The esplanade smells all over of hot tar. But they all say that of course this will not last.

Wednesday

Tomorrow I shall be going. Because this is my last whole day, Mrs Heccomb and Cecil's mother are going to take me to see a ruin. We are to pack our tea and go in a motor bus.

Clara is going to drive me in her car to the Junction tomorrow, to save the having to change. Clara says she feels really upset. Because this will be my last evening, Dickie and Clara and Cecil are going to take me to the Southstone rink, so's I can watch them skate.

I cannot say anything about going away. I cannot say anything even in this diary. Perhaps it is better not to say anything ever. I must try not to say anything more to Eddie, when I have said things it has always been a mistake. Now we must start to take the bus for the ruin.

Thursday

I am back here, in London. They won't be back till tomorrow.

Part Three

THE DEVIL

I

THOMAS and Anna would not be back from abroad till Friday afternoon.

Everything was ready for them to come back and live. That Friday morning, 2 Windsor Terrace was lanced through by dazzling spokes of sun, which moved unseen, hotly, over the waxed floors. Vacantly overlooking the bright lake, chestnuts in leaf, the house offered that ideal mould for living into which life so seldom pours itself. The clocks, set and wound, ticked the hours away in immaculate emptiness. Portia – softly opening door after door, looking all round rooms with her reflecting dark eyes, glancing at each clock, eyeing each telephone – did not count as a presence.

The spring cleaning had been thorough. Each washed and polished object stood roundly in the unseeing air. The marbles glittered like white sugar; the ivory paint was smoother than ivory. Blue spirit had removed the winter film from the mirrors: now their jet-sharp reflections hurt the eye; they seemed to contain reality. The veneers of cabinets blazed with chestnut light. Upstairs and downstairs, everything smelt of polish; a clean soapy smell came out from behind books. Crisp from the laundry, the inner net curtains stirred over windows reluctantly left open to let in the April air with its faint surcharge of soot. Yes, already, with every breath that passed through the house, pollution was beginning.

The heating was turned off. Up the staircase stood a shaft of neutral air, which, upon any door or window being opened, received a tremor of spring. This morning, the back rooms were still sunless and rather cold. The basement was still colder; it

smelled of scrubbing; the light filtered down to it in a ghostly way. City darkness, a busy darkness, collected in this working part of the house. For four weeks, Portia had not been underground.

'Gracious, Matchett, you have got everywhere clean!'

'Oh – so that's where you've been?'

'Yes, I've looked at everywhere. It really *is* clean – not that it isn't always.'

'More likely you'd notice it, coming back. I know those seaside houses – all claptrap and must.'

'I must say,' said Portia, sitting on Matchett's table, 'today makes me wish only you and I lived here.'

'Oh, you ought to be ashamed! And mind, too, you don't get a place like this without you have a Mr and Mrs Thomas. And then where would you be, I should like to know? No, I'm ready for them, and it's proper they should come back. Now don't give me a look like that – what is the matter with you? I'm sure Mr Thomas, for one, would be disappointed if he was to know you wished you were still at that seaside.'

'But I never did say that!'

'Oh, it isn't only what's *said*.'

'Matchett, you do fly off when all I just said was –'

'All right, all right, all right.' Matchett tapped at her teeth with a knitting needle and marvelled at Portia slowly. 'My goodness,' she said, 'they have taught you to speak up. Anyone wouldn't know you.'

'But you go on at me because I have been away. After all, I didn't go, I was sent.'

Sitting up on the table in Matchett's basement parlour, Portia stretched her legs out and looked at her toes, as though the change Matchett detected (was there a change really?) might have begun there. Matchett, knitting a bedsock, sat on one of the chairs beside the unlit gas stove, feet up on the rung of another chair – she had unbuttoned the straps across her insteps, which were puffy today. It was twelve noon: the hands of the clock seemed to exclaim at the significant hour. Twelve noon – but everything was too ready, nothing more was to come till an afternoon train steamed into Victoria and a taxi toppling

with raw-hide luggage crossed London from s.w. to n.w.1. Therefore, there had happened this phenomenal stop. In the kitchen, the cook and Phyllis tittered to one another, no doubt drinking tea. In here, the two chairs now and then creaked with Matchett's monolithic repose.

She had had her way like a fury. Tensed on the knitting needles (for she could not even relax without some expense of energy) her fingers were bleached and their skin puckered, like the skin of old apples, from unremitting immersion in hot water, soda, soap. Her nails were pallid, fibrous, their tips split. Light crept down the sooty rockery, through the bars of the window, to find no colour in Matchett: her dark blue dress blotted the light up. She looked built back into the half darkness behind her apron's harsh glaze. In her helmet of stern hair, a few new white threads shone – but behind the opaqueness of her features control permitted no sag of tiredness. There was more than control here: she wore the look of someone who has augustly fulfilled herself. Floor by floor over the basement towered her speckless house, and a reckoning consciousness of it showed like eyes through the eyelids she lowered over her knitting.

Portia, looking through the bars of the window, said: 'It was a pity you couldn't wash the rockery.'

'Well, we did spray the ivy, but that doesn't go far, and those tom cats are always after the ferns.'

'I did imagine you busy – but not so busy, Matchett.'

'I don't see you had call to imagine anybody, not with all you were up to with them there.' (This, though worded sharply, was not said sharply: all the time Matchett spoke she was knitting; there was something pacific about the click-click-click.) 'You don't want to be in two places, not at your age. You be at the seaside when you're at the seaside. You keep your imaginings till you need them. Come a spring like this one we've been having, out of sight out of mind should be good enough. Oh, it has been a lovely spring for the airing – down at Mrs Quayne's, I'd have had my mattresses out.'

'But I thought about you. Didn't you think of me?'

'Now when do you suppose I'd have had a minute? If you

had have been here, you'd have been under my feet one worse than Mr and Mrs Thomas if they hadn't gone away. No, and don't you say to me that you went round moping, either: you had your fill of company where you were, and I've no doubt there were plenty of goings on. Not that you've got much to tell; you keep it all to yourself. However, that's always your way.'

'You didn't ask me; you were still so busy. This is the first time you've listened. And now I don't know where to begin.'

'Oh, well, take your time: you've got the rest of the summer,' said Matchett, glancing at the clock. 'I must say, they've sent you back with a colour. I can't see that this change has done you harm. Nor the shake-up either: you were getting too quiet. I never saw such a quiet girl, for your age. Not that that Mrs Heccomb, poor thing, could teach anyone to say no. All I've ever heard her say to Mrs Thomas was yes. But the rest of them down there sound a rough lot. Did you have enough stockings?'

'Yes, thank you. But I'm afraid I cut the knees out of one pair. I was running, and I fell smack on the esplanade.'

'And what made you run, may I ask?'

'Oh, the sea air.'

'Oh, it did, did it?' said Matchett. 'It made you run.' Without a pause in her knitting, she half lifted her eyelids, enough to let her look stay tilted, through space, at nothing particular. How far apart in space these two existences, hers and Portia's, had been for the last weeks; how far apart they still were. You never quite know when you may hope to repair the damage done by going away. Removing one foot cumbrously from the rung of the chair, Matchett hooked with it at the ball of pink knitting wool which had been rolling away. Portia got off the table, picked the ball of wool up, and handed it back to Matchett. She said boldly: 'Is that bedsock for you?'

Matchett's half nod was remote, extremely unwilling. No one *knew* that she slept, that she went to bed: at nights she just disappeared. Portia knew she had trespassed; she said quickly: 'Daphne knitted. She used to knit at the library. Mrs Heccomb could knit, but she used to paint lamp shades more.'

'And what did you do?'

'Oh, I went on with my puzzle.'

'That wasn't much of a treat.'

'But it was a new puzzle, and I only did that when I wasn't doing anything. You know how it is –'

'No, I don't, and I'm not asking, and I don't want mysteries made.'

'There's no mystery, except what I've forgotten.'

'You don't have to say; I'm not asking you. What you do's all one on a holiday. Now it's all over, get it out of your head – I see you've worn the elbows out of that blazer. I told Mrs Thomas that wouldn't be wearing stuff. Did you use your velvet, or was I wrong to pack it?'

'No, I wore my velvet. I –'

'Oh, they dress for their dinner, then?'

'No, I wore it for their party. It was a dance.'

'I did ought to have packed your organdie, then. But I didn't want it to crush, and sea air limpens the pleats out. I daresay your velvet did.'

'Yes, Matchett: it was admired.'

'Well, it's better than they'd see: it's got a nice cut.'

'You know, Matchett, I did enjoy myself.'

Matchett gave another sideways look at the clock, as though admonishing time to hurry for its own sake. Her air became more non-committal than ever; she appeared to be hypnotized by the speed of her knitting, and, at the same time, for her own private pleasure, to be humming an inaudible tune. After about a minute, she receipted Portia's remark with an upward jerk of the chin. But the remark had, by that time, already wilted in the below stairs dusk of this room – like, on the mantelpiece, the bunch of wild daffodils, some friend's present, thrust so sternly into a glass jar. These, too, must have been a gift that Matchett no more than suffered.

'You're glad, aren't you?' Portia more faintly said.

'The things you do ask. . . .'

'I suppose it may have been just the sea air.'

'And I daresay the sea air suited Mr Eddie?'

Unarmoured against this darting remark, Portia shifted on the table. 'Oh, Eddie?' she said. 'He was only there for two days.'

'Still, two days are two days, at the seaside. Yes, I understood him to say he felt fine there. At least, those were his words.'

'*When* were they his words? What do you mean?'

'Now don't you jump down my throat in such a hurry as that.' Running the strand of pink wool over a rasped finger, Matchett reflectingly hummed a few more unheard bars. 'Five-thirty yesterday, that would have been, I suppose. When I was coming downstairs in my hat and coat, just off to meet your train with no time to spare, my lord starts ringing away on the telephone – oh, fit to bring the whole house down, it was. Thinking it might be important, I went and answered. *Then* I thought I should never get him away – chattering on and on like that. However, no doubt that's what Mr Thomas's office telephone's for. No wonder they've got to have three lines. "Excuse me, sir," I said, "but I am just on my way to meet a train." '

'Did he know it was my train?'

'He didn't ask, and I didn't specify. "I am just off to meet a train," I said. But did that stop him? Trains can wait while some people have to talk. "Oh, I won't keep you," he said – then ran on to something else.'

'But what did he run on to?'

'He seemed quite put out to hear Mrs Thomas was not back yet, and that neither were you. "Oh dear, oh dear," he said, "I must have muddled the days." Then he said, to be sure to tell Mrs Thomas, and to tell you, that he would be out of London from the following morning (today morning, that was) but would hope to ring up after the weekend. Then he said he thought I'd be glad to hear that you had looked well at the sea-side. "You'd be so pleased, Matchett," he said, "she's really got quite a colour." I thanked him and asked if there would be anything more. He said just to give his love to Mrs Thomas, and you. He said he thought that would be all.'

'So then you rang off?'

'No, he did. It was his tea time, no doubt.'

'Did he say he'd ring up again?'

'No, he left what he had to say.'

'Did you say I was on my way back?'

'No, why should I? He didn't ask.'

'When did he *think* I'd be back?'

'Oh, I couldn't tell you, I'm sure.'

'What made him be going away on a *Friday* morning?'

'I couldn't tell you that, either. Office business, no doubt.'

'It seems to me very odd.'

'A good deal in that office seems to me very odd. However, it's not for me to say.'

'But, Matchett – just one thing more: did he realize I'd be back that very night?'

'What he realized or didn't realize I couldn't tell you. All I know is, he kept chattering on.'

'He does chatter, I know. But you don't think –'

'Listen: I don't think: I haven't the time to, really. What I don't think I don't think – you ought to know that. I don't make mysteries, either. I suppose, if he hadn't thought to say, *you'd* never have thought to tell me he'd been there at Mrs Heccomb's? Now, you get off my table, there's a good girl, while I plug in the iron: I've got some pressing to do.'

Portia said, in a hardly alive voice: 'I thought you said you had finished everything.'

'Finished? You show me one thing that is ever finished, let alone everything. No, I'll stop when they've got me screwed into my coffin, but that won't be because I've got anything finished . . . I'll tell you one thing you might do for me: run up, like a good girl, and shut Mrs Thomas's bedroom window. That room should be aired now, and I won't have any more smuts in. Then you leave me quiet while I get on with my pressing. Why don't you go in the park? It must be pretty out there.'

Portia shut Anna's windows, and gave one blank look at herself in Anna's cheval glass. Before shutting the windows she heard the wooing pigeons, and heard cars slip down the glossy road. Through the fresh net curtains, she saw trees in the sun. She could not make up her mind to go out of doors, for she felt alone. If one is to walk alone, it should be with pleasant thoughts. About this time, Mrs Heccomb, alone today, would be getting back to Waikiki after the morning shopping . . . She lagged downstairs to the hall: here, on the marble-topped table, two stacks of letters awaited Thomas and Anna. For the third

time, Portia went carefully through these – it was still possible
that something for Miss P. Quayne could have got slipped in
among them. This proved not to be so – it had been not so before ... She went through the letters again, this time for interest purely. Some of Anna's friends' writings were cautious,
some were dashing. How many of these letters were impulses,
how many were steps in some careful plan? She could guess at
some of the writings; she had seen these people already, stalk-
ing each other. For instance, here was St Quentin's well-cut
grey envelope. Now what had *he* got to add to what was already
said?

Personal letters for Thomas were not many, but to balance
Anna's pile back was quite an affair of art. Portia tried to
imagine getting out of a taxi to find one's own name written so
many times. This should make one's name mean – oh, most
decidedly – more.

With a stage groan, Anna said: 'Now will you look at those
letters!'

She did not, at first, attempt to pick them up: she read one or
two messages on the telephone pad, and looked at a florist's gilt
box on the chair – there was no room on the laden table for it.
She said to Thomas: 'Someone has sent me flowers,' but he had
already gone into the study. So Anna, smiling at Portia, said
nicely to her: 'One can't attempt to open everything, can
one? ... How well you're looking: quite brown, almost fat.'
She looked up the stairs and said: 'Well, we certainly are clean.
You got back yesterday evening, didn't you?'

'Yes, yesterday.'

'And you enjoyed yourself frightfully?'

'Oh yes, I did, Anna.'

'You said so, but we did hope you did. Have you seen Matchett?'

'Oh, yes.'

'Yes, you naturally would have: I was forgetting you got
back yesterday ... Well, I must look round,' said Anna picking
up the letters. 'How odd I do feel. Will you open those flowers
and tell me who they're from?'

'The box looks nice. I expect the flowers are lovely.'

'Yes, I'm sure they are. But I wonder who they are from.'

Anna took her letters up, and went up to have a bath. Five minutes later, Portia came to tap on the bathroom door. Anna was not yet quite into the bath; she opened the door, showing a strip of herself and letting out a cloud of scented steam. 'Oh hullo?' she said. 'Well?'

'They are carnations.'

'What colour?'

'Sort of quite bright pink.'

'Oh God – Who are they from?'

'Major Brutt. He says on the card that they are to welcome you home.'

'This would happen,' Anna said. 'They must have cost him the earth; he probably didn't have lunch and this makes me hysterical. I do wish we had never run into him: we've done nothing but put ideas into his head. You had better take them down and show them to Thomas. Or else give them to Matchett; they might do for her room. I know this is dreadful, but I feel so unreal ... Then you might write Major Brutt a note. Say I have gone to bed. I am sure he would much rather have a note from you. Oh, how was Eddie? I see he rang up.'

'Matchett answered.'

'Oh! I thought you probably would. Well, Portia, let's have a talk later.' Anna shut the door and got into her bath.

Portia took the carnations down to Thomas. 'Anna says these are the wrong colour,' she said. Thomas was back again in his armchair, as though he had not left it, one foot on a knee. Though only a dimmed-down reflection of afternoon came into the study, he had one hand near his eyes, as though there were a strong glare. He looked without interest at the carnations. 'Oh, are they the wrong colour?' he said.

'Anna says they are.'

'Who did you say they were from?'

'Major Brutt.'

'Oh yes, oh yes. Do you think he's found a job?' He looked more closely at the carnations, which Portia held like an unhappy bride. 'There are hundreds of them,' he said. 'I suppose

he has found something. I hope he has: we cannot do anything ... Well, Portia, how are you? Did you really have a good time? – Forgive me sitting like this, but I seem to have got a headache – How did you like Seale?'

'Very much indeed.'

'That's excellent: I'm really awfully glad.'

'I wrote and said I did, Thomas.'

'Anna wondered whether you did really. I should think it was nice. I've never been there, of course.'

'No, they said you hadn't.'

'No. It's a pity, really. Well, it's nice to see you again. Is everything going well?'

'Yes, thank you. I'm enjoying the spring.'

'Yes, it is nice,' said Thomas, 'It feels to me cold, of course ... Would you care to go for a turn in the park, later?'

'That would be lovely. When?'

'Well, I think later, don't you? ... Where did you say Anna was?'

'She's just having her bath. She asked me to write something to Major Brutt. I wonder, Thomas, if I might write at your desk?'

'Oh yes, by all means do.'

Having discharged himself of this good feeling, Thomas unostentatiously left the study while Portia opened the blotter to write to Major Brutt. He got himself a drink, carried the drink upstairs, and took a look round the drawing-room on his way. Not a thing had been tweaked from its flat, unfeeling position – palpably Anna had not been in here yet. So then he carried his drink into Anna's room, and sat on the big bed till she should come from her bath. His heavy vague reflections weighted him into a stone figure – Anna jumped when she came round the door at him, her wrapper open, the bunch of steam-blotched opened letters in her hand. Superfluously, she said: 'How you made me jump!'

'I wondered if there were letters. ...'

'There are letters, of course. But nothing at all funny. However, darling, here they all are.' She dropped the letters on to the bed beside him, and went across to the mirror, where she

took off the net cap that kept the waves in her hair. Making a
harsh face at her reflection, she began to rub in complexion milk
with both hands. Tapping about among the pots and bottles, she
had found everything in its known place – the familiarity of all
these actions made something at once close in on her: the mood
of her London dressing-table. With her back to Thomas, who
sat raking through letters, she said: 'Well, here we are back.'

'What did you say?'

'I said, we are back again.'

Thomas looked all round the room, then at the dressing-table.
He said: 'How quickly Matchett's unpacked.'

'Only the dressing-case. After that, I turned her out and told
her to come back and finish later. I could see from her face she
was going to say something.'

Thomas left the letters and sat leaning forward. 'Perhaps she
really had got something to say.'

'Well, Thomas, but what a moment – really! Did you hear
me say just now that here we were, back?'

'I did, yes. What do you want me to say?'

'I wish you would say something. Our life goes by without
any comment.'

'What you want is some sort of a troubadour.'

Anna wiped complexion milk off her fingers on to a tissue,
smartly re-tied the sash of her wrapper, walked across, and gave
Thomas's head a light friendly unfriendly cuff. She said: 'You
are like one of those sitting images that get moved about but
still always just sit. I like to feel some way about what happens.
We're *home*, Thomas: have some ideas about home –' More
lightly, less kindly, she hit at his head again.

'Shut up: don't knock me about. I've got a headache.'

'Oh dear, oh dear! Try a bath.'

'I will later. But just now, don't hit my head ... I thought
Portia gave us a welcome.'

'Poor child, oh poor child, yes. She stood about like an angel.
It was we who were not adequate. I wasn't very, was I?'

'No, I don't think you were.'

'But you think you were? You bolted into the study. What's
in your mind, I suppose, is, why should you rise to occasions

when I don't? Let's face it – who ever is adequate? We all create situations each other can't live up to, then break our hearts at them because they don't. One doesn't have to be in love to be silly – in fact I think one is sillier when one's not in love, because then one makes a thing about everything. At least, that is how it is with me. Major Brutt sending those carnations has made me hysterical. Did you see them? They were cochineal pink.'

'I don't create situations, I don't think.'

'Yes, you do; you're creating one by having a headache. Besides you are making creases in my quilt.'

'I'm sorry,' said Thomas rising. 'I'll go down.'

'Now you are making another situation. What I really want to do is to dress and not have to talk, but I can't have you walk out into the night. And Matchett is simply waiting to pop back and rustle about and spring something on me. I know I am disappointing you, darling. I'm sure you would be happier in the study.'

'Portia's down there, writing to Major Brutt.'

'And if you go down, you'll feel you will have to say, "Well, Portia, how are you getting on with your letter to Major Brutt?" '

'No, I shouldn't see the least necessity to.'

'Well, Portia would look up until you did. Now, Major Brutt having sent me those carnations is just the sort of thing that Portia really enjoys,' said Anna, sitting down by the dressing-table, unrolling and putting on a pair of silk stockings. 'Yes, it often does seem to me that you and I are not natural. But I also say to myself, well, who is natural, then?'

Having put his glass down on the carpet, Thomas boldly swung his legs up on to the bed and stretched out on the immaculate quilt. 'I don't think that bath has done you much good,' he said. 'Or is this the way you talk most of the time? We so seldom talk; we're so seldom together.'

'I must be tired; I do feel rather unreal. As I keep saying, all I want is to dress.'

'Well, do dress. Why can't you just dress and why can't I just lie? We don't have to keep on saying anything. However much

of a monster you may be, I feel more natural with you than I feel with more natural people – if there are such things. Must you put on those beastly green suède shoes?'

'Yes, because the others aren't unpacked. How hot the afternoon sun is,' said Anna, drawing the curtains behind the dressing-table. 'All the time we were *there*, I kept imagining England coolish and grey, and now we land into this inferno of glare.'

'I expect the weather will break. You don't much like anything, do you?'

'No, nothing,' said Anna, smiling her nice fat malign smile. She finished dressing in the gloom of the curtains, through whose yellows and pinks the afternoon sun beat. The vibration of traffic came through the shut window, through the stiff chintz folds. She gave one more look at Thomas and said: 'I suppose you do know that that ruins my quilt?'

'It can go to the cleaners.'

'The point is, it has just come back from there ... How do you think Portia is?'

Thomas, who had just lighted a cigarette (the worst thing for a headache) said: 'She says she's enjoying the spring.'

'Now whatever makes her do that? Little girls of her age don't just enjoy weather. Someone must have been fussing her up.'

'She may not have been enjoying the spring really, but just felt she must say something polite. I suppose it's possible she enjoyed Seale – in which case, we might have left her there longer.'

'No, if she's to be with us she's got to be with us, darling. Besides, her lessons begin on Monday. If she's not enjoying the spring (and I can't make out if your impression was that she wasn't or that she was) there must be something wrong with her, and you had better find out what it is. You know she will never talk to me. If someone's let her down that would be Eddie, of course.'

Thomas reached down to knock ash off into his empty glass. 'Anyhow, it's high time the lid was put on that. I don't know why we have let it go so far.'

'Oh, it's stationary: it's been like that for months. Evidently you don't know what Eddie is. He doesn't have to go far with anybody to fail them: he can let anyone down at any stage. And what do you expect me to say or do? There are limits to what one can say to people and it isn't really a question of doing anything. Anyhow, she's your sister. As for speaking to Eddie, you must know how touchy he is with me. And she and I feel so shy, and shyness makes one so brutal ... No, poor little Eddie's not a ravening lion.'

'No, he's not a *lion*.'

'Don't be malicious, Thomas.'

Glad, however, to find herself dressed again, Anna gave herself a sort of contented shake inside her green dress, like a bird shaking itself back into its preened feathers. She looked for her case and lighted a cigarette, then came over to sit on the bed by Thomas. Rolling his head round, he at once pulled her head down to pillow level. 'All the same,' said Anna, after the kiss, sitting up and moulding back with her fingers the one smooth curl along the nape of her neck, 'I do think you'll have to get off that quilt.' While she went back to the dressing-table to screw the caps back on to her pots and bottles Thomas rose and, meticulous and gloomy, tried to smooth the creases out of the satin. 'After tea', he announced, 'Portia and I are going for a turn in the park.'

'But do. Why not?'

'If you were half as heartless as you make out, you would be an appallingly boring woman.'

After tea, Thomas and Portia dodged two lines of traffic, successfully crossed the road, and went into the park. They crossed the bridge to the far side of the lake. Here stood the tulips just ready to flower: still grey and pointed, but brilliantly veined with the crimsons, mauves, yellows they were to be. Late afternoon sunshine streamed into the faces of people sitting in deck chairs, along the lake or on the bright grass – shading their eyes or bending their heads down or letting the sun beat on their closed lids, these people sat like reddening stones.

The water was animated: light ran off blades of oars or struck

through the coloured or white sails that shivered passing the
islands. Bending rowers crossed the mirroring view. The ether-
ealization of the early morning had lifted from the long narrow
wooded islands, upon which nobody was allowed to land, and
which showed swans' nests at the edge of their mystery. Light
struck into the islands' unvisited hearts; the silvery willow
branches just shifted apart to let light glitter through. Reflections of trees, of sails, made the water coloured and deep, and
water birds lanced it with long ripples.

People approaching each other, beside the lake or on the
oblique walks, looked into each other's faces boldly, as though
they felt they should know each other. Thin hems of women's
dresses fluttered under their coats. Children shuttled about, or
made conspiracies that broke up in shouts. But this vivid evening, no grown-up people walked fast: the park was full of
straying fancies and leisure.

Thomas and Portia turned their alike profiles in the direction
from which the breeze came. Portia thought how inland the air
smelled. Looking unmoved up at the turquoise sky above the
trees burning thinly yellow-green, Thomas said he felt the
weather would change.

'I hope not before these tulips are out. These are the tulips
father told me about.'

'Tulips – what do you mean? When did he see them?'

'The day he walked past your house.'

'Did he walk past our house? When?'

'One day, once. He said it had been painted; it looked like
marble, he said. He was very glad you lived there.'

Thomas's face went slowly set and heavy, as though he felt
the weight of his father's solitary years as well as his own. He
looked at Portia, at their father's eyebrows marking, here, a
more delicate line. His look made it clear he would not speak.
Across the lake, only the parapet and the upper windows of
Windsor Terrace showed over the trees: the silhouette of the
stucco, now not newly painted, looked shabby and frail. 'We
paint every four years,' he said.

In the traffic, half way across the road, Portia suddenly looked
up at the drawing-room window, and waved. 'Look out!'

Thomas said sharply, gripping her elbow – a car swerved past them like a great fish. 'What's the matter?'

'There was Anna, up there. She's gone now.'

'If you don't take better care in the traffic, I don't think you ought to go out alone.'

2

HAVING been seen at the window, having been waved to, made Anna step back instinctively. She knew how foolish a person looking out of a window appears from the outside of a house – as though waiting for something that does not happen, as though wanting something from the outside world. A face at a window for no reason is a face that should have a thumb in its mouth: there is something only-childish about it. Or, if the face is not foolish it is threatening – blotted white by the darkness inside the room it suggests a malignant indoor power. Would Portia and Thomas think she had been spying on them?

Also, she had been seen holding a letter – not a letter that she had got today. It was to escape from thoughts out of the letter that she had gone to the window to look out. Now she went back to her *escritoire* which, in a shadowed corner of this large light room, was not suitable to write more than notes at. In the pigeonholes she kept her engagement pad, her account books; the drawers under the flap were useful because they locked. At present, a drawer stood open, showing packets of letters; and more letters, creased from folding, exhaling an old smell, lay about among slipped-off rubber bands. Hearing Thomas's latch-key, the hall door opening, Portia's confident voice, Anna swept the letters into the drawer quickly, then knelt down to lock everything up. But this sad little triumph of being ready in time came to nothing, for the two Quaynes went straight into the study; they did not come upstairs.

They did not come up to join her, though they knew where she was. Looking at the desk key on the palm of her hand,

Anna felt much more cut off from the letters: one kind of loneliness hammers another in. Directly the two had gone out after
tea, she had gone to this drawer with the clearly realized intention of comparing the falseness of Pidgeon with the falseness of
Eddie. There are phases in feeling that make the oddest behaviour quite relevant. She had said what was quite true, at least
of herself, when she had told St Quentin, last January, that experience means nothing till it repeats itself. Everything in her
life, she could see now, had taken the same turn – as for love,
she often puzzled and puzzled, without ever allowing herself to
be fully sad, as to what could be wrong with the formula. It
does not work, she thought. At times there were the moments
when she asked herself if she could have been in the wrong: she
would almost rather think that. What she *thought* she regretted
was her lack of guard, her wayward extravagance – but had she
all the time been more guarded than she imagined, had she been
deceitful, had she been seen through? For what had always happened she could still not account. There seemed to be some way
she did not know of by which people managed to understand
each other.

All I said to Thomas was, to get off my quilt. After that he
takes her for a walk in the park.

Ease and intelligence seemed to her to lead to a barren end.
Thoughtfully, she put the key of the locked drawer into the
inner pocket of her handbag, then snapped the bag shut. Anybody as superficially wounded, but at the same time as deeply
nonplussed as Anna seems to themselves to be a forlorn hope.
This is what one gets for being so nicely nonchalant, for saving
people's faces, for not losing one's hair. She could not think why
she fussed so much with this key, for the drawer held no secrets:
Thomas knew everything. It was true, she had never shown
him these letters; though he knew *what* had happened he did
not know how, why. Supposing she were to throw this pack of
letters at Portia, saying: 'This is what it all comes to, you little
fool!'

At this point, Anna lighted a cigarette, sat down by her bag
on the yellow sofa, and asked herself why she liked Portia so
little. The *idea* of her never leaves me quiet, and by coming into

this room she drives me on to the ice. Everything she does to me is unconscious: if it were conscious it would not hurt. She makes me feel like a tap that won't turn on. She crowds me into an unreal position, till even St Quentin asks why do I over-act? She has put me into a relation with Thomas that is no more than our taunting, feverish jokes. My only honest way left is to be harsh to them both, which I honestly am. This afternoon, directly she heard our taxi, she had to snatch open the door and wait for us, all eyes. I cannot even stand in my own window without her stopping to wave, among those cars. She might have been run over, which would have been shocking.

But, after all, death runs in that family. What is she, after all? The child of an aberration, the child of a panic, the child of an old chap's pitiful sexuality. Conceived among lost hairpins and snapshots of doggies in a Notting Hill Gate flatlet. At the same time she has inherited everything: she marches about this house like the Race itself. They rally as if she were the Young Pretender. Oh, I know Matchett's conspiratorial mouth. And it's too monstrous of Eddie; really it's so silly. As far as all *that's* concerned – well, Heaven help her: I don't see why I should.

Well, she'll never find any answer here, thought Anna, lying with her feet up on the sofa, unrestfully clasping her hands behind her head, asking herself what that brother and sister found to say to each other down there. It's no use her looking everywhere like that. Who are we to have her questions brought here?

Pulling the telephone towards her, Anna dialled St Quentin's number. She heard the bell ringing for some time – quite clearly St Quentin was out.

On Monday morning, Thomas went back to the office, Portia went back to her classes in Cavendish Square. Mild grey spring rain set in and shivered on the trees. Thomas, who liked to be right about small things, liked having foretold this change in the weather. The first week the tulips were out, no sun shone on them; they stood in their mauves, corals, and crimsons, fleshily damp, with no one by to see. No, this May afternoon was not

like that May afternoon when old Mr Quayne had crept about in
the park. Portia did not see Eddie till the end of that week, when
she came in on Saturday afternoon to find him at tea with Anna.
He seemed very much pleased, greatly surprised to see her,
jumped up, smiled all over, took her hand, and exclaimed to
Anna: 'Doesn't she look well, still!' He made her sit down
where he had been sitting, while he sat on the arm of the chair.
Meanwhile, Anna, with just the hint of a flicker, rang for another cup. Portia was in the wrong: she was not expected; she
had said she would have tea with Lilian that afternoon. 'Do you
know,' went on Eddie, 'it must be months since we have all
three met?'

St Quentin, the previous Wednesday, had been more en-
thusiastic. Portia had met him walking briskly, aimlessly along
Wigmore Street – black Homburg hat cocked forward, gloves
tightly clasped in both hands behind his back. Half stopping
now and then, and turning his whole body, he gave the luxury
objects in dark polished windows glances of a distracted intensity. His behaviour was, somehow, not plausible: Portia felt uncertain, as she approached him, whether St Quentin really did not
see her, or did see her and wished to show that he did not. She
hesitated – ought she to cross the street? – but then made on
down the pavement, swinging her dispatch case, like a too light
little boat before a too strong wind: she could find no reason to
stop. Something about her reflection in a window caught St
Quentin's eye, and he turned round.

'Oh, hullo,' he said rapidly, 'hullo! So you're back, too: how
nice! What are *you* doing?'

'Going home from lessons.'

'How lucky you are – I am not doing anything. That's to say,
I am putting in time. Do you go down Mandeville Place? Shall
we walk down Mandeville Place?'

So they turned the corner together. Portia shifted her dispatch
case from one hand to the other and said: 'How is your new
book?'

Instead of replying, St Quentin looked up at the windows.
'We'd better not talk too loud: this is full of nursing homes.

You know how the sick listen . . . Have you had a nice time?' he continued, pitching his voice low.

'Yes, very,' she said almost down to a whisper. She had an inner view of white high beds, fever charts, waxy flowers.

'I'm afraid I can't remember where you were.'

'At Seale. The seaside.'

'Delightful. How you must miss it. I wish I could go away. In fact I think I shall; there is no reason why I shouldn't, but I'm in such a neurotic state. Do tell me about something. How is your diary?'

He saw Portia's face flash his way; she at once threw him a look like a trapped, horrified bird's. They pulled up to let someone, stepping out of a taxi, cross the pavement and carry a sheaf of flowers up the stark steps of a nursing home. When they walked on again, St Quentin was once more up to anything, while Portia looked ahead steadily, stonily, down the overcast canyon of the street that was threatening in this sudden gloom of spring. He said: 'That was just a shot in the dark. I feel certain you should keep a diary. I'm sure you have thoughts about life.'

'No, I don't think much,' she said.

'My dear girl, that is hardly necessary. What I'm certain you do have are reactions. And I wonder what those are, whenever I look at you.'

'I don't know what they are. I mean, what are reactions?'

'Well, I could explain, but must I? You do have feelings, of course?'

'Yes. Don't you?'

St Quentin bit at his upper lip moodily, making his moustache dip. 'No, not often; I mean, not really. They're not so much fun for me. Now what can have made me think you kept a diary? Now that I come to look at you, I don't think you'd be so rash.'

'If I kept one, it would be a dead secret. Why should that be rash?'

'It is madness to write things down.'

'But you write those books you write almost all day don't you?'

'But what's in them never happened – It might have, but never did. And though what is felt in them is just possible – in fact, it's much more possible, in an unnerving way, than most people will admit – it's fairly improbable. So, you see, it's my game from the start. But I should never write what had happened down. One's nature is to forget, and one ought to go by that. Memory is quite unbearable enough, but even so it leaves out quite a lot. It wouldn't let one down as gently, even, as that if it weren't more than half a fake – we remember to suit ourselves. No, really, er, Portia, believe me: if one didn't let oneself swallow some few lies, I don't know how one would ever carry the past. Thank God, except at its one moment there's never any such thing as a bare fact. Ten minutes later, half an hour later, one's begun to gloze the fact over with a deposit of some sort. The hours I spent with thee dear love are like a string of pearls to me. But a diary (if one did keep it up to date) would come much too near the mark. One ought to secrete for some time before one begins to look back at anything. Look how reconciled to everything reminiscences are ... Also, suppose somebody read it?'

This made Portia miss one step, shift her grip on her case. She glanced at St Quentin's rather sharklike profile, glanced away, and stayed silent – so tensely silent that he peered round for another look at her.

'I should lock it up,' he said. 'I should trust no one an inch.'

'But I lost the key.'

'Oh, you did? Look here, do let's get this straight: weren't we talking about a hypothetical diary?'

'Mine's just a diary,' she said helplessly.

St Quentin coughed, with just a touch of remorse. 'I'm so sorry,' he said. 'I've been too smart again. But that does me no good, in the long run.'

'I'd rather not have it known. It is simply a thing of mine.'

'No, that's where you're wrong. Nothing like that stops with oneself. You do a most dangerous thing. All the time, you go making connexions – and that can be a vice.'

'I don't know what you mean.'

249

'You're working on us, making us into something. Which is not fair – we are not on our guard with you. For instance, now I know you keep this book, I shall always feel involved in some sort of plan. You precipitate things. I daresay', said St Quentin kindly, 'that what you write is quite silly, but all the same, you are taking a liberty. You set traps for us. You ruin our free will.'

'I write what has happened. I don't invent.'

'You put constructions on things. You are a most dangerous girl.'

'No one knows what I do.'

'Oh, but believe me, we feel it. You must see how rattled we are now.'

'I don't know what you *were* like.'

'Neither did we : we got on quite well then. What is unfair is, that you hide. God's spy, and so on. Another offence is, you have a loving nature; you are the loving nature *in vacuo*. You must not mind my saying all this. After all, you and I don't live in the same house; we seldom meet and you seldom affect me. All the same –'

'Are you teasing me now, or were you teasing me before? You must have been teasing one or the other time. First you said you felt sure I kept a diary, then you told me I mustn't, then you asked where it was, then you pretended to be surprised when you knew there was one, after that you called me an un-kind spy, now you say I love everyone too much. I see now you knew about my diary . . . *I suppose Anna found it and told you?* Did she?'

St Quentin glanced at Portia from the tail of his eye. 'I don't come out of this well,' he said.

'But did she?'

'I am perfectly able to tell a lie, but my trouble is that I have no loyalty. Yes, Anna did, as a matter of fact. Now what a fuss this will make. Now, can I trust your discretion? You see that nobody can rely on mine.'

Pushing her hat brim further back from her forehead, Portia turned and sized St Quentin up boldly. She believed he had a malignant conscience; she did not feel he was really indiscreet. 'You mean,' she said, 'not tell Anna you told me?'

'I would as soon you didn't,' said St Quentin humbly. 'Avoid scenes; in future keep an eye on your little desk.'

'She told you I had a little desk?'

'I supposed you would have one.'

'Has she often –?'

St Quentin rolled his eyes up. 'Not so far as I know. Don't be at all worried. Just find some new place to keep your book. What I have always found is, anything one keeps hidden should now and then be hidden somewhere else.'

'Thank you,' said Portia, dazed. 'It is very kind of you.' She was incapable of anything past this: her feet kept walking her on inexorably. The conversation had ended in an abyss – impossible to pretend that it had not. Like all shocked people, she did not see where she was – they were well down Marylebone High Street, among the shoppers – from the depth of her eyes she threw wary, unhuman looks at faces that swam towards her, faces looking her way. She was aware of St Quentin's presence only as the cause of her wish to run down a side street. They had been walking fast, in this dreadful dream, for some time, when he cried loudly: 'These *lacunae* in people!'

'What did you say?'

'You don't *ask* what made me do that – you don't even ask yourself.'

She said, 'You were very kind.'

'The most unlikely things one does, the most utterly out of character, arouse no curiosity, even in one's friends. One can suffer a convulsion of one's entire nature, and, unless it makes some noise, no one notices. It's not just that we are incurious; we completely lack any sense of each other's existences. Even you, with that loving nature you have – In a small way I have just ratted on Anna, I have done something she'd never forgive me for, and you, Portia, you don't even ask why. Consciously, and as far as I can see quite gratuitously, I have started what may make a frightful breach. In me, this is utterly out of character: I'm not a mischievous man; I haven't got time; I'm not interested enough. You're not even listening, are you?'

'I'm sorry, I –'

'I've no doubt you're upset. So you and I might be at different

ends of the world. Stop thinking about your diary and your Anna and listen to me – and don't flinch at me, Portia, as though I were an electric drill. You ought to want some key to why people do what they do. You think us all wicked –'

'I don't, I –'

'It's not so simple as that. What makes you think us wicked is simply our little way of keeping ourselves going. We must live, though you may not see the necessity. In the long run, we may not work out well. We attempt, however, to be more civil and kindly than we feel. The fact is, we have no great wish for each other – no spontaneous wish for each other, that is to say. This lack of *gout* makes us have to behave with a certain amount of policy. Because I quite like Anna, I overlook much in her, and because she quite likes me she overlooks much in me. We laugh at each other's jokes and we save each other's faces – When I give her away to you, I break an accepted rule. This is not often done. It takes people in a lasting state of hysteria, like your friend Eddie, for instance, or people who feel they have some higher authority (as I've no doubt Eddie feels he has) to break every rule every time. To keep any rule would be an event for him: when he breaks one more rule it is hardly interesting – at least, not to me. I simply cannot account for his fascination for Anna –'

'Does he fascinate Anna?'

'Oh, palpably, don't you think? I suppose the deduction is that she really must have a conventional mind. And, of course he has some pretty ways – No, with me there has to be quite a brainstorm before I break any rule, before speaking the truth. Love, drink, anger – something crumbles the whole scene: at once one is in a fantastic universe. Its unseemliness and its glory are indescribable, really. One becomes a Colossus ... I still don't know, all the same, what made that happen just now. It must be this close spring weather. It's religious weather, I think.'

'You think she's told Eddie about my diary, then?'

'My dear, don't ask me what they talk about – Why turn down here?'

'I always go through this graveyard.'

'The futility of explaining – this is telling you nothing. Some

252

day, you may hear from somebody else that I was an important man, then you'll rack your brains to remember what I once said. Where shall you live next?'

'I don't know. With my aunt.'

'Oh, you won't hear of me *there*.'

'I think I am to go and be with my aunt, when I'm not with Thomas and Anna any more.'

'Well, with your aunt you may have time to be sorry. No, I am being unfair to you. I should never talk like this if you weren't such a little stone.'

'It is what you've told me.'

'Naturally, naturally. Do you like to walk through the grave-yard? And why has it got a bandstand in the middle? As you're quite near home, do something about your face.'

'I don't have any powder.'

'I'm not really sorry that this has happened: it was bound to happen sooner or later – No, I don't mean powder: I just mean your expression. One thing one must learn is, how to confront people that at that particular moment one cannot bear to meet.'

'Anna's out to tea.'

'If we had not said all this, I'd get you to have tea with me in a shop. But anyhow, I'm due somewhere at a quarter to five. I think I ought to go back now. I suppose you're sorry we met?'

'I suppose it's better to know.'

'No, truly it is not. In fact I've done something to you I could not bear to have done to myself. And the terrible thing is, I am feeling the better for it. Well, good-bye,' said St Quentin, stopping on the asphalt path in the graveyard, among the tombs and the willows, taking off his hat.

'Good-bye, Mr Miller. Thank you.'

'Oh, I shouldn't say that.'

That had been on Wednesday. This Saturday, Portia soon moved out of Eddie's chair, which he slipped gladly back to, to take her accustomed place on the stool near the fire. A pallid flare and a rustling rose from the logs; the windows framed panoramas of wet trees; the room looked high and faint in rainy afternoon light. Between Portia and Anna extended the still life

of the tea-tray. On her knees, pressed together, Portia kept balanced the plate on which a rock-cake slid. Beginning to nibble at the rock-cake, she sat watching Anna at tea with Eddie, as she had watched her at tea with other intimate guests.

By coming in, however, she had brought whatever there was to a nonplussed pause. The fact that they let her see such a pause happen made her the accessory she hardly wanted to be. Eddie propped an elbow on the wing of his chair, leaned a temple on a palm, and looked into the fire. His eyes flickered up and down with the point of flickering flame. Desultorily, and for his private pleasure, he began to make mouths like a fish – curling his lower lip out, sucking it in again. Anna, using her thumb-nail, slit open a new box of cigarettes, then packed her tortoise-shell case with them. Portia finished her cake, approached the tray, and helped herself to another – taking his eyes from the fire for one moment, Eddie accorded her one irresponsible smile. 'When do we go for another walk?' he said.

Anna said: 'Are you ready for more tea?'

'A fortnight ago,' said Portia, for no reason, going back for her cup, 'I was having tea at Seale golf club with Dickie Heccomb and Clara – a girl there that he sometimes plays golf with.'

Anna ducked in her chin and smiled vaguely and nodded. Absently, she said, 'Was that fun?'

'Yes, the gorse was out.'

'Yes, Seale must have been fun.'

'There's a picture of you there, in my room.'

'A photograph?'

'No, a picture holding a kitten.'

Anna put her hand to her head. 'Kitten?' she said. 'What do you mean, Portia?'

'A black kitten.'

Anna thought back. 'Oh, that black kitten. Poor little thing, it died . . . You mean, when I was a child?'

'Yes, you had long hair.'

'A chalk drawing. Oh, is that in her spare room? But who is Clara? Tell me about her.'

Portia did not know how to begin – she glanced at Eddie. He came to himself and said with the greatest ease: 'Clara? Clara's

position was uncertain. She was hardly in the set. All the same, she haunts me – perhaps because of that. She spends ever so much money hoping to marry Dickie – Dickie Heccomb, you know. Besides money, she keeps inside her handbag a sort of mouse's nest that she dives into whenever things get too difficult. Doesn't she, Portia? We saw Clara do that.'

Anna said: 'I wish I could.'

'Oh, you would never need to, Anna darling ... Well, we made Clara pop into her handbag that night at the E.C.P. When we all behaved so badly. I was the worst, of course. It was really dreadful, Anna: Portia and I had been for a nice walk in some woods, then I ruined the day by getting tight and rowdy. I had made a fine impression when I first got to Waikiki, but I'm afraid that spoiled it.' Eddie gave Portia an equivocal sidelong look, then turned his head and went on talking to Anna. 'Clara's position was really trying, you see: she had eyes only for Dickie, and Dickie had eyes only for Portia here.'

She made a dumbfounded movement. 'Oh, Eddie, he *hadn't*!'

'Well, there were goings-on – they were perfectly one-sided, but there were goings-on as far as Dickie does go. I heard him breathing over you at the movies. He breathed so much that he even breathed over me.'

'Eddie,' Anna said, 'you really are very common.' She looked remotely, sternly down at her finger-nails, but after a minute could not help saying: 'Did you all go to the movies? When?'

'That first evening I got there,' Eddie said fluently. 'Six of us. All the set. I must say, I really was shocked by Dickie: not only is he an old Fascist, but he does not know how to behave at all. At the seaside, they really do go the pace.'

'How dreadful for you,' said Anna. 'And so, what did you do?'

'It was in the dark, so I could not show how I felt. Besides, his sister was holding my hand. They really are a fast lot – I do think, Anna, you ought to be more careful where you send Portia off to another time.'

This did not go down well. 'Portia knows how to behave,' said Anna frigidly. 'Which makes more difference than you would ever think.' She gave Portia what could have been a

kindly look had there been the least intention behind it. To Eddie she said, with enraged softness: 'For anybody as clever as you are, you are really not good at describing things. To begin with, I don't think you ever know what is happening: you are too busy wondering what you can make of it.'

Eddie pouted and said: 'Very well, ask Portia, then.'

But Portia looked down and said nothing.

'Anyhow,' Eddie said, 'it has been an effort to talk, when I don't feel in the mood to. But one has got to be so amusing here. I'm sorry you don't like what I say, but I have been more or less talking in my sleep.'

'If you are so sleepy, you had better go home.'

'I can't see why the idea of sleep should offend you as much as it seems to, Anna. It is the natural thing on a rainy spring afternoon, when one's not compelled to be doing anything else, especially in a nice quiet room like this. We ought all to sleep, instead of talking away.'

'Portia has not said much,' said Anna, looking across the fire.

At the very sound, on Eddie's lips, of the word, desire to sleep had spread open inside Portia like a fan. She saw reflections of rain on the silver things on the tray. She felt blotted out from the room, as little present in it as these two others truly felt her to be. She moved a little nearer the fireplace, so as to lean her cheek on the marble upright, with as little consciousness of her movement as though she had been alone in some other place. Behind shut eyes she relaxed; she refreshed herself. The rug under her feet slid and wrinkled a little on the polished floor; the room, with its image of cruelty, swam, shredded, and slowly lost its colour, like a paper pattern in water.

Since the talk with St Quentin, the idea of betrayal had been in her, upon her, sleeping and waking, as might be one's own guilt, making her not confront any face with candour, making her dread Eddie. Being able to shut her eyes while he was in this room with her, to feel impassive marble against her cheek, made her feel in the arms of immunity – the immunity of sleep, of anaesthesia, of endless solitude, the immunity of the journey across Switzerland two days after her mother died. She saw that tree she saw when the train stopped for no reason; she saw in

her nerves, equally near and distant, the wet trees out there in the park. She heard the Seale sea, then heard the silent distances of the coast.

There was a pause in the drawing-room. Then Anna said: 'I wish I could just do that; I wish I were sixteen.'

Eddie said: 'She looks sweet, doesn't she?' At some later time, he came softly across to touch Portia's cheek with his finger, to which Anna, though still there, did not say anything.

3

'REALLY, Anna, things *have* gone too far!' Eddie, out of the blue, burst out on the telephone. 'Portia has just rung me up to say you've been reading her diary. And I could say nothing – someone was in the office.'

'Are you on the office telephone now?'

'Yes, but it's lunch time.'

'Yes, I know it is lunch time. Major Brutt and two other people are here. You are ruthlessly inconsiderate.'

'How was I to know? I thought you might think this urgent. I do. Are they in the room?'

'Naturally.'

'Well, good-bye. *Bon appétit,*' added Eddie, in a loud bitter tone. He hung up just before Anna, who returned to the table. The three guests, having heard in her voice that note of lover-like crossness, tried not to look askance: they were all three rather naïve. Mr and Mrs Peppingham, from Shropshire, had this Monday been asked to lunch because they were known to have a neighbour in Shropshire who was known to be looking for an agent, and it seemed just possible Major Brutt might do. But during lunch it became clearer and clearer that he was only impressing the Peppinghams as being the sort of thoroughly decent fellow who never, for some reason, gets on in the world. Tough luck, but there you are. He was showing a sort of amiable cussedness; he ignored every hoop that Anna held out for him.

The Peppinghams clearly thought that though no doubt he had done well in the War, he had not, on the whole, been unlucky in having *had* the War to do well in. It became useless for Anna to draw him out, to repeat that he had grown rubber, that he had had – for he had had, hadn't he? – the management of a quite large estate. In Malay, of course, but the great thing was – wasn't it? – to know how to manage men.

'Yes, that is certainly so,' agreed Mr Peppingham, safely.

Mrs Peppingham said: 'With all these social changes, I sometimes fear that's a lost art – managing men, I mean. I always feel that people work twice as well if they feel they've got someone to look up to.' She flushed up the side of her neck with moral conviction and said firmly: 'I'm quite sure that is true.' Anna thought: These days, there's something dreadful about talk; people's convictions keep bobbing to the surface, making them flush. I'm sure it was better when people connected everything of that sort with religion, and did not talk about religion at meals. She said: 'I expect one thinks about that in the country more. That is the worst of London: one never thinks.'

'My dear lady,' said Mr Peppingham, 'thinking or not thinking, there are some things that you cannot fail to notice. Destroy tradition, and you destroy the sense of responsibility.'

'Surely, for instance, in your husband's office –' Mrs Peppingham said.

'I never go to the office. I don't think Thomas inspires hero worship, if that's what you mean. No, I don't think he'd know what to do with that.'

'Oh, I don't mean hero worship. I'm afraid that only leads to dictators, doesn't it? No, what I mean', said Mrs Peppingham, touching her pearls with a shy but firm smile and flushing slightly again, 'is *instinctive* respect. That means so much to the people working for us.'

'Do you think one really inspires that?'

'One tries to,' said Mrs Peppingham, not looking very pleased.

'It seems so sad to have to try to. I should so much rather just pay people, and leave it at that.'

Phyllis inhibited Mrs Peppingham from any further talk about class by firmly handing the orange *soufflé* round. PAS

AVANT LES DOMESTIQUES might have been carved on the Peppinghams' dining-room mantelpiece, under HONI SOIT QUI MAL Y PENSE. Mrs Peppingham helped herself and, with a glance at Phyllis's cuff, was silent. Anna, plunging the spoon and fork into the *soufflé* with that frank greed one shows in one's own house when there is enough of everything, said: 'Besides, I thought you said that it was instinctive. Whose instincts do you mean?'

'Respect's a broad human instinct,' said Mr Peppingham, letting one eye wander to meet the *soufflé*.

'Oh yes. But do you think it is still?'

The two Peppinghams' eyes, for less than a second, met. They share the same ideals, thought Anna. Do I and Thomas? Perhaps, but what ever are they? I do wish Major Brutt would say something or contradict me: the Peppinghams will start thinking *he* is a Red. What a misleading reputation my house has – the Peppinghams must have come here for Interesting Talk, because they feel they don't get enough of that in Shropshire. The yearnings of the County are appalling. They forget Major Brutt has come here to get a job; they probably are offended at meeting only him. If I had asked an author, which they must have expected, things could not be more hopeless than they are now, and it might have put the Peppinghams into a better mood – besides showing Major Brutt up as the practical man. I thought that my *beaux yeux* should be enough to send Major Brutt and the Peppinghams into each other's arms. But these Peppinghams are not nice enough to be flattered. No, they are full of designing hardness; all they think is that I'm making use of them. Which I would do if I could, but they are impossible. They despise Major Brutt for being nicer than they are and for not having made good in their line. If he would only flush and argue, instead of just sitting. Oh dear, oh dear, I shall never sell him at all.

'You disapprove of my ideas, don't you?' she threw out to Major Brutt with a frantic summoning smile.

But he only crumbled his bread and quietly ate the crumbs. 'Oh, I don't think I'd venture to. Not wholesale. I don't doubt for a moment there's a great deal in what you say.' Looking

kindly at her with his straight grey eyes, he added: 'One reason I should like to settle down is that then I might begin to think things out for myself. Not knowing exactly what may turn up is inclined to make one a bit unsettled, and often when I've intended to have a think – for after all, I've got a bit of time on my hands – I find I am not in form, so I don't get much thinking done. Meanwhile, it's a treat to listen to a discussion, though I don't feel qualified to shove my oar in.'

'My only quarrel with this charming lady', said Mr Peppingham (who was becoming odious), 'is that she will not tell us what her ideas *are*.'

Anna (now throwing up the sponge completely) replied: 'I could if I knew what we were talking *about*.'

Mr Peppingham, tolerant, turned to dig in the cheese. Anna wanted to reach along the table, grip Major Brutt's hand and say: No good. I've drawn you another blank. I've failed to sell you and, to be perfectly honest, you really don't do much to sell yourself. No good, no good, no good – we can't do any more here. Back with you to *The Times* advertisement columns, and the off-chance of running into a man who has just run into a man who could put you on to a thing. You ran into us. Well, that hasn't got you far. Better luck next time, old boy. *Je n'en peux plus.*

In fact, he constituted – today, by so mildly accepting, with his coffee, that there would be nothing more doing about this Shropshire thing, and at all times by the trustfulness of his frequentation of the Quaynes as a family – the same standing, or, better still, undermining reproach as Portia. He was not near enough their hearth, or long enough at it, to take back to Kensington with him any suspicion that the warmth he had found could be illusory. His unfulfilled wishes continued to flock and settle where the Quaynes were, and no doubt he thought of them in the lounge of his hotel, or walking along the Cromwell Road. No doubt he stayed himself on the idea of them when one more thing fell through, when something else came to nothing, when one more of his hopeful letters was unanswered, when yet another iron went stone cold, when he faced that the money was running out. He gave signs that he constantly thought of

them. Does it make one more nearly good and happy to be thought good and happy? The policy of pity might keep Anna from ever pointblank disappointing him. He was the appendix to the finished story of Robert. Useless, useless to wish they had never met – they had been bound to, apparently. In a sort of sense, Major Brutt had been legated to her by Robert. Or, was it that she felt she found in him the last of Robert's hurting, hurting because never completely bitter, jokes – one of those hurting exposures of her limitations, to obtain which he seemed able to hire fate?

Major Brutt outstayed the Peppinghams – thus giving her no chance to sing his merits in private, to say that whoever got him would be lucky, or to repeat that he was a D.S.O. Ready to say good-bye after a few minutes, he stood up and looked round the drawing-room.

'Those were lovely carnations you sent me the other day. I got Portia to send you a line because I was tired, and because I hoped I should see you soon. You know how one feels when one gets back. But that makes it all the nicer to find flowers.'

He beamed. 'Oh, good,' he said. 'If they cheered you up –'

Some obscure wish to bestir herself, to be human, made her say:

'You did not, I suppose, hear any more of Pidgeon since we've been away?'

'Now it's funny your asking that –

'Funny?' said Anna.

'Not that I heard *from* him – that's the devil, you know, about not having a fixed address. People soon give up buzzing letters along. Of course, I've got an address, at this hotel, but when I write from there it never looks permanent. People take it you'll have moved on – at least, so I find. But if I'd had an address I might not have heard from Pidgeon. He never was one to write.'

'No, he never was – But what were you going to say?'

'Oh yes. Now that really was very funny. It's the sort of thing that's always happening to me. About a fortnight ago, I missed Pidgeon by about three minutes – literally, by just about that. A most extraordinary thing – I mean, only missing him by about an inch when I didn't know he was in the country at all.'

'Tell me about it.'

'Well, I happened to go into a fellow's club – with the fellow, I mean – and run into another fellow (I hadn't seen him for years, either) who'd been talking to Pidgeon about three minutes ago. Talking to Pidgeon in that very club. "By Jove," I said, "that's funny. Is he in the club still?" But the other fellow said not. He said he'd gone. I said, which way did he go? – having some idea that I might make after him – but the other fellow of course had no idea. It seemed to me an amazing coincidence and I made up my mind I must tell you about it. If I had got there three minutes earlier ... It's simply chance, after all. You can't foresee anything. Look, for instance, how I ran into you. In a book, that would sound quite improbable.'

'Well, it was improbable, really. *I* never run into people.'

Major Brutt drove his hands down slowly into his pockets, considering something rather uncertainly. He said: 'And of course, that week you were abroad.'

'Which week?'

'The week I just missed Pidgeon.'

'Oh yes, I was abroad. You – you heard no more? He's not in London still?'

'That I can't tell; I wish I could. It's the very devil. He might be anywhere. But this other fellow seemed to get the idea that Pidgeon was just off somewhere – "on the wing", as we always used to say. He's generally just off somewhere. He never liked London much.'

'No, he never liked London much.'

'And yet, do you know, though I cursed missing him, it seemed better than nothing. When he's once turned up, he may turn up again.'

'Yes, I do hope he'll turn up – But not where I ever am.'

Fatalistically, she faced having got this out at last. She looked at herself in the glass with enormous calm. Major Brutt, meanwhile, turning his shoulder against the mantelpiece, investigated a boat-shaped glass of roses, whose scent had disturbed him for some time. Reverently, with the tip of a finger, he jabbed at the softness of the crimson petals, then bent over to sniff exhaustively. This rather stagy, for him rather conscious, action showed

he knew he stood where she might not wish him to stand – outside a shut door, a forgotten messenger for whom there might be an answer and might not. Perplexity, reverence, readiness to be sad or reliable showed in every line of his attitude. He would be glad to move, if she gave him the word. It was not his habit to take notice of flowers, or of any small object in a room, and by giving the roses such undue attention, he placed himself in an uneasy relation to them. He jabbed once more and said: 'Do these come from the country?'

'Yes. And your nice carnations have just died.'

Or was it likely he could be missing a cue, that Anna might have created this special moment in which it was his business to ask bluntly: Look here, just what *did* happen? Where's the whole thing gone to? Why are you not Mrs Pidgeon? You are still you, and he still sounds like himself. You both being you was once all right with you both. You are still you – what has gone wrong since?

He looked at her – and the delicate situation made his eye as nearly shifty as it could ever be. He looked, and found her not looking at him. Instead, she took a handkerchief from her bag and blew the tip of her nose in a rapid, businesslike way. If she ever did seem to deliberate, it was while she put away the handkerchief. She said: 'I should not be such a monster if Pidgeon had not put the idea into my head.'

'My dear girl –'

'Yes, I must be; everyone thinks I am. That horrid little Eddie rang me up at lunch to tell me I was unkind to Portia.'

'Good heavens?'

'You don't really like Eddie, do you?'

'Well, he's not much my sort. But look here, I mean to say –'

'Robert thought nothing of me,' said Anna laughing. 'Did you not know that? He thought nothing of me at all. Nothing really happened; I did not break his heart. Under the circumstances – you see now what they were, don't you? – we could hardly marry, as you must surely see.'

He mumbled: 'I expect it all turned out for the best.'

'Of course,' said Anna, smiling again.

He said quickly: 'Of course,' looking round the handsome room.

'But how I do skip from one thing to another,' she went on, with the greatest ease in the world. 'The past is never really the thing that matters – I just thought I'd clear that up about Robert and me. No, if I do seem a little rattled today, it is from being rung up in the middle of lunch and told by a stray young man that Portia is not happy. What am I to do? You know how quiet she is; things must have gone really rather a long way for her to complain to an outside person like that. Though, of course, Eddie is very inquisitive.'

'If I may be allowed to say so,' said Major Brutt, 'it sounds to me the most unheard of, infernal cheek on his part. And that is to put it mildly. I must say I really never –'

'He always is cheeky, the little bastard,' she said, reflectively tapping the mantelpiece. 'But it is Portia that I'm worried about. It all sounds so unlike her. Major Brutt, you know us fairly well as a family: do you think Portia's happy?'

'Allowing, poor kid, for having just lost her mother, it never struck me she could be anything else. She seemed to fit in as though she'd been born here. As girls go, she has quite the ideal life.'

'Or is that the nice way you see things? We do give her more freedom than most girls of sixteen, but she seemed old enough for it: she took care of her mother. But I see now that a girl has to be older before she can choose her friends – especially young men.'

'You mean, there's been a bit too much of *that* little chap?'

'It looks rather like that now. Of course, I blame myself rather. He has always been a good deal at this house – he's lonely, and we've tried to be nice to him. Except for that, I do think during the winter Portia got on very happily here. She seemed to be settling down. Then, as you know, she went away to the seaside, and I'm afraid some trouble may have begun there. My old governess is an angel, but I'm afraid her step-children are not up to much, and they may have upset Portia. She has not been quite the same since she came home. Even our old housemaid notices it. She isn't nearly so shy, but at the same time she is less

spontaneous. No, I suppose we were wrong in ever making that break – in going away, I mean – while she was settling down with us. That came too soon; it unsettled her; it *was* silly. But Thomas really needed a holiday; he's had a fairly hard winter in the office.'

'She's such a dear girl. She *is* a sweet little kid.'

'If you were me, then, you'd just tell Eddie to go to the devil?'

'Well, more or less – Yes, I certainly would.'

'And just have a word with Portia?'

'I'm sure *you* could manage that.'

'Do you know, Major Brutt, I'm most stupidly shy?'

'I feel certain', he said with vigour, 'she'd be most upset if she thought she's upset you. I'd be ready to swear she hasn't the least idea.'

'She hasn't any idea how Eddie talks,' Anna said with a sharpness she simply couldn't control. 'Major Brutt, this has been a wretched afternoon for you: first those dreadful people at lunch, and now my family worries. But it cheers me up to feel you feel Portia's happy. You must come back soon and we'll have a much nicer time. You will come again soon?'

'There's nothing I'd like better. Of course, as you know, my plans are rather unsettled still. I shall have to take up whatever may come along, and the Lord only knows where that might involve being sent.'

'Not right away, I do hope. I am so glad, at any rate, that you're not going to Shropshire. Thomas and I were mad to consider that idea; I see now that it would not have done at all. Well, thank you for listening: you have been an angel. It's fatal', she concluded, holding her hand out, 'to be such a good friend to a selfish woman like me.' With her hand in his, being wrung, she went on smiling, then not only smiled but laughed, looking out of the window as though she saw something funny in the park.

Upon which he took his leave. She, not giving herself a moment, sat down to dash off that little letter to Eddie.

Dear Eddie: Of course I could not say so at lunch but I should, if I were you, be rather more careful about using the office tele-

phone. It must be hard to know when is the once too often, but I'm afraid the once too often may have been passed. The fact is, I hear that Thomas and Mr Merrett are going to have a drive about all these personal calls that get put through and taken. The girl at the switchboard must have ratted, or something. You must not think this unkind of Thomas and Mr Merrett; they seem to feel it is a matter of principle. Even though you are getting on so well at the office, I should be a little careful, just for a week or two. I feel it is more considerate to tell you: you know I do want you to get on well.

However much your friends may have to say to you, I should ask them to wait till you get back to your room. And if I were you I should ring them up from there. I'm afraid this may send up your telephone bill, but that seems a thing that simply cannot be helped.   Yours,

                                                        ANNA

When Anna had written this, she glanced at the clock. If she were to send this to post now, it could only reach Eddie to-morrow morning. But if it went round by special messenger, he would find it when he came in, late. That is the hour when letters make most impression. So Anna rang up for a special messenger.

At half past four, that same Monday afternoon, Lilian and Portia came up Miss Paullie's area steps into Cavendish Square. Lilian had taken some time washing her wrists, for her new bangles, though showy, left marks on them. So these two were the last of a long straggle of girls. After the silence of the class-room, the square seemed to be drumming with hot sound; the high irregular buildings with their polished windows stood glaring in afternoon light. The trees in the middle tossed in a draught that went creeping round the square, turning the pale undersides of their leaves up. Coming out from lessons, the girls stepped into an impermeable stone world that the melting season could not penetrate – though seeing the branches in metallic sunlight they felt some forgotten spring had once left its mark there.

Lilian cast a look at those voluptuous plaits that hung over her

shoulders, down her bosom. Then she said: 'Where are you going now?'

'I told you: I am meeting someone at six.'

'That's what I mean – six is not now, you silly. I mean, are you going home for tea, or what?'

Very nervous, Portia said: 'I'm not going home.'

'Then look, we might have tea in a shop. I think some tea might be good for your nerves.'

'You really are being very kind, Lilian.'

'Of course, I can see you are upset. I know myself what that is, only too well.'

'But I've only got sixpence.'

'Oh, I've got three shillings. After what I've been through myself,' said Lilian, guiding Portia down the side of the square, 'I don't think you ever ought to be shy of me. And you can keep my handkerchief till this evening, in case you need it again when you meet whoever it is, but please let me have it back tomorrow; don't let them wash it, because it is one with associations.'

'You are being kind.'

'I go right off my food when I am upset; if I try to eat I simply vomit at once. I thought at lunch, you're lucky not to be like that, because of course it attracts attention. It was a pity you had attracted attention by being caught using Miss Paullie's telephone. I must say, I should never dare do that. She was perfectly beastly, I suppose?'

'She was scornful of me,' said Portia: her lip trembled again. 'She has always thought I was awful since last term, when she found me reading that letter I once got. She makes me feel it's the way I was brought up.'

'She is just at the age when women go queer, you know. *Where* did you say you had got to meet your friend?'

'Near the Strand.'

'Oh, quite near your brother's office?' said Lilian, giving Portia a look from her large near-in gelatinous dark grey eyes. 'I do think, Portia, you ought to be careful: an untrustworthy man can simply ruin one's life.'

'If there wasn't *something* one could trust a person about, surely one wouldn't start to like them at all?'

'I don't see the point of our being such bosom friends if you don't confess to me that this is really Eddie.'

'Yes, but I'm not upset because of him; I'm upset about something that's gone on.'

'Something at home?'

'Yes.'

'Do you mean your sister-in-law? I always did think she was a dangerous woman, though I did not like to tell you so at the time. Look, don't tell me about this in Regent Street, because people are looking at us already. We will go to that A.B.C. opposite the Polytechnic; we are less likely to be recognized there. I think it's safer than Fuller's. Try and be calm, Portia.'

Actually, it was Lilian who commanded attention by looking sternly into every face. Beside her goddess-like friend, Portia walked with her head down, butting against the draughty air of the street. When they came to the crossing, Lilian gripped Portia's bare arm in a gloved hand: through the kid glove a sedative animal feeling went up to Portia's elbow and made the joint untense. She pulled back to notice a wedding carpet up the steps of All Souls', Langham Place – like a girl who has finished the convulsions of drowning she floated, dead, to the sunny surface again. She bobbed in Lilian's wake between the buses with the gaseous lightness of a little corpse.

'Though you are able to eat,' said Lilian, propping her elbows on the marble-topped table and pulling off her gloves by the finger-tips (Lilian never uncovered any part of her person without a degree of consciousness: there was a little drama when she untied a scarf or took off her hat), 'though you are able to eat, I should not try anything rich.' She caught a waitress's eye and ordered what she thought right. 'Look what a far-off table I got,' she said. 'You need not be afraid of saying anything now. I say, why don't you take off your hat, instead of keeping on pushing it back?'

'Oh Lilian, I haven't really got much to tell you, you know.'

'Don't be so humble, my dear; you told me there was a plot.'

'All I meant was, they have been laughing at me.'

'What made them laugh?'

'They have been telling each other.'

'Do you mean Eddie, too?'

Portia only gave Lilian an on-the-run look. Obedient slowly, she took off the ingenuous little hat that Anna thought suitable for her years, and put the hat placatingly down between them. 'The other day,' she said, 'that day we couldn't walk home together, I ran into Mr St Quentin Miller – I don't think I told you? – and he very nearly gave me tea in a shop.'

Lilian poured out, reproachful. 'It does no good', she said, 'to keep on going off like that. You are only pleased you nearly had tea with St Quentin because he is an author. But you don't love him, do you?'

'Eddie *has* been an author, if it comes to that.'

'I don't suppose St Quentin's half so mean as Eddie, laughing at you with your sister-in-law.'

'*Oh*, I didn't say that! I never did!'

'Then what's the reason you're so mad with her? You said you didn't want to go home.'

'She's read my diary.'

'But good gracious, Portia. I *never* knew you ever –'

'You see, I never did tell a soul.'

'You are a dark horse, I must say. But then, how did *she* know?'

'I never did tell a soul.'

'You swear you never did?'

'Well, I never did tell a single soul but Eddie. . . .'

Lilian shrugged her shoulders, raised her eyebrows, and poured more hot water into the teapot with an expression Portia dared not read.

'We-ell,' she said, 'well, good gracious, what *more* do you want? There you are – that's just what I mean, you see! Of course I call that a plot.'

'I didn't mean him. I don't mean a plot like that.'

'Look, eat some of that plain cake; you ought to eat if you can. Besides, I'm afraid people will look at us. You know, I don't think you're fit to go all the way down the Strand. If you didn't eat any cake, we could afford a taxi. I shall go with you, Portia: I don't mind, really. I think he ought to see you have got a friend.'

'Oh, he *is* a friend. He is my friend all the time.'

'And I shall wait, too,' Lilian went on, 'in case you should be too much upset.'

'You are being so kind – but I'd rather go alone.'

There is no doubt that sorrow brings one down in the world. The aristocratic privilege of silence belongs, you soon find out, to only the happy state – or, at least, to the state when pain keeps within bounds. With its accession to full power, feeling becomes subversive and violent: the proud part of the nature is battered down. Then, those people who flock to the scenes of accidents, who love most of all to dwell on deaths or childbirths or on the sick-bed from which restraint has gone smell what is in the air and are on the spot at once, pressing close with a sort of charnel good will. You may first learn you are doomed by seeing those vultures in the sky. Yet perhaps they are not vultures; they are Elijah's ravens. They bring with them the sense that the most individual sorrow has a stupefying universality. In them, human nature makes felt its clumsy wisdom, its efficacy, its infallible ready reckoning, its low level from which there is no further drop. Accidents become human property: only a muffish dread of living, a dread of the universal in our natures, makes us make these claims for 'the privacy of grief'. In naïver, humbler, nobler societies, the sufferer becomes public property; the scene of any disaster soon loses its isolated flush. The proper comment on grief, the comment that returns it to poetry, comes not in the right word, the faultless perceptive silence, but from the chorus of vulgar unsought friends – friends who are strangers to the taste and the mind.

In fact, there is no consoler, no confidant that half the instinct does not want to reject. The spilling over, the burst of tears and words, the ejaculation of the private personal grief accomplishes itself, like a convulsion, in circumstances that one would never choose. Confidants *in extremis* – with their genius for being present, their power to bring the clearing convulsions on – are, exceedingly often if not always, idle, morbid, trivial, or adolescent people, or people who feel a vacuum they are eager to fill. Not to these would one show, in happier moments, some secret spring of one's nature, the pride of love, the ambition, the sus-

taining hope: one could share with them no delicate pleasure
in living: they are people who make discussion impossible.
Their brutalities, their intrusions, and ineptitudes are, at the
same time, possible when one could not endure the tender touch.
The finer the nature, and the higher the level at which it seeks
to live, the lower, in grief, it not only sinks but dives: it goes
to weep with beggars and mountebanks, for these make the
shame of being unhappy less.

So that, that unendurable Monday afternoon (two days after
Portia had seen Eddie with Anna, nearly a week after St
Quentin's revelation – long enough for the sense of two allied
betrayals to push up to full growth, like a double tree) nobody
could have come in better than Lilian. The telephone crisis, before lunch at Miss Paullie's, had been the moment for Lilian to
weigh in. To be discovered by Lilian weeping in the cloakroom
had at once brought Portia inside that subtropical zone of feeling: nobody can be kinder than the narcissist while you react
to life in his own terms. To be consoled, to be understood by
Lilian was like extending to weep in a ferny grot, whose muggy
air and clammy frond-touches relax, demoralize, and pervade
you. The size of everything alters: when you look up with wet
eyes trees look no more threatened than the ferns. Factitious
feeling and true feeling come to about the same thing, when it
comes to pain. Lilian's arabesques of the heart, the unkindness
of the actor, made her eye Portia with doomful benevolence –
and though she at this moment withdrew the cake plate, she
started to count her money and reckon up the cost of the taxi
fare.

'Well, as you feel,' she said. 'If you're crazy to go alone. But
don't let the taxi stop where you're really *going*. You know, you
might be blackmailed, you never know.'

'I am only going to Covent Garden.'

'My dear – why ever not tell me that before?'

4

EDDIE did not think Covent Garden a good place to meet, but he had had no time to think of anywhere else – his telephone talk with Portia had been cut off at her end while he was still saying they might surely do better. He had to be thankful that there had, at least, been time to put the lid on her first idea: she had proposed to meet him in the entrance foyer of Quayne and Merrett's. And this – for she was such a good, discreet little girl, trained to awe of Thomas's office – had been enough to show her desperate sense of emergency. She would arrive distraught. No, this would never have done.

Particularly, it would not have done this week. For Eddie's relations with the firm of Quayne and Merrett were (apart from the telephone trouble, of which, still unconscious, he was to hear from Anna) at the present moment, uncertain enough. He had annoyed many people by flitting about the office as though he were some denizen of a brighter clime. There had been those long weekends. More, the absence of Thomas, the apparent susceptibility of Merrett to one's personal charm had beguiled Eddie into excesses of savage skittishness: he had bounced his weight about; he had been more nonchalant in the production of copy, at once more coy and insolent in his manners than (as it had been borne in on him lately) was acceptable here. He had lately got three chits of a damping nature, with Merrett's initials, and the threat of an interview that did not promise to take the usual course. There had been an unseemly scene in a near-by bar, with a more than low young man recruited by Mr Merrett, when Eddie had been warned, with a certain amount of gusto, that one could not go to all lengths as Mrs Quayne's fancy boy. This had been a time when a young man in the tradition should have knocked the speaker's teeth down his throat: Eddie's attempt to look at once disarming, touchy, tickled, and not taken aback had just not come off, and his automatic giggle had done nothing to clear the air. Mr Quayne's kid sister sitting in the foyer would, without doubt, have been the finish of him.

Covent Garden just after six o'clock, with its shuttered arcades, was not gay. Across the façades, like a theatre set shabby in daylight, and across the barren glaring spaces, films of shade were steadily coldly drawn, as though there were some nervous tide in the sky. Here and there, bits of paper did not blow about but sluggishly twitched. The place gave out a look of hollow desuetude, as though its desertion would last for ever. London is full of such deserts, of such moments, at which the mirage of one's own keyed-up existence suddenly fails. Covent Garden acted as a dissolvent on Eddie: he walked round like a cat.

Then he saw Portia, waiting at the one corner he did not think they had said. Her patient grip on her small case, her head turning, the thin, chilly stretch of her arms between short sleeves and short gloves struck straight where his heart should be – but the shaft bent inside him: to see her only made him breezily cross.

'Well, you have come a way,' he said. 'I do feel so flattered, darling.'

'I came in a taxi.'

'Did you? Listen, whatever happened? You seemed to have some sort of fit on the line, just when I was thinking about some much better place to meet.'

'I don't mind here; it's all right!'

'But you did rattle me, ringing off like that.'

'I was using the telephone in Miss Paullie's study, and she came in and caught me. We're not allowed to telephone from that place; we may only ask to send messages.'

'So then you got hell, I suppose. Who would be young!'

'I'm not so young as all that.'

'Well, *in statu pupillari*. Where now?'

'Can't we simply walk about?'

'Oh, all right, if you like. But that isn't much fun, is it?'

'How can this be fun?'

'No, it's not very promising,' said Eddie, starting to walk rather faster than she could. 'But now, look here, darling, I'm ever so sorry for you but really you must not work yourself up like this. I think it's *dingy* of Anna to read your diary, but I always told you not to leave it about. And what a good thing,

now, that I made you promise not to write about us. You didn't, of course?' he added, flicking a look at her.

She said, all in a gasp: 'I see now why you asked me not.'

A perceptible twitch passed over Eddie's features. 'What on earth are you getting at *now*?' he said.

'Please don't be angry, please don't be angry with me – Eddie, you told Anna about my diary?'

'Why in God's name should I?'

'For some sort of a joke. Some part of the joke that you always have with her.'

'Well, my poor dear excellent lamb, as a matter of interest – no, I didn't ... As a matter of fact ...'

She looked dumbly at him.

'As a matter of fact,' he went on, '*she* told *me*.'

'But I told you, Eddie.'

'Well, she had told me first. She's been at that book for some time. She really is an awful bounder, you know.'

'So when I told you, you knew.'

'Yes. I did. But really, darling, you make too much of things, like keeping this diary. It's ever so honest and it's beautifully clever, and it's sweet, just like you, but is it extraordinary? Diaries are things almost all girls keep.'

'Then, why did you pretend it meant something to you?'

'I loved to have you tell me about it. I am always so moved when you tell me things.'

'And all this time you've let me go on with it. I did write down *some* things about you, of course.'

'Oh God,' said Eddie, stopping. 'I did think I could trust you.'

'Why are you ashamed of having been nice to me?'

'After all, that's all between you and me. I can't have Anna messing about with it.'

'You don't mind, then, about all the rest of my life? As a matter of fact, there's not much rest of my life. But my diary's me. How could I leave you out?'

'All right, go on: make me hate myself ... By the way, how did you find this out?'

'St Quentin told me.'

'*There's* a crook if you like.'

'I don't see why. He was kind.'

'More likely, he was feeling bored with Anna. She goes on with the same joke far too long ... Now for God's sake, darling – you really *must not* cry here.'

'I only am because my feet do hurt.'

'Didn't I say they would? Round and round this hellish pavement. Look, shut up – you really *can't*, you know.'

'Lilian always thinks people are looking. Now you are just like Lilian.'

'I must get a taxi.'

On the crest of a sob, she said: 'I've only got sixpence. Have you got any money?'

Portia stood like a stone while Eddie went for a taxi, came back with one, gave the address of his flat. Once they were in the taxi, with Henrietta Street reeling jerking past, he miserably took her in his arms, pushing his face with cold and desperate persistence into the place where her hair fell away from her ear. 'Don't,' he said, 'please don't, darling: things are quite bad enough.'

'I can't, I can't, I can't.'

'Well, weep if it helps. Only don't reproach me so terribly.'

'You told her about our walk in the wood.'

'I was only talking, you know.'

'But that wood was where I kissed you.'

'I can't live up to those things. I'm not really fit to have things happen, darling. For you and me there ought to be a new world. Why should we be at the start of our two lives when everything round us is losing its virtue? How can we grow up when there's nothing left to inherit, when what we must feed on is so stale and corrupt? No, don't look up: just stay buried in me.'

'*You're* not buried; you're looking at things. Where are we?'

'Near Leicester Square Station. Just turning right.'

Turning round in his arms to look up jealously, Portia saw the cold daylight reflected in Eddie's dilated eyes. Fighting an arm free, she covered his eyes with one hand and said: 'But why can't we alter everything?'

'There are too few of us.'

'No, you don't really want to. You've always only been playing.'

'Do you think I have fun?'

'You have some sort of dreadful fun. You don't want me to interfere. You like despising more than you like loving. You pretend you're frightened of Anna: you're frightened of me.' Eddie pulled her hand from his eyes and held it away firmly, but she said: 'You're like this now, but you won't let me stay with you.'

'But how could you? You are so childish, darling.'

'You say that because I speak the truth. Something awful is always with you when I'm not. No, don't hold me; let me sit up. Where are we now?'

'I wanted to kiss you – Gower Street.'

Sitting up in her own corner of the taxi, Portia knocked her crushed hat into shape on her knee. Flattening the ribbon bow with her fingers, she moved her head away a little and said: 'No, don't kiss me now.'

'Why not now?'

'Because I don't want you to.'

'You mean', he said, 'that I didn't once when you did?'

She began to put on her hat with an immune little smile, as though all that had been too long ago. The tears shed in that series of small convulsions – felt by him but quite silent – had done no more than mat her lashes together. Eddie noted this while he examined her face intently, while he with one anxious finger straightened her hat. 'You're always crying now,' he said. 'It's really awful, you know ... We're just getting there. Listen, Portia, how much time have you? When do they expect you home?'

'That doesn't matter.'

'Darling, don't be sappy – if you're not back, someone will have a fit. Is there really any good in your coming into my place? Why don't I see you home, instead?'

'It's *not* "home"! Why can't I come in?' Knotting her hands in their prim, short gloves together she screwed her head away and said in a muffled voice: 'Or have you invited somebody else?' The taxi drew up.

'All right, all right then: get out. You must have been reading novels.'

The business with the taxi fare and the latch-key, the business of snatching letters from the hall rack, then of hustling Portia quietly upstairs preoccupied Eddie till he had turned a second Yale key and thrown open the door of his own room. But his nerves were at such a pitch of untoward alertness that he half expected to find some fateful figure standing by his window, or with its back to the grate. In the state he was in, his enemies seemed to have supernatural powers: they could filter through keyholes, stream through hard wood doors. The scene with Portia had been quite slight so far, but the skies had begun to fall – like pieces of black plaster they had started, still fairly gently, flaking down on his head. However, there was no one. The room, unaired and chilly, smelled of this morning's breakfast, last night's smoke. He put the two letters (one was 'By Hand', with no stamp) down on the centre table, threw open a window, knelt to light the gas fire.

With the crane-like steps of an overwrought person, Portia kept going round and round the room, looking hard at everything – the two armchairs with crushed springs, the greyish mirror, the divan with its scratchy butcher-blue spread, pillows untidily clipped into butcher-blue slips, the foreign books overcrowded, thrust with brutality into the deal shelves. She had been here before; she had twice come to see Eddie. But she gave the impression of being someone who, having lost their way in a book or mistaken its whole import, has to go back and start from the beginning again.

Only a subtler mind, with stores of notes to refer to, could have learned much from Eddie's interior. If this interior showed any affection, it was in keeping the bleakness of college rooms – the unadult taste, the lack of tactile feeling bred by large stark objects, tables, and cupboards, that one does not possess. The concave seats of the chairs, the lumpy divan suggested that comfort was a rather brutal affair. Eddie's work of presenting himself to the world did not, in fact, stop when he came back here, for he often had company – but he chose by all kinds of negligence to imply that it did. Whatever manias might possess him in solitude, making some haunted landscape in which cupboards and tables looked like cliffs or opaque bottomless pools, the effect

(at least to a woman) coming in here was, that this was how this fundamentally plain and rather old-fashioned fellow lived when *en pantoufles*. On the smoky buff walls and unpolished woodwork neurosis, of course, could not write a trace. To be received by Eddie in such frowsty surroundings could be taken as either confiding or insolent. If he *had* stuffed a bunch of flowers (never very nice flowers) into his one art vase, the concession always seemed touching. This was not all that was touching: the smells of carpet and ash, of dust inside the books, and of stagnant tea had a sort of unhopeful acquiescence about them. This was not all phony – Eddie did need to be mothered; he was not aesthetic; he had a contempt for natty contrivances, and he did sincerely associate pretty living with being richer than he could hope to be. To the hideous hired furniture and the stuffiness he did (with a kind of arrogance) acquiesce. Thus he kept the right, which he used, to look round his friends' room – at the taste, the freshness, the ingenuity – with a cold marvelling alien ironic eye. Had he had a good deal of money, his interior probably would have had the classy red Gallic darkness of a man-about-town's in a Bourget novel – draperies, cut-glass lamps, teetering bronzes, mirrors, a pianola, a seductive day-bed, and waxy *demi-monde* flowers in *jardinières*. Like the taste of many people whose extraction is humble, what taste he had lagged some decades back in time, and had an exciting, anti-moral colour. His animal suspiciousness, his bleakness, the underlying morality of his class, his expectation of some appalling contretemps which should make him have to decamp from everything suddenly were not catered for in his few expensive dreams – for there is a narrowness about fantasy: it figures only the *voulu* part of the self. Happily he had to keep what taste he had to himself. For as things were, this room of his became a *tour de force* – not simply the living here (which he more or less had to do) but the getting away with it, even making it pay. He was able to make this room (which was not even an attic) a special factor, even the key factor, in his relations with fastidious people ... There were some dying red daisies in the vase, which showed he had had someone to tea last week.

'Your flowers are dead, Eddie.'

'Are they? Throw them away.'

Portia, lifting the daisies from the vase, looked with a sort of unmeaning repulsion at their slimy rotting stalks. 'High time, too,' said Eddie. 'Perhaps that was the stink – In the waste-paper basket darling, under the table, there.' He took up the vase and prepared to make off with it to the lavatory. But there was a dripping sound as Portia went on holding up the daisies. She said: 'Eddie. . . .'

He jumped.

'Why don't you open that letter from Anna?'

'Oh God! Is there one?'

'I mean the one you've just brought up. It hasn't got any stamp.'

Eddie stood with the vase and gave a tortured giggle.

'Hasn't it?' he said. 'How extraordinary! She must have sent round by special messenger. I thought that looked like her writing. . . .'

'Surely you must know it,' said Portia coldly. She put down the daisies and watched them make a viscous pool on the cloth, then she took up the letter. 'Or, I will.'

'Shut up. Leave that alone!'

'Why? Why should I? What are you frightened of?'

'Apart from anything else, that's a letter to me. Don't be such a little rat!'

'Well, go on, read it. Why are you so frightened? What are the private things you and she say?'

'I really couldn't tell you: you're too young.'

'Eddie. . . .'

'Well, leave me alone, damn you!'

'I don't care if I'm damned. What do you and she say?'

'Well, quite often we have talks about you.'

'But you used to talk a lot before *you* got to know me, didn't you? Before you had said you loved me, or anything. I remember hearing you talking in the drawing-room, when I used to go up or down stairs, before I minded at all. Are you her lover?'

'You don't know what you're saying.'

'I know it's something you're not with me. I wouldn't mind

what you did, but I cannot bear the things I think now that you say.'

'Then why keep asking?'

'Because I keep hoping you might tell me you were really saying something not that.'

'Well, I am Anna's lover.'

'Oh ... Are you?'

'Don't you believe me?'

'I've got no way of telling.'

'I thought it didn't seem to make much impression. Why make such a fuss if you don't know what you do want? As a matter of fact, I'm not: she's far too cautious and smart, and I don't think she's got any passion at all. She likes to be far more trouble.'

'Then why do you – I mean, why –?'

'The trouble with you has been, from the very start, that you've been too anxious to get me taped.'

'Have I? But *you* said we loved each other.'

'You used to be much gentler, much more sweet. Yes, you used to be, as I once told you, the one person I could naturally love. But you're all different, lately, since Seale.'

'Matchett says so too – Eddie, will you turn out the fire?'

'What's the matter – do you feel funny? What's made you feel funny? Why don't you sit down, then?' He came hurriedly round the table pinning her with a hard look, as though he dared her to crumple, to drop down out of sight. Then he put one stony hand on her shoulder and pushed her down into an armchair. His high-pitched insensibility was not being acted – he sat on the arm of the chair, as he so often used to do, stared boldly into the air above her head, and giggled, as though the scene were as natural as it could ever be. 'If you pass out here, darling, you'll lose me my job,' he said. He took off her hat for her and put it down on the floor. 'There, that's better. I do wish to God you smoked,' he said. 'Do you still not want the fire? And why should you pass out?'

'You said everything was over,' Portia said, looking straight up into his eyes. They stayed locked in this incredulous look till Eddie flinched: he said: 'Have I been unkind?'

'I've got no way of telling.'

'I wish you had.' Frowning, pulling his lip down in the familiar way, that made this the ghost of all their happier talks, he said: 'Because I don't know, do you know? I may be some kind of monster; I've really got no idea ... The things I have to say seem never to have had to be said before. Is my life really so ghastly and so extraordinary? I've got no way to check up. I do wish you were older; I wish you knew more.'

'You're the only person I ever –'

'That's what's the devil; that's just what I mean. You don't know what to expect.'

Not taking her anxious eyes from his face – eyes as desperately concentrated as though she were trying to understand a lesson – she said: 'But after all, Eddie, anything that happens has never happened before. What I mean is, you and I are the first people who have ever been us.'

'All the same, most people get to know the ropes – you can see they do. All the other women I've ever known but you, Portia, seem to know what to expect, and that gives me something to go on. I don't care how wrong they are: it somehow gets one along. But you've kept springing thing after thing on me, from the moment you asked why I held that tart of a girl's hand. You expect every bloody thing to be either right or wrong, and be done with the whole of oneself. For all I know, you may be right. But it's simply intolerable. It makes me feel I'm simply going insane. I've started to live in one way, because that's been the only way I can live. I can see you get hurt, but however am I to know whether that's not your own fault for being the way you are? Or, that you don't really get hurt more than other people but simply make more fuss? You apply the same hopeless judgements to simply everything – for instance, because I said I loved you, you expect me to be as sweet to you as your mother. You're damned lucky to have someone even as innocent as I am. I've never fooled you, have I?'

'You've talked to Anna.'

'That's something different entirely. Have I ever not spoken the truth to you?'

'I don't know.'

'Well, have I? If I weren't innocent to the point of deformity, would you get me worked up into such a state? Any other man would have chucked you under the chin, and played you up, and afterwards laughed at you for a silly little fool.'

'You have laughed at me. You've laughed at me with them.'

'Well, when I'm with Anna you do seem pretty funny. I should think, in fact I'm certain that you'd seem funny to anybody but me. You've got a completely lunatic set of values, and a sort of unfailing lunatic instinct that makes you pick on another lunatic – another person who doesn't know where he is. You know I'm not a cad, and I know you're not batty. But, my God, we've got to live in the world.'

'You said you didn't like it. You said it was wicked.'

'That's another thing that you do: you pin me down to everything.'

'Then why do you say you always tell me the truth?'

'I used to tell you the truth because I felt safe with you. Now –'

'Now you don't love me any more?'

'You don't know what you mean by love. We used to have such fun, because I used to think that we understood each other. I still think you're sweet, though you do give me the horrors. I feel you trying to put me into some sort of trap. I'd never dream of going to bed with you, the idea would be absurd. All the same, I let you say these quite unspeakable things, which no one has the right to say to anyone else. And I suppose I say them to you too. Do I?'

'I don't know what is unspeakable.'

'No, that's quite clear. You've got some sense missing. The fact is, you're driving me mad.' Eddie, who had been chain-smoking, got up and walked away from the armchair. He dropped his cigarette behind the gas fire, stopped to stare at the fire, then automatically knelt down and turned it out. 'Apart from everything else, it's time you went home,' he said. 'It's going on for half past seven.'

'You mean you would be happier without me?'

'*Happy!*' said Eddie, throwing up his hands.

'I must make some people happy – I make Major Brutt happy,

I make Matchett happy, when I don't have secrets; I made Mrs Heccomb rather happy, she said . . . Do you mean, though, that *now*, you feel you could be as happy without me as you used to be with me when you thought I was different?'

Eddie, with his face entirely stiff, picked up the forgotten dead daisies from the table, doubled their stalks up, and put them precisely into the waste-paper basket. He looked all round the room, as though to see what else there was out of place; then his eyes, without changing, without a human flicker, with all their darkness of immutable trouble, returned to Portia's figure, where they stopped. 'I certainly do feel that at the moment,' he said.

Portia at once leaned down to reach her hat from the floor. The titter of the silly chromium clock, and a telephone ringing on and on in some room downstairs filled up the pause while she put on her hat. To do this, she had to put down Anna's letter, which, unconsciously, she had been holding all this time: she got up and put it down on the table – where Eddie's unseeing eyes became fixed on it. 'Oh,' she said, 'I haven't got any money. Can you lend me five shillings?'

'You won't want all that just to get back from here.'

'I'd rather have five shillings. I'll send you a postal order for it tomorrow.'

'Yes, do do that, darling, will you? I suppose you can always get money from Thomas. I've run rather short.'

When she had put her gloves on, she slipped the five shillings in small silver, that he had rather unwillingly collected, down inside the palm of her right glove. Then she held out her hand, with the hard bulge in the palm. 'Well, good-bye, Eddie,' she said, not looking at him. She was like someone who, at the end of a too long visit, conscious of having outstayed their welcome, does not know how to take their leave with grace. This unbearable social shyness of Eddie, her eagerness to be a long way away from here, made her eyes shift round different parts of the carpet, under their dropped lids.

'Of course I'll see you down. You can't wander about the stairs alone – this house is lousy with people.'

Her silence said: 'What more could they do to me?' She

waited: he put the same stone hand on her shoulder, and they went through the door and down three flights like this. She noted things she had not seen coming up – the scrolls, like tips of waves, on the staircase wallpaper, the characters of scratches on the olive dado, the chaotic outlook from a landing window, a typed warning on a bathroom door. For infinitesimal moments in her descent she paused, under Eddie's hand, to give these things looks as though it helped to fix her mind on them. She felt the silent tenseness of other people, of all those lives of which she had not been conscious, behind the shut doors; the exhausted breath of the apartment house, staled by so many lungs, charged with dust from so many feet, came up the darkening shaft of the stairs – for there were no windows down there near the hall.

Down there, Eddie glanced once more at the letter-rack, in case the next post should have come in. He swung open the hall door boldly and said he had better find a taxi for her. 'No, no, no, don't: I'll find one easily ... Good-bye,' she said again, with a still more guilty shyness. Before he could answer – while he still, in some reach of the purely physical memory, could feel her shoulder shrinking under his hand – she was down the steps and running off down the street. Her childish long-legged running, at once awkward (because this was in a street) and wild, took her away at a speed which made him at once appalled and glad. Her hands swung with her movements; they carried nothing – and the oddness of that, the sense that something was missing, bothered him as he went back upstairs.

Here he found, of course, that she had left the dispatch case, with all her lessons in it, behind. And this quite small worry – for how on earth, without comment, was he to get it back? this looked like further trouble for the unlucky pupil at Cavendish Square – pressed just enough on his mind to make him turn for distraction to the more pressing, dangerous worry of Anna. He got bottles out of a cupboard, made a drink for himself, gave one of those defiant laughs with which one sometimes buoys up one's solitude, drank half the drink, put it down, and opened the letter.

He read Anna's note about the office telephone.

5

THE Karachi Hotel consists of two Kensington houses, of great height, of a style at once portentous and brittle, knocked into one – or, rather, not knocked, the structure might hardly stand it, but connected by arches at key points. Of the two giant front doors under the portico, one has been glazed and sealed up; the other up to midnight, yields to pressure on a round brass knob. The hotel's name, in tarnished gilt capitals, is wired out from the top of the portico. One former dining-room has been exposed to the hall and provides the hotel lounge; the other is still the dining-room, it is large enough. One of the first-floor drawing-rooms is a drawing-room still. The public rooms are lofty and large in a diluted way: inside them there is extensive vacuity, nothing so nobly positive as space. The fireplaces with their flights of brackets, the doors with their poor mouldings, the nude-looking windows exist in deserts of wall: after dark the high-up electric lights die high in the air above unsmiling armchairs. If these houses give little by becoming hotels, they lose little; even when they were homes, no intimate life can have flowered inside these walls or become endeared to them. They were the homes of a class doomed from the start, without natural privilege, without grace. Their builders must have built to enclose fog, which having seeped in never quite goes away. Dyspepsia, uneasy wishes, ostentation, and chilblains can, only, have governed the lives of families here.

In the Karachi Hotel, all upstairs rooms except the drawing-room, have been partitioned up to make two or three more: the place is a warren. The thinness of these bedroom partitions makes love or talk indiscreet. The floors creak, the beds creak; drawers only pull out of chests with violent convulsions; mirrors swing round and hit you one in the eye. Most privacy, though least air, is to be had in the attics, which were too small to be divided up. One of these attics Major Brutt occupied.

At the end of Monday (for this was the end of the day unless you were gay or busy) dinner was being served. The guests

could now dine in daylight – or rather, by its unearthly reflections on the façades of houses across the road. In the dining-room, each table had been embellished some days ago, with three sprays of mauve sweet peas. Quite a number of tables, tonight, were empty, and the few couples and trios dotted about did not say much – weighed down, perhaps, by the height of the echoing gloom, or by the sense of eating in an exposed place. Only Major Brutt's silence seemed not uneasy, for he, as usual, dined alone. The one or two families he had found congenial had, as usual, just gone: these tonight were nearly all newcomers. Once or twice he glanced at some other table, wondering whom he might get to know next. He was learning, in his humble way, to be conscious of his faint interestingness as a solitary man. On the whole, however, he looked at his plate, or at the air just above it; he tried hard not to let recollections of lunch at Anna's make him discontented with dinner here – for, really, they did one wonderfully well. He had just finished his plate of rhubarb and custard when the head waitress came and mumbled over his ear.

He said: 'But I don't understand – "Young lady –?" '

'Asking for you, sir. She is in the lounge.'

'But I am not expecting a young lady.'

'In the lounge, sir. She said she would wait.'

'Then you mean she's there now?'

The waitress gave him a nod and a sort of slighting look. Her good opinion of him was being undone in a moment: she thought him at once ungallant and sly. Major Brutt, unaware, sat and turned the position over – this *might* be a joke, but who would play a joke on him? He was not sprightly enough to have sprightly friends. Shyness or obstinacy made him pour himself out another glass of water and drink it before he left the table – rhubarb leaves an acid taste in the teeth. He wiped his mouth, folded his table napkin, and left the dining-room with a heavy, cautious tread – conscious of people pausing in what they were hardly saying, of diners' glum eyes following him.

One's view into the lounge, coming through from the other house, is cut across by the row of shabby pillars that separate the lounge from the entrance hall. At first, in those dregs of day-

light, he saw nobody there. Glad there was no one to see him standing and looking, he challenged the unmeaning crowd of armchairs. Then he saw Portia behind a chair in the distance, prepared to retreat further if the wrong person came. He said: 'Hullo, hul-*lo* – what are *you* doing here?'

She only looked at him like a wild creature, just old enough to know it must dread humans – as though he had cornered her in this place. Yes, she was terrified here, like a bird astray in a room, a bird already stunned by dashing itself against mirrors and panes.

He pushed on quickly her way through the armchairs, saying, more urgently, less easily, lower – 'My dear child, are you lost? Have you lost your way?'

'No. I came.'

'Well, I'm delighted. But this is a long way from where *you* live. At this time of night –'

'Oh – is it night?'

'Well, no: I've just finished my dinner. But isn't this just the time when you ought to be having yours?'

'I don't know what time it is.'

Her voice rang round the lounge which, whatever despair it may have muffled, cannot have ever rung with such a homeless note. Major Brutt threw a look round instinctively: the porter was off duty; nobody was arriving; they had not begun to come out from dinner yet – there would be the cheese, then the coffee, always served at table. He went round the chair that barricaded her from him and kept them in their two different worlds of uncertainty: he felt Portia measuring his coming nearer with the deliberation of a desperate thing – then, like a bird at still another window, she flung herself at him. Her hands pressed, flattened, on the fronts of his coat; he felt her fingers digging into the stuff. She said something inaudible. Grasping her cold elbows he gently, strongly held her a little back. 'Steady, steady, steady – Now, what did you say?'

'I've got nowhere to be.'

'Come, that's nonsense, you know ... Just stay steady and try and tell me what's the matter. Have you had a fright, or what?'

'Yes.'

'That's too bad. Look here, don't tell me if you would rather not. Just stay still here for a bit and have some coffee or something, then I'll take you home.'

'I'm not going back.'

'Oh, come . . .'

'No, I'm not going back there.'

'Look, try sitting down.'

'No, no. They all make me do that. I don't want to just sit down: I want to stay.'

'Well, *I* shall sit down. Look, I'm sitting down now. I always do sit down.' Having let go of her elbows he reached, when he had sat down, across the arm of his chair, caught her wrist and pulled her round to stand like a pupil by him. 'Look here,' he said, 'Portia, I think the world of you. I don't know when I've met someone I thought so much of. So don't be like a hysterical little kid, because you are not, and it lets me down, you see. Just put whatever's the matter out of your head for a moment and think of me for a minute – I'm sure you will, because you've always been as sweet as anything to me, and I can't tell you what a difference it's made. When you come here and tell me you're running off, you put me in a pretty awful position with your people, who are my very good friends. When a man's a bit on his own, like I've been lately, and is marking time, and feels a bit out of touch, a place like their place, where one can drop in any time and always get a warm welcome, means quite a lot, you know. Seeing you there, so part of it all and happy, has been half the best of it. But I think the world of them, too. You wouldn't mess that up for me, Portia, would you?'

'There's nothing to mess,' she said in a very small voice that was implacable. 'You are the other person that Anna laughs at,' she went on, raising her eyes. 'I don't think you understand: Anna's always laughing at you. She says you are quite pathetic. She laughed at your carnations being the wrong colour, then gave them to me. And Thomas always thinks you must be after something. Whatever you do, even send me a puzzle, he thinks that more, and she laughs more. They groan at each other when you have gone away. You and I are the same.'

Steps in the hall behind him made Major Brutt crane round automatically: they *were* beginning to come out from dinner now. 'You must sit down,' he said to Portia, unexpectedly sharply. 'You don't want all these people staring at you.' He pulled another chair close: she sat down, distantly shaken by the outside force of what she had just said. Major Brutt intently watched four other people take their own favourite seats. Portia watched him watch; his eyes clung to these people; their ignorance of what he had had to hear made his fellow hotel guests the picture of sanity. There are moments when one can comfort oneself by a look at the most callous faces – these have been innocent of at least one crime. When he could not look any more without having to meet their looks, he dropped his eyes and sat not looking at Portia. It was she, for the moment, who felt how striking their silence, their nearness here had become – anxiety, and the sense of being pursued by glances still more closely than she had been all day made her sit stone still, not even moving her hands.

There seemed no reason why Major Brutt should ever raise his eyes from the floor: he had begun, in fact, to stroke the back of his head. She interposed, in a low voice: 'Is there no other place –?'

He frowned slightly.

'Haven't you got a room here?'

'I've been a pretty blundering sort of fellow.'

'Oh, *can't* we go upstairs? Can't we go somewhere else?'

'I don't know what made me think they would have time for me ... What's that you're saying?'

'Everyone's listening to us.'

But that still did not matter. He watched, with an odd grim sort of acquiescence, three more people come between the pillars, sit down. Then older ladies in semi-evening dresses cruised through the hall and upstairs: they were the drawing-room contingent. Major Brutt's grey eyes returned to Portia's dark ones. 'No, there's nowhere else,' he said. He waited: a conversation broke out at the other end of the lounge. He pitched his voice underneath this. 'You'll just have to talk more quietly. And mind what you say – you've no business to talk like that.'

She whispered: 'But you and I are the same.'

'Besides, anyhow,' he went on frowning at her, '*that* doesn't alter – nothing alters – anything. You've got no right to upset them: can't you see that's a low game? I'm going to take you right back – now, pronto, at once.'

'Oh no,' she said, with startling authority. 'You don't know what has happened.'

They sat almost knee to knee, at right angles to each other, their two armchairs touching. Their peril, the urgent need to stop him from this mistake, made the lounge, the rest of the world not matter – ruthless as a goddess, she put a small sure hand on the arm of his chair. So he wavered more when he said: 'My dear child, whatever's happened, you'd so much better go home and have it out.'

'Major Brutt, even if you hated them you couldn't possibly want me to do anything worse. It would never stop at all. Having things out would never stop, I mean. Besides, Thomas is my brother. I can't tell you down here ... Do you like this hotel?'

He readjusted to this in two or three seconds, hummed slowly at her, said: 'It suits me all right. Why?'

'If you left tomorrow, what they thought would not matter: you could tell them I was your niece who had got a pain and had got to lie down, then we could talk in your room.'

'That would still not do, I'm afraid.'

But she interposed: 'Oh, *quickly*! I'm starting to cry.' She was: her dilated dark eyes began dissolving; with her knuckles she pressed her chin up to keep her mouth steady; her other fist was pressed into her stomach, as though here were the seat of uncontrollable pain. She moved her knuckles, to mumble: 'There've been people all day ... I just want half an hour, just twenty minutes ... Then, if you say I must ...'

He shot up, knocking a table, making an ash-bowl rattle, saying loudly: 'Come, we'll look for some coffee.' They went through the dining-room arch to the other stairs – there was no lift – then she darted up ahead of him like a rabbit. He followed, stepping heavily, ostentatiously, whistling nonchalantly a little flat, fumbling round all the time for his room key,

passing palms on landings with that erect walk of the sleep-walker – his usual walk. Her day had been all stairs – all the same, her look became wilder, more unbelieving as, whenever she turned her head, he kept signalling: 'Up up.' This house seemed to have no top – till she came to the attic floor. At Windsor Terrace, that floor close to the skylight was mysterious with the servants' bodily life; it was the scene of Matchett's unmentioned sleep. Under this hotel skylight he came abreast with her: whistling louder, he unlocked his own door. Till now, she had not seen him approach anything with the authority that comes from possession. After that second, she was looking doubtfully over a lumpy olive sateen eiderdown at a dolls' house window dark from a parapet.

'I fit pretty tight,' he said. 'But, you see, they give me cut price terms.'

His anxious nonchalance, and his caution – for he went out again to knock on the other doors, to be certain there was nobody on this landing – made her not speak as she passed the end of the bed to sit, facing the window, on the edge of his eiderdown. He said: 'Well, here we are,' with an air of solemn alarm – he had just fully realized their position. His chair back grated against the chest of drawers: on the mat there was just room for his feet. 'Now,' he said, 'go on. What made you cry just now?'

'All those people everywhere, the whole time.'

'I mean, what brought you here? What is this you say you are running from?'

'Them all. What they make happen –'

He interrupted, austerely: 'I thought there was something special; I thought something had happened.'

'It has.'

'When?'

'It always has the whole time; I see it has never stopped. They were cruel to my father and mother, but the thing must have started even before that. Matchett says –'

'You ought not to listen to servants' talk.'

'Why? When she's the person who sees what really happens? They did not think my father and mother wicked; they simply

despised them and used to laugh. That made all three of us funny, I see now. I see now that my father wanted me to belong somewhere, because he did not: that was why they have had to have me in London. I hope he does not know that it has turned out like this. I suppose he and my mother did not know they were funny: they went on feeling upset because they thought they had once done an extraordinary thing (their getting married had been extraordinary) but they still thought life was quite simple for people who did not do extraordinary things. My father often used to explain to me that people did not live the way we did: he said ours was not the right way – though we were all quite happy. He was quite certain ordinary life went on – yes, that was why I was sent to Thomas and Anna. But I see now that it does not: if he and I met again I should have to tell him that there is no ordinary life.'

'Aren't you young to judge?'

'I don't see why. I thought when people were young that they were allowed to expect life to be ordinary. It did seem more like that at the seaside, but as soon as Eddie came it all got queer, and I saw even the Heccombs did not believe in it. If they did, why were they so frightened by Eddie? Eddie used to say it was he and I who were mad, but he used to seem to think we were right, too. But today he said we were wrong: he said I gave him the horrors and told me to go away.'

'That's it, is it? You two have had a quarrel?'

'He's shown me all my mistakes – but I have not known what to do. He says I've gone on taping him too much. I never could stop asking him why he did some things: you see, I thought we wanted to know each other.'

'We all take these knocks – this is your first, I daresay. Look here, my dear child, do you want a handkerchief?'

'I have one somewhere.' Automatic, compliant, she pulled a crushed one out of a buttoned pocket, held it up to please him, then, in a hand that went on sketching vague motions, held it crunched up tight. 'How can you say "first"?' she said. 'This can't happen again.'

'Oh, one forgets, you know. One can always patch oneself up.'

'No. Is this being grown up?'

'Nonsense. This is no time to say so, and you'll bite my head off, but you'll do better without that young man. Oh, I know I've got no business to chip bits off him, but –'

'But it isn't just Eddie,' she said, looking amazed. 'The thing was, he was the person I knew. Because of him, I felt safer with all the others. I did not think things could really be so bad. There was Matchett, but she got cold with me about Eddie; she liked me more when she and I were alone: now she and I are not the same as we were. I did not mean to be wrong, but she was always so angry; she wanted me to be angry. But Eddie and I weren't angry: we soothed each other. But I find now, he was with them the whole time, and they knew. I can't go back there now I know.'

'One's feelings get hurt; one cannot avoid that. One really can't make a war out of that, you know. A girl like you, Portia, a really good girl, ought not to get her back to the wall. When people seem to give you a bad deal, you've got to ask what sort of deal they may have once got themselves. But you are still young enough –'

'I don't see what age has to do with it.'

He swivelled round on his chair, as wretchedly as a schoolboy, to look, in glum, dumb, nonplussed communication at his own rubbed ebony hairbrushes, his stud-box, his nail-scissors – as though these objects, which had travelled with him, witnessed to his power somehow to get through life, to reach a point when one says, It doesn't really much matter. Unhappy on his bed, in this temporary little stale room, Portia seemed to belong nowhere, not even here. Stripped of that pleasant home that had seemed part of her figure, stripped too, of his own wishes and hopes, she looked at once harsh and beaten, a refugee – frightening, rebuffing all pity that has fear at the root. He tried: 'Or look at it this way –' then spoilt this by a pause. He saw what a fiction was common sense.

However he had meant to finish, she would hardly have listened. She had turned to grasp his bed-end, to bend her forehead down on her tight knuckles. Her body tensely twisted in this position; her legs, like disjointed legs, hung down: her thin

lines, her concavities, her unconsciousness made her a picture of premature grief. Happy that few of us are aware of the world until we are already in league with it. Childish fantasy, like the sheath over the bud, not only protects but curbs the terrible budding spirit, protects not only innocence from the world but the world from the power of innocence. Major Brutt said: 'Well, cheer up; we're in the same boat.'

She said, to her knuckles: 'When I thought I'd be older, I thought Eddie'd be the person I would marry. I saw I'd have to be different when that happened, but not more different than I could be. But he says he knew I thought that; it is that that he does not like.'

'When one's in love –'

'Was I? How do you know? Have you been?'

'In my time,' declared Major Brutt, with assertive cheerfulness. 'Though it may seem funny to you, and for one or another reason I never cut much ice. For the time being, of course, that queers everything. But here I am, after all. Aren't I?' he said, leaning forward, creaking the cane chair.

Portia almost gave him a look, then turned her head to lay the other cheek on her knuckles. 'Yes, *you* are,' she said. 'But today he said I must go. So what am I to do now, Major Brutt?'

'Well, it may seem tough, but I still don't see why you can't go home, after all. We've all got to live somewhere, whatever happens. There's breakfast, dinner, so on. After all, they're your people. Blood's thicker –'

'No, it isn't; not mine and Anna's. It, it isn't all right there any more: we feel ashamed with each other. You see, she has read my diary and found something out. She does not like that, but she laughs about it with Eddie: they laugh about him and me.'

This made Major Brutt pause, redden, and once more turn his head to look out of the window behind his chair. He said, to the parapet and the darkening sky: 'You mean, they're quite hand in glove?'

'Oh, he's not just her lover; it's something worse than that ... Are you still Anna's friend?'

'I can't get over the fact that she's been very good to me. I

don't think I want to discuss that ... But look, if you feel, if you *did* feel there was anything wrong at home, you should surely stick by your brother?'

'He's ashamed with me, too: he's ashamed because of our father. And he's afraid the whole time that I shall be sorry for him. Whenever I speak he gives me a sort of look as much as to say, "Don't say that!" Oh, he doesn't want me to stick. You don't know him at all ... You think I exaggerate.'

'At the moment –'

'Well, this sort of moment never really stops ... I'm not *going* home, Major Brutt.'

He said, very reasonably: 'Then what do you want to do?'

'Stay here –' She stopped short, as though she felt she had said, too soon, something important enough to need care. Deliberately, with her lips tight shut, she got off the bed to come and stand by him – so that, she standing, he sitting, she could tower up at least a little way. She looked him all over, as though she meant to tug at him, to jerk him awake, and was only not certain where to catch hold of him. Her arms stayed at her sides, but looked rigid, at every moment, with their intention to move in unfeeling desperation. She was not able, or else did not wish, to inform herself with pleading grace; her sexlessness made her deliver a stern summons: he felt her knocking through him like another heart outside his own ribs. 'Stay here with you,' she said. 'You do like me,' she added. 'You write to me; you send me puzzles; you say you think about me. Anna says you are sentimental, but that is what she says when people don't feel nothing. I could do things for you: we could have a home; we would not have to live in a hotel. Tell Thomas you want to keep me and he could send you my money. I could cook; my mother cooked when she lived in Notting Hill Gate. Why could you not marry me? I could cheer you up. I would not get in your way, and we should not be half so lonely. Why should you be dumbfounded, Major Brutt?'

'Because I suppose I am,' was all he could say.

'I told Eddie you were a person I made happy.'

'Good God, yes. But don't you see –'

'Do think it over, please,' she said calmly. 'I'll wait.'

'Its no good beginning to think, my dear.'

'I'd like to wait, all the same.'

'You're shivering,' he said vaguely.

'Yes, I am cold.' With a quite new, matter-of-fact air of possessing his room, she made small arrangements for comfort – peeled off his eiderdown, kicked her shoes off, lay down with her head into his pillow and pulled the eiderdown snugly up to her chin. By this series of acts she seemed at once to shelter, to plant here, and to obliterate herself – most of all that last. Like a sick person, or someone who has decided by not getting up to take no part in a day, she at once seemed to inhabit a different world. Noncommittal, she sometimes shut her eyes, sometimes looked at the ceiling that took the slope of the roof. 'I suppose', she said, after some minutes, 'you don't know what to do.'

Major Brutt said nothing. Portia moved her head on the pillow; her eyes roved placidly round the room, examined things on the washstand. 'All sorts of pads and polishes,' she said. 'Do you clean your own shoes?'

'Yes. I've always been rather fussy. They can't do everything here.'

She looked at the row of shoes, all on their trees. 'No wonder they look so nice: they look like chestnuts ... That's another thing I could do.'

'For some reason, women are never so good at it.'

'Well, I'm certain I could cook. Mother told me about the things she used to make. As I say, there'd be no reason for you and me to always live in hotels.'

The preposterous happy mirage of something one does not even for one moment desire must not be allowed to last. Had nothing in Major Brutt responded to it he would have gone on being gentle, purely sorry for her – As it was, he got up briskly, and not only got up but put back his chair where it came from, flat with some inches of wall, to show that this conversation was closed for good. And the effort this cost him, the final end of something, made his firm action seem more callous than sad. To stop any weakening pause, he kept on moving – picked up his two brushes, absently but competently started to brush his hair. So that Portia, watching him, had all in that moment a

view of his untouched masculine privacy, of that grave ab-
stractedness with which each part of his toilet would go on being
performed. Unconscious, he could not have made plainer his
determination always to live alone. Clapping the brushes together, he put them down with a clatter that made them both
start. 'I'm sure you will cook,' he said, 'I'm all in favour of it.
But not for some years yet, and not, I'm afraid, for me.'

'I suppose I should not have asked you,' Portia said – not
confusedly but in a considering tone.

'I feel pleased,' he admitted. 'In fact, it set me up no end.
But you think too much of me, and not enough of what I'm
trying to say. And, at the finish of this, what I still ask you to
do, is: forget this and go home.' He dared hardly look at the
eiderdown, under which he still heard no stir. 'It's not a question of doing the best you can do, it's a question of doing the
only thing possible.'

Portia, by folding her arms over it tightly, locked the eiderdown, her last shelter, to her chest. 'That will do no good, Major
Brutt. They will not know what to say.'

'Well, let's hear what they do say. Why not give them a
chance?' He paused, bit his upper lip under his moustache, and
added: 'I'll come with you, of course.'

'I can see you don't really want to. Why?'

'I don't like to spring this on them – your just turning up
with me, I mean, when they've had hours to worry. I've got to
telephone – Why, you know', he added, 'they'll be calling out
the police, the fire brigade.'

'Well, if you so much want to, you may tell them I'm with
you. But, please, you are not to tell them I'm going back. That
will all have to depend.'

'Oh, it will, will it? On what?'

'On what they do then.'

'Well, let me tell them you're safe.'

Without any further comment, she turned over and put her
hand under her cheek. Her detachment made her seem to
abandon being a woman – she was like one of those children
in an Elizabethan play who are led on, led off, hardly speak, and
are known to be bound for some tragic fate which will be told

in a line; they do not appear again; their existence, their point of view has had, throughout, an unreality. At the same time, her body looked like some drifting object that has been lodged for a moment, by some trick of the current, under a bank, but must be dislodged again and go on twirling down the implacable stream. He picked up her hat and hung it on the end of the bed: as he did this, she said: 'You'll come back when you've telephoned?'

'You will wait, like a good girl?'

'If you'll come back, I will wait.'

'And I'll tell them that you are here.'

'And you'll tell me what they do then.'

He took one more look round the darkening room with her in it, then went out, shut the door, started down to go to the telephone – his somnambulist's walk a little bit speeded up, as though by some bad dream from which he still must not wake. As he went down flight after flight he saw her face on the pillow, and saw in a sleep-bound way how specious wisdom was. One's sentiments – call them that – one's fidelities are so instinctive that one hardly knows they exist: only when they are betrayed or, worse still, when one betrays them does one realize their power. That betrayal is the end of an inner life, without which the everyday becomes threatening or meaningless. At the back of the spirit a mysterious landscape, whose perspective used to be infinite, suddenly perishes: this is like being cut off from the country for ever, not even meeting its breath down the city street.

Major Brutt had a mind that did not articulate: he felt, simply, things had changed for the worse. His home had come down; he must no longer envisage Windsor Terrace, or go there again. He made himself think of the moment – he hoped that the Quaynes would have some suggestion ready, that something could be arranged about Portia crossing London, that he would not have to go with her to their door. But as he went into the upright telephone coffin, he did not doubt for a moment that he was right to telephone, though they might laugh, they would certainly laugh, again.

6

ST QUENTIN, drawn to the scene of his crime – or, more properly, to its moral source – was drinking sherry at Anna's when the alarm broke. St Quentin had been, up to then, in good spirits, relieved to find how little guilty he felt. Nothing was said on the subject of diaries.

The trouble began on the ground floor of 2 Windsor Terrace and moved up. While St Quentin and Anna were at their sherry, Thomas came home, happened to ask for Portia, was told she was not back. He thought no more of this until Matchett, in person, came to the study door to say Portia was still not in yet, and to ask Thomas what he meant to do. She stood in the doorway, looking steadily at him: these days they did not often confront each other.

'What I mean,' she said, 'twenty to eight is late.'

'She must have made some plan, and then forgotten to tell us. Have you told Mrs Quayne?'

'Mrs Quayne has company, sir.'

'I know,' said Thomas. He almost added: Why else do you think I am down here? He said: 'That's no reason not to ask Mrs Quayne. She may quite likely know where Miss Portia is.'

Matchett gave Thomas a look without any quiver; Thomas frowned down at his fountain pen. 'Well,' he said, 'better ask her, at any rate.'

'Unless you would wish to, sir. . . .'

Under this compulsion, Thomas heaved himself up from his writing-desk. Evidently, Matchett was thinking something – but was Matchett not always thinking something? If you look at life one way, there is always cause for alarm. Thomas went upstairs, to gain the drawing-room landing enough infected by whatever Matchett did think to open the door sharply, then stand on the threshold with a tenseness that unnerved the other two. 'Portia isn't back,' he said. 'I suppose we know where she is?'

St Quentin at once got up, took Anna's glass to the tray, and gave her some more sherry. The business with this enabled him

to stay for some time with his back to the Quaynes: he gave himself more sherry, then filled a glass for Thomas. Then he strolled away and, looking out of the window, watched people calmly rowing on the lake. He told himself that if this had been going to happen it would have happened before: the argument therefore was that it could not be happening now. Five days had elapsed since he had lifted his hat to Portia in the graveyard, having just said to her what he had just said. At the same time – he had to face it – you cannot be sure how long a person may not take to react. Shocks are inclined to be cumulative. His heart sank; he loathed his renewed complicity with the child's relations and wanted to leave their house. He heard Thomas agree with the quite disconcerted Anna that it might be well to telephone to Lilian's home.

But Lilian's mother said that Lilian was out with her father: quite certainly, Portia was not with them. 'Oh dear,' Lilian's mother said, with a touch of smugness, 'I'm so sorry. What a worry for you!' Anna at once hung up.

Then Thomas started, on a sustained note that soon became rather bullying: 'You know, Anna, no one but us would let a girl of that age run round London alone.' 'Oh, shut up, darling,' said Anna, 'don't be so upper class. At her age, girls are typists.' 'Well, she is not a typist; she's not likely to learn to be anything, here. Why don't we send Matchett to fetch her, in the afternoons?' 'We don't live quite on that scale: Matchett's rather too busy. One thing Portia can learn here is to look after herself.' 'Yes, in theory all that is excellent. But in the course of learning she might, perhaps, get run over.' 'Portia takes no chances: she's much too scared of the traffic.' 'How can you know what she's like when she's alone? Only the other evening, just outside here, I had to pull her back from right under a car.' 'That was because she suddenly saw me.' Anna with a bold and frightened little inflection, said: 'Well, do we start to ring up the hospitals?'

'Before that,' said Thomas, impervious, 'why not ring up Eddie?'

'Because, for one thing, he is never in. Also, why on earth should I?'

'Well, you quite often do. I grant that Eddie's not bright, but he might have some idea.' Thomas picked up the glass of sherry St Quentin had left poured out, and drank it. Then he said: 'After all, they are quite thick.'

'By all means let's try everything,' Anna said, with the perfect smoothness of ice. She dialled Eddie's number, and for some time waited. She had been right: he was out. She hung up again and said: 'What a help telephones are!'

'What other friends has she got?'

'I can't really think of any,' said Anna frowning. Taking a comb from her bag, she ran the comb through her hair – and this nonchalant action only proclaimed her utter lack of indifference. 'She ought to have friends,' she said. 'But we can do that for her?' Her eye travelled round the room. 'If you were not here, St Quentin, I could telephone you.'

'I'm afraid I should not be much help, even if I were not here ... I'm so sorry I can't think of anything to suggest.'

'Well, do try. You're a novelist, after all. What *do* people do? But, after all, Thomas, it isn't eight o'clock yet: it's not really so late.'

'Late for her,' said Thomas relentlessly. 'Late if there's never any place you do go.'

'Well, she may have gone to a movie. . . .'

But Thomas, whose voice had become legal – obdurate, tough, tense – bore this down without considering it. 'Listen, Anna,' he said, 'has anything special happened? Had she been upset about anything?'

The sort of blind dropping over the others' faces made it clear that they were not prepared to say. The air immediately tightened, like the air of a court. Thomas cast a second look at St Quentin, wondering how he came to come in on this. Then, looking back at Anna, he saw that behind her face, with its non-committal half smile and dropped eyelids, Anna clearly believed she was alone. An individual deep guilty knowledge isolated her and St Quentin from each other – she did not even see St Quentin's fishy look; *she* had no idea he had anything on his mind. This split in the opposite party encouraged Thomas, who just allowed Anna to finish saying: 'I didn't see her this

morning, as a matter of fact,' before, himself, going on saying: 'Because, of course, in that case she might just be staying out. It's a thing one's inclined to do.'

'Yes, you are,' agreed Anna. 'But Portia's almost unfairly considerate. However, how can one know what people might do?'

St Quentin, amiably putting down his glass, put in: 'She's quite a mystery to you, then?' Ignoring this, Anna said: 'Then, Thomas, you mean she may just be trying it on?'

'We all have our feelings,' he said, looking oddly at Anna.

St Quentin said: 'Possibly Portia really hasn't got much talent for home life.'

'What you both really mean', said Anna, from her end of the sofa, a handsome image, not turning a hair, 'is, that I am not nice to Portia? How little it takes to bring things to the top. No, it's all right, St Quentin: we're not having a scene.'

'My dear Anna, do if you want. The thing is, I don't feel I am being very much use. Unless I can be, hadn't I better go? If I can do anything later, I'll come back. If I go, I'll go back and sit by my telephone.'

'Goodness,' she said tartly, 'it's not such a crisis yet. It won't be even nearly a crisis for half an hour. Meanwhile, it's eight – the whole point is, are we to have dinner? Or don't we want to have dinner? I don't know, really: this sort of thing has never happened before.'

Neither St Quentin nor Thomas seemed to know how they felt, so Anna rang downstairs on the house telephone. 'We'll have dinner now,' she said. 'We won't wait for Miss Portia, she'll be a little late ... I'm sure that is best,' she said, 'there are no half measures. We either have dinner or telephone the police ... The best thing you can do, St Quentin, is, stay and support us – that is, if you're not dining anywhere else?'

'It would not be that,' said St Quentin, quite frankly at bay. 'But the point is, *is* there much point in my being here?'

'The point is, you're an old family friend.'

The evening became more gloomy and overcast. Clouds made a steely premature dusk, and made the trees out in the park

metallic. Anna had had the candles lit for dinner, but, because it should still be light, the curtains were not drawn. The big shell of columbines on the table looked theatrical in a livid way: out there on the lake the people went on rowing. Phyllis served dinner to Thomas, Anna, St Quentin: no one looked at the time. Just after the duck came in, the dining-room telephone started ringing. They let it ring for some seconds while they looked at each other.

'I'll answer,' said Anna – but not moving yet.

Thomas said: 'No, I think I'd better go.'

'I could, if you'd both rather,' St Quentin said.

'No, nonsense, said Anna. 'Why shouldn't I? It may not even be anything at all.'

St Quentin steadily ate, his eyes fixed on his plate: Anna kept shifting her grip on the receiver. 'Hullo?' she said. 'Hullo? ... Oh, *hullo*, Major Brutt. ...'

'Well, he says she's there,' she said, sitting down again.

'Yes, I know, but *where?*' said Thomas. '*Where* does he say she is?'

'At his hotel,' said Anna, with no expression. 'That sort of hotel that he stays at, you know.' She held out her glass for some more wine and then said: 'Well, that is that, I suppose?'

'I suppose so,' said Thomas, looking out of the window. St Quentin said: 'Does he say what she's doing there?'

'Just being there. She turned up.'

'Now what, then?' Thomas said. 'I take it he's going to bring her home?'

'No,' said Anna, surprised. 'He wasn't suggesting that. He –'

'Then what *did* he want?'

'To know what we meant to do.'

'So you said?'

'You heard me – I said I'd ring up again.'

'To say – I mean, what are we meaning to do?'

'If I had known, I'd have told him, wouldn't I, Thomas dear?'

'Why on earth not tell him, just bring her straight round? The old bastard's not as busy as that. We could give him a drink

or something. Or why not just let him put her into a taxi? What could be simpler?'

'It's not so simple as that.'

'I don't see why not. What are the complications? What in God's name *was* he chattering on about?'

Anna finished her wine, but after that only said: 'Well, it *could* be simpler, if you know what I mean.'

Thomas picked up his table napkin, wiped his mouth, glanced once across at St Quentin, then said: 'What you mean is, she won't come home?'

'She doesn't seem very keen to, just at the minute.'

'Why just at the minute? Do you mean she'll come later?'

'She is waiting to see whether we do the right thing.'

Thomas said nothing. He frowned, looked out of the window, and rapped his thumbs on the table each side of his plate. 'Then you mean, something *is* up?' he finally said.

'Major Brutt seemed to think so.'

'Damn his eyes,' Thomas said. 'Why can't he keep out of this? What is it, Anna? *Have* you any idea?'

'Yes, I must say I have. She thinks I read her diary.'

'Does she keep a diary?'

'Yes, she does. And I do.'

'Oh! Do you?' said Thomas. Having seemed not to think of this for some time, he began to rap with his thumbs again.

'Darling, must you do that? You make all the glasses jump – No, it's not at all odd: it's the sort of thing I do do. Her diary's very good – you see, she has got us taped. Could I not go on with a book all about ourselves? I don't say it has changed the course of my life, but it's given me a rather more disagreeable feeling about being alive – or, at least, about being me.'

'I can't see, all the same, why that should send her right off at the deep end. His hotel's right off in Kensington, isn't it? And why Brutt? Where does he come in?'

'He has sent her puzzles.'

'Still, even that could be something,' said St Quentin. 'Even that, I suppose, could be quite encouraging.'

'I've got housemaid's tricks,' Anna went on, 'and more spare time than a housemaid. All the same, I should like to know how

she knew I'd been at her diary. I put it back where it lives; I don't leave finger marks: I should have seen if she'd tied a thread round it. Matchett cannot have told her, because I never touch it unless I know Matchett is out ... That's what puzzles me. I really should like to know.'

'Would you?' St Quentin said. 'Well, that's simple: I told her.' He looked at Anna rather critically, as though *she* had just said some distinctly doubtful thing. The pause, through which Thomas made his steady aloofness felt, was underlined by the swimming entrance of Phyllis, who changed the plates and brought in a strawberry *compote*. St Quentin, left face to face with what he had just said, stayed composedly smiling and looking down. Meanwhile: 'Oh, Phyllis,' said Anna, 'you might tell Matchett Miss Portia has rung up. She has been delayed; we're expecting her back later.'

'Yes, madam. Should cook keep her dinner hot?'

'No,' said Anna. 'She will have had dinner.' When Phyllis had gone, Anna picked her spoon up, looked at the strawberries, then said: 'Oh, did you really, St Quentin?'

'I suppose you want to know why?'

'No, I'd much rather not.'

'How like Portia – she took no interest, either. Of course, Portia had had a shock, too, and though I felt very much moved to tell her about myself, she was in no mood to listen. As I said to her in Marylebone High Street, how completely closed we are to one another ... But what *I* should like to know is, how do you know she knows?'

'Yes, by the way,' said Thomas, coming alive abruptly, 'how do you know she knows?'

'I quite see,' said Anna, slightly raising her voice, 'that whatever anyone else may have done – betray confidences, or run off to Major Brutt – it is *I* who have been to blame, from the very start. Well listen, St Quentin, listen, Thomas: Portia has not said a word about this to me. That would not be her way. No, she simply rang up Eddie, who rang me up to complain how unkind I'd been. That happened today. When did you tell her, St Quentin?'

'Last Wednesday. I so well remember, because –'

'— Very well. Since Wednesday, something else must have happened to bring all this to a head. On Saturday I did think she looked odd. She came in and found Eddie here at tea. Possibly he and she blew off in some way when they were down at Seale. Perhaps Eddie got a fright.'

'Yes, he's sensitive,' said St Quentin. 'Do you mind if I smoke?' Having lighted cigarettes for himself and Anna, he added: 'How I do hate Eddie.'

'Yes, so do I,' said Thomas.

'*Thomas* – you never said so!'

With a gigantic air of starting to ease himself, Thomas said: 'Yes, he is such a little rat. And his work's been so specious. Merrett wants to fire him.'

'You can't do that, Thomas: he'd starve. Why should Eddie starve simply because you don't like him?'

'Why should he not starve simply because you do? That principle seems to me the same throughout, and bad. Worse things happen to better people.'

'Besides,' St Quentin said gently, 'I don't think Eddie would starve. He'd turn up for meals here.'

'No, you can't do that, Thomas,' Anna wildly repeated, pulling her pearls round. 'If he is being slack, simply give him a good fright. But you can't sack him right out of the blue. You've got nothing against him, except being such a donkey.'

'Well, we can't afford donkeys at five pounds a week. When you asked me to put him in, you insisted he was so bright – which I must say he was, for the first week. Why did you say he was bright if you say he is such a donkey, and if he's such a donkey, why is he always here?'

Anna looked at St Quentin but did not look at Thomas. She left her pearls alone, ate a spoonful of *compote*, then said: 'Because he is running after her.'

'And you think that's a good thing?'

'I really could not tell you. After all, she's your sister. It was you who wanted to have her here. No, it's all right, St Quentin, we're not having a scene – If you didn't like it, Thomas, why didn't you say so? It seems to me we have talked about this before.'

'She seemed to know what was what, in her own way.'

'In fact, you wouldn't cope, but you always hoped I might.'

'Look, what did you mean just now about them blowing off at Seale? What business had he down there? Why couldn't he stay in London? Was that old fool Mrs Heccomb running a *rendezvous*?'

Anna went very white. She said: 'How dare you say that? She was my governess.'

'Oh, yes, I know,' said Thomas. 'But was she ever much of a chaperone?'

Anna paused, and looked at the candle-lit flowers. Then she asked St Quentin for one more cigarette, which he with the discreetest speed supplied. Then she returned and said very steadily: 'I'm afraid I don't quite understand you, Thomas. Am I to take it you don't trust Portia, then? It is you, I suppose, who should know if we're right to trust her or not. You knew your father: I really never did. I never saw any reason to spy on her.'

'Except by reading her diary.'

St Quentin, sitting with his back to the window, turned round and had a good look out. He said: 'It's getting pretty dark outside.'

'St Quentin means that he wishes he wasn't here.'

'Actually what I do mean, Anna, is, didn't you say you would telephone Major Brutt?'

'Yes, he'll be waiting, won't he? So, I suppose, will Portia.'

'Very well, then,' said Thomas, leaning back, 'what *are* we going to say?'

'We should have kept to the point.'

'We've kept a good deal too near it.'

'We must say something. He'll think us so very odd.'

'He's got every reason,' said Thomas, 'to think us odd already. You say, he says she'll come home if we do the right thing?'

'Do we know what the right thing is?'

'I suppose that's what we're deciding.'

'We shall know if we don't do it. It will be quite simple: Portia will simply stay there with Major Brutt. Oh, heaven keep me', said Anna, sighing, 'from insulting a young person again!

But it hasn't simply been me – you know, we are all in it. We know what we think we've done, but we still don't know what we did. What did she expect, and what is she expecting now? It's not simply a question of getting her home this evening; it's a question of all three going on living here ... Yes, this is a situation. She's created it.'

'No, she's just acknowledged it. An entirely different thing. She has a point of view.'

'Well, so has everybody. From the outside we may seem worthless, but we are not worthless to ourselves. If one thought what everyone felt, one would go mad. It does not do to think of what people feel.'

'I'm afraid', St Quentin said, 'in this case we may have to. That is, if you are anxious to get her home. Her "right thing" is an absolute of some sort, and absolutes only exist in feeling. There they both are, waiting in Kensington. Really you will have to do something soon.'

'Even supposing one wanted to for a moment, how is one to know how anyone else feels?'

'Oh, come,' said St Quentin. 'In this case, none of us are so badly placed. I am a novelist; you, Anna, have read her diary; Thomas is her brother – they can't be *quite* unlike. However much we may hate to, there's no reason, now we have got to face it, why we should not see more or less what her position is – or, I mean more, see things from her position ... May I go on, Anna?'

'Yes, do. But really we must decide. What are you doing, Thomas?'

'Drawing the curtains. People are looking, in ... Are we not to have any coffee?'

'St Quentin, wait till the coffees come.'

The coffee was brought. St Quentin, one elbow each side of his cup of coffee, continued slowly to rub his forehead. At last he said : 'I think you're jealous of her.'

'Does she know that? If not, it can't be called her position.'

'No, she's not properly conscious of enjoying everything you are so jealous of. She may not enjoy it herself. Her extraordinary wish to love –'

'– Oh, I'd never want *that* back –'

'Her extraordinary expectation that whatever offers offers to lead you somewhere. What she expects to get at we shall never know. She wanders around you and Thomas, detecting what there is not and noting clues in her diary. In a way, of course, she has struck unlucky here. If you were much nicer people, living in the country –'

'What proof have you', said Thomas, breaking in for the first time, 'that much nicer people do really exist?'

'Suppose that they did, and you were those much nicer people, you would not be bothered with her – what I mean is, you would not be so concerned. As it is, you are both unnaturally conscious of her: anybody would think she held the clue to the crime . . . Your mother, for instance, Thomas, must have been a nice person living in the country.'

'So, as a matter of fact, was my father, until he fell in love. All there is to nice easy people, St Quentin, is, that they are fairly impermeable. But not impermeable the whole way through. Yes, I know just the sort of people you've got in mind – you're a novelist and you've always lived in town – but my experience is that they've all got a breaking-point. And my conviction is that a thorough girl like Portia would be bound to come to it in them pretty soon. No, the fact is that nobody can afford to have a girl as thorough as that about.' Thomas refilled his glass with brandy and went on: 'I don't say we might not have kept the surface on things longer if we had lived in some place where we could give her a bicycle. But, even so, could she keep on bicycling round for ever? She'd be bound, sooner or later, to notice something was up. Anna and I live the only way we can, and it quite likely may not stand up to examination. Look at this conversation we're having now, for instance: it seems to me the apogee of bad taste. If we were nice easy people living in the country we should not for a moment tolerate you, St Quentin. In fact, we should detest intimacies, and no doubt we should be right. Oh, no doubt we should be a good deal jollier than we are. But we might not do Portia better in the long run. For one thing, we should make her feel pretty shady.'

'Which she is,' said Anna. 'Throwing herself at Eddie.'

'Well, what did you do, at not much more than her age?'

'Why always bring that up?'

'Why always have it in mind? ... No, she is growing up in such a preposterous world that it's quite natural that that little scab Eddie should seem as natural to her as anyone else. If you, Anna, and I had come up to scratch, she might not –'

'Yes, she always would. She wanted to pity him.'

'Victimized,' said St Quentin. 'She sees the victimized character. She sees one long set of attacks on him. She would never take account of the self-inflicted wrong – the chap who breaks his own arm to avoid going back to school, then says some big bully has done it for him; the chap who lashes himself to his bedroom chair so as not to have to go and cope with the burglar – oh, she'd think he was Prometheus. There's something so showy about desperation, it takes hard wits to see it's a grandiose form of funk. It takes nerve to make a fuss in a big way, and our Eddie certainly has got nerve. But it takes guts not to, and guts he hasn't got. If he had, he'd stop Anna having him on. Oh, he won't stop baying the moon while he's got someone to listen and Portia'll listen as long as anyone bays the moon.'

'How right you must be. All the same, you are so brutal. Does one really get far with brutality?'

'Clearly not,' said St Quentin. 'Look where we all three are. Utterly disabused, and yet we can't decide anything. This evening the pure in heart have simply got us on toast. And look at the fun she has – she lives in a world of heroes. Who are we to be sure they're as phony as we all think? If the world's really a stage, there must be some big parts. All she asks is to walk on at the same time. And how right she is really – failing the big character, better (at least, arguably) the big flop than the small neat man who has more or less come off. Not that there is, really, one neat unhaunted man. I swear that each of us keeps, battened down inside himself, a sort of lunatic giant – impossible socially, but full-scale – and that it's the knockings and batterings we sometimes hear in each other that keeps our intercourse from utter banality. Portia hears these the whole time; in fact she hears nothing else. Can we wonder she looks so goofy most of the time?'

'I suppose not. But how are we to get her home?'

St Quentin said: 'How would Thomas feel if he were his own sister?'

'I should feel I'd been born in a mare's nest. I should want to get out and stay out. At the same time, I should thank God I was a woman and did not have to put up one particular kind of show.'

'Yes,' Anna said, 'but that's only because you feel that being a man has run you in for so much. Your lack of gusto's your particular thing. If you were Portia, let off being a man, you would find something else to string yourself up about. But that's not what St Quentin is getting at. The point is, if you were Portia this evening, what would be the only thing you could bear to have us do?'

'Something quite obvious. Something with no fuss.'

'But my dear Thomas, in our relations with her nothing has ever seemed to be obvious. It's been trial and error right from the start.'

'Well, I should like to be called for and taken away by someone who would not make any high-class fuss. They could be as cross as they liked if they'd cut the analysis.' Thomas stopped and looked sternly at Anna. 'She's not fetched from places nearly enough,' he said. 'When she is fetched, who generally fetches her?'

'Matchett.'

'Matchett?' St Quentin said. 'You mean Matchett your housemaid? Are they on good terms?'

'Yes, they're on very good terms. When I am out for tea I hear they have tea together, and when they think I am out say good night. They say a good deal more – but what, I have no idea. Yes, I have though: they talk about the past.'

'The past?' said Thomas. 'What do you mean? Why?'

'Their great mutual past – your father, naturally.'

'What makes you think that?'

'Their being so knit up. They sometimes look like each other. What other subject – except of course, love – gives people that sort of obsessed look? Talk like that is one climax the whole time. It's a trance; it's a vice; it's a sort of complete world.

Portia may have defaulted lately because of Eddie. But Matchett will never let that drop; it's her *raison d'être*, apart from the furniture. And she is least likely of all to let it drop with Portia about the house. Portia's coming here was a consummation, you see.'

'Consummation my aunt. Has this really been going on? If I'd had any idea, I'd have fired Matchett at once.'

'You know quite well Matchett stays with the furniture. No, you inherited the whole bag of tricks. Matchett thinks the world of your father. Why shouldn't Portia hear about her father from someone who sees him as *someone*, not just as a poor ignominious old man?'

'I don't think you need say that.'

'I've never said it before ... Yes, St Quentin: it's Matchett she talks to chiefly.'

'Matchett – is that the woman with the big stony apron, who backs to the wall when I pass like a caryatid? She's generally on the stairs.'

'Yes, she's generally up and down ... Why not Matchett, after all?'

'It's "why not" now, then, not "why"? Well, how would you feel, Anna?'

'If I were Portia? Contempt for the pack of us, who muddled our own lives then stopped me from living mine. Boredom, oh such boredom, with a sort of secret society about nothing, keeping on making little signs to each other. Utter lack of desire to know what it was about. Wish that someone outside would blow a whistle and make the whole thing stop. Wish to have my own innings. Contempt for married people, keeping on playing up. Contempt for unmarried people, looking cautious and touchy. Frantic, frantic desire to be handled with feeling, and, at the same time, to be let alone. Wish to be asked how I felt, great wish to be taken for granted –'

'This is all quite new, Anna. How much is the diary, how much is you?'

Anna quieted down. She said: 'You said, if I were Portia. Naturally, that's impossible: she and I are hardly the same sex. Though she and I may wish to make a new start, we hardly

shall, I'm afraid. I shall always insult her; she will always persecute me ... Well then, it's decided, Thomas – we are to send Matchett? Really, we might have thought of that before, without dragging all this up.'

'Decidedly we send Matchett. Don't you agree – St Quentin?'

'Oh, by all means –

> We'll send Matchett to fetch her away,
>   Fetch her away, fetch her away,
> We'll send Matchett to fetch her away,
>   On a cold and frosty –'

'St Quentin, for *heaven's sake* –!'

'Sorry, Anna. I felt quite outside myself. So glad this is all arranged.'

'We've still got to think. What are we to tell Matchett? Which of us is to ring up Major Brutt?'

'No one,' said Thomas quickly. 'This is a *coup* or nothing. We don't talk; we do the obvious thing.'

Anna looked at Thomas: her forehead smoothed out slowly. 'Oh, all right,' she said. 'Then I'll tell her to get her hat.'

Matchett said: 'Yes, madam.' She stood waiting till Anna turned back into the dining-room. Then she started heavily up the silent staircase: by the time she came to the second landing she was undoing her apron at the back. She stopped to open the door of Portia's room and, in the dusk, take a quick look round. Though the bed was turned down, the nightdress lying across it, the room seemed to expect nobody back. An empty room gets this look towards the end of an evening – as though the day had died alone in here. Matchett, holding the unfastened straps of her apron together in the small of her back with one hand, switched on the electric fire. Standing up again, she took one look out of the window: steel-green under the sky the tree tops were in their order, the park was not shut yet. Matchett then went on up, to her own room that no one saw but herself.

When she came down in her hat, her dark overcoat, still holding her black suède-finish gloves, with her morocco handbag pressed to her ribs, Thomas was in the hall, holding the door open. He was looking anxiously for her, up the stairs. A taxi

ticked outside so near the step that it seemed to be something in the hall.

'Here's your taxi,' Thomas said.

'Thank you, sir.'

'I'd better give you some money.'

'I carry all I shall need.'

'Then all right. Better get in.'

Matchett got into the taxi; she shut the door after herself. She sat upright, took one impassive look out of each window, then unfolded her gloves and started putting them on. Through the glass, she watched Thomas give some direction to the driver – then the taxi croaked into gear and lumbered off down the terrace.

Matchett not only buttoned her gloves but stroked the last wrinkle out of them. This occupied her to half way up Baker Street. *Then*, she electrically started, paused, one thumb over the other, and said, aloud: 'Well, to think ...' She looked anxiously through the glass at the driver's back. Then she put down her bag beside her, heaved herself forward and began to try to slide open the glass panel – but her gloved fingers only scrabbled on it. The driver twitched his head once or twice. Then the lights went against him; he pulled up, slid open the panel, and looked obligingly in. 'Ma'am?' he said.

'Here, do you know where you're to go to?'

'Where he just said, don't I?'

'Well, so long as you do know. But don't you come asking me. It's not my business. You've got to know your own way.'

'Ho, come,' said the driver, nettled. 'I didn't start this, did I?'

'None of that, young man. You mind your own business, which is to know what address the gentleman said.'

'Ho, so that's what you want to know? Why not ask me out straight?'

'Oh, *I* don't want to know. I just wanted to know you did.'

'Rightie-o, auntie,' said the driver. 'Then you chance it. Isn't life an adventure?'

Matchett sat back, not saying another word. She did not even attempt to shut the panel: the lights changed and they shot forward again. She picked up her bag from the seat, crossed her

hands on it, and thereafter sat like an image. She did not even look at a clock, for she could do nothing about time. Crossing the great wasteful glare of Oxford Street, they took a cut through Mayfair. At corners, or when the taxi swerved, she put one hand out and stiffly balanced herself.

Inside her, her spirit balanced in her body, with a succession of harsh efforts, as her body balanced inside the taxi. When at moments she thought, she thought in words.

I don't know, I'm sure.

Mrs Thomas certainly never thought to mention, and I never thought to ask. Whatever came over me? All Mr Thomas said, when he put me in the taxi, was, did I need money outside of what I had. No, Mr Thomas didn't mention, either, taking it Mrs Thomas would be sure to have said. And there, you see, if I'd just left that door open I'd have heard what he said to the man. But I shut the door. Whatever came over me? No, I never thought to notice what he said to the man. And I wouldn't ask *him* right out, not after all that sauce. You don't know what drivers are. Not a nice class.

Oh well, it does seem queer. I ought to say to myself, well, things will get overlooked. What with all that hurry and that. The hotel was all she said, the hotel. But one of those might be anywhere. I can't but worry – oh, I am vexed with myself, not thinking to ask like that. How am I to know the place is the right place? He might stop and put me down anywhere, well knowing that not knowing I wouldn't know. I had no call to let on I didn't know. That did make me look wrong . . . Not one of the drivers off our stand.

And what do I say if they say, Oh no, Major Brutt's not *here*, or Oh no, we know no one of that name. How am I to say, none of that, now: this is the place I was told, this is where I've orders to wait. Oh, they could put me right out, now I don't know the address. Any little buttons could put me wrong. Oh, he might say to me, and as saucy as anything, but you've come to the wrong place.

Let alone they ought to have said, I should have had it in writing.

It was Mrs Thomas being all in a rush. She quite put me

about. If she was to be in a hurry, why did she not send down and give the order before? When Phyllis came down and said, Well, they've heard all right, but she's to be in late, I was only waiting to go and put on my hat. Phyllis said, they *are* talking away in there. They beat all, tonight, she said, it must be that Mr Miller.

If they was to talk less and make up their minds more. I've never seen Mrs Thomas in such a rush. She couldn't hardly wait till she'd got it said. It was as if she didn't half like to ask. Well, I'm used to taking her orders, I'm sure. Take a taxi both ways, she said, we've just sent for the taxi. She kept looking at me, for all she didn't quite look. At the same time, she spoke as if she was there to tell me to do some sort of a conjuring trick. Then how she did run back into that dining-room, yes, and shut the door. They were all in there.

Oh, Hyde Park, is it? ... Well, I don't know, I'm sure.

I know I said to myself, as I went up for my hat, well now, there's *something* she hasn't said. It was in my mind while I got my hat. Then when I came down and there was Mr Thomas, I looked at him and said to myself, now, there's *something* I ought to ask. If I'd just have taken notice of what he said to the driver. But I was put about with my gloves to put on and all that hurry and that. It didn't come to mind not till we were in Baker Street. Then I said to myself, well, we're off to – and I stopped. Oh, I did feel queer. It all came over me.

Just fancy me just going off like that. Fancy me going off to where I've got no idea. Fancy going off just like an image. Fancy going off when you don't know the address.

Well, he does know, I suppose. I've no reason to think he doesn't. But fancy me depending on a fellow like him. Oh, they should have thought to have told me, one of them or the other. They did ought to have thought. Forgetfulness is one thing. But this isn't natural, really.

It puts me wrong. Why, there's not a thing I can say.

That's them all over. That's where they're different, really. That's where they're not like Mr Quayne.

Not like Mr Quayne. He would always think of a thing. He'd tell you, but he would say why. He wouldn't never put you in

that sort of position, not with a taxi man. He wouldn't leave you to be put in the wrong. Oh, he was fair, he was fair in all that he did. For all there were many worse that would point him down.

Yes, and what would he think of *you*, out all over London at this time? No, it wasn't right of you, not to give me a turn like that. What would your father say, I should like to know? To start with, you never said you would not be back for your tea. I'd got a nice tea for you, I was keeping it. It wasn't till half past five that I thought to myself, oh well! She's with that Lilian, I thought, but she did ought to have said. So then I expected you round six. No, you did give me a turn. I couldn't hardly believe the clock. When I did hear the front door, it was nothing but Mr Thomas.

I couldn't believe the clock. It didn't seem like you, really. Not like what you was. Whatever's come over you? Oh, you have got a silly fit, these days. First one thing, then it's another. Stuffing nonsense under your pillow – I could have told you then. You'll do yourself no good. You're not like what you were. And when it's not that Eddie, it's those Heccombs, and this that and the other off at the seaside. You didn't ought to have gone to the seaside; it was there you came back from with that silly fit. You did ought to know better, after all what I told you. No good ever came of secrets – you look at your father. And you didn't ought to have gone to a gentleman's hotel.

South Kensington Station ... Well, I don't know, I'm sure.

Well, and did you get a good supper? Wholesome, was it? You never know at those places; they're out to make what they can. And that Major Brutt's just an innocent: he would never know. Him and his puzzles. However ... No, what I'm on about is, you staying out like this, you coming right off here, you giving me such a turn. No, it's high time you came out of this silly fit. You stay quiet, now, and remember what I said. I've got your fire on; it looks nice in your room now; and I've got those biscuits you like. You'd be all right if you'd only be like you were.

No, I'm not going on at you. No, I'm done now. I've said what I've said. Don't you be upset and silly. You come back with Matchett and be a good girl.

My, the hotels in this street! They're like needles in hay.

Now, what does he think he's up to? Oh, so we're stopping are we? Well, I don't know, I'm sure.

The driver, slowing into the kerb, looked boldly at her through the panel. He pulled up, then pottered round to open the door – but Matchett was out already standing and looking up. The sad gimcrack cliff of the hotel towered above her, with colourless daylight showing over the top. 'Well, ma'am,' said the driver, 'here's our little surprise.' With a movement of implacable dignity she drew herself up and read *The Karachi Hotel*. Her eyes travelled stonily down the portico to the glass door, the dull yellow brass knob, then down the steep steps blowsy from many feet. Not looking round, she said: 'Well, if you've brought me wrong, don't think you'll get your money. You can just drive right back and I'll speak to the gentleman.'

'Yes, and how'm I to know you'll be coming back out of here?'

'If I don't come out of here with a young lady, that'll be because you'll have brought me wrong.'

Matchett straightened her hat with both hands, gripped her bag more firmly, mounted the steps. Below the steps the grey road was all stucco and echoes – an occasional taxi, an occasional bus. Reflections of evening made unlit windows ghostly; lit lights showed drawing-rooms pallid and bare. In the Karachi Hotel drawing-room, someone played the piano uncertainly.

All the same, in the stretched mauve dusk of the street there was an intimation of summer coming – summer, intensifying everything with its heat and glare. In gardens outside London roses would burn on, with all else gone in the dusk. Fatigue but a sort of joy would open in all hearts, for summer is the height and fullness of living. Already the dust smelled strong. In this premature night of clouds the sky was warm, the buildings seemed to expand. The fingers on the piano halted, struck true notes, found their way to a chord.

Through the glass door, Matchett saw lights, chairs, pillars – but there was no buttons, no one. She thought: 'Well, what a place!' Ignoring the bell, because this place was public, she pushed on the brass knob with an air of authority.

READ MORE IN PENGUIN

In every corner of the world, on every subject under the sun, Penguin represents quality and variety – the very best in publishing today.

For complete information about books available from Penguin – including Puffins, Penguin Classics and Arkana – and how to order them, write to us at the appropriate address below. Please note that for copyright reasons the selection of books varies from country to country.

In the United Kingdom: Please write to *Dept. EP, Penguin Books Ltd, Bath Road, Harmondsworth, West Drayton, Middlesex UB7 ODA*

In the United States: Please write to *Consumer Sales, Penguin USA, P.O. Box 999, Dept. 17109, Bergenfield, New Jersey 07621-0120.* VISA and MasterCard holders call 1-800-253-6476 to order Penguin titles

In Canada: Please write to *Penguin Books Canada Ltd, 10 Alcorn Avenue, Suite 300, Toronto, Ontario M4V 3B2*

In Australia: Please write to *Penguin Books Australia Ltd, P.O. Box 257, Ringwood, Victoria 3134*

In New Zealand: Please write to *Penguin Books (NZ) Ltd, Private Bag 102902, North Shore Mail Centre, Auckland 10*

In India: Please write to *Penguin Books India Pvt Ltd, 706 Eros Apartments, 56 Nehru Place, New Delhi 110 019*

In the Netherlands: Please write to *Penguin Books Netherlands bv, Postbus 3507, NL-1001 AH Amsterdam*

In Germany: Please write to *Penguin Books Deutschland GmbH, Metzlerstrasse 26, 60594 Frankfurt am Main*

In Spain: Please write to *Penguin Books S. A., Bravo Murillo 19, 1° B, 28015 Madrid*

In Italy: Please write to *Penguin Italia s.r.l., Via Felice Casati 20, I–20124 Milano*

In France: Please write to *Penguin France S. A., 17 rue Lejeune, F–31000 Toulouse*

In Japan: Please write to *Penguin Books Japan, Ishikiribashi Building, 2–5–4, Suido, Bunkyo-ku, Tokyo 112*

In Greece: Please write to *Penguin Hellas Ltd, Dimocritou 3, GR–106 71 Athens*

In South Africa: Please write to *Longman Penguin Southern Africa (Pty) Ltd, Private Bag X08, Bertsham 2013*

BY THE SAME AUTHOR

The Heat of the Day

Wartime London and Stella's lover, Robert, is suspected of selling information to the enemy. Harrison, shadowing Robert, is none the less prepared to bargain, and the price is Stella.

'Rarely, to my knowledge, has the late flowering of love in war-time been more poignantly described in fiction' – John Hayward in the *Observer*

Eva Trout

'Resonant, beautiful and often very funny . . . Eva is triumphantly real, a creation of great imaginative tenderness' – Julian Jebb in the *Financial Times*

'Rarely have I come across a novel in which sexual frustration (and sexuality) have been so richly and powerfully conveyed' – *Books and Bookmen*

Friends and Relations

In *Friends and Relations*, through nuances of drawing-room comedy, the absurd – potentially explosive – interplay of propriety and passion, Elizabeth Bowen richly earns V. S. Pritchett's tribute that she was 'Daring by nature and intellect and passionate in imagination, compassionate in heart'.

The Last September

'Miss Bowen is amusing and satirical . . . her biting little sketches of social awkwardness or shallowness, her rendering of character by the idiocies of abbreviated conversation, show extraordinary discernment and are extraordinarily funny' – *Observer*

and:

Collected Stories	**The Little Girls**
The Hotel	**To the North**
The House in Paris	**A World of Love**

Oral Epics from Africa

African Epic Series

Thomas A. Hale and John Wm. Johnson, General Editors

Oral Epics from Africa
*Vibrant Voices from a Vast Continent*_____

edited by

John William Johnson
Thomas A. Hale
Stephen Belcher

Indiana University Press
Bloomington and Indianapolis

The paper used in this publication meets the minimum requirements of
American national Standard for Information Sciences—Permanence of
Paper for Printed Library Materials, ANSI Z39.48-1984.

Manufactured in the United States of America

Library of Congress Cataloging-in-Publication Data

Oral epics from Africa : vibrant voices from a vast continent / edited by
John William Johnson, Thomas A. Hale, Stephen Belcher.
p.   cm. — (African epic series)
Includes bibliographical references, map, and index.
ISBN 13: 978-0-253-21110-1

1. Epic literature, African. I. Johnson, John William, date.
II. Hale, Thomas A. III. Belcher, Stephen Paterson, date. IV. Series.
PL8010.072   1997
896—dc21   96-47367

1   2   3   4   5   02   01   00   99   98   97

To the memory of Goosh Andrzejewski
To the memory of Nouhou Malio
And to all our Teachers

And gladly would he learn, and gladly teach . . .

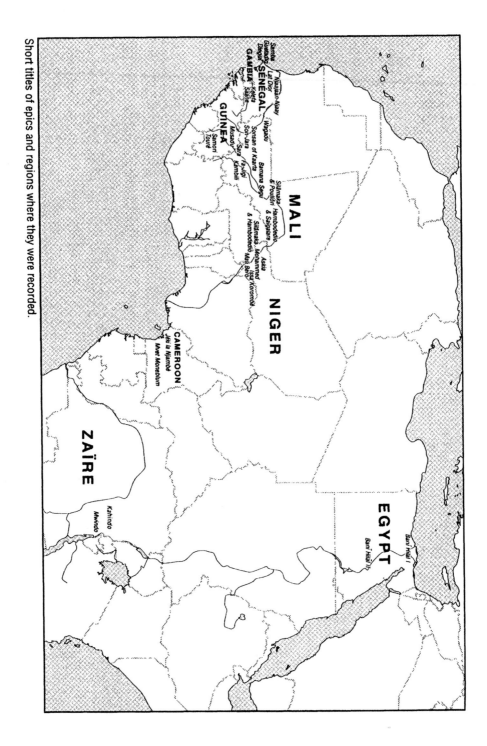

Short titles of epics and regions where they were recorded.

Contents

THIS ANTHOLOGY OF EXCERPTS from twenty-five African epics is the first of its kind to appear in the world and the third volume in the African Epic Series launched by Indiana University Press. It marks a significant step forward in the effort to shift the notion of epic from a Western to a global context. We hope that this volume will inspire readers to delve more deeply into epic traditions in Africa. The purpose of the present text is to offer a broad sample of the extensive epic traditions in Africa and to provide an overview of this important genre on this vast continent.

Books in this series provide affordable volumes of epic texts for a variety of uses. Teachers will find these books helpful for classroom use, and they will prove beneficial in a wide variety of courses where epic texts are needed at both the university and high school levels. Literary scholars who teach courses on the genre of epic will be pleased to have readable, authentic, linear translations of some of the world's great epics. Folklore and anthropology scholars who study the social use of text-based traditions and oral literature will also appreciate these volumes. Scholars of African written literature, who like to begin their courses with the flavor of oral performance, will find this book, and others in the series, inexpensive enough to include on their reading lists. Indeed, students in a wide range of related courses, such as mythology, history, communications, and linguistics will find an astonishing diversity of symbols, images, metaphors, and themes in these excerpts. We hope that all readers will encounter in these texts the same fascination that they hold for us.

Finally, for those who want to examine a particular African epic more thoroughly, scholarly editions of most of these texts exist. Two epics in this series, for example, *The Epic of Son-Jara* (collected, translated, and annotated by Johnson) and *The Epic of Askia Mohammed* (collected, translated, and annotated by Hale), provide complete texts and detailed descriptions. Two other studies that are now very close to completion, a detailed study of African bards (*griots* and *griottes*) by Hale, and another on African epic by Belcher, promise to provide even broader perspectives for the specialist and for the really curious reader with a more complete understanding not only of texts but also of their regional literary contexts and their narrators. When all these publications become available, a really thorough knowledge of epic in Africa will be available to Western reading audiences, long ignorant of the oral performance of this vibrant genre on that vast continent.

At the end of this volume, we have included a general bibliography on the African epic, and for each regional series of epics, the reader will also find short and more specialized listings of sources for further study. The general bibliography will give the reader a more extensive overview of the genre than we can supply here. The specialized listings include titles of more culture-specific works for the reader who wants to examine more closely what lies behind one of the epic traditions. The epic is a multi-functional genre not only for the societies that are reflected in the verbal mirror of its narrative, but also, we

think, for readers outside of Africa. The generalist interested in literature will discover here an extraordinary universe of heroes, battles, and intrigues that matches anything produced elsewhere in the world.

For an anthology as varied and complex as this one, we have many people to acknowledge. We would like to thank the narrators of these texts as well as the collectors, translators, and editors who undertook the difficult task of conveying the oral performance to the print medium. Many of these texts are appearing in print for the first time. We are especially grateful to John Gallman, Director of Indiana University Press, for his sustained encouragement as well as for his patience, which must surely approach that of Job.

Just as the epic is a vast and interactive verbal form, so too we would like readers to consider this book as an opening statement in a continuing and expanding dialogue about the oral epic in Africa. Subsequent editions, with an even more diverse collection of excerpts, will depend on the responses of current and future scholars interested in this form. We would like to hear from you, and we may be reached via Indiana University Press, 601 North Morton Street, Bloomington, Indiana 47401-3797.

John William Johnson, Indiana University
Thomas A. Hale, The Pennsylvania State University
Stephen Belcher, The Pennsylvania State University

Acknowledgments

THE EDITORS GRATEFULLY ACKNOWLEDGE THE KINDNESS of the following individuals and publishers for granting permission to reprint previously published materials, as well as for permission to publish several original texts. It is through their generosity that this book has been made possible.

The Epic of Wagadu translated by Thomas Hale from mimeographed documents, by permission from Guy Sabouret and Youssouf Tata Cissé for the Fondation SCOA.

The Epic of Son-Jara reproduced from the published version of John William Johnson by permission from John William Johnson and Indiana University Press.

The Epic of Fa-Jigi from unpublished work by David Conrad, reproduced by permission from David Conrad.

The Epic of Bamana Segu reproduced from the published work of David Conrad by permission from David Conrad and the British Academy.

The Epic of Sonsan of Kaarta from unpublished work by David Conrad, reproduced by permission from David Conrad.

The Epic of Almami Samori Touré from unpublished work by David Conrad, reproduced by permission from David Conrad.

The Epic of Musadu from unpublished work by Timothy Geysbeek, reproduced by permission from Tim Geysbeek.

The Epic of Kelefa Saane from published work by Gordon Innes, reproduced by permission from Gordon Innes and the School of Oriental and African Studies, University of London.

The Epic of Kambili from published work by Charles Bird, reproduced by permission from Charles Bird and the African Studies Program at Indiana University.

The Epic of Sara from unpublished work by Charles Bird, reproduced by permission from Charles Bird.

The Epic of Askia Mohammed from published work by Thomas Hale, reproduced by permission from Thomas Hale and Indiana University Press.

The Epic of Mali Bero from unpublished work by Thomas Hale, reproduced by permission from Thomas Hale.

The Epic of Issa Korombé from unpublished work by Ousmane Mahamane Tandina, reproduced by permission from Ousmane Mahamane Tandina.

The Epic of Hambodedio and Saïgalare from published work by Christiane Seydou, translation and reproduction authorized by the Association des Classiques Africains.

The Epic of Silâmaka and Poullôri from published work by Lilyan Kesteloot; translation and reproduction authorized by L'Harmattan.

The Epic of Silâmaka and Hambodedio from published work by Christiane Seydou; translation and reproduction authorized by the Association des Classiques Africains.

The Epic of Samba Gueladio Diegui from unpublished work by Amadou Ly; translation and reproduction authorized by Amadou Ly.

Acknowledgments

The Epic of Njaajaan Nyaay from published work by Samba Diop; reproduced by permission from Samba Diop.

The Epic of Lat Dior from published work by Bassirou Dieng; translation and reproduction authorized by Bassirou Dieng and Editions Khoudia.

The Epic of Banī Hilāl: The Birth of Abū Zayd I from unpublished work by Dwight Reynolds; reproduced by permission from Dwight Reynolds.

The Epic of Banī Hilāl: The Birth of Abū Zayd II from unpublished work by Susan Slyomovics; reproduced by permission from by Susan Slyomovics.

The Epic of Mvet Moneblum from published work by Samuel Martin Eno-Belinga; translation and reproduction authorized by Samuel Martin Eno-Belinga.

The Epic of Jéki La Njambè Inono from published work by Tiki a Koulle a Penda; translation and reproduction authorized by the College Libermann.

The Mwindo Epic from published work by Daniel Biebuyck; reproduced by permission from Daniel Biebuyck and the University of California Press.

The Epic of Kahindo from published work by Daniel Biebuyck and Kahombo Mateene; translation and reproduction authorized by the Académie Royale des Sciences d'Outre-Mer.

The editors would also like to express their gratitude to Nicole Paulin for her assistance with preparation of the index and to David Barnes of Deasey GeoGraphics Laboratory at The Pennsylvania State University for his assistance in the preparation of the map facing the table of contents.

The Existence of Epic in Africa

AFRICAN EPIC TRADITIONS have not attracted much recognition from scholars in literature until recently because of the many barriers, intellectual and physical, that stood between the oral sources and their potential readership. For example, few people outside of Africa know any of the more than 1,000 languages on the continent. Even when a researcher knows one of these languages, it is difficult to transcribe an epic as it is being narrated. One must copy it on audiotape, a technology that came into wide-spread use only in the last few decades. Early collecting efforts, such as those of Leo Frobenius and others, may present the story but do not accurately reflect the performances. The consequence of these obstacles is that African traditions remain less well documented than those of Europe and Asia.

The epic is recognized as a primary genre of world literature. The earliest examples, such as the *Epic of Gilgamesh* or the Greek *Iliad* and *Odyssey*, attest to its age; the Greek literary tradition makes this genre almost equivalent to scripture. The influence of the classical literary tradition has associated the epic with written forms and until recently obscured its occurrence in the oral tradition. Unlike more universal forms of oral folklore, epics do not appear in the literatures of every culture, but they are far more widespread than is generally recognized. Readers will probably be acquainted with the written epics of Europe such as *Beowulf*, the French *chansons de geste*, and the German *Nibelungenlied*; they may also know the Sanskrit monuments of India, the *Ramayana* and the *Mahabharata*, or the Persian *Shahnama* of Firdausi. They are less likely to have firsthand acquaintance with the more recent textual versions of oral traditions, the result of an effort which began in the early nineteenth century with Elias Lönnrot's compilation of the Finnish *Kalevala* and Vuk Karadzic's compilation of Serbo-Croatian heroic narratives and continues to the present day with extensive research into the vast Turkic traditions, the discovery of epics among the Ainu of northern Japan, and the study of vernacular epic traditions in India. They are even less likely to know of African epic traditions, since a number of scholars, in spite of available evidence, have doubted their existence.

An early influential statement on the subject came from Ruth Finnegan in 1970. At the end of a chapter on "Poetry and Patronage" in her landmark study, *Oral Literature in Africa*, she offered a note on epic. She observed that "in the more obvious sense of a 'relatively long narrative poem,' epic hardly seems to occur in sub-Saharan Africa" (p. 108). Her objections were based on current assumptions, some of which were reasonable at the time but have since proven to be inaccurate. At the time of the publication of her book, there was very little evidence for the occurrence of epic in Africa for a number of reasons. First, compared to later decades, few epic texts had yet been collected and published; and second, almost all had been reconstructed into "novel-like" prose. Moreover, a number of collectors had published poems that purported to be epic but that were in fact panegyric, one of the dominant

forms of African folklore, related but not identical to epic. Finnegan was also attempting to lay to rest the Western prejudice, born in theories of social evolution, that "epic is often assumed to be the typical poetic form of non-literate peoples . . . at a certain stage" (p. 108), and she concluded that "epic poetry does not seem to be a typical African form" (p. 110).

Finnegan's objection raised immediate protests. In successive order, Daniel Biebuyck ("The African Heroic Epic"), Isidore Okpewho (*The Epic in Africa*), and John Wm. Johnson ("Yes, Virginia, There Is an Epic in Africa") provided diverse critical responses. The best answer, of course, has been the publication of the evidence for African epics. In the past two decades scholars from Africa, Europe, and North America have recorded, transcribed, translated, and published many epic texts. Many of these texts, however, are inaccessible to a general public or only available in languages other than English. This volume represents the first attempt to assemble a representative selection of examples from the epic traditions of Africa. Our hope is to acquaint readers with the wealth of material available and to open the door for further recognition and study.

African Literature

Before focusing on the nature of African epic, we must place the study of the genre in the broader context of African literature. For many people, the notion of "African literature" still seems curious: they envision the Darkest Africa of Henry Stanley, an impenetrable jungle inhabited by isolated "tribes" speaking incomprehensible "dialects" and endowed with the most primitive level of material culture. It is an image reinforced by writers as diverse as Edgar Rice Burroughs, author of *Tarzan*, and Joseph Conrad, whose *Heart of Darkness* survived for generations on the reading lists of freshman English courses in the United States. If African peoples did not appear to have a literature, then it followed that they had no history either. Such a view was expressed by Hegel in the nineteenth century and was affirmed as late as 1963 by the historian Hugh Trevor-Roper.

Today, as both African literature and history emerge from behind a veil of ignorance maintained by the West, there are still questions about the definition of oral literature. Literature, after all, is based on the notion of "letters" and thus of writing. For some, the formulation "oral literature" is an offensive oxymoron. Modern African literature has found a more hospitable reception in the last three decades. Produced in the languages of the colonial powers (English, French, Spanish, Portuguese) and shaped in the genres of their European models (poetry, novels, plays), these literatures often appear as an extension or a variant of the respective European literature. In the last decade three writers from Africa have won the Nobel Prize for Literature (Soyinka in

1986, Mahfouz in 1988, Gordimer in 1991). The names Achebe, Ngugi, Sembène, Senghor, Kourouma, and Bâ now appear frequently on reading lists in universities around the world. But the relation of these emerging new literatures to their African roots and their accessibility to African audiences remains a subject of much discussion.

There are also literatures in Arabic produced in North and West Africa that draw on a variety of traditions. Written literatures in Swahili, Hausa, Amharic, and Fulfulde predate the arrival of Europeans. In many cases these literatures grew out of the introduction of Islam and the spread of literacy for local needs. But the elements of African verbal art most invisible to the outsider are those forms still transmitted through the oral tradition—in person, on the radio, and via cassettes. They do not necessarily conform to the accepted genres of European literature, for they exist within different social constructs and world views. To fully appreciate them, one must know their original languages and study the social organizations from which they emerge. All too often, anthropologists and folklorists are the only ones to invest the required time and effort to accomplish these goals.

To grasp the truly African element of African literature, we must turn to the oral forms of their verbal art and respect the diversity produced on a continent-wide scale. We cannot rely upon isolated, anecdotal images of single groups; nor should we be guided by our preconceptions or the familiarity of certain forms. And we must not be influenced by the poorly translated and highly selective publication of children's oral literature published by missionaries and others in the nineteenth and early twentieth centuries.

The African Epic Belt

Epics do not occur everywhere. They are the products of a combination of social and historical circumstances and various verbal genres. The opportunity to explore the roots of such a phenomenon is one of the great contributions Africa can make to the world-wide study of oral epic traditions. In various works, John Wm. Johnson has studied the documented appearances of epic across Africa (Johnson 1978, 1981). He has postulated the existence of an "African Epic Belt," running across the Sahel and down into Central Africa. The epics collected within this region possess features that link them with each other, although not necessarily in a continuous and historically related tradition. These traits set them apart from the widely documented panegyric tradition of Eastern and Southern Africa, as well as from the Arabic traditions of North Africa. Within this volume, however, we have been able to expand the boundaries of the epic belt as originally conceived, a process which we hope will continue as more and more information about the existence of this genre in Africa becomes available.

The term epic has often been applied to any tradition that is

"national" or "heroic," regardless of form and length. The texts included here do not reflect this wider usage of the term. For instance, the Akan drum histories of their kings have not been included, although they may be viewed by some scholars as epics. We hope that our volume may inspire continuing lively discussions on the meaning of this term, as well as the publication of more texts recorded from the oral tradition.

Sources

Researchers encounter many difficulties in the translation of oral performances to book form. Some have proposed solutions ranging from variations in typography to extensive annotation. This volume offers no radically innovative solutions. Ideally, one should expect a "text" to represent the accurate transcription of an artist's production at a "natural" or "induced natural" performance (i.e., an occasion for which such a performance would be expected within the culture of origin). The printed text should reproduce faithfully the various elements of the performance: principal narrator, supporting personnel—backup singers, respondents, patrons, and intrusive audience members—as appropriate. But such texts are not always available; nor, often, are they accessible to a foreign audience unacquainted with the local idioms, norms, and expectations. One must strike a balance between the ideal representation of a communal event and the literary and textualized presentation of a verbal tradition. Such a balance requires the audience, in this case the readers, to attempt to recreate the performance context in their own minds.

Our concern has been to provide texts whose origin from the oral tradition can be reliably traced. We should know the name of the performer and the circumstances of the performance. We should have available the original language transcription (if not a tape). But our concern is also to recognize the material already available and the research of the scholars who have worked so hard to process these texts. In a few cases we have translated from a French version of the original transcription. Where possible, we have checked these translations with the collectors and editors who worked with the original recording in an African language. We feel that our inclusion of these selections justifies itself from the intrinsic merits and importance of the material, as well as from the stature as African men-of-letters of the individuals involved: Amadou Hampaté Bâ, in one case, and Samuel-Martin Eno-Belinga in another. We have also drawn on the recent collection efforts of scholars and their unpublished texts, for example the epic of Samori collected by David Conrad.

But the principal concern that has been respected is that the selections be traced, by whatever route, to an original performance. We do not present reconstructed conflations of variants or the transcriptions

of anonymous informants. We wish to credit the original artists whose performances we are attempting to bring before a wider public.

Regional Similarities

Through this collection, we wish to lead the reader to an appreciation of the nature of local, regional, and universal traditions. For example, within the vast Mande world of West Africa, and in its neighboring and related areas (the Songhay, for example), one finds considerable cultural continuity as the result of two thousand years of contact through wars, trade, migrations, famines, and droughts. One is entitled to describe the features of this region, in Paul Stoller's term, as elements of a "Deep Sahelian Civilization." We must recognize that one feature common across this space is the narrator, the bard or *griot*, known by a variety of local names: *gewel, gawlo, jali, jeli, mabo, geseré, jeseré,* and others.

The Central African traditions are somewhat different. The link with human social and political institutions is less prominent. Instead, the epics present prodigious heroes with supernatural powers who move through an essentially mythical landscape. There are some exceptions—for example, the Mvet Moneblum reveals concerns that are also purely human. The style of performance is also distinctive. In this general region, the performances are far more dramatic and involve a wider cast. The lead performer will move about, miming the actions of his subjects, and he will be accompanied by musicians and singers as well as by the audience.

The contrast of the intercalated lyrics and the ongoing narrative has led some collectors in the region to present their material as prose rather than in set lines, as is the standard practice for West African texts. This difference raises a number of questions about textualizing epics, and needs to be studied in more detail. On a deeper and so for unexplored level, one can perceive similarities between the precocious heroes, Mwindo of the baNyanga or Lianja of the Mongo, and the troublesome children of the Sahel, such as Maren Jagu of *La dispersion des Kusa* or even Sun-Jata, bone-breaker and uprooter of baobabs. Within the local context, these Central African narratives also present an image of the past that is in many ways the functional equivalent of what we see in the Sahelian epics.

Inclusion of the North African epics opens the door to comparisons of the Arabic and sub-Saharan epic traditions. We offer no hypotheses here on influences or parallels, but we invite study of the question. The geographic proximity and elements of the narrative material—for example, Abū Zayd, like another Arabian hero, Antar, is black—suggests that such study might be richly rewarded.

Women and Epic

The world of the epic appears at first to be dominated by men. One soon discovers, however, that the heroes of many of these epics—Son-Jara and Askia Mohammed, for example—depend on women both in childhood and later at key points in their lives. One question emerges from the role of women in the epic: do women griots also recount epics? When asked if women narrate epics, male griots usually respond that the role of women is to sing songs, not epics. The man may sing or speak the narrative, while women contribute songs at the appropriate points during the same performance. In Central Africa, the very sketchy evidence available to us at this point suggests that women there may fit more easily into the role of performers of long narrative poems.

There is a growing debate, led by Lucy Durán, over this apparent gender division in the epic. The discussion is in some ways clouded, because local sources do not distinguish clearly between praises, sung by both men and women, and narrative, traditionally the province of men. Durán argues that women will sing an entire epic if no man is available for the task. Although no epic by a woman has appeared in print, Durán reports that some songs by women extend over long periods of time—as much as two hours—and contain in essence all of the elements of epic. The short narrative by the late Siramory Jabaatè, one of the most famous Malian griottes, or *jelimusow*, that we have included, gives some idea of the nature of epic songs by women. Future research on this question by Durán and other scholars will provide, we hope, evidence to explain more clearly the role of female bards in relation to the epic.

Definitions of Epic

Ruth Finnegan based her skepticism about the epic in Africa on formal criteria. She felt, essentially, that in many regards the examples she had examined of African epic at the time did not match the characteristics displayed by Eurasian examples of the genre. We do not wish to assert that African epic is identical to Eurasian traditions—such an assertion, in fact, would diminish the interest of these texts for a wider community. John Wm. Johnson has outlined features which he finds common to African epic and useful for analysis. Epics are poetic narratives of substantial length, on a heroic theme (so far we are on familiar territory); they are also multigeneric and multifunctional, incorporating more of a community's diversity than might have been expected; and they are transmitted by culturally "traditional" means. They are not the overnight creation of visionaries, whatever the role of individual creativity in the generation of a specific performance version.

The term epic, deeply rooted in the Western literary tradition, certainly fits the texts we present here; but readers need to keep in mind that the peoples who produced these African epics have their own words and generic boundaries for this genre. Just as we have employed the regional and global words griot and bard along with more ethno-specific terms such as *jali* to identify the narrators of some epics, we feel it is time for scholars to learn more about the particular ethno-poetic features represented in local terms for these texts. The Wolof term for epic is *cosaan* or *woy jallore*, praise song, tale of great exploits, and gene-alogical song (Kesteloot and Dieng, 1989, 13). For the Fulbe, it is *hoddu* (epic story as well as the lute played to accompany it; Seydou, 1972, 47). Among the Moors, who have a very rich and complex tradition of both oral and written poetry produced by different members of society, *thaydina* is a musical and poetic form of some length that contains both praises and accounts of deeds. It is sung mainly by *iggawen*, griots from the sub-Saharan oral tradition (Guignard, 36; Norris, 41). For the diverse peoples of the Mande world, there are many different terms. In the Mandinka region of The Gambia, *tariko* refers to spoken narratives. In Upper Guinea, David Conrad reports that *tariku* is commonly applied to long narratives. Both of these words come from the Arabic term for history, *tārīkh*. Elsewhere, for example among the Bamana and Maninka, the most common words for epic are *wasala* or *maana*. *Wasala* suggests completeness, inclusion, and thorough interpretation of all events and people in the narrative. *Maana*, a more typical term for epic, does not imply such great detail. In Songhay, the noun for a long narra-tive is *deeda*, or story about the past that often involves a blend of gene-alogy and narrative. Other terms in Central Africa include the *mvet* among the Fang and related peoples of Cameroon and Gabon, *munia* for the Jéki tradition of the Douala in coastal Cameroon, and *karisi* for the baNyanga performances. The variety of terms for long poetic narratives suggests that we need to redefine the notion of epic from a global rather than a Western perspective. Let us read the texts first and then derive the definitions.

Epic and History

Many of the heroes portrayed in epics have been described in documents ranging from medieval chronicles written in Arabic (*Askia Mohammed*) to French colonial reports from the late nineteenth century (*Lat Dior*). Those who read these texts for the first time, as well as Afri-canist historians who are quite familiar with the societies portrayed, often want to know what is of historical value in them. Attempts to reconstruct the past from these oral epics are severely limited, however, by a wide range of factors influencing the performance—the origin of the narrator, his or her knowledge of the different traditions, patterns of migration in the region, the location of the performance, the relation-

ship of the bard to the audience, and the biases of the listeners. A version of the Sunjata epic in Kita, Mali, may differ considerably from one recounted in Brikama, The Gambia, for all the reasons cited above.

A more productive approach to the question of historicity is to view these epics as windows on the past that reflect contemporary values conveyed by one group in society, the narrators, who have a vested interest in promoting a particular version of events. That interest is closely tied to the patrons of these wordsmiths and to complex clan relationships. If we frame the question of historicity in a much broader temporal and geographical context, where the image of the past may change from generation to generation (example: African American history today versus that which appeared in textbooks half a century ago) or from people to people (example: British versus Russian views of who won World War II), then we can begin to understand why there may be such variability among performances of the same epic.

Our view of the historicity of epics may differ from that of many African listeners for whom the version of the past recounted by a griot constitutes the accepted representation of events. But we share both a common appreciation of the verbal art displayed by the narrators and a keen awareness that at bottom all historical accounts, written or oral, are interpretations of events subject inevitably to variation, revision, and reinterpretation, depending on who is telling the story and to whom it is recounted.

Terminology

The reader of these epics will quickly discover a confusing inconsistency in terminology and spelling for ethnic groups, places, and other terms. There are several reasons for this lack of a common nomenclature. First, the parts of Africa represented in this anthology reflect various external influences. The Wolof, Mande, and Songhay texts, for example, all come from French-speaking Africa, but Mandinka texts tend to come from English-speaking Africa. We have adopted French or English spellings depending on the country of origin of the text. But some of our contributors, notably Conrad, an American, have used English spellings in place of French when editing texts from French-speaking countries—for example Segu instead of Ségou. At other points, readers will note several different spellings for spirits known in English as genies—djinns, jinns, etc. Again, we have decided to maintain the original spelling in the text. A more complex problem arises with the names of peoples. The Bamana have long been known as Bambara to the outside world. The Fulbe are sometimes called Fulani, Fula, Poular, and Peulh, and they speak the Fulfulde language. The Maninka, a Mande people, are called Malinké by the Fulbe, a term that has been adopted by the French for that people. Within these groups, there is considerable variation depending to a large extent on who is talking

and the distance between his or her maternal language and the local lingua franca. The Zarma, for example, speak a dialect of Songhay that is fully understandable by anyone who speaks that language. But the Zarma refer to their language as Zarma not Songhay. For comparison, note that Americans say they speak English, but when a French translator translates an American novel into French, the cover page reads "traduit de l'américain"—translated from American.

Another variation occurs in the names of clans. Diarra, a province of the ancient empire of Ghana as well as the name of a clan, is also spelled Jarra. The Keita clan is sometimes spelled Keyta by English speakers, and the village of Kéla in Mali is often spelled Keyla by anglophones. The profession of griots not only has different names, as indicated above under regional similarities, but also different spellings—for example *dieli, djeli,* and *jeli* for griot in the central Mande area, and *djali* or *jali* in the western Mande.

Another kind of vocabulary that may be confusing at first falls into the category of ideophones, which we have not attempted to translate. These are words that convey movement or action by their sound. An example in English would be "plop" for when something falls on the floor. The reader will find many different ideophones from a variety of languages in these excerpts—*bilika* (sound of weeping), *faat* (sound of an arrow striking), *bari* (sound of speed), *wuu* (sound of musket firing), and *farak* (sound of a horse drinking). In nearly every case, the context will help the reader to understand the ideophone. We might have modified all of these diverse terms to fit a uniform linguistic pattern. But such an approach would have done violence to the texts that we are including and would have robbed the reader of a full appreciation of the great diversity that marks the world of epic in Africa.

Finally, a few words of explanation about the use of the word tribe are necessary. "Tribe" is one of those anthropological terms that has taken on an extraordinarily wide range of meanings outside that field. Anthropologists cannot agree on just what it means, though the terms "common language" and "common ancestor" turn up often in attempts to define it. In the historical context, a people living as a tribe were usually viewed as fairly low on the scale of social development. Thus, until recently, it was quite common for scholars and journalists to use tribe in referring to Africans. Tribalism still appears in the media as the bane of African countries. In some parts of Africa a space for tribe is included on passports, and many Africans use tribe to describe their own peoples. The Bedouins, who are the source of the Banī Hilāl epics, refer to their own people as members of tribes. But today tribe is too vague a descriptor for most other contexts. The extent of the controversy over the use of tribe can be seen in the large number and generally negative tone of message postings in May and June 1995 on the H-Africa electronic network based at Michigan State University (H-Africa@ MSU.EDU). The British Broadcasting Corporation and the Library of Congress have dropped the term as a descriptor for Africans. With few

exceptions, then, we have adopted other words such as clan, people, ethnic group, or nation, to refer to the extraordinarily diverse collectivities that have produced these epics.

Presentation of the Texts

With such a diverse collection of texts, we have not imposed a particular format on our contributors. For many of the epics, a series of excerpts linked by transitional paragraphs written by the collectors or translators provides the flavor of the narrative in the few pages available. For shorter narratives, the entire text has been included. In a few cases—Charles Bird's excerpts from *Kambili* and the full text of *Sara*—the commentary is somewhat more extensive than for others because of the density or unusual nature of the narrative. Throughout, we have attempted to respect the original format. For some epics, the breaks between lines or sections simply indicate a pause. In other cases, however, these spaces reflect a shift from one episode to another or the omission of lines. The reader can judge from the sequence of line numbers whether the break indicates a pause or a shift to a new section of the epic.

We have adopted the same line numbers that appear in the original, but with a few exceptions—for example, the prose texts from Central Africa are not numbered. Two of the three Fulbe epics (*Silâmaka and Poullôri* and *Silâmaka and Hambodedio*) did not have line numbers in the original, so we have added them for the excerpts. The third Fulbe text, *Hambodedio and Saïgalare*, carries line numbers in the original, but for typographic reasons they do not distinguish between lines and line fragments. In the excerpts provided here, we have chosen to recount runover fragments as part of the line to which they belong rather than as separate lines. For this reason, our numbering system does not match the original. The problems of line numbering reflect in microcosm the highly complex task of transforming a recording of an epic to the print medium. Our goal is to facilitate the activities of reading, discussion, and analysis of these narratives.

We hope that this brief introduction to the issues rooted in the study of African oral epics, as well as the excerpts from the texts that follow, will inspire readers to explore in more depth both the general subject of this relatively unknown form and the particular traditions presented here. We believe that the excerpts and the references in the bibliography at the end of the volume will enable the reader to discover what we have learned during the past two decades: that the oral epic in Africa represents one of the most vibrant voices from this vast continent today.

PART ONE

WEST AFRICA

The Soninké Epic

THE SONINKE KINGDOM OF GHANA IS THE OLDEST KNOWN West African kingdom on the written record. It was described by Arab travelers in the ninth century a.d. as "the land of gold." With its capital in southeastern Mauritania, Ghana controlled trade in gold, ivory, salt, and slaves between North Africa and the forest region to the south. By the eleventh century, Ghana had declined and was eventually replaced by Mali in the thirteenth century under the rule of Sunjata (Son-Jara). The decline of Ghana had many causes, including wars and draught. Groups of Soninké began to disperse from the eleventh century onward over a large area of the Sahel and Savanna regions. These people, their descendants, fragments of their oral tradition, and in some cases just echoes of their language may be found today from Senegal to Niger. There is some evidence to suggest that Soninké oral traditions may well underlie many of the royal traditions of origin throughout the area.

The Soninké epic tradition, one of the oldest in the region, is not as well recorded as one might wish. At the start of the century, the German anthropologist Leo Frobenius collected a number of traditions on Wagadu and Dama Ngille of Jaara. He believed that he had uncovered a West African *Heldenbuch,* or book of heroes, but his sources, and indeed the language of his texts, are open to question.

The story of Wagadu is the central moment for Soninké history, a period of unity before its fall and dispersal. We have many short versions recorded over the past century. In a recent study, Germaine Dieterlen republished some older accounts, along with an annotated, 453-line text recorded from Diarra Sylla. Our principal lengthy example of Soninke oral performance is excerpted from a 1,220-line narrative by Diaowa Simagha entitled *Légende de la dispersion des Kusa.* It was published by Claude Meillassoux and Lansana Doucouré and gives the origin of a subordinate group of Soninke speakers who are not directly connected with Wagadu. Otherwise, we are left with more fragmentary and regional traditions: the story of Dama Ngille and the kingdom of Jaara, the history of the Kagoro, which in current form appears to reflect historical narration rather than epic performance, and a variety of tales, legends, and songs edited by Oudiary Makan Dantioko and published in often hard-to-obtain formats in 1978, 1982, and 1987.

These and many other examples of the Soninké oral tradition mentioned above convey parts of the legend of Wagadu, the story of how the empire was founded, the role of the Bida snake in providing wealth for its peoples, and the incident that led to the destruction of Ghana. This legend is known among many Soninké-speaking peoples from the Guidimaka region in Mauritania to the Borgu region in northern Benin. In many cases, however, it has been replaced by local oral traditions. We may still recognize historical elements in this legend—the production of gold, the decrease in rainfall, and the migration south toward the Senegal River and then eastward. In some versions, we also encounter historicized myth, incidents borrowed from the Judeo-Islamic tradition, and a unique twist on the pattern of the dragon-slayer story.

3

1. The Epic of Wagadu
Narrated by Diarra Sylla and Jiri Silla

Diarra Sylla text recorded in 1977 in Yéréré, Mali, transcribed and translated into French by Mamadou Soumaré. Jiri Silla text recorded in 1965 in Yéréré by Malamine Cissé, transcribed and translated into French by Abdoulaye Bathily. Each published in separate mimeograph form by the SCOA Foundation for the 1977 Colloquium at Niamey, Niger. This excerpt edited and translated into English by Thomas A. Hale.

THESE EXCERPTS ARE FROM TWO NARRATIVES about the rise and fall of the Ghana Empire, known locally as Wagadu because the first city was the home of the Wago, one of the three main peoples who claim descent from the empire and the group that is most closely associated with its founding.

Although no one has published an epic that gives the full story of the Ghana empire, the following two excerpts from two different versions of shorter narratives, the first by Diarra Sylla, 257 lines, and the second from Jiri Silla, 800 lines, taken together, give the reader the outline of what happened to the people of Wagadu. These texts constitute a partial reconstruction of what must have been a somewhat longer epic about events nine centuries ago.

Because the excerpts from the 1977 texts presented here are divided into separately numbered chapters and come from two different sources, the line numbers do not follow sequentially. But the shift from the first narrator to the second will be indicated below.

[Diarra Sylla first tells his listeners about Dinga Khoré, ancestor of the descendants of the Ghana empire. In this version, they came from India via Yemen and Israel to an unidentified place in Africa approximately 1,000 miles east of present-day Mauritania. Toward the end of his life, Dinga left a message for a vulture to convey to his descendants:]

75 . . . I have a message I would like to entrust to you.
   The vulture replied, "We are at your service."
   Dinga spoke again: "After my death, when all the sacrifices have
      been made, you will tell my descendants to go toward the
      West.
   "There is a place there called Kumbi, there is a well at that place,
      and there is something in the well, people talk with that
      creature, for it is not an ordinary creature, they only settle
      down there after they have reached an understanding with the
      creature in question."

[The vulture transmitted the message to one of Dinga's sons, Djabé Cissé.]

Djabé Cissé asked, "How can one find this place? "

The vulture replied, "You will kill forty fillies for us, one a day.
125 "The lungs and the liver are for me, the vulture, and the remainder
of the meat you will give to the hyena "

[After the sacrifices were made, the vulture explained what the
descendants of Dinga would find at Kumbi.]

... after their arrival at Kumbi, they will find there a well and inside the well a monster.
15 They will be called upon to make a contract with this creature.

[Djabé Cissé and his people set off with the hyena and the vulture for
Kumbi.]

They walked for forty days before reaching Kumbi. At their arrival
the hyena stopped at the edge of a well and the vulture
perched at the top of a tree near the well.
20 The vulture said then to the children of Dinga, "Here is Kumbi,
here is the well."
Then a loud noise arose from the well.
The voice asked who was there, and the vulture replied that they
were the children of Dinga and that they had come to settle
there.
At these words, an enormous snake rose out of the well. He was
very black, he had a crest on his head like that of a rooster, and
the crest was very red.
He said, "No one will settle here."
25 Djabé replied, "We will settle here, for our father at the end of his
life ordered us to come to Kumbi. And this is certainly Kumbi:
here is the well! We shall settle here."
"Agreed!" said the snake called Bida. "But there are conditions for
that."
Djabé declared then, "We are ready to listen to these conditions."
"Fine!" replied Bida.
"Each year," he said, "in the seventh month, on the seventh day of
the seventh month, you will offer me 100 heifers, 100 fillies,
and 100 girls."
30 "Agreed," said Djabé, "but each year, the loss of 100 heifers, 100
fillies, and 100 girls will amount to the ruin of the country."
They bargained and finally agreed on one filly and one girl—but
the filly will be the best in the entire country and the girl the
most beautiful in the entire country.

[Djabé won the title of King of Wagadu as the result of a competition to
lift four heavy drums. The snake then gave him conditional power to
rule.]

47 When Djabé was installed as ruler, Bida declared to him that he
   would be supplied with people and goods as long as he honors
   the contract that linked them together.

[The Jiri Silla version follows from here on. When the time for the
sacrifice came next year, the people prepared themselves.]

15 At the end of the rainy season, in the seventh month and on the
   seventh day, all the people gathered and the sacrifice was
   carried out.
   The morning of the sacrifice, the morning of the solemn day, everyone turned up before the door of the ruler, drummers as well as
   citizens, all gathered in this spot.

18 As for the girl, she was already dressed, dressed in such an extraordinary way that you had to see it to appreciate it.
   The filly was so fat that it was beyond commentary.

25 When they arrived near the well, the cortege divided in two.
   The griots were always in front of the ruler, competing with each
   other in turn until they arrived at the edge of the well.

28 Before the griots could return to the ruler with their songs, Bida the
   snake suddenly surged out of the well and made a terrifying
   loud noise.

[After coming out and going back into the well twice, the snake
appeared again for a final time.]

30 He wrapped himself around the girl and the filly; he carried them
   into his lair.
   The ruler and his people returned to the town.

[The snake kept his promise. Gold rained down on the country and the
people prospered. But during the annual sacrifice to Bida another year,
after the third appearance of the snake from the well, a man attacked
it.]

690 Mahamadu the Taciturn cut off his head with his saber.
   At the very moment his head fell away, the serpent cried out:
      "Seven stars, seven luminous stars,
   "Seven famines, seven great famines,
   "Seven rainy seasons, seven entire rainy seasons,
   "No rain will fall in the country of Wagadu.
695   "And even less gold.
   "People will say that Mahamadu the Taciturn ruined Wagadu!"

[After the flight of the Wagadu people from the land, some of them returned home to see what was left.]

    They found that everyone was dead.
775 Wagadu emigrated.
    It divided into three groups.
    One went along the banks of the river.
    One group headed toward the Sahel.
    And the third left by the middle way.
780 The one that left by the middle maintained the use of the Soninké language.

[Today, all that remains at Kumbi are some ruins. But the Soninké people live on in many parts of the Sahel from Senegal to Niger. An archaic form of their language has become the occult tongue of Songhay sorcerers and griots.]

Mande Epics

THE MANDE PEOPLES MAY BE DEFINED either linguistically, as a group of peoples speaking closely related languages, or historically, as a group of peoples defined by belief in a common origin, generally centered on the towering figure of Sunjata (Son-Jara in the version presented in this anthology), the thirteenth-century hunter-warrior-hero who founded the empire of Mali. The epic of Son-Jara is the best known example of this rich epic tradition and may be the most important piece in some respects, but it hardly represents the full range of possibilities found from The Gambia to Segu, from the Sahara to the forests of Côte d'Ivoire and Sierra Leone.

Some distinctions apply within the corpus. Most of the pieces are performed by *jeliw*, musicians who are members of hereditary status groups; the jeli functions within the community as a repository of shared, public, historical and genealogical knowledge (as opposed to private, familial traditions) and verbal arts. In the past, specific alliances linked noble and jeli clans and lineages, and the patron-retainer relationship was personal as well as commercial; the jeli served as confidential advisor as well as entertainer. Those days and patterns of patronage are gone, and the jeli now seeks a living where it may be found, though some jeli clans cling to old ways and claim a relationship to a noble clan, as do the Jabaatè clan of Kela, who remain loyal to the Keytas.

Another entirely separate epic tradition also exists among Mande peoples, that of the *dònsòn-jeliw* or hunters' bards, who are not jeliw by birth; they serve as bards for initiatory societies such as the hunters' groups or the Komo; such a one was Seydou Camara, the blacksmith, singer of *Kambili* and *Makantaga Jigi (Fa-Jigi)* in this anthology. In such a case, talent, practice or training, as well as knowledge of the occult and loyalty to a specific group or groups, define the role of the bard.

A similar distinction may apply to the corpus of performed pieces. Many are said to be historical in reference. These epics and songs are generally the product of the hereditary performers, the jeliw. Others are less time-bound and perhaps more popular both as to the story line and to a performance style which will readily incorporate songs and even some forms of dancing.

The selection of texts presented here offers a geographical and generic sampler of the Mande epic traditions. The tradition of Son-Jara is represented by a Maninka version from Kita in present-day Mali. Kelefa Saane comes out of The Gambia; this hero is typical of the bellicose aristocracy of the nineteenth century, remembered across West Africa as a time of tumult and war. Almami Samory Turé, coming on the scene somewhat later, was a war-leader from Upper Guinea and undoubtedly the fiercest opponent of French colonial penetration. He was indeed the most effective ruler the region had seen for some time. Musadu comes from a region lying southwest of Samory's territory, in modern Sierra Leone; the epic is comparable to that of Kelefa Saane in its local focus

and style of presentation. The same is true of the epic of the Kaarta, which, together with the epic of Bamana Segu, takes us to the eastern fringe of the Mande world.

The epic of Bamana Segu is but a small portion of a wide and rich epic cycle dealing with the history of the kingdom that arose along the middle Niger in the early eighteenth century, under Biton Kulibali, and lasted some 150 years until it fell to the advance of the Islamic Fulbe and Tukolor. The cycle may be divided into many discrete episodes (particularly for the stories of the conquests of Segu), but is also presented as a grand and finite unit by its performers. Tayiru Banbera was a widely recognized and talented performer, and his version of the cycle is perhaps the most circumstantial and detailed available.

Seydou Camara, blacksmith, French army veteran, and hunters' bard extraordinaire, was a well-documented performer and a widely respected master of occult lore. The pieces presented here come from his adopted function of singer; *Kambili* is a classic hunters' tale which involves mastering the bush not through physical strength, but through the proper regulation of social relations and the discovery of secrets of power. *Makantaga Jigi (Fa-Jigi)* is, in some sense, the legend of origin for the occult power, which moves so much of Mande spiritual thought. The legend serves as a myth of origin for blacksmiths but is recognized beyond that group as an account of the introduction of magical knowledge into the Sahel.

The world of Mande oral tradition goes well beyond the canonized figure of Son-Jara, and we are fortunate that it has been relatively well documented so that we can provide such a diversity of texts. Each of the following texts, of course, is but the tip of a greater tradition. Beyond Kelefa Saane one finds a generation of Mandinka heroes in The Gambia. Accompanying Samori one finds his generals and his brother. In Segu we have a series of four kings and innumerable conquests. And finally, the corpus of the hunters' bard is potentially infinite. The traditions of performance and content change in response to new conditions brought about by recording technology and the transformation of the micro-economy, but they are not dying. They remain vital and enthralling.

While on one level, the Mande world is marked by broad cultural unity over great space and time, one should also note a number of tensions and divisions within the society, identified by analysts and recurring within the texts that follow. Within the frequently polygynous family, two tendencies may be observed: *badenya*, or 'mother-childness,' a spirit of unity and cooperation which marks the children of the same mother and binds them together; and *fadenya*, or 'father-childness,' which points to two sources of rivalry and tension—against the half-siblings, with whom one competes, and also, in the case of the sons, with the father whom one will strive to surpass. *Fadenya* is seen as a spirit of competition and ambition; it may lead to success, but it may also be socially disruptive.

9

Within the society at large, a number of other distinctions recur. The nobles, *hòròn*, will consider themselves above all others; their ancestry is free of the taint of servility or of professional status. The professional status groups, known collectively as *nyamakalaw*, have elicited copious analysis and discussion. The term "caste" has been used in reference to these groups, as a consequence of their endogamy; but we consider it inappropriate. The names of the different groups involved describe professions or economic activities, and these recur throughout the epic selections presented below. The *jeli*, or bard/griot, is the master of verbal arts, the praise-singer, the loremaster, genealogist, and mediator between troubled parties—and the source of our texts. The *numu* is the blacksmith, a figure of great occult power and authority. The *garangè*, or leatherworker, is less visible and claims a Soninké origin; the *kule*, woodworkers, are equally low profile. Finally, one should mention the *finè* (*funè*), who appear to be professionally related to the jeliw in that they are bards of a sort; but their specialization is not local genealogy but Islamic lore outside the recognized Muslim lines of authority.

2. The Epic of Son-Jara
Narrated by Fa-Digi Sisòkò

Recorded in Kita, Mali, on March 9, 1968, by Charles Bird. Transcribed and translated into English by John Wm. Johnson with the assistance of Charles Bird, Cheick Oumar Mara, Checkna Mohamed Singaré, Ibrahim Kalilou Téra, and Bourama Soumaoro. Edited by John Wm. Johnson, published by Indiana University Press in 1986 as The Epic of Son-Jara: A West African Tradition, *and reprinted with a new introduction in 1992 as the first volume in the African Epic Series. This excerpt edited by John Wm. Johnson.*

THE EPIC OF SON-JARA (SUNJATA, SOUNDIATA) KEYTA celebrates the exploits of the founder of the empire of the Manden, Old Mali, some 750 years ago. It is recited in several languages, among which are Mandinka, Bamana (Bambara), Jula, Khasonke, Wangara, and Maninka (Malinké). Professional bards (*jeli, jali*), well known to some readers by their French designation *griot*, recite this epic over a widespread area in West Africa: Mali, Senegal, The Gambia, Guinea, Guinea-Bissau, northern Côte d'Ivoire, northern Liberia, southern Mauritania, and anywhere else the well-traveled bard can find an audience of Mande language speakers in the commercial centers of West Africa and Europe.

Running some 3,084 lines of poetry, this version was recited in 1968 by the renowned bard Fa-Digi Sisòkò in the town of Kita in west central Mali. The plot opens with a remarkably similar structure to that of the book of Genesis in the Bible. It begins in heaven with the creation of Adam and Eve (*Adama* and *Hawa*) and proceeds through genealogies of Islamic and Mande families down to Son-Jara's father, thus establishing his royal heritage. The plot then shifts to another part of Old Mali to pick up the hero's mother's clan and his heritage of occult power from her, later to become the key to his successes as a ruler. The narrative goes on to describe Son-Jara's miraculous birth, his sibling rivalry, his exile and return to power through the defeat of his major adversary, Sumamuru Kantè. A final episode describes the conquest of The Gambia by Tura Magan Tarawere (Traoré), one of Son-Jara's generals.

In the following excerpts, we have selected passages which will take the reader through the career of Son-Jara, who is the most important culture hero of the Mande peoples. Indeed it is the recitation every seven years of a long variant of this epic, which lasts over several days, in the village of Kaaba (Kangaba) in the Mande heartland that acts as a "cultural cement" to many Mande peoples of West Africa by celebrating their common origin.

[The origin of Mali is recounted by the bard from the beginnings of humankind and recounted through the birth of the Prophet Muhammad. The Prophet's third convert and personal servant sired three sons, who go from Mecca to a strange new land and found the kingdom of the Mande. Note the italicized pronouncements to the right of the page.

11

These comments are spoken by the *naamu*-sayer, sometimes an apprentice bard, who represents the audience to the bard by responding after most lines, as is common in speech. Such pronouncements indicate atteniveness to the speaker.]

	Our grandparent Eve and our ancestor Adam,	*Indeed*
155	Conceived some forty times,	*Mmm*
	And begat eighty children!	
	Ben Adam,	*Indeed*
	His first grandchild was Noah,	*Indeed*
	And he had three sons,	
160	Ah, Bèmba!	*Indeed*
	Noah begat three sons:	*Indeed*
	Ham, Shem, and Japheth.	*Indeed*
	Japheth went forth and crossed the sea.	*Indeed*
	His descendants became the Masusu and the Masasa.	*Indeed*
165	Ham, black people descended from him, my father.	*Indeed*
	Shem, the twelve white clans	*Indeed*
	Descended from him.	*Indeed*
170	The Messenger of God, Muhammad, was born,	*Indeed*
	On the twelfth day of the month of Dònba.	*Indeed*
	On the thirteenth day,	
	Tuesday, Bilal was born in Samuda.	*Indeed*
	Ask the ones who know of this.	*Mmm*
175	That Bilal,	*Indeed*
	His child was Mamadu Kanu.	
	That Mamadu Kanu,	*Mmm*
	He had three sons:	*Indeed*
	Kanu Simbon,	*Indeed*
180	Kanu Nyògòn Simbon,	
	Lawali Simbon.	*Indeed*
	That Kanu Simbon and Kanu Nyògòn Simbon,	*Indeed*
	Settled in Wagadugu.	*Indeed*
235	They left Wagadugu,	*Indeed*
	And they went to Jara.	*Indeed*
	They left Jara	*Mmm*
	And went forth to found a farming hamlet,	*Mmm*
	Calling that village Farmtown.	*Indeed*
240	That Farmtown is Manden Kiri-kòròni,	*Indeed*
	The very first Manden village was Manden Kiri-kòròni.	*Indeed*
250	Kanu Nyògòn Simbon	*Indeed*
	Begat King Bèrèmu,	*Mmm*
	King Bèrèmu begat King Bèrèmu Dana.	*Indeed*
	King Bèrèmu Dana begat King Juluku, the Holy.	*Indeed*

255	King Juluku, the Holy, begat King Belo Komaan.	*Indeed*
	Belo Komaan begat Juruni Komaan.	
	Juruni Komaan begat Fata Magan, the Handsome.	
	That Fata Magan, the Handsome,	*Indeed*
	Went forth to found a farm hamlet called Kakama,	*Indeed*
	And they called that place, my father, Bintanya Kamalen.	*Mmm*

[The king's second wife, the ugly Sugulun Kutuma, descendant of a powerful sorceress, has come from the faraway land of Du, where she has been given as a prize for the defeat of the same sorceress by a pair of hunters. Fata Magan's personal fetish has told him that the offspring of this wife will bear the most powerful king the Manden will ever know, but he must first convince the hunters to give her to him. He trades her for his sister, Nakana Tiliba. A struggle for the throne ensues, as Fata Magan's two wives, Saman Berete and Sugulun Kutuma, both bear him sons nearly at the same time.]

	That Fata Magan, the Handsome,	
	He married the daughter of Tall Magan Berete-of-the-Ruins,	
	Called Saman Berete, the Pure.	*Mmm*
265	They called her Saman Berete.	*Indeed*
	She had not yet borne a child at first.	*Indeed*

[Speaking to the hunters, King Magan, the Handsome, says:]

	"You must give me your ugly little maid."	
	That token was added to Nakana Tiliba,	
	Exchanging her for Sugulun Kòndè.	*Indeed*
	It is said that Fata Magan, the Handsome,	
1045	Took the Kòndè maiden to bed.	*Mmm*
	His Berete wife became pregnant.	*Indeed*
	His Kòndè wife became pregnant.	*Indeed*
	One day as dawn was breaking,	*Indeed*
	The Berete woman gave birth to a son.	*Indeed*
1050	She cried out, "Ha! Old Women!	*Indeed*
	"That which causes co-wife conflict	
	"Is nothing but the co-wife's child.	*True*
	"Go forth and tell my husband	*Indeed*
	"His first wife has borne him a son."	*Indeed*
1055	The old women came up running.	*Indeed*
	"Alu kònkòn!"	*Mmm*
	They replied to them, "Kònkòn dògòsò!	
	"Come let us eat."	*Mmm*
	They fixed their eyes on one another:	
1060	"Ah! Man must swallow his saliva!"	*True*
	They sat down around the food.	*Indeed*
	The Kòndè woman then bore a son.	*Indeed*

	They sent the Kuyatè matriarch, Tumu Maniya:	*Indeed*
	"Tumu Maniya, go tell it,	*True*
1065	"Tell Fata Magan, the Handsome,	
	"Say, 'the Tarawere trip to Du was good.'	*True*
	"Say, 'the ugly maid they brought with them,'	
	"Say, 'that woman has just borne a son.'"	*True*
	The Kuyate matriarch came forward:	*True*
1070	"Alu kònkòn!"	*Mmm*
	They replied to her, "Kònkòn dògòsò!	*Indeed*
	"Come and let us eat."	

[The female bard Tumu Maniya goes to find the king and, like the old women who preceded her, is also invited to eat; but she rejects the food until her message is delivered. The announcing of the birth of Son-Jara first, though he was actually born second, causes the father to designate him as first-born. The old women then burst out their message of the Berete woman's child, but alas, they are too late. The reversal of announcements is viewed as theft of birthright; the Berete woman is furious at the old women, and co-wife rivalry is born for all time.]

	Saman Berete,	
1100	The daughter of Tall Magan Berete-of-the-Ruins,	
	Saman Berete,	*Indeed*
	Still bloodstained, she came out.	*Indeed*
	"What happened then?	
	"O Messengers, what happened?	*Indeed*
1105	"O Messengers, what became of the message?"	*Indeed*
	The Kuyate matriarch spoke out:	
	"Nothing happened at all.*Indeed*	
	"I was the first to pronounce myself.	*Indeed*
	"Your husband said the first name heard,	
1110	"Said, he would be the elder,	*Indeed*
	"And thus yours became the younger."	*Indeed*
	She cried out, "Old women,	*Indeed*
	"Now you have really reached the limit!	*True*
	"I was the first to marry my husband,	
1115	"And the first to bear him a son.	*Indeed*
	"Now you have made him the younger.	*Indeed*
	"You have really reached your limit!"	
	She spoke then to her younger co-wife,	*Indeed*
	"Oh Lucky Karunga,	*Indeed*
1120	"For you marriage has turned sweet.	*Indeed*
	"A first son birth is the work of old,	
	"And yours has become the elder."	*That's the truth*
	The infants were bathed.	*Indeed*
	Both were laid beneath a cloth.	*Indeed*
1125	The grandmother had gone to fetch firewood.	*Indeed*

	The old mother had gone to he . . . , to fetch firewood.	*Indeed*
	She then quit the firewood-fetching place	
	And came and left her load of wood.	*Indeed*
	She came into the hut.	*Indeed*
1130	She cast her eye on the Berete woman,	*Indeed*
	And cast her eye on the Kòndè woman,	*Indeed*
	And looked the Berete woman over,	
	And looked the Kòndè woman over.	*Indeed*
	She lifted the edge of the cloth	
1135	And examined the child of the Berete woman,	
	And lifted again the edge of the cloth,	
	And examined the child of the Kòndè woman.	*Indeed*
	From the very top of Son-Jara's head,	*Indeed*
	To the very tip of his toes, all hair!	*Indeed*
1140	The old mother went outside.	*Indeed*
	She laughed out: "Ha! Birth-givers! Hurrah!	
	"The little mother has borne a lion thief."	*That's true*
	Thus gave the old mother Son-Jara his name.	*Indeed*
	"Givers of birth, Hurrah!	
1145	"The little mother has borne a lion thief.	*That's true*
	"Hurrah! The mother has given birth to a lion thief."	

[At the death of King Magan Fata, the Berete wife's son is declared heir to the throne, disregarding the earlier declaration of Son-Jara as heir. The Berete woman summons a Muslim holy man and has a hex placed on Son-Jara, which causes him to be lame for nine years. In spite of her efforts, however, sign after sign portends that Son-Jara will one day rule the Manden. Finally, the day comes when Son-Jara must overcome the hex and stand on his own two legs.]

	For nine years, Son-Jara crawled upon the ground.	*Indeed*
	Magan Kònatè could not rise.	*Indeed*
1255	In the month of Dòmba,	*Indeed*
	The very, very, very first day,	*Indeed*
	Son-Jara's Muslim jinn came forward:	*Indeed*
	"That which God has said to me,	*Indeed*
	"To me Tanimunari,	*Indeed*
1260	"That which God has said to me,	*Indeed*
	"So it will be done.	*Indeed*
	"When the month of Dòmba is ten days old,	*Indeed*
	"Son-Jara will rise and walk."	*Indeed*
	In the month of Dòmba,	*Indeed*
1265	On its twelfth day,	*Indeed*
	The Messenger of God was born.	*Indeed*
	On the thirteenth day,	*Indeed*
	Jòn Bilal was born.	*Indeed*

15

	On its tenth day,	*Indeed*
1270	Was the day for Son-Jara to walk.	

1290	On the tenth day of Dòmba,	*Indeed*
	The Wizard's mother cooked some couscous,	*Indeed*
	Sacrificial couscous for Son-Jara.	
	Whatever woman's door she went to,	*Indeed*
	The Wizard's mother would cry:	*Indeed*
1295	"Give me some sauce of baobab leaf."	*Indeed*
	The woman would retort,	
	"I have some sauce of baobab leaf,	
	"But it is not to give to you.	
	"Go tell that cripple child of yours	
1300	"That he should harvest some for you.	*Mmm*
	"'Twas my son harvested these for me."	*True*
	And bitterly did she weep: *bilika bilika*.	
	She went to another woman's door;	*Mmm*
	That one too did say:	*Mmm*
1305	"I have some sauce of baobab leaf,	
	"But it is not to give to you.	
	"Go tell that cripple child of yours	
	"That he should harvest some for you.	
	"'Twas my son harvested these for me."	*True*
1310	With bitter tears, the Kòndè woman came back, *bilika bilika*.	

	"King of Nyani, King of Nyani,	
	"Will you never rise?	*Mmm*
	"King of Nyani, King of Nyani,	
	"Will you never rise?	*Mmm*
1315	"King of Nyani with helm of mail,	
	"He says he fears no man.	
	"Will you never rise?	
	"Rise up, O King of Nyani!"	*That's true*

	"King of Nyani, King of Nyani	
1320	"Will you never rise?	
	"King of Nyani with shirt of mail,	
	"He says he fears no man.	
	"Will you never rise?	
	"Rise up, O King of Nyani!"	*True*

1325	"O Wizard, I have failed!"	*True*
	"Ah, my mother,	
	"There is a thickener, I hear, called black *lele*.	*True*
	"Why not put some in my sauce?	
	"'Tis the thickener grown in gravel."	
1330	She put black *lele* in the couscous.	

	The Wizard ate of it.	
	Ma'an Kònatè ate his fill:	*True*
	"My mother,	*Indeed*
	"Go to the home of the blacksmith patriarchs,	*Indeed*
1335	"To Dun Fayiri and Nun Fayiri.	*Indeed*
	"Have them shape a staff, seven-fold forged,	
	"So that Magan Kònatè may rise up."	*Indeed*
	The blacksmith patriarchs shaped a staff, sevenfold forged.	*Indeed*
	The Wizard came forward.	*Indeed*
1340	He put his right hand o'er his left,	
	And upwards drew himself,	*Indeed*
	And upwards drew himself,	
	He had but reached the halfway point.	*Indeed*
	"Take this staff away from me!"	
1345	Magan Kònatè did not rise.	*True*
	In misery his mother wept: *bilika bilika*:	*Indeed*
	"Giving birth has made me suffer!"	*Mmm*
	"Ah, my mother,	*Mmm*
	"Return to the blacksmith patriarchs.	*Indeed*
1350	"Ask that they forge the staff anew,	*Indeed*
	"And shape it twice again in size.	*Mmm*
	"Today I arise, my holy man said."	*Mmm*
	The patriarchs of the smiths forged the staff,	
	Shaping it twice again in size.	*True*
1355	They forged that staff,	
	And gave it to Ma'an Kònatè.	*Indeed*
	He put his right hand o'er his left,	*Indeed*
	And upwards Son-Jara drew himself.	*Indeed*
	Upwards Nare Magan Kònatè drew himself.	*Indeed*
1360	Again he reached the halfway point:	*Mmm*
	"Take this staff away from me!"	
	Ma'an Kònatè did not rise.	
	He sat back down again.	*Indeed*
	His mother wrung her hands atop her head,	
1365	And wailed: "*dendelen*!	
	"Giving birth has made me suffer!"	*True*
	"Ah, my mother,	*Mmm*
	"Whate'er has come twixt you and God,	*Indeed*
	"Go and speak to God about it now!"	*Indeed*
1370	At that, his mother left	
	And went to the east of Bintanya,	*Indeed*
	To seek a custard apple tree.	*Indeed*
	Ah! Bèmba!	*Indeed*
	And found some custard apple trees	*Indeed*
1375	And cut one down.	*Indeed*

	She cut down that staff,	
	Going to give it to Nare Magan Kònatè,	
1405	To the Kòndè woman's child, the Answerer-of-Needs!	*True*
	The Wizard took the staff,	*Mmm*
	And put his right hand o'er his left,	*Indeed*
	And upwards drew himself,	*Indeed*
	And upwards drew himself.	
1410	Magan Kònatè rose up!	*Mmm*
	Running, his mother came forward,	
	And clasped his legs	
	And squeezed them,	*Indeed*
	And squeezed them:	*True*
1415	*"This home of ours,*	
	"The home of happiness.	*Indeed*
	"Happiness did not pass us by.	
	"Magan Kònatè has risen!	*Indeed*
	"Oh! Today!	*Indeed*
1420	*"Today is sweet!*	*Indeed*
	"God the King ne'er made today's equal!	*Indeed*
	"Ma'an Kònatè has risen!"	*Indeed*
	"There is no way of standing without worth.	
	"Behold his way of standing: danka!	
1425	*"O Kapok Tree and Flame Tree!"*	*Fa-Digi, that's true*

[Even more potent signs follow, foretelling that Son-Jara will one day rule the Manden. Finally, Saman Berete convinces her weakling son, the king, that Son-Jara must be exiled from the Manden. He is forced to flee with his mother and his younger sister and brother. After passing through several lands, they settle in Mèma, where eventually messengers come from the Manden to beg his return. In his absence, the sorcerer king of Susu, Sumamuru Kantè, has conquered the Manden and driven his weak brother from the throne. It is at this point that Son-Jara's mother dies, some say in order to enter the next world to better serve him through powerful occult. Son-Jara asks Prince Birama Tunkara of Mèma to give him a place to bury his mother. The king is at first reluctant, but gives in after a veiled threat. Actually, Son-Jara has buried his mother in a secret place so that her amulets will not be stolen by those who would steal her power.]

	Son-Jara looked on the Kòndè woman,	*Indeed*
2450	But the Kòndè woman had abandoned the world.	*Indeed*
	He washed his mother's body,	*Indeed*
	And then he dug her grave,	*Indeed*
	And wrapped her in a shroud,	*Indeed*
	And laid his mother in the earth,	*Indeed*
2455	And then chopped down a kapok tree,	*Indeed*
	And wrapped it in a shroud,	*Indeed*

	And laid it in the house,	*Indeed*
	And laid a blanket over it,	*Indeed*
	And sent a messenger to Prince Birama,	
2460	Asking of him a grant of land,	*Indeed*
	In order to bury his mother in Mèma,	
	So that he could return to the Manden.	*Indeed*
	This answer they did give to him	
	That no land could he have,	
2465	Unless he were to pay its price.	*Indeed*
	Prince Birama decreed,	*Indeed*
	Saying he could have no land,	*Indeed*
	Unless he were to pay its price.	*Indeed*
	He took feathers of Guinea fowl and partridge,	*Indeed*
2470	And took some leaves of arrow-shaft plant,	*Indeed*
	And took some leaves of wild grass reed,	*Indeed*
	And took some red fanda vines,	*Indeed*
	And took one measure of shot,	*Indeed*
	And took a haftless knife,	*Indeed*
2475	And added a cornerstone fetish to that,	*Indeed*
	And put it all in a leather pouch,	*Indeed*
	Saying to give it to Prince Birama,	*Indeed*
	Saying it was the price of the land.	*Indeed, ha, Fa-Digi*

[Prince Birama summons his three sages, All-Seeing-Sage, All-Saying-Sage, and All-Knowing-Sage, to read the signs.]

2495	They untied the mouth of the pouch,	
	And shook its contents out.	*Indeed*
	The All-Seeing-Sage exclaimed,	*Indeed*
	"Anyone can see that!	*Indeed*
	"I am going home!"	*Indeed*
2500	The All-Knowing-Sage exclaimed,	*Indeed*
	"Everybody knows that!	*Indeed*
	"I am going home!"	*Indeed*
	All-Saying-Sage exclaimed,	*Indeed*
	"Everybody knows that?	*Indeed*
2505	"That is a lie!	*Indeed*
	"Everybody sees that?	*Indeed*
	"That is a lie!	*Indeed*
	"There may be something one may see,	
	"But if ne'er explained to him,	
2510	"He will never know it.	*Indeed*
	"Prince Birama,	*Indeed*
	"Did you not see feathers of Guinea fowl and partridge?	
	"They are the things of ruins.	*Indeed*
	"Did you not see the leaf of arrow-shaft plant?	
2515	"That is a thing of ruins.	*Indeed*

"Was not your eye on the wild grass reed?	*Indeed*
"That is a thing of ruins.	*Indeed*
"Did you not see those broken shards?	*Indeed*
"They are the things of ruins.	*Indeed*
2520 "Did you not see the measure of shot?	*Indeed*
"The annihilator of Mèma!	*Indeed*
"Did you not see the haftless knife?	*Indeed*
"The warrior-head-severing blade!	*Indeed*
"Was not your eye on the red fanda vine?	*Indeed*
2525 "The warrior-head-severing blood!	*Indeed*
"If you do not give the land to him,	*Indeed*
"That cornerstone fetish your eye beheld,	
"It is the warrior's thunder shot!	*Indeed*
"If you do not give the land to him,	
2530 "To Nare Magan Kònatè,	
"The Wizard will reduce the town to ruin.	*Indeed*
"Son-Jara is to return to the Manden!"	*That's the truth*
They gave the land to the Sorcerer.	*Indeed*
He buried his mother in Mèma's earth.	

[Son-Jara returns to the Manden and does battle with Sumamuru but cannot overcome him, because his adversary's occult power is stronger than that of Son-Jara. Finally, Son-Jara's sister steals into Sumamuru's camp, seduces him, and learns the key to his power. She returns to Son-Jara and reveals the secret, which Son-Jara uses to overcome Sumamuru.]

Son-Jara's flesh-and-blood-sister, Sugulun Kulunkan,	*Indeed*
She said, "O Magan Son-Jara,	*Indeed*
2670 "One person cannot fight this war,	*Indeed*
"Let me go seek Sumamuru,	*Indeed*
"Were I then to reach him,	
"To you I will deliver him,	*Indeed*
"So that the Manden folk be yours,	*Indeed*
2675 "And all the Mandenland your shield."	*Indeed*
Sugulun Kulunkan arose	*Indeed*
And went up to the gates of Sumamuru's fortress.	*Indeed*
2690 "Come make me your bed companion!"	*Indeed*
Sumamuru came to the gates:	*Indeed*
"What manner of person are you?"	*Indeed*
"It is I, Sugulun Kulunkan!"	*Indeed*
"Well, now, Sugulun Kulunkan,	*Indeed*
2695 "If you have come to trap me,	*Indeed*
"To turn me over to some person,	*Indeed*
"Know that none can ever vanquish me,	*Indeed*
"I have found the Manden secret,	*Indeed*

20

	"And made the Manden sacrifice.	*Indeed*
2700	"And placed it in five score millet stalks,	*Indeed*
	"And buried them here in the earth,	*Indeed*
	"'Tis I who found the Manden secret,	*Indeed*
	"And made the Manden sacrifice,	*Indeed*
	"And in a red piebald bull did place it,	*Indeed*
2705	"And buried it here in the earth.	*Indeed*
	"Know that none can vanquish me,	*Indeed*
	"'Tis I who found the Manden secret,	*Indeed*
	"And made the sacrifice to it,	*Indeed*
	"And placed it in a pure white cock.	*Indeed*
2710	"Were you to kill it,	*Indeed*
	"And uproot some barren groundnut plants,	*Indeed*
	"And strip them of their leaves,	
	"And spread them round about the fortress,	*Indeed*
	"And uproot some more barren peanut plants,	*Indeed*
2715	"And fling them into the fortress,	*Indeed*
	"Only then could I be vanquished."	*Indeed*

2730	He lay Sugulun Kulunkan down on the bed.	*Indeed*
	After one week had gone by,	
	Sugulun Kulunkan spoke up:	*Indeed*
	"Ah, my husband,	*Indeed*
	"Will you not let me go to the Manden,	*Indeed*
2735	"That I may get my bowls and spoons,	
	"For me to build my household here?"	*Indeed*
	From that day to this,	
	Should you marry a woman in Mandenland,	*Indeed*
	When the first week has passed,	
2740	She will take a backward glance,	*Indeed*
	And that is what this custom means. *Yes, Fa-Digi, that's the truth*	
	Sugulun returned to reveal those secrets	
	To her flesh-and-blood-brother, Son-Jara.	*Indeed*
	The sacrifices did Son-Jara thus discover.	*Indeed*
2745	The sacrifices did he thus discover.	*Indeed*

[With these secrets, and with the assistance of Sumamuru's nephew Fa-Koli, from whom Sumamuru has stolen a wife, Son-Jara defeats Sumamuru by neutralizing his occult power. After fleeing Son-Jara's army through several villages, Sumamuru, with his favorite wife, arrives at the banks of the Niger River, where so many significant events take place in Mande folklore. Even in defeat, this great sorcerer cannot die a natural death. And if you go to Kulu-Kòrò even today, you may find the spirit of Sumamuru dwelling in a sacred stone, to which you may pray for a favor.]

	Sumamuru crossed the river at Kulu-Kòrò,	*Indeed*

	And had his favorite wife dismount,	*Indeed*
	And gave her a ladle of gold,	
2865	Saying that he would drink,	*Indeed*
	Saying else the thirst would kill him.	*That's the truth*
	The favored wife took the ladle of gold,	*Indeed*
	And filled it up with water,	*Indeed*
	And to Sumamuru stretched her hand,	
2870	And passed the water to him.	*Indeed*
	Fa-Koli with his darts charged up:	
	"O Colossus,	*Indeed*
	"We have taken you!	*That's the truth*
	"We have taken you, Colossus!	
2875	"We have taken you, Colossus!	
	"We have taken you!"	*Indeed*
	Tura Magan held him at bladepoint.	*Indeed*
	Sura, the Jawara patriarch, held him at bladepoint.	*Indeed*
	Fa-Koli came up and held him at bladepoint.	
2880	Son-Jara held him at bladepoint.	*Indeed*
	"We have taken you, Colossus!	*That's the truth*
	"We have taken you!"	*Indeed*
	Sumamuru dried up on the spot, *nyɔnyɔwu!*	*Indeed*
	He has become the fetish at Kulu-Kòrò.	*Indeed*
2885	The Bamana worship him now, my father.	
	Susu Mountain Sumamuru,	
	He became the sacred fetish.	*That's the truth, indeed, father, yes, yes, yes, yes!*

[Son-Jara now returns to the Manden in glory and governs the land until his death, when his descendants continue to rule over the empire. At this point a number of episodes may follow, describing how Son-Jara's generals conquer vast lands around the Manden, incorporating them into the empire. Son-Jara's own death is a secret that bards of today are not likely to discuss in public but rather keep as a secret. His burial place, which is reported to be in more than one location, is also kept a secret for the same reason that he kept his mother's grave site a secret: so that greedy power-seeking people would not come there and steal his powerful amulets and fetishes.]

3. The Epic of Fa-Jigi
Narrated by Seydou Camara

*Recorded in Bamako, Mali, on September 29, 1975, by David Conrad.
Transcribed and translated into English by David Conrad with the
assistance of Sekou Camara, son of the performer. This excerpt edited by
David Conrad.*

DURING THE CENTURIES WHEN ISLAM was gradually being integrated
into societies of the western Sudan and becoming "Africanized," the
bards or griots, specialists in the oral arts of peoples such as the Soninke
and Malinké, were assimilating elements of Islamic tradition. At the
same time that Islamic elements from across the Sahara Desert were
finding their way into local oral accounts, the western Sudan was
engendering its own Muslim heroes, among whom were some early
Malian kings (*mansaw*) who undertook the arduous trans-Saharan
pilgrimage to Mecca. One of the most prominent of these was Mansa
Musa, who made his historic journey in 1324. The general outline of the
Fa-Jigi legend is probably based on rural, non-Muslim people's
perceptions of pilgrimages to Mecca by high government officials, and
it could have been engendered as early as the fourteenth century,
though the earliest accounts probably differed greatly from those we
know. Pilgrimage stories were recorded in writing by the
mid-seventeenth century, but no traditions mentioning the name Fa-Jigi
were recorded before the colonial era in the late nineteenth century.

In its most general form as presented in many variants, this
narrative begins with Fa-Jigi desiring to atone for a sin, often described
as incest or murder, that sometimes involves his mother. He undertakes
a pilgrimage to Mecca where he acquires the spiritually powerful
medicines, amulets and sacrificial objects of important Mande secret
societies, including the prestigious Komo power association which
serves as a regulatory agency in traditional village life. As the hero
returns through the lands of Mande he distributes various potions and
amulets to the people who help him. Upon reaching the rivers of Mali,
Fa-Jigi uses a magic canoe to transport his spiritually powerful baggage.
When the canoe encounters rough waters, some of the cargo falls into
the water and is transformed into various creatures such as fish and
scorpions. Arriving at home, the location of which varies according to
the informant, the canoe sinks to the bottom of the lake or river where it
remains to this day, itself a spiritual object that receives sacrificial
offerings. It is interesting to note that *jigi*, which means "hope" in
Bamana, is used in a number of word plays in this text, beginning with
Fa-Jigi ("the father of hope").

The narrator of this variant of the Fa-Jigi tradition is the late
Seydou Camara (d. 1983), of Kabaya in the Wasulu region of southern
Mali. He was from a family of blacksmiths that has worked with iron for
many generations. From 1937 to 1945 he was in the French army,
serving in Morocco during World War II. Following the war and many
years of apprenticeship with a master singer, Seydou Camara became

famous in Mali as one of the great singers of hunters' praise music. In the 1960s and 70s, he could often be heard on Radio Mali, which had recorded his music. In some of his performances he would occasionally interrupt his singing to offer an explanation, but all of the lines presented here were sung as he played the hunter's *ngoni*, a large six-stringed harp. In this performance, Seydou Camara was accompanied by his wife, Numuso, who played the *narinya*, a small, ridged, cylindrical, iron percussion instrument.

       The blacksmith,
       The blacksmith ancestor was called Old Fande.
       His first wife was called Fanbukudi.
       No, no blacksmith is older than Old Fande,
5   No blacksmith is older than Old Fande.

       Koroma Numuso,[1]
255   I speak of the smiths.
       Ah, people!
       Eternal life is not possible.
       Kuda Jan Kali[2] gave birth,
       He sired Numuso who plays the *narinya*.
260   Play the *narinya* for me, Numuso.
       Let us look for success and fame in this world, Numuso.
       Death is inevitable, Numuso.
       The other world allows no debts, Numuso.
       Nufaramba is dead, Numuso.
265   Camara Jan[3] has gone back, Numuso.
       Eh! Allah is powerful.
       Ah, people!
       Kali Jan has left the world.
       Koroma-Jigi,[4]
270   Jigi was a smith at Nora.[5]

305   Heeee!
       Koroma-Jigi got up,
       Fa-Jigi.[6]
       Fa-Jigi was handsome as a genie.
       Fa-Jigi was pretty as a European.
310   Fa-Jigi was prettier than a woman.
       Koroma-Jigi,
       The first woman who fell in love with Jigi was his mother.
       She wailed, "Jigi is so handsome,

---

1. The performer's wife. 2. The father of Numuso. 3. Late father of narrator.
4. "Hope of the Koroma." 5. Large town in upper Guinea. 6. "Father of hope."

Jigi's mother had a passion for him.
315 "They say he could not have come from my loins!"
Ah, people!
It was a miracle.
Ah, eh!
Nighttime is bad,
320 Nighttime is bad!
The night is a serious thing.
Fa-Jigi,
Leave the millet beer alone, Fa-Jigi!
Do not drink the millet beer, Fa-Jigi!
325 Do not get drunk, Fa-Jigi!
It is risky to drink, Fa-Jigi!
Koroma-Jigi filled himself with millet beer.
Jigi had no lover at Nora except for one girl.
This girl had gone to a hamlet for millet.
330 She had gone with her father,
Away for the night.
Before Fa-Jigi came home,
His mother took a supporter and fastened it to her breasts.
What else did she do before Fa-Jigi came home?
335 She took a bracelet and attached it to her wrist,
She took some waist-beads and put them around her waist.
On a dark and rainy night,
She went and stretched herself on Jigi's bed.
Ah, people!
340 Man is not equal to Allah.
Koroma-Jigi came home from the millet-beer hut,
And he lay with his mother.
He made her his wife, Fa-Jigi!
Ah, people!
345 Fa-Jigi had an accident.
Heeee!
Jigi did a very bad thing.
Aaah!
Fa-Jigi was upset.
350 Koroma-Jigi had made his mother his wife,
So he decided to go and see the village almami.[7]
Fa-Jigi said "Listen, village almami.
"Almami, I have lain with my mother.
"Almami, how can I avoid the darkness of hell?"
355 "Koroma-Jigi,
"Clear a field beside the road.
"Farm for three years, Fa-Jigi.

---

7. Muslim cleric.

"Give your harvest to the beggars without touching a single
    grain, Fa-Jigi.
"Then your sin will be absolved.
360   "If you cannot farm,
"Go and dig a well in the bush, Fa-Jigi.
"Fill a jar with cool water and put it by the well, Fa-Jigi.
"The thirsty people will come to drink, Fa-Jigi,
"And this will absolve your sin.
365   "Ah, Fa-Jigi,
"You have done wrong.
"If you cannot do that, Fa-Jigi,
"I do not know how to help you."
Fa-Jigi said he was no well-digger.
370   He said he could not farm or make a jar.
The almami said, "Eh!
"Fa-Jigi, if you cannot do all this,
"You must go to Mecca.
"Go to Mecca and wipe out your sin."
375   If it is said that Fa-Jigi went to Mecca,
He did not do it by chance.
Ah, people!
Fa-Jigi did not play around.

Heee!
Allah is a *faama*.[8]
460   Allah refuses to do some things,
But he is never unable to do those things.
They made the necessary sacrifices for Jigi, who must go to
    Mecca.
[His uncle] said, "Heee!
"Koroma-Jigi, go to Mecca,
465   "For you will not meet any danger."
Koroma-Jigi began his trip to Mecca with a ram.
He accepted everything [his uncle] told him.
[His uncle] gave one hundred and fifty bags of gold for Fa-Jigi's
    journey.
"Go on your journey, Fa-Jigi,
470   "The trip to Mecca will be a source of happiness, Fa-Jigi."

Heee!
Koroma-Jigi walked and walked.
Soso Bala Sumanguru told Fa-Jigi to go to Mecca
    and sacrifice four *jigiw*.[9]
Fa-Jigi had only one, the *saka-jigi*,[10]
510   But his uncle said he would find the others along the way.

---

8. King. 9. "(Animals of) hope." 10. "Ram."

Koroma-Jigi walked until he saw a male baboon,
Sitting in the dust of the road.
When the baboon looked up and saw Koroma-Jigi,
It said, "Jigi of men,
515   "You face the east and go *makasi, makasi*.11
"Where are you going?
"Ngon-Jigi,
"Bring your head near me," said Fa-Jigi.
"Anybody who has lain with his mother,
520   "If they do not go to Mecca,
"They will be unhappy, Ngon-Jigi.
"They will begin with hell, Ngon-Jigi.
"They will end with hell, Ngon-Jigi.
"Let us go to Mecca and wipe out our sins, Ngon-Jigi."
525   The baboon said, "Have you not heard about Ngon-Jigi?
"All the children around me were born of the love between my
        mother and me.
"Koroma-Jigi, do not take another step without me,
"Let us go together."
So Ngon-Jigi followed Koroma-Jigi,
530   And the number of *jigiw*12 were three.
The baboon *jigi* walked ahead of the ram *jigi*,
And the man *jigi* followed on the way to Mecca.
Fa-Jigi's journey to Mecca is not a lie, my dear.
It is not a lie,
535   It is not a fiction.
It is not just a song by a player of the hunter's harp.
Koroma-Jigi walked and walked until he found a male
        porcupine,
Crouched in the dust of the road.
Fa-Jigi said, "Eh,
540   "Man of thorns."
The porcupine looked at the *jigi* of men.
He said, "*Jigi* of men,
"Where are you going so fast, *marata, marata*,13
"In the direction of the East?"
545   "Heee, good fellow porcupine,
"I am not lying to you.
"Anybody who has lain with his mother,
"If he does not make a journey to Mecca,
"He will begin with hell, Bala-Jigi,
550   "He will end with hell, Bala-Jigi.
"We are going to Mecca to wipe out our sins, Bala-Jigi.
"We are cursed."
"Ah, people!

11. Sound of footsteps. 12. "Hopes." 13. Sound of footsteps.

The porcupine told his children to choose a *jigi* among them,

555 A new family leader.
He said, "Awa, Koroma-Jigi.
"Do not take another step without me.
"All my children were born of the love between my mother
   and me.
"I will go to Mecca to wipe out my sins."

560 The *jigiw* of Koroma-Jigi were then three,
And he himself was the fourth.
They walked and walked until they met Nkonkodon-Jigi in a
   grassy plain,
Browsing on the fresh grass.
The antelope raised its head to look at Fa-Jigi.

565 "*Jigi* of men you walk quickly.
"Where are you hurrying to, Fa-Jigi?"
"I am going to Mecca," said Fa-Jigi.
"I have lain with my mother and made her my wife;
"I am going to wipe out my sins at Mecca."

570 "Eh, Fa-Jigi," said the antelope.
"You will not go without me,
"Thank you very much.
"My mother has seven children and they are all by me.
"I will go with you to wash away my sins."

575 Ah, people!
Thank the Father of the world for that walk.
They walked until they arrived at Mecca,
On the day of the *boli*[14] market.
There were amulets[15] everywhere in that market,

580 The *boliw*[16] were everywhere that day.
The *boliw* wandered through the market,
And the *Komo*[17] played at tripping them.
Ah!
Fa-Jigi and his people were astonished.

585 There was no sorcery in Mande,
There were no powerful sorcerers in Mande,
There was no Nama Komo in Mande,
The bird dance did not exist in Mande,
There were no stilt-dancers in Mande,

590 There was no Komo in Mande,
There were no magic powders in Mande.
All these things were brought from Mecca by Koroma-Jigi.
Salute the Fula patriarch for clearing many dark ways.

---

14. Power object, fetish. 15. Charms made of knots in a string. 16. "Fetishes."
17. Esoteric initiation society.

The burning deadly things would not have filled
    a red duiker's[18] horn.
595   Eh, weii!
Since Jigi died,
The world has calmed down.
Koroma-Jigi exchanged the antelope for magic powder.
Ah, *naamu*-sayer![19]
600   The porcupine was traded for magic powder.
The ram was traded for magic powder.
Fa-Jigi returned from Mecca with nine horns of magic powder.
Nine birds' heads dangled from his bonnet when he came from
    Mecca.
Fa-Jigi had a bark-dyed sorcerer's bonnet,
605   He had the mud-cloth sorcerer's bonnet,
And he had the sorcerer's shirt.
Fa-Jigi got all those things in Mecca.
Eeeh!
He who imitates a thing is different from the one who really
    owns it.
610   Fa-Jigi did not play around.
Patron, do not play around with the blacksmith's art.
Do your work well for the blacksmiths.
Sorcery came from smithing.
Ah, people!
615   Blacksmithing is no joke.
Eh, wei!
Numu Kulumba,
Jigi who went to Mecca,
He bought so many *boliw* that he could not carry them alone.
620   He asked the people of Mecca to help him find a canoe.
He said "Ah, people!
"There are too many *boliw* for me to carry alone."
They felled a *kolokolo* tree
To make a canoe for Fa-Jigi.
625   He put the *boliw* in the canoe,
Including the *ntamani* drum. [20]
The griot's *ntamani* drum was given to Fa-Jigi,
As well as the stick for playing it.
The *boliw* talk a lot, Fa-Jigi.
630   They are too talkative, Fa-Jigi.
If they break your eardrum,
Play the *ntamani* drum, Fa-Jigi,
Then the *boliw* will shut up, Fa-Jigi.
Hear how Koroma-Jigi's *boliw* chattered:

---

18. Dwarf antelope. 19. Respondant who encourages the narrator. 20. Hour-glass-shaped drum.

635   "Eh, Koroma-Jigi,
    "You have done well.
    "When I arrive at your father's yard,
    "I will fight your enemies.
    "I will make them swell up, Fa-Jigi.
640   "They will not be able to get out the door, Fa-Jigi.
    "I will give someone a hernia,
    "I will cut the heads off the penises of others,
    "I will cut off the testicles of many.
    "What will I do, Fa-Jigi?
645   "Do you not know, Fa-Jigi?
    "I will put worms in the living bodies of your enemies."
    That is how the *boliw* spoke.
    The *marabout* [21] vocation began at Mecca.
    The Komo began at Mecca.
650   The first Komo owner at Mecca was called Yamusa.
    There is a mountain east of Mecca.
    Even today,
    If a bee from this mountain stings you,
    You will die before you can open your mouth to scream.
655   This is the mountain of magic powder near Mecca.

    Heee!
    Bila Fa-Koli!
    Everything has lost its mystery,
    But the blacksmith things cannot be revealed.
660   Heee, wei!
    They have turned everything upside down,
    But the secret of Komo cannot be betrayed.
    People of the country,
    Everything has been scattered.
665   Heee, wei!
    People have revealed many secrets,
    But the darkness of the grave cannot be revealed.
    Heee, nowadays people scatter everything,
    But *sayasila* [22] cannot be scattered.
670   People of the country have finished scattering everything,
    But the hunters' things cannot be scattered.

675   Koroma-Jigi put the *boliw* into the canoe.
    He took the paddle himself and embarked from Jeddah.[23]
    From Jeddah he paddled to the Bagwe River,
    From the Bagwe he went to Lake Debo,[24]
    From Lake Debo he entered the Joliba.[25]

---

21. Muslim holy man. 22. Sacrificial object for the Komo. 23. Seaport near Mecca.
24. Lake on the inland delta of the Niger River. 25. Bamana name for the Niger.

680   The *boliw* chattered constantly.
       If they break your eardrums, Jigi,
       Play the *ntamani* and they will shut up.
       Ah, *naamu*-sayer!
       When Jigi arrived at Keka,
685   The *ntamani* drumstick was dropped there.
       Nobody could lift it but Turamakan;
       He picked it up and placed it on a tamarind tree.
       If the war was won they spoke of Turamakan.[26]
       If the battle was lost they spoke of Turamakan.
690   If the river flooded they spoke of Turamakan,
       On the other side of the river.
       If the river was dry they spoke of Turamakan.
       The Battle of Dibuntu had heated up.
       This is no lie,
695   Jigi Koroma returned from Mecca.
       Koroma-Jigi slowly returned to Nora.
       The journey had gone well for Fa-Jigi.
       Sad to say,
       The enemies had laid a curse on Fa-Jigi with a louse.
700   The louse was stuck into the mud of the river.
       The day Koroma-Jigi arrived on the lake,
       There would be a great whirlwind.
       The wind would enter the water and cause a hurricane.
       The wind would make Fa-Jigi's canoe disappear in Nora Lake.
705   The whirlwind entered the water near the main entrance of
          Nora town.

       There was a great struggle,
       But the canoe turned over in the flooded lake.
       The Somono came quickly to rescue Jigi,
730   And Jigi was not drowned.
       They fished for the *boliw* for days,
       The *boliw* completely filled a house.
       Jigi brought special divination from Mecca,
       Jigi brought the magic pebbles from Mecca.
735   Jigi had a special amulet on his toe,
       And this amulet became a scorpion.
       Fa-Jigi had a magic powder called "wasp sting" in his armpit,
       And this powder became a wasp.
       If it stings you,
740   You will run in place.
       Jigi had a magic powder[27] called "To-make-unconscious,"
       And this was given to the white men.
       Eeeh!

---

26. One of Son-Jara's greatest generals. 27. Apparently an anesthetic.

	Fa-Jigi brought a powder called "Beware,"
745	And this became a bee that made excellent honey.
	Eeeh!
	The rescued *boliw* were distributed all over the Mande.
	Koroma-Jigi brought the Komo from Mecca.
	Fa-Jigi brought the dust-divining from Mecca.
750	He brought the divination pebbles from Mecca.
	He brought the divination cowries,
	He brought sorcery,
	Sorcery for eating people.
	He brought sorcery with him,
755	Sorcery for saving people.
	He brought the magic powders from Mecca.
	Even now Jigi's bonnet is at Nora,
	And they make sacrifices to it.
	Every Wednesday of the month of November they make those sacrifices.
760	This cap fits all the legitimate descendants of Fa-Jigi.
	Ah, people!
	Fa-Jigi was an unbeliever.[28]
	Koroma-Jigi brought the power of preventing cannibalism.
	Fa-Jigi gave that to the old women.
765	Fa-Jigi,
	Koroma-Jigi took the sorcery of cannibalism,
	He gave it to the evil sorcerers so they could eat people.
	Fa-Jigi took the magic powder,
	He gave it to the Komo masters,
770	He gave medicine to the great healers.
	He gave *marabouts* the power to enfeeble.
	He gave the Komo masters power to transform themselves.
	He said, "Protect yourselves with this.
	"However long the course of life,
775	"The last day will arrive."
830	Heee!
	Naamu-sayer,
	Koroma-Jigi threw deadly powder on his mother,
	And before morning lice had invaded that woman's entire body.
	Her head,
835	Her armpits,
	Her pubic hair,
	Everything was full of lice.
	His mother swelled up so bad she could not get through the door.

---

28. He followed a local religion instead of Islam.

Eeeh, wei!
840 *Naamu*-sayer,
Jigi's mother left the earth.
She died,
And Jigi shouted like this:
"If destiny has chosen that you must go to hell,
845 "Do everything you can to be the little sister of Diahanama
        Malikiba."[29]

Eeeh, wei!
Naamu-sayer,
They dug a grave for Jigi's mother.
860 Eeeh!
The shade-tree has fallen,
Death has removed it from me.
My mother was a shade-tree,
Death has taken her from me.
865 Bard of the Komo,
Death has taken the shade-tree from me.
Numu Camara Jan was a shade-tree,
Death has taken him from me.
I am not telling lies,
870 The shade-tree has fallen,
Death has removed it from me.
Numu Faraban was a shade-tree,
Death has removed him from me.
Aaayi!
875 Death has taken the shade-tree from me.
Sele of Koulikoro was a shade-tree,
Death has removed him from me.
Numu Kulumba the shade-tree has fallen,
Death has taken him from me.
880 Numu Camara Jan was one of the shade-trees,
Death has removed him from me.
Death is bad,
The shade-tree has fallen,
Death has removed it from me.
885 Heee, wei!
Kuda Jan Kali was a shade-tree,
Death has removed him from me.

---

29. Angel who escorts sinners to hell.

4. The Epic of Bamana Segu
Narrated by Tayiru Banbera

Recorded in Segu, Mali, between February 28 and March 11, 1976, by David Conrad. Transcribed and translated into English by David Conrad with the assistance of Soumaila Diakité. Edited by David Conrad and published in A State of Intrigue: The Epic of Bamana Segu *by Oxford University Press, 1990. This excerpt edited by David Conrad.*

THE DECLINE OF THE MALI EMPIRE by the fifteenth century and the fall of Songhay in the late sixteenth left a power vacuum on the upper Niger River that eventually came to be filled by a number of smaller states. One of these which flourished from the late seventeenth to the mid-nineteenth century was the Bamana Empire, whose capital of Segu (as the state was also known) is some 150 kilometers downriver (northeast) from where Bamako, the present-day capital of Mali, is located.

This version of *The Epic of Bamana Segu* was narrated by the late Tayiru Banbera, a famous jeli of Segu. Jeli Tayiru's performance was recorded during six sessions at Segu between February 28 and March 11, 1976, by David Conrad who, with the assistance of Soumaila Diakité, later translated it into 7,942 lines of English.

In one of the longest epics recorded in Africa, Jeli Tayiru describes the deeds of many memorable characters, including the hero Bakari Jan, the villain Bilisi, the heroine Sijanma, the bard Tinyètigiba Danté, and several rebellious chiefs such as Desekoro of Kaarta and Basi Samanyana. He also frequently interjects discussions on topics of Bamana culture ranging from beer drinking and cooking to hair styles and seduction. At irregular intervals, Jeli Tayiru would pause, either to collect his thoughts or for dramatic emphasis, while he continued playing the *ngoni*, a small four-stringed lute on which he accompanied himself. These pauses are marked in the text as "musical interludes."

In the interest of continuity, the excerpts presented here focus on kings (*mansaw*) of Segu. There were at least nineteen mansaw of Segu before it was conquered by the Tukulor Army of Al-hajj Umar Tal in 1861. However, Jeli Tayiru mainly talks about only four of those, whose deeds are most memorable: Mamari (Biton) Kulubali (c. 1712-55), Ngolo Jara (c. 1766-87), Monzon Jara (c. 1787-08), and Faama Da Jara (1808-27).

Jeli Tayiru was a Muslim, so his narrative begins with a blessing as part of his traditional introduction, which is followed by some ancestral legends. He then describes Biton Kulubali's rise to power (in which the new king's mother figures prominently), the origin of taxes, and how Biton acquires a slave child named Ngolo, future founder of the next ruling dynasty.

May Allah bless our master Muhammad,
Grant peace to him and his family,

34

Peace to our master Muhammad.
This knowledge is older than any other knowledge.
5   A slave[1] must know the Being who made him,
He must know the messenger of the Being who sent him,
If he wants to be blessed.
If he does this,
He will accomplish what he came to do.

                        MUSICAL INTERLUDE

10   I, Jeli Tayiru, I come from Ngoin.
Eh the stories I will tell you here in Segu,
They are stories of long ago.
The *mansaw* who performed these deeds,
They are now in *lahara*.[2]
15   They have gone to lie in their own shady places.
The dust from each of their heads could fill a calabash scoop.

                        MUSICAL INTERLUDE

What *mansa* and what *mansa* do we talk about in Segu,
In Segu of the *si* tree,
Place of the Jara,
20   Segu of the *balansa* trees?
Four thousand *balansa*,
And four hundred *balansa*,
And four *balansa*,
And one humpbacked *balansa*.
25   Not every native understands their significance,
To say nothing of a stranger.

                        MUSICAL INTERLUDE

In those days Segu was not named "Segu,"
It was called "Sekoro."
There was only one entrance and one exit,
30   Segu was enclosed by a special wall.
Nzan the dog merchant was in the market,
The Bamana sold dogs.
If someone did not sell his dog by mid-afternoon,
The market did him wrong.
35   His dog would be served to the *faama*[3] for breakfast.
The Bamana ruled in Segu for 200 years, less twenty years and
     four months.

                        MUSICAL INTERLUDE

1370 When Biton Kulubali, the man-killing hunter, was in power,
His people ruled for forty years.
His people in power for thirty years were six in number:
Biton himself and his son Bakari and Cekoro,

---

1. Slave here means servant of God. 2. Paradise. 3. "King."

Pelenkene Kanubanyuma and Gasi Kalfajugu and Ngoin Ton
    Mansa.[4]
1375   They ruled for forty years.
    At that time Ngolo was at Nyola,
    At that time Ngolo had not come into this land.
    He was really a native of Nyola.
    Balikoro Jara's grandson was not yet in this land.
1380   If the world were a human being,
    All its hair would now be gray.
    Many great things have happened since it was created.

[Through divination Biton Kulubali and his supporters learn that the slave child Ngolo, who is not of the Kulubali lineage, is destined to become *mansa* of Segu. Plots to kill the child repeatedly fail, so he is sold to Moorish salt traders, who take him north to Walata in the Sahara desert. Ngolo goes from there to the powerful Muslim Kunta Family of Timbuktu, from whom he eventually acquires the blessings that assure his accession to kingship.]

2130   Finally Ngolo came to Segu.
    When the time came for Ngolo to return, Biton's day was done.
    After Biton's day there was an old man in Sebugu whose name
        was Donbila Nsan.
                    MUSICAL INTERLUDE
    When Ngolo returned to Segu his rival was Donbila Nzan at
        Sebugu.
    Donbila Nzan was older than Ngolo,
    But Ngolo came to live at Segu earlier than Donbila Nzan.
    People said, "If we decide according to age, Donbila Nzan will
        become master of the land.
2140   "But if we decide according to the order of arrival, Ngolo will
        become master of the land."
    Finally they decided to place Ngolo in power.
    On the matter of Ngolo coming to power, the councilors said,
        "All right,
    "Very well, how will this be done?"
    Banbugu Nce was Ngolo's first son.
2145   He said, "Is it possible for someone to sit in power without
        calling the slaves?"
    "No one can sit in power if he does not call the *sofaw*."[5]
    Then Banbugu Nce organized the power to follow his father.
    He assembled the Bamana here to cross the river.
    On that day the Bamana swore an oath.
2150   They said, "Until the death of Ngolo,

4. Slave chiefs who ruled Segu during a time of turmoil, c. 1757-66. 5. Mounted warriors.

"Until the end of Ngolo's descendants,
"Nobody will step between them.
"They will have the power until their line has ended,
"No one can interfere with them."

2155 The Bamana went across the river to swear that oath.
They chewed red kola nut,
They cut their arms to make the blood flow,
They put the red kola in the blood.
Everyone swore on the kola and chewed it:

2160 "If anyone spoils this alliance, may the four great *boliw* 6 of Segu
not spare him.
"May Bakungoba not spare him,
"May Nangoloko not spare him,
"May Kontara not spare him,
"May Binyejugu not spare him."

2165 After everybody swore they came home to Segu.
MUSICAL INTERLUDE
Ngolo settled his first son Nce in Banbugu.
His next son was Monzon and he settled him at Npeba.
His sons Jokele Nyankoro, Seri, and Mamuru were settled at
Sebugu.
Ben settled at Kirango, and Denba settled at Masala.

2170 Nalukuma and Torokoro Mari, all these were his sons.
MUSICAL INTERLUDE
He gave each of them a place to settle.
When each of them was settled, Banbugu Nce had something
on his mind.
He went to his father and said, "Baba."
Ngolo said, "I hear you."

2175 Nce said, "Baba the thing that has been said is indeed true."
He said, "It is said that before dying and going to *lahara*,
"Every old man strikes an axe-blow in his homeland.
"This is indeed true."
Ngolo said, "Why, *Cemogo*?"7

2180 Nce said "Eh, you divided up your sons and gave them each a
place to settle.8
"Where did you settle me, your son Nce?"
Ngolo said "I settled you at Banbugu."
"Where did you settle Monzon?"
"I settled Monzon at Npeba."

2185 "What about Jokele, Nyankoro Seri, and Mamaru?"
Ngolo said, "They are settled at Sebugu,
"Ben is at Kirango, and Denba is at Masala."

6. Objects of power, fetishes. 7. Literally "man," but here a nickname. 8. Each of
the king's sons ruled over a garrisoned town.

37

Nce said, "Ah yes, let us look at the problem together.
"The mouth can fail to say something but the thoughts show it
anyway."

MUSICAL INTERLUDE

2190   Ngolo said, "Cemogo, why do you say that?"
Nce said, "What about the distance between Banbugu and the
riverbank?"
Ngolo said, "It is far from the riverbank."
Nce said, "What about the distance between Npeba and the
river?"
Ngolo said, "It is close to the river."

2195   "What about the distance between Sebugu and the river?"
"It is close to the river."
"Oh," said Nce, "This is why I said the mouth can fail to say
something but the behavior shows it.
"You have shown that you prefer your other sons over me."
Then Ngolo said to Banbugu Nce, "Segu is a group of four
villages,

2200   "Marakadugu is a group of nine villages,
"Dodugu is a group of twelve villages,
"Six of them on one side of the river and six on the other side.
"Segu is a group of four villages,
"Marakadugu is a group of nine villages,

2205   "Dodugu is a group of twelve villages.
"We believe that Marakadugu begins at Kuku not far from
here.
"From there you reach Marakaduguba,
"And from there you go to Busen, then Koke.
"Oh the Fula come from Macina.

2210   "They ride horses and can easily come to Segu.
"Marakaduguba is an old town where believers, learned, wise
and worthy people live.
"If the Fula of Macina come here two more times, they will ally
themselves with Duguba.
"If they ever become allied with Duguba, Segu will spend the
night peering at shadows.
"This is why I settled you at Banbugu.

2215   "I want you to be our bulwark for Segu against Duguba and
the Macina Fula."
(Eh, we *nyamakalaw*[9] say, "Nce" and the Fula say "Hamadi" to
describe the first son.)
Ngolo said, "There are three kinds of Nce in Bamana land.
"Nce the sauce-eater is one of them,
"Nce the dog-seller is one of them,

2220   "Worthy Nce is one of them.

---

9. Craft specialist and artists, including bards, blacksmiths, and leatherworkers.

"You are the worthy Nce."

MUSICAL INTERLUDE

Nce said, "This is all right, Baba, I hear it."
Ngolo calmed the heart of the eldest son.
Banbugu Nce went back to Banbugu.

[Urged on by a famous female bard of the time, Nce constructs a canal
reaching seven kilometers from the Niger River to Banbugu. Ngolo
dies and his son Monzon comes to power, but his younger brothers
insist that the kingdom must be divided among them. Monzon refuses,
saying, "a hundred heads can wear the same cap only if they do it one
at a time." The brothers start a war, which Monzon wins before
embarking on a series of conquests, including the famous battle of Koré,
which expand the empire.]

2710   At the time that Monzon fought against Koré, things were not
        like they are now.
    The young *marabout* who did the blessings for the battle of Koré
        was Mamadu Bisiri.
    He was a *dafin*[10] master.
    The people of Segu went to tell him that they wanted to attack
        Koré.
    They asked Mamadu Bisiri to give them a blessing.
2715   He agreed to do the blessing,
    He raised a lighted straw to the sky.
    The people heard a noise coming from the sky.
    The *marabout's* novice began to moan.
    The *marabout* said to the novice, "Child do not bring misfortune
        on yourself and choose me as the cause of it."

MUSICAL INTERLUDE

2720   The *marabout* did the blessing and gave it to Monzon.
    Then Monzon left here with two times forty companies of
        warriors.
    They went to station themselves there.
    What a spectacle it was.
    They spent the day at the gates of Koré.
2725   They sent word to Dugakoro that war had come to his town.
    Dugakoro put a basket of kola nuts on somebody's head and
        sent it with a message to Monzon:
    "If you plant these and wait until they sprout and wait until
        they bear fruit,
    "If you wait that long you will be able to conquer Koré."
    He said, "If you cannot do so,
2730   "You had better go about your other business.

---

10. Form of Muslim divination.

"I am not sure you will ever be able to conquer Koré."
The town was so big that if some people fired gunpowder all
    day in one part of the town,
And if some others beat wedding drums all day in another
part,
Nobody knew what the others were doing.
2735   Oh this had nothing to do with the failure of the three-month
siege.
The siege began.
The expression "Koré siege, Koré siege" was first spoken that
    day.
They tried every tactic but were unable to enter Koré.
They were unable to enter Koré though they tried every tactic.
2740   Monzon himself was frustrated.
He said, "Hey, the day Koré is captured,
"The first man to bring me the news will be made a chief of
    something."
That day Nangoyi Koné was here.
That day Jeli Gorogi Koné was here.
2745   The leadership of the *nyamakalaw* belonged to them at that time.
                                     MUSICAL INTERLUDE
Little by little the sacrifices and the blessings were answered.
One day Koré was captured and destroyed like an old calabash,
Like an old clay pot.
The man called "Possessor of truth" ran *bara-bara-bara* to where
    Monzon was sitting.
2750   He said, "What was said has been realized.
"The prayers have been answered.
"We have destroyed Koré like an old calabash.
"We have smashed it like an old clay pot.
"Things inside the houses are now things outside the houses."
2755   Monzon said, "Then I give to you leadership of the *nyamakalaw*
    of Segu.
"It was my own mouth that said the first man to tell me Koré
    was conquered would be made a chief."
Tinyètigi, "Master of truth," ran to tell Monzon that Koré was
    captured.
That day Monzon made Tinyètigiba Danté chief of the bards.
Before that there had been some people above him.
2760   That was the end of the war with Koré.

2925   Oh, a day came with the sickness that would send Monzon to
    lahara.
He sent for Jeli Tinyètigiba Danté.
Monzon told him to go and call his favorite son.
Oho, when that was done, when the son came,
Jeli Tinyètigiba began to recite the genealogy.

40

2930 He started praising Da with Wanasi and his nine generations.
He ended with how the Koné left Sankaran.
"Eh," people said, "there is no limit to the word of this man!
"Is his word not accurate?
"Is his word not true?
2935 "Is the form of his word not just right?
"We cannot choose one of these at the expense of the rest.
"Your word has no limit.
"The word from your mouth is good.
"You are also the possessor of truth.
2940 "You are the possessor of truth,
"The word from your mouth is good,
"Your word has no limit."
Dan t'i ka kuma na, "There is no limit to your word."
That became a family name,
2945 The word of this man was good.
There was no limit to his word.
Tinyètigiba Danté, "Big possessor of limitless truth."
                                        MUSICAL INTERLUDE
The sickness bit Monzon.
He said, "Go and call my favorite son."
2950 Tinyètigiba Danté said, "Who is your favorite son?"
Monzon said, "Faama Da."
"Where is he?"
"He is at Banankoro!"
Tinyètigiba Danté went to call Faama Da,
2955 To say his father had called him.
Faama Da came.
He said, "Father?"
Monzon said, "I hear you."
Da said, "Father?"
2960 Monzon said, "I hear you."
Da said, "Is it true you are calling me?"
Monzon said, "Yes, I am calling you."
Da said, "Why are you calling me?"
2965 Monzon said, "The reason for calling you is not serious.
"I, Monzon, have been caught by the illness that will take me
        to *lahara.*
"This illness will not go away without me.
"It will take me to *lahara.*
"I have destroyed every town I had to destroy.
"I have conquered every town I had to conquer.
2970 "But when I was in my prime there were three towns I failed
        against.
"I want to tell you about those three towns.
"Here are the keys to Segu.

41

"They are one hundred twenty and ten in number.
"Among them is the key of the old dog,
2975 "Among them is the key of the female dog,
"Among them is the key of the four slaves.
"Hers is the key to the four big *boliw*.
"These are the substance of power in Segu.
"Never lose them after I am gone.
2980 "If you lose them you will be separated from Segu ahead of
    your time.
"If you keep them in your hands you and Segu will spend your
    life together.
"The people of Segu will not oppose your power.
"Ah, as for those three towns,
"I will die with my regret.
2985 "Except for those few towns,
"I defeated every one my eyes saw.
"But I do regret those three towns!"
                                  MUSICAL INTERLUDE
Faama Da said, "Very well Father.
"I hear your word.
2990 "What town and what town are these?
"Name for me the towns you could not conquer."
Monzon said, "Nwenyekoro is at Npebala.
"Desekoro is at Kaarta.
"Basi is at Samanyana.
2995 "These are the three towns.
"I could not conquer them.
"If you are able to conquer them after I am gone,
"Bakungoba will bless you,
"Kontara will bless you,
3000 "Binyejugu will bless you,
"The four big *boliw* of Segu,
"The remains of Cekolo will bless you.
"I myself will bless you from *lahara*,
"I failed to conquer them."
3005 Da said, "So be it."
Then Da went out.
He went to see Tinyètigiba Danté.
He said, "Danté."
"I hear you."
3010 "Danté."
"I hear you."
"Eh, my father's illness is getting more serious but he will not
    die.
"Father's illness is getting more serious but he will not die."
Da was impatient for his father to die because he wanted the
    power here in Segu.

3015 He had that in his heart.
A week passed.
Within that week the illness became more serious.
In the second week the illness became 'Go and meet me.'
In the third week Monzon set down his burden here in Segu.
3020 They began to beat the big ceremonial drum.
Men gathered together,
Women went into their houses.
The *nyamakalaw* were shouting that the world had become
    troubled and confused:
        The goat is sick,
3025   The goat owner is ailing.
        The knife is dull,
        The goat's throat is tough.
        The day is drawing to a close,
        The ground is hot.
3030 We have no basket to sit on in the sky while we tell our
    troubles to the angels of Allah.
Where will we go to bathe?
Where will we go to dry off?
Our bathing place is gone,
Our drying place is gone,
3035 All that was left of Segu was one forked post.
Now that forked post is broken.
The crossbeams, roof timbers, and wall posts have fallen.
Cemogo Monzon has set down the baggage.
We *nyamakalaw* had nothing before,
3040 But now our whole life is gone.
The one who gave us our riding horse is gone.

[Despite Monzon's wishes, the Segu elders repeatedly refuse to recognize Da as the next *mansa*. Finally, in an organized plot, Da's hatchetmen swarm into a council meeting and begin to massacre the elders. The surviving councilors accept Da, who soon launches military campaigns against the rebellious chiefs whom his father, Monzon, had failed to conquer. One of these is the formidable Basi Diakité of Samanyana, who is defeated when the slave girl Sijanma seduces him to learn the secret of his power. Among Da's other conquests is his destruction of Kaarta, a neighboring Bamana state founded by Kulubali ancestors who are thought to have been related to Biton's forebears (see l. 5598).]

They moved on with their war and crept ahead as slowly as a
    bad marriage.
(Once a marriage turns bad, there is much discussion about it.)

43

5505   Oh world, father of astonishing things,
They took the war to the gate of Desekoro's Kaarta.
When the war arrived at the gate of Desekoro's Kaarta,
They fired a warning shot at the walls.

                                MUSICAL INTERLUDE

They were sending a message to Desekoro.

5510   At Kaarta in those days Desekoro had two men.
They did the divining for him on matters related to his wars or
    his power.
The name of the first diviner was "Nobody-knows-himself-but-
    you-will-see-someday."[11]
The name of the second diviner was "A-willful-person-with-his-
    mouth-open-is-bad."
After the warning shot was fired at the town wall, there was
    turmoil everywhere from sky to earth.

5515   No one had to tell another that the mounted warriors of Segu
    were coming.
Finally, master, 'the name of the child is Marabout.'[12]
At that time Desekoro had a new calabash.
His seers did their divining using the water in that calabash.
The calabash was filled with water and placed on the ground.

5520   Then the grooms brought out their war horses.
They pulled some hair from under the saddles.
The wind blew it into the calabash of water.
Then on the day that the amount of hair increased to more than
    any other day,
They would take that as a sign and say,"Hum!

5525   "Something is coming near us today."
They made the sacrifice that was required against the
    approaching thing.
Then they could deal with whatever war that was.

                                  MUSICAL INTERLUDE

Oh, when this had been done "A-willful-person-with-his-
    mouth-open-is-bad" went to Desekoro of Kaarta.
"Ha!" he said, "Today."

5530   Desekoro said, "What happened?"
"Ha, very well," he said.
"Dese, the horsehair has darkened the top of the calabash."
Desekoro said, "Aha, very well, pour it out and put in fresh
    water."
He poured out the water and refilled the calabash.

5535   Before he could begin to say, "The name of the child is
    Marabout,"

---

11. This sort of descriptive name usually indicates slave status. 12. An oath
confirming the truth of one's words.

More horsehair made the calabash look like there was no water
    in it.
"Aha, very well Desekoro," said the diviner.
"The matter has become worse than before."
Desekoro said, "Very well pour out that water."
5540   They did that three times.
Desekoro said, "Go out and look at the road."
                                MUSICAL INTERLUDE
He climbed a high tree and craned his neck.
He looked at the road and saw mounted Segu warriors every-
    where.
There were hammermen among them,
5545   There were hatchetmen among them,
There were spearmen among them,
There were musketeers among them.
Turmoil was everywhere,
People could not even see each other.
5550   Then "A-willful-person-with-his-mouth-open-is-bad" rode his
    horse back to Desekoro, *bari, bari, bari.*
He said, "Aha, very well, is this not Desekoro of Kaarta?"
Desekoro said, "Yes it is."
He said, "Today we have arrived at the matter of war."
Desekoro said, "What has happened?"

5555   "Hmm," said the diviner. "Very well,
"You must know that the matter of today,
"Hmmm, bwa! bwa!
"It is not like anything before."
He said the mounted warriors of Segu had arrived.
5560   He thought that Kaarta was smashed.
The diviner said, "Very well, Kaarta is smashed."
Desekoro said, "Hey!
"'A-willful-person-with-his-mouth-open-is-bad.'"
He said, "I hear you."
5565   Dese said, "Eh, have you gone crazy?
"Indeed is the smashing of a town the size of Kaarta something
    to be spoken of?
"Aha, very well, seize him!"
Finally they seized "A Willful Person With His Mouth Open Is
    Bad,"
They cut his head from his neck.
5570   His two shoulders became milk brothers,[13]
The rest of his body ran away.
The blood poured out like a sacrificial cow of Mande.

---

13. Children of the same mother; very close.

45

War is not good for a coward.

MUSICAL INTERLUDE

Desekoro said, to his other diviner, "Aha, very well,

5575 "Nobody-knows-himself-but-you-will-see-someday," get up.

"Go look at the road and see about what has been said."

MUSICAL INTERLUDE

Oh, "Nobody-knows-himself-but-you-will-see-someday" went out.

He climbed a high tree and craned his neck.

There could not have been more turmoil.

5580 It extended from sky to ground.

He cast his eye as far as possible but could not see the end of the crowd of warriors.

He climbed down and went to Desekoro.

He said, "Very well, Dese,

"It is the little warriors of the warrior Monzon.

5585 "They are approaching fearfully, *yoli, yoli.* . . .

"We will capture them all but we must have courage."

MUSICAL INTERLUDE

The diviner said, "Hah, very well Desekoro, we must have courage."

Desekoro said, "For that I give you two baskets of millet.

"I give you two bars of salt,

5590 "I give you two male slaves to attend to your horse."

The mounted warriors of Segu were everywhere outside the walls of Kaarta.

Only the sand of the river separated them from Kaarta.

The Kaarta horsemen dashed boldly out.

Mansa and Moriba,[14]

5595 Nya Ngolo and Barama Ngolo,

Mansa and Moriba Kurubari.

Oh, that Desokoro, his family name was Kurubari.

He and Biton Kulubali of Segu came from the same father,

But they did not share the same mother.

MUSICAL INTERLUDE

5600 Finally they met on the sand of the river.

They were not in Kaarta,

They were not in Segu.

Hard things and difficult things,

They clashed nine times.

5605 Painful things and porcupine quills,

When mature men meet in battle there is no mercy.

Men were fighting so the winner would soon be known.

In those days a Bamana musket would fire only one shot at a time.

---

14. Praise-names of inspirational ancestors.

But once the battle started the warriors on both sides stood fast
    in their positions,
5610   They were ready to go to *lahara*.
                                      MUSICAL INTERLUDE

When the battle companies came together,
When the Kaarta muskets spoke *wuu!*
There were so many Segu muskets.
5635   The Kaarta bullets, powder, and wadding flew into the mouths
    of some Segu muskets
When the Segu muskets spoke *wuu!*
The bullets, wadding, powder, and smoke flew into the mouths
    of some Kaarta muskets.
Between them was river sand.
                                        MUSICAL INTERLUDE

Hah, it became a very serious matter.
5640   The men took each other,
They took each other,
They took each other.
At one point Segu took Kaarta,
Then Kaarta took Segu.
5645   Segu would take Kaarta,
Then Kaarta would take Segu.
When the battle heated up,
Faama Da said, to Tinyètigiba Danté, "Danté!"
He said, "I hear you."
5650   "Tell them to let the battle rest."
Segu let the battle rest.
Da came to them and said, "Segu!
"Gather round while I give you a message about *lahara*.
"Hot bullets can take somebody to *lahara*,
5655   "Or a cold sword can take somebody to *lahara*.
"You will have to choose which one is better for you.
"If Segu takes Kaarta, I am not talking about that.
"But if Kaarta pushes Segu all the way back to me,
"I, Da, will take the men at the back and send them to *lahara*
    with a cold sword.
5660   "You know if I am able to do that or not.
"There are plenty of others to take your place.
"I do not want to take all day attacking one town.
"I will not spend a whole year laying siege to one town."
Then the warriors discussed this among themselves.
5665   That day the Bamana swore an oath to one another.
They said, "Well, from now on a hot bunch taking somebody to
    lahara,
"That is better than the throat cut with a cold sword.
"From now on any man who runs away,

"A dog has spent the night with his mother.
5670 "Any man of Segu who runs away after this,
"A dog has spent the night with his mother."
The Bamana carried their insult to this extent.
Oh, after that, death would find people there.
For any man they said this to, retreat became shameful.
5675 After that Segu pushed Kaarta and Kaarta pushed Segu.
Segu pushed Kaarta and Kaarta pushed Segu.
Segu pushed Kaarta and Kaarta pushed Segu.
Segu faltered but nobody retreated toward Da.
                                        MUSICAL INTERLUDE

Oh some were impervious to bullets,
5680 Some were impervious to bullets.
Those who did not need muskets used axes.
Some who did not need muskets used battle hammers.
Oh, the hammermen finally said, "Hey musketeers!
"You are slowing our battle.
5685 "Get out of our way.
"We will look for them word for word.[15]
"This battle will soon be settled."
The musketeers stayed behind the hammermen.
                                        MUSICAL INTERLUDE

Eh, when the hammermen seized someone by the shirt, they
        would ask him:
    "Elder brother are you one of us?"
5690 You would hear him, "Eh, little brother, are you going crazy?"
You would hear him, "Yes, all right, these are Segu words."
When they seized someone by his shirt and forced him to stop,
His eyes would pop out,
You would say like those of a frog carrying a clay pot on his
        head.
5695 You would hear them, "Elder brother are you one of us!"
You would hear him, "Yes, *i lanbè*, I am one of you."
"Among us you say *i lanbè*?
"That is not all right.
"*I lanbè* is not of Segu!"
5700 Pow! They would hammer him on the head.
He would go to *lahara*. . . .
The hammermen did this again and again.
5715 They were doing to people, you would say, like breaking
        chicken eggs.
They were doing to people, you would say, like breaking
        guinea fowl eggs.
They were doing to people, you would say, like breaking par-
        tridge eggs.

---

15. Recognizing them by their idiomatic speech.

They were doing to people, you would say, like breaking
    chicken eggs again and again.
A skillful horseman came riding *ban, bari, bari.*
5720   He went and said, "All right, is this Desekoro?"
"Yes it is."
"Are you just sitting here?"
"I am sitting here."
"Huh, all right, if you are sitting you must get up.
5725   "Get up!"
"What is the matter?"
"Ah, ayee, the Segu people have a weapon called a hammer.
"Aha, all right, many people have amulets against muskets,
"But they have nothing against the hammer.
5730   "Oh, they will break your head, you would say, like that of a
    dog.
"We are going.
"No one has amulets against the hammer.
"We are going."
Finally Segu took things inside the house of Kaarta,
5735   They made them things outside the house of Kaarta.
They came and sat down and snuffed tobacco.

[After more campaigns Da succeeds in conquering all of the towns
Monzon had named on his deathbed. Later Segu is troubled by the
slave-raider Bilisi and by invading Fula warriors from the kingdom of
Macina to the north. In additional episodes totalling more than 1,850
lines, Jeli Tayiru Banbera's narrative concludes with his story of how
the great hero Bakari Jan rides to the rescue on his wondrous horse,
Nyoté. There is no mention of the last seven rulers or of the conquest of
Segu by Al-hajj Umar Tal in 1861.]

5. The Epic of Sonsan of Kaarta
Narrated by Mamary Kuyatè

Recorded in Kolokani, Mali, August 19-21, 1975, by David Conrad. Transcribed and translated into English by David Conrad with the assistance of Sekou Camara and Jume Diakité. This excerpt edited by David Conrad.

ROUGHLY CONTEMPORARY TO BAMANA SEGU was a second Bamana state known as Kaarta, which for a time played a less significant role in filling the power vacuum left by the sixteenth-century decline of the Songhay Empire. Because Kaarta was much less successful than Segu, it left very little in the way of a historical record. It was apparently located in an area northwest of Segu in the general area of today's Beledugu region north of Bamako. The prosperity of the neighboring Bamana state of Segu can in great measure be attributed to its advantageous location, with many towns strung along the Niger River on the trade route between the land of Manden to the southwest and the inland Niger Delta to the northeast. Some north-south trade must have gone through Kaarta, but this state never had the level of prosperity that allowed Segu to maintain a powerful army and expand its borders in all directions. Indeed, despite the fact that the founders of Segu and Kaarta are said to have descended from the same distant ancestor (they were both of the Kulubali clan), the oral sources indicate that Segu attacked Kaarta on more than one occasion, and some informants believe that Kaarta was soundly defeated by its stronger neighbor during the reign of Desekoro Kulubali (1788-99).

The excerpt presented here is a rare example of epic discourse about Kaarta, and it focuses on a single character, the ancestor Sonsan, who is credited with founding the town of Sonsana. Sonsan's origins go back to the earliest ancestor of both Kaarta and Segu, recalled as the great hunter Kalajan, who is identifiable as one of three brothers known as Simbon, said to have come from "the east." Among Kalajan's descendants, two brothers, Nya and Barama, are usually recalled as important ancestors, and the performer of this text says Barama was the father of Sonsan. Sonsan's own son was Massa, whose descendants became the ruling lineage of Kaarta, including Desekoro who appears in the Bamana Segu epic.

The narrator of this discourse is Jeli Mamary Kuyatè of Kolokani, Mali, a sightless jeli who accompanies himself on the *ngoni* or four-stringed harp-lute like the one used by Tayiru Banbera, narrator of the Segu epic. His narrative is frequently punctuated by songs and musical variations. Jeli Mamary's text reflects the dangerous rivalry that can develop in Bamana society between brothers of the same father but different mothers. Also important here is the fact that unlike many cultures in this part of West Africa, the Bamana resisted conversion to Islam until long after the events of this story. However, for the past century Islam has been an important presence in Bamana society, which is why the bard (who is himself a Muslim) commences his tale by asso-

ciating early Kaarta and Segu ancestors with the Prophet Muhammad. Nevertheless, he makes it clear that while they were willing to fight for the Prophet (in a battle that the bard locates in Kayes, Mali, rather than in Arabia), these fierce hunter-warriors were not interested in adopting a religion that would require them to "bob up and down" in prayer.

If you hear "Kulubali,"
The first village they settled here at Beledugu was Kulikòròba.[1]
In those days of the Kulubali, nobody had a family name.
There were twelve families in Mande.
5   They were headed by sons of the same parents.
These twelve men helped our king [the Prophet Muhammad]
    in the battle of Kaybara.
When people hear "Kaybara," they think it means another
    town.
They think Kaybara is another town far away.
Kaybara is not a remote town, it is Kayes.
10   Even today the sun has more force at Kayes than at any other
    place.
After the battle of Kaybara,
Only seven of the twelve men remained.
Among them, three were named Simbon.
When the country had been destroyed the leader asked them if
    they wanted a place in paradise.
15   This was not just any king,
This was the Prophet.
They had helped him in the battle of Kaybara.
He said, "Do you not want a place in paradise?"
They replied, "Bobbing up and down all night,
20   "Bobbing up and down all day to gain such a reward,
"We have no time for that."
So the Prophet said, "Very well,
"What would you like instead?"
"We want powder and bullets," they said.
25   "Very well, they are yours," said the Prophet,
"And good luck to you."
The three Simbon traveled to the Somono country on the bank
    of the river.
They were hoping to get across.
The Somono and Bozo fishermen said this would be no prob-
    lem.
30   "We will take you across," they said,
"On the condition that you unpack your loads and divide them
    among us.

---

1. Historic town on the Niger near Bamako.

"Then we will take you across the river."
But the Simbon did not want to do this so they refused.
In those days there was very dangerous sorcery.

35   This sorcery was very powerful.
Such a thing still exists, but it is not as strong.
On that day of sorcery the Joliba[2] was full to its banks,
But the three Simbon walked across it and the water was not up
    to their hips.
There were many people on the riverbank and they were
    astonished by this deed.

40   Ah! Those three men went ahead of the canoe,
They did not bother to use a canoe.
Ah! Those three men went ahead of the canoe.
Where the mountain sits by the river,
They built three houses near that mountain.

45   They cut down groves of trees to build three houses.
When you go out,
When you go out to those houses,
When you are asked, "Where are you going?"
You who go to those houses,

50   You say, *"mun ye kurun beli,"* 'those who precede the canoe,'
"I am going to their place."
Later that was shortened.
They just said *"Kurun beli"* or Kulubali.
That is how they got their name.

55   They got that name at Tufin Kumbe,
The shady place.
The Malinke call Kulikoro "the shady place."
It was there that they got their names.
The names of those three Simbon became famous.

60   There was Lawali Simbon,
Kanu Simbon,
And Furu Simbon,
All of the same parents.
In those days children were called by the father's or mother's
    names.

[Before they come by the name of Kulubali, Sonsan's ancestral lineage is identified as Wolo. Soro Wolo and his wife Nya give birth to the brothers Nya (named after his mother) and Barama Wolo. Seeking less populated lands, Nya and Barama go off in different directions to establish new communities. Sonsan is born and begins to mature at Gwegwa, where his charisma soon arouses the potentially deadly jealousy of his step-brothers, led by Kuntu, the eldest.]

---

2. "River of Blood." Bamana name for Niger River.

310

[Barama] passed near Banamba[3] and went on north of there.
They cleared the trees and founded a village called Gwere-
gwena.
This was hard for the Maraka of the area to say,
So later it became known as Gwegwa.
Barama Wolo had seven sons in that place.
The first of them was Kuntu.

315

The second son was Banfo,
Then there were Gweneke and Sonsan.
Sonsan and his sister were the only two children of one of
Barama's wives.
But the seven boys and the girl all had the same father.
There were seven boys in all,

320

But Sonsan was the favorite because of his ways.
He was loved by everyone.
From the time he knew his right hand from his left,
Even if he was just walking through the village in the morning,
Even if he was on his way to wash his face,

325

He would be accompanied by a group of friends,
Sometimes as many as ten of them.
Even now you will see children doing this.
If you want to send a child on an errand to another compound,
The father of the house can explain to the child where he wants
him to go,

330

Just by telling him the name of the boy his age who lives there.
Then he will make no mistake.
If the child did not know the place from the name of its family
head,
He would say, "Oh yes, the father of my friend."
He would always know it by the boy in his own age group.

335

It was like that until Sonsan had been circumcised,
But even when that was done,
The other boys and girls of the village would go around with
him.
At night the children of his age would meet at Barama Wolo's.
They would enliven his compound.

340

When a Fula would come to Gwegwa,
He would be sent to stay with Sonsan's family.
When a Maraka came,
He would also be lodged with Sonsan's family.
When the blacksmiths came,

345

They would stay with Sonsan's family.
When the griots came to Gwegwa,
They would stay with Sonsan's family.
When the *funew*[4] came,

3. Town north of Bamako. 4. Bards specializing in Islamic oratory.

They would be sent to stay with Sonsan's family.
350 When the Suraka[5] came,
They would be lodged with Sonsan's family.
This had an effect on Sonsan's brothers.
In those days the way that they built houses in Bamana
    country,
They had small and large houses.
355 One day Sonsan's elder brother,
The one named Kuntu,
He called his five younger brothers into the small house.
He said, "There is something for which we must find a remedy.
"That is Sonsan.
360 "The back feet have passed up the front feet.
"Eh!
"The Fula,
"The blacksmiths,
"The griots,
365 "The *funew*,
"The leatherworkers,
"The Kakolo,[6]
"All the strangers who come and go,
"They stay at the house of Sonsan.
370 "The father is not yet dead,
"But if it is like this while he still lives,
"When he dies Sonsan will surely become head of the family.
"Let us go after Sonsan and kill him.
"Otherwise, when our father dies and things are like this,
375 "The way these strangers come and go,
"I will not be head of the family."
The rival brothers collected 6,000 cowries and gave them to
    Kuntu.
This was so Kuntu could see the diviners and learn how to kill
    their brother Sonsan.
They went to see the diviner.
380 The diviner sat down.
He smoothed the dust in front of him to trace his magic signs.
He would search in the dust for a message,
An omen that would guide the step-brothers.
The diviner cast some dust in different directions and chanted.

450 "The mouth begins by saying bad things,
"It ends by saying good things.
"Speak to Kuntu who respects his father's customs,
"Speak to Kuntu who respects his mother's customs,

---

5. Bamana term for Moors or Berbers from the Sahara. 6. Mande-speaking people,
east of Beledudu in Mali.

"Those who know Kuntu speak of him,
455   "Those who have seen Kuntu speak of him.
"He has taken his father's wealth and his mother's wealth,
"He has gone away from his father's family and his mother's
     family.
"He has put his right foot in front of his left foot.
"He needs eight genies and eight humans to work as slaves
     and nobles.
460   "He is doing harm to his younger brother, Sonsan, today,
"He will be doing harm to him tomorrow,
"Because he wants to kill him.
"If Kuntu is impatient,
"If he is impatient,
465   "He must be patient,
"He must be patient.
"He cannot do anything against Sonsan today,
"He cannot do anything against Sonsan tomorrow.
"He will just shake his head in regret,
470   "Slap his thigh in regret.
"He will regret it all night and be angry all day.
"When I move my hand up and down,
"Good sit and good rise.
"If the dust is good may the eight genies make it look good.
475   "If the dust is good may the eight humans make it look good.
"Show me if Kuntu's desire will be realized.
"Only a small omen in the dust can reveal the truth of the dust.
"May the truth of the dust grow so I can see it and speak of it.
"The bird flies, but not the tree where he perches.
480   "A little bad news is better than a lot of lies."
The diviner traced sixteen houses of *lateru*,[7]
The signs for the near future.
Then he said "Eh, Kuntu!
"You can do nothing against your younger brother.
485   "Allah has chosen Sonsan,
"So leave him in peace."
Kuntu was angry at this.
He said, "That big-headed diviner knows nothing.
"He sits in the dust and the dust is worthless."

[Frustrated at the unsatisfactory divination, Kuntu leads the step-brothers in a direct attack on Sonsan, lowering him into a well and then dropping large rocks which, unknown to them, fail to hit the boy who shelters under a ledge. They lower a white chicken on a rope, and when it comes back bloody (Sonsan cuts his finger and drips blood on it), they rejoice at his death and return home with the news.]

---

7. Divination signs.

610   The six enemy brothers held their heads in mock grief.
They said, "Oh, father!
"We are a long time finding our way back because we are so
     sad."
They returned to Barama Wolo like that,
Crying and rolling on the ground.
615   Barama Wolo said, "What is going on?"
The brothers replied, "Father,
"When we were at the well we let Sonsan down into it.
"The sides broke away and fell down on Sonsan."
The father said, "Didn't I tell you not to let your little brother
     down into the well?
620   "Your son has died, but not mine.
"Go back to that well and get Sonsan out.
"Why don't you get going?"
Kuntu said, "Father,
"Now the mud of the well is still falling inside.
625   "If somebody goes in again, there will be two dead instead of
     one."
They went to tell the mother of Sonsan.
She had Sonsan's sister with her.
The sister ran crying between the well and the house.
Messages were sent to tell everyone of Sonsan's death.
630   Sonsan's mother said, "Ah,
"Big well, you have had me.
"The bird has taken my only grain of millet and dropped it
     where it can be eaten.
"That was my son,
"He was the reason that I came to Gwegwa.
635   "But big well, you have had me."
People who came for the funeral said,
"May Allah not add to this tragedy any more of our village's
     strength."
For a long time there had been jealousy between the parents.
From the time the sun was high in the sky,
640   The mother and sister had no place to rest until night.
Until after the evening meal,
Sonsan's mother had no place to rest.
She also ran between the well and the house.
She let herself fall into the mud by the well,
645   She knelt there and wailed pitifully.
"Oh, the big well of Gwegwa,
"You have had me,
"Truly you have had me."
The mother continued to mourn like that into the night.
650   Even when a goat came into the mud with her,
She continued to wail:

"Big well of Gwegwa,
"If you have eaten Sonsan,
"If you have taken my only seed,
655   "You must also take us,
"You must also eat my daughter and me."
Sonsan heard what she said from down in the well.
He climbed onto a rock and said from the well,
"Is that Mama?"
660   The mother said, "It is me."
Sonsan said, "Ah, I am not dead."
As soon as his mother heard that,
She turned and ran to her house.
She had twelve meters of new cloth.
665   She called her daughter and said, "Come on,
"We are going to get your brother out."
They went with the twelve meters of cloth.
They stopped at the side of the well and unrolled the cloth.
They let it down to Sonsan in the well.
670   When it got to Sonsan he held on tight.
His mother and sister pulled him out of the well.
When they had lifted him out of the well and he was safely
      with them,
His mother said, "Is it really you, Sonsan?"
He said, "It is me."
675   His mother said, "Oh, Sonsan!
"Have you escaped the jealousy of the Kulubali?
"Sonsan, go wherever you want, my son.

"Wherever you put down and raise your feet,
"Where your brothers would find nothing,
"May you win good fortune there.
"Go, my son,
695   "Now that you have survived the jealousy of your brothers.
"My son,
"Go with my blessings and not my curses.
"If Allah brings you to manhood while I still live,
"I will come and join you."
700   Sonsan left Gwegwa and headed north.

[Sonsan travels to Dorko, a town of the Soninke people (whom the
Bamana know as Maraka), where he receives a warm welcome. At a
council of elders it is agreed that Sonsan may join their community.]

755   When the chief of the Maraka town had welcomed him,
Sonsan told him the story of his brothers' attempt to kill him.
Sonsan said, "Maraka,
"If that was not the end of life,

"Then death cannot happen.
760 "We the Bamana say, 'Death is hard,
"'But it still leaves somebody to sit around the dinner bowl.'"

[Having no land of his own, Sonsan is unable to farm. Outside the town he encounters his spirit guide, the genie king (Jinna Magha). It is noteworthy here that the sacred grove to be destroyed in pursuit of Sonsan's destiny is the dwelling place of the same spirits who require him to do it. Also, note that although the Maraka people were among the earliest converts to Islam in this part of West Africa, they have protected the sacred grove out of respect for (and fear of) the indigenous spirits. This excerpt includes one of the bard's many songs.]

There was a grove of trees at Dorko.
It was known as the Jinna Mansa's grove.
That place was the grove of the genies.
Nobody could defecate there because it was a sacred place.
850 It was forbidden to gather chewing sticks[8] there,
And nobody could enter that grove with an axe.
As Sonsan passed near this grove on his way to the bush,
The Jinna Mansa saw him.
The Jinna Mansa said to his wife,
855 "When that Bamana man returns past here,
"Change yourself into a Maraka woman
"And meet him along the way.
"After he greets you,
"Tell him to ask the Maraka to give him this sacred land where
          our grove is standing.
860 "If they agree,
"He will have to cut down the grove to clear his field for
          planting.
"His destiny, his fame, and his life,
"They are all contained in the earth of this grove."
The genie wife did as she was told.
865 In those days we had good genies,
But the corruption of man's innocence has spoiled all that.
At the beginning of their friendship with genies men were
          good,
But at the end they turned bad.
The miser must die near his shop.
870 If the thief recognized the informer,
He would not give him his daughter.
A free woman asks Allah to let no evil come between her and
          her absent husband,

---

8. Sticks with soft, fibrous ends, used as toothbrushes.

Otherwise something worse than evil can happen between
them.
    Ha, if you kill your wicked dog,
875   Another man's dog will bite you.
    If you kill your wicked dog,
    Another man's dog will bite you.
    If wicked neighbors urge Nyenenkoro to divorce his
        worthless wife,
    Someone else's wife will kick him.
880   If people urge you,
    If wicked neighbors urge you to chase your brother
        away,
    Someone else's brother will give you a kick.
    If people urge him,
    If wicked neighbors urge Nyenenkoro to disown his
        son,
885   The son of another will give him a kick.
    Kill a wicked dog,
    If you kill your wicked dog
    Somebody else's dog will bite you.
    Kill a wicked dog,
890   If you kill your wicked dog,
    Somebody else's dog will bite you.
    Ah, those blacksmiths were brave.
    We play for the brave blacksmiths.
    The fly sits on the dunghill of someone he does not
        respect,
895   But young blacksmiths put dung near the hearth all
        day,
    And the flies pass it by every time.
    Termites build their house on the dunghill of those they
        do not respect,
    Otherwise the dung may lie on the rubbish heap for
        ten years,
    Untouched until uncircumcised boys throw it on little
        girls' heads.
900   Salute the elephant,
    The bravest of the elephants is a great elephant.
    Salute the elephant,
    The bravest of the elephants is a great elephant.
    Salute the elephant,
905   The bravest of the hyenas is a great hyena.
    Salute the elephant,
    The bravest of the warriors is a great warrior.
    Two brave men do not know each other until they
        meet.
    Two heroes do not know each other until they meet.

910   The bravest of the elephants is a great elephant.
Sonsan went out to cut the soft *nuan-nuan* bark for trimming his
      mats,
He loaded it on his head and started home.
When he got near the grove of the genies,
The wife of Jinna Mansa changed herself into a beautiful
      Maraka woman on the path.
915   Sonsan approached wearing a big sun hat on his head.
She greeted him, "*i ni ce*, Bamana man."
Sonsan replied, "*i ni wula* , 'good afternoon,' Maraka woman."
Then the Maraka woman said *nuwari*.
That is a Maraka greeting.
920   Sonsan said, "Maraka woman,
"I do not understand that language.
"I am Bamana and I do not know Maraka."
The Maraka woman said, "Bamana man,
"If you hear the Maraka say *nuwari*,
925   "It means the same as *i ni ce*.
They greeted each other in Maraka,
But Sonsan repeated that he was a Bamana.
He asked the woman to speak that language.
She said, "Bamana man,
930   "You are afraid!"[9]
Sonsan said, "No, I am not afraid.
"I, Sonsan,
"If I suspected that any part of my body was afraid,
"I would take my knife and cut off that part,
935   "So do not say that again."
Then the woman said, "Very well, Bamana man.
"I am not really a Maraka woman,
"I am a genie.
"Do you see that grove of trees?
940   "That is the dwelling place of my husband,
"He is chief of the genies.
"He told me to come and tell you to ask the Maraka for that
      grove.
"If they agree to give it to you,
"You must return and cut it down to clear your field.
945   "That is how you will gain your destiny, your fame and your
      life.
"All of this you will find in the earth of that place, oh Bamana
      man.
"That is what my husband has sent me to tell you."
Sonsan said, "That is all right.
"When you go back, tell your husband that I understand,

---

9. A stranger met in the bush may be dangerous.

950 "That I will ask the Maraka to give me the land.
"If they agree to let me have it that is all right,
"But if they will not give it to me it is the end of the matter."

Sonsan returned from gathering his *nuan-nuan* bark.
He stored it in the rafters of his house.
1085 He passed that night and the following day without speaking of
    the genie grove.
Toward evening he went to see the Maraka village chief
And asked him to assemble the elders.
After the evening meal the elders came to the chief's house.
Sonsan said to them, "The reason you have been called today is
    not a serious matter.
1090 "It is I who asked for this meeting.
"I have seen something you have here.
"I would like you to give it to me,
"Nothing else will do.
"Because I am a Bamana,
1095 "Nothing pleases me so much as a good piece of land.
"I like your sacred grove very much, Maraka people.
"I pray that you will give me that grove of trees.
"I want to clear a field for planting."
"Safuru lai!" shouted the elders.
1100 "Do not say that again!
"Do not say that again!
"Leave it alone!
"Take care that your thoughts are not dried by the wind.
"You escaped your jealous brothers,
1105 "You came here asking for our protection,
"And yet you want us to give you that place?
"Since the time when our ancestors lived,
"Both fathers and brothers,
"That grove has stood there.
1110 "Nobody can defecate there,
"Nobody can cut chewing sticks there,
"Nobody can even enter it with an axe.
"Bamana man,
"That is the sacred grove of the spirits and it must remain
    untouched.
1115 "You look again in the bush,
"And if you find another place that you like,
"If it has nothing to do with that grove,
"Bamana man,
"Even if you decide to found a village there,
1120 "We will give you that place and everything around it.
"But we cannot give you that grove."

61

[Sonsan eventually convinces the elders of Dorko that they will be protected from the genies' wrath if he is allowed to cut down the sacred grove. He clears and farms the land, harvests his crops, and builds houses at the new location, which becomes the village of Sonsana. Next the genie chief directs him to choose Duba Sangarè for his wife, no matter how bad she looks to him. Sonsan rides to Dambala, home of his prospective father-in-law, a Fula chief named Alu Sangarè. Six daughters are exhibited for Sonsan's inspection, but none of them is Duba, who is regarded as too worthless for consideration.]

At that time, Duba Sangarè had been suffering from an open
    sore for seven years.
The only way she could move about was to scoot along on her
    buttocks.
She could not even go out to urinate without scooting on her
    buttocks.
1690   When somebody brought her meals they would hold their
    nose,
They would slide the food into the room and hurry away.
Sonsan went to Duba's room, where she was sitting on a mat.
He sat down and greeted her.
He said, "Are you the daughter of Alu Sangarè?"
1695   Duba said, "I am."
Sonsan said, "You see me here today,
"But I do not bring any problems with me.
"I have come seeking you to marry,
"So tell me if you like me or not."
1700   Duba began to weep.
She said, "Bamana,
"Everyone who mocks a person does not say *kete kete*.[10]

"You do not really want to marry me,
"You only come to mock me."
1725   Sonsan said, "Duba,
"I truly have not come to mock you,
"I have come to marry you.
"If you like me, say so.
"If you do not like me, say so."
1730   Duba said, "Bamana,
"If I say I like you, how will I go with you?"
Sonsan said, "That is no problem.
"Everybody knows I have a horse."
"Very well," said Duba,
1735   "Go and tell my father that I like you."
Sonsan went to Alu Sangarè.

---

10. Sound of laughter.

He said, "Your daughter says she is fond of me."
Alu Sangarè said, "Very well, Bamana.
"I thank you very much.
1740 "You will relieve me of a burden if you take that filth out of my
    house.
"It will please me very much."
Sonsan saddled his horse and removed its hobbles.
He asked for somebody to carry Duba out and put her up
    behind him.
Alu said to his slaves, "Get up and get that obscenity,
1745 "Put her on the horse behind Sonsan.
"Sonsan has relieved us of a big problem."
Duba was placed on the horse,
And Sonsan galloped away with her.
When they arrived at Sonsan's compound,
1750 He carried her into his house and placed her on a mat.
Sonsan took care of his horse,
Then he heated water and began to bathe Duba.
Before he had finished, the genie chief arrived with special
    medicines.
There was a red powder for cleaning Duba's sore,
1755 There was a white powder to heal it.
The genie's wife showed Sonsan how to use them.
Under this treatment the sore improved quickly.
After two weeks Duba could walk with a cane.

1810 When Duba had been with Sonsan for six weeks,
Her wound had healed and left only a white scar.
Duba could now fetch her own water and bathe herself.
She was ready for Sonsan,
But so far they had not shared a sleeping mat.
1815 When they had been at Dorko for three months,
Duba's sore had healed so completely that there was not even
    the trace of a scar.
Duba had changed.
Anybody who did not know she was a Fula,
They would have thought she was a Maraka woman.
1820 She gained weight and learned to speak the Maraka language.
One afternoon Sonsan and the genie chief were talking.
Sonsan said, "I have something on my mind.
"Tomorrow I want to take Duba and present her to her father,
"Then he can name the bride-price.
1825 "If he will not accept bride-price from me,
"I cannot appreciate Duba as I should.
"I am not a Muslim,
"I will not take a wife without paying the proper bride-price."
The genie chief agreed that this should be done because

1830   "A woman's power comes from the marriage."
       That night when it was time for bed Sonsan said to Duba,
       "Get ready to leave tomorrow morning.
       "I am going to return you to your father so he can name a
           brideprice.
       "If he does not do this I cannot hold you in proper esteem.
1835   "I would never accept a wife like a Muslim, without bride-
           price."
       "There, Bamana," said Duba.
       "I said you were only mocking me,
       "That you never intended to marry me.
       "My father has already told you he would not accept even a
           piece of kola for me,
1840   "And now you say you are taking me back to him.
       "I will not go."
       Sonsan said, "Wait until tomorrow."

[Returning to Dambala they astonish Duba's family with her recovery and affirm her honor by paying the bride-price. Later she bears three sons, the eldest of which is Massa, future ancestor of the Massasi ruling lineage. In the final episode the Maraka capture a group of Bamana men, which leads to conflict between Sonsan and his former benefactors. Involving his wife Duba in the plot, Sonsan lays a trap for the Maraka. Finally, the three sons depart in search of new lands and establish the settlement known as Kaarta.]

2010   The genie chief came one day.
       He told Sonsan to buy some muskets.
       Sonsan bought fifty muskets and stored them in his compound.
       In those days the villages were always preparing for war.
       Sonsan had built a secure enclosed compound,
2015   And he had those fifty muskets.
       One day fifty lost men were wandering near the Maraka
           village.
       The Maraka took them captive.
       They tied them together by the necks with rawhide
       And locked them in Sonsan's compound.
2020   Captives were told that those who accepted slavery would be
           turned loose,
       And those who refused slavery would be killed.
       One afternoon Sonsan sat down where he could see the fifty
           men.
       They were tied by the neck with ropes attached to the house
           beams.
       When Sonsan looked at the fifty men,
2025   He lowered his head and wept.

When he raised his head and saw their eyes,
He lowered his head and wept.
Some of the captives saw this.
One of them said to Sonsan,

2030 "Why are you weeping?
"You are the owner of this house,
"So why do you weep?"
Sonsan said, "I must weep.
"I must weep because you are Bamana.

2035 "The only reason I am here myself,
"Is because of the greed of my brothers,
"The same sort of greed that touches you now.
"There are my three sons who are still young and can do
    nothing for themselves.
"If the Maraka decide to confiscate my property,

2040 "They will do the same thing to me that they have done to you,
"And my sons will have no chance in the world,
"For they will never benefit from my legacy.
"You are Bamana and I am Bamana,
"Yet they have captured you and imprisoned you in my com-
    pound.

2045 "This is the same kind of greed that brought me here.
"If you see me weeping it is because I am reminded of my own
    suffering.
"I have a plan.
"If you will agree to it I will be glad.
"I want us to plan together as Bamana."

2050 The captives wanted to know what they should do.
Sonsan made them swear an oath of loyalty before he told them
    his plan.
Sonsan put a spell on some water,
And all the men drank it and swore their oaths.
Any man who broke his oath would die.

2055 Sonsan said, "I have my own musket,
"But I also have fifty muskets for you men,
"And I have powder and ball.
"Tomorrow morning I will set you free,
"I will give you each a musket and a pouch with powder and
    ball.

2060 "After I have gone to greet the Maraka chief,
"You must send Duba to find me."

Then Sonsan went into the village of Dorko and greeted the
    Maraka chief.
The chief said, "Good morning.

2080 "Do you still have the fifty captives there?"
Sonsan said they were there,

But while they were talking Duba Sangarè came along and
    said,
"I have told you the Maraka are doing you wrong.
"You live alone in your compound while they are in their
    village,
2085   "But they have taken the fifty captives and tied them in your
    compound.
"Now the fifty captives have cut their bindings.
"I and the children are left in the house with them.
"Why do you allow this?"
Sonsan said, "Leave me in peace,
2090   "Leave me in peace.
"How can men tied with fresh cowhide cut themselves free?
"Leave me in peace,
"Get away from me.
"You women think men must sit all day watching you.
2095   "Leave me in peace.
"What kind of nonsense is this?"
Duba went back home and the captives killed the horse.
They cut off the tail and gave it to her.
Duba went weeping back to the chief's house.
2100   She stopped at the door and threw the horsetail at Sonsan.
She said, "You say that during the day I want you to do
    nothing but sit and watch me.
"Now they have killed your horse.
"Now you know you are mistaken!"
Ah, Sonsan began to wail.
2105   He said, "Chief, how can this be?
"I thought her words were nothing,
"And now I am truly unhappy because of it."
As the chief shouted for his men,
Sonsan ran to his compound and locked himself inside.
2110   Each of the fifty men took his musket,
They sat on top of the wall with their weapons ready.
The Maraka chief told the village men to go after the fifty
    captives at Sonsan's,
He told them to leave nobody alive.
They were going to kill them like chickens.
2115   When the first men tried to open Sonsan's gate, the muskets
    suddenly fired.
The villagers shouted, "It is a Bamana plot!
"Sonsan has betrayed us,
"Sonsan has betrayed us."
By the time the sun was high overhead the Maraka agreed to
    Sonsan's demands.
2120   He told them they must change the name of the village.
They must call it Sontiana, which they did.

This is the same Sontiana that is north of Kolokani.
That is how it was named.
Sometime later Massa, Bakari, and Ceba Mana left Sontiana.
2125   They went west from Kolokani to settle.
They called their new settlement Kaarta.
All of those who are Kulubali at Kaarta,
They are descendants of Sonsan.
They came from Sonsan.
2130   Sonsan's father was Barama Wolo,
Barama Wolo's father was Tontigi.

There then, is the story of Sonsan.
Ah, my listeners,
2140   That brings us to the end of the Kulubali story.
I have told you all that I can remember.
That story ends here.

6. The Epic of Almami Samori Touré
Narrated by Sory Fina Kamara

Recorded in Kissidougou, Guinea, April 4, 1994, by David Conrad. Transcribed and translated into English by David Conrad with the assistance of Jobba Kamara and Lansiné Magasouba. This excerpt edited by David Conrad.

AMONG THE MANY AFRICAN LEADERS who resisted the nineteenth-century European conquest of Africa, Almami Samori Touré (c. 1830-1900) was one of the most determined and successful. Samori waged war against invading French forces from 1882 until they captured him in 1898. In 1861 Samori had acquired the Mande people's status of *kèlètigi* (war chief, war lord, commander). He was soon invading neighboring territories, conquering local rulers, and taking control of their lands and people. By 1876 Samori had established his first empire, mostly in what is now the Republic of Guinea, but extending into southern Mali to Bamako and Sikasso and into today's northern Sierra Leone and western Côte d'Ivoire. In 1892, as a consequence of his wars and failed treaties with French colonial forces, Samori moved eastward with many of his people. By 1886 he had succeeded in conquering a new empire extending over a large area of what is now northern Côte d'Ivoire. In 1899 the French exiled Samori to Gabon, where he died in 1900.

Sory Fina Kamara, a *fina* or traditional Mande bard specializing in Islamic subjects, is well known in Guinea for his fine vocal performances, especially his song and narrative of Almami Samori. In this performance Sory Fina is accompanied by two guitarists. The tune played by them is that of a praise-song, not for Samori, but for Samori's brother Kèmè Brèma, another important figure in this text. One of the guitarists, Sekou Kantè, also functions as the *naamu*-sayer, or respondent, interjecting remarks between some of the lines, as seen in other texts. *Naamu* may be translated as 'indeed' or 'yes.' Sory Fina's version of the Samori epic reflects the local African perspective rather than that of European observers. The narrator is mainly interested in describing Samori's imperial conquest against neighboring peoples rather than his battles with the French invaders.

> Good evening,
> Big men of the blackskin's land,
> Good evening.
> We are performing today at Kissi Faramaya.
> 5   This morning Sory Fina Kamara of Banko Wuladala is
>   speaking to you.   (Mm, hm)
> He is living at Kissi Faramaya.
> Sekou Kantè is playing the strings,
> Fadama Kantè is playing the accompanying strings,
> Because there is not such a performance every day,
> 10   There is not such speaking done every day.

[Before Samori is born, a diviner predicts that Kèmo Lanfia will sire a "doer of great deeds." Competing for the honor of bearing the future hero, Lanfia's three wives make sacrifices of their most valuable possessions. Ma Sona Kamara becomes the mother of Samori, winning out over her co-wives, Ma Kèmè and Manigbè. In these lines the bard employs some of Samori's praise-names, such as Manju and Sanakoro Faama (King of Sanakoro). The frequently repeated song lines about the "three big brides" of Samori's brother Kèmè Brèma refer to Brahima's wife, Mariama Sire, his horse, Joro, and his sword, Ju'ufa ("Enemy killer").]

        Allah blessed Ma Sona Kamara with that good fortune.
115   Ma Sona Kamara,
        Ma Kèmè,
        Manigbé.
        She gave birth to Almami.
        When he was born,
120   He was born with birthmarks.
        He had marks on both wrists,
        And over the eyebrow.
               Kèmè Brèma had three big brides,
               Joro and Mariama Siré and Ju'ufa,
125   When Almami was born he grew up a headstrong child,
        But some wise people observed him carefully.
        Almami was popular,
        With many children following him,
        Manju.
130   He and the other youth formed different societies.
        The children would collect around Manju to play.
        Some days they would catch chickens and make it their
           society's sauce.
        They kept catching domestic animals until they got up to cows.
        People went and complained to ancestor Kèmo Lanfia:
135   "Your son who is called Almami,
        "He has been doing bad things.
        "He often catches our cows and makes them into the society's
           sauce."   (Naam)
        Allah caused it, Manju!
        Sanankoro Faama said, "I'm going to become an itinerant *marabout*,
140   "In fact I'm going to become a trader,
        "I don't want to offend my father any more,   (Naamu)
        "I have to start trading."
        He loaded up his bundle of goods.
        His friends used to sell bolts of white cloth,

145   The cloth that used to be made in the *koré*.[1]
He said to his friends, "Let's travel together,
"I also want to sell white cloth."
They went to one town and then came to Albadariah.
Albadariah is what they refer to as Bakadayi.

150   They passed there and went on to Banko Wuladala.   (Naam)
They met the *ilimunu bajana*.[2]
Sèdinu Kulubali.
Ancestor Mori Soumaila,
He was the master of the prayer beads at Banko Wuladala.
         (Naam)

155   He was the Almami's very first *marabout*.
They came and lodged with ancestor Mori Soumaila.
He had done his eight o'clock and bedtime prayers to Allah.
         (Naam)

At three o'clock in the morning,
He came and questioned the strangers.

160   He pointed at Almami, saying,
"The boy among you whose left foot is sore,
"Where does this youth come from?"
Almami's friends woke him up.
They told him, "Our host is waiting for you."   (Mmm)

165   The host said, "My son, where do you some from?"
He said, "I come from Sanankoro."
"Very well, you stay with me because your left foot is injured,
"So I can heal your foot, my son.
"It is Allah who has caused me to love you, Manju."   (Naamu)

170   Sanankoro *faama* said, "Very well."
Tis Allah who causes his slaves to love one another.
         (That's right)

Almami's wound finally healed.
Ancestor Mori Soumaila told him,
"This is what I have seen in you

180   "You must stop trading.
"Trading is not for you.   (Hm)
"You have spent three months here and you haven't sold ten
     dalasi[3] worth of cloth.
"Let me exchange this cloth of yours for one cow.
"A cow is easier to sell than cloth."

185   Almami agreed and exchanged his white cloth for a bull.
He took the bull by its lead rope and went to Saraya Wuladala.
He tied his bull outside the town of Saraya,
Then he entered to greet the people in traditional fashion.
The cow got loose and ate some of the people's crops.

---

1. Esoteric initiation society. 2. A powerful Muslim cleric. 3. Five franc coin equivalent to a penny.

190   "Aah!"
They said to Almami,
"This cow is no longer yours.
"Your cow has eaten many people's crops."
He begged those people and begged them
195   But they refused to return his cow.

[Samori loses more cows in a similar fashion and suffers additional humiliation in other communities. These incidents provide the narrator's motives for Samori's later behavior when he returns with his army and brutally conquers each of the towns that gave him trouble. But Samori must also have the genies' approval, because for a hero to accomplish memorable deeds, he must be in accord with the spirit world. One sign of the genies' approval is Samori's possession of firearms, which are said to have been provided by twin female genies. Firearms were one key to Samori's success against both the French and the people he incorporated into his empires.]

Almami Samori said, "A slave who depends on Allah is never poor."   (That's right, mm)
He said, "The old man told me at Banko Wuladala that I should withdraw from business."   (That's right)
285   He went back to Mara at Kuriya.
He said, "I have lost my investment three times."
Mara took four bundles of kola nuts.   (Naamu)
He said, "Go and wander the land, my son."
In early times, people did not give grudgingly. (Never, walayi)
290   He took the four bundles of kola and headed for Sirin Setigiya.
He went to Namanji Kamara at Setigiya.   (Mmm)
Namanji Kamara was a big man at Sirin.   (Son of Kaman, mm)
Kèmè Brèma had three big brides,
Joro and Mariama Siré and Ju'ufa.   (Naamu)
295   Before people realized it, Manju . . .
Manhood had its *sabu*.[4]
Great deeds are not accomplished without a *sabu*.   (That's right)
Eeeyoooo,
Everybody has his special *sabu*.   (That's right, Sory)
300   Nobody must overlook his *sabu*.
He remained in Setigiya for three months.
Nobody picked up ten *dalasi*,
He did not sell ten *dalasi* worth of kola.   (Naam)
When people worry, they sleep too much.
305   Almami was worried.   (Ah, Allah! Naamu, mm)
He lay in the hammock,
Stretched out his legs,

---

4. Cause, foundation, source of good things.

71

Took off his white cap and set it on his chest.   (Naamu)
As Almami began to fall into deep sleep,
310   Two young female genies came.
Their home was Takirini.
At that time Samawurusu . . .
Samawurusu was the ancestor of all the genies   (Naam)
Samawurusu sent for all twelve genie families to come at the
        same time.
315   "Let's have a meeting,
"Let's look for one trustworthy person,
"Let's give him the first musket in the blackskin's land."
                                        (*Djassaow*, mm)
It was that genie who authorized Almami to go to war.
                                        (That's right)
He did not attack people just for nothing.
                                        (That's right, mm, mmm)
320   Samawurusu's first son is Jumanjujan.   (Naamu)
"Send for your two twin sisters,
"Let them go all over Africa land,
"So we can entrust the musket to one trustworthy person."
                                        (Naamu)
[Samori is not the genie's first choice as the person who deserves to
receive the musket. The genie twins first approach other leading people
of the time, but they fail the tests of worthiness. In the following passage Samori makes the correct ritual sacrifice and passes his test but
receives the genies' blessing and the musket only on the condition that
he swear never to attack three other rulers who are specially protected
by genies. Meanwhile, Sere Brèma, powerful chief of the Sise clan,
whose army already possessed firearms, has conquered Sanankoro and
enslaved Samori's mother. Historically we know that Samori captured
Sere Brèma and annexed his territory in 1881.]

620   A message arrived from Kankan:
"Those who are wise should build walls around their towns.
"If war comes and you don't have walls, you can become slaves
        in a single day.
"Everyone must build walls around their towns."
All the youths passed the word that nobody should go to
        market the next day:
625   "We are going to build a wall tomorrow."
Almami heard this while he was still in Basando Moribaya,
                                        (Naamu, naamu)
Not knowing that it was for fear of Almami [himself] that the
        walls were being built.
At that time Almami had not yet acquired the musket.
At that time Sere Brèma was commanding,
630   He was the first one to acquire the musket in this land of ours,

La Guinée.
Karisi Manden Mori of Bakonko,   (Aaaaah)
Sere Brèma was the war lord.
When Almami set out to leave in the morning,
635   He met the youths on the road.   (Naamu)
The youths asked him, "Where are you going?
"Didn't you hear the announcement?"
He said, "Ah!
"I'm a stranger, that's why I was leaving."
640   They told him, "Go back to where the mud is being made,
"The law is not for only one person."
There was one hot-tempered man who hit Almami with a
        switch.   (Eeeh, beat him?)
Almami Samori smiled and went into the mud at Moribaya.
They were dancing in the mud until midday.
645   Almami asked them, "Is the work finished?" (Allah, mm, mm)
Almami had three bundles of ten kola nuts in his load.
He gave one to his host.
He took ten kola nuts and gave them to the workers.
He said, "Workers benefit everybody."
650   One old man called Kèmo Musa was there.
They told Kèmo Musa.
They said, "There was a stranger here who helped us dance in
        the mud,
"He had birthmarks on his wrists and above his eyebrows.
                                                            (Mm)
"He helped us mix the mud.
655   "He has also given ten kola nuts to the workers.
"He said they don't work only in the interest of one person."
                                                            (That's right)
"Haaa!" said Kèmo Musa,
"It was not a good thing for you to accept those ten kola nuts.
"We have been told about that man's signs.
660   "Anybody whom he helps to build a wall,
"He will break down that wall.
"Go after that Almami."   (Naam)
            Kèmè Brèma had three big wives,
            Joro and Mariama Sire and Ju'ufa,
665   The people searched for him.
            Descendant of the war lord.
            Good evening,
            It's Allah who makes a man the leader.   (That's right)
            The musket has its *sabu*.
670   Trading has its *sabu*.
            Expertise has its *sabu*,
            It is not just for nothing.   (That's right, Sory)
            Almamiiii!

They went after Almami.
675 There was one old man called Suba Musa,
He was also a war lord.
He opened his closet and put Almami inside.
The Bananso people came searching for Almami,
They did not see Almami again.
680 After they went away,
Suba Musa let Almami out.
He said, "My son, go on."
"Aaaah!"
He met some people pounding grain with their mortars and
pestles.
685 He said, "I need to sacrifice a white cock."
He said to Suba Musa, "Loan me your musket,
"I want to go outside the town."   (Naamu)
He went and shot one antelope,
Put it on his shoulder and carried it back to town.   (Naamu)
690 He gave the animal to his host Suba Musa.
He took one of the legs and showed it to the women who were
pounding outside.
He asked, "Who can trade me a white cock for this?"
"Aah," he said, "this has more meat than a chicken."
[One woman said], "My workers will go to the farm tomorrow,
695 "Come and I will give you one white cock."   (Naamu)
He took the cock and tied its two feet together.   (Mm)
The genie twins said,
"Go to Kerouane,
You must go to Kerouane,
700 Arrive there between Thursday night and daybreak Friday,
When both sides of the night are equal,
When nobody is awake in Kerouane.
You must meet us by the Jigbé River at Kerouane.
Bring this white cock to offer as a sacrifice.   (Allahu akbar)
705 Almami said, "Very well."
At midnight Almami took the cock by its two feet and
departed.
He said, "Fear is not the companion of manhood."   (Never)
He arrived at the bank of the Jigbé at midnight.
The water changed to the color of fresh milk,
710 The water changed to the color of fresh blood,   (Naamu)
The color changed as if the water had been dyed.
The genie twins rose out of the water.   (Hetch . . . mm)
They called to Almami,
"We are the ones calling to you,
715 "Don't be frightened."   (Eh, Allah)
Almami went into the water.
"Aah!" he said, "the water is not the place for me,

74

"I am afraid."
They made a rope bridge for Almami.
720 They told him not to be afraid. (Weii)
Almami walked and walked until he came to the genie twins.
They gave Almami the musket. (Naamu)
They said, "We are giving you the musket,
"But it is accompanied by three conditions:
725 "Thirty years, three months and three days,
"That's the time of your leadership in blackskins' land.
"Stranger in the morning,
"Host to strangers by evening."[5]
This is what they told Almami,
730 Almami said, "Very well."
Almami Samori climbed a *sida* tree.
There was a *sida* tree called Omisira. (Naamu)
The genie twins told Almami to climb that *sida* tree.
Almami Samori climbed the *sida* tree.
735 The genie twins transformed themselves.
One of them transformed herself into a python.
It started swallowing Almami from the hand to the armpit.
Almami Samori was not frightened.
The other one transformed herself and started licking his face.
(Naamu)
740 Almami Touré was not frightened of them. (Mmm)
"*Mba*,"[6] they said,
"We are giving you the musket for thirty years, three months
and three days.
"That's how long you will enjoy leadership in the blackskins'
land,
"But there are three conditions attached to the musket:
745 "When the war favors you, you must never attack Karamogo
Daye at Kankan.
"Karamogo Daye is our old friend. (Weiii)
"When the war favors you, you must not attack Sikasso Kèba.
"Our aunt does his genie work.
"When the war favors you, do not attack Gbon.
750 "Our sister does the genie work for the chief of Gbon.
"We have warned you about those three places,
"Do not attack Gbon.
"We have given you the rest of the Africa land."
Almami Samori said, "Very well."
755 He said, "Now that this is done,
"Let me go and see my old mother."
I want to go and see my old mother in Sanankoro,
Kabako! (Naam, naam, naam)

---

5. Standard praise for a conqueror. 6. Response to a greeting.

Sona Kamara,
760   Ma Kèmè Kamara,
Maningbè,
Kamara woman's son Sankun,
Mori the savior of everyone.
Before he could get there,
765   The warriors of Sere Brèma had already captured Sanankoro,
Including his mother Sona Kamara.   (Hmm)
Haaa!   (Hmm)
Almami went there and asked for his old mother.
"Aah!
770   "The warriors of Sere Brèma have taken your mother."
Blessings are good,
A blessed house is never empty.
Allah made the sky with abundant blessings,
Allah made the earth with abundant blessings,
775   And made the moon with abundant blessings,
He made the stars with abundant blessings.   (Sory, that's right)
He went to Sere Brèma,
Karisi Manden Mori,
He said, "I came for my old mother,
780   "Her name is Fani Sona.
"My father is living like a bachelor at Sanankoro.
"He was with Sere Brèma for three months,
"Then it became seven months.
"After those seven months it became seven years with Sere
        Brèma."
785   Ahah!
He had faith in Sere Brèma,
Sere Brèma had faith in Almami.
Whatever place Sere Brèma decided to attack,
Almami would go and capture it.
790   They would come and tell Sere Brèma. "Heeh!
"This stranger of ours is very powerful."
Sere Brèma became suspicious of Almami.   (Hmm)
Lack of confidence does not accomplish anything.
                                        (There's truth in that)
He asked Almami Samori,
795   He said, "What do you want from me?"
Almami said, "I 'm worried about my old mother.
"My father is living like a bachelor at Sanankoro."
"I will give you back your mother plus seven muskets. (Weiii)
"If you wish, when you come back I will divide the army into
        two.
800   "You will have one division and I will have one division.
"I have come to like your ways very much Almami." (Naamu)
Almami Samori said, "Very well."

A long time passed and Sere Brèma did not see Almami again.
He heard that Almami had organized some troops in Sanan-
    koro.   (Naam)

805   Almami said to the young men of Sanankoro,
"There is no special amulet for winning a battle."
He said, "Let's organize our own army."
Some of the young warriors were suspicious,
Some of them hesitated.

810   Those who were not afraid,   (Naamu)
Almami took them and attacked some people.
They captured three towns.
All the young warriors who were not married were each given
    a girl.
The word traveled from person to person:

815   "An army has been organized in Sanankoro,
"You can get a wife without paying any money."
Almami's army became popular.

[With his newly formed army, Samori launches a series of military
campaigns, beginning with the towns that had humiliated him when
he was a wandering merchant.]

When Almami's army was complete,
He said, "I still feel angry about the cow incident at Wasulu."
They mounted their horses and marched toward Wasulu.

915   At Wasulu they had put Almami's leg in shackles
Because he had gotten so furious about the cow,
But he was made exempt from the law.
Some had said, "Let's kill him."
There was one old man who said,   (Naamu)

920   "If one drop of this man's blood falls on the ground,
"Rain will not fall for seven years.
"Our eyes will not see rain fall in this land."
They had said, "Release him."
People are not alike.   (People are not alike)

925   Almami did not forget this,
Manju Touré.   (Naamu)
He said, "Since my army is ready,
"Let's go and ask them for the cow I loaned them.
"When I left there I told them I was only leaving it,

930   "Because I was unable to get it back from them,
"But that I was not satisfied."   (That's right)
He went and said to the people of Ton,
"Let me pass on the road through town,
"I am going to Wasulu."   (Naamu)

935   They said, "You can't use the road through the center of town,
"You must go around the outside of the town."

He said, "Nobody should disrespect a warlord, (That's right)
"Ancestor of the warlord." (Naamu)
He requested passage in the traditional way,
940 They did not allow passage to Almami.
In the morning he woke them up with muskets and gunpow-
der,
What an amazing thing.
He took the road through the center of town, (Paki)
He went on to Wasulu.
945 He told the Wasulu people, "I did not come to fight.
"The cow you took from me when I was a trader,
"That's the cow that I have come after." (Hmm)
They asked him, "What did your cow look like?
"Was it a white cow?
950 "Or was it red?
"Was it a black cow?"
He said, "There is blood on my cow's face,
"And smoke is rising in front of it." (Battle has come)
Everyone knows there is no cow like that.
955 He surrounded Wasulu with nineteen ranks with their gun bar-
rels overlapping.
Whoever witnessed it saw a very big thing.
Anybody who failed to witness it missed something wonderful.
Good evening warlord,
Grandson of the warlord,
960 Manju Touré.
Good evening,
My presentation does not get interesting until late at
night,
Mm, hmm,
There is a *sabu* for excellence.
965 There is a *sabu* for kingship. (That's right, Sory)
Everyone has his time.
After a time Almami asked the Wasulu people one question.[7]
He started destroying Wasulu,
He destroyed it like an old pot,
970 Like an old calabash.
That's why there are so many village ruins in the Wasulu
country. (There are many ruins)
If you can't help someone,
At least don't do him wrong. (It's not good)

[Continuing his campaigns, Almami Samori violates his oath by attacking all three of the men who were protected by the genies. In one case
he ignores the genies' warning that if he attacks Sikasso (where Kara-

---

7. About the cow they took from him, ll. 185ff.

78

mogo Daye, one of the protected men has taken refuge), his army will suffer great losses. Kéba, king of Sikasso, has a sister known as "One-breasted Demba." (Physical deformity signifies special power.) She falls in love with Samori's brother Kémé Brèma and sends him food every day. Learning of this, Samori wrongly accuses his brother (who is one of his greatest fighters) of treachery and strips him of his weapons. In an earlier falling out, Kémé Brèma had sworn that he would never again argue with his brother, so he removes his protective medicine before the next battle and is killed. This motivates the one-breasted woman to emerge as a heroine of Mande epic.]

<blockquote>

Kémé Brèma stripped off his protective amulets during the battle of Sikasso.
He purposely faced the gunfire without his medicine and was hit by musket balls.
They went and told the one-breasted woman.
1255 They said, "Kémé Brèma did not survive the battle at Sikasso."
In his lifetime Kémé Brèma was never captured and abused by the enemy.
He gave himself up to the gunfire
Because of what his brother did to him.
People of early times lived up to their oaths,
1260 One-breasted Demba was told what happened.
The one-breasted woman said, "At dawn I will ask my brother."
She did not sleep.
She went and asked Sikasso Kéba.
She said, "I want to know if it's true that Kémé Brèma has been killed."
1265 She took off her *lapa*[8] and threw it at her brother.
She said, "Give me your trousers."
He took her *lapa* and wrapped it around himself,
And gave the trousers to his sister.
She put on his trousers.
1270 She said, "I invite you and Almami to the bank of the Kokoro,
"So you and Almami can settle the account of Kémé Brèma."
They let Karamogo Daye escape to Bamako.
Sikasso Kéba said to Karamogo Daye,
"You were here under my protection.
1275 "I don't want you to suffer from this turn of events."
The Kokoro is in the region the Maninka call Woyowayanko.
The battle at Woyowayanko was not sweet.
Even up to tomorrow morning
Musket barrels can be found in the Woyowayanko.
1280 It was that woman who organized the battle at Woyowayanko.
</blockquote>

---

8. Wraparound cloth skirt.

7. The Epic of Musadu
Narrated by Moikè Sidibe

Recorded in Kankan, Guinea, on December 1, 1993, by Timothy Geysbeek. Transcribed and translated into English by Ansu Cisse and Faliku Sanoe with the assistance of Timothy Geysbeek. This excerpt edited by Timothy Geysbeek.

MANY MANDE PEOPLE OF SOUTHEASTERN GUINEA and western Liberia narrate a popular story of how a slave named Zo Musa founded the town of Musadu near the provincial capital of Beyla in Guinea. They also tell how a powerful Mande warrior named Foningama (Kamara) later took control of the town. "Zo Musa" may have founded Musadu between the thirteenth and fifteenth centuries during the time of the Mande or the Mali empire. Most of the "Foningama" episodes seem to date to a later period, perhaps during the sixteenth century or a little earlier. The stories about Zo Musa and Foningama began as separate accounts, but over time the Mande have compressed them into one narrative. The Musadu epic is as important to many of the Mande peoples in this region for defining social, cultural, and historical relationships between themselves and other peoples as the Sunjata epic is for the Mande in Mali and neighboring lands.

Moikè Sidibe, the narrator, is Professor of History at the University of Kankan, Guinea. Sidibe's father is of the Fula ethnic group from Futa Jallon, and his mother is a Kamara-Mande from Damaro in Kerouane province. The speaker can trace his ancestry through his mother's father's line over ten generations to Foningama's son Fajala (Fènjala). Moikè Sidibe thus provides a Kamara view of the Musadu epic.

Timothy Geysbeek recorded Moikè Sidibe in Lai Makula Mammadi Kamara's yard in Kankan on December 1, 1993. Toligbè Braima Kamara and Fata Jiba Kamara encouraged Sidibe like *naamu*-sayers throughout the narrative. Ansu Cisse and Faliku Sanoe helped Geysbeek translate the text. Sidibe divided his narrative into three major parts: the Kamara migrations from the Mande to Côte d'Ivoire and southeastern Guinea, Foningama's flight to Musadu after his father died, and Zo Musa's founding of Musadu and exile after the Mande forced him out of town. Sidibe usually said Masa instead of Musa and Misadu instead of Musadu.

[The growth of Misadu.]

105	Damaro came from Misadu.	(Uhun)
	How did it come from Misadu?	(Uhun)
	Misadu was a town all by itself.	(Uhun)
	The Koniya people,	(Uhun)
	Loma,	(Uhun)
110	Kpelle,	(Uhun)
	Kono,	(Uhun)

80

They all lived in Misadu.   (That is right)
Misadu was a small town,   (Uun)
But Misadu later became a big town.   (Uun)

[The Kamara began to migrate south as the Mande became less secure. The Kamara ancestor's sons dispersed to different areas, and one, Foningama, traveled down to the town of Siyanò in Côte d'Ivoire. Foningama sired a son named "Small Foningama," who is the Kamara hero in this story.]

[The Kamara dispersal from the Mande.]

115	Later, Misadu	(Uun)
	The first Kamara who were there	(Uhun)
	Were not the same as the Kamara who came from up north,	
		(Uum)
	In Côte d'Ivoire.	(Uum)
	Foningama	(Uhun)
120	Came from Côte d'Ivoire.	(Uum)
	He came from a town,	(Uhun)
	From Siyanò.	(Uhun)
	They called it Silana.	(Uhun, Silana)
	How they came,	(Uhun)
125	Lets talk about that.	(Uhun)
	History	(Uum)
	Did not happen today.	(Uhun)
	Eh—Foningama,	(Uhum)
	Miakèdè Kamara,	(Uun)
130	Sonkoli Kamara,	(Uhun)
	Friki Kamara,	(Uhun)
	All came from one man.	(Uun)
	They came from Sibi,	(Uhum)
	From the north.	(Uum)
135	At that time,	
	There was trouble in Mande.	(Uum)
	The old people	(Uum)
	Say that many things were happening in Mande	(Uum)
	At that time.	
140	That did not happen in our presence.	(Uum)
	We only heard about it.	(Uhum)
	When they came from the north,	
	Some Kamara went and settled in a town in Côte d'Ivoire.	(Uun)
	It is called Siyanò.	(Siyanò)
145	The others went to Kouroussa.	(Uun)
	Sonabale	(Uun)
	Was founded on that side of Kouroussa.	(Uun)
	The other two went and settled, èh—near Fria.	(Uum)

The other went and settled in the Sigidi[1] region. (Uhun)

[Kamara medicine, *saakèle.*]

150	The one who went left to the northern part of Côte d"Ivoire,	
		(Uhun)
	That was Foningama.	(Uhun)
	Foningama lived in Silana	(Uhun)
	And sired many children.	(Uhun)
	He died after his grandchildren were born.	(Uhun)
155	Those grandchildren were here.	(Uun)
	The name of an ancestor can be given	(Uhun)
	To a child.	(Uhun)
	After Small Foningama was born,	(Uhun)
	Confusion arose among his father's children.	(Uhun)
160	What was the nature of this confusion?	(Uhun)
	There was something in their family	(Uhun)
	That was called *saakèle.*[2]	(Uhun)
	The secret thing	(Uhun)
	Of the Jomani	
165	Was that *saakèle.*	
	After the father died,	(Uhun)
	It would be given to the first son.	(Uhun)
	That *saakèle*	
	Was medicine.	
170	It was a symbol of power.	(Uuun)
	The person who had it would rule.	(Uun)
	You would rule a region.	(Uun)

[The Kamara patriarch traditionally gave *saakèle,* or medicine-imbued sheep horn, to the oldest son in the family. Foningama's father, however, gave the *saakèle* to Foningama because of their close relationship. This caused resentment among Foningama's older brothers, particularly Kònsava. So, Foningama fled to his mother's family, the Kromah, who lived in Nèlèkòlò near Misadu. Foningama and the Kromah later moved to Misadu to secure more protection against Kònsava.]

[Foningama inherits the Kamara *saakèle.*]

	Concerning Small Foningama,	
	Eh, they said that Kònsava	(Uhun)
175	Was one of his father's children.	(Uhun, the Kònsava people)
	Tension rose between them	(Uhun)
	Because they were not near their father	(Uhun)
	And because they wanted to get their father's blessing.	(Uun)

---

1. Siguiri.   2. Sheep horn.

	The son who went near the father and was blessed	(Uun)
180	Was Foningama.	(Uun)
	That Kònsava	(Uhun)
	Left and went far away,	(Uhun)
	From his father.	(Uun)
	Life became difficult for his father.	(That is right)
185	His father got sick	
	And died later on.	(Uhun)
	Now after his death	
	Before he died,	
	He told his son [Foningama],	(Uhun)
190	"My son, you are the youngest of my children.	(Uhun)
	"I am not supposed to give the thing to you	(Uhun)
	"That I am going to give to you.	(Uum)
	"You are not the oldest,	(Uun)
	"But I am going to give it to you	(Uum)
195	"Because you have taken care of me,	
	"Because a good relationship developed between father and child.	(Uum)
	"I am giving this thing [to you],	(Uum)
	"And God will bless you in this world.	(Uun)
	"God will bless you at the time of judgment.	(Uun)
200	"If God agrees,	(Uhun)
	"And if there is nothing [bad] between the father and the child,	(Uun)
	"Nothing bad	(Uun)
	"Will come your way."	(Uhun)

[Foningama flees to his Kromah uncles in Koniya.]

	After they announced that he died,	(Uhun)
205	They sent a message for all the father's children to come.	
	They were thinking about . . .	(Uhun)
	They were thinking about	(Uhun)
	The *sani-saakèle,*	(Uhun)
	That medicine.	(Uhun)
210	But the man left the medicine with his son,	(Uhun)
	Small Foningama,	(Uhun)
	So the others went and tried to kill him.	(Uhun)
	He fled	(Uun)
	And went	
215	To his mother's home.	(Uum)
	He said, "If a child	(Uhun)
	"Can't be in his father's home,	(Uhun)
	"He should go to his mother's home."	(Uun)
	That did not happen recently.	(Uhun)
220	That happened a long time ago.	(That is right)

	That is the parable that Konava gave.	(Uhun)
	Layi Mako himself	(Uhun)
	Said that if you see a man who is able to carry a load,	
	It means that he respects his mother's people.	(Uum)
225	If you respect your mother's people,	(Uum)
	There are some things that you can do that others cannot do.	
		(Uhun)
	You can become strong and powerful and have a good reputa- tion.	(That is right)

[Tumani Kromah and Foningama move from Nèlèkòlò to Misadu.]

	Foningama fled and went to his uncles,	(Uum)
	Who were the Kromah,	(Uhun)
230	The Kromah of Koniya.	
	His mother,	
	Her name was Dama Soloba.	
	His uncle was Tumani Kromah.	
	Tumani Kromah	
235	Ruled Koniya at that time.	
	The Koniya	
	Was divided into twelve regions,	(Uhun)
	And the Kromah ruled the whole area.	(Uhun)
	In Koniya,	
240	Foningama went to Nèlèkòlò,	(Uhun)
	Which was Tumani Kromah's home.	(Uhun)
	His uncle said, "I am happy that you came,	(Uhun)
	"But I want us to flee	(Uhum)
	"From the war	(Uhum)
245	"That is following you.	(Uhum)
	"Let's go to Misadu	(Uhun)
	"And settle in Misadu.	(Uhun)
	"It is better than living in Nèlèkòlò."	(Uuhun)
250	That is why Foningama and his uncle went to Misadu.	(Uhun)
	Many people lived there.	(Uhun)
	"[Let's move to Misadu] in case Kònsava decides to come and fight.	(Uhun)
	"They say they want to take the *saakèle* from you	(Uhun)
	"And fight you."	(Uum)

[Plot to kill Foningama. This harks back to an earlier moment when
Foningama still lived with his family (l. 212).]

	They had dug a hole	(Uhun)
255	In the house	(Uhun)
	Even before he left,	
	And they put a spear and many other dangerous things	

	In the bottom of the hole.	(Uhun)
	When Foningama came [into the house],	(Uhun)
260	They asked him to sit in the middle [of the room].	
	They hoped	
	That when he came and sat in the middle of the room	(Uhun)
	He would fall into the hole	(Uum)
	And that that would be the end of him.	(Uhun)
265	When he arrived,	(He came)
	He said, "Uun, this	(Uhun)
	"Is not my place."	(Uun)
	One old woman had warned him about the plot	
	Before he went to sit in the middle [of the room].	(Uhun)
270	Foningama listened and remembered what she said.	(Uum)
	When he went there,	
	They said, "Here is your seat."	
	He replied, "No, that place is reserved for important people."	
		(Uum)
	He went and sat at the back of the room,	(Uun)
275	And those who came in after him	(Uum)
	Went and fell into the hole.	(Uum)
	That is why Foningama fled to his uncle's place.	(Uun)
	That is what I have said today.	
	They left Nèlèkòlò	(Uhun)
280	And went to Misadu.	(Uun)

[As the Kamara were emigrating from Mande, a slave named Zo Masa ('chief') founded Musadu. Zo Masa acquired some powerful medicine and established a secret (*doo*) society to organize his followers against the Mande in a hilly area outside of Musadu called Doofatini. A *moli* or 'cleric' named Beyan Bèlète from Musadu finally defeated Zo Masa. Bèlète placed a more powerful medicine on a frog, and the frog swallowed Zo Masa's medicine. Zo Masa and the Loma, Kpelle, Kono, and Mano peoples associated with him later fled after Foningama defeated them in battle. Zo Masa moved to the town of Zota near N'Zerekore. The Kromah had granted Foningama the chieftancy of Musadu after he repulsed an attack from Kònsava. Foningama then extended his power and put his sons in control over twelve neighboring regions. Some of his sons, however, were executed for breaking a law. The survivors left and ruled other areas.]

[Zo Musa Kromah or Zo Masa Kòlò. Many say that Masa was a slave of the Kromah, and that his "last name" was Kòma.]

When they reached Misadu,	(Uun)
Zo Masa Kromah was there.	(Uun)
The people used to call him Zo-Zo Masa Kòlò.	(Uum)
He was the owner of Misadu at that time.	(Uhun)

285	He had medicine that could do anything.	(Uhun)
	The Kromah,	(Uhun)
	Bèlète,	(Uhun)
	Fofana,	(Uun)
	Zozo [Donzo],	(Uun)
290	Sumaro [Dole],	(Uum)
	They had all settled in Misadu by that time.	(Uhun)
	Misadu was mixed up by that time.	

[Kònsava attacks Foningama in Misadu.]

	Eh, when they attacked Misadu—	(Uhun)
	Kònsava and his people,	(Uhun)
295	Foningama fought very hard,	(Uhun)

[The Kromah make Foningama the *masa*³ of Misadu.]

	And the Kromah appreciated what he did.	(Uhun)
	His older . . .	
	His uncle	(Uun)
	Helped him	(Un)
300	And said that they should make him that thing—the masa.	
		(Uhun)

[Moli Beyan Bèlète destroys Zo Masa's medicine.]

	But he asked how they would defeat Zo Masa and his people.	
		(Uhun)
	There was a *saakèle*,	(Uhun)
	Which Zo Masa had for medicine,	(Uhun)
	And it used to kill and do other big things there.	(Uhun)
305	They made medicine	(Uhun)
	From a frog.	(Uhun)
	The frog . . .	
	When it [Zo Masa's *saakèle*] swallowed the frog,	(Uhun)
	It was ruined.	(Uhun)
310	That is how Zo Masa lost his power.	(Uhun)
	That is how it is explained,	(Uhun)
	For the medicine was ruined.	(Uhun)
	Moli Beyan Bèlète	(Uhun)
	Was the one who fixed that medicine.	(Uhun)
315	He made the medicine.	(Uhun)
	He was a *moli*—	(Uhun)
	Somebody: [From] Misadu there.	
	Sidibe: [From] Misadu there.	
	The other person's power	(Uhun)

---

3. Chief.

320	Was destroyed	(Uhun)
	After he fixed that medicine.	(Uhun)

[Zo Masa's people go to Man, Bosu, and Lola.]

	Zo Masa Kòlò	(Uhun)
	Left	(Uhun)
	With his people.	(Uhun)
325	One group went	(Uhun)
	To Man in Côte d'Ivoire,	(Uhun)
	And they fought the people of Man	(Uun)
	When they reached Man.	(Uun)
	It was called Man.	(Uum)
330	That is what the people of Man did.	(Uum)
	Some went	(Uhun)
	To Zòò,	(Uum)
	All the way down to the region of Lola,	(Uhun)
	And settled in Bosu and Lola.	(Uhun)
335	Those are the Mano who live there.	(Uhun)

[Zo Masa takes water, roots, and rocks from Misadu.]

	The Kpelle,	(Uun)
	When Zo Masa Kòlò	(Um)
	Left Misadu,	(Uum)
	He took some water from Misadu,	(Uhun)
340	From the surrounding streams.	(Uhun)
	He also took some of its tree roots	(Um)
	And some of its rocks.	(Um)
	There were some rocks.	(Um)

[Foningama's sons are executed for breaking a law.]

	They passed a law	(Uhun)
345	And said that anybody who violated the law	(Uum)
	Would be killed.	(That is right)
	The persons who violated the law	(Uhun)
	Were Foningama's children.	(Uum)
	They killed them	(Uum)
350	At the rock near Misadu's mosque.	(Uum)
	That is their grave.	(They are there)
	They are the ones who were killed because they violated the law.	(Uum)
	[They said,] "We have passed a law.	(Uum)
	"How can your children violate the law?	(Uhun)
355	"What should be done to them?"	
	Braima: Kill them.	

	Sidibe: They were killed.	(Uhun)
	Was there sympathy for anybody else?	(Uun)

[Zo Masa travels to Boola and Wenzu.]

	They left.	(Uhun)
360	When they reached the road,	(Uhun)
	They said, "*Kanikwekoe.*"	(Uhun)
	[When they reached] the river near Damaro,	(Uhun)
	Zo Masa stood up and said,	(Uhun)
	"*Kanikookwe.*"	(Uhun)
365	That means,	(Uhun)
	"God has saved me	(Uhun)
	"From Foningama and his people	(Uhun)
	"And separated me from them."	(Uhun)
	He passed	(Um)
370	And went to the region of Boola.	(Uhun)
	There are many mushrooms in the area	(Uhun)
	That are named *kpoola*.	(Um)
	They named Boola	(Um)
	After *kpoola*.	(Uhun)
375	The Kpelle settled there.	(Uum)
	They went to Wenzu.	(Um)

[Zo Masa settles in Zota.]

	After they left Wenzu,	(Uum)
	They went to Zèlèkole.	(Uum)
	They went and established a town	(Uhun)
380	There called Zota.	(Uhun)
	That Zota,	(Uhun)
	Ta,	(Uun)
	In Kpelle means 'town,'	(Uum)
	And Zo was Zo Masa Kòlò's name.	
385	That is why they call it Zo Masa Kòlò's town.	(Uum)
	Zèlèkole	(Uhun)
	Is not the real name of Zèlèkole.	
	The real name is Zaakolè.	(Uhun)
	Zaakolè	(Um)
390	Was a name given	(Um)
	To a small stream.	(Um, that is right)
	That is [Zota] where he [Zo Masa] went and settled.	
	He poured some water.	(Uhun)
	That water was like the water in Misadu.	(Uhun)
395	He put down the rock that he had,	(Uhun)
	And it became like the rock in Misadu.	(Uhun)
	The hill rose like the hill in Misadu.	(Uhun)

The big tree also grew like the big tree in Misadu.	(Um)
Even if that had not happened,	(Um)

400 The people knew that Zo Masa Kòlò left Misadu with his
medicine (Uum)
And came here. (Uun)

[Zo Masa, scarification, and *doo* in Misadu.]

Scarification formed the basis of the *doo*.[4]	(Uum)
Doo started in Misadu,	(Uum)
In the Gbèi area.	(Uum)

405 The hill [Doofatini] (Uum)
Is by the road that leads to Sinkò. (Uun)
That is where *doo* was started. (Uum)
That is where they started to cut people's skin. (Uum)
His name was Zo Masa Kòlò. (Uum)
410 Do you understand? (Uum)

[The Mande people meet the Loma, Kpelle, Kono, and Mano in Koniya.]

Foningama lived in Misadu. (Uhun)
Didn't I tell you that this area was divided into twelve regions?
(Koso-Kosobè)
He put the Kamara[5] to rule over these regions. (Uum)
Braima: Now we come to Koniya.
Sidibe: Now we come to Koniya.
415 What does Koniya mean? (Uhun)
Say, "Kòniya." (Uhun)
Kòni, (Uum)
Water, èh—'rock.' (Uhun)
Ya means this thing—
420 *Braima:* 'Water.'
Sidibe: 'Water.'
That is where the name Koniya comes from. (Uum)
Otherwise, the children of the land of Koniya, (Uhun)
They are the Loma, the Kpelle, the Kono. (Uum)
425 The people of Mani[6] came and met them there. (Uum)
All of the [Mande] people who can say, (Uum)
"*Ngo* (I say)," came and met them there. (Uum)
Do you understand? ... (Uum)

[Zo Masa Kòlò founds Misadu.]

How was Misadu founded?

---

4. Secret. 5. His sons. 6. The Mande.

	A man was there	(Uhun)
950	Whose name was Masa.	
	Some people called him Musa,	(Uhun)
	And some people called him Masa.	(Uuhun)
	Do you understand?	(Uhun)
	Masata Zo	(Uhun)
955	Was Loma.	

It is *masa so*,[7]
Masa kèla so.[8]
Musata Zo, Musa's town, Misadu.
The town of Musa.

960	How was it established?	
	You know that a stream was there.	(Uhun)

Now, Musa was a slave.
He used to go fishing there.
After he caught fish,
965 He would go and make a mat and put the fish on it.
People went and bought them.
People went and bought them a little at a time.
He built a house there.
After he built his house,
970 People started to go and settle there as his business became
      more prosperous.
The Dukule settled there.
The Kromah settled there.
The Sware settled there.
The Fofana settled there.
975 All of them went there and made the place become big.
But the Loma, Kpelle, èh-èh—Kono, Konè,
Braima: Mano [in the background].
Sidibe: They all lived—all lived in Misadu town.

[The Loma, Kpelle, Kono, and Mano flee when Foningama defeats Zo
Masa.]

	That is why they say	
980	That all of the towns in the forest came from Misadu.	
	All of them came from Misadu.	(Uhun, Uhun)
	Many people left Misadu when Foningama	
	Went to Misadu	(Uhun)
	And fought, èh-èh—Zo Masa Kòlò.	
985	They fought Zo Masa Kòlò.	
	That is what happened.	
	Now, the people left.	
	Some people went to the east.	

---

7. Chief's town. 8. The chief man's town.

Some people went to the south.
990   Some went toward Macenta and Zèlèkole and Lola and Liberia
        and Côte d'Ivoire.
Do you understand?   (Uhun)
That is how Misadu was established.
That is how Misadu came to be.

8. The Epic of Kelefa Saane
Narrated by Shirif Jebate

Recorded for Radio Gambia sometime in the 1960s. Transcribed by Bakari Sidibe. Translated into English by Gordon Innes with the assistance of Bakari Sidibe. Edited by Gordon Innes and published in 1978 by the School of Oriental and African Studies, University of London. This excerpt edited by John Wm. Johnson.

KELEFA SAANE WAS A MID-NINETEENTH CENTURY WARRIOR of the aristocracy of Kaabu, a confederation of Mandinka states whose influence extended from the Gambia River southward as far as the Rio Corubal, but whose heartland was the state of Kaabu, which was located in the northeast of what is now Guinea-Bissau. It is puzzling that an epic is today recited by Mandinka bards about this figure, for he had no influence on events in which he was involved and in no way affected the course of history. Indeed, he loses the battle which is recounted in the epic and is killed. Moreover, he is described by the Mandinka bards as being a Jola, who are linguistically and culturally quite distinct from the Mandinka. The bards' practice of referring to Kelefa as a Jola is made even more puzzling by the fact that Kelefa's family name is Saane, the name of one of the lines of warrior aristocrats of the Mandinka state of Kaabu. Yet, in The Gambia, the story of Kelefa's career is one of the best-known and best-loved items in the bards' repertoires, and his principle praise-poem is traditionally the first piece a young bard learns to play on the kora, the twenty-one-stringed lute-harp so popular among the Mande peoples.

The text presented here is a transcription of a performance by a highly respected elderly Gambian, Jali Shirif Jebate who, like other Gambian bards, possesses a repertoire of historical narratives falling into two main parts. The first of these is the Sunjata epic, which recounts the career of Sunjata Keita, culminating in the defeat of his great adversary, Sumanguru, about the year 1235 and his establishment as ruler of Manding (or Mali), which expanded under his successors to become the most influential of all the medieval Sudanic empires. The second part of the bards' repertoire comprises accounts of the careers of various outstanding local figures of the second half of the nineteenth century who were active in The Gambia valley and in the area stretching south from there into Guinea-Bissau. The epic of Kelefa Saane falls in this second category.

Kelefa's military career can be briefly told. When war between Niumi and Jokadu appeared inevitable on the north bank of the River Gambia, King Demba Sonko of Niumi, a member of one of the three lineages which held the kingship of Niumi in rotation—the others were the Saanes and the Maanes—sent a request for help to Badora, one of the states in the Kaabu confederation. Kelefa Saane responded to the call and set off to Niumi. His arrival in Niumi seems to have been an embarrassment to the king, who had been forewarned by his Muslim diviners that he would be ill advised to have Kelefa by his side when

he joined battle with Jokadu. King Demba Sonko therefore sent Kelefa off across the river on a pretext while the Niumi forces launched their attack. When Kelefa returned and caught up with his allies, who had gone off without him, he was not of great assistance. He certainly did not help the Niumi forces to victory, for the war was a disaster for both sides. In the fighting, Kelefa was rather ingloriously shot by a deformed leper (or albino) who lay in wait for him up a tree in the shade of which Kelefa rested from time to time.

Whatever the reality may have been, the princely ideal still has a powerful emotional appeal for the Mandinka. Kelefa seems to be the embodiment of the highest princely ideals, and in this lies much of his popularity with Mandinka audiences. Kelefa displays unselfishness of the highest order; he responded to the king of Niumi's call for help, because the king was in trouble, and it therefore behooved a prince to respond, regardless of his own circumstances. Kelefa clearly did not go to Niumi for personal gain; on the contrary, he repeatedly rejected the offer of generous gifts by the various rulers through whose territory he passed if he would abandon his intention of going to fight in Jokadu. These same rulers reminded him that war brings sudden death to many, but Kelefa remained resolute in his resolve to go and do battle on behalf of the king of Niumi, rejecting all offers of wealth. It would have been a betrayal of the princely ideal if he had chosen wealth rather than battle. The story of how Kelefa resisted all the offers of wealth and instead pressed forward to the hazards of battle to assist a friend in need must make a powerful impact on a Mandinka listener. Here are displayed loyalty to a friend, courage and unselfishness of the highest order. The popularity of the Kelefa story with Mandinka audiences must surely be due in large measure to the fact that Kelefa embodies in their highest form not only the ideals of the princes, but also ideals of everyday life such as unselfishness, loyalty to a friend, and courage.

> Kelefa summoned his men
> And said to them, "Let's go!"
> Kelefa took some wine and drank it.

> *Mm yee ee*, sit down and wait for me.
300 Ah, you seized him and you slew him.
> Yammadu the warrior, you are successful in war.

> When Kelefa Saane
> Arrived, he found all the Niumi forces assembled at the Mem-
>   meh bridge.
> They were arguing with each other;
305 Some were saying,

"Let's go to Dasilami," but Kelefa said to them, "The people
there are Muslims, so don't let's go there."
Some said,
"Let's go to Tambana," but Kelefa said, "The people there are
caste members."
Some said,

310 "Let's go to Bali."
But Kelefa said to them, "That area is upriver; if our attack fails,
it will not be possible to get back to Niumi."
Some said,
"Then what are we to do?"
Kelefa told them,

315 "The best place for us to wage war is a place called Baria Koto.
"Let's go there."
As you approach Kuntair,
The small valley which you see
Marks the line of march of Kelefa Saane and the forces of
Niumi; it is their passage which produced that valley.

320 They went to Madina Jiikoi,
Then they crossed the upper reaches of the creek at Fatakoo.
At the spot where the horses crossed, their hooves, which made
the rock dry,
Have left prints which are visible to this day at low tide.
They crossed over and came to Baria Koto.

325 Saane Balaamang lies at Baria, Bobo Tuma, and Bobo
Sankung.
Great man of Tambana, a bee in sorghum wine, warrior in
a foreign land.
Not every child inherits his father's estate; I-haven't-got-it's
griot is unfortunate, a mean man's griot is unfortunate.
For what great men have I sung this? For great men, both
friendly and hostile.
But a Mandinka with his fickleness, if you do him a good
turn, that will be noised abroad; if you do him a bad
turn, that too will be noised abroad.

330 Kelefa said that they should not go to Tambana
Because the people there were caste members; but there were
many men of high distinction there,
For at that time Mang Bandi was in Tambana,
Keni was in Tambana,
Keni Kumba was in Tambana,

335 Ngaali was in Tambana,
Kali Meta Suuko was in Tambana,
Jeenung Meta Suuko was in Tambana,
Hama Demba was in Tambana, Seeku Nufung was in Tam-
bana, there were griots too in Tambana.

94

Mootang Maane,
340 Jata Banna Karte Was,
All of these were men of high distinction.
That was why
Kelefa Saane said that they should not go to Tambana.

They advanced,
345 The Niumi forces advanced,
They reached Baria Koto.
But before the Niumi forces reached Baria Koto,
King Demba took the mahogany writing board
Upon which the *marabout* had written
350 And he gave it to a messenger, who went and stood on the
     bank
Of the creek at Memmeh;
He took the mahogany writing board and threw it into the
     creek.
When he threw it in, a great sound filled the air,
A great noise was heard.
355 The Jokadu men shouted, "The men of Niumi are coming by
     river!"
Those who were first off the mark flung themselves into canoes
     and set off in the direction of the noise, but the canoes cap-
     sized with their occupants and they were drowned; they
     never arrived,
And they were not present on the field of battle.
The Jokadu men went
And manned the fence; Hamadada Seeka Ndemba and all the
     Jokadu forces
360 Along with the men from Bali manned the fence.
Kelefa Saane
And King Demba
Stood in front, side by side,
With all the Niumi forces behind them.
365 They launched their attack
On a Monday.
When Kelefa Saane
Fired his gun,
Three men, four men, ten men
370 Were laid low
With a single shot.
When Hamadada Seeka Ndemba
Fired his gun,
Five men, six men
375 Were laid low.
But when Kelefa Saane was fired upon,
The bullets failed to penetrate his body;

He picked them up, examined them and dropped them into his
    bag.
They fought
380   On Monday,
And on Tuesday,
And on the third day
The female jinn came to Hamadada Seeka Ndemba and said to
    him, "Hamadada!" and he answered, "Yes."
She said, "This Jola who confronts you," and he said, "Yes." "A
    bullet," she said, "Won't kill him."

385   When the two armies had met,
On the third day
The fighting was still going on;
On the fourth day
The fighting was still going on,
390   And the female jinn came and said, "This Jola who confronts
    you will not be killed by a bullet. But this Jola fellow—
"Before six days are up,

"This Jola." Hamadada said, "Mm. You must kill a one year
    old cock on Monday
"And remove its spur
"And soak it in poison.
395   "When you have soaked it in poison,
"You must put it in a gun.
"You must send a deformed leper without fingers
"Up a tree onto a platform.
"When you have sent him up onto a platform,
400   "Before he shoots Kelefa Saane on Monday morning,
"He must bend down with his back to him.
"But before you do all that,
"You must take a bead of a pure Fula
"And put it in a gun and shoot him with it."
405   They went to Hamadi Fall
And got a bead of a pure Fula
And put it in a gun.
They shot Kelefa with it,
But it made no impression on Kelefa.
410   They moved from there,
And the female jinn said to them,
"Ah, look, this bead of a pure Fula has made no impression on
    Kelefa.
"Now take the one-year-old cock."
On Sunday evening
415   They took the spur of the one-year-old cock
And soaked it in poison.

They sent a deformed man up a tree onto a platform
And told him,
"When dawn breaks,
420   "Before you shoot Kelefa,
"You must bend down with your back to him three times,
"And the fourth time,
"You fire."

Kelefa Saane—
425   On the Monday morning,
When the female jinn
Had given them those instructions,
They put the spur of the one-year-old cock in a gun.
The deformed man climbed up into a tree,
430   He bent down with his back to Kelefa Saane.

When the deformed man had bent down three times with his
    back to Kelefa Saane, the fourth time he took the spur of the
    one-year-old cock
And shot Kelefa Saane with it.
When Kelefa was shot,
The bullet hit him;
435   And he swayed forward,
And he declared, "This bullet which has hit me will be the
    death of me."
He said, "King Demba!" and the king said, "Yes."
Kelefa asked him, "Who are the men who are giving you most
    trouble in this battle? Tell me who they are, so that they
    can be my hosts in the next world when I have killed
    them."
Kelefa clutched the bridle.
440   When he was leaving Badora, his mother had given him a little
    horn,
And that horn now fell to the ground.
It went back to Badora.
If you remember, I have already told you about that. When
    Kelefa was leaving Badora, I told you about the horn; I said
    that his mother gave him a little horn. She said that he was
    to take that little horn with him to war;
If he died, it would return and report his death, but if he did
    not die, he would return home with the horn.
445   Kelefa Saane
Moved forward
And almost fell from his horse; but he did not altogether fall,
    for several men rushed to his aid.
When he had been helped to sit firmly in the saddle,

Those men who had been giving King Demba most trouble in
    the battle
450   Were shot by Kelefa
And carried off by him to the next world,
Where they became his hosts.
He suddenly fell from his horse
And his followers lifted him up;
455   And the spot where they were going to lay him down
Was under a mango tree.
Kelefa asked them, "What tree is this?"
And they told him, "This is a mango tree."
He said, "This tree is very cold.
460   "Don't bury me here,
"Because this is a mango tree
"And this is what children practice their climbing on."
He left there;
They bore him away
465   And laid him under a *santang* tree.
He asked them, "What tree is this?"
And they told him, "This is a *santang* tree."
He said, "If the ash of a *santang* tree is not bitter, it is still not
    palatable."
He left there,
470   And they carried him under a *sinjang* tree.
He asked them, "What tree is this?"
And they told him, "This is a *sinjang* tree."
He said, "Dig up its root and examine it.
"What is it like?"
475   They said, "It is bitter."
"What about its seeds?"
They said, "They are bitter."
He told them, "You must bury me here.
"But when you bury me here,
480   "At the head of my grave and at the foot,
"A termite mound will rise up,
"But upon my grave
"No grass will grow
"Till the end of time."
485   And to this very day,
Upon Kelefa Saane's grave
No grass grows.
The war was a disaster.

Then Kelefa Saane's spear was removed.
490   His spear is at Niumi Jufureh at the present time.
Whoever can do so should go and see his spear.
But in any case Kelefa's spear is at Jufureh at the present time.

The maternal grandfather of Alkali Nufung who died
    recently—
When Kelefa Saane and his followers arrived,
495   There was great poverty—
Was trading in European goods.
Some men took the spear
And pledged it with him.
That spear was pledged
500   And to this day it has never been redeemed.
It belonged to
Alkali Nufung Taali's maternal grandfather.
He died,
And the Alkali's father took it over.
505   He in turn died,
And Alkali Nufung took it over.
He in turn died,
And it is his son who is there now—
Mamadi Taali.
510   He has the spear.
The war was a disaster.
There was no one who could take
Kelefa Saane's place.
One Fula
515   Thought that he could take Kelefa's place.
That Fula—
Hamadada Seeka Ndemba
Took a spear against him,
And they wounded each other with their spears.
520   Hamadada wounded him with his spear
And drove him across the river,
And he entered Senegal.
He fled.
The war was a disaster.
525   Wounded men
Crawled back
To Niumi.
Wounded men
Crawled back
530   To Jokadu.
Ah, the nobles are finished,
War has finished the nobles
Civil war has finished the nobles.

9. The Epic of Kambili
Narrated by Seydou Camara

Recorded in Bamako in 1968 by Charles Bird. Transcribed and translated by Charles Bird with Mamadou Koita and Bourama Soumaoro. Published by the African Studies Program, Indiana University. This excerpt edited by Charles Bird.

> I've seen a hunter; I've seen my friend.
> I've seen a hunter; I've seen my brother.
> I've seen a hunter, I've seen my sharer of pleasures.
> Heroes, let's be off!
> Eating the traditional dish is not an evil deed.
> A man's learning and his ability are not the same.
> Harp-playing Seydou from Kabaya has come.
> Falsity is not good, Master.
> Look to the Camara tree for the sacred tree of Mecca.
> The wing descends, the wing and its captives.
> The wing ascends, the wing and its captives.
> Bow, Ancestor, your enemy-striking arrow!
> You hit a *balenbon* tree.
> From that day to this,
> One side of the *balenbon* has yet to recover.
> Should the wing move to the east,
> You will hear its sound.
> Should the wing move to the west,
> You will hear its sound.
> Ah! It's the voice of harp-playing Seydou!
> The thing is not easy for all.
> It's the sound of harp-playing Seydou from Kabaya.
> Dugo's Kambili! The lion is evil!
>
> The opening lines of Seydou Camara's *Kambili*

THE PRECEDING SELECTION IS FROM THE BEGINNING OF *KAMBILI*, an extended heroic epic of the Wasulu hunters in Mali. The published version available through Indiana University's African Studies Center consists of 2725 lines. The full narrative opens with events leading up to the birth of the hero, Kambili, during the reign of the Imam Samori Touré, whose rule in the nineteenth century extended over much of today's southern Mali and Guinea. The middle portion deals with aspects of Kambili's adolescence and the end deals with his marriage to the beautiful Kumba and his battle against the lionman, Cekura.

When the recording of Kambili was made in the spring of 1968, Seydou was about fifty years old. He had begun playing indigenous instruments of the Wasulu region as a young boy and had shown considerable promise, particularly on the *dan*, a six-stringed lute. He began his interest in the *donsonkòni*, the hunter's lute-harp, through his initiation and extensive interest in the Komo societies of the Wasulu region. In his early twenties, he was conscripted into the French army and went

to serve in Morocco with the Free French Forces during World War II. After the war, he transferred to the Civil Guard in Mali and was stationed in Timbuktu, where he married his first wife, Kariya Wulen. While in Timbuktu, according to Seydou, he was poisoned by his enemies in the local community, the result of which was what we would probably call a nervous breakdown; Seydou said he was possessed by jinns. As a consequence, he was dismissed from the service and returned to his native village. Under the care of the famous Kankan Sekouba, Seydou gradually regained his health and devoted himself exclusively to playing the hunter's lute-harp, serving as a singer for the Wasulu hunters and as a bard for the Komo society. By 1953 he had developed his art to such an extent that he drew the attention of the influential deputy, Jime Jakite. Jakite brought him to a major political rally in Sikasso, where Seydou won the hunters' bard competition, which elevated him to national celebrity.

> *Speaking is not easy;*
> *Not being able to speak is not easy.*
> *I'm doing something I've learned,*
> *I'm not doing something I was born for.*

He recorded a number of songs for the national radio and his voice was frequently heard on Radio Mali's broadcasts when I was first in Mali in the mid-1960s. When I first met him, Seydou earned his living performing for hunters and their associations at their festivals, funerals, weddings, and baptisms, traveling to many of the major towns in southern Mali: Segu, Kutiala, Sikaso, Buguni. He got little for his services, usually receiving a *worosongo*, the price of kola nuts (about 500 to 1,000 francs, between one and two dollars), a traditional gift usually given as a greeting gesture. He performed wherever and whenever he could, often up to twenty times per month.

The most important part of Seydou's poetics was rhythm. He created his lines, unfolded his narratives against the rhythm of his *donsonkòni*, which itself was dependent on the forceful drive of the iron rasp scraper, among whom the best were his wives, Kariya Wulen and Nunmuso. Seydou's apprentices played the bass lines on their *donsonkònis* and Seydou played across the top. Seydou laid his language over the top of this as if his voice were the lead instrument in the ensemble, sometimes locking into the rhythm, sometimes in counterpoint, sometimes somewhere in between. In an effort to have the text reflect something of this rhythmic richness, I present the text in three different ways. Songs mark his performances like in a Broadway musical and are represented by indented lines with the choral responses further indented following them. Seydou delivered much of the narrative in a mode in which he organized the accented syllables of his language to coincide with the accented beats of the music, a variation of 4:4. This narrative mode is represented by an indentation. In a mode of delivery that

Seydou used to start his performances or to break between parts of performances, Seydou sang in a sprung rhythm, usually at breakneck
speed. The content of this mode of delivery consists mainly of proverbs,
aphorisms, wisdom of the hunters, and praise-lines. I represent this
praise-proverb mode in italics.

> Mother Dugo the Owl!
> I play my harpstrings for you.
> > *Master, you filled us with knowledge.*
> > *Ah! You've filled us with sorcery.*
> Man, I can't hear the sound of your harp.
> Is your harp not playing?
> > *Master, you filled us with knowledge.*
> > *Ah! You've filled us with sorcery.*
> Ah! Should you see a man with bad habits.
> You see a man who will die young.
> > *Master, you filled us with knowledge.*
> > *Ah, you filled us with sorcery.*
> Man, tighten that string!
> Tighten that string a bit!
> > *Master, you filled us with knowledge.*
> > *Ah, you filled us with sorcery.*
> All hunters go off to the bush,
> All are not masters of the powder.
> > *Master, you filled us with knowledge.*
> > *Ah, you filled us with sorcery.*
> Ah! Harpist, you're slowing down
> My words.
> > *Master, you filled us with knowledge.*
> > *Ah, you filled us with sorcery.*
> Some women give birth to sons,
> But all don't give birth to kings.
> > *Master, you filled us with knowledge.*
> > *Ah! You filled us with sorcery.*
> Hurry your hand on the strings!
> You make it hard for me to speak!
> > *Master, you filled us with knowledge.*
> > *Ah! You filled us with sorcery.*
> Ah! Dugo's Kambili, can't you stop
> The man-eating lion?
> > *Master, you filled us with knowledge.*
> > *Ah! You filled us with sorcery.*
> Ah! Rhythm man! Rhythm man!
> Slow down a little!
> > *Master, you filled us with knowledge.*
> > *Ah, you filled us with sorcery.*
> > > An excerpt from Kambili's wedding song

Seydou was always enigmatic to me. He was a consummate musician. I have yet to hear another lute-harp player with the mechanical mastery, rhythmic drive, and lyrical lilt that Seydou gave to his music. To some, Seydou was like a court jester, a buffoon. He loved to clown, to tell off-color jokes and stories that made his audience roar with laughter. Seydou loved women. He had two wives and would have had many more if he could have afforded it. He liked booze of all kinds and he could frequently be found at the local millet beer hall when he had a few francs in his pocket. He would say, from time to time, that he was a Muslim, but he loved to ridicule the Muslim clergy, whose hypocrisy he saw as ludicrous. I never did see him pray.

> Ah! All the holy men are by the mosque,
> But all of them are not holy men!
> > Master, you filled us with knowledge.
> > Ah! You filled us with sorcery!
> Ah! Some are studying at the mosque,
> But they all don't give birth to saints.
> > Master, you filled us with knowledge!
> > Master, you filled us with sorcery!
> All the holy men are by the mosque,
> But they all don't know how to read.
> > Master, you filled us with knowledge!
> > Master, you filled us with sorcery!
> Of all those who make the pilgrimage,
> They all don't know what it means.

He had a twinkle in his eyes that let you know, more than anything, that Seydou was having a good time doing what he was doing. To others, Seydou was like a priest. His services for the hunters were often of ritual nature, singing songs that empowered his hunter clients to overcome the obstacles of the bush and the wild game they sought to kill. On a number of occasions while I was sitting in his hut talking or listening to him play, a hunter would come in with dried or smoked parts of an antelope as Seydou's part of the kill. He sang the songs that calmed the unleashed spirits of those slaughtered beasts.

> *Born for a reason and learning are not the same.*
> *A man doesn't become a hunter if he cannot control his fear.*
> *A coward does not become a hunter,*
> *Or become a man of renown.*
> *Death may end the man; death doesn't end his name.*

To some, he was a traditional medicine man. His tiny hut was crammed full of powdered roots, leaves, dried unidentifiable animal parts and bones. He had a steady stream of clients to whom he delivered medicines for such ills as menstrual cramps or examination anxi-

ety. He cast divination stones to guide people on new voyages, marriages, business ventures, and hunts. I was in awe of Seydou's effortless expertise and the efficacy of his arts. I came to see Seydou as my protector. In a place full of things I didn't and perhaps couldn't understand, Seydou was always there with talismans, poultices, incantations, and divinations, assuring me that I would be all right.

The extended text which follows is from the end of the epic.

> A hunter's death is not easy for the harp-player, Allah!
> A hunter dies for the harp-player.
> A farmer dies for the glutton.
> A holy man dies for the troubled.
> A king dies for his people.
> To each dead man, his funeral song, Kambili.
> And should an old bard die,
> Call out the hourglass drummer,
> Call out the iron rasp scraper,
> Call out the jembe drummer.
> Have them sing my funeral song.
> To each dead man, his funeral song, call Kambili!

Seydou Camara died in his village, Kabaya, in 1981.

	The Jimini nobles made a plan.
1900	Cekura had a wife.
	His wife's name was Kumba.
	They changed her mind, taking her from Cekura.
	Ah! They took Cekura's wife from him.
	And Cekura was a man who could change into a lion!
1905	Ah! *Naamu*-sayers!
	He sent word to all the lion people.
	He said, "Lionmen!" "Yes?" the reply.
	"Let us eat all the people of the village.
	"Let us eat all the cows of the village.
1910	"Let us eat all the sheep of the village.
	"Let us eat all the dogs of the village.
	"Let us make this a fight for my wife."
	The slave's wife had been taken from him.
	The fight for his wife wasn't sweet in Jimini.
1915	Don't you know Cekura was deeply hurt?
	So he sent word to the lionmen.
	Whoever went to defecate,
	He was made a toothpick.
	Whoever was going out to the fields,
1920	They turned him into a toothpick.
	Whoever went to water the garden,

	They turned into a toothpick.
	And made it hot for the village people,
	And made it hot for the cowherd,
1925	And made it hot for the sheep flock.
	Yes, they made it hot for the people.

Ah! There seemed no end to the bits of people around Jimini.
When night had fallen, Master,
As soon as you had closed the door of your hut,
1930 He would pull out his sticklike tail
And bang on the door with it,
And do the best of greetings, Kambili.
No sooner would you say, "Welcome,"
And open the door a crack,
1935 He would jump in and grab one of you.
He would turn him into a toothpick, Kambili Sananfila.
Ah! The Jimini man-eating lion was really playing in Jimini.
    The lion was going to eat the whole army.
    He had already finished the water carriers.
1940   He had finished the best of the farmers.
    The lion had finished the horsemen.
    The lion had finished the learned holy men.
    The lion had finished the king's children.
    Ah! It was an awful situation in Jimini.
1945 The voice of death was in Jimini.
Lots of noise was in Jimini.
It's a story about Dugo the owl, the soul-seizing angel.
There was no joy in the Jimini lion business,
And the lion's name was Cekura.
1950 His apprentice's name was Faberekoro.
Cekura was seizing people in Jimini.
Faberekoro was finishing up their remains.
This created a serious problem for Samori,
And so he advised the hunters' group,
1955 "If you don't apply yourselves, if you don't apply yourselves,
"I will come to doubt the hunters."
This warning given once,
This warning given twice.
It was given before the harp-player, Yala the smith.
1960   Yala the smith took his harp
    And went straight to Kambili,
    The son of Dugo, the Owl Bird,
    The son of Dugo, the Night Bird.

Ah! *Naamu*-sayers!
1995 At this time, kolas had been sent out for Kambili's wife.
And what was Kambili's first wife's name?
Her name was said, Kumba.

They tied up ten kolas,
And went off to marry the beloved Kumba.
2000 And brought her and gave her to Dugo's Kambili.
It was the way of doing a marriage.
Man, pay attention to the rhythm!
Don't miss the rhythm whatever you do!
To each slave his reason for coming.
2005 *To each his destiny.*
Putting tradition aside for one day's pain is not good.
Hot Pepper of the Game, Kambili Sananfila!
Speaking is not easy;
Not being able to speak is not easy.
2010 *I'm doing something I've learned.*
I'm not doing something I was born for.

[Seydou sings the wedding songs.]

They finished the wedding procession.
2110 The wedding speeches had been given, Allah!
When the message had been given to Kambili,
He spoke out saying,
"This man-eating lion, Allah!
"If this man-eating lion is going to die,
2115 "Pay attention to the rhythm!
"Ah! If this man-eating lion is going to die in Jimini,
"That lion will die with one shot in Jimini."
Look to the cat for the wild hunting cat.
The dancers of the war dance have decreased.
2120 *The dancer of the warriors' dance has gone to rest.*
Soloba Jantumanin has gone to Last Judgment.
No reason was given for the powderman's going to rest.
Soloba Jantumanin has gone to Allah.
The bullet master has gone back for sure.
2125 *The darkness of Last Judgment is never empty of strangers.*
It's the call for Dugo the Owl, Kambili Sananfila.
Greet the tracking dog as the hunting dog.
Look to the chair for seizing all the smells.
A sandal that's stepped in dung leaves its bits behind.
2130 They finished with the wedding ceremony.
Toure ni Manjun came out.
He came out with ten red kolas
And went to give them to Kanji.
He said, "Kanji!" "Yes?" the reply.
2135 "Go tell the hunters in Jimini,
"If the man-eating lion doesn't die in Jimini,
"The vulture will settle on the hunters' children."
"Ah! The totem of the man-killer king is not broken

106

"If the Jimini man-eating lion doesn't die!"
2140   The vulture will finish eating the children;
       The beast will finish all the good children;
       The beast will finish the grass cutters,
       The beast has finished the horsemen;
       The beast has finished the wood gatherers,
2145   The beast has finished all the good farmers.
       The beast will finish all the good children;
   Don't you see there's no way to get to the market?
       The beast finished eating all the market people.
   Don't you see that this powder business has heated up.
2150   The Jimini battle was no pleasure, Kambili.
Greet the tracking dog as the hunting dog.
Greet the chair for seizing all the smells.
Look to the drying sun for the sun of midday meal.
Greet the loincloth as breeze-catching cloth.
2155 *The man's totem cannot be the loincloth.*
Neither can it be the women's totem.
The loincloth is but breeze-catching cloth.
Look to the undryable for the unburnable.
Mother Dugo, it's the call for early death in the Terende bushes.
2160 *The brave, seated, a dangerous thing.*
The brave standing, a dangerous thing.
A small deadly thing burned up wouldn't fill a horn.
Although the great snake makes like to coil,
He can't be used as a head coil.
2165 *Who has ever seen a snake as a head coil?*
It's the call for the Hot Pepper of the Game.
It's the call for the Hot Pepper of the Beast.
Buffalo fighting is not easy for the coward.
Buffalo fighting is not easy for the trembler.
2170 *The voice of the wild dog of the plain, "Arise and fight!"*
The wild dog's voice in the plain, "To the attack!"
Great stallion of the plain without saddle,
His belly great; it's not from begging.
His mouth, white, but not from the worthless one's mother's flour.
2175 *His tail, close to the ground, not to be seized by the worthless one's*
      hand.
His ear, great, it will never be the worthless one's mother's scoop.
My hand is now in my traditional thing.
Kabaya Seydou's hand is now in his traditional thing, no lie.
A man dies for his sharer of secrets, Father.
2180 *A man dies for his sharer of hopes, Allah.*
A man dies for his sharer of wealth, Man.
A man dies for his sharer of secrets, no lie.
Kanji took his harpstrings there.
Kanji took his harpstrings to Jimini,

2185	And presented himself to Dugo's son.
	He said, "Dugo's Kambili!
	"The king brought out the man-killing kolas,
	"Saying to give them to my men,
	"To give them to my hunters' group,
2190	"Saying, if the Jimini man-eating lion doesn't die,
	"Come next Thursday,
	"The vulture will descend on the hunters, Kambili."
	Ah! The speech was bad!
	Ah! I'm afraid of the widow's headband, Kambili.
2195	I'm afraid of one blast of the whistle, Kambili.
	I'm afraid of one blast of the whistle, Kambili.
	I'm afraid of cold tears, Kambili.
	"Ah! That's no lie!" said Kumba.
	"I don't ever want to become a widow. Allah!
2200	"There is no one to inherit me, father.
	"I don't want to get mixed up in it.
	"Ah! Do your best, Kambili. Do your best!"
	Born for a reason and learning are not the same.
	Putting tradition aside for one day's pain is not good.
2205	*Hot Pepper of the Game!*
	The brave sat down and thought.
	He said, "Kumba! Beloved Kumba!" "Yes," she replied.
	She said, "Kambili, the Hunter, Kambili Sananfila!
	"The man-eating lion will die in Jimini.
2210	"I will go to the hair-dressing place at my namesake's house.
	"With Cekura's mother, Marama.
	"I was once the loving wife of Cekura in Jimini.
	"I grew up by the side of his robe in Jimini.
	"The wife of Cekura's host was my tutor.
2215	"I know Cekura himself.
	"No other is seizing the people,
	"If it is not Cekura."
	So they called Bari the Omen Reader.
	Bari began to read the signs.
2220	"Namusa
	"Naburuma
	"Woro dogolen
	"Woro faransan
	"Jitumu Mansa
2225	"Jitimu Forokoro
	"Filanin Fabu
	"Kenken Mamuru
	"Jonyayiriba
	"Twenty-four parts of the bow.
2230	"This is sigi.
	"This is maromaro.

"This is karalan.
"This has become teremise.
"This has become regret,
2235 "Another regret.
"This is Nsorosigi.
"This, Yeremine.
"Here again is Karalan.
"Ah! This sign has become Maromaro, Man!
2240 "The omen has become a longbow sign.
"The earth-shaking reason has come out.
　　"Bring me a head hair.
　　"Yes, bring a hair of the lion's head.
　　"And bring some hair from under his arm,
2245 　　"And bring some hair from his crotch,
　　"And bring the sandal off his foot,
　　"And bring a pair of his old pants,
　　"And lay them on the omen board.
　　"And when we find a means to the man-killer lion,
2250 　　"Should we do that, the man-eating lion will die."
Sleep has made your eyes heavy. Pay attention to the rhythm!
The debt of Last Judgment is never forgotten for the living.
A slave spends a late evening.
A slave doesn't stay long among you.
2255 *The omen for staying here is not easy on things with souls.*
A name is a thing to be bought: a name is not to be forced.
My hand is dipped in my habitual thing.
The thing is not easy for all.
Ah! It was none but Kumba's voice.
2260 "Kambili the Hunter," she said, "Kambili Sananfila!
"I will go have my hair done at Marama's place.
"I will never betray you."
　　She took ten kolas,
　　And came with the ten white kolas,
2265 　　And put them in a little calabash,
　　And brought out greeting gifts,
　　And put them in a little white calabash.
"I'm doing this for my man, Kambili.
"Please forgive me, Kambili.
2270 "I'm going for the hair on his head, Kambili.
"I'm going for the underarm hair, Kambili.
"I'm going for the sandal, Kambili.
"I'm going for the old pants, Kambili.
"That done, the man-eating lion will die, Kambili."
2275 *If you are not afraid of females, Master,*
If you are not afraid of females,
You're not afraid of anything.
The woman's hand knows how to strike a man's desires in any case.

	Beloved Kumba went to meet Cekura,
2280	Entering his place at about two o'clock.
	She called, "Cekura!" "Yes?" the reply.
	"I have come to the hair-dressing place."
	Don't you know this made Cekura happy?
	It was none but the lionman's voice.
2285	He said, "The hunters will surely kill you this time,
	"And I, Cekura, will cry.
	"Ah! Little hypocrite, didn't I tell you
	"Marrying a hunter will never succeed?
	"A hunter is nothing!
2290	"When a hunter enters the bush,
	"He may spend a whole week.
	"He has no need for his wife.
	"When a hunter sees some antelope,
	"He has seen the game he will kill.
2295	"It's a case of coveting the game.
	"He has no concern for having children, Allah."
	This put Kumba in a difficult situation, beloved Kumba.
	Kumba responded, saying, "So it is.
	"You have just said my reason for coming.
2300	"Cekura, that's my reason for coming.
	"I'm no longer in this hunter's marriage.
	"I'm fed up with this hunter's business.
	"Him and his shoulder talismans!
	"The hunter and his side talismans are never far apart.
2305	"Saying you shouldn't touch the hunter's bag;
	"A woman's taboo is inside it.
	"Don't put your hand on his shirt;
	"A woman's taboo is on it.
	"When he has gone off to the bush,
2310	"He can come back and spend three nights,
	"Without touching his wife;
	"He has no desire for his woman."
	She went on, "Cekura!" "Yes?"
	"There's just one thing about what I've said,
2315	"I beg of you
	"That you hurry up this matter between us
	"So that I can go back soon.
	"Kambili's funeral, I don't want to miss that."
	So he called out, "Marama, Kumba's here to have her hair done."
2320	He went and bought some grains of rice,
	And went and bought some white chickens,
	And went and bought ten white kolas,
	And came and gave them to beloved Kumba.
	He had some rice prepared,

2325	And had those chicken's meat cooked up,
	And went and poured out some milk,
	And soaked the fresh milk with honey,
	And gave it to beloved Kumba.
	"Kumba, don't you see this drinking water?
2330	"As for me, I'm doing well these days.
	"What need have I for any of this?
	"As for me, I'm after these people, for vengeance."
	When night had fallen,
	As soon as they had finished eating,
2335	They lay down together.
	He put his leg over Kumba,
	But she said, "Get your leg off me!"
	He laid his hand on her,
	But she said, "Get your claws off me!"
2340	Ah! Cekura was in a hurry.
	"I have found the way,
	"I have found the way to destroy Kambili.
	"Those nights between Kambili and me,
	"I can count them.
2345	"They do not go beyond ten.
	"None of them ever accomplished anything beyond hunting
	game,
	"Charging off to game hunts.
	"I have no desire to be married to a hunter.
	"If you give me an old pair of pants,
2350	"They'll be used as a means against Kambili.
	"Bring me some hair off your head,
	"We'll find a means to Kambili today.
	"Bring me some hair from under your arm,
	"And get me some from your crotch,
2355	"And take off your old sandals,
	"Take those sandals off your feet.
	"We'll use them as a means to get the tough one, Master.
	"When all that is done, he'll be a corpse,
	"And I will begin marriage to Cekura once more.
2360	"Ah! Take up the weapon!
	"Don't you fail! Do not hesitate!"
	Words are like the writing of a holy man;
	They don't suit the heart of every young man.
	Speech is something to be learned in every day of this world.
2365	*Intelligence has become a thing hard to find, Master.*
	Look to Mother Dugo's ogre for that which scares the children.
	Cekura gave some of the hair off his head,
	And gave the hair from under his arm,
	And gave the hair from off his crotch,
2370	And gave the old pair of pants,

111

And gave the sandals off his feet,
 And went and took an old, used hat,
 And put it all in one calabash,
 An old cloth, wrapped around it for good.
2375 "After that, there is only me."
She said, "Cekura, oh, Cekura!
 "My hair has been dressed,
 "I am going right off with these means,
 "So that no one does it before me.
2380 "As soon as the hunter is killed,
 "I will come and marry Cekura.
 "There is no other person I want in this world,
 "If it is not Cekura."
These words were sweet in the old hyena's ears.
2385 He hunched back his shoulders.
 He tried to hold back his joy.
 He gave a little chuckle.
He said, "Don't betray me." He said,
"Don't betray me between this world and Last Judgment."
2390 And she replied, "I would never betray you in this world."
 Kumba brought back the things for her means
 And came to give them to Bari of the Omens.
 He laid them in the omen dust,
 And made an offering to the omen,
2395 An Earth-shaking Reason sacrifice,
 And went to bury it in the old market in Jimini,
By the old *nere* tree there.
Ah! Mother Dugo the Owl,
 Kambili took the magic black Nyaji powder.
2400 Kambili had become an expert, old hunter.
 Kambili took out a kola of red hue,
 And took out a white pullet,
 And went to sit at the crossroads.
 "If we are to go toward the east, Nyagi,
2405 "For me to kill the man-eating lion, Nyagi,
 "Turn the kola halves face to the ground."
 The two halves turned face to the ground.
 "If we are to go to the south, Nyaji,
 "For me to kill the man-eating lion, Nyaji,
2410 "Turn the two kola halves face to the sky."
 The two kola halves turned face to the ground.
 "If we are to go to the west, Nyaji,
 "For me to kill the man-eating lion, Nyaji,
 "Turn the two kola halves face to the sky."
2415 "The two kola halves turned face to the ground."
 "Should we go to the north, Nyaji,
 "For me to kill the man-eating lion, Nyaji?

"Turn the two kola faces to the sky."
"The two kola halves turned face to the ground."
2420   "Should I sit in the old market, Nyajij,
"To kill the Jimini man-eating lion, Nyaji,
"Have the kolas turn face to the ground."
And the two kola halves turned face to the ground.
Look to the talisman's Angel of Death for that's not easy for all.
2425   *The praise for Tears of the Game, Nyaji.*
No man becomes a hunter if he has no good talismans.
You don't become a hunter if you have no knowledge of magic.
Nothing is pleasing to a man without a reason.
Nothing is displeasing to a man without a reason.

[Kambili sets a trap for the lionman, tying a small boy to the base of the *nere* tree in the market. Kumba leads the lionman into the market. The lionman comes up, circles the young boy, and is about the devour him, but Kambili has fallen into a deep sleep under the influence of Cekura's sleep talisman. The young boy, however, sings a song invoking Kambili to awake. In the nick of time, he raises his musket, pulls back the hammer, and fires straight and true, killing the lionman with a single shot. The epic ends with Kambili's victory songs, the principle one of which sings the praises of Kumba.]

Ah! Kumba has charm, Jimini Kumba.
Kumba has charm.
2695   The gracious, the beautiful Kumba.
You've killed the man-eating lion!
The gracious, the beautiful Kumba.
A woman to surpass all women.
Kumba has no match among women.
2700   The gracious, the beautiful Kumba.
She lies beside a hunter brave.
The gracious, the beautiful Kumba.
Kumba did not betray the hunter brave.
The lion was left in the dust.
2705   The gracious, the beautiful Kumba.

Kumba was given to the hunter brave.
The lion cried in despair.
The gracious, the beautiful Kumba.
2725   Ah! The Jimini man-eating lion has been killed.
The reason was Kumba!
The gracious, the beautiful Kumba.

10. The Epic of Sara
Narrated by Sira Mori Jabaté

*Recorded in Kéla, Mali, in 1968 by Charles Bird. Transcribed and trans-
lated into English by Charles Bird and Kassim Kònè. This excerpt edited
by Charles Bird.*

SIRA MORI JABATÈ WAS ONE of Mali's GREAT FEMALE BARDS. She was especially renowned for *Sara*. For this version, she was accompanied by her
brother, Yamuru Jabatè, and a chorus of adolescent females. Sira Mori
passed away in 1989, and fifteen head of cattle were sacrificed at her
funeral ceremony.

We include this as an example of epic for a number of reasons.
Sira Mori uses the formal style of the traditional bards to deliver this
story of the heroic behavior of Sara, whose promise would not be denied. The form she uses is more melodic than the typical Mande male
bard's narrative mode. As such it sounds more like praise song (*faasa*),
of which Sira Mori was one of the great Mande masters. This is not,
however, at all typical of praise song from the point of view of content.
Praise songs do not tell stories. This is clearly poetic narrative, and
heroic, and therefore, by any definition, it qualifies as epic. From the
point of view of Maninka speakers, *Sara*, like the Sunjata epic, is called
maana, the term they use when talking about poetic narratives.

The theme of *Sara* recurs in virtually all societies where marriages are arranged. In the Mande world marriages are officially arranged and sanctioned by the male authorities, often in conflict with the
wishes of the bride and sometimes of the groom. In this story Sara has
given the promise of her undying love to another, her "promise-
sharer." The story is about the importance of that promise and what
Sara does to protect it. The poetic density of this text requires detailed
explanation and commentary.

"Ah! Sara! Sara is sung for those of one voice./Ah! Long-necked
Sara!" 'Those of one Voice' translates *kankelentigi*, 'voice-one-master.' It
means roughly 'someone who is true to his/her word.'

Mande poetry exploits polyphony. The word Sara itself is poly-
phonic. Sara is an Islamic woman's name probably borrowed very early
with the introduction of Islam in West Africa in the eighth and ninth
centuries. It is an Old Testament name, the wife of the patriarch Abraham. It is also a traditional Mande name given to the first-born girl.
Sara is also the word for 'charm, grace,' and in this story, Sara's charm
and grace constitute much of its understood content. *Sara* is also the
word used to refer to 'payment, salary, reward.' This too is a subtheme
of this story. Sara is rewarded for keeping her word.

> Chorus: Ah! Sara is sung for those of one voice.
> Don't you see it?
> Sira Mori: Sara! Sara is sung for those with promises.
> Long-necked Sara!

5   Chorus: Ah! Sara is sung for those of one voice.
            Don't you see it?
       Sira Mori: Sara! Sara is sung for those with promises.
            Long-necked Sara!
            Don't you see it?

10   Chorus: Sara is sung for those of one voice.
            Don't you see it?
       Sira Mori: Sara is not sung for "Money's in my pocket."
            Sara is not sung for "My name is gold."
            Sara is not sung for beauty.

15   Sara is sung for a person's behavior, Allah!
                  (Yes! It's the truth! It's a matter of behavior. Sara
                  was sung for the promise, for those who have seen
                  tough days, for those who looked into fiery things.)

[The above paragraph presents Yamuru Jabatè's commentary on the story. It is not uncommon to have commentators who may from time to time contribute pieces to the performance. The phrase, *minw ye lon ye* translates literally as 'those who have seen the day,' which is used in Maninka to convey the sense of 'having met a challenge, having faced difficult times and come through them.' We used 'fiery things' to translate *ko wulen*, literally 'red thing.' *Wulen* has polyphonies extending from 'red' to 'hot, fiery, fierce.' As we read it, it refers to those who have suffered for a cause. An important theme introduced here is that the bards sing of a person's deeds. Their praise cannot be bought.]

       Sara is not sung for beauty.
       Sara is sung for a person's behavior.
       Sara is not sung for the charming.
       Sara is sung for a person's behavior

20   Behaving is hard!
                  (Amazing! Amazing, Sira Mori!)
       Why union happens is that love is of paradise.
       Why union happens is that union is of paradise.
       No one should shame their sharer of secrets.
       Why union happens is that union is of paradise.

25   Why union happens is that union is of paradise.

[We have translated *yomali kiyama* as 'paradise.' It could be translated as 'heaven, the hereafter.' It is not difficult to see that Sira Mori's story constructs a strong argument for love and for marriage based on love. Love, she argues, is Allah's will. It is something of the hereafter, the eternal, something of paradise. The union of two people is first and foremost the will of Allah.]

       No one should shame their sharer of secrets
       Do not say your inner words to a gossip.

No slave knows Allah.

['Slave' (*jon*) is here understood as 'slave of God,' a human being. No one can claim to know the ways of God.]

Giving your word is misery.
30   Ah! Giving your word is hard.
Giving your word is hard.
Nobles must hold to their word.
Ah! Giving your word is hard.
Nobles must hold to their word.
35   If you are not a bastard,
Then giving your word is your misery, Allah!

[Sira Mori here is using *horon* to refer to a kind of noble behavior which is not limited to social structural categories. Anyone may be called *horon* if they behave in a certain way. As Yamuru said, a person becomes a slave by his or her behavior. *Horon* are those who can trace their patrilineal descent and be proud of it. This is opposed to *nyamogoden*, literally 'before-person child,' 'the child of someone who came before' (the wedding, we assume), hence, a bastard. Bastards cannot trace their ancestors through their fathers and are thus cursed by a biological lack of dignity and are therefore untrustworthy.]

The wedding people came,
Sara's wedding people came.
Sara's husband-to-be did not please her,
But she said, "I will not shame my fathers.
40   "I will not shame my grandfathers.
"I will not shame my uncles.
"If Allah is not in the matter
"It does not happen,
"Because my word has been spoken to another."
45   Sara's bride-price had been taken.
The wedding cows had been taken.
Sara's wedding date had been set.
Oh Sara, Allah!

(This part calls to Sira Mori Nana.
They did not break their promise.)

The wedding escort rose up.
50   Sara's promise-sharer spoke.
He said: "Ayi! Giving your word is hard. Oh, la, la!
"Oh, oh! Giving your word is hard.
"Your bride-price has been taken.
"Your wedding cows have been taken today.
55   "Your wedding escort has risen up.
"Long-necked Sara, giving your word is hard.

"Do not think about those cows, my twin-alike.
"Do not think about this marriage, my pair-alike."

[We have translated *filanin-nyogon* as 'twin-alike,' which is a literal
translation of the Maninka. It is a term of endearment used for someone
who is like a twin to you, someone with whom you giggle, laugh, and
cry. The meaning of *ma-nyogon* is 'person-alike,' roughly 'each other's
person.' We wanted to preserve Sira Mori's Maninka parallelism in our
translation which explains the idiosyncratic English.]

         I will not shame my grandfathers.
60   Giving your word is hard.
         Do you not take me at my word?
         Do not hurry so.
         Giving your word is hard.
                (Amazing! If you spit out your saliva, it can
                  not be gathered up again. That's the truth!)

[The following section describes the wedding party leaving Sara's village for the village of her husband-to-be, where she will reside. The
wedding party will be met outside the new village by a party consis-
ting mostly of her new female in-laws.]

         The wedding arrangers rose up, Sara.
65   They all went off passing the boundary.
         The birds in the trees were crying.
         The *ko-n-kan-ko* birds all were crying, Sara.

[*Ko-n-kan-ko* is held to be the cry of the messenger bird. It is a way of
gaining the floor when you have something to say: "Say, my voice
says. . . ."]

         The wedding arrangers said: "This is amazing!"
         This is what the *ko-n-kan-ko* birds sang:
70   "No slave knows Allah.
         "Giving your word is hard."
                (Your father makes you noble. You mother
                makes you that. You make yourself a slave.
                   This calls to Sira Mori Nana's child. Bati
                Hayidara, this must call to him. He is noble.)
         Sara arrived outside the village.
         Those meeting the wedding party came.
         The *jembe*-drummers began.
75   The balafon-players began.
         The gong-playing bard women began.
         The bride who was being met . . .
         When those meeting the wedding party saw Sara,

She said her belly was in pain,
80   Ah! Those meeting the wedding came up.
She said: "Laila! Laila! Mahamadarasurudilahi!"

[The above expressions are Arabic and mean, "There is no God but Allah, and Mohammad is His Prophet." In Maninka, it is used in situations similar to those in which an English speaker might say in swearing, "Jesus Christ Almighty God." We have not broken the expression up into its Arabic words, because we do not believe that the majority of Maninka who use it do so.]

She said: "Ah! Allah! My belly pains me."
The wedding arrangers said: "It's amazing!"
Those meeting the wedding party having come,
85   They said: "Sara says her belly pains her."
"Get away from me!
"My belly pains me, lalala layi!
"My belly won't cool down.
"Ah! My belly pains me!"
90   One old brave spoke up:
"Calm down!
"Let the *jembe*-drummers return,
"Let the bard women return."
He took the end of Sara's staff to lead her.

[The image here is of Sara debilitated by her illness, leaning on a staff like a blind person who is often led around by a young boy or girl holding the end of the staff. There is a very material sense of language in this story. Sara's promise is embodied; it is in her belly. Words are things that enter into people and cause them to behave in particular ways. Some phrases, like the Arabic expressions above, are known only by their use, by their potential effects on one's life. They have no analyzable meanings independent of that.]

95   They went to her groom's compound, Allah!
They went there with Sara,
Ah! World!
The belly-pain men came up to her.
The medicine-powder men came up to her.
100   The string-knotters came up to her.
The belly-spitters came up to her.

[There are hundreds, if not thousands, of practitioners of traditional medicine in the Mande world. They are brought into the story named for the devices they use. Some medicines, like ours, involve the use of powders: ground roots, bark, or leaves. Some medical interventions involve the knotting of string which may then be wrapped around the

problem. The knots draw the badness out. They say that some of these knotted strings wrapped around a fetish can kill your enemies.]

<blockquote>

She said: "My belly pains me.
"If you don't get away from me,
"My belly will not cool down, lalala layi!
105   "My belly pains me."
(Amazing! Her stomach does not pain her.
It is the sound of her promise that pains her.)
Sara's man said: "Laila, eee! Laila!
"Mahamadarasurudilahi!"
He said: "Ah! World! My bride who has come thus,
"Three days, her belly does not cool.
110   "Four days, her belly does not cool.
"Five days, a headache is added to it.
"Ah, Sara! What will cool your belly?
"Long-necked Sara!
"The medicine powder men have failed on you.
115   "The string-knotters have failed on you.
"The belly-spitters have failed on you.
"Ah! Long-necked Sara!
"What will cool your belly then?"
She said: "My belly pains me.
120   "If you don't leave me alone,
"My belly will not cool. Laila!
"Ayi! My belly hurts me. Allah!
"My belly will not cool."
Sara's man-to-be said: "Laila,
125   "No slave knows Allah.
"The wedding arrangers are troubled.
"Sara's bride-price should go back.
"I am shamed before my ill-wishing *faden*.
"I am shamed before my ill-wishing *baden*."

</blockquote>

[*Faden* is literally 'father-child.' *Baden* is literally 'mother-child.' These terms, as you might expect, are polyphonous. Perhaps early meanings referred, in the case of *faden*, to the children of the same father but not the same mother in polygamous households. *Baden* refers from this point of view to children of the same mother. Perhaps by extension, *faden* came to refer to those people with whom you compete, against whom you measure yourself. *Baden* refers to those people with whom you cooperate, with whom you subordinate your self-interest and suppress matters of ego. Your *faden* pushes you away. Your *baden* pulls you close. We have translated the Maninka word *jugu* as 'ill-wishing.' As a noun, it can mean 'enemy.' Modifying a noun, it can translate 'mean, cruel, dangerous, bad,' and 'ill-wishing.']

130   "My bride having come
        "Three days, her belly does not cool.
        "Four days her belly does not cool.
        "Five days, a headache is added to it.
        "Let the wedding arrangers go back."
135   Two young boys had run up *biribiribiri*.
        And climbed out on a branch of a *dubalen* tree
        To look out on the world.
        "Well, the world is thus!"
        The two boys ran *biribiribiri*.
140   They came to stop before the promise-sharer's door.
        One said: "Cool off my mouth!
        "Sara's wedding is dead!
        "Those ten kola nuts in the container there,
        "That is the mouth-cooler, my father.
145   "Thus a promise is not paid just once."

[The expression *n da lafige*, literally, 'fan/blow on my mouth,' is used by the bringer of news, which, it is said, makes his or her mouth hot. The heat dispels with a gift. Thus, *n da lafige* means, in Wittgenstein the Elder's sense of the word, 'give me a tip.']

        Sara stood before her father.
        She said: "It's Allah's work."
        "Mama, this child of yours,
        "Long-necked Sara! . . . and her belly will not cool."
150   Sara's mother said: "Laila, no slave knows Allah.
        "Will your belly not cool?"
        She said: " Mothers do not cry!
        "Ayi! Mother, do not cry, ay!
        "King White Guts did this to me."

['King White Guts' translates word for word the expression *Mansa nagal-agwe*. This is a metaphor for God, whose white, gutlike clouds pass across his great belly, the sky.]

155   Sara said to her father:
        "Baba won't you gather the men for me today?
        "Gather the riverbank village men for me today.
        "Gather the men in the village for me.
        "Whoever will cool my belly today,
160   "Father, that will be my husband
        "And get you out of this talk.
        "Won't you gather the men?"
                (Amazing! Her belly does not hurt her. It's the spoken
                   words that hurt her. Her spoken words are hurting her.)
        Iyo! He gathered the men,

165   Gathered the men in the village.
       The medicine-powder men came.
       The men of importance came.

[We have translated *cebakoro* as 'men of importance.' In some contexts,
one might think of a *cebakoro* as a seasoned brave, a mature warrior.]

       The big money men came.
       The Koran men came.
       The *nasi*-writing men all came.

[Islamic holy men are heavily involved in traditional medical practices.
Some specialize in writing verses of the Koran on a chalkboard, which
is then washed and the water collected. This *nasi* water can be used for
washing or drinking, and its uses extend to all manners of illness and
social problems.]

170   Three days, Sara's belly was hurting.
       They all had failed. Sara remained in it.
       Sara's mother said: "How is it going to go today, Sara?"
       "Mother, hush up, my mother.
       "King White Guts did this to me.
175   "Do not hurry Allah, my mother."
       With the night half gone,
       With the night half gone,
       She stopped before her promise-sharer's door.
       "Is there no one in the house, my twin-together?"
180   "There is someone in the house, my mother.
       "Whose voice is that in the deep, dark night?
       "Whose voice is that in the dawn?"
       "It's the voice of your embrace-together.
       "It's the voice of your sharer of inner words."
185   "Well, won't you sit, Long-necked Sara?"
       "I am sitting down, my father.
       "The powder medicine men have failed on me.
       "The string-knotters have failed on me.
       "The belly-spitters have failed on me.
190   "What will cool this belly,
       "If there is no meaning to it?
       "You should find ironstone tomorrow,
       "And put it in the fire and embers.
       "I say, when the ironstone gets hot,
195   "You should put it in drinking water, my promise-sharer.
       "Wiii! My belly will cool tomorrow,
       "Because of my spoken words, Allah!"

> (Yes! That is just the answer she was looking for. Her
> belly was not hurting her. The promise that she gave
> him, that was what was hurting her. That is the reason
> for this part, to detail it and show to the people. The
> children of Adam must stick to their word.)

[There is certainly an interpretation of this story in which Sara is con-
strued to be duplicitous, faking her illness to avoid her marriage; but
both Sira Mori and Yamuru go to considerable pains to show that her
pain was real, coming from the promise she had given to another man.
The ruse that she constructs to allow her "promise-sharer" to cure her
and win her hand may, in the view of some readers, detract from her
moral standing somewhat, but her *horonoya*, her nobility, comes from
her keeping her promise; and it must be pointed out that the ruse is in
fact a way for her father to save face. Sara does not defy authority in this
story. Rather, like Brer Rabbit, she finds ways to use it to her
advantage.]

	From the time the cock cried,
	When the first cock cried,
200	He went to find the ironstone.
	Allah came to lay the stone before him. Iyo!
	Mid-morning prayer time arrived,
	He took the ironstone *co!*
	And put it in the fire and embers.
205	When the ironstone boiled,
	He put some in drinking water.
	He was off with the water an hour later.
	The men of importance said:
	"No one should even speak with you.
210	"The thing that caused the medicine powder to fail,
	"The thing that caused the *nasi*-waters to fail,
	"And you think it's just dead water that will cool it for you!"
	"I beg your pardon, big money men.
	"I beg your pardon, medicine men.
215	"Let her try the water for me.
	"Sara should try my fresh water for me."
	Ah! Sara! Sara drank the water, unnnh!
	She drank the water at midmorning.
	As the early afternoon prayer was called,
220	She went before her birth father.

[In the Mande social world, there are many people that you call *n fa*,
'my father.' To refer to the biological father, the Maninka use the expression, *wolo-fa*,' birth father.']

"Ah! Baba!" She said: "My belly has cooled,
"Baba, ah, my belly has cooled, lalala! Woyi!
"My belly has cooled today.
"I passed the night my belly did not rise up.
225   "Baba, my belly has cooled.
"Make this my true wedded husband."
Sara's mother said: "Won't you calm down?
"The late afternoon prayer has not been called.
"And you say your belly has cooled?"
230   "Mama, won't you prepare the baggage today?
"Prepare my wedding baggage today.
"Let my wedding arrangers come forward.
"This one will be my true wedded husband."

    Sira Mori: Ah! Sara! Sara is sung for those of one voice.
235   Ah! Long-necked Sara!
        Chorus: Ah! Sara is sung for those of one voice.
            Don't you see it?
    Sira Mori: Ah! Sara! Sara is sung for those of one voice.
        No slave knows God.
240   Chorus: Ah! Sara is sung for those of one voice.
            Don't you see it?

Songhay and Zarma Epics

THE SONGHAY AND THEIR COUSINS THE ZARMA constitute two related groups that are part of a much larger and more complex assemblage of diverse peoples who speak different dialects of a single language. These peoples—the Songhay, the Zarma, the Kourthèye, the Wogo, the Dendi, and others—live in an unusually elongated space that follows the Niger River for about 1,200 kilometers from Goundam, in the Timbuktu region of north central Mali, down to the Kandé-Parakou region in northern Benin. This area once stretched farther west to the ancient city of Djenné in Mali and east to include communities in the Agadez-In Gall region of northern Niger. Today, one can find Songhay and Zarma speakers in parts of northeastern Burkina Faso and northwestern Nigeria. Zarma is linguistically a dialect of Songhay, but the Zarma refer to their language simply as Zarma.

Some of these peoples trace their roots to the Songhay empire. It developed in the fifteenth century under the rule of Sonni Ali Ber (1463-1492), reached its apogee in 1493-1528 during the reign of Askia Mohammed Touré, and then declined during the sixteenth century before falling on April 12, 1591, to an invading force of 3,000 soldiers sent by the Sultan of Morocco. After the defeat of the Songhay, the leadership retreated southward from the capital in Gao, 443 kilometers upriver from Niamey, Niger, into western Niger and regrouped in small principalities. They mounted a sustained resistance against the colonial regime installed in Timbuktu by the Moroccans. In this effort, they were aided by their Zarma neighbors, who had migrated from Mali at some point in the distant past to the left-bank region of the Niger River in western Niger.

The Songhay and the Zarma share, then, a language and some common experiences in the past. One of those experiences is recurring conflict with some of their other neighbors in the region, the Tuareg and the Fulbe. The result is an oral tradition that often turns out to be a blend of heroes and events known by both peoples. In the *Epic of Askia Mohammed*, we find descriptions of the aid provided by the Zarma. In *The Epic of Mali Bero*, there are also descriptions of that mutual assistance. Both *The Epic of Mali Bero* and *The Epic of Issa Korombé*, narratives that describe events separated by several centuries, feature conflict with the Fulbe and the Tuareg. For those who seek to understand the rebellion of some Tuareg groups against the governments of Mali and Niger in the 1990s, the epics reveal early episodes of those conflicts.

Scholars in Niger, Mali, the United States, and Europe have recorded narratives about some of these heroes, but much of the published material is available only in mimeograph form from local research centers. In the 1960s and 1970s, the late Boubou Hama and Diouldé Laya published a series of short studies on the oral traditions of the Songhay and Zarma that included prose versions of *The Epic of Askia Mohammed* and *Mali Bero*. More recent poetic versions appear in Ousmane Mahamane Tandina's doctoral thesis on Issa Korombé, cited later, as well as in *Le mythe et l'histoire dans la Geste de Zabarkane* (Niamey:

Centre d'Études Linguistiques et Historiques par Tradition Orale, 1988) by Fatimata Mounkaila, a study that includes several fragments of the Mali Bero story, and in Thomas A. Hale's *Scribe, Griot, and Novelist: Narrative Interpreters of the Songhay Empire,* which contains Songhay and English versions of *The Epic of Askia Mohammed* (Gainesville: University of Florida Press, 1990). Indiana University Press published a slightly revised version of the English translation of that epic in 1996.

11. The Epic of Askia Mohammed
Narrated by Nouhou Malio

Recorded in Saga, Niger, on December 30, 1980, and January 26, 1981, by Thomas A. Hale. Transcribed by Mounkaila Seydou Boulhassane Maïga, Ousmane Mahamane Tandina, Moussa Djibo, and Thomas A. Hale. Translated into English by Thomas Hale with the assistance of Mounkaila Seydou Boulhassane Maïga, Ousmane Mahamane Tandina, Moussa Djibo, Fatimata Mounkaila, Abdoulaye Dan Louma, and Abdoulaye Harouna. Edited by Thomas A. Hale, published as part of Scribe, Griot, *and* Novelist: Narrative Interpreters of the Songhay Empire *by the University of Florida Press in 1990, and reprinted in 1996, with a new introduction, as the second volume in the African Epic Series by Indiana University Press. This excerpt edited by Thomas A. Hale.*

THANKS TO THE AGGRESSIVE LEADERSHIP of Sonni Ali Ber, the Songhay empire, based at Gao on the Niger River in southeastern Mali, expanded to absorb a part of Mali as that kingdom, founded by Son-Jara, declined in the fifteenth century. From 1463 to 1492, Sonni Ali Ber laid the foundation for Askia Mohammed Touré, a ruler of Soninké origin who, in turn, built a vast and complex empire from 1493 to 1528. At its apogee in the early sixteenth century, Songhay appears to have controlled in one way or another peoples and territory covering over 400,000 square kilometers, from eastern Senegal 3,000 kilometers eastward to central Niger, and from Upper Guinea 1,500 kilometers northward to the Mali-Mauritania-Algeria frontier region.

Our knowledge of Songhay history comes both from the Timbuktu chronicles, written in Arabic by Muslim scribes close to the ruling elite, and from griots, known in Songhay as *jesere*, a term derived from the Soninké word *geseré*. Songhay oral narratives were originally chanted in Soninké, probably because griots from the dispersed peoples of the much earlier Ghana empire gravitated toward a powerful ruler whose clan name, Touré, indicated a Soninké link. Today, some Soninké phrases survive in archaic and often untranslatable form in narratives and incantations from Songhay *jesere* and *sohanci* (sorcerers).

Askia Mohammed spread Islam to new areas of West Africa by force and by other means. He also offered support to Islamic scholars in Timbuktu, made a pilgrimage to Mecca in 1497-98, and corresponded with the North African theologian al-Maghili. It is not surprising, then, that Islam has a much higher profile here than in epics about earlier periods. But traditional Songhay beliefs and magic play equally significant roles in the story of Askia Mohammed. Like Son-Jara and other epic heroes, Askia Mohammed was born under extraordinary circumstances and had to overcome great obstacles. Called Mamar Kassaye (the dimunitive of Mohammed, son of Kassaye), he appears in the epic as the killer of Sonni Ali Ber, referred to here as his uncle Si. These excerpts come from a 1602-line version recounted in Songhay by Nouhou Malio and accompanied by Soumana Abdou, who played the three-stringed *molo*, a type of lute.

Kassaye is the woman.

It is Si who is the man, it is he who is on the throne, it is he who
is the chief.

Kassaye is his sister, she is in his compound.

Any husband who marries Kassaye, and if she gives birth,

10   The seers have said "Listen"—they told Si it is Kassaye who
will give birth to a child who will kill him and take over
the throne of Gao.

It is Kassaye who will give birth to a child.

That child will kill Si and will take the position of ruler.

Si also heard about this.

Each of the children that Kassaye gave birth to,

15   As soon as Kassaye delivered it, Si killed it,

Every child that Kassaye delivered, as soon as it was born, Si
killed it.

Until she had given birth to seven children,

Which her brother Si killed.

Kassaye had enough, she said she would no longer take a
husband.

20   She stayed like that.

Si is on his throne,

While Kassaye remained like that.

Until, until, until, until one day, much later, in the middle of
the night,

A man came who was wearing beautiful clothes.

25   He was a real man, he was tall, someone who looked good in
white clothes, his clothes were really beautiful.

One could smell perfume everywhere.

He came in to sit down next to Kassaye.

They chatted with each other, they chatted, they chatted.

He said to her, "It is really true.

30   "Kassaye, I would like to make love with you.

"Once we make love together,

"You will give birth to a boy,

"Whom Si will not be able to kill.

"It is he who will kill Si and will become the ruler."

35   Kassaye said to him, "What?"

He said, "By Allah."

She said, "Good, in the name of Allah."

Each night the man came.

It is during the late hours that he came,

40   Each time during the coolness of the late evening,

Until Kassaye became pregnant by him.

Kassaye carried her pregnancy.

Kassaye had a Bargantché captive.

It is the Bargantché woman who is her captive, she lives in her
house, and she too is pregnant.

127

45   They remained like that,
         Kassaye kneeled down to give birth.
         The captive kneeled down to give birth.
         So Kassaye, Kassaye gave birth to a boy.
         The captive gave birth to a girl.
50   Then Kassaye took the daughter of the captive, she took her
             home with her.
         She took her son and gave it to the captive.
         So the people left for the palace.
         They said to Si:
         "The Bargantché captive has given birth."
55   He said, "What did she get?"
         They said, "A boy."
         He said, "May Allah be praised, may our Lord give him a long
             life and may he be useful."
         Then they were thoughtful for a moment.
         They got up and informed him that Kassaye had given birth.
60   They asked, "What did she get?"
         They answered, "A girl."
         He said, "Have them bring it to me."
         They brought it to him, he killed it.
         It is the boy who remained with the captive and Kassaye.

[By this subterfuge, Kassaye saves her son, who becomes a servant working for his uncle. Of noble origin, he must nevertheless pass as a slave.]

         He became a young man, tall and very strong, a tall young
             man.
         The children in the compound,
         They are the ones who insult him by saying that they don't
             know his father.
         Also, they call him the little slave of Si.
110   "The little slave of Si, the little slave of Si."
         They called him "little slave of Si," and said, "We don't know
             your father, you don't have a father.
         "Who is your father?"
         Then he came home to his mother's house and told her that the
             children in the compound were really bothering him.
         They say to him, "Who is your father?"
115   She told him, "Go sit down, you'll see your father."
         He stayed there until the celebration at the end of Ramadan.
         It is going to take place the next day.
         Tomorrow is the celebration.
         Soon they will look at the moon.
120   The moon will appear in a short while, and they will celebrate
             the next day.

It is in the night that the jinn came to her,
For the man is a jinn.
He is also a chief of the town under the river, his land that he
    rules.
It is under the river that lies the country he rules.
125   That night he called her.
He came, the man came to Kassaye's house.
He took a ring off his middle finger.
He said to her that when daylight comes,
"Give it to your son."
130   He should hold it in his hand.
If he gets to the edge of the river, then he should put the ring
    on his finger.
He will see his father.
She said, "So it will be."
Daylight came.
135   The sun was hot, I think, the sun was hot.
Then Kassaye called Mamar.
She said, "Mamar."
He said, "Yes."
She said, "Come."
140   He came.
She said to him, "Look, take this ring in your hand.
"But don't put it on your finger
"Until you get to the river.
"Then you put it on your finger.
145   "At that moment, you will see your father."
Mamar took the ring to the river.
Then he put the ring on his middle finger.
The water opened up.
Under the water there are so many cities, so many cities, so
    many cities, so many villages, and so many people.
150   It is his father too who is the chief.
They too get themselves ready, they go out to go to the prayer
    ground.
He said, "That's the way it is."
His father greets him with an embrace.
There is his son, there is his son.
155   Yes, the prince whom he fathered while away,
The chief's son whom he fathered while away has come.
He said to him, "Now go return to your home, you do not stay
    here.
"Go return home."
His father gave him a white stallion, really white, really, really,
    really, really, really, really, really white, like, like percale.
160   He gave him all the things necessary.
He gave him two lances.

He gave him a saber, which he wore.
He gave him a shield.
He bid him good-bye.

[Armed by his real father from the underwater spirit world, Mamar
Kassaye sets out to take power from his evil uncle. He chooses to do so
on a Muslim holy day. Pretending to demonstrate his loyalty to Si, he
races his horse up to the ruler three times in succession, stopping each
time just before reaching his uncle.]

165   Si too and his people,
       Si too has a daughter, two boys and one daughter that he has
          fathered.
       He and his people go out, they went to the prayer ground.
       They are at the prayer ground.
       Then Mamar went around them and headed directly for them.
170   They were about to start the prayer.
       They said, "Stop, just stop, a prince from another place is
          coming to pray with us.
       "A prince from another place is coming to pray with us."
       The horse gallops swiftly, swiftly, swiftly, swiftly, swiftly,
          swiftly he is approaching.
       He comes into view suddenly, leaning forward on his mount.
175   Until, until, until, until, until, until, until he touches the prayer
          skin of his uncle, then he reins his horse there.
       Those who know him say that he is the little captive of Si.
       Actually, he does resemble the little captive of Si, he has the
          same look as the little captive of Si.
       Did you see him! When I saw him I thought that it was the little
          captive of Si.
       He retraced his path only to return again.
180   Until he brought the horse to the same place, where he reined
          it again.
       Now he made it gallop again.
       As he approaches the prayer skin of his uncle,
       He reins his horse.
       He unslung his lance, and pierced his uncle with it until the
          lance touched the prayer skin.
185   Until the spear went all the way to the prayer skin.

[Mamar Kassaye decides to atone for the killing of his uncle by making
a pilgrimage to Mecca. On his way, he forces many peoples to accept
Islam.]

       In each village where he stopped during the day, for example,
          this place,

If he arrives in mid-afternoon, he stops there and spends the
 night.
Early in the morning, they pillage and they go on to the next
 village, for example, Liboré.
The cavalier who goes there,
280 He traces on the ground for the people the plan for the mosque.
Once the plan for the foundation is traced,
The people build the mosque.
It is at that time,
Mamar Kassaye comes to dismount from his horse.
285 He makes the people—
They teach them verses from the Koran relating to prayer.
They teach them prayers from the Koran.
Any villages that refuse, he destroys the village, burns it, and
 moves on.

[After his return from Mecca, Mamar Kassaye continues to impose Islam
on the territories he conquers. But he does not always succeed. He cannot escape the fact that when he was an infant he was nursed during
the day by a woman from another people, the Bargantché, who live in
northern Benin. This milk tie is as strong as the tie of blood that links
people together in families and clans. For this reason, when Mamar
Kassaye sets out to conquer the Bargantché, he encounters difficulty
and must call upon his mother for help. He sends a *sohanci*, who flies
through the air, to see his mother and ask advice.]

His mother, Kassaye, had told him, "Long ago,
"I told him not to fight against the Bargantché.
"He cannot beat them, for he has in his stomach the milk of a
 Bargantché."
435 However, she told him,
Now, she took some cotton seeds in her hand and said, "Take."
She took an egg, a chicken egg, and she said to him, "Take."
She took a stone, a river stone, she told him, "Take."
"If you go," if he goes to the Bargantché,
440 If the Bargantché chase him,
He should put all his horses before him and he should be the
 only one behind.
He should scatter the cotton seeds behind him.
They will become a dense bushy barrier between him and
 them.
If they chop it down,
445 This dense bush will not prevent anything.
They will clear the bush in order to find him.
If the bush does not help at all,
This time, if they are still hunting him,
He should put all his cavalry in front of him.

450 He should throw the stone behind him.
It will become a big mountain that will be a barrier between
them.
If the big mountain does not help them,
And if they chase him again,
He should put all his cavalry in front of him again,
455 Leaving himself in the rear.
He should throw the egg behind him.
The egg will become a river to separate them.
The river cannot—they will stop at the river.
That egg will become a river that will be a barrier between
them.
460 Before the cocks crow at dawn,
When dawn has really come,
The *sohanci* returns, he lands on the earth.
He said, "By Allah, when I passed by Sikiyay I heard them say
that Sana had given birth.
"Then I said that if Sana gives birth—since Sana had given
birth,
465 "They should name the child Daouda."
He is the one who is Daouda Sana.
They continued until they . . .
He escaped from the Bargantché, the Bargantché who live along
the river.
He never again fought against them.
470 Now, he just passed through their country, to go and start again
his reign.

[Nouhou Malio does not tell us what happened to Mamar Kassaye. But
we know from the Timbuktu chronicles that he was overthrown by one
of his sons, Askia Moussa, in 1528, and exiled to an island in the Niger
River. He died ten years later. For the remainder of the century, the
empire experienced a series of rulers descended from Askia Mohammed. A few, for example Askia Daouda, mentioned at the end of this
excerpt, were extremely effective leaders, but most were not so talented.
On April 12, 1591, an army sent across the Sahara by the sultan of
Morocco defeated the Songhay, an event that destroyed not only their
empire but marked the final chapter in the rise of a great Sahelian
civilization whose stories still echo across the region in the narratives of
modern griots.]

12. The Epic of Mali Bero
Narrated by Djibo Badié, known as Djeliba

Recorded by Thomas A. Hale on December 17, 1980, and April 1, 1980, at the home of Djibo Badié in Niamey, Niger. Transcribed and translated in first draft into French by Mounkaila Seydou Boulhassane Maïga. Translated into English by Thomas A. Hale. These excerpts edited by Thomas A. Hale.

MALI BERO, OR MALI THE FIRST OR ELDEST, is a legendary leader of the Zarma people of Western Niger who guided them in their migration from an unspecified region in Mali eastward to Western Niger several centuries ago. The story of Mali Bero has appeared in a variety of forms —poems, songs, and oral narratives. No one, however, has published a linear version of Mali Bero that is more than a few hundred lines long. Many of the shorter texts about him were assembled or collected and published by Fatima Mounkaila in the study cited in the introduction to this section. There, Mali Bero is framed in the broader context of a mythic Arab ancestor of all Zarma people who went to Mecca to convert to Islam and became a warrior fighting on behalf of the Prophet Mohammed before migrating to West Africa. Depending on the version, either Zabarkane or his son returned to Mali. One of his children or grandchildren was Mali Bero, known also as Zarmakoy [Zarma king] Sombo.

The following excerpts come from a 1,236-line epic narrated by Djibo Badié in two parts on two rather separate occasions. The long break between the two recordings was due in large part to his busy schedule. At the time of the recordings, he was the *jesere* most in demand in Niamey because of his great talent, the frequent broadcast of his songs on the radio, and his ancestry. He comes from one of the most respected *jesere* families in western Niger. It was very difficult for the researcher to arrange a recording session with him because he was either on the road every evening or performing at a special event in the capital.

The epic contains two episodes. The first is the story of the migration, an event that occurs in the distant past, though modern scholars now see it as taking place in the sixteenth century as the result of both a migration of Mande-speaking peoples from the West and the shift of a Songhay group to Zarmaganda, northwest of Niamey. The result of these two movements was the creation of the Zarma people. The second episode, occurring some time later, probably in the seventeenth century, tells of how the Zarma came to the aid of Songhay resistants who were fighting the Moroccan-led army that had defeated them in 1591 north of their capital, Gao, on the Niger River north of the Niger-Mali border. This episode also appears in *The Epic of Askia Mohammed*. In *The Epic of Mali Bero*, the migration and the support of the Songhay are separated by hundreds of lines of genealogy, a key part of the epic that links the heroes of the past to noble families today.

For the Zarma, the most important passage in this epic is the story of their migration eastward via a flying millet silo bottom. This is a flat and round surface perhaps two or three meters in diameter made of woven straw that serves as a foundation for a temporary silo. More permanent egg-shaped silos are crafted over a longer period of time out of mud. The incident that prompts the migration, the fight between Zarma, Tuareg, and Fulbe children, reflects the history of an off-and-on conflict that marks relations between these three groups until the present.

1	Mali the Great,
	Zarmakoy Sombo, he is the ancestor of all the Zarma people.
	One Friday,
	When Mali
10	Found some Tuareg children
	And some Fulbe children
	Who were taking a bath,
	Mali Bero
	Told each Zarma boy to steal his father's spear.
15	They arrived at the edge of the pond.
	Mali Bero
	Dug into the sand.
	He buried his spears in the sand.
	He told all the other Zarma children to do the same.
20	Mali,
	He and all the Zarma children went into the pond.
	They wash themselves.
	The Tuareg children
25	And the Fulbe children
	Run up to the edge of the pond.
	The Tuareg prince
	Grabs the cloth wrapper of Mali Bero
	And wipes his own body with it.
30	Mali Bero comes out of the pond.
	He tells him that he may lose his life.
	The Tuareg prince thinks that Mali Bero will grab the cloth from him.
	Mali slips his hand into the sand.
	He reaches the Tuareg prince
35	Who has taken his wrapper.
	Mali pierces him with his spear
	And kills him.
40	Mali Bero

Goes to look for his second spear.
He says to the Zarma children,
"Whoever among you allows the one who has taken your cloth
"To reach the dune,
45   "Know that I will strike you with my spear."
On that day, the Zarma children
Caused many lives to be lost at that pond.
"You, too, take your spear
50   "And strike the one who takes your wrapper."
Until they killed all the Tuareg children,
And all the Fulbe children around that pond.
Mali,
Whom they call Sombo,

57   On that day he came to the village.
He ordered that the drum named Sambonkon be beaten.
At that time, the Zarma had seven drums.

66   Sombonkon is the biggest of them all.

On that day the Zarma,
70   When the Sonbonkon is beaten,
Nobody asks why it is beaten
They simply come armed and ready for war.

75   On that day they had thirty horsemen.
He told the Zarma,
"I killed the Tuareg children,
"And the Fulbe children.
"And all the children of nobles who will follow a chief to war."
80   On that day, even those who arrived with courage
Found that their ardor cooled.
Those who arrived with *gris-gris*[1]
Found that their *gris-gris* no longer worked.
Going out in front will not work.
85   Hiding in the sand will not help.
Sombo, who is Mali Bero,
Had a man
Named Alamin.
Alamin is a sorcerer.
90   He is Mali Bero's slave.
On that day Alamin said to the Zarma people,
"Everybody should dismount."
Everybody dismounted.
He told everybody to go look for straw.

---

1. Charms.

135

95   They went and got straw and returned.
       He said that they should construct the bottom of a millet silo.
       He told everybody to climb on to it.
100   Only the cow should not get onto it.
       In those days it was only Alamin
       Who had a cow in Mali.

       Now, everybody climbed on board the millet silo bottom.
       The goats got in.
       The sheep got in.
110   The horses got in.
       The people got in.

       Alamin has a stick with a ring on it.
       Alamin strikes the millet silo bottom on the side facing the East.
       He says some words, he spits.
145   He strikes the millet silo bottom on the side facing the West.
       He strikes the millet silo bottom on the side facing the North.
       He says some words, he strikes it on the side facing the South.
       And the millet silo bottom begins to tremble with the people in
          it.
       He sits down in the center of the millet silo bottom.
150   Alamin makes the millet silo bottom rise.

[The flying millet silo bottom makes many stops on its trip eastward. During a stop at Andéramboukane, a small town 225 kilometers northeast of Niamey, on the Niger side of the Niger-Mali border, Mali Bero's jealous younger brother Bolonbooti informs the local Tuaregs that his older brother has killed Tuareg children in Mali. Thanks to his own *gris-gris*, Mali Bero becomes aware of his younger brother's betrayal. He awakens the other Zarma, and they attack the Tuareg, who flee along with his brother. The Zarma then take off on the millet silo bottom without Bolonbooti. After more stops, it comes to a final rest at Sargan, where the tomb of Mali Bero is located today. Sargan is a village seven kilometers south of Ouallam, a provincial capital seventy-five kilometers north of Niamey. The narrator lists the many descendants of Mali Bero, tracing the lineage of some down to the present, including Abdou Aouta, then the Zarmakoy, or chief Zarma, of Dosso, the best known of the traditional Zarma chiefs in Niger. Djibo Badié then shifts back to the narrative and to the period of Songhay resistance against the Moroccan invaders who had toppled the empire in 1591. The Zarma contribute to that resistance, and in so doing join their own history to that of their neighbors. One of Mali Bero's descendants, Hawayzé Mali, goes to the aid of the Songhay.]

       On that day, the Arabs of Morocco
       They swept through all of the Songhay region.

	They destroyed Gao.
	They captured Gao.
755	Until they entered the Zarma land.
	Until they arrived here.

	On that day he rose up at Dosso,[2]
	He came out to meet the Arabs.
	He took his army from Dosso.
	He gathered together the charlatans.
770	He gathered together the *marabouts*.
	He said to them, "Everyone will die in this battle except
	Yefarma Issaka."
	Yefarma Issaka is the son of his sister.
	On that day Yefarma Issaka
	Was sent to the Kebbi region in order to purchase a horse.

[Yefarma Issaka often appears in the oral tradition either as the nephew of Mali Bero or as the leader of the Golé people, a Zarma subgroup of Tuareg origin. Here, the narrator tells us he is a descendant of Mali Bero via his uncle, Hawayzé Mali. While Yefarma Issaka travels eastward, his uncle Hawayzé heads West with the army of Dosso to challenge the Moroccan-led force. He defeats them, forcing the invaders back to the Niger River, 100 kilometers westward. But the battle continues to rage along the river just south of present-day Niamey. Finally, Yefarma learns from a captive woman at a well that he has been sent away from the combat because he will die if he participates in it. Yefarma turns around and catches up with the Zarma army in the Niamey area.]

	He asks his uncle, "What are the fires on the edge of the river?"
	He replies, "They are the Arabs whom we are fighting."
905	Yefarma Issaka,
	He says, "Then you did not come here for war.
	"You came to get warm.
	"How is it that their fires are lit?
	"Your fires are also lit.
910	"But one fire must be extinguished."

	The uncle said, "Stop your mockery.
	"Stop your bravado.
915	"The people whom you will find here tomorrow,
	"You will find Zaw Zaw, he is a great Arab warrior.
	"You will find Bayero, he is a great Arab warrior.
	"You will find Sigsi, he is a great Arab warrior.
	"You will find here Mossoro, he is a great Arab warrior.

---

2. Provincial capital 107 kilometers east of Niamey.

137

920 "Among them all, one alone and his clan could fight both the
   Songhay and the Zarma for an entire day."
  Yefarma Issaka,
  He said, "Fine, tomorrow one fire will go out."

  The next morning the war began.
  Yefarma Issaka mounted his horse.
930 The Arab warrior named Zaw Zaw
  Mounted with his battalion.
  He chased all the enemies toward the dune.
  He found Yefarma Issaka who had stopped.
  They pierced Yefarma Issaka with two spears.
935 Yefarma Issaka cut off his head with a sword.
  He died.

[Bayero does the same thing, but is also beheaded by Yefarma. After
the Zarma has killed six of the enemy, the Arabs take to dugout canoes.
Yefarma goes after them on his horse and tries to capture one of them.
He and the Arab end up in the water. He captures the young warrior,
gives him to his uncle, and then goes back to the battle. By the end of
the day, his body is full of spears.]

  Early in the morning they left,
990 They said that they wanted to remove the spears from the body
   of Yefarma Issaka.
  Yefarma said that they should not try to remove the spears
  Because if they are all removed, he will die.
  He spent the day fighting with the Arabs.
  They stopped to spend the night under the great baobab tree at
   Boubon.[3]
995 It is there that they removed the spears from the body of
   Yefarma Issaka.

1006 Under the great baobab tree of Boubon,
  Yefarma Issaka,
  His tomb is under the great baobab tree of Boubon.

[The battle continues as Hawayzé Mali and his army advance north up
the left bank of the Niger River and defeat the invaders. From the
Zarma perspective, it is they who saved the Songhay.]

1018 On that day the griots said of Hawayzé Mali,
  You are the one who freed the Songhay from their burden.

---

3. Town on the left bank of the Niger twenty-five kilometers north of Niamey.

[At this point, the narrator turns briefly to another hero of the Songhay-Zarma world, Issa Korombé, subject of the following epic, and links him to Mali Bero.]

1032   Issa Korombé,
        He is the descendant of Mali Bero.

1051   The mother of Issa Korombé is of blacksmith origin.

        Daouda Bougar
        He too is a warrior.
1055   He was the teacher of Issa Korombé.
        When Issa Korombé was a child,
        He learned to fight from him.

[The narrator continues the story of Mali Bero's descendants by evoking, a few lines at a time, the names of other heroes, towns, and villages where battles took place, and of peoples against whom the Zarma fought. He ends the narrative with the the oft-repeated question:]

1236   Who asks again about the deeds of Mali?

13. The Epic of Issa Korombé
Narrated by Samba Gâfisso

Recorded, transcribed, and translated into French by Ousmane Mahamane Tandina. Reproduced in "Une épopée Zarma: Wangougna Issa Korombeïzé Modi ou Issa Koygolo, 'Mère de la science de la guerre'" (Ph.D. diss., University of Dakar, 1984). These excerpts edited and translated by Thomas A. Hale.

A NINTEENTH CENTURY HERO OF THE GOLÉ, one of the Zarma-speaking peoples of Niger, Issa Korombé was born around 1810 in Koygolo, a town in the Boboye region of western Niger about 100 kilometers east of the modern capital of Niger and 50 kilometers north of the provincial city of Dosso. The Boboye is a dry riverbed that flows into the much larger Dallol Bosso, another dry riverbed that runs for 1,000 kilometers from the Aïr Mountains in the Sahara of northern Niger south to the Niger River.

Fulbe migrants began to settle in the Boboye region in the eighteenth and early nineteenth centuries. According to Zarma oral sources, many of the Fulbe lived peacefully as herders and as Muslim religious leaders until some time between 1804 and 1808. Bambakar Louddouji, a Fulbe chief and an ally of the great Fulbe empire builder Ousman Dan Fodio in Sokoto, 250 kilometers southeastward in present-day Nigeria, began to impose his will on the region at that time, a move that generated resistance among Zarma warriors. They united to drive Louddouji into exile in Sokoto. But his son, Abdoul Hassane, returned to defeat the Zarma in 1831, reestablishing control over them and also over the Tuareg in the region.

The Zarma suffered not only from Fulbe hegemony but also from drought, raids by the Tuareg, and wars between different Zarma chiefs. Issa Korombé, like so many other epic heroes from the Sahel, left home around 1840 to learn the arts of war with the hope of returning some day to help his people. He fought against the Tuareg and the Fulbe in the Songhay area on the right bank of the Niger River 200 kilometers to the west as well as in the northern Zarma region of Zarmaganda on the left bank nearer the current Niger-Mali border.

In 1854, he returned to the Boboye, settling with his brother Daudu in Karma, a village about twenty-five kilometers northwest of Dosso. He then appealed to all Zarma *wangaari* ('war chiefs') in the region to join him in a sustained effort to defeat both the Tuareg and the Fulbe. His successful campaign to free the Zarma from external hegemony lasted for ten years and ended in 1866 with the signing of a peace treaty that guaranteed the independence of Zarmatarey, the land of the Zarma.

Because of his great skill as a military strategist, Issa Korombé was accorded the title of *wangougna*, "mother of the science of war," by his people. He was typical of a class of war chiefs of his epoch who did not seek political power but lived instead for combat and the opportunity to drive traditional enemies out of their region. For the next thirty

years, he offered his services as a skilled commander to a series of clients in the region and participated in wars against the western Zarma, whom he considered to be the allies of the Fulbe. In 1895, at the age of eighty-five, he decided to return to Koygolo. But Bayero, son of the Fulbe leader Abdoul Hassane, who had reestablished control over the Zarma in 1831, set out to reassert his family's influence in the region. With support from other Fulbe leaders being pushed eastward by the French from Senegal and Mali, his army defeated the Zarma force of Issa Korombé in August 1896 at Boumba, located at the confluence of the Niger and the Dallol Bosso. The attackers were armed with rifles while the Zarma were still fighting with spears, swords, and arrows. Issa Korombé died of gunshot wounds in that battle. The victory of his enemies was short lived, however, because the French soon moved into the region to establish their own colonial empire for the next six decades.

This 805-line text from which the following excerpts are taken is one of a collection of four narratives about Issa Korombé assembled for comparative study by Ousmane Mahamane Tandina. Two are in prose while two others are in linear form. One of the linear texts is 2,355 lines long and is recounted by an elder based on his memory of a written account owned by his father. The shorter version that serves as the source here came from an elder in the home town of Issa Korombé. None of the four texts was recounted by a griot because the Zarma people do not have griots who recount long epics, only genealogists and town criers. But the Golé people are known locally to share many of the traits of griots. For example, they are seen as particularly talented with words to describe their heroes. For this reason as well as because of the content and form of the text, Tandina argues that the narrative by Samba Gâfisso is indeed an epic.

	Issa in reality
	Is not a prince.
10	Nobody was a prince
	In those days when the Whites had not yet come here.
	But one used to become a chief and was succeeded in turn by others.
	Korombé[1] was a big producer of millet.
	He became a chief because of the quantity of millet he produced.
15	The mother of Issa was of blacksmith origin.
21	She ask Korombé to marry her.
	They got married and produced Issa.

---

1. The father of the hero.

Daudu[2] came to ask Korombé for the boy.
Daudu said to him:
"Korombé, will you allow me to take your son?"
30   "What will you do with him?" he asked.
"My child, you see, does not work with his hands.
"He does not farm.
"I don't want him for farming.
"I will take him at the risk of sacrificing him
35   "Because I, I only fight wars,
"And it is in war that I will engage him.
"So that he can become my squire.
"Is he capable of it?"
"Discuss it with him," replied Korombé
40   He called him to talk about it.
"My boy, do you like me?
"I want to make you my follower.
"But you must know that I have no other occupation except war
"If you want to join me, say so."
45   "Yes," agreed the boy.
"Do you understand all the consequences?"
"I accept them," replied Issa.
So then they went off on the warpath against the Tuareg, who
        were bothering them.

[Issa and Daudu go off in different directions, fighting their own separate wars against the various enemies of the Zarma. Issa returns from one war with much booty.]

Issa alone brought back forty horses.
"All these forty horses," he explained,
"Come from warriors who abandoned their mounts
85   "And from warriors whom I killed."

[The chief of Kolman invited all of the warriors to march through the village to his palace to choose among the eligible young women. Suffering from an unexplained sense of unhappiness, Issa declined the offer and then left for Wanzerbé, a town in the Songhay region near the Niger-Mali-Burkina Faso border that is known as the capital of Songhay magic. He seeks help from a single-breasted woman who is widely known for her powers. She proposes to solve his problems by placing his head on her knees and having him suckle her breast.]

150   He suckled, he suckled, and then fell asleep.
She wanted to remove his head from her knees.
But he gripped her breast.

---

2. A warrior friend of the family.

He suckled again, suckled until he went back to sleep again.
She wanted to free his head from her knees again.
155   He again grabbed his breast.
"My child," she said, "this, my breast,"
"I have not given it a single time to someone
"Who suckled it, fell asleep,
"And I wanted to sleep,
160   "And he tried to stop me, continuing resolutely to hold on to
        it."
"My mother," replied Issa, "it is because I suffer from a great
        problem."
"If that is the way it is, continue to suckle."
After six more sessions with her, she tells him that he does not
    need to suckle anymore.

196   "If it is the world that you desire,
"Everything that you want,
"Know that you will have it.

200   "The only thing left, I think,
"Is to give you a few small things."
She made him some *gris-gris*.[3]
She made him
Some magic powders.

[She warns him that when he leaves he will encounter a woman with a calabash containing seven measures of food. He must take the food, eat four measures of it, give the other three to his horse, and destroy the calabash. He then encounters some Tuareg, engages them in combat, defeats them, and continues on his way. He arrives at a village where the chief wants to buy his horse for the price of ten captives. Issa demands twenty. When the two fail to agree on a price, the chief then bars the gates of the village to prevent Issa from escaping. Issa simply jumps with his horse over the walls and goes on his way, eventually meeting up with his old patron, Daudu. When the two decide to settle down, no city or town will accept them. Only after they arrive at the town of Bankassam are they finally accepted by threatening violence to the local people. Later, after an incident in which they kill a Fulbe boy who insulted them, the Fulbe in the region set out to attack Issa Korombé.]

Issa posted scouts in the bush.
To warn him of the first sign of their arrival.
410   They saw the dust far away.
They came to warn Issa,

---

3. Charms.

To warn him that the Fulbe were coming.
He then ordered
That a horseman remain with him,
415   That ten others go out on the road
To wait for them,
That the ten horsemen go off a little distance,
To a point where they could see the enemy,
And that they should wait for them there.
420   The assailants arrived.
They encountered the ten horsemen.
Issa and the one horseman are hiding in ambush.
The skirmish takes place.
It goes on, it goes on.
425   When anger arose in him, Issa shouted.
He shook the magic gourd
(Provided by the woman of Wanzerbé)
And the Fulbe retreated.
They pursued them.
430   They harassed them.

[Some time after the victory, Daudu dies, Issa Korombé attends his funeral, and then assumes the leadership of the Zarma military forces.]

He looted here,
He pillaged there.
460   He destroyed such and such a city
He consumed another city
Until he gained control of the entire region.
Now the ancestor of the Fulbe,[4]
As soon as Issa heard of him,
465   He[5] was forced to retreat to the right bank of the river.
To spend three months there,
Four or five years,
Before returning.
Issa did not accept the idea of coexisting with him.

[The Fulbe plan to attack Issa Korombé. His *marabout* recommends that he retreat some distance to a tree on the horizon because the religious leader and diviner foresees danger that day.]

"May Our Lord save me from doing that," declared Issa.
"Nobody will ever say that behind my back!"
485   He stood up and made several leaps forward,
About five steps forward,
And sat down.

---

4. Bayero. 5. Bayero.

-" Me, I am your *marabout*," continued Gounou.
"I have spoken to you,
490 "Because today is not your day.
"If ever the opposing army possesses a *marabout* of my talent
"They will attack shortly,
"If they don't, you will be spared,
"But I repeat that if they have one of them,
495 "In an instant, they will find us here."
Before this meeting was over,
The people of Ziji[6] betrayed Issa
Because they declared:
"We thought that
500 "You came to fight and then run,
"When actually you came to deliver us as prey to the enemy.
"We, we will no longer follow you."
As soon as the Ziji people had turned in the opposite direction,
The Fulbe attacked.
505 The battle started,
Mayatchi Téko[7] and Marou[8]
Charged into the melée,
Made a path among the attackers,
Sent them into retreat,
510 Pushed them back.
Mayatchi Téko returned, Marou continued,
Mayatachi Téko returned, then he said,
"Father of Bibata,"[9]
"Naam!"[10]
515 "Let's withdraw, today's encounter
"Is turning out as Alfa Gounou had predicted.
"Let's retreat.
"A man, if he does not flee one day, does not return another
    day!"

520 Issa said that he would not know how to flee,
That he would never flee.

[After his son Marou dies in battle and Mayatchi Téko and other warriors counterattack, Issa Korombé single-handedly chases the enemy
down to the edge of the Niger River. The retreating Fulbe decide that
only a hunter's child who has not reached puberty will be capable of
killing Issa Korombé. He hides in a tree and succeeds in shooting Issa
Korombé with a poisoned arrow that penetrates the forearm and the
armpit. The child reports his feat but also says that the hero did not

6. Region to southeast of Boboye. 7. Chief lieutenant of Korombé. 8. Son of
Korombé. 9. Term of respect normally used by the first wife to her husband.
10. "Yes."

fall. The Fulbe decide to wait until the poison takes effect. When Issa Korombé weakens, he lies down on his shield and wraps himself in a white sheet. When the Fulbe approach, he transforms himself first into an elephant and then into one lion, two lions, and three lions in order to pursue them till late at night. At this point, a hunter takes the initiative to take a closer look. He discovers green flies all over the trees near Issa Korombé.]

	"Really!" he exclaimed.
	"It is a cadaver that is chasing us!"
595	He went off to tell everyone else.
	They got up.
	"We are the victims of a hallucination," they declared.
	"It is not a living person,
	"Let's reassemble and go there.
600	"If it is a lion, let him eat all of us at once.
	If it is an elephant, may we all be fodder for him."
	So, they got together and marched off
	To the cadaver.
	He transformed himself into a lion without hunting them.
605	He transformed himself into an elephant without pursuing
	them.
	Finally, they came closer.
	Then
	They cut off his head.

[After displaying his head, the Fulbe are shamed into burying it and they also spare the life of his *marabout*. Soon thereafter, the French arrive and demand that all wars cease.]

700	"No more war.
	"We have come to stay.
	"So that you listen to us from now on,
	"Anyone who doesn't want to listen to us,
	"Must know that he has no place here on earth.
705	"Because we, our fire,[11]
	"No fire can equal it.
	"May everyone here follow our orders,
	"For we are here."
	Since that time, they submitted to the Whites;
710	The Whites became their masters.

[The presence of a small French force does not prevent the Tuareg from harassing the Zarma after the death of Issa Korombé during a period of some instability that lasts until the First World War.]

---

11. That is, guns.

Fulbe Epics

THE FULBE ARE A CATTLE-HERDING PEOPLE who are now to be found across the Sahel, that region of Africa just south of the Sahara desert from the Atlantic coast of Senegal, Mauritania, and Guinea in the west, to Cameroon, Chad, and southern Sudan in the east. Pastoralists and nomads in origin, they have followed their herds over vast distances. They have also followed their faith. The nineteenth century saw several outbreaks of religious fervor among the Fulbe in various portions of West Africa and the establishment of Islamic states: Ousman dan Fodio in northern Nigeria (where the Fulbe established their rule over the Hausa); Cheikou Amadou in the Macina; and later and most spectacularly Al-hajj Umar Tal in Senegal. This latter's career brought him into conflict with the French, so that he was forced east and into conflict with both Cheikou Amadou (a sectarian struggle within Islam) and with the Bamana state of Segu (a holy war against unbelievers). He perished in 1864 when his conquered subjects revolted; he took refuge in a cave and someone set fire to the gunpowder.

Over this vast sweep of West Africa, there are many subgroups of Fulfulde-speakers who go by many different names. Their language remains recognizable, and so do certain of their traditions: Muslim and non-Muslim, the Pullo (singular) and cattle raising are intertwined. They have settled down and formed states, most notably in Guinea (the Futa Jallon) and in Senegal/Mauritania (the Futa Tooro), or attached themselves to other groups as herdsmen and neighbors. But cattle-herding (and cattle-raiding) are an essential element of Fulbe tradition, as one sees in their epic poetry.

The literature, oral and written, of the Fulbe is abundant and complex. Pre-Islamic initiatory traditions are represented by *Kaydara* or *Koumen*, poems collected and presented originally by Amadou Hampaté Bâ and Lilyan Kesteloot, and by an abundant tradition of songs and poems. Evidence suggests that the Fulbe of Macina took their epic-singing tradition from their neighbors, the Bamana of Segu, or possibly from the Soninké. The various linguistic traditions become intimately connected in the area north of the Niger, in the former Bamana kingdom of the Kaarta.

Among the Fulbe, as elsewhere in the Niger River valley, epic narration is the function of professionals known by a variety of names. Musicians in general are *awluube* (sing. *gawlo*); the specialized singers of epic are *mabuube* (sing. *mabo*), a term that also refers to weavers. The sedentarized Fulbe appear to observe the professional status groups common in the Mande world, including such occupations as blacksmith, leatherworkers, woodcarvers, and others. For example, one repeated poetic passage describes a hero mounting his horse by using the names of these professions as metonymies for the products of their labor: the blacksmith represents the stirrups and the bit, the leatherworker the reins and parts of the saddle, the woodcarver the saddle-frame. The musicians are generally considered to be of foreign origin.

In the process of appropriation, the epic as a borrowed form

loses its historical value. Where the Malinké traditions of Sunjata, who founded the Empire of Mali, or the Bamana traditions of Segu deal with purportedly historical events, the Fulbe songs deal fairly consciously with an admitted never-never land of heroic deeds and gestures, and their purpose is entertainment. There is, however, a nuance to this statement. Early in the first epic (*Hambodedio and Saïgalare*), we hear of "praise-names" (*jammoore* or *noddol* in Fulfulde), which are traditional praises associated with celebrated individuals or, through them, with their clans. These praises are a source of self-identification for the individual Pullo; to hear them is to be sent into a paroxysm of family pride, to be swept up into the glory of one's tradition (see Seydou 1977). Besides the praises, the epics serve also as the classic demonstration of *pulaaku*, the quintessential quality of the Pullo hero in his (or her?) former arrogance and prowess. These qualities are demonstrated through a variety of heroes, all significantly pre-Islamic. Hambodedio and Silâmaka, neighbors and contemporaries in Macina, are associated with the Bamana kingdom of Segu of the late eighteenth century, before the establishment of an Islamic *dina*, or rule of faith, by Cheikou Amadou; Samba Gueladio, a hero of the Futa Tooro, is dated by Senegalese scholars to the early eighteenth century.

14. The Epic of Hambodedio and Saïgalare
Narrated by Hamma Diam Bouraima

Recorded in Douentza, Mali, February 23, 1970, by Christiane Seydou. Transcribed and translated into French by Christiane Seydou. Edited by Christiane Seydou and published in La geste de Hambodedio ou Hama le rouge *by Armand Colin in 1976. This excerpt edited and translated into English by Stephen Belcher.*

HAMBODEDIO AND SAÏGALARE IS AN EPIC POEM from the region of Macina, in the modern republic of Mali, and it tells, in Fulfulde, of the legendary hero Hammadi Paté Yella, also known as Hambodedio or Hama the Red. There are many stories about Hambodedio; this is only one of them, and perhaps one of the least historical. It is also one of the most delightful, and versions of this story are reported in other regional languages.

The historical Hambodedio lived at the time of Monzon and Da, kings of Segu between 1790 and 1828. Legend and epic performances attach him to the time of Da (c. 1808-18), and he is said to have been the ally and son-in-law of the king of Segu. He probably lived somewhat earlier; we can date him by reference to the battle of Noukouma in 1818, between Segu and Islamic Macina. Around that time, his son, Gueladio, was the leader of the Fulbe of the Kunaari and eventually came into conflict with Cheikou Amadou, founder of the Fulbe Islamic state of Macina. Gueladio then led a migration of Fulbe to the southeast, across the arc of the Niger bend, to what is now Niger and Burkina Faso, around 1818. A German traveler met Gueladio (Gelaajo) there in 1853, and his descendants are still to be found there.

The story is a long and episodic one, revolving essentially around Hambodedio's quest for reputation (through "his" tune "Saïgalare") and the consequences of that quest; he shares the stage with his griot, who acquires the tune from the jinns, and with his wife Fadia, who incites him to great deeds. As the story starts, we consider the praise-names of the hero.

> Now, we—Hamma Diam Bouraïma and Ousmane Amadou
>   Ousso are from Time,
> But I, Hamma Diam Bouraïma, I am from Koysa—
> We are going to record a little.
> We will record Saïgalare of Hambodedio Hammadi Paté Yella.
> 5   This is the tune for Nyanyi Hammadi, for Wel-Hore Hammadi,
> For Fadia Hammadi, Kummbo and Umma Haani!
> Hammadi rose and trampled through the dew.
> At noon he had made the land a dark waste,
> The stranger-guest in the morning, the master of the house at
>   noon.
> 10   He said, "Oh, no! Don't name me by those worthless praise-
>   names!

149

"Those are the praise-names of the low-rumped hyena!
"I, Hammadi, am no hyena."
They told him, "Well, shall we call you the Peredio
"Who gathered no monkey-bread fruit with his pole,
15   "Who gathered no wild duck eggs,
"Who drank no watered milk in Barbe,
"Who drank no water from Hoore-Gennde!
"You are the Pullo who rules Bumaani and Budaande,
"And Aada-Wadda and Nama Nawre and Kanel Jeeje and
     Wandu Jeeje and Humbaldu-Jeeje and Ngappere Wumbere
     Jeeje,
20   "Or yet that you are the Pullo of Delbi and of Bubdo Njaree.
"You are the man who, if he goes to Segu, is the son of a red
     Pullo; if you squeezed his throat, the man would spit sour
     milk.
"But back in Kunaari he is the son of a Bambara and the grand-
     son of Da Monzon."
He said, "Ha! Now you have spoken God's truth of me.
"The night when I, Hammadi, am no longer in this world,
25   "Then for sure Saïgalare will be sold across the counter,
"And Saïgalare will be played for any peanut seller."

[Hambodedio then tells of the only three times he had felt fear: once
when a snake crawled over him while he was sitting with a woman;
again when he encountered a woodcutter whom he mistook for a jinn at
night; and a third time when he forded a river filled with wild beasts to
punish a shepherd who had insulted him. The last two incidents
occurred while he was fulfilling a request by his wife Fadia that he raid
some cattle for her from Samba Bongouel Samba, her old beau, and
while he was accompanying her on a boat ride: these incidents intro-
duce characters and themes which will reappear.]

And when did Saïgalare come down here?
It was on a Wednesday night that Saïgalare came into this
     world.
At the time, there was no Saïgalare, so that one might speak of
     the Saïgalare of Hambodedio Hammadi Paté Yella.
295   From Yeli to Yelikapa,
That is where people had settled.
One Wednesday night, a male genie,
An elder, came out of Yelikapa, over there,
And was brought into the entrance hall of Hambodedio, here in
     Gundaka.
300   He sat, plucking out Saïgalare.
It was a Wednesday, in the night.
While he was playing Saïgalare, Hammadi was upstairs, lying
     down.

He woke up with a start, he heard Saïgalare being played.
Hammadi rushed down, armed with his wide spear, he tum-
    bled down the stairs and came into his entrance hall.
305   The genie stopped playing his music
And called "silence."
Hammadi returned upstairs immediately;
He lay down again.
Once again, the genie began to play Saïgalare.
310   Hammadi rose up with a double-barreled rifle of tempered steel
    and moving breech; he loaded it with powder and ball; it
    never left him by night or day.
He came down again to the entrance hall.
The genie stopped playing Saïgalare.
He went back upstairs
No sooner was he back upstairs
315   Than the sun was driven by sticks, pushed from the East,
    drawn over the lands of China.
He turned over Karsana, he spread himself over Baghdad, he
    came down over Hanjiwa
And Hadeijiya
And Doogonduci and Kaedi, the little *guiguili* trees of Tamba-
    counda.
In Dakar they say that he is slow to come but that shading your
    eyes will not hide him.
320   Hammadi rose, sounded the great drum
From Kassa
To Kuna,
From Denga
To Mondio.
325   Everyone in the country assembled in Gundaka.
He declared that he needed none but the pluckers of strings.
All he needed was a player of the lute.
So the musicians who were there that day assembled,
Numbering a thousand.
330   He said, "Musicians!" The musicians answered, "Yes."
He said, "Last night,
"I heard a tune.
"Never, since God made me,
"Never have I heard its like.
335   "I do not know if it was one of you musicians who played,
"I don't know if it was a genie playing,
"I don't know if it was the Devil playing, but in any case I
    heard it.
"And all I know is that if, when the time comes around
"For the prayer of *salifana*[1] on the next Thursday,

---

1. Noontime.

340   "If I have not heard it again,
"Then that evening, there will be no live musicians in this
     world.
"If I have not heard it,
"Then that evening, no musicians will be left in the world."
The musicians asked, "What is it named?"

345   He said, "Eh!
"Exactly! I don't know what it is named.
"All I know is that if I have not heard it again
"By the time of the prayer of *salifana* on the next Thursday,
"Then that evening there will be no musicians living in the
     world."

350   The musicians asked, "How is it named, Hammadi?"
He said, "We have talked enough!
"Let each of you decide which way he will go,
"And leave at once to look for it.
"I do not know how it is named."

355   The musicians dispersed.
Each left, looking for what he did not have at his fingertips,
Without knowing how it was called.
They left that Thursday morning,
None of them having found it then,

360   And by the time of the *salifana* prayer on the next Wednesday,
Not a single one of them had yet found it.
Each one of them came back. Then came the turn of Ko Biraïma
     Ko, alone.
Each on his return played for Hammadi what he had found.
     Hammadi said it was not the tune he had heard.
As for Ko Biraïma Ko,

365   That Thursday, God's sun had already risen and he still had
     not found it.
And when the time for the *salifana* prayer came and the people
     played,
Then that evening not one would be left alive in the world.
And Ko Biraïma Ko himself that Thursday
Found nothing the whole day long.

370   He said, "Well, I will go back now. This is bad luck."
Ko left
And prepared to return to Gundaka.
Soon he came where the Black River and the White River join.
There was a rise of wooded land;

375   A termite mound stood on it.
Soon he came, and he was going past
When the genie came out and hailed him.
As soon as he hailed him, Ko turned his head to see.
The genie hid.

380   Ko said, "Ho! You!

"You, who called me, whoever you are! If you would stop then
    I could see you.
"Nothing can bother a man who is doomed to die today!
"The rice will be well cooked tomorrow.
"As for me, what awaits me in Gundaka terrifies me far more
    than you, who called me and then hid."

385   He went on his way. The genie called to him again.
He turned his head and saw him.
He touched heaven with his head, with his feet still on earth.
He did not falter, did not waver,
Did not turn, did not retreat,

390   But went on until he touched him.
The genie sat up, and they were face to face.
They greeted each other.
The genie said, "Ko Biraïma Ko!" He answered, "Yes!"
He said, "I am the one who called you."

395   He added, "As for why I called you,
"It is just that I have in my hands the thing you are looking
    for."
He said, "What is it that I must look for?"
He said, "A tune that was played in the entrance hall of
    Hambodedio,
"Last Wednesday night," he said. "That is what you seek."

400   He said, "That's true, that is what I must find."
The other said, "Come, here it is in my hand."
He said, "Sit down." He sat.
The genie pressed on the termite mound, and the lute came
    out. They tuned their instruments.
They began to play Saïgalare again and again.

405   He said, "That is what you are seeking." He said, "Rise and go.
"We the genies call it Saïgalare.
"All of God's creation living here below, all the sons of Adam,
    will only hear the tune from you. Rise and go."
Ko rose.
He went off a bit further.

410   He sat and began to pluck the strings.
He realized that what he had learned by heart had slipped
    from his fingers, and even more so with Saïgalare. He
    realized that nothing was left.
Ko turned around,
He came back
Where he had left him. He came and said, "Peace upon you."
    The old man answered, "And upon you, peace." He said,
    "If you are not a joker,

415   "Then, for that gift you gave me,
"Help me to know it,

"Give me back what I had before, let me once again play my
    instrument."
The genie said, "Ko!" And he said, "Yes!"
The genie said, "Raise your lute above your head and break
    it."
420   Ko struck his lute on the ground. It split.
The genie pressed on the termite mound.
A lute came out.
He pressed upon the termite mound, and another lute came
    out.
He pressed the mound, and a spring flowed out.
425   He pressed on the mound,
A bag of magic charms came out. He pressed the mound,
A calabash came out.
He took the calabash, he drew water,
He took the charms,
430   He undid them over the calabash, he told Ko to drink. Ko
    drank.
He told Ko to wash; Ko washed.
He told Ko to take up . . .
One of the lutes. He took one of the lutes.
Together, they played the first chords of Saïgalare.
435   Then they played Saïgalare again and again.
He said, "Ko!"
Ko said, "Yes!"
He said, "Rise and go home."
He said, "Rise and go home. Now you have it!
440   "No one will ever now be able to take Saïgalare from you; even
    I could not, no other could take it from you now.
"As for any one of God's creation,
"It is from you he will hear the tune."
Ko rose.
He took the hem of his robe in his teeth,
445   He gave himself to God, hoping he would reach Gundaka as
    noon came.
From point to point, from point to point, at last he reached Gun-
    daka just at noon.
He arrived.
They received him with open arms, they greeted each other,
    they announced, "Ko Biraïma has come! Ko Biraïma has
    come!
"He was the last we were expecting."
450   He came.
You know, one Jawando in a village is a cure.[2]

---

2. Someone skilled in diplomacy and intrigue.

Two Jawandos in a village are a sickness, and if the number
    rises to three, then it's an epidemic.
Hambodedio had one Jawando.
He said, "Now, Ko has come!
455   "Bring him food,
"And dry onion,
"And those little yellow things,
"And fish oil: it slips into the hand, it slides, it's swallowed,
"It sends the food down smoothly and sweetly. Bring him
    some!"
460   He asked for curdled milk and fresh milk; they were brought.
He asked to have a white kola nut, and he was given one.
He collected his wits.
Ko picked up his lute, he went to the entrance hall of Hambo-
    dedio,
He came and he found sitting there nine hundred—I tell you
    the truth—and ninety-nine men, all musicians.
465   The musicians said, "Well, well! Ko, come! Play us whatever
    you may have found, and let us all die. Because certainly
    you, all by yourself, cannot have found whatever we all
    together could not find."
Ko sat down, tuned his *hoddu*[3]
Began to play Saïgalare,
And played Saïgalare over and over again.
Hambodedio said, "That is it! That is the tune I heard last
    Wednesday night!"
470   The musicians said that as for them, they had never heard any-
    thing like that tune.
Hammadi said to him, "Ko!" He said "Yes!"
He said, "What you have accomplished just now is magnificent.
"I will make you a gift of a ten-count of everything, even the
    base of stew."
What is the base of stew?
475   He meant even ten chickens.
And with that, Hammadi picked up the double-barreled rifle,
    which he loaded with bullets.
He said that any musician he came across just then would travel
    to the next world, except for Ko Biraïma Ko.
The musicians pushed and shoved each other, struggling to be
    the first through the door.
The powder charge coughed.
480   Four slipped into that everlasting slumber; most succeeded in
    escaping
And returned to Gouyel.
Ever since those musicians left Gundaka to get back to Gouyel,

---

3. A four-stringed lute.

Any musician you see who claims to come from Gouyel,
They really come from here, from Gundaka, even though they
    may have settled in Gouyel later.
After that, Saïgalare belonged to Hammadi and to him alone,
    and no other could listen to Saïgalare as a piece of music.
Hammadi said, "Ko!" and he answered, "Yes!"

515   He said, "Saïgalare
"Has become my very own particular Saïgalare.
"You must not play Saïgalare for any of God's creatures
"Except for me.
"If ever I learn that you have played Saïgalare for anyone but
    myself,

520   "I will make of you a cold corpse."
He said, "I have two wives:
"I have one named Fadia,
"I have another named Tenen, daughter of Da Monzon.
"I also have two sons: I have one named Gueladio Hambodedio
    Hammadi Paté Yella,

525   "And one named Ousmane Hambodedio. Even for them,
"Let me not hear that you have played the tune. If I learn
"That you have played it for them, I will make of you a cold
    corpse."
He said, "Truth!"
He said, "I have heard, I agree.

530   "For none of God's creatures, whoever it may be, will I play the
    tune."
And from that moment on, it was for Hammadi alone that it
    was to be played,
There in his entrance hall.
Fadia lived upstairs, on the second story.
Tenen Da Monzon was here, on the ground floor.

535   But there! For Hammadi, the music was played in the entrance-
    way here,
When a little old woman servant who was on the ground floor
    heard it being played.
The little old woman servant climbed upstairs, she found Fadia.
She said, "Fadia!" Fadia said, "Yes!"
She said, "They have made up a tune for Hambodedio."

540   Fadia said, "Really? They have composed a tune for Hambode-
    dio?" She said, "Yes, they have composed a tune, in truth."
Fadia said, "And yet I have not heard this tune."
The old woman said, "If you haven't heard it, that means you
    are not the preferred wife.
"Tenen Da Monzon, the concubine, is dearer than you; she
    hears it every day, while you have not yet managed to
    hear it."

156

Fadia answered; she said, "Old servant," and the other said
    "Yes!"
545   She said, "As for me, since they have composed a tune for
        Hambodedio, I will hear it!
    "Whether because I have earned the right, or because money
        enables me to hear it,
    "But nevertheless, I will hear it."
    The servant went back down.
    At length, one fine morning,
550   Ko left the ground floor
    And climbed upstairs to the second story.
    He greeted Fadia, and Fadia answered him.
    Fadia said, "Ko Biraïma Ko!" He said "Yes!"
    She said, "I hear that you have composed a tune for Hambo-
        dedio."
555   He said, "Indeed, I have composed a tune."
    She said, "But won't I get to hear it?"
    He said, "You will not hear it."
    She said, "And why not?"
    He said, "Hammadi has said that if he learns I have played the
        tune for any other person, whoever it may be, he will kill
        me and the other person."
560   Fadia told him, "Well, Ko, if you have composed a tune for
        Hammadi, I will hear it,
    "Whether I am worthy of hearing or not,
    "I will hear it.
    "And meanwhile, as for you, Ko,
    "Take these fifty *mithqal*[4] of gold!
565   "By God, I will hear it!"
    Ko took the fifty *mithqal;*
    He made a hole in his trousers, he placed them there;
    Ever since that time there have been pockets in the pants.
    Ko went downstairs.
570   On Saturday, Hammadi was launching a campaign.
    All evening long, Ko drowned Hammadi in music.
    Hammadi said, "Tomorrow, when the morning rises,
    "I launch my campaign,
    "I go off to get the tawny cattle of Bongouel Samba,
575   "Drank-no-dust, Never-walked-on-foot, the Little Man of
        Gaïssoungou.
    "I wish to bring them back here to Gundaka."
    The morning rose.
    They were busy harnessing the horse
    When Ko rose up alone in his place.

---

4. Thirty grams.

580   He put ashes into the water, and pepper, and then splashed it
        into his eyes.
    At the last moment, as the horsemen were leaving,
    They realized he had not left, that his eyes must be treated.
    And so he would have a way to play Saïgalare for Fadia,
    So that Fadia could hear the tune at that time.

585   When morning came, all the horses were harnessed.
    Ko Biraïma Ko was the only one who did not come.
    They asked, "How is Ko today?
    "He hasn't yet come, has he?"
    They said, "Someone should go look in his sleeping place."

590   They found him wide awake, but his eyes—as you
        know—were sick.
    They said that his eyes were sick.
    They said, "And now what?
    "We aren't going to put off the departure
    "Because Ko isn't feeling well."

595   Hammadi told the riders to saddle their mounts; they saddled
        them.
    They set off, they left on the raid noiselessly, before the dawn,
        and rode through Kunaari.
    As soon as she was sure they were really off and away,
    Fadia came down
    From the upper story. No one was left in Gundaka,

600   Save for Ko; he was the only man left behind.
    Fadia came down,
    She took some sour milk, she splashed his eyes and rinsed
        them out,
    And the eyes were completely healed.
    Ko took his *hoddu*,

605   Slipped up to the upper story and found Fadia there.
    He seated himself across from Fadia,
    And began to beat out Saïgalare as best he could, while Fadia
        drank in Saïgalare.
    Hammadi's horsemen had ridden out on their raid.
    Soon they came to Dena.

610   Hammadi turned about.
    He did not hear Saïgalare.
    He looked far away before him, and he heard no Saïgalare.
    Hammadi told the riders to turn around immediately;
    On that day, he knew that if he met Bongouel, Bongouel would
        defeat him; he said that he had not heard Saïgalare all
        morning.

615   He told the horsemen to go back;
    On that day, the other would defeat them.
    If ever he met Bongouel on that day, Bongouel would defeat
        him.

He told them to return.
He said the rearguard should lead the way, and this was one.
He said the vanguard should take up the rear.

620 They turned about face and lined up to ride back to Gundaka.
Soon they reached the outskirts of Gundaka.
Soon, they came and entered Gundaka,
And as they entered, the griots began to praise them. He said, "No!"
Not one should praise him.

625 "I have not seen Ko Biraïma Ko, my own griot, the only one I care for, for some time. He is not in good health.
"Let each of you other griots go home to his house, while I in turn return to my own house."
Hammadi went straight to his house,
And as his steps led him there, he heard Saïgalare
Being played above on the upper story.

630 You might think that pepper juice had been dropped into his eyes.
Here, Hammadi comes to the door of the entrance hall, dismounts,
Leaves Mad Mane,
Leaps forward with his broad spear,
Takes the stairs.

635 He had almost reached the upper story:
They heard his feet pounding the stairs.
Ko Biraïma Ko leaped to his feet, dropping his *hoddu*.
Fadia said, "Sit down! Where are you going?
"No matter how high the Lord may have raised you, you are only his dog, while I am his wife. You're playing for me here. Sit down.

640 "You may curse me, if he kills you today."
Hammadi burst into the upper story rooms.
He said, "Ko!" Ko said, "Yes." "Didn't I tell you that you should not play Saïgalare
"For any of God's creatures? Didn't I tell you?" He said, "Yes, you said that."
He said, "And why then?"

645 He said, "Fadia told me to play for her.
"She gave me fifty *mithqal* so that . . .
"That is why I was playing for her."
He said, "If God wills, you will pass on right now."
He brandished his broad spear. The crested cranes screamed,

650 They spoke with Dibi.
He said, "Where will they land?
"Where should this spear fall? Will it fall on the woman, or will it fall on Ko?"
The woman said, "Really, Hammadi!

159

"It's not proper for it to fall on Ko.
655   "Ko is your griot. He composed Saïgalare for you.
"Your spear can only fall on me."
He brandished it again.
He asked, "Where must it fall?
"Will it fall on the woman, or on the griot?"
660   The woman answered more strongly, "Heavens, really,
     Hammadi!
"It is not proper to it to fall on Ko, for he is your griot.
"It must fall on me, yes, on me. It's on me, your wife, that it
     must fall."
He brandished it again.
He told her to show him where it should fall.
665   The woman drew back her skirt.
Showed him her thigh.
He pierced it through to the straw mat, and he withdrew it.
He said, "That is not the only blow!
"Where should it strike for the second?
670   "Will the second blow fall on the griot, or will it fall on my
     wo . . . , my woman?"
The woman said, "The second blow must fall here, on me. It
     would be wrong if you struck him on the second blow."
He said to show him where this second blow should fall. The
     woman drew back the skirt from her left thigh and showed
     it to him.
He struck and he hit the bone.
He pulled.
675   He pulled so hard that he fell over.
Fadia did not stop chatting and laughing.
Ko Biraïma Ko had not stopped playing the *hoddu*.
The blood streamed out.
The blood streamed so much that it was going to trickle down
     the stairway,
680   The sound was that of a punting pole that sobs.
He said, "Ko!" Ko said, "Yes!"
He said, "What is that I hear now? Is it rain falling?"
Ko said, "No."
Ko said, "It is your wife's blood dripping."

[Hammadi then sends for holy men and healers, and makes of them the
same demand he made of the griots: cure her, or else. The most notable
among them succeeds; the others are dispersed with gunfire. Once
healed, Fadia twits Hambodedio. "Brrrrr!" she cries. All you can do, she
says, is stab women and griots, and she challenges him to attend the
market at Kuna where the heroes meet on market day to drink beer.

    Hambodedio sends Ko first, and Ko comes to Kuna and is re-
fused beer by Nyamoy, the woman who brews and sells the beer

drunk by the heroes. One after another, the heroes come: Djenne Worma Djenne, Hama Alseini Gakoy, Silâmaka, and especially Bongouel Samba 'Drank-no-Dust,' Fadia's former suitor. Each of them intercedes on Ko's behalf, but Nyamoy remains adamant: she does not know Hambodedio, still less his griot. Ko returns and reports his mission. Hambodedio rides off to Kuna. On the way, he consults the omens; riding into town, he shoots a pair of lovers emerging at dawn. He comes to the market-place and settles down. The other heroes ride in, learn who is sitting in the market, and ride off without drinking beer, except for Bongouel. He buys some beer for Hambodedio, and then they play "tioki," a local board game. Hambodedio beats Bongouel, and he responds by cuffing Hambodedio. Finally, of course, they come to a duel. Neither can injure the other with weapons: swords, guns, spears all fail. At last, Hambodedio pulls out a hobble and begins to beat Bongouel with it, and Bongouel flees, leaving Hambodedio the field.

And so Hambodedio accomplishes the boast he had made to Fadia: he has gone to the market, he changes the market-day for Kuna, and he marries Nyamoy to Ko.]

15. The Epic of Silâmaka and Poullôri
Narrated by Maabal Samburu

Collected by Amadou Hampaté Bâ. Published by Amadou Hampaté Bâ and Lilyan Kesteloot in "Une épopée peule: 'Silâmaka,'" L'homme 8 (1969), 1-36. Reprinted in Lilyan Kesteloot, Da Monzon de Segu: L'épopée bambara (Paris: Fernand Nathan, 1972; reissued by l'Harmattan, 1993). English version by Stephen Belcher.

THE STORY OF SILÂMAKA IS A MAJOR ELEMENT OF THE TRADITIONS of Macina, where it seems to have become the common property of the Fulbe and the Bamana: the epic is sung (with differences) in both languages. Historically, the narrative places itself in the time of Da Monzon, ruler of Segu in the early nineteenth century, but this connection is hardly essential. While the story fits the pattern of revolt and conquest typical of many elements of the Bamana tradition, the most interesting dynamic is the relationship of the master, Silâmaka, with his retainer Poullôri, and the questions of social status and human worth involved.

A number of versions were collected in the colonial era by Leo Frobenius and Gilbert Vieillard. The following excerpts are taken from a version collected by Amadou Hampaté Bâ from the *mabo* Maabal Samburu, about whom we know nothing except that Hampaté Bâ (himself a figure of some importance) considered him the greatest *mabo* he knew. This version was published in French translation by Hampaté Bâ and Lilyan Kesteloot in 1969 and thus marks one of the first salvos before the explosion of collecting and publishing of African epic of the 1970s and 1980s.

[The Ardo Hammadi and his household captive Baba both marry; their wives conceive on the same day and give birth on the same day. The noble son is named Silâmaka; the captive is Poullôri.]

> Da Monzon was the lord of Ardo Hammadi.
> He sent one day for the "price of the honey-beer."[1]
> The tax gatherers were three young Bambaras.
> They went to Hammadi and told him why they had come.
5 > The Ardo went into the chamber where he kept his cowries.
> He saw his son's mother nursing the boy.
> He called to Aissa; she put the baby on a mat
> Near the three emissaries who stood waiting.
> The baby was then exactly forty days old.
10 > A horsefly suddenly landed on his forehead
> And began to suck his blood.
> The three messengers from Da Monzon
> Watched this infant, barely forty days old,
> Who didn't even bother to raise his eyes.

---

1. The tribute.

15   Silâmaka did not move.
He did not blink.
He did not weep,
Before the horsefly, sated with blood, fell off him.
Then blood flowed over the face of Silâmaka.
20   When the father and mother returned,
They gave the emissaries a measure of gold for the "price of
       honey-beer."
Hammadi said to his wife, "See the naughty boy!
"A horsefly drinks all his blood,
"And he doesn't even cry to warn us."
25   Silâmaka's mother crushed the insect.
The three emissaries observed this scene.
The three emissaries returned to Segu,
They told their master, "We are afraid,
"That son of Hammadi, as we saw him,
30   "Will certainly give us grief."
And they told him the story of the horsefly.

[Da Monzon summons diviners and they tell him that a terrible child
has been or will be born in that year; they tell him what magical measures to take against him, but these involve conditions almost impossible to fulfill. The *jeli* of Da Monzon comforts him.]

    So Da understood that on the horizon of Macina,
A black cloud rose to threaten
35   The throne of the Master of Waters in Segu.
Silâmaka and his captive grew up;
Soon they were old enough to spend their afternoons at *niallo*.[2]
Within the chiefdom of Ardo Hammadi was a woman,
The most beautiful of the land.
40   One hundred young Fulbe horsemen came every afternoon
To spend some time with her.
Silâmaka was among them, and the young woman
Showed him more favor than others.
Each time he appeared with Poullôri,
45   The young Pullo woman set out two mats,
Finely woven and well adorned;
She set one on the ground for herself,
The other was for Silâmaka and his captive.
The two friends sat comfortably,
50   While everyone else was crushed together like faggots of wood.
One day Silâmaka and the young woman had a lover's spat.
They reproached each other and spoke hard words.
The woman said to Silâmaka, "You make me mad.

2. In dalliance.

"People say you are brave, and so you claim to be,
55   "But all those who flatter you in this way
"Have no choice about it.
"Because you are a chief's son, they eat from your bowl
"They are clothed in your robes!
"If you really are brave, you should not prove it through me,
60   "But rather go and prove your valor to Da Monzon.
"It is to him your father pays a measure of soft gold,
"The price of your breathing.
"Da Monzon only uses it to buy honey-beer."
Poullôri came between them and reconciled them.
65   The next day, the horseman and his captive came back to the
            niallo,
But as soon as the woman recognized the tread of Silâmaka,
She hid a sharp thorn under his usual mat
So that the point rose just where Silâmaka would sit down.
The mat bulged from the thorn.
70   When the Fula arrived, he saw the bump,
But instead of moving aside, he sat directly on it,
There in his usual place,
Without even bothering to look and see why the mat was mis-
            shapen.
So he sat down on the thorn as though it were a tuft of wool;
75   The point entered his buttock,
But Silâmaka did not blink or flinch.
He chatted as though nothing were wrong
And never stopped chewing his kola.
Blood stained his trousers and his robe,
80   As well as the mat on which he was seated;
Poullôri saw it and cried, "Silâmaka!
"Blood is running from under you!"
Silâmaka said, "Continue pouring out your words,"
And they bantered until the usual time.
85   When Poullôri wished to leave,
His master wanted to wait until the time of *lasara.*[3]
When *lasara* came, Poullôri said, "Let's go."
Silâmaka said, "Then you go first."
The captive rose, and then Silâmaka.
90   The thorn and the mat came with him,
Stuck to his behind and clotted with blood.
With a single motion, Silâmaka tore them away.
Poullôri said, "Wait, let me treat you."
Silâmaka replied, "No need.
95   "My horse's saddle will bind my wound,

---

3. The evening prayer.

"And tomorrow I shall find the master to make me invulner-
    able."

[Silâmaka consults a diviner who tells him he must make a talisman
from the skin of the black snake of Galamani, king of the bush spirits.
Silâmaka sends warriors to kill the snake, but they fail. He goes himself.]

Soperekagne was saddled.
Soperekagne was a pure white horse.
Silâmaka trod on the blacksmith,
100 He seized the leatherworker,
He sat on the woodcarver,
He spurred his mount and made him rear,
The tail swept the sand,
The hundred horses started to move.
105 See the stallions, the strong males,
So handsome when grazing in the pasture,
But changed to murderers in the battle!
They set off, growling like the thunder.
What was high, they flattened.
110 What was low, they bestrode.
What was green, they tore up.
What was dry, they broke.
They galloped, *kerbekerbe*,[4]
The blades of grass bent over.
115 Silâmaka was on the move.
The young animals knew some great deed was to come,
And wildly ran to their mothers for shelter.
A griot sang the praise-song for Gueladio:
    Samba, should a man dare say your eye is white
120   You split his skull on the spot.
    You cannot see the cartilage
    Which separates the hippo's nostrils.
    You cannot see Gueladio
    When he charges the hippo!
125   Gueladio, he rides the horse,
    Ummu Latoma,
    The mare who crushes vermin,
    Who tramples and flattens termite hills.
When Silâmaka came to the grove,
130 He found the snake in its favorite spot,
For already it was used to killing a man each time.
Silâmaka said, "Stop the horses."
He dismounted and handed the animal to faithful Poullôri.

---

4. Onomatopoeia for speed.

The snake was facing the group.
135   Silâmaka went around the grove,
He walked with quiet little steps.
He seized the beast suddenly by the neck;
The snake wrapped itself around his arm,
And beat his ribs with its tail.
140   Then Silâmaka rejoined his horsemen.
All of them fled, except Poullôri.
The valiant Pullo mounted his horse,
Still holding the great black snake by the neck.
All Poullôri had to do was tell the others
145   That Silâmaka had captured the snake of Galamani.

[They make belts out of the snakeskin and test them at a village: the population is terrified. Then follows an extended interlude in which three griots visit the Fulbe heroes of the region, asking who is considered bravest. Djenne Vere names four: Silâmaka, Hambodedio, himself, and Hamma Alaseyni Gakoy; Silâmaka claims to be braver and says he will visit Hambodedio. When he visits Hambodedio, he is insulted, and to take revenge he and Poullôri raid Hambodedio's cattle. When Hambodedio rides after them, he also listens to the advice of an old man and approaches Silâmaka peacefully. The two heroes make up and Silâmaka returns home. Da Monzon sends for the tribute; Silâmaka takes the gold from the messengers and tells them Macina will no longer pay tribute. The messengers return and tell Da Monzon that the child they had warned him about has grown up. Da Monzon sends the three men to capture Silâmaka, but they are beaten and mutilated: one loses a tongue, the other an ear, the third an eye. They inform Da Monzon and he sends cavalry.]

The horses flew through Segu like arrows
And their hooves pierced the ground.
The news reached Silâmaka.
"How many are they?" asked the son of Hammadi.
150   "Fifty," he was told.
Silâmaka exclaimed, "Allah blast Da Monzon!
"He cannot write me off with fifty horses!"
Silâmaka could count on men of solid worth in Kekei,
They were divided in five companies, each of a hundred
        bridles,
155   All members of his age group,
All members of the Ferobe clan.
But Silâmaka told his five hundred riders,
"You may rest today,
"Poullôri and I can handle this.
160   "Do not worry, your turn shall come."
He ordered that Soperekagne be saddled;

It was done so well the noble horse raised its hoof in greeting.
Silâmaka trod on the blacksmith,
He seized the leatherworker,
165 He sat upon the woodcarver;
Poullôri did the same,
Together they rode down the hill from the village.
Silâmaka was wearing his talismans of war.
West of Kekei is a tamarind tree.
170 Silâmaka's magic charm is buried at the foot of the tree.
Before it grows a thorn tree, facing the plain.
It was on that plain that Silâmaka was accustomed
To draw his enemies if he wanted a sure victory.
So the Pullo waited in the shade of the tamarind tree.
175 The horses of Segu crossed the plain of Wougouba.
Silâmaka was smoking his pipe
When he saw the horses racing toward him.
He placed his pipe in his mouth and drew,
He blew out the smoke and made a cloud
180 Which divided into three other clouds.
Then he rode forward, with Poullôri close behind.
As soon as the warriors of Segu saw them,
They drew up into battle array and charged.
Their arrows pierced the air,
185 The echo came whistling in answer.
Silâmaka and Poullôri sat leaning on their mounts,
As though listening to tuneful music,
And Silâmaka continued to smoke his pipe.
Their enemies shot so many times
190 That the powder made a cloud, blocking their sight,
A fog which masked them from their opponents.
But the wind blew, dispersed the cloud,
And the fighters were face to face.
Silâmaka and Poullôri went through the horsemen
195 Like a needle through cotton.
They tore the column, as a *pirogue*[5] parts the waters.
The horses of Segu panicked and ran together.
Silâmaka and Poullôri scattered them a first time
And then returned to the plain of Wougouba.
200 The horsemen reunited but could not control their mounts;
They fled to the village of Gandekorbo
And were forced out.
The Bambara piled up like flies in Kobikoboro;
Silâmaka and Poullôri winnowed them there.
205 They pursued them and flayed them
As far as the village named "Skinning."

---

5. A dugout canoe.

The horses of Segu fled to Kondo,
But the Fula followed after to thrash them
With their fish-bodied spears and their barbed arrows.
210 The horses of Segu hid in Nene,
But found no peace there.
They entered the village and got lost.
With difficulty they found their way,
They fled to Dierma, they fled to Temougou,
215 But nothing good awaited them there.
All night through they marched,
To the village of Goumougatchamare,
The village of defeats.
That is where Silâmaka and Poullôri defeated them,
220 Silâmaka who feared shame but not spearheads.
Poullôri killed thirteen and Silâmaka twenty-seven.
Only ten returned to Segu to bear the news to Da Monzon.

[They return and give the news. A warrior of Da Monzon, trained in Fulbe warfare, rides against Silâmaka. On the first day he puts him to flight by brandishing a tether, i.e., by threatening to beat him like a slave. On the second day, Silâmaka seizes him and cuts off his head, which he brings back to his sister. Meanwhile, Poullôri has defeated the other riders. Da Monzon sends a thousand horsemen against Kekei.]

Silâmaka asked, "How many are there?"
His griots began to sing his praises.
225 Da Monzon has sent many horses.
Silâmaka, you are *Garba mama*,[6]
Segu has crossed the river
With large and agile horses;
Their number blackens the bush.
230 We ask God to watch over Kekei in the night,
For the daytime, we shall take over, we shall guard.
Segu has crossed Senokorbo.
Segu has crossed Gande Korbo.
Segu has crossed Kondomodi.
235 Segu has crossed Siromodi.
Segu has crossed Konotamamodi.
Segu has crossed Kuma Wedu.
Oh, Kuma, pond of lily pads,
Segu has crossed you too.
240 Where we used to collect the bulbs,
We find the heads of Segu's warriors.
Where the women would do the wash,
On the banks where the white clothes were spread,

---

6. The name of a tune.

Today we spread the fat flesh of the men of Segu
245   On the banks of the pond of Kuma.

[The first force of Segu is defeated by Silâmaka and Poullôri. Da Monzon sends another army. Silâmaka anticipates the end and consults a diviner who foresees his death. Da Monzon fetches *marabouts* (Muslim holy men) who instruct him in the occult measures to take to defeat Silâmaka. Da Monzon takes the measures, which involve sacrificing a bull in a tree and entrusting a weapon to an albino boy. He then sends another army. Silâmaka sends Poullôri away to Hambodedio to inform him of their revolt.]

       When day came, the army of Segu had just reached Kekei.
       Silâmaka ordered his horse saddled as usual,
       He went out as he was used to go,
       He placed himself in the shade of the tamarind tree.
250   He faced Segu, he puffed on his pipe,
       Then he charged the enemy cavalry,
       Which he put to flight as usual.
       Then he came to rest under the tamarind tree.
       Then the horsemen of Segu wondered
255   Why the child hidden in the tree
       Had not fired at Silâmaka.
       All began examining the tamarind tree under which he was.
       The Fula understood there was something unusual.
       The child had indeed tried three times to shoot the arrow,
260   But fear paralysed him.
       Then Silâmaka raised his eyes.
       He saw the child, the child trembled.
       The arrow fell from his hands.
       It wounded Silâmaka.
265   It struck his hip.
       It pierced through to the saddle.
       The child fell like a ripe fruit.
       Soperekagne trampled his body.
       When the arrow touched Silâmaka,
270   The poison entered his veins.
       He felt dizzy
       But his horse raced for the village,
       As though it knew its master would die,
       So his body would not fall into enemy hands.
275   It carried him to the door of his compound.
       That is where the dying Silâmaka collapsed.
       The enemy horsemen, rejoicing, returned to Da Monzon in
          Segu.
       They told him, "Silâmaka is dead.
       "Macina is ours once again."

280   When Hambodedio had read the letter,
And Poullôri had understood its content,
He immediately took off for Kekei.
He cried out, "My disgrace! Silâmaka goes
"And will spend his first night without me in the other world."

285   When he arrived, he found the irreparable.
He said, "Today, I have lost my master.
"The one to whom I belonged,
"But who never made me feel that I was his captive,
"His whole life long—save for three times.

290   "The first came when we went to greet Djenne Vere at Borigo-
      ral.
"Djenne Vere was a renowned hero,
"Owner of many goods.
"Silâmaka's greeting made him exuberant.
"He bought boots worth fifty thousand cowries.

295   "He gave them to my master, who entrusted them to me.
"I was going to try them on, but Silâmaka said,
"'Don't stretch my boots!'
"That day, Silâmaka showed me
"That mine was not the small foot of a noble.

300   "The second time, we had gone to bathe,
"And we saw arriving men of rank,
"Before whom we must show modesty.
"Silâmaka told me, 'Hide your sex with your hands,
"'And fetch my clothes.' There again,

305   "He made me feel that I was a captive:
"I had to expose myself, while he remained in the water.
"And the third time is today.
"Silâmaka knew he was to die.
"He did not want me to witness his death,

310   "And sent me to Hambodedio.
"He showed me that I am his captive,
"He stopped me from sharing his fate."
Da Monzon sent a thousand horses
And ordered them to plunder Kekei.

315   Poullôri saddled his steed;
He went to thank his master's family
And to take leave of his relatives.
He wept. He said, "It is time now
"For me to join Silâmaka."

320   He took their two sons and mounted them with him,
Silâmaka's son before, his own son behind.
He took Silâmaka's enchanted spear.
He charged the thousand horsemen of Segu,
He divided them into two groups.

325   He pursued five hundred and five hundred pursued him.

Thus he was in the midst of the thousand horses.
This was at the time the sun was setting,
And night swallowed them all. No one ever learned
Where this procession disappeared.
330   Those thousand horses, in legend,
Rose to the sky with Poullôri.
And today, as clouds march by
As thunder strikes and the rains pelt down,
When lightning flashes and the echo answers,
335   The Bambara say, "There is Poullôri,
"Still chasing the horsemen of Segu."
Ardo Hambodedio went to Segu.
He begged Da Monzon, so that Macina
Would not be enslaved; the king agreed.
340   This is how the *Masinanke*[7] escaped their captivity
Under the empire of Segu.

---

7. The people of Macina.

16. The Epic of Silâmaka and Hambodedio
Narrated by Boubacar Tinguidji

Published by Christiane Seydou in Silâmaka et Poullôri *(Paris: Armand Colin, 1972), pp. 175-213. English version by Stephen Belcher. N.B. Seydou's published text incorporates elements from a second performance by Tinguidji; these elements are indented in what follows.*

BOUBACAR TINGUIDJI, THE PERFORMER, WAS A *MABO* from the region of Niamey; for much of his life he was the retainer of Mossi Gaïdou, a local chief, and he recalls those days as the proper manner for a *mabo* to live (see Seydou 1972 for his career). He accompanies himself on the *hoddu*, the four-stringed lute.

Sometimes incorporated into the longer account of Silâmaka's revolt (see the previous text), this epic tells the lighter story of his encounter with Hambodedio. This piece is representative of a wider genre of narratives concerning cattle-raiding confrontations between two heroes of substantial reputation, and is well represented in Macina and in the Futa Tooro. The following piece was performed by Boubacar Tinguidji as a piece separate from the fuller story. It presents virtually the same emotional range as the longer narrative, beginning with the pride and valor of the two heroes and ending with Poullôri's statements of outrage about Silâmaka's deception.

Here is another story about Silâmaka, *ardo*[1] of Macina, and
  Poullôri, *ardo* of Macina.
Silâmaka's father had become old; he had no strength any
  more.
Poullôri had become Poullôri and Silâmaka, Silâmaka.
They learned that a great war was about to start between
  Macina and the people of Bandiagara.
5   Silâmaka set off, Poullôri set off.
They mounted their horses.
They dressed in light-colored clothes, they headed for Gun-
  daka.
They said they were going to put themselves under the protec-
  tion of Hambodedio, Lord of Gundaka.
"I want to entrust to you my father, the Lord of Macina, who is
  very old.
10   "I am just the son of a village chieftain, not the son of a king.
"I entrust my father to you."
A war was about to start; they did not know if they could with-
  stand it.
A king is more powerful than all the village chiefs in the world
  united.
If he lost, in that war, Amiiru Gundaka would assist him.

---

1. Ruler.

15 If he didn't lose, no harm done, it would be to Amiiru's credit.
  They straddled their horses in the first rains.
  They talked to a *marabout*, asked him to divine for them at
   home.
  This war about to start—how should they wage it that year?
  The *marabout* consulted the table, and after a long moment de-
   clared that he couldn't see anything.
20 The only thing he saw was that this year, Macina would flee.
  Every last man would die.
  He couldn't see a single one of them standing up!
  The dead and the fleeing—that was what he saw!
  Poullôri slapped the *marabout*; he fell.
25 Poullôri said, "Rise and speak!" He got up.
  He continued. "Speak. If you miss again, we will kill you."
  The *marabout* said, "By God, if you must kill, kill me.
  "I did not see a single one alive; everyone flees.
  "Some die in the bush, others are killed in the village."
30 Silâmaka slapped the *marabout*, and he fell down again.
  He said, "Look! You didn't examine all the squares.
  "Look again, maybe you'll see."
  He said, "And now, if you make a mistake, I'll send you where
   you'll make no more mistakes. You'll see where I take
   you."
  That is what Poullôri said to him,
35 So spoke the slave.
  He looked for a long time at his divining table.
  He said, "That day,
  "Poullôri and Ardo Silâmaka, I see you in the cemetery, I see
   you dead and buried."
  Then they said, "That's what we wanted you to say.
40 "But us, fleeing with the others—that, you didn't see."
  They got on their horses and left for Gundaka.
  The road was long enough to dry out.
  They arrived and found Hambodedio's herdsmen behind the
   village, a bit further. There were seven.
  They said, "Hey, you, whose are those cows?"
45 The others, all seven, answered, "The cattle
  "Of Hambodedio, Lord of Gundaka."
  They went on, and when they arrived at Hambodedio's gate
   they called, "Peace be with you."
  Hambodedio said, "And on you, peace.
  "Oh, you strangers!
50 "Is it you they call Poullôri?" He said, "That's me."
  "Is it you they call Silâmaka?" He said, "That's me."
  Amiiru Gundaka asked, "Do you really come in peace?"
  They said, "That is our only desire."

One of Hambodedio's slaves said, "Bah! Even if you hadn't said
'*Salaam*,'[2] we knew you came in peace.
55   "No one among you could come here and cause trouble.
"Whoever comes here to bring trouble, for sure, trouble comes
    on him.
"Here, trouble is named Gundaka."
For slaves to talk that way
And Amiiru Gundaka didn't rebuke the slaves,
60   He didn't reprimand them—
That he did not rebuke or reprimand them—
That inflamed Silâmaka and inflamed Poullôri.
If your wife insults someone,
Or your child insults someone,
65   And you sit there laughing,
Without shutting them up,
Then you have insulted the person, not your wife or your child,
What a shame!
When the slaves told them they could not cause trouble, the
    heart of Silâmaka leapt, the heart of Poullôri leapt.
70   They said, "We came filled with deference, but you have made
    this deference a duty.
"Well, now you will learn that we can bring trouble.
"Doing evil is not hard; doing good is."
Silâmaka signaled Poullôri, and they went back without saying
    a word to Amiiru Gundaka of what brought them.
The evening was cooling, the sun was about to set but hadn't
    yet.
75   They went back to the herders
Who were guarding Amiiru Gundaka's cattle.
They went to Hambodedio's cattle;
There were seven herds,
Each of a hundred head.
80   They arrived and dismounted; they told Hambodedio's
    herders, "Come here to us."
Of the seven herdsmen,
They killed five.
They cut off their heads.
They left two.
85   They took a spear.
They took the eye of one
And cut off one hand.
With the other, they cut off an ear
And cut off one hand.
90   To the two mutilated survivors,
They said, "You survivors,

---

2. Peace.

"Report to Amiiru Gundaka
"I, Silâmaka Ardo Macina,
"And I, Poullôri Ardo, we are here.
95 "Tell him we will spend the night here with his cattle!
"We are the evening visitors
"Whom his slaves insulted—
"And he didn't say a word—
"They said we couldn't cause any trouble.
100 "That's who we are.
"And that is why we have taken your eye and his hand.
"Tell him we are here and we won't move, we will go no
    further. We will wait for all of Gundaka, we will wait for
    him here.
"Tell him that he will not drink his cow's milk until the day he
    dies.
"We heard his slaves insult us and he laughed."
105 One left with one eye and one hand,
The other left with one ear and one hand,
To show themselves to Hambodedio.
They spent the night there, drinking their milk till dawn.
Amiiru Gundaka left in the early morning.
110 He set off with his horsemen,
A hundred horsemen; he reached them, he found Silâmaka and
    Poullôri.
These two rose, they pounced upon them.
They killed and they killed,
Until few were left
115 To reach Gundaka.
Only a few survivors reached Gundaka.
Silâmaka told Poullôri to collect all the cattle, as many as there
    were,
The cattle of the seven herdsmen,
And to take them away,
120 To go a bit further,
And to stay there with them.
He should make a big corral.
He should wait there with them.
And then Gundaka,
125 And even beyond Gundaka—
Up to ten villages—
If they found him there,
Himself, Silâmaka Ardo Macina,
They would have to kill him to get by "and reach you, Poullôri,
130 "I myself say this,
"If you see people come to you, then you will know,
"You can swear by the Book, that I am dead."

175

There was a young woman whom Silâmaka had courted. To-
    gether they had flirted and talked since they were teen-
    agers.
Her name was Bandado Abdoulaye,
135   Bandado Suleimana.
Silâmaka courted this woman,
Hambodedio courted this woman.
Hambodedio
Drove off Silâmaka Ardo Macina.
140   He married her.
The king of the land, he drove off Silâmaka and married the
    woman.
Silâmaka courted her, but didn't get her.
Amiiru Gundaka married her.
She was in his house
And he still did not know
145   That Silâmaka had courted the young girl he had married.
As for Silâmaka, he was very touchy about the whole thing.
If a woman comes between two men, they'll never ever agree
    again.
All the horsemen who came, Silâmaka slaughtered them.
All the horsemen who came, Silâmaka slaughtered them.
150   And that lasted
Seven days.
In the morning at dawn,
Poullôri would set off.
He brought milk where Silâmaka was.
155   Then he went back to the cows.
He was named Poullôri Benana, the slave who died without
    being anyone's thing.
A pile of blue *bougue* cloth for him alone!
Let his neck bend beneath the weight of the *bougue* cloth!
A shelter of unshattering steel!
160   Gorbal
Ali Mansore! The most cunning of the cunning!
Katiel says, "Milk."
Poullôri answers, "Mildew!"
He would tear something,
165   To have God sew it up again.
He would dry something,
To make God wet it.
Poullôri said, "Two things can't stand a third.
"Generosity and war
170   "Cannot stand deliberation.
"If you deliberate
"Then generosity and war will be hindered."
So spoke Poullôri.

Amiiru Gundaka's *mabo* said,
175   "You want your cows, don't you, Amiiru Gundaka?" He said,
        "I want them."
He asked, "You want them?" He said, "I want them."
He said, "If you want them, tomorrow I'll bring them. No need
        for spear or gun; they will come tomorrow."
Amiiru Gundaka said, "You lie."
He said, "By God! They will come tomorrow—my lute and my
        quality of *mabo* will bring them."
180   He said, "Go."
The next morning at dawn—
Amiiru Gundaka
Had not spent the night with Bandado Abdoulaye.
Bandado Abdoulaye had belts made of what you call coins:
185   Two
Of silver.
You go to jewelers.
They melt them.
They make a sort
190   Of rosary.
The two belts
Were hung over her bed.
She said, "Silâmaka was my suitor. He courted me when I was
        young.
"He and the king were rivals for my hand.
195   "That king—I didn't love him. He held power.
"That's why he carried me off and married me
"So tomorrow at dawn—since Hambodedio won't spend the
        night in my room—
"Take what hangs over the bed in my room,
"My two belts.
200   "Take down my two belts from above the bed: two belts of
        silver.
"Take them down.
"Take a strip of cotton—"
Her head-scarf—
"Take it down and roll it up like a turban. I give it to you.
205   "Take the belts, carry them to Silâmaka Ardo Macina—
"You will find him in the bush.
"Ask him if he knows these belts—my belts—or not.
"If you show them to him, he'll give you the cattle and you will
        come back.
210   "He will understand that none other than I send him those
        belts;
"He will understand from them that you do come to him from
        me.

"At any rate, if you don't take them, the cattle won't come
    back. No spear will bring them back."
The *mabo* got up early, and at dawn he came.
The *mabo* went into Amiiru Gundaka's hut.

215   He stole the two belts
He stuck them in his pocket.
He left to find Silâmaka.
He followed the road alone, with his little lute, and soon he
    arrived as though begging before Silâmaka Ardo Macina.
He greeted Silâmaka and he greeted Silâmaka.

220   "Dikko, did you have a good night? Dikko, did you have a
    good night? The night was propitious for you! You are like
    a fine winter season without growls or claps of thunder; you
    are like a harvest without chaff or nettles. You will come
    down
"Where there is no softness;
"Where it is otherwise
"You are not to be found.
"You have no bad luck, no unfortunate days, no ill-omened
    times.

225   "Fortunate Lord of Macina!
"I call down peace on you.
"I am only a messenger; I did not come on my own account."
Silâmaka said to him, "Heh!
"Man, did you come to lie?"

230   He said, "By God! I did not lie! If I lied, cut my throat,
"Silâmaka."
He said, "Be careful. If you lied, I will cut your throat."
"By God," he said, "If I lied, cut my throat." So spoke the *mabo*.
He said, "I hear this past month that you have only been kil-
    ling *mabos*.

235   "Don't you care for killing free men?"
He answered, "What! Come on!
"Who would kill you?
"You aren't worth the effort. Would one kill a dog?"
He came up to Silâmaka, bowed to him.

240   Silâmaka bent his legs
And sat down on his cloth.
The *mabo* said, "Well, I was sent."
Silâmaka asked, "Who sent you?
"Shouldn't I rather believe that you and Hambodedio agreed
    that you would come here to mock me?"

245   He said, "Bandado Abdoulaye sent me,
"Hambodedio's wife."
Silâmaka said, "What did she say to you?"
"She told me to tell you that her neck hurts,
"That she drinks no milk,

250 "That her hair is falling out,
 "That she has no butter.
 "She will not take the butter from another man's cows; she will
     not take the milk of another man's cows.
 "The cows you took
 "Do not belong to her husband, they belong to her.
255 "Her father and mother brought them behind her; she brought
     them here.
 "And so these days she is ready to die!
 "She does not want Hambodedio's butter!
 "She does not want Hambodedio's milk!
 "Those are her cows you stole.
260 "She said, 'Can't you find someone other than me to rob?'"
 Silâmaka laughed.
 For sure, then, the cows would return to their pen. Of course!
 There are things one cannot resist!
 He said, "Hey, little dog!
265 "You're still lying. You have no proof."
 And he heaped abuse on the *mabo*.
 He said, "By God's will! Praise be to God! If you don't stop
     your lies, I'll kill you on the spot."
 The *mabo* answered, "Bandado Abdoulaye told me to show you
     proof.
 "If it's a lie you may kill me."
270 He put his hand in his pocket,
 He pulled out the two belts—
 They were of silver.
 Silâmaka had known them well, once upon a time
 When the world was sweet to him.
275 He said, "Bandado said that if you didn't know them, you
     should kill me, but if you knew them you would know the
     cows are hers."
 As soon as he showed them to Silâmaka, Silâmaka smiled.
 He said, "You know that when you go back Hambodedio will
     certainly kill you.
 "Here you are, involved in trickery."
 That is what he said to the *mabo*.
280 He said, "When you go back, tell
 "Bandado Abdoulaye
 "That cattle are not my affair, I don't want any cattle.
 "My cattle
 "Are at my spear point,
285 "Any man I see is mine, him and his cattle.
 "I came to pay my respects to him,
 "But a black does not appreciate respect.
 "I stopped at the gate of his house, Poullôri and I, we wanted to
     tell him that we were entrusting my father to him.

"He is very old.
290   "Nobody knows if he will win or lose.
       "And when I greeted him, the slaves said to me,
       "'Is it peace,
       "'Or is it not peace?'
       "And since I answered, 'Peace,'
295   "And his slaves insulted me, he should at least rebuke them.
       "If he had rebuked them, I would have been satisfied, I would
              have said why I had come.
       "His slaves offended me, and he laughed!
       "He did not abuse them!
       "He did not rebuke them!
300   "That is what angered me.
       "So I will show him
       "That anyone can cause trouble.
       "That is why I have turned back, and why I tell him
       "That anybody who wants can cause trouble.
305   "Evil is hardly as difficult as good.
       "Anyway, as for his cattle, tell him that tomorrow morning,
              whenever he wants, he can come get them.
       "For my part, I will stop this fighting.
       "If he comes,
       "I will give him
310   "The means.
       "The cattle—
       "There are seven hundred cows—
       "I gave them to Poullôri Benana.
       "He took them on,
315   "To the Tree of the Captives.
       "Poullôri went on with them, he went ahead.
       "Poullôri is far away.
       "But Poullôri is mean, you know, and he doesn't think.
       "If I don't go,
320   "The cattle won't return.
       "He will think that I was killed.
       "So let come to me,
       "Hambodedio in person.
       "Tell him that his cattle are over there, further on. I will give
              him a letter and he can go get his cattle. I didn't want cattle!
325   "I just came to make arrangements with him for my father, who
              is old."
       The *mabo* went back to tell this to Hambodedio.
       Hambodedio didn't know that the cattle were coming back
              because his wife's belts were gone!
       He told the *mabo* he was a trickster, he said to him: "You're
              lying! You want me to go out there and be killed! All you
              do is plot!

"I know your trickery very well!"
330 The next morning at dawn,
Amiiru Gundaka went riding off with a hundred horsemen,
The *mabo* was the leader.
As he was leading them, the *mabo* said, "Come on!
"We'll have no trouble with Silâmaka."
335 Soon they came to the place where Silâmaka was.
Amiiru Gundaka stopped.
He said, "Come, let's go."
He stopped and waited until the *mabo* had reached
Silâmaka Ardo Macina. Silâmaka stood up; he wore only his
cloth
340 And his pants,
He had no spear
Or staff.
He said, "You are permitted! Approach!"
He said, "I have called you.
345 "I am not a traitor.
"I will not betray your trust."
Amiiru Gundaka came near, they vied in greetings. When the
greetings were at last ended,
Silâmaka said, "I don't need cows, but your slaves offended me,
and you didn't answer them—because a slave is dear to
you!
"You should have rebuked them a bit,
350 "Even if it annoyed you.
"If you had rebuked them, I would have calmed down.
"This is why I showed my anger. But I don't need your cows
any more, I have no claim to your cows.
"I don't even want your cows.
"But Poullôri is further on there, with the cattle.
355 "I'll send one of my boys on,
"He will go ahead and tell him that we have come to terms.
"If he is informed, he will bring back the cows.
"If you went yourself, or one of your men, things would not
work out.
"He who knows nothing is aggressive!
360 "So let me give you a spear, let me give you a messenger;
"You will go find Poullôri—
"He is my captive—
"You will tell him that I said to give you your cattle, that I per-
mit it, that he should let you lead them back to their pen.
They are a woman's cattle. I do not want cattle taken from a
woman."
Hambodedio said, "No! Since you know, by God! that we
agree, and since you are frank with me, I am content. A
slave is merely a rope's end.

181

365   "Show him the rope, and that's enough for him!
        "You are the one that we fear."
        He said, "What, Poullôri?"
        Silâmaka said, "Take my offer." Hambodedio said, "No!"
        He said, "Silâmaka, since you have agreed,
370   "The one over there doesn't concern us.
        "Isn't Poullôri a slave? A slave means nothing to us."
        He said, "All right. I warned you, but have it your way.
        "Since you set no store by my warnings and call him a rope's
            end,
        "Take my spear and go your way."
375   Here is the drumbeat of Silâmaka Ardo Macina and Poullôri
            Ardo Macina!
        For the day they defeated Amiiru Gundaka and his men!
        These are the vultures devouring the bodies!
        It is that morning . . . Tinguidji plays that tune today!
        Silâmaka had told Poullôri,
380   "The day you see Hambodedio's men,
        "You will know that I have died.
        "They cannot pass unless they kill me. No horseman will come
            to you.
        "The day you see them, you will know that I am dead."
        Poullôri had a spear named "Gaping Wound."
385   Silâmaka had a spear named "Evil Doer."
        One had a horse named Golden Scarab.
        The other had a horse named Lethal Hoof.
        Hambodedio continued, walked, walked, walked.
        Poullôri, standing in the middle
390   Of the enclosure,
        He looked behind him, his head turned; he was named Poul-
            lôri, he was the slave who would die being no man's thing!
        A pile of blue *bougues* for him alone!
        His head bows beneath the weight of *bougue* cloth!
        Shelter of unshattering steel!
        Gorbal!
395   Ali Mansore! Most cunning of the cunning!
        Premier piper!
        God tears
        And he sews it up behind him.
        Poullôri makes dry,
400   God makes wet!
        He said, "Generosity and fighting can do without thought and
            advice.
        "To action! To deeds!"
        When Poullôri saw Amiiru Gundaka and his men come up,
        Coming to get the cattle,
405   With that spear held high,

He said, "God is great! A slave acts as a slave!
"Whatever a slave does will have no end.
"Silâmaka must have been killed, since they brandish his
    spear.
"No doubt they come to show me they have killed Silâmaka."
410   He opened the cattle pen.
He paid no more attention to the cattle.
He charged straight at the men of Gundaka and at Hambo-
    dedio.
Hambodedio
Brandished
415   Silâmaka's spear.
He said, "Listen! We did not kill him! It is he who sends us!
    Silâmaka sends us!"
The men who were coming—
The men of Gundaka—
Called out, "We don't come to fight!
420   "We don't come to fight!
"We have reached an agreement! We have made peace!"
Poullôri wasn't listening.
He was charging.
He was coming straight at them!
425   He reached them, he attacked them furiously!
Poullôri never dismounted.
He thrusts his spear and withdraws it.
Driving them like a herd,
He runs them on.
430   When they reached Silâmaka,
Of the two hundred horsemen,
Poullôri has vanquished a hundred and fifty, he has beaten
    them down.
Silâmaka cannot see them.
The fifty others manage to reach Silâmaka,
435   They stop exhausted.
Hambodedio's horse is running away, the rein is slack,
He doesn't check it.
Each man, reaching Silâmaka, leaps from his horse, falls to the
    ground,
Lets the horse run on, for the horses are runaways!
440   They drop!
Come what may!
Poullôri comes up, he reins in his horse suddenly before Silâ-
    maka.
He says, "Silâmaka, shame on you!
"This lie is your making! You said that if I saw people coming
    to me, you would be dead!
445   "You are not dead!

"You are alive, but now you will live a life of shame.
"You knew that if I saw your killer, he wouldn't have—this you
    knew—the time to tell me why he came."
Silâmaka answered, "By God! I warned them!"
Hambodedio said, "By God! You did! Everything happened as
    you said!"
450   Then he sent his men to get the cattle, to return them to Gun-
    daka.
That time, they understood at last.
That is how Silâmaka and Poullôri dealt with Hambodedio.
That is what I know. This is the end of their story.

17. The Epic of Samba Gueladio Diegui
Narrated by Pahel Mamadou Baila

English translation by Amadou Ly and Stephen Belcher from unpub. work of Amadou Ly. French translation by Amadou Ly, L'épopée de Samba Gué-ladiégui (Paris: Editions Nouvelles du Sud, I.F.A.N./U.N.E.S.C.O., 1991).

THE STORY OF SAMBA GUELADIO BELONGS TO THE FUTA TOORO, the Ful-fulde-speaking area on the middle reaches of the Senegal River. Various dates have been proposed for the confrontation of Samba Gueladio and the uncle who usurped his place on the throne, and the most likely historical identification appears to be with a Samba Galadiegui who appears in French commercial records of the early eighteenth century. Some time later in the 1790s, an Islamic government, the Almamate, was established in the Futa Tooro. Samba's story is considered historical by some scholars, but we should note that it contains the classic pattern of the dragon slayer which goes back to Perseus and before, and that the same story is widely told of Hambodedio, a hero of Macina in Mali. Clearly, legend has gone to work on the historical material.

Samba Gueladio may have a claim to be the earliest recorded West African epic; in 1856, Commandant Anne Raffenel provided a lengthy prose version of the story, which has had a remarkable literary life. It is only relatively recently that Senegalese scholars have begun to record their oral traditions, and the following excerpts are taken from one of several recent versions.

[Pahel Mamadou Baila begins with the early ancestry of Samba, and the origin of the Deniyanke dynasty in the Futa Tooro. A noble named Tenguella asked the Malian emperor Sunjata for gifts and was given Sunjata's pregnant wife. She became the mother of Koli, known as Koli Tenguella, who led a migration from Mali into the Futa Tooro. Then he tells how Gueladiegui, father of Samba, was without children. His slave, Doungourou, performed a divination and identified the sort of woman his master should marry. But the child would be born after Gueladiegui's death. Gueladiegui assigned to Sewi Malal, his griot, the task of finding the woman, and eventually he did: Coumba Diorngal, a hunchback. She became pregnant and Gueladiegui died. His brother, Konko Boubou Moussa, succeeded him. He ordered that any of his brother's wives who was pregnant should be put to death, to avoid giving birth to a future king. Sewi Malal, the griot, tricked him by bloodying a cloth so that he thought Coumba Diorngal was menstruating. Coumba Diorngal gave birth, and Konko Boubou Moussa's daughter Rella (aged seven) discovered this.]

> The baby whined; at the cry,
> Rella came and leaned over them.
> She said, "What! But you,
> "You said no woman in this house was pregnant.
515   "But my aunt Coumba was certainly pregnant,

185

"And now she has given birth to a boy-child!
"I shall go and tell my father."
The *gawlo*[1] said to her,
"Well, go and tell your father!
520   "I know I am only a *gawlo*—
"You see, here is my instrument.
"But if you tell your father, and he kills this child, he will have
    killed your brother!
"As for me, I will go to the court of some other king and pay
    suit to some other noble who will grant me gifts.
"But if this child—your brother—grows up,
525   "And if one day he becomes king, then you can profit together
    from his success.
"And if he becomes rich, then you can enjoy the wealth to-
    gether,
"And if he becomes famous, he will owe his fame to you."
Rella said, "Yes, but I have a small condition,
"That you should give me your word"—
530   We in the East say *laayidu*,[2]
It is something extremely important for us,
Giving your word—
"Give me your word that you promise me that if he grows up
    he shall have no other first wife than me,
"And that even though I am several years older than him,
535   "It is I he will make his first wife.
"I shall be his *diewo*."[3]
"Bah!" said Coumba Diorngal, "that isn't so hard.
"God willing, we swear by God, we swear this to you—
"If he grows up he shall have no other first wife than you!"
540   Then Rella said,
"Leave it in my hands,
"I will take care of it."
She went back to her father.
She said, "Father, you know, that man Sewi really has no idea
    what a pregnant woman is!
545   "As it happens, my aunt Coumba Diorngal was pregnant!
"But she had a girl!"
Konko Boubou Moussa said, "What did you just tell me?" And
    she said, "She had a girl."
He said, "Well! Go tear off a piece of cloth,
"And tie it to the baby
550   "In the name of your brother Samba Konko.
"Tell him he has found his future wife,
"That they are sort of engaged."
Rella tore off a piece of cloth,

---

1. Bard. 2. To swear. 3. Senior wife.

	And she tied it to the child's wrist.
555	A week went by.
	Konko Boubou Moussa kills ten times ten of all sorts of animals for Samba's naming ceremony.
	But instead of Samba, he called him Fatimata Gueladiegui,
	Since Rella had told him he was a girl.
	That is why he named him Fatimata Gueladiegui.
560	Gueladiegui had never had a child,
	And since this was the first born to him, they called the child Fatimata.
	They dressed him in *belefete*,[4]
	They pierced his ears and put gold in them,
	They put bracelets on his wrist.
565	After that, Rella would carry him on her back all day long.
	When she had carried him all day, until the evening, she would bring him home to sleep,
	Until the time he learned to walk and could accompany Rella.
	Then they dressed him in *biftoje*[5] such as Rella wore.
	They used to go have their hair plaited at a woman blacksmith's house;
570	She was named Thiedel the blacksmith.
	She was their hairdresser.
	When they came, Rella had planned things out.
	She would lie down first and have her hair plaited.
	After her, Samba would lie down in his turn.
575	While he was lying there, she would arrange the folds of his *biftoje*.
	When the job was done, they left and went off.
	But Samba had no idea
	Why he was wearing bracelets, or why his ears were pierced. He thought it was simply an old Denianke custom.
	So things went until he reached his seventh year.
580	One day they went off to have their hair done at the blacksmith's.
	"Well," said the attendants on Samba son of Konko, "your betrothed is having her hair done at the blacksmith's house; let's go there for a chat."
	And the others agreed, "Let's go!"
	When they got there, they found that Rella had finished having her hair done and that Samba, in fact, was lying there.
	They said, "We've come to talk with our fiancée."
585	Our fiancée? But since Rella was a young girl,
	Samba thought that perhaps they were talking of Rella.
	In old times, young warriors carried bows and arrows,

---

4. A short skirt. 5. A fancier skirt.

And it happened that Samba Konko had his bow and arrows
    with him.
A cat chased a mouse.
590   He drew the bow and struck the cat with an arrow, *fatt!*
The cat fell.
Meantime, the mouse had climbed up on a beam,
And from where Samba was lying having his hair plaited, the
    mouse was just overhead.
He said, "My brother, lend me your bow and arrows."
595   When Samba Konko hit the cat,
He said, "Enemy of the heir of Konko Boubou Moussa!"
He meant, 'Enemy to me, heir of Konko Boubou Moussa.'
He had extolled himself, he had praised himself.
Samba borrowed the bow and arrows from Samba Konko.
600   The mouse was right above his belly.
He hit it with an arrow and it fell on him.
He said, "Me too, enemy of the heir of Gueladiegui!"
They said, "What? You're saying that, but you're a girl!"
"It's a girl!" "It's a girl!" The questions filled his ears.
605   He rose and stood.
He said, "Who said I was a girl?"
He took his *biftoje* and broke the belt. He took his gift from God
    and showed it to Samba Konko.
He said, "Who told you I was a girl?"
The other said, "My father told me you were a girl."
610   He said, "Your father lied!
"I am no girl!
"Ah! That is why he gave me all this[6] and named me Fatimata
    Gueladiegui!
"Well! I strip off the braids that were made,
"And I will do my own hair.
615   "Yesterday I was named Fatimata Gueladiegui,
"Today I name myself Samba Gueladiegui,
"Samba Konko Boubou Moussa,
"Samba Gueladiegui Konko Boubou Moussa
"Samba Wouri Tjilmang Gadiaga,
620   "Samba Coumba Diorngal Ali Hamadi Bedinki."
He also named himself "Samba-among-the-bandits, Samba
    Lion's-tooth."
The hero is my Samba. The toads may croak as loud as they
    wish, they will not stop the elephant going down to the
    pond.

[He goes angrily to his mother and she explains that he was disguised
as a girl to save his life. He says that henceforth there will be no doubt

---

6. His ornaments.

about his manhood. Konko Boubou Moussa learns of the revelation and sends people to see; Samba shoots the first man to look into the compound. Sewi the *gawlo* calms him down. Konko Boubou Moussa then plans how to kill Samba, and it is decided that there shall be an accident at the circumcision ceremony. Sewi the *gawlo* forestalls this plot by having a smith perform the circumcision at Samba's house. Samba goes into retreat with the other boys. At the end of the retreat, in a mock attack, Samba kills Hamadi Konko, a son of Konko Boubou Moussa. Despite this tendency to violence, Samba is a good boy; he brings food to an old woman, and she warns him that Konko Boubou Moussa is preparing a magic dish; whoever eats the marrow bone in it will succeed him as king. The next day, at the meal, Samba seizes the bone and eats it. On the following day, Konko Boubou Moussa divides his wealth. Rella tells Samba that her father is doing this, and he asks for his share.]

        Konko asked him, "Where were you?"
        He said, "I was sleeping."
        Konko said, "Well then, I give you sleep."
        He came back, told his mother, and his mother began to weep.
1045   He spoke to Doungourou, and Doungourou began to weep.
        He said, "Why are you weeping? My father has granted me sleep?
        "Well, if you are given something you become its master!
        "So tonight no one will sleep.
        "Let us go into the bush."
1050   They went into the bush and cut *kelli sticks*.
        After eight-thirty, whenever he found anyone in bed,
        He stripped off the bedclothes to bare his head,
        And putting his back into it, whacked him with the sticks.
        Doungourou and he did this throughout the town,
1055   And complaints rose up all around the town.
        People got up and came outside.
        They asked, "What? What does this mean?" and he answered them, "My father gave me sleep,
        "So I am master of sleep.
        "No one will sleep unless I allow it."
1060   His father called him and asked, "Why are you doing this?"

[Konko Boubou Moussa takes back sleep and offers Samba all things of beauty; Samba immediately takes one of his wives, and Konko takes this gift back. He gives Samba handfuls of gunpowder and bullets, saying that is how his father became king. Samba says that he will regret this gift. He marries Rella, and then he leaves. He has with him his horse, Oumou Latouma, his mother, Doungourou, and Sewi. He asks Sewi who furnished the magical protection to his father, and Sewi tells him it was a jinn. Samba goes to the jinn, and obtains magical

protections from him, as well as a rifle named Boussi Larway, which never misses. He then kills the jinn, to prevent him giving such protection to anyone else. They then leave town.]

1325   They traveled all day, they traveled until evening time.
       A storm threatened.
       It was a bit before dusk; they slipped under a tree of the sort
           named *tialli*.
       This is when he gets the *Lagya*, his tune.
       Some, who do not know, call it *Lagya*,
1330   But *Lagya* isn't a name.
       When they had slipped under the tree—and at that time, they
           played the *Ana* for them—
       The *gawlo* women sang the song *Ana*, which is also called the
           Alamari!
       The *Alamari* was the tune for the Denianke.
       Those are the tunes that were played or sung for them.
1335   So when they had slipped under the tree,
       A green woodpecker—it's a bird with a long beak—
       Yes, the Wolof call it *toxxo*, and we Poular call it *lori*—
       This bird was at the top of the tree calling out the *Lagya*.
       "I made my nest in the *dieri*,[7] and I was rousted out.
1340   "I made my nest in the *waalo*,[8] and I was rousted out.
       "This time when I make my nest, I shall not be displaced."
       He also sang, "*Diala Waali Ndende,*
       "*Diala Waali Ndende,*
       "Between the Poure waters and the Manimani waters!
1345   "*Diala Waali!*
       "He who dares not cause trouble will not rule."
       The bird said that and played the tune.
       Samba had his staff, he was beating out the time on the tree.
       Sewi had fallen asleep.
1350   His mother had fallen asleep,
       And Sewi's mother had fallen asleep.
       He called out, "Father Sewi! Father Sewi!" His father Sewi
           answered, "Yes?" and he said, "Quick, wake up!"
       Sewi got up.
       Samba said, "Listen carefully to this."
1355   Sewi said, "I've listened carefully."
       He said, "Have you heard what is happening?"
       Sewi said, "I have heard."
       He asked, "Can you play that on your lute?"
       "Well," said Sewi, "I shall see, my Samba."
1360   Sewi stretched his strings and tuned them to the words of the
           bird

---

7. Rarely flooded land. 8. Floodplain.

Until he was able to play the tune.
Then Samba said, "Do you know it?" "I know it," he said.
"You can play it?" "Yes, I can play it."
Samba asked, "You know it?" He said, "I know it."
1365   Samba said, "Every task must have its wage.
"I offer the bird up to you."
Sewi said, "Now? In this night, my Samba?"
He said, "I'll bring it right down."
He touched his brow and said, "Enemy of the heir of Gueladie-
    gui!"
1370   He fired a shot!
And the *lori* fell to earth.
Samba said, "Collect the blood and moisten the strings with it."
Sewi collected the blood and moistened the strings.
Samba said, "Well, I have just offered a sacrifice in your honor."

[He then says that he will return and kill Konko Boubou Moussa that
night. Sewi expresses some doubts. Konko Boubou Moussa is listening
to his *gawlo* name the great heroes; the *gawlo* does not name Samba, and
so Konko Boubou Moussa sings Samba's praises. He does so just as
Samba is creeping up on him, and so Samba refrains from killing him:
one may not kill someone who sings one's praises. He returns to Sewi.
They continue on their way. Samba leaves a half-*muid* [a measure] of
gold with the ruler of Tiyabu to take care of the two mothers, his own
and Sewi's, and continues with his retainers. In a clearing, he and Sewi
exchange wishes, and Samba then engages in a horse race with a Moor,
for which the stakes are the loser's life. The Moor loses. The Moor's
father acknowledges that his son was arrogant and hotheaded, and
gives Samba his daughter as wife; Samba eventually becomes restless,
mutilates his pregnant wife, burns her father's village, and goes on his
way. He comes to the land of El Bil Djikri and he and his retainers put
up with an old woman, Mint Hobere.]

She brought them water; the water was twelve months old.
It stank.
Samba leaned over the water to drink; the stench filled his nos-
    trils and he threw the gourd away.
He said, "We asked you to bring water, and you have brought
    us piss!"
1705   She said, "Alas, my son.
"You are doing me wrong!
"If we weren't just about to come on the time—
"Tomorrow we must give the king's daughter to the Crocodile.
"He will eat her and give us water—
1710   "You would have done me a great wrong!"
He said, "How is that?"

She said, "A crocodile lives there in our river; unless we adorn
   a princess every twelve months, and give her to him as
   food—

"And that is how we get our water; everyone takes enough for
   twelve months—

"Otherwise, we have no water, Samba."

1715   He said, "And this river right here?"
       She said, "One cannot touch it!"
       He said, "Doungourou, lead Oumou Latoma.
       "Father Sewi, wait for us."
       They put a halter on Oumou Latoma.

1720   They walked to the river.
       When they came to the river—
       Oumou Latoma couldn't drink unless her hocks were entirely
          in the water, and her belly touched the water.
       Only then would she drink; otherwise, she would refuse to
          drink.
       Doungourou led her into the water as far as she was accustomed
          to go—

1725   For we all have our habits,
       And her habits had to be satisfied before she would drink.
       She began to drink, *farak!* as horses do,
       And already the *Caamaaba*⁹ came out of the depths of the river,
       And the whole river went up in flames.

1730   The *Caamaaba* came toward them.
       Samba was behind the mare, Oumou Latoma.
       Doungourou held her by the bridle.
       Doungourou didn't blink.
       Samba didn't blink.

1735   Oumou Latoma didn't blink.
       When the *Caamaaba* was some five to ten meters from him,
       Samba pulled out Boussi Larway.
       He touched the middle of his forehead.
       He said, "Enemy of the heir of Galadiegui!"

1740   He shot at the *Caamaaba*.
       The bullet found that the *Caambaaba* wasn't fully protected.
       The *Caamaaba* dove, but without its soul.
       Already, Doungourou had closed his fist—
       We say *womre*,

1745   The Whites say "fist"—
       He struck the *Caamaaba* on the head,
       And his hand went through to the water and withdrew.
       He said, "My Samba, if I had known that you didn't even want
          me to kill it,
       "When you told me to come, I wouldn't have come,

---

9. Here, a crocodile.

1750 "For you should have left this to me.
"I am the *Diagaraf*,
"I am he who gets angry and reigns,
"I am he who gets angry and establishes reigns,
"I am he who gets angry and dethrones.
1755 "I do not butcher,
"Or trap,
"Or hunt lizards.
"I am *Doumbooy Daali*, Hunts-no-lizards."
In Macina, they are called *maram marooji*.
1760 In the East, the lizard is called *maram mara*.
We in the Futa call it *gunndo*.
He said, "I do not butcher, or trap, or hunt lizards.
"I am the one who has noble parents—
"Meaning that noble parents give birth
1765 "And noble women carry children on their back,
"But these are gift giving nobles; these are the women who
    carry me on their back and with whom I spend my child-
    hood."
He really praised himself fully, did Doungourou, as he struck
    the head of the *Caamaaba* with his fist.
They drew the *Caamaaba* up on the bank,
And Samba cut off fifty centimeters of his tail.
1770 He took off one of his shoes
And left it near the beast.
They went back to the house.
Oumou Latoma had been watered and groomed.
They filled the old woman's calabash up to the rim with fresh
    water,
1775 And they brought it back to the Moorish woman. . . .
The next morning, at dawn,
The daughter of El Bil Djikri,
Named Soueina,
Soueina was adorned
1780 And covered with gold.
"Your sister died in such and such a year, without fear;
"Another sister died, in such and such a year, without fear,
"We were given our water.
"Your other sister died here. . . . All told, seven princesses.
1785 "And you, today.
"And if you show no fear, we shall have water.
"But if you run away,
"The town will die of thirst!"
They sang her praises, and she sang her own praises as well.
1790 She said, "When I get there today,
"I shall give myself first to him,
"And you shall know me for a king's daughter,

193

"For the daughter of a hero,
"As a descendant of Someone, son of Someone, son of Someone,
     going back to the Arabs."
1795   They came and were twenty meters from the river.
They saw, floating on the surface, the Crocodile.
"Ha!" they said, "Today,
"Today, he is impatient.
"Today, if you show no fear,
1800   "The people will have water early!
"In the past people had to wade into the water to their waist,
"Only then would he appear. But today he is already out!"
The young girl Souëina was so brave
That she leaped from her horse
1805   And walked to the Crocodile.
She came to him, climbed over him, and began to trample him.
Her clothes were stained with blood.
She came back and said, "That one is dead!"
Then all sorts of people like us sat up:
1810   "It was me, Someone son of Somebody!
"I came last night with the thought that a young Moorish
     woman like you
"Should not die in this way in front of everybody.
"I am the one who fought with him in the night,
"And I inflicted insults worse than death upon him,
1815   "So that you wouldn't die."
And everyone boasted about themselves.

[They inspect the carcass and notice the missing piece of tail and the shoe. Mint Hobere suggests the hero might be her lodger; when they try to wake Samba in Moorish fashion, however, by pinching him, the attendants are killed. Finally he rises and is identified as the slayer of the Crocodile. Samba asks El Bil Djikri for an army with which to regain his kingdom. El Bil Djikry imposes some other tasks first. Samba breaks a wild horse that no one could tame and is lost for a time in the bush. The Moors enslave Doungourou and Sewi while Samba is gone. When Samba and the horse emerge, the Moors quickly buy the silence of Samba's retainers. He then battles various Moorish groups and finally encounters a great hero named Baayo, who has famous herds of cattle. At first Samba only takes a fraction of the herds, but El Bil Djikry complains, and so Samba returns and kills Baayo. El Bil Djikry fulfills his promise and gives Samba an army: enough horsemen so that the procession, passing over three large logs, cuts through them. On the way back Samba and Sewi encounter their mothers, who have been evicted by the ruler of Tiyabu and are living in poverty in the bush.]

2250   Then Sewi sang, "Has-no-herdsman,
"Sire Gansiri Sawalamou Ndioubou Diom Koli Tenguella!

"Those who saw Samba leave in the morning will see him re-
turn
"Samba did not leave in vain, Samba has not labored for
nothing, Samba!
"The hero, the son of Gueladiegui!
2255 "Samba!
"Samba was best at the court of the Wali Counda, Samba was
the best at the court of El Bil Djikry!
"Samba goes with purebloods, and so does Oumou Latoma!
"So come out in the morning, admire the departure of Samba
Galadiegui, Samba who must be greeted as an equal!"
"My God!" said Tourou Tokossel, "Is it possible?
2260 "Oh, welcome! Beloved voice!"
Sewi's mother called out, "Coumba Diorngal?"
Coumba answered, "Yes?" She asked, "Did you hear Sewi's
voice?" She said, "Which Sewi?" She said, "Sewi my son!"
Coumba said, "What are you saying?" She said, "That voice I
heard,
"That voice—I bore it.
2265 "That voice is the voice of my Sewi!"
"Bah!" said Coumba Diorngal. "Let's try to sleep, all right?
"Do you imagine the Tounka would have treated us so badly,
"If he hadn't learned of Samba's death?
"Sleep!"
2270 The next morning,
Sewi said again, "Has-no-herdsman! Come out and admire the
departure of Samba Galadiegui-Konko Boubou Moussa!
"Let all who thought that Samba was dead learn that he is
alive!"
"Ah!" said Coumba Diorngal, "You were right!
"That is the voice of Sewi,
2275 "And Sewi sings for no one but Samba Galadiegui!"
After eight days, the vanguard of the purebloods
Broke into the clearing which they had come through.
Sewi had forgotten it!
But Samba was a prince
2280 And a hero: he forgot nothing.
He said, "Father Sewi?
"Do you remember this clearing?"
"Ah," said Sewi, "I have forgotten, my Samba."
He said, "When we were coming here, me alone with you and
Doungourou and our three horses,
2285 "And today we lead five thousand purebloods—
"Not counting the goats, the sheep, and the cattle,
"When we came through here, what did you tell me about this
clearing?"

195

Sewi said, "I said, about this clearing, that I would be happy if
    it were full of cattle, of goats, and of sheep that someone
    was giving me."
Of each sort, Samba selected some:
2290   A flock of goats,
A flock of sheep,
A herd of cattle,
And even a herd of horses.
He said, "This, Sewi, is a gift to you.
2295   "But what I wished for,
"God has not granted me here.
"I wished for someone to try to compete with me!
"What you asked for, God has granted you. But what I wanted
    God has not granted."
The next morning they went on
2300   Until they found Tourou standing in the middle of the road.
She said, "You have no reason to sing your praises,
"You have no cause for pride!
"It is now two years, two months, and ten days
"That we have been living next to an anthill."
2305   Samba, on Oumou Latoma, faltered and fell to the earth.
Pieces and pieces of cloth—
They took a hundred to make tents.
We call them *gidwar*, some say "tent."
They were comforted warmly; Samba asked his mother's for-
    giveness,
2310   And he asked forgiveness from the mother of Sewi,
Saying, "Mother, I am the cause of this,
"Please accept my apologies and forgive me."
They stayed there for eight days.
Meat was cooked for them, and they ate it.
2315   They were washed, with good water.
They were given milk to drink.
They were rubbed and consoled for all the troubles they had
    suffered, which were completely erased.
They put soft pillows on camels for them.

[They come to Tiyabu and are told by the townspeople that their mothers have died. Samba punishes the town by demanding, as tribute, a
pile of cloth as tall as he can reach while standing on Oumou Latoma's
back. The *Tounka* of Tiyabu dies of his punishment. While his army is
crossing the river, Samba shoots a hero, Boisigui. On the other side, he
gathers allies for the battle with Konko Boubou Moussa. The night before the battle, Samba rides into the enemy camp to sleep with Rella,
his wife. His presence is discovered, but Konko Boubou forbids any
action against him. The next day comes the battle.]

In Poular, a proverb says that if your father cleared an acre, you
    should clear a furlong more.
That is true.
Do you know there are three sorts of sons?
"You aren't worth your father,"
2535   "You're as good as your father,"
And "You are worth more than your father."
"You're worth more than your father,"
That's a good state to be in, but it's not nice to hear "You are
    worth more than your father."
"You're as good as your father," that is a good state,
2540   And it's nice to hear it said:
"You're as good as your father."
"You aren't worth your father"—
That's not a good state, and it's not nice to hear.
So Samba had three forms of protection:
2545   The protections of his father,
The ones he had gotten himself,
And those he had snatched from the hands of the heroes killed
    by him, Samba Gueladio, Samba Konko Boubou Moussa,
    Samba Coumba Diorngal Ali Hamadi Bedinki,
Samba-among-the-bandits, Samba Lion's-tooth, Samba the hero,
    my hero,
Grandson of Birama Ali and Dianga Ali and Bira Mbaba
    Ndiouga Dianga Youman Bele. . . .

[They come to fight on the field of Bilbassi. Over several days there is a
series of single combats].

Sewi called: "Has-no-herdsman! Courage! Courage!"
2650   He said, "Cheer him! Cheer him!"
He said, "The master of the town has met his equal.
"You can tell! Samba has met Mawndo Gali Coumba Kagnina!"
Samba slew Fouybotako Ali Maham Daouda Mbarya Sokoum
    Ya Allah
At Bilbassi.
2655   As he advanced on Fouybotako,
Samba said, "Ford the pond at Gawdoule!"
Fouybotako said, "I will not ford the pond at Gawdoule!
"My clothes are white,
"My rifle stock is of white *dabadji* wood,
2660   "My thoroughbred has a white coat.
"If I dipped into the pond at Gawdoule,
"You might wash them, but they would not be clean.
"You might perfume them, but they would stink.

197

"People would ask me, 'What happened to you?' and I would
answer, 'I was running away from Little-Samba-won't-
rule.'"

2665 He tied his pants legs together.
Samba fired a shot at him—*karaw*!
And said, "I've killed a Mbegnoughanna!"
That was Fouybotako Ali Maham Daouda Mbarya Sokoum Ya
Allah.
Samba killed him at Bilbassi.

2670 He gave no work to the washers,
He did not wear out the mourners;
The fish carried him off.
Samba fought with Sam Maïram Molo Baroga, who might have
trouble with the beauties but always makes a day of deeds.
They met in a deadly duel.

2675 Samba killed him.
He fell at Bilbassi.
He didn't tire out the mourners or the washers; the fish carried
him away.
Samba did the same with Biram Gaal Segara Ali Mousse.
He was so tough that when he went into battle he would only
take a single bullet.

2680 He would say, "When I've killed someone, I'll take his bullets
and powder."
That's the sort of man Biram Gaal was.
Samba met him in deadly duel, and fired a shot at him—*tall!*
Biram fell, without his soul.
Samba slew him at Bilbassi.

2685 He didn't tire out the mourners or the washers, the fish carried
him away. . . .

[Samba continues his deeds. The battle ends on the seventh day.]

Samba advanced on his father,
2760 Konko Boubou Moussa.
He chased him into a pumpkin field.
He shot at a pumpkin.
The pumpkin flew into the air and landed on the father's head.
Samba said, "I shall not kill you, but with that squash.
2765 "I've given you a green pumpkin hat."

[Samba becomes king and kills Konko Boubou Moussa's children—except for his own wife, Rella—and grandchildren to establish his own
position. Samba rules for ten years, plundering his neighbours; Konko
Boubou Moussa lives on by begging. Samba moves into the Fulbe
kingdom of Bondou and lives there for a time; Sewi and Rella, traveling, are captured by Moors from the northeast. Samba eventually res-

cues them. There are other minor adventures. Finally, Samba dies as the jinn had foretold, from eating a forbidden food. And there is a story that a man who threw a stone onto his tomb later died. Even in death, Samba is terrible.]

Wolof Epics

THE WOLOF CONSTITUTE THE LARGEST ETHNIC GROUP IN SENEGAL, with nearly forty percent of the population. Their history is rooted in the Jolof empire, which flourished from approximately the twelfth century to the sixteenth century and covered much of what is known as modern Senegal on the western coast of West Africa. Jolof was heavily involved in trade beween the Moors of Mauritania to the north and the Mali empire to the south and east. With the arrival of the Portuguese in the mid-fifteenth century, Jolof began to decline, a process that led to the independence of successor states Baol (Bawol), Walo (Waalo), Kayor (Kajoor, Cayor), Sine (Siin), Ñaani, and Wuli (Woulli) in the sixteenth and seventeenth centuries. Kayor became the strongest of these new states, dominating a coastal strip of land from the Senegal River in the north to Rufisque in the south. These states experienced internal conflicts, wars between each other as well as against other states farther east, and resistance against the French, who conquered the region in the latter half of the nineteenth century.

The oral memory of that tumultuous past remains quite vivid today, especially the events of the nineteenth century. Jacques François Roger's *Fables sénégalaises recuéillies de l'ouolof* (Paris: 1828), Jean Baptiste Bérenger-Féraud's *Recuéil de contes populaires de la Sénégambie* (Paris: Leroux, 1885), and Victor-François Equilbecq's *Contes populaires d'Afrique occidentale* (Paris: Maisonneuve et Larose, 1913) are among the early collections by Europeans. By the twentieth century, the Senegalese were beginning to record their own oral tradition, especially the veterinarian Birago Diop (published as *Les Contes d'Amadou Koumba* [Paris: Présence Africaine, 1961], in English as *The Tales of Amadou Koumba*, trans. Dorothy Blair [London: Oxford, 1966]). But it is not until relatively recently that scholars have managed to record, transcribe, translate, and publish major examples of the Wolof epic tradition.

The two texts that follow convey interpretations of the founding of the Walo kingdom and the last days of resistance of the Kayor state at the end of the nineteenth century. The richness of these texts, and in particular the many episodes of Kayor from which *The Epic of Lat Dior* is taken, suggest that we have much more to learn about the Wolof epic from the other states that developed after the fall of Jolof.

18. The Epic of Njaajaan Njaay
Narrated by Sèq Ñan

Recorded in six sessions starting January 12, 1990, in Rosso, Senegal, by Samba Diop. Transcribed and translated into English by Samba Diop. Edited by Samba Diop and published in The Oral History and Literature of the Wolof People of Waalo, Northern Senegal: The Master of the Word (Griot) in the Wolof Tradition *by Mellen Press, Lewiston, 1995. This excerpt edited by Thomas A. Hale.*

THE HISTORY OF THE WOLOF PEOPLE of Senegal is marked by the rise and fall of several empires, kingdoms, and states. Waalo, based at the mouth of the Senegal River, developed rapidly in the seventeenth century as the result of the slave trade. Many European countries vied for control of the region, but the French and the British were the principal competitors. By the late eighteenth century, the French had outlasted the English and gained a trade monopoly in the area that served as the foundation for the nineteenth-century colonial conquest of Senegal.

This 975-line epic about the founding of the Waalo empire was recorded in Wolof by the Senegalese scholar Samba Diop from the griot or *guewel* Sèq Ñan during a series of sessions beginning on January 12, 1990. Diop also translated the epic into English. A retired veteran and truck driver of *guewel* origin, Ñan lived in Xuma, a village fifteen kilometers east of the town of Richard-Toll, 150 kilometers upriver from Saint-Louis near the mouth of the river. The recording took place in the home of Mapaté Diop, the father of Samba Diop, in Rosso, Senegal, a town on the left bank of the Senegal River just east of Richard-Toll. The audience was composed of Mr. Diop and his son Samba, two other men, and occasional visitors who dropped in from time to time. According to Samba Diop, Sèq Ñan sometimes stopped the narrative to play the *xalam*, a five-stringed lute, eat meals, drink tea, and pray during recording sessions that lasted from 5 p.m. to midnight on the first day and from 10 a.m. to 5 p.m. the next day (Diop, 33-34).

As with any epic, the genealogy of the hero is particularly important. At the outset the narrator traces Njaajan Njaay's heritage back to a past that has echoes from Islam, Judaism, and Christianity. These excerpts also emphasize the role of the hero in creating both political and family relationships with other peoples in the surrounding region, from the Serer to the Peul. Finally, the *guewel's* narrative refers often to the importance of transmission of knowledge from father to son.

	Tradition says that,
75	One day,
	Noah fell asleep;
	Ham the eldest son was laughing.
	Sham asked him:
	"Why are you laughing?
80	"Are you laughing about our father?"
	Right at that moment,

Noah woke up.
Noah said:
"From today on,
85   "You,
"Ham!
"You will be the precursor of the black race.
"You,
"Sham!
90   "You will beget all white people."
Thus Sham begot two persons called Yajojo and Majojo.
Ham begot a son called Anfésédé.
Anfésédé addressed Ham his father in these terms:
"Noah is my grandfather,
95   "You are my father.
"I am asking for your grace to fall upon me."
Anfésédé himself begot a son called Misrae.
Misrae himself is the founder
Of a town called Misrae.
100   Ham also begot two black children:
One male and one female.
One day, Ham went into exile.
He arrived at the shores of the River Nile
When he went into exile,
105   Ham said to his wife:
"These two children are not mine."
The wife replied: "What? You are the father.
"Remember that it takes two people
"To make a child: me and you."
110   Ham went into exile.
That was the beginning of the black race.
Thus, Ham went into exile.

115   Ham's children grew up.
They became very strong.
They didn't know their father.
They asked their mother:
"Mother, where is our father?"
120   The mother replied:
"I don't know where your father is."
The two children left in their turn.
They journeyed for many many months
Until they arrived at the banks of the River Nile.
125   There they met Ham.
The latter asked them:
"Where are you going?"
They answered: "We are looking for our father."
Ham said: "What is your father's name?"

130   They replied: "Our father's name is Ham;
        "We were told that Noah is Ham's father;
        "Noah is then our grandfather.
        "We were also told that
        "Our father went into exile;
135   "He went to exile just after our birth.
        "Now we are fully grown up.
        "That's why we are journeying;
        "We want to find him."
        Ham replied:
140   "The man you have in front of you is your father.
        "I am Ham."
        Ham created a settlement on the banks of the Nile.
        The settlement was called Nobara.

[A descendant of Ham named Bubakar Umar, father of the hero, along with a retainer named Mbaarik Bô, migrated first to the Ghana Empire and then to the Waalo Kingdom in the lower Senegal River of northern Senegal.]

        They arrived in the River Senegal area,
        More precisely, up the river.
        There, they found Abraham Sal;
        They converted Abraham to Islam.
270   Abraham thought that Bubakar was Bilal.
        Bilal himself was the companion of the prophet Muhammad;
        (Peace upon him)
        That's why Abraham didn't fight Bubakar.
        Abraham Sal is the ancestor
275   Of all the people bearing the name Sal.
        Among the Lamtoro, the Tukulor people.
        Thus, Bubakar was the one
        Who converted Abraham to Islam.
        Abraham begot Fatumata Abraham Sal.
280   Fatumata was Abraham's daughter.
        Her father gave her in marriage to Bubakar.
        She became Bubakar's wife.
        Thus, Bubakar converted the Serere people.

[But some leaders were reluctant to convert.]

        Bubakar called on Hamar-the-scolder-of-old-people.
300   He said to him: "Come here!
        "I am going to shave your head;
        "I am going to convert you to Islam."
        "Hamar-the-scolder-of-old-people replied:
        "Can you let me go to the outhouse first?"

305   Bubakar said:
      "Yes, you can."
      Hamar-the-scolder-of-old-people did not enter the outhouse.
      He went behind a nearby tree.
      His bow and quiver were hanging there
310   With many arrows inside.
      He took the bow;
      He adjusted an arrow;
      He then hit Bubakar on the forearm.
      The latter quivered, quivered, and quivered;
315   He was in pain.
      He went to his wife Fatumata and told her:

      I am going to die,
      As a result of the wound
330   Caused by Hamar-the-scolder-of-old-people.
      The arrow is poisoned;
      I don't want to die here.
      I want to die back East where I am from.
      I am going back East

[Bubakar then leaves his wife.]

345   At that time, Fatumata was pregnant with Njaajaan Njaay,
      His given first name was Muhamadu;
      It wasn't Njaajaan.
      A few days later Bubakar left the village.
      He headed back East to his native homeland.
350   He didn't make it back east;

355   He died halfway through his journey.

[His son, the hero, then accomplishes what his father failed to do.]

      Muhamadu, Njaajaan was born.
380   When he was eleven,
      He fought Hamar-the-scolder-of-old-people
      In a very celebrated combat;
      Njaajaan smote him with his swift hand behind the ear;
      He smashed both jaws killing him instantly.

[But the hero continues to enjoy a normal childhood, playing with other children, until his mother remarries his father's retainer, Mbaarik Bô. Njaajaan Njaay's friends make fun of him for this reason.]

450   Njaajaan Njaay was playing in the river.
      He was with his young friends.

They were splashing water on each other;
They were running after each other.
On the bank of the river.
455 The playmates started teasing him;
They said to him:
"Oh! Poor boy!
"Your mother couldn't find any man to marry;
"That's why she fell back on the man
460 "Who accompanied your father.
"What a shame!"

[Njaajaan Njaay becomes so upset by this taunting that he leaves home,
goes into the river and becomes a water spirit. He reenters the human
world when he finds children fighting over fish. He demonstrates his
wisdom, kindness, and concern for others by helping resolve the dispute over the fish.]

580 After seven days and three days,
He came out of the river.
In those days in Waalo,
The children went fishing in the river.
When one caught a fish,
585 He would throw it several feet away from the bank.
In those days,
They had not yet learned the technique
Of taking a rope,
Of running it through the gills of each fish,
590 Of linking all the fish onto a single rope.
After they finished fishing, they would gather the fish;
They would start fighting.
For no one would recognize his fish.
One would say: "This is my fish";
595 Another would say: "No;
"It's not your fish,
"It's mine."
They would keep quarreling and fighting.
When Njaajaan saw the children quarreling,
600 He came out of the river.
He walked toward them.
When the children saw him,
They were scared.
They started running away.
605 He raised his hand;
He signaled them to stop.
He reassured them that
He wouldn't do them any harm.
When the children stopped,

610   Njaajaan came.
He took all the fish;
He divided them in equal piles.
After that, he took a rope.
He ran it through the gills of the fish of one pile;
615   He then put it down.
He did so until all the piles were done.
My father told me that
He would look straight into the eyes of one child;
He then would point to a pile;
620   The child would grasp the rope,
The rope from which the fish were dangling.
He would then walk away.
He would do so
Until all the children had their fish
625   And peacefully walked home.
For three days.
He divided the fish in this manner.
He did so after the children had finished fishing.
If you add the three days to the previous three,
630   You come to a total of six days.
The older people were amazed at the children's behavior.
They asked: "Well! Whenever you went fishing,
"You used to quarrel and fight about the catch.
"Now, you come back here in peace,
635   "Each one holding an equal amount of fish.
"What's happening?"
The children answered in unison:
"There is a man who comes out of the river.
"He equally divides the fish among us.
640   "He has been doing so for the past three days.
"He has hair all over his body,
"Except on his palms and around his eyes."
The older people held a council.
One of them said:
645   "We are going to set a trap;
"We should catch that man;
"We want to know more about him.
"Some of you are going to take reeds.
"Get them from the river bank.
650   "Then make a round fence near the fishing place.
"When he comes to divide the fish among the children,
"You should step inside the fence.
"He will certainly follow you.
"If he is a noble man,
655   "He will not jump over the fence
"Once he steps inside it."

A few strong men were chosen to do the job.
After setting up the fence,
They hid behind a nearby tree.
660   After the children caught some fish,
They went inside the round fence;
Then they started quarreling.
Njaajaan was watching them.
After a while,
665   He stepped inside the fence.
He calmed the children down.
He then proceeded to divide the fish.
He wanted to divide them equally among the children.
After he finished,
670   He was walking back to the exit door.
At that moment, a gang of men jumped on him;
They immobilized him.
After that,
The old people were called to see the prisoner.
675   My father told me that
Njaajaan had killed three men among
Those who were trying to catch him.
He was a very strong man;
He had supernatural powers.
680   After they caught him,
They tied his hands behind his back.
A man of the Council of the Elders asked him:
"What's your name?"
Njaajaan didn't answer;
685   He was silent.

Maramu Gaaya came to the council and said:
"If you give me this man,
"I'll take him to the kitchen.
"If you give me two stones,
705   "A cauldron,
"Some flour,
"Water,
"And fire,
"I'll make him talk."
710   What Maramu asked for was given to him.
Njaajaan sat on a low stool;
He was staring at Maramu.
Maramu mixed the water and the flour;
After he finished the mixing,
He took the two big stones;
He then put them half a foot apart.
720   He then lit the logs

In order to make a cooking fire.
He then took the cauldron;
He filled it with water;
He then put it on the two stones.
725 But as soon as he put the cauldron down,
It fell and the water spilled out.
He started again;
He filled the cauldron with water;
He then put it on the two stones;
730 But the cauldron fell on the ground;
The water splashed all around.
Njaajaan was very hungry.
He said to Maramu in Peul:
"You need three stones,
735 "Not two,
"In order to hold the cauldron straight above the fire."
Maramu replied:
"Oh, really?"

[After several other incidents in which Njaajaan Njaay offers advice to Maramu, the "cook" announces the news.]

Maramu Gaye left the kitchen.
He ran out;
775 He called the people and said:
"My dear villagers, come here;
"Come and witness the man speaking."

[The discovery that the strange mute can speak prompts the elders of Waalo to seek advice from the King of the Serere, who advises that they should make Njaajaan Njaay chief of the army and ruler. Njaajaan later rediscovers a long lost younger brother named Mbarak, whom he designates as his successor. Njaajaan Njaay establishes a democratic government and expands his influence over the region.]

When the white Europeans came here long ago
895 They found here, in Waalo,
A true model of government,
A democracy.
They also found here a well-organized
And very efficient army headed by the Mbarak.
900 Njaajaan was the first Mbarak:
He was the first chief of the army.
Njaajaan begot Gèt Njaajaan,
Saré Njaajaan,
Dombur Njaajaan,
905 Nafaye Njaajaan,

Fukili Njaajaan.
All in all,
He had five children.
Fukili went to the Saalum region.
910 Njaajaan left Gèt in Tundu Gèt
On his way to Jolof.
When he arrived in Warxox,
His horse was very tired,
That's why he named the place Xoox.
915 He named the place Xoox.
After that,
Njaajaan arrived in Yang-Yang.
He got there at sundown,
At the time darkness was covering the land.
920 There,
He was given in marriage a Peul woman called Këyfa.
They spent the night together.
At the break of dawn,
Njaajaan left the room.
925 He left Këyfa and Yang-Yang.
He really did not want to have her as a wife.
But Këyfa was pregnant.
She is the ancestor of all the Peul people
Who bear the name Njaay.

Njaajaan had been chief of the army for sixteen years in Waalo
Before he was transferred to Jolof.
945 Before he came to the Waalo region,
The Waalo Empire had been in existence
For four hundred and thirty years, before Njaajaan came into
 existence

950 There,
In Jolof,
He begot Biram Njèmé, Kumba, and Albury Njaay.
Albury was later going to be ruler of the Jolof kingdom;
But when Njaajaan got to Jolof,
955 It was unsettled.
There was no authority,
No chiefdom,
No kingdom,
960 Njaajaan installed authority in Jolof.
In the same order of things,
The region of Bawol,
Of Kayor,
Jolof and Siin were part of the Waalo Empire.

965 That empire covered a vast area going from Ganaar to Casa-
   mance.
  This is how the story of Njaajaan Njaay
  Was handed down to me
  By my father and my ancestors.
  This is also how I learned the traditions,
970 Customs,
  Events,
  And history of the Waalo Empire.
  This is exactly
  How my father narrated to me
975 The story of Njaajaan Njaay.

19. The Epic of Lat Dior

Narrated by Bassirou Mbaye

Recorded in 1985 in Sakh, Senegal, by Bassirou Dieng. Transcribed and translated into French by Bassirou Dieng. Edited by Bassirou Dieng and published in L'épopée du Kajoor by Editions Khoudia in Dakar in 1993. This excerpt edited and translated into English by Thomas A. Hale.

LAT DIOR DIOP (1842-1886), ONE OF THE MOST FAMOUS HEROES of Senegal, was the last great *damel*, or ruler, of the Wolof kingdom of Kayor in the northwest part of the country. He died in battle during the final French drive to conquer Senegal. He is viewed as the hero who incarnated both traditional values and the newer beliefs of Islam at a time of great change. The Senegalese government has designated him as a national hero for his resistance against the French conquest of Senegal. After the breakup of the Jolof empire in the sixteenth century, Kayor, Baol, Sine, and Saloum developed as smaller states in the area near the frontier between the Arab-Berber cultures north of the Senegal River and the black African cultures in Senegal. Each maintained its own identity until the French conquest.

A French commercial presence in the region dates back to the seventeenth century, although it was only in the nineteenth century that French colonial expansion began to impact more directly on these kingdoms. But the story of the conflict between Lat Dior and the French is rooted in a rather complex family history that reflects the importance of women in the Wolof political system. Birima Ngoné Latir, son of a woman of royal origin and a man named Makodou, ruled Kayor from 1855 to 1859. He and the French administration in Saint-Louis, the colony's capital located on an island at the mouth of the Senegal River, signed the first of several agreements for the construction of a railroad that would link Saint-Louis with Dakar, a growing port 300 kilometers to the south. After Birima Ngoné Latir's death, his father, Ten Makodou, was elected ruler of Kayor against the opposition of those who preferred Lat Dior, a son of Ngoné Latir and another man. Lat Dior withdrew from the political arena to build a powerful army. In the meantime, Makodu renewed the railroad construction treaty, violated it at one point, and came into conflict with the French at the battle of Mekhé. He was defeated by the invaders, who replaced him on the throne of Kayor with Madiodio and a resident French supervisor in 1861.

At this point Lat Dior reasserted his claim to the kingship by unseating Madiodio in 1862 and forcing the French to recognize him as the Damel. They responded by driving him into exile in 1864. He retreated south to the Saloum region where a Muslim leader, Maba Diakhou Ba, was fighting both the French and other non-Muslim peoples in the area. It was during his stay there that Lat Dior converted to Islam, a process that included circumcision. He and Maba then mounted a fierce campaign of resistance against the French and forced them to retreat at the battle of Pathébadiane in 1865. Maba was killed in 1867

211

and Lat Dior retreated to Kayor. With new Muslim allies he defeated the French at Mekhé in 1869 but then had to retreat after a split with his closest ally. He reached an agreement with the French in 1871 and reassumed the kingship of Kayor. In 1874, he was defeated by his former allies and then joined the French and a Jolof ally, Albury, to defeat Al-hajj Umar Tal, leader of the Tukulor empire. Two years later, Lat Dior expanded his kingdom to include Baol, a neighbor to the south of Kayor. When construction began in 1883 on the long-planned Saint-Louis-Dakar railroad, a project that would cut through Kayor, Lat Dior scrapped earlier agreements, fought the French, and then retreated. He was killed in battle in 1886 by the French and their allies, including some of his former supporters, at a place called Dékhelé.

The Wolof epic that includes the story of Lat Dior differs from the earlier forms in several ways. Instead of the sweeping history of a single hero who marks a turning point in history (for example, Son-Jara), *The Wolof Epic of Kayor*, collected from two griots and edited by Bassirou Dieng, is composed of a series of episodes that cover four centuries and the major political developments of this long period. Each episode focusses on a particular ruler and his effort to solve a political, institutional, or social crisis. Power in the region was originally based on ownership of land as well as the concept of the master hunter, a source of both magic and military strength. Kayor came into being as the result of the merger of these two notions. But the growth of Islam in the region and the impact of European colonization led to the destabilization and eventual collapse of the Kayor kingdom.

This 1074-line version of *The Epic of Lat Dior* was recounted in Wolof by Bassirou Mbaye, a thirty-five-year old royal *guewel* of Kayor, in 1985 at Sakh, a small village two miles from Mboul, a town that was the capital of the kingdom. Mboul is approximately halfway beween the cities of Thiès and Louga in eastern Senegal. In the larger *Epic of Kayor* it appears as text number twelve of a series of thirteen that, collectively, tell the story of the Kayor Kingdom from the early sixteenth to the late nineteenth centuries. Given the importance of the maternal lineage in the transfer of power from one generation to the next, it is not unusual that Lat Dior is often referred to as the child of his mother, Ngoné Latir. In the text the original spellings of names and places from the French translation are maintained.

> The son of Ngoné Latir,
> We lost him in order to become solders for the Whites.
> We lost him in order to pay taxes to the Whites.
> Ngoné Latir, his mother,
> 5   Commanded in the battle of Ngangaram for her father, the
>   Damel Maysa Tend.
> It is the mother of Birima Ngoné Latir and of Khourédia Mbodj.
> She fought for her father, the Damel Maysa Tend,

The master of cavalrymen Darnde, Goreel, and Nambaas.
After the battle of Ngangaram,

10 All of Kayor spoke only of her.
All of Baol spoke only of her.
All of Jolof spoke only of her.
Troublemakers paralyzed one of her legs;
Thus, since she could not find in Kayor a nobleman from the
same lineage,

15 They gave her to Sakhward Faatma Mbaye, a freeman landowner.
But Njibi Koura, his mother, is the sister of Tiam Mbaye.

Ngoné Latir told them:

25 "Even if you give me to the Lawbé,
"I will give them a *Maalaw*.[1]
"That is why Lat Dior will make 'Maalaw' the name of his
horses."
Some say that a Maalaw does not have to be big, provided that
he be instead a skillful woodcutter.
Others say: "As skilled a woodcutter as he may be, he should
never cut the trunk of his father."

30 Ngoné Latir had affirmed that
"Even among the Lawbé,
"I will give birth to a *Maalaw*."
Maalaw will be therefore the last warhorse of Lat Dior.
When Birima Ngoné Latir died,

35 Madiodio Déguène Kodou took power.
He conquered all of Kayor brought together at Loro;
Conquered them at Diadji Daaro;
Obliged them to work in his fields in the middle of the dry
season;
He made all of Kayor flee across the Tan stream.

40 Birima Ngoné Latir
Had made a gift of a horse to Lat Dior, then an adolescent.
He spurred it,
And the horse threw him.
Birima predicted then that "You will never become king.

45 "The day I leave this world
"The Gedj lineage will lose power forever.
"When a prince
"Is incapable of controlling a horse,
"He will not be able to govern an entire country."

50 The son of Ngoné Latir left the royal court
And went to Koki, the land of Amadou Yalla,

---

1. Chief of the woodcutters.

The fiefdom of his father, in order to learn the Koran.
Madiodio Déguène Kodou, he moved into the capital,
    Nguiguis,
Where he kept a vulture spirit named Njëbb.

55   When the vulture flew over the houses,
Madiodio interpreted the event: "He still would like some
    human flesh.
"Call the people to a meeting."
He stared for a long time at someone in the assembled crowd
Before killing him with a gunshot.

60   "Throw him out for Njëbb to feed on," he added.
The vulture opened the chest of the victim
To feed on his innards.
Kayor was deeply shocked,
Without any means to remedy the situation.

65   Demba War Dior Mbaye Ndéné said one day:
"I can no longer put up with the tyranny of Madiodio Déguène
Kodou;
"I, the eldest of the Gedj lineage,
"I can no longer endure this:
"I am therefore going to look for Lat Dior."

70   He found the son of Ngoné Latir with Serigne Koki
Who was teaching him the Koran.
Lat Dior still had his hair done in the three-tuft style of Diop
adolescents.
The tablet of wood for learning the Koran was between his
hands.
Demba War greeted Serigne Koki

75   And said to him, "Entrust Lat Dior to me.
"I will install him at Mboul.
"Thus, tomorrow he will make you the *Barget*[2] of Guet."
"I cannot do it because Lat Dior is a religious chief and you are
still non-believing warriors."
"Entrust Lat Dior to me," insisted Demba War.

80   "Take him, if that is the way it is," concluded Sérigne Koki.
With Lat Dior mounted behind him,
Demba War rode to Nguiguis
And proclaimed, "Here is the new king."
Kayor replied, "No Damel named Diop,

85   "With his three tufts of hair,
"Will spend the day here."
Madiodio Déguène Kodou said to them,
"You, Demba War with Lat Dior mounted behind you,
"Don't spend the day at Nguiguis,

---

2. Governor.

90   "Or else I will reduce you to ashes."
Demba War left with him on his horse called Kuddu, "the
     spoon,"
Repeating all the while, "One who has a spoon doesn't get
     burned while cooking."

[Next comes Lat Dior's circumcision.]

     They brought Lat Dior into the "men's house"
     At Khabnane.
     Laba[3] sat down.
     They told this to Madiodio Déguène Kodou:
125   "Some blood of a noble has been spilled on your land."
He commented, "One who dares to spill the blood of a noble on
     my land without my authorization
"Will not set up his compound for circumcised men here."
Demba War said then to the son of Ngoné Latir: "After all,
     Madiodio Déguène is your grandfather."
Madiodio sent to him a final emissary bearing this threat:
130   "I will come to burn down his compound for circumcised men."

160   Demba War sent the emissary back with this message:
"Even if he is riding a wooden mortar, he will find me here."
The first name of the horse of Lat Dior is "Dondo-Neeri."
It is not a Wolof adage, rather it is Tukulor and means:
"Let someone else take care of your bleeding wound."
165   This was the motto of his first horse.
He was still circumcised
When Demba War told him:
"They should saddle a horse for you
"So that you can train it yourself."
170   They saddled a horse for him and handed him the reins.
"Dondo-Neeri" he named it,
"Let someone else take care of your bleeding wound."
He rode it and spurred it;
His blood of a newly circumcised man wet him all the way
     down to the stirrups.
175   Demba War said to him:
"You are now capable of fighting any king."

     They followed Lat Dior
     And booed him all the way to Kër-Madiop,
215   The frontier between Kayor and Baol.
     Lat Dior said to them:

---

3. Praise-name for Lat Dior.

"You could have installed an exit door for the future,
"Because I will come back soon."
*Laba*⁴ continued his quest.

[Dressed in the clothing of a young man who is circumcised at the age
of seventeen, Lat Dior wins his first battle but loses the second against
Madiodio, who has the support of the French. He then goes off into
exile. His itinerary includes battles against the armies of neighboring
kingdoms. A victor over Baol, he is defeated at Sine. Finally, he arrives
at his destination, the kingdom of Maba Diakhou Ba, who gives him an
army.]

| | The son of Ngoné Latir continued on his way |
| 315 | And went to Maba Diakhou in the Saloum region. |

325	He sent emissaries to Maba Diakhou,
	Telling him that it was Lat Dior who greeted him.
	Maba, who was in the middle of a big meeting,
	Spoke to the assembled in these terms: "I have a great dilemma today.
	"For Lat Dior, who has just asked me for asylum here,
330	"Seeks only power on earth.
	"While I, I lead a holy war,
	"Only for the greatness of God.
	"Morever, he who fights for God
	"Must be neither an ingrate
335	"Nor someone who disappoints hopes.
	"How could I give asylum
	"To Lat Dior, who is fighting for worldly benefits?
	"I who fight for the glory of God?
	"One remembers that Makodou Yandé Mbarou asked me for asylum here, in the same circumstances.
340	"I fought with him
	"In order to advance him to the throne
	"And surprised him afterward drinking wine!
	"That is why I don't trust Kayor people."
	An elder stood up in the assembly and proposed:
345	"Ask him to convert,
	"To cut his hair
	"And to present it as a sign of humility.
	"In that way you will give him exile.
	"And when he will be strong enough,
350	"You will let him return to Kayor."
	Lat Dior remained for a long time at that place and said one day:

---

4. Praise-name for Lat Dior.

"A disciple must go look each Wednesday for the pittance he
    gives each week to his master."
The son of Ngoné Latir assembled his army.
365   And raided Sasa Ndoukoumanae,
Raided Waliyaar,
Raided Sabakh
Raided Diaba Kounda
Before going to find Sàmba Diabaye at Ndiaw Mame.
370   He refused to convert.
Lat Dior put his foot on his head and slit his throat.
In fact he asked for Demba War Dior Mbaye Ndéné, and told
    him,
"Go greet Mame Samba Diabaye."
This man, at that time, had pierced one of his nostrils, where he
    hung a golden chain.
375   And at his feet was a vessel full of wine.
When he shouted "The nobles have heard,"
They pulled on the golden chain and he took a long drink of
    wine.
When he got up, his eyes bulged from his head.
He replied to the emissary, "I thought there was no other king
    but me,
380   "And you speak to me of a certain Lat Dior, king of Kayor."
Demba War said, "I will not reply to him before consulting
    with Lat Dior."
He went to report to Lat Dior,
Who said, "Nobody ever showed his own death to the door.
"Return and present my greetings to Mame Samba Diabaye
385   "And point out to him that it is Lat Dior, king of Kayor, who
    greets him."
He returned,
And said to Mame Samba Diabaye, "Lat Dior greets you.
"The king of Kayor also demands from you hay and water for
    his horses."
He cried out, "The nobles have heard."
390 .   They pulled on the chain and he took a long drink of wine;
He stood up, saying:
"I thought there was no other king but me."
Demba War returned to report to Lat Dior.
The people of Kayor said to Lat Dior:
395   "For three days, we are feeding only on *nduur*[5] plants
"While drinking water from the stream.
"We rustle some sheep from herds
"That we encounter.

---

5. A kind of bush.

"We will slaughter them, we will roast them to satisfy our
    hunger,
400   "Before meeting Mame Samba Diabaye at Ndiaw."
Then a *jeli*[6] named Samba Koumba Kalado
Played on his *xalam*[7] the tune *lagya*, while seated on the ground,
And composed that day this song: "Niani refuses to be subjec-
    ted.
"O descendant of Dior Saala Faatma Khourédia,
405   "The son of Ngoné Latir swept down on Mame Sàmba Diabaye
"And burned Ndiaw.
"He knocked down all the stockades
"And burned the entire country,
"Bringing everything there back as booty.
410   "He finally returned."

[In the service of Maba Diakhou, Lat Dior leads a series of battles
against non-Muslim peoples and French-led armies.]

Maba Diakhou, the Foutanké,[8] warned him, nevertheless:
455   "I taught you the letter 'B,'
"Which should remind you of my taboos.
"I taught you the letter 'S,'
"Which should remind you never to fight against the people of
    Sine;
"These are peaceful people,
460   "Living by the sweat of their brow,
"Who never commit aggression against anyone.
"I will give you, too, two kinds of land:
"This red earth,
"And this white earth.
465   "If the soil of the field where you must fight is red,
"You will not survive this campaign."
Maba, who had to fight a battle, looked at the white earth that
    had become red.
He decided nevertheless to follow his destiny;
But he called Lat Dior
470   And said to him, "I know you very well;
"A noble has a sense of honor;
"You will want to follow me till death.
"I am undertaking my last campaign against the ruler of Sine.
"With Sayeer Mati, my elder,
475   "To the Sayaan of Somb.
"You, Lat Dior,
"Today you are the elder of the Gedj lineage,
"And you have still not yet been installed at Mboul.

---

6. Mande griot. 7. Lute. 8. Someone from the Fouta Toro region.

"Many people have followed you into exile,
480 "Abandoning women, children, and goods;
"Thus, if you die with me in this war,
"They will not know how to return to Kayor.
"I order you to saddle a mare when we go to the Sayaan of
    Somb."
That is why Lat Dior did not die during that battle.
485 Maba Diakhou was killed, with Sayeer Mati, his eldest son.
Lat Dior came back to Kayor.

The son named Lat Dior finally returned.
505 It was the beginning of the rainy season.

On the third day of the rainy season,
510 The people of Kayor were going to sow peanuts and millet.
He declared, "From Koki, fiefdom of Amadou Yalla,
"To Kër-Madiop, the frontier between Kayor and Baol,
"I plugged all of the wells,
"I burned all the villages.
515 "I burned all of the silos.
"Today the country is called 'Diop'
"Or 'Ndiour'
"Where the forest returned for seven years."
Madiodio Déguène Kodou
520 Supported, by the *Jawrin-Mboul*[9] Mador Diagne,
Also said, "The country will answer to 'Faal,'
"Or 'Ndiour,'
"Or will become forest for seven years."
That is the cause of the battle of the wells of Kalom.
525 The battle raged for a full day.
On that day, at Ndande,
The Madior lineage was decimated.
Madiodio Dior Lobé fell at Ndandé;
Ten Lat Déguène Kodou was killed with An, "The luncheon."
530 Ma Bigué Faati Lobé was killed with Boo-dëdde-nuul.[10]
All the great compounds of Ndiémbale on that day.

535 They are lineage of Madior.
The night before, Madiodio Déguène Kodou had proclaimed:
"Tomorrow, I will eat my own flesh!"
"Why?" he was asked.
"When one speaks of the Madior lineage," he explained,
540 "One refers to Dior who had come from Njiguène.
"I will kill them at the Wells of Ndande."

9. Ruler of Mboul. 10. "You-turn-black-when-you-turn-around."

219

"While tomorrow, Weyndé Nakk and Tanor Nakk,
As soon as the sun rises,
Madiodio Déguène Kodou killed Weyndé Nak and Tanor
    Nakk.
545   As for the *Jawrin-Mboul* Madior Diagne,
The heroes of the army of Madiodio Déguène Kodou,
As brave as Demba War in the army of Lat Dior,
The lineage of Demba Tioro cast a spell on him,
Magically plunging his body into the well,
550   Maintaining it between the bottom and the curb. His body had
    no more strength.
He could neither fight nor raise his gun.
He who, like Demba War at the side of Lat Dior,
Was the pillar of the army of Madiodio Déguène Kodou.
Lat Dior conquered Madiodio Déguène Kodou.
555   Who took refuge in Saint-Louis, with many relatives.
Lat Dior returned
And called again to the people of Kayor, "What is your deci-
    sion?"
"We refuse," replied the people of Kayor.
He was going to slit the throat of Sérigne Gatiratte,
560   Exterminating all those who were on the surrounding hills.

[The hero thus completes the cycle of traditional heroes of the Sudan that is made up of a conquest or reconquest of power. Son-Jara is the model for this type. The tragic epic of the hero's resistance against the French and the colonial penetration into the region follows next. Lat Dior fights unceasingly against both the French and the Muslim Tukulors who want to build a federation of traditional kingdoms. He will die alone in combat against the French and part of his own original army, led by his general Demba War, whom the invaders have succeeded in bringing over to their side.]

785   He returned to Kayor.
That is why, when one talks about the battles of Lat Dior
One can estimate that there were forty or thirty of them,
But to tell about each one, where it took place and what he did,
Nobody would dare recount in detail.
790   He encountered, for example, Sidiya Ndaté Yalla at Bangoye.
It was a lightning battle.
Bouba Mbaye succeeded in killing rapidly Sidiya Ndaté Yalla,
Who raised himself up on an arm and moaned,
"God All Powerful!"
795   Ngoté Niasse in his turn fired his gun at Bouba Mbaye,
Who was projected into the air,
Sticking his tongue completely out:
His heart came out of his arm;

Lat Dior turned his head and cried.
800 Nevertheless, that didn't stop the son of Ngoné Latir.
He encountered Cheikhou Amadou at Tiowane.

825 Lat Dior called for the French to help
—this is the origin of their long conflict—
And said to them:
"Help me to conquer Amadou Cheikhou.
"If he leaves my kingdom for good,
830 "What you ask from me,
"The railroad from Ndar to Dakar,
"I will grant it to you."

Kayor betrayed him, one man after another.
910 Some of his closest men
Said to him goodbye.
Others advised him to go into exile:
"Lat Dior, why don't you go into exile?
"Why not go to the Sine Kingdom?" they asked him.

930 "I can't go there!
"What should I do with you?" he asked himself;
"Anyone who does not want to die should not follow me."
One cavalryman said goodbye to him on that day.
And Lat Dior took his horse and said:
935 "There is *licin*—the Hawk—take him!"
"What does *licin* mean?" he asked him.
"One flies easily with him," he replied.
The son of Ngoné Latir got himself ready at Thilmakha.
The tamarind tree where they hang their guns
940 Is still full of nails.
He took off all of his magic charms
And buried them at the foot of the tamarind tree.
He went to greet Khadimou Rassoul,
Who said to him, "You have had all of the powers of this world.
945 "Come prepare with me your rule in the other world!"
He replied, "If people ask me for protection,
"And if I begin to look for protection myself,
"That will seem like cowardice.
"A noble must never retreat.
950 "I don't want to tarnish the honor of my lineage.
"But there is Mbakhane, my son,
"I make him your disciple."
The Marabout said, "Mbakhane, I name you Abdou Khafor,
"'The pardoned slave.'"
955 That is why Sérigne Bamba never cursed Mbakhane.

He took off his *boubou*[11] and gave it to Lat Dior
And prayed for him.
Lat Dior got ready and ordered,
"Saddle my companion."
960   Every horse that they presented to him,
He said, "That one is not my companion."
Until there were none left except Maalaw,
Who pawed the ground with his right foot.
"Have you understood this augury of Maalaw?" he asked.
965   "No," they replied.
"He pawed with his right foot; it is my tomb that he is digging.
"I will pray the *tisbaar*[12] prayer today with Maba Diakhou,
    my guide, in the world beyond."
At daybreak they arrived at Dékhélé.
Khadim had recommended one thing to him:
970   "However rough the combat may be,
"Don't sing your praises.
"Always say, 'God is All Powerful!'
"As long as you praise him, you will not fall."
He left with many relatives from our village.
975   None returned.
That is why the village is so barren.
All those who left here on that morning
Fell on the field of battle.
Even we griots.
980   At daybreak,
Lat Dior went out of Dékhélé.
When the Whites arrived,
The White placed his hand on the shoulder of Demba War and
    asked him:
"Who is Lat Dior?"
985   "Lat Dior? There are the tracks of his horse," he replied.
"Lat Dior has fled!" he said to him.
"Lat Dior does not flee!
"I witnessed his birth, I educated him!"
"By the way, what is your tie with Lat Dior?"
990   "We were together for a long time," he replied.
"Are you relatives?"
"To be linked for a long time suffices for a family relationship.
"I saw Lat Dior born:
"I brought him up;
995   "It was I who had him initiated into the 'house of men.'
"We participated together in twenty-nine battles.
"This is the thirtieth and we are fighting against each other.
"What is turning white down there,

---

11. Robe. 12. Early afternoon prayer.

"We Wolof call the sun.
1000 "When it reddens, I will see his blood.
"You will know then that Lat Dior does not flee."
They advanced again, arriving near the well;
They planted their flag and decided to prepare a meal.
It was at this moment that the son of Ngoné Latir swept down
   upon them
1005 And cried "*Tuuge waaye!*"[13]

[Lat Dior's enemies now carefully prepare to kill him.]

They had prepared the bullet magically
Before giving it to the one who was to kill Lat Dior.
A bit of gold,
A bit of silver,
1025 A bit of copper,
A bit of iron.

1030 They had prepared two bullets.
Lat Dior never looked behind him.
The first bullet hit his horse Maalaw on the white spot on his
   forehead.
The second cut down Lat Dior,
Tearing out his right eye.

1051 The son of Ngoné Latir
Is the only one for whom the people of Kayor say:
"We lost you in order to become soldiers for the whites.
"We lost you in order to pay taxes to the whites."

1070 But the great deeds of Lat Dior
No one has equaled them.
To be the last born
And to have the greatest reputation,
If it is not due to virtues, it is certainly the sign of greatness.

---

13. Exclamation when catching a criminal.

PART TWO

NORTH AFRICA

Egyptian Epics

AT LEAST A DOZEN ORAL EPICS have existed at different times in the Arab world. Some, such as *Sīrāt ʿAntar ibn Shaddād* (the *sīra* of the pre-Islamic black poet-knight, ʿAntara son of Shaddād), *Sīrat Dhāt al-Himma* (the *sīra* of the heroine Dhāt al-Himma and her wars against the Byzantines), and *Sīrat al-malik Sayf ibn Dhī Yazan* (the *sīra* of the Himyarite king, Sayf ibn Dhī Yazan and his wars against the Abyssinians) have ancient, pre-Islamic roots. Others, such as *Sīrat al-amīr Ḥamza al-Bahlawān* (the *sīra* of Ḥamza, uncle of the Prophet Muhammad), and *Sīrat al-Zīr Sālim* (the *sīra* of the Bedouin warrior, al-Zīr Sālim) are set at the beginning of the Islamic era. Still others, such as *Sīrat al-Ẓāhir Baybars* (the *sīra* of the thirteenth-century Egyptian ruler and folk hero, al-Ẓāhir Baybars) and *Sīrat Banī Hilāl* (the *sīra* of the Banī Hilāl Bedouin tribe and their eleventh-century conquest of North Africa) are tied to more recent historical events. Several of these were still performed up to the nineteenth century; today, however, only *Sīrat Banī Hilāl* exists in the oral tradition.

Arabic written literature has left us a fragmentary record of the emergence of these epics, their stories, and the poets who performed them. The epics are often cited in medieval collections of religious sermons in which the devout are warned not to waste time with such frivolous pastimes and are encouraged instead to devote themselves to prayer and the study of religious works. Occasionally, a scholar or a market-place scribe would record a fragment of one of the poems: such is the case of Ibn Khaldūn, the famous fourteenth-century Arab historiographer, who quoted pages of *Sīrat Banī Hilāl* in his treatise on the nature of history, *al-Muqaddimah* ("The Introduction"). In later centuries we even find versions of the oral epics in Classical Arabic, part of the "popular literature" of the day. These texts, however, were usually written on inexpensive materials which have not easily weathered the passing years. For this reason, it is very difficult to determine what role these "pulps" may have played in the development or preservation of the epics.

Since *Sīrat Banī Hilāl* is the last of these epics to survive, it has received more attention from modern scholars than the other epics. This epic, though well known in much of the Arab world, is now sung as a versified epic poem in only two regions, northern and southern Egypt. Elsewhere it is currently found as a cycle of folktales occasionally punctuated with lines of poetry.

Dwight Reynolds

227

20. The Epic of the Banī Hilāl
Narrated by Shaykh Tāhā Abū Zayd

Recorded in June 1987 in al-Bakātūsh, Egypt, by Dwight Reynolds. Transcribed and translated into English by Dwight Reynolds. This excerpt edited by Dwight Reynolds.

The Birth of the Hero Abū Zayd

THE FOLLOWING EXCERPT IS FROM THE ARABIC ORAL EPIC POEM *Sīrat Banī Hilāl*, the epic history of the Arab Bedouin tribe of the Banī Hilāl (literally "sons of the crescent moon"). This recording was made in the village of al-Bakātūsh in the Nile Delta region of northern Egypt. The poet was Shaykh Tāhā Abū Zayd, who was about seventy at that time. Since Tāhā is an epithet of the Prophet Muhammad and Abū Zayd is the central hero of the epic as it is sung in Egypt, the poet's name itself is emblematic of the connection between the Islamic nature of the epic and the close bond which is understood to exist between epic singers and the epic heroes of whom they sing. The performance was held in the home of Ahmad Bakhtātī and was the first of a series Shaykh Tāhā Abū Zayd sang over a period of two months in which he provided a full rendition of the epic as he knew it. The resulting version was fifty-four hours long; it numbers well over 12,000 verses of *qasīda*-style poetry, a form in which each verse is twenty-eight to thirty syllables long with a medial caesura and closes with a mono-endrhyme. In this tradition the poet can maintain the same rhyme for a hundred verses or more before moving on to a different rhyme. The poet accompanies himself musically on the *rabāb*, a two-stringed, spike-fiddle, the same instrument on which the heroes in the epic perform, providing a tangible link between epic singer and epic hero.

At the beginning of this performance the audience consisted of six men from the village and myself; several more men, however, arrived after verse 68. Had they been high-status guests the poet would have interrupted his singing to greet them in improvised poetry; this group, however, consisted of men who regularly attend all epic performances in the village, aficionados of the tradition, and as "regulars," they were greeted simply with a nod. The beginning of most performances is rather sedate, with audience members providing only desultory comments and sounds of approval. As the scene foretelling the birth of the hero, Abū Zayd, approaches, the listeners begin shouting comments at the end of every line; and from verse 95 onward many verses are even interrupted and one listener makes a display of placing a handful of cigarettes in front of the poet, which elicits the poet's thanks. The epic opens on a common theme: the most valiant warrior of the tribe does not yet have a son. He has married nine women before he encounters a Sufi dervish who predicts the birth of a son if only he marries the daughter of the ruler of Mecca.

[Spoken:]

After praise for the Prophet of the tribe of ʿAdnān, and we do not gather but that we wish God's blessings upon Him, for the Prophet was the most Saintly of the Saintly, the Seal of God's Messengers, and on the Day of Resurrection He shall smile on the faces of all who wish God's blessings upon Him.

The author of these words tells of Arabs known as the Arabs Banī Hilāl, and their Sultan at that time and that era was King Sarhān, and their Warrior was Rizq the Valiant, Son of Nāyil, for every age has its nation and its men. And the guardian of the maidens was a stalwart youth, his name was Prince Zayyān, and the protector of the Zaghāba clan was the courageous Ghānim, warrior among warriors.

Rizq had married women, yes, eight maidens, but he had not yet sired a male heir. He sat in his pavilion and some lads passed by him (lads, that is, of the Arabs, the lads, that is to say, the little boys, if you'll excuse me). His soul grew greatly troubled over the lack of an heir, so Rizq sat and sang of the lack of a male heir, words which you shall hear; and he who loves the beauty of the Prophet increases his wishes for God's blessings upon Him.

All: *May God Bless and Preserve Him!*

Voice: *You mean you're not going to have supper tonight?*
Shaykh Tāhā: *Why do you say that, brother?*
Voice: *The food!* (gesturing to the food being laid out in the next room.)
Shaykh Tāhā: *Praise be to God!*[1]

[Music on the spike-fiddle.]
[Sung:]

I am the servant of all who adore the beauty of Muhammad,
All: *May God Bless and Preserve Him!*
Tāhā, for whom every pilgrim yearns.

Listen to what said Rizq the Valiant, Son of Nāyil;
Tears poured forth from the orb of his eye, flowing.

Ah! Ah! the World and Fate and Destiny!
All I have seen with my eyes shall disappear.

5   Fate make peace with me, 'tis enough what you've done to me,
I've cast my weapons at thee, but my excuse is clear.

---

1. That is, We have already eaten.

I do not praise among the days one which pleases me
    But that its successor comes along, stingy and mean.

My wealth is great, O men, but I am without an
        heir;   *Voice: Allah!*
    And wealth without an heir after a lifetime disappears.

I look out and find Sarhān when he rides,
    His sons ride with him, princes and prosperous.

I look out and find Zayyān when he rides,
    His sons ride with him and fill the open spaces.

I look out, ah!, and find Ghānim when he rides,
    And his sons ride with him and are princes, prosperous.

10   And I am the last of my line, my spirit is broken,
    I have spent my life and not seen a son, prosperous.

I have taken of women, eight maidens,
    And eleven daughters followed, princesses true!

This bearing of womenfolk, ah!, has broken my spirit,
    I weep and the tears of my eyes on my cheek do flow.

So Ghānim said to him, "O Rizq I have a maiden daughter,
    "Marry her today and you shall achieve your desires."

He signed the marriage contract with the maiden Jallās,
             Shaykh Tāhā: Wish God's blessings on the Prophet!
                  All: May God Bless and Preserve Him!
    They held the wedding, O Nobles, and slaughtered
      slaughtering beasts.

15   The first year Jallās bore him a daughter,
    That rounded out a dozen daughters for him, true!
                                     [Laughter]
But Ghānim said, "Be patient! There is benefit in patience,
    "With patience, Royal One, you shall achieve your desires.

"One who bears a daughter may also bear a son,
                             Voice: That's right!
    "And if my Lord God wills, from her will come children to
      people the open spaces."

The second year passed and the third she became pregnant,
    At the pregnancy of the Zaghāba girl perfumes were
      released.   Voice: *Allah!*

Her months went by, ah!, and she bore him a boy!
    But his two arms were crippled and his legs were lame.

20   It became a wonder amongst the Arabs,
    And those coming and going did speak of it.

So Rizq said to the maiden Jallās: "Take your son and move off
    from here, "I want no women, by God, in this camp."

She took her son on her arm and her daughter, O Nobles, with
    her,
    And this is the way of the husband when he is mean.

So Sarhān said, "Let us go, O Rizq, you and I, out into the des-
    ert and wilderness,
    "To hunt gazelles, O Friend, in the wide, open spaces."

They set out, then, the two of them,
                Shaykh Tāhā: *Wish God's blessings on the Prophet!*
                        All: *May God Bless and Preserve Him!*
    And they found a man, a shaykh, in the wilds wandering.
                                  Voice: *Allah!*

25   They found this man, a shaykh, in the desert and the wilder-
    ness,
    The foam on his chest was like the billowing sea.

"O Rizq, my son, your need, ah yes, is clearly for a boy,
    "Who will, after your lifetime, honor those coming and
      going.

"The day the pilgrims set forth from Egypt to the Prophet,
                        All: *May God Bless and Preserve Him!*
    "Pack up the Hilālī Arabs and offer up slaughtering beasts.

"Go marry Khadra, daughter of Qirda the Sharīf, Son of
    Hāshim,
    "From her shall come a lad, O Courageous One, who shall
      prosper.

"From her shall come a lad, God shall cause his memory to live
    on.
    "He shall be a strong boy of ominous determination."

30   They took in the <u>sh</u>eik<u>h</u> and invited him for three full days,
         And each night, O Nobles, the *dhikr*[2] rang out.

The day the pilgrims set out from Egypt to the Prophet,
      Rizq said to them, "O Hilālī Arabs, I intend to Visit the
         Prophet, Possessor of shining light."
                 All: *May God Bless and Preserve Him!*

The Hilālī nobles then packed up with the Son of Nāyil,
      O fortunate is he who yearns and then makes pilgrimage.
         <u>Sh</u>ay<u>kh</u> Tāhā: *Wish God's blessings on the Prophet!*
                 All: *May God Bless and Preserve Him!*

[Spoken:]

      Said the *Rāwī* [reciter]: After praise for the Prophet of the tribe
of ʿAdnān, they reached the land and the country of Mecca. They erec-
ted their tents and their pavilions and hoisted their banners, and they
occupied the country from every side and direction. Then Qirda [the
<u>Sh</u>arīf of Mecca] welcomed them with the warmest of welcomes and
showed them every consideration. He invited them to rest for three
days. After three days he asked them about their origins. So King Sarhān said, "We are Arabs from the land of <u>Sh</u>arīfa the High-born . . .
[<u>Sh</u>eik<u>h</u> Tāhā corrects himself] . . . from the land of Najd, O Warrior
among warriors, and our desire is the hand of <u>Sh</u>arīfa the High-born.
Our goal is a maiden of noble descent and good lineage, O Warrior
among warriors." So Qirda said to them, "Welcome to you, O Arabs of
Hilāl. You have honored us and graced us in our land and our country." Then he moved them to his own area of the camp and placed
them in tents of honor and hospitality. Then the Hilāl *Qādī* [religious
judge] came forth, Fāyid, father of Badīr, and Sarhān said to him,
"Speak, Qādī, speak of the brideprice for the maiden" [aside to audience: The brideprice, that is, the dowry]. See what the Qādī will say,
and he who loves the beauty of the Prophet wishes God's blessings
upon Him.
                 All: *May God Bless and Preserve Him!*
[Music.]
[Sung:]

      I am the servant of all who adore the beauty of Muḥammad,
         Tāhā, who asked for intercession and obtained it.

      Listen to what the Qādī Fāyid said and what he sang:
         "My *eye* aches and sleep frequents it not in this state.[3]

---

2. Sufi chanting. 3. Metaphor for the soul.

35   "It goes to sleep with good intention, but awakes filled with
         caution,
         "As if all the hooks of life lay in sleep's domain.

"If my burdens lean, with my own hand I set them straight,
         "But if the world leans, only God can set it straight.

"Happy is the eye which sleeps the whole night through,
                         Shay<u>kh</u> Tāhā: *Ah yes, by God!*
         "It passes the night in comfort, no blame is upon it.

"But my eye is pained and keeps vigil the whole night
         through,
         "It passes the night troubling me with all that has befallen
         it.

"Listen to my words, O Qirda, and understand,
         "These are the words of princes, not mere children.

40   "We wish from you a maiden, high-born,
         "Of noble ancestry from both grandfathers, paternal and
         maternal uncles, too.

"We shall give her a dowry, a dowry of nobles, O Hero,
         "We shall dress her in the finest and purest of silks.

"Perhaps she'll bear a son, a prince awe inspiring,
         "He shall emerge from the vessel whose waters are pure.

"If he comes and speaks in the mosque a word, they will say,
         "'That is the son of Rizq who came to us and said it.'

"We'll take not the fair maid for the fairness of her cheek,
         "If the fair one goes astray, her menfolk are blamed.
                                     Voice: *True!*

45   "We'll take not the dark maid for the greatness of her wealth,
         "If her wealth decreases she'll blame you for her loss.
                                     [Laughter]

"We'll take not the foolish maid or the daughter of a miser,
         "Flustered on the day of the feast, we won't even approach
         her.

"We'll take not one who scrapes the pot with her hand,
                                     [Laughter]

"If a few days of want come,
   "She'll vie with her own children [for the food]!   [Laughter]

"We shall only take the high-born princess,   Voice: *Allah!*
   "Who honors the guest of God, yes, when he comes to her.

50   "She who receives the guest of God with welcome and greet-
               ings,
   "So that her man may sit honored among men.

"We shall give you, O Qirda, a hundred horses, and a hundred
         sheep,
   "And a hundred slave girls, and one hundred camels.

"And a hundred slaves, O Kindest-of-the-Arabs,
   "And one hundred fair slave girls to serve their men.

"And on top of all of this, one thousand pieces of gold,
   "Wealth is useful and the years are long.

"This is our dowry, O paternal uncle, in our country,
   "And we are Arabs, the poorest of its men.   [Laughter]

55   "Have pity on us, ah!, O Son of Hashing,   Voice: *Allah!*
   "Nobles are not thanked except for their actions."

Then Qirda said, "Write this down, too, O Qādī of the Arabs,
   "From me, I give its equal for the Lady Khadra.

"Perhaps Fate will change toward her;
   "And if she sets aside her wealth,   Voice: *Allah!*

"Even if Fate and Destiny and Time change toward her,
   "She need not rely on the least of her menfolk." [Laughter]

The Courageous One signed the wedding contract,
               Shaykh Tahā: *Wish God's blessings on the Prophet!*
                     All: *May God Bless and Preserve Him!*
   They slaughtered young camels and they invited all her
         men.

60   The Arabs packed up that very day and travelled,
   They placed the heavy loads on their camels.

They went home, ah, ah, to their land and their territory,
   Their land was that of Taifa, may its men always thrive!

They brought the burdens, all the men, every single one of
    them,
    They brought the burdens to Rizq in their entirety.

But then there was Ghānim, who felt wronged,
    O Hero, that Rizq had left Jallās and left her children with
    her.

The first year went by the Lady Khadra,
    And the second passed, and the third just the same.

65   And the fourth passed by the Lady Khadra,
    And the fifth passed without the fulfillment of her desires.

And the sixth passed and was finished,
    The elders spoke of it, as did even their children.

Seven years were completed with the Son of Nāyil,
    She neither gave birth nor grew pregnant, nor fulfilled her
    desires.

Ghānim heard the talk and he grew light hearted.
    He was the bringer of evil, Ghānim, among the men of the
    tribe.

He came to Rizq in order to tell him,
    "Listen to my words," so hear now what he said to him:

70   "You married al-Sharīfa,[4]
    "O Rizq, to increase your honor. It turns out she's barren,
    cannot fulfill her desires."

[Music while additional guests enter and are seated.]

"You married al-Sharīfa, O Rizq, to increase your honor,
    "It turns out she's barren, cannot fulfill her desires.

"You've taken a line of barren women, O Rizq, what a pity,
        Shaykh Tāhā: *Your line of barren wives is a pity, O Rizq!*
    "Rizq, divorce this one and take yourself another."

Rizq heard these words and his mind grew greatly troubled,
    "O fire of my heart whose flames are not slackened!"

---

4. Literally "the honorable."

He went to Khadra as she sat in her pavilion,
　　O how beautiful were her features.

75　　As soon as she saw Rizq,
　　　　　　　Shaykh Tāhā: *Wish God's blessings on the Prophet!*
　　　　　　　All: *May God Bless and Preserve Him!*
　　Tāhā, the pilgrims pelerinated and came [to Him].

She stood up on her feet, her hand lovely,
　　Her face fair and oh so comely.

So he said to her, "Khadra, you're a whore,
　　"By God I married you but there are no sons in you.

"I married you an honorable woman[5] to increase my honor,
　　"It turns out you are barren, in you there are no offspring.

"Seven years, O Khadra, you have been in my dwellings,
　　"And I have not seen from you any sons."

80　　"She heard this fury from him, she gestured to speak to him,
　　　"Stop there, man, and put your faith in God!　　　All: *Ah!*

"By God, the bearing of children is not in my hands,
　　"Everything, O Rizq, comes about by the will of God."

He heard from her these words and gestured and said to her,
　　"My mind from me, O Sharīfa, has strayed.

"I am like a crazy man in the desert and the wastelands,
　　"Woe to him whose strength Fate has destroyed!"

He struck her with his palm upon her comely cheek,
　　Her fair cheek, its sweetness fled.

85　　So Khadra began to complain to those in the encampment,
　　　"By God I am a stranger, I have no dignity of rank."

She passed by Shamma, wife of King Sarhān,
　　She was also a stranger with little dignity of rank.

And Shamma was the daughter of King Zayd the Virtuous
　　From the land of Tubbaʿ, from righteous men.

---

5. Sharīfa.

She said to her, "O <u>Kh</u>adra, who has caused you to weep?
   "Who is capable of this to a stranger, to cause you such suf-
      fering?"

She said to her, "Rizq reproaches me about offspring,
   "About the lack of a son and heir."   All: *Ah!*

90   She said to her, "You are barren, and I am just like you,
           "My sustenance [*rizq*] and your sustenance are both up to
              God.

      "Come, come, you and I, let us go out into the wilderness,
         "Let us go out and wander beneath the face of God."
                                                        Voice: *Ah!*

      They passed a short night, the two of them,
         While Sarhān kept Rizq company.

      And it was Friday morning,
                  <u>Sh</u>ay<u>kh</u> Tāhā: *Wish God's blessings on the Prophet!*
                           All: *May God Bless and Preserve Him!*
         As for the oppressed, God hears their prayers.

      She said to her: "Let us go, you and I, to the sea in the wilder-
            ness,
         "Let us go calm our blood in its emptiness.

95   "When you look at the salten sea you shall encounter wonders,
           "You shall encounter wonders, by the will of God."

      They set out, the two of them along with their slave,
         Saʿīda, wife of Najjāh, oh so beautiful.

      Suddenly a white bird . . .   Voice *Yes!*
                           . . . from the distance came to them,
         A white bird, beautiful to behold.

      He landed and did not take flight again, the bird in the waste-
            land,
         All the other birds flocked round him.

      Said <u>Sh</u>amma, "O Lord, the One the Everlasting,   Voice: *Allah!*
         "Glory to God, there is no god but He.

100   "Grant unto me a son, like unto this bird,
           "And may he be handsome and the Arabs obey his [every
              word]."

237

Her request was completed, O Nobles, and the bird rose up,
    The bird took flight, it climbed up toward the heights.

Then suddenly a dark bird from the distance came to them,
                Laughter—Voice: *This is Abū Zayd!*
    A dark bird . . .   Voice: *Yes!*
        . . . frightful to behold.   Voice: *Heavens!*

He beat his wings at the other birds,
    And each one he struck did not [live to] smell his supper.

Said Khadra, . . .   Voice: *Yes!*
    . . . "O how beautiful you are, O bird, and
      how beautiful your darkness.
                            Voice: *Allah!*
    "Like the palm date when it ripens at its leisure on the tree.

105   "O Lord, O All Merciful, O One, O Everlasting,
                Voice: *May God be generous to you!*
                Shaykh Tāhā: *May God reward you!*
    "Glory to God, veiled in His Heaven!"

[Audience member lays cigarettes in front of poet.]

                Shaykh Tāhā: *Wish: May you always have plenty!*
                May you always have plenty, we wish you!

"Grant unto me a son, like unto this bird,
    "And may each one he strikes with his sword not [live to]
      smell his supper."   Voice: *My heavens!*
              Voice shouting: *That's Abū Zayd!*

The two of them requested. Then Saʿīda said, "O Lord, grant
    unto me a son like my mistresses,
    "He whose satisfaction is with the Most Generous fears
    nought."

They went home, O Nobles,
          Shaykh Tāhā: *Wish God's blessings on the Prophet!*
              All: *May God Bless and Preserve Him!*
    O how fortunate is he who requests, and the Most Generous
    [grants] its fulfillment.

Said King Sarhān to Rizq the Hero,
    "O Cousin, listen to my words and to their meaning,

110   "Make peace with Sharīfa, Rizq, O Kindest-of-the-Arabs,
        "Honor her for she is of the line of God's Messenger.

      "Honor her, O Rizq, or escort her back to her people
        "For honor is like tilled land, honor is dear, honor is dear,
          and the Arabs know this."   Voices: *Allah! Allah!*

      He made peace with her and escorted her to her pavilion,
        And the Most Generous willed that he be rightly guided, O
          how beautiful!

      And on this night the three became pregnant,   Voice: *Allah!*
        O how fortunate is he who requests, and the Most Generous
          grants its fulfillment.

      Her months passed, Shamma of noble ancestry,
        she gave birth to a son, O Nobles,
        Of rare features, a boy handsome of face, O how beautiful!

                Shaykh Tāhā: *Wish God's blessings on the Prophet!*
                      All: *May God Bless and Preserve Him!*
                        Voice: *May God provide for you!*
                   Shaykh Tāhā: *May God reward you!*
                          Voice: *Listen . . . .*
                   Shaykh Tāhā: *May God bless you!*

      [Tea break]

21. The Epic of the Banī Hilāl

Narrated by 'Awadallah 'Abd al-Jalāl 'Ali

Recorded in 1983 in Gūrna (Qēna Governorate), Egypt, by Susan Slyomovics. Transcribed and translated into English by Susan Slyomovics. This excerpt edited by Susan Slyomovics.

Milād Abū Zēd: The Birth of Abū Zayd

'AWADALLAH 'ABD AL-JALĪL 'ALI IS AN ILLITERATE EPIC POET and singer who recites in Sai'idi Arabic, the dialect of his native Upper Egypt. He was born in the village of Naj' al-Hajis, Aswan Governorate, in southern Egypt, and at the time of this recorded performance on January 23, 1983 (ll. 1-414) and March 5, 1983 (ll. 415 to the end), he gave his age as sixty-three or seventy-three years old. He is the son and grandson of epic singers and he accompanies himself on the large Nubian frame drum (*ṭār*), following the musical tradition of his family. He sings during weddings, circumcisions, Ramadan fast-breaking ceremonies, in local cafes for public audiences, and in private homes for evening command performances. For additional material on the poet, see Susan Slyomovics, *The Merchant of Art: An Egyptian Hilali Oral Epic Poet in Performance* (Berkeley: University of California Press, 1988), and her article "Arabic Folk Literature and Political Expression," *Arab Studies Quarterly* 8:2 (1986), 178-85.

An epic poet characteristically recites isolated tales and episodes either according to audience request or by prior economic arrangement with a patron. 'Awadallah claims he has never performed the birth sequence, because listeners prefer the love stories or the battle sequences. However, even when reciting to a Western ethnographer, he follows performance protocol in opening with a praise-poem (*madīḥ*) and closing by invoking the Prophet Muḥammad. Opening praise-poems occur at ll. 1-14, 81-84, 179-84, and 310-31.

This section is from "The Birth of Abū Zayd," the first part of the traditional tripartite division of the epic. Part one begins the Banī Hilāl cycle with an account of the marriage of Rizq, the Hilāli Bedouin, to Khaḍra Sharīfa, daughter of the Sharīf of Mecca, and the miraculous circumstances surrounding the birth of their baby, the hero Abū Zayd. When the Hilāli Bedouin Arabs discover his black skin color, mother and infant are banished to the desert. There they meet al-Khiḍr (literally, "the Green Man"), called the "Pillar of the Turbaned Ones" (l. 249). In Egyptian and much other Islamic folklore, he is a man who achieved immortality in this life. He is thought to be without a bone in his right thumb, and if this is discovered as one shakes hands with him, one may demand that he grant a wish. Al-Khiḍr protects Abū Zayd from early exile in the wilderness until his first youthful battle against the Koranic schoolteacher (*faqi*). This first part of the cycle ends with Abū Zayd battling his father until the hero is accepted back into the Banī Hilāl tribe. Note how the poet uses the term "tribe" (*qabila*) to evoke the particular ethos and glory of the Bedouin desert peoples.

240

How happy are you who praise the Prophet
Ahmad Muhammad, Who dwells in the city of Yathrib.
I took as my heavenly merit a poem of praise to the
    One with kohl-darkened eyes.
I adore the beauty of the Prophet while praising Him.

5   I adore His beauty, I adore the beauty of the Prophet to
    whom we utter "peace."
O Protector of the oppressed against those who oppress,
I praise a Prophet Ṭāhā;[1] His light is consummate,
Muhammad of the ʿAdnān, clouds came sheltering
    Him.
My next words, my words, about the Prophet of good
    lineage,

10   Ahmad was led by Gabriel on the night of Rajab.
I create and make art about the Arab horsemen,
With my art esteemed only by clever minds,
With my art esteemed only by perfect minds:
The community of our Prophet, the Hashemite, peace
    be upon Him.

15   Said the horseman, Rizq son of Nayil, emir of valiant men:
"I want to wed, O bold ones of Hilāl,
"I want to wed because I am perfect.
"I wish to have a girl or a boy."
Said the horsemen who are the brave Hilāl:

20   "The daughter of S̲h̲arīf Gurḍa, king in his house,
"The daughter of S̲h̲arīf Gurḍa, from perfect people,
"A descendant of our Prophet, the Chosen One, peace be upon
    Him."
The brave horsemen of Hilāl saddled up.
Rizq headed to S̲h̲arīf, to Mecca, made straight for S̲h̲arīf Gurḍa,

25   "I am S̲h̲arīf," and Rizq journeyed to his place.
They were prosperous nobles, fortunate people of times past.
When S̲h̲arīf saw the horsemen descending upon the *diwan*,[2]
He slaughtered for them a plump she-camel for their supper,
He slaughtered for them a she-camel, even honored them more:

30   At S̲h̲arīf's, they attained happiness and their desire.
S̲h̲arīf Gurḍa said: "Welcome, O Arabs,
"What you request, God will provide,
"What you request, we will bring you in excess,
"It will be brought to you, whether near or far."

35   Said Rizq the Hilāli: "I come to you desiring
"Kinship with you, O you the spring pasture for passers-by,
"Kinship with you, O you who give spring pasture to guests,
"And your lineage will increase my honor above the rest."

---

1. Another name for the Prophet Muhammad. 2. Special meeting room where men
share coffee, talk, and listen to oral performances.

So said the Hilāli, Rizq son of Nayil.

40 Sharīf Gurḍa said: "I want four thousand in money,
"Five hundred strong camels and two hundred young she-camels,
"Five hundred choice horses
"And four hundred to carry the loads.
"All these, O clever-minded ones,

45 "All are gifts for the servants and envoys,
"All are gifts for the servants and slaves.
"This as a dowry for Khaḍra Sharīfa—to meet her is a joy:
"A hundred Abyssinian women from the land of Upper Egypt,
"A hundred Mamlukes must come to us here,

50 "These hundred Mamlukes to meet the need
"To serve the emirs who have high rank.
"If, O Hilāli, these lineages are linked,
"Khaḍra's dowry in wealth is a full coffer,
"Khaḍra's dowry in wealth is a coffer of gold

55 "Like the dowry of her mother. Ask the Arab elders.
"If, O Hilāli, your intention is kinship
"On the wedding night, the meal is my duty,
"On the wedding night, by God, dinner is my duty—
"The dowry of Khaḍra, who came from my loins.

60 "If she gives birth to an infant and he grows and matures,
"He will grow to be a brave youth, lionlike, he will vex the enemy,
"He will grow to be a brave youth, of good descent, he will vex valiant men,
"A descendant of our Prophet, peace be upon Him."
Said Rizq the Hilāli, emir of valiant men:

65 "Were you to say something more, God would requite;
"Were you to say something more, I must say to you, it would be my duty."
They brought him the *maʾzūn*[3] and they counted the gold.
She became his wife, from among the women,
The daughter of Sharīf Gurḍa became his wife,

70 Khaḍra Sharīfa, her honor was pure.
They set up for her an elegant royal litter.
From atop a high palace whose heights are decorated,
From atop a high palace spaciously built,
She passed the night telling him: "Your company is a delight, O love."

75 The white chemise was stained with blood,
O night,
The white chemise was drenched with blood.
A descendant of the Prophet, praise be upon Him.

---

3. Official authorized to perform marriages.

Khadra Sharīfa lived there an entire year. She bore and gave
   birth to Shīha, with God's leave.
80   Muhammad let us pray for Him.

[Pause.]

Praise for Tāhā, a poem of praise for the Messenger
To whom his Lord gave happiness and acceptance of
   prayers.
One who praises Ahmad, my Beloved, the Prophet, I
   start to tell,
My art esteemed by clever minds.
85   Khadra gave birth, she gave birth to Shīha,
May happiness increase!
She remained with Rizq the Hilāli in harmony,
But she spent eleven years
Barren. This is the destiny intended by God.
90   Barren—this is the destiny intended by my generous Lord—
Imposing His judgment, light or heavy.
They requested horses for Rizq and Hilāli, the prince
To meet with the princes, horsemen and warriors
To meet with the horsemen of the Banī Hilāl.
95   Their children came out
      [The Arabs were seated in the *diwan*.]
Happy and prosperous. Their sons delighted him,
Their sons upon the cushions playing
Like leopards in the vast desert,
Like lions in the vast plains.
100   Their fathers' happiness and delight grew greater.
Rizq and Hilāli eyed them and his wound increased.
Inside his tent tears poured again.
Inside the tent tears poured again.
He cried, wet his cheeks and his handkerchief.
105   Khadra Sharīfa left, her tears a canal.
Beautiful as she was, she loved him to the point of death,
Beautiful as she was, by God, unique,
She cried and felt hardship each night he was absent:
"Tell me, what is the reason for laments, O love,
110   "O Rizq, you cry, why, why?
"What good has weeping done you?
"O Rizq, O you so dignified, why do you cry?
"The tears upon your cheek are flowing swiftly."
He said to her, "O Khadra I beheld during the day
115   "There is no warrior, knight, nor courageous horseman who has
      not his son to play with him—
"No knight, nor horseman who has not his son beside him on
   the cushions.

"I looked, I found myself among them, worthless."
"Khadra Sharīfa's tears fell like hissing droplets.
"Rizq son of Nayil's turmoil was so great, this answer softened
    her,
120   "Rizq, son of Nayil's turmoil was so great, he gave this answer.
"Khadra had had reason in her head, but reason departed.
"Then came Shamma, a maiden of noble descent and lofty
    lineage.
"She gathered her robes, with cheeks resembling roses touched
    by dew,
"With cheeks resembling roses but touched by dew,
125   "She entered and found Khadra weeping, tormented.
"She said, O Sharīfa why are you like this?
"You have lost nothing, my cousin, and none has gone astray.
"You lost nothing from the exalted homeland.
"O Khadra, why do you weep, why do you have tears
    flowing?"
130   Khadra said to her, "O Shamma, I have a problem,
"It rends the core of my heart and my womb aches,
"It rends the core of my heart and the tears are flowing—
"I, if I complain, I, if I complain, O the nights!
"If I complain to the mountain so that it bends,
135   "If I complain to the river so that its waters stop,
"Saddened for my sake, and my tears a riverbed,
"My tears pour down upon the bed, O Shamma, they wet my
    cheeks."
"O my cousin, O Khadra, your Lord feels compassion and He
    will bestow.
"Whoever abandons something lives without it,
140   "Whoever seeks something of God, he will obtain.
"My Lord is to be trusted to grant bountifully."

> *He is to be trusted with what? With the*
> *granting of supplication. When one says,*
> *"O lord" he is entrusting Him with ample*
> *supplication, that is the one who invokes*
> *Him, may He be praised and exalted.*

She said to her: "O Khadra, arise and cast aside burdens!
"Tomorrow we go to this river, we will see its clarity,
"Tomorrow we go to the crossing, O coquettish woman,
145   "We will show you waters that are limpid."
She gathered ninety maidens from the daughters of Hilāl
They walked alongside Khadra like sentinels,
They walked alongside Khadra until they reached the rivers;
They found translucent water surrounded by birds.
150   But among them was a bird, black and disturbing.
He scattered all the kinds of birds, and cleared them away,
He scattered all the birds and kept them dispersed,

He was black, and in his coloring were all the qualities.
Shamma says:

155 "Supplicate, O maidens, the Lord provides for His worshippers
though they have no eyes to see.
"He provides for his worshippers though they have no eyes to
see Him,
"The Lord provides for His worshippers from the beginning of
the world.
"He knows the drops of dew and the walk of ants."
Khadra says: "Give me a lad like this bird,
160 "Black like this bird!
"I swear to make him possess Tunis and Wadi Hama,
"I swear to make him possess Tunis by the blade of the sword."
From this they say she bore a lad
To Rizq and Hilāli fulfilling God's favor.
165   O You who cured Job,
     O You who cured Job, he recovered from his affliction,
     O You who cured Job, he recovered from affliction,
     O You who opened Jacob's eyes from blindness,
     O You who raised Enoch to the highest heaven,
170   O You who called to our Lord Moses, O my God,
     When Pharaoh came and his army was with him,
     When Pharaoh came and his army was cut down.
     Moses lay his staff upon the ocean and it parted.
     My generous Lord, You have neither associate nor son,
          there is only You, O Knower of the waters' course,
175   There is only You, O my Lord, who knows what is in
          the wilderness.
     You subdue the wind, the clouds, and the rain.
     I beseech Thee, O light, O radiantly beautiful.
     I adore the beauty of the Prophet, let us Praise Him.

[Pause.]

How happy are you who praise the Messenger,
180 Whose God gave Him joy and granted supplications,
A praise-poem for Husayn's beauty, I begin to say.
I praise the Hashemite,
I adore His beauty to whom we utter "peace,"
O Protector of the oppressed against those who oppress.
185 Supplicate, O daughters and servants of the Hilāli Arabs!
Khadra Sharīfa—her reason failed, lost—
Khadra Sharīfa stopped bearing, but weak with desire
She came to the royal bed yearning.
Rizq son of Nayil came to her after the evening prayer.
190 Khadra wore silk brocade, she sat with him.
She wore brocade of silk, her best clothing.

Rizq asked for union with her.
She was happy! And the Lord of the Throne sent her
An infant who vexes the enemy!
195   She bore an infant who vexes valiant men!
Khaḍra passed the full nine months.
They approached the Emir Abū Zayd, emir of valiant men,
They found the Emir Abū Zayd was blue-black, not resembling
    his father,
They found the hero, Abū Zayd the Hilāli, the color of a black
    slave.
200   They found the boy coal black, a strange color,
Black, as if from distant Upper Egypt.
Prince Sirḥān said: "God's decrees are obdurate,
"With God's mercy who shields sinners,
"With God's mercy who shields the guilty,
205   "His mother and father are both fair, whom does he take after?"
It was an insult, so the Arabs convened.
"O, the wrong of Khaḍra, she loves a cloak-bearing slave,
"O, the wrong of Khaḍra, she seduced a purchased slave."
They said "Sharīfa is from the best lineage."
210   When he heard these words, Rizq was overcome.
Azgal said to his people: "Listen, O tolerant ones,"
Azgal said to his people: "Listen, O valiant men,
"The killing and death of a son of adultery is lawful,
"No good is expected from an infant who does not take after his
    father,
215   "No good is expected from an infant born in adultery!
"Divorce Khaḍra, O Rizq, so that you can obtain your desire.
"Divorce Khaḍra, O Hilāli, during this year.
"I will give you a Zughba woman—much is said about her.
"I will give you a Zughba woman, a pleasing one,
220   "She has necklaces of silver and bracelets of gold."
When Rizq the Hilāli heard these words he was overcome.
He swore an oath and a vow. In anguish he said:
"I will not receive Khaḍra again nor do I want the child."
The Hilāli Arabs pleaded with Rizq,
225   They pleaded with Rizq but he did not consent.
They pleaded with Rizq but he refused to consent.
Their bold men cursed him but they returned in vain.
Then came Shīha moving slowly.
To her father, Rizq, she said these words:
230   "My mother Sharīfa is from the Prophet's lineage.
"O Rizq, you mistreat Khaḍra, whose sin is unseen.
"O Rizq, O father, you mistreat Khaḍra, who has not sinned.
"My mother Sharīfa does not know the paths to tread.
"Graciously grant Khaḍra a single companion,
235   "Graciously grant Khaḍra, by God's truth,

"Graciously grant Khadra, by His truth, the One, the Unique—
"He who is my Lord knows the true state of the boy."
When he heard these words, patience came to Rizq;
When he heard these words, he called out: "O Najāh,
240 "Listen to my words, for my thoughts are sound:
"Take the lance and the sword and depart for the vast plain,
"Cast the lance across my wealth, and your eyes will see,
"Cast it across my wealth, may your will be strong.
"Rely upon God, generous and adept,
245 "Wherever the lance falls from afar
"Give to Khadra, O slave, as charity—
"Lest my son among Arabs be shamed."
Najāh took the lance. While he rode
The pillar of turbaned ones[4] hovered and came to him.
250 The pillar of turbaned ones said to him, "Where do you go?
"I will plead for your sake, O slave."
Khidr took the lance from Najāh as he cast—
Half the wealth of Sirhān, his wealth divided equally—
He took half of Sirhan's wealth, O listeners.
255 Praise Tāhā we have a guarantor!
He said to him: "O prince of the Arabs, in the name of the
       Prophet, the Guarantor,
"He took your wealth and half of Sirhan's to be divided
       equally,
"Half of Sirhan's wealth though not demanded."
Then came the Arabs:
260 "Find us a guardian engaged for hire
"Find us a guardian from the land of Hejaz
"He will take Khadra's clothes and even her trousseau
"From here to accompany her to the land of Hejaz
"For the sake of her father whose domain we have entered,
265 "For the sake of her father whose generosity is vast."
They summoned the judge, his name is Manī.
When he heard these words, he came to them obediently.
They said, "Here are the ones behind whom people pray,
"Here are the ones wanting an *imām*."[5]
270 They said, "We are with him, we will not oppose his words."
They awoke in the morning, they spread out the wide tent.
Khadra approached the judge and kissed his hands,
She approached the judge and said, "I am Sharīfa.
"I cannot descend to my father for this whole year,
275 "If I told him Rizq the Hilāli has abused us.
"I cannot say these words while I am in Rizq's custody,
"I cannot say these words nor speak of it,

---

4. Khidr, a man who achieved immortality in this life and grants wishes to those who discover his identity. 5. Religious leader and judge.

"Were Rizq to concede generously that I am still his wife."
"Then find me a guardian, I will go to his side.
280   "Let me raise the prince Abū Zayd in his custody.
"Find us a good man, I will raise the prince Abū Zayd with
    him.
"Let me raise Abū Zayd while he is young.
"O how fate rules over many people!
"He who has ordered our separation from each other, O prince,
285   "May he be destitute among the Arabs and his women led
    astray,
"May he be dropped from the bold ones and may he have
    children
"Who are assaulted by the vanguard Hilāl."
The judge struck his palms and said,
He said, "The land is Zahlān and I am their great enemy."
290   He said, "The land is Zahlān, I cannot pass through.
"Even if a thousand were with me they must die."
The judge accompanied them, they returned silently.
Then the Atwān Arabs came upon Khadra brandishing spears.
He said: "Attack the tent and bring it down."
295   Khadra Sharīfa emerged veiled:
"Shame on the horsemen who dishonor women,
"Shame on the horsemen who dishonor ladies.
"This deed is evil, only the wicked do it.
"Whoever is pure and his body sound,
300   "He never does hateful things,
"He never does hateful things throughout eternity.
"Whoever traverses the region travels in safety.
"I considered you a tribe with leaders of good lineage.
"You turned out to be Atwān Arabs, vile and worthless,
305   "You turned out to be Atwān Arabs, vile and greedy,
"The most cowardly of the region, you do not honor a guest!
"I beseech Thee, O Knower of languages and wild beasts,
"O Provider of the birds in the vast desert."
    Muhammad let us praise Him.

[Pause.]

310   God is noble, His coffers full. After my words about His Beauty
I begin and make art about the Hilāli Arabs,
I turn my words to the hero Abū Zayd,
His turban tilted, his side fringe aslant,
Defender of the Zughba and the Dirayd
315   And of the horsemen of Najd Hilāl.
From his birth, a child of strength,
Abū Zayd, Abū Zayd, a courageous man,
Lacking brothers and siblings,

With his sword he vexes enemies.
320 From his birth the prince is blessed,
In the fray he thrashes his rivals,
And he enters his wars eagerly,
The battlefield, his feastday.
From his birth he descends to the fray
325 In the vanguard with a mighty armspan,
When horses clash together
He opens the gates to misfortune.
O the nights, O the night!

[The poet repeats ll. 297 to 308.]

Abū Zayd grew up a horseman riding steeds,
He seizes fools with iron hands,
He reaches his goal against his greatest enemies,
345 He reaches his goal with noble people,
I swear by the life of our beloved Prophet, the Imam of the
Sacred Precincts.
When he heard about Abū Zayd, Daghīr became angry.
He said to his tribe: "Hear me, O listeners,"
He said to the Atwān Arabs, "Hear me, O valiant men,
350 "Let us plunder her horses and even the camels.
"Do not leave with the woman or child.
"I will abandon her alone in the wild,
"I will abandon her alone in the vast desert,
"O how she will suffer humiliation and disgrace!"
355 Then there came a lion, invisible, peace be upon Him,
Khiḍr, Khiḍr, may God be pleased with Him.
Then came a lion, invisible, from the open country,
Walking, quickening his steps,
Walking, quickening, he went to her.
360 He found Sharīfa weeping; beside her, her son.
The bold Khiḍr dispersed and beat the Atwān Arabs with
swords.
He knew their schemes with the aid of God the One,
He knew their schemes with the aid of God the One, the
Unique,
He turned to Khaḍra and said, "Bring me the boy."
365 She gave him the hero, Abū Zayd,
She gave him the Hilāli, Abū Zayd,
But the strength to endure did not come to her.
"Name him *Barakat*,[6] my secrets will be his;
"Though I become annoyed with him, I will be of use to him."

---

6. "Blessed."

370   The Pillar of Turbaned Ones, peace be upon Him, from that
        time armed him.
    Khaḍra Sharīfa peered about, she beheld Khiḍr not.
    Khaḍra Sharīfa peered about, she did not see him—
    She stared with her eyes, but she could not see him.
    Then came Prince Zahlān. He saw an army;
375   He identified a green pavilion and around it banners,
    He identified a green pavilion and around it tents.
    They were not Arabs of his tribe and not northerners.
    "I will send four horsemen to her, to the mother of the lad."
    She said, "I am a guest of the king, under his protection."
380   She said, "A guest, O slaves, go bring him the news.
    "Tell him guests have arrived, O generous countenance."
    The slaves went to him right away. They told him the news.
    He came to her and said, "Arise." She entered his tent.
    He came to her and said, "Arise, you enter safety,
385   "Raise Abū Zayd in happiness and perfection."
    They remained among the Zahlān a long time.
    The hero Abū Zayd grew and God made him robust.
    The hero Abū Zayd grew up and was brought to a *faqi.*[7]
    He was clever in writing and in prayers devout.
390   He was advanced in writing before he could read.
    He was advanced in writing, he had the best answer,
    People of the Koran, because he was upright.
    There were other young lads among the Zahlān.
    From the day they went to Koran school they were together.
395   From the day they went to Koran school together, they were
        with each other.
    Then came the Emir Abū Zayd. The teacher intended to harm
        him.
    The teacher began and said to the lads:
    "Hold him down, I will give him thirty blows,
    "Hold him down, I will give it to this naughty Abū Zayd."
400   They all encircled him, even the teacher.
    Abū Zayd fled from them, no one beheld him.
    Abū Zayd fled from them, O listeners,
    He ransacked the corners of the house, left and right,
    When suddenly he found a spear many years old.
405   It weighed eighty pounds. Abū Zayd held it level in his hand.
    It weighed eighty pounds, including its spear-point.
    The Emir Abū Zayd carried it in the palm of his hand.
    Then came Khaḍra and kissed him:
    "You distract me, my son, from private sorrows."
410   She said, "You distract me from lasting passions."
    He said to her: "I will not retreat until I kill the teacher."

---

7. Koranic school teacher.

She said: "That would be villainous."
While they were talking, the teacher arrived.
   Muḥammad let us praise Him.

[Pause.]

415   While they were talking, the teacher came intending to betray
      him.
    Abū Zayd brought him a meal that they gave him to eat.
    The teacher behaved shamefully, his sin his punishment,
    The teacher behaved shamefully, and his sin overcame him.
    Abū Zayd went to him, to the Koranic school, as earlier
      ordained.
420   The teacher said to Abū Zayd, "O ill-mannered slave."
    The teacher tried to seize Abū Zayd. Abū Zayd hit him with a
      spear, he threw him down.
    The teacher tried to seize Abū Zayd. Abū Zayd hit him with
      the spear, he was thrown,
    His breath left him, and blood flowed.
    Then came the teacher's brother Ruyan and wrapped him in
      cloth.
425   He went to Zahlān, he requested rescue.
    He went to Zahlān, he said: "O emir,
    "Abū Zayd killed the teacher, the Shaykh."
    The emir said: "But he is a small child!
    "Go now, attend to the school, for your memory is great."
430   Abū Zayd's knowledge was perfected by God, his Lord,
    And his knowledge was perfected out of piety.
    Abū Zayd became the schoolteacher, and the brother, a
      monitor.
    If a child entered school late, he called to God,
    Fearing the hero Abū Zayd would cut short his life.
435   Muḥammad let us praise Him.

[Abū Zayd kills Daghīr, leader of the Atwān Arabs who tried to humil-
iate Khadra Sharīfa when she was banished to the desert. The defeated
Atwān Arabs join forces with an Arab prince, Emir Jayel, and his tribe
to attack the Zahlān, the protectors of Abū Zayd and his mother. Emir
Jayel is invincible, because he possesses a magic necklace capable of
summoning a fighting genie. Abū Zayd flees, but when assured of divine protection by Khidr, who captures the genie, he returns and defeats his enemies. Abū Zayd and the Zahlān tribe depart for the Hilāli
Arabs. There Abū Zayd provokes a fight with the Hilāli leaders who
call upon their strongest warrior, Rizq, who battles Abū Zayd while his
mother, Khadra Sharīfa, rejoices. It is only at the intervention of Shīḥa
(Rizq and Khadra Sharīfa's daughter, Abū Zayd's sister) that Abū
Zayd's identity is revealed. The family and tribe are reunited.]

PART THREE

CENTRAL AFRICA

Central African Epics

QUESTIONS OF PERFORMANCE STYLE AND HISTORICAL REFERENCE may serve to distinguish Central African epic traditions from those of West Africa. History is essentially absent from the stories of Jéki, Mwindo, Kahindo, and the Mvet tradition of the Cameroon-Gabon region, except insofar as the epics reflect and preserve images of the past embedded in their social descriptions and narrative construction. Instead, we find cycles of stories centered on a given figure such as Jéki, or others not represented in this anthology, such as Lianja and Ozidi; in the case of the *mvet* tradition, an entire fictive world lies at the performer's disposal.

Performances are more visibly associated with ritual than in the Sahelian traditions, although the occasions remain overwhelmingly secular. Performers are often initiates in spirit cults, and their art is the product of apprenticeship rather than genealogy and birth to a status group as with the *jeli* of the Mande (although some Sahelian performers do claim a relation with the spirit world and one should not belittle the importance of training in the Sahel). A performance is in some sense the occasion of spirit possession, and certainly a focus of occult energy; descriptions of apprenticeship and training always include mention of the magical preparation of the performer. Women may also perform, although there is little documentation available of their performances and training, if different from that of the men.

More significant, however, are the performative differences between the two areas. In this region, epic performance becomes in a sense a group effort: the lead performer is accompanied by a team of musicians and singers (the backup chorus). Performances take place not in the private space of a courtyard but in open and public spaces; the performer him- or herself is not stationary and impassive but is passionately and dramatically involved in the reenactment of the story. The audience will participate in the songs and dances which punctuate the narrative. All these features combine to provide grounds for a general regional distinction in performance traditions between the Sahel and central Africa, although one must note that the distinction is not rigid; one may find counter examples in each region. The division reflects a sense of the prevailing performance mode for the region.

The various groups represented in the following selections may be classified as belonging to the Bantu language family, that broad label which covers the southern third of the continent; they are concentrated in the upper tier of that region (Cameroon, Gabon, northeastern Zaire), in the dense equatorial forests. The economic activities described center on hunting and fishing, although there is some mention of agriculture. The political traditions of the groups do not include states and great kingdoms, although on the local level there is a clear hierarchy of authority derived most probably from patterns of migration in which the first settlers in a region subsequently become the chiefs.

Exposure to the outside world varies considerably among the groups. The Douala of Cameroon (*Jéki la Njambè*) have been trading

middlemen for centuries. The baNyanga of Zaire have been relatively isolated, having migrated southwest from the region of Uganda into their present territory.

22. The Epic of Mvet Moneblum, or The Blue Man
Narrated by Daniel Osomo

*Recorded in 1967 in Yaoundé, Cameroon, on the occasion of the inaugura-
tion of the Faculté de lettres of the University of Yaoundé. Transcribed by
Arthur Sibita. French translation by Samuel Martin Eno-Belinga. First
published as S. M. Eno-Belinga, Mvet Moneblum (n.p.), Yaoundé, 1978.
This excerpt translated and edited by Stephen Belcher.*

Mvet is the term used in Central Africa, among the Fang and Bulu populations of Cameroon and Gabon, for a narrative performance style and
for the instrument which accompanies it. Performances by the *Mbom-
mvet* are public and highly animated, incorporating songs and dances
in which the audience may participate. The subject matter of the *mvet* is
not historical but imaginary or mythical: the world evoked is one of the
distant past in which the mortal men of the clan of Oku struggle with
the immortals of Engong who are ruled by the great man of power,
Akoma Mba. Stories typically develop a conflict, a complex intrigue of
mobile and airborne characters, and finally a resolution through the
decisive intervention of Akoma Mba. The knowledge required of the
performer is one of geography and genealogy, necessary for a proper
description of clan relations, but there is little evidence for standard
story lines. The performer is free to shape his or her story in this mythical landscape as he or she wills, and the results are highly creative.

The modern nation of Cameroon is a highly diverse one, prid-
ing itself on representing Africa in microcosm. Before World War I, it
became a German colony; after the war, it was divided between the
French and the British. The forced labor on the road, to which the hero
is subjected, echoes the colonial experience. The expressions of magic
and power the various warriors exhibit may also recall external mecha-
nisms. The family conflict between a son and a father over the question
of a wife is an ordinary sort of domestic tension. Fathers are expected to
provide the bride-price for a son, but they need not be eager to incur
the sometimes heavy expense.

Canto 1

  This is what happened.
  The man, Ondo Mba, had a son.
  He named him Mekui-Mengômo-Ondo.
  As soon as Mekui-Mengômo-Ondo was old enough to marry,
5 He asked his father, "When shall I marry?"
  His father answered him, "A son of Ekañ never asks his father
    when he will marry."
  His father swore an oath. "May I disappear and meet the dead
    while I mourn Ngema!
  "If you dare to ask me such a question again,
  "I will cut off your head,
10 "Or I will banish you."

Canto 2

That is why his son stayed sitting for two days,
Until again he came to ask his father, "When will you get me
married?"
To! His father growled,
And a violent storm shook the sky nine times.
15   The courtyard was plunged into thick darkness.
And there, Ondo himself took his horn and blew it, *ko-o-o!*
The sky once again became as clear as a new dawn.
Now we sing and dance!
Let us sing of the deeds and exploits of the Ekañ. Hey!
20   I have come to hear you. The ears are listening.
In truth, they are listening!

Canto 3

Then his father dressed his lower half.
He dressed his upper half.
He put on his iron armor.
25   He put on the shoes which speak of war.
He took his iron helmet, and *to!* placed it on his head.
Then he seized the great sword named *Abe-Nleme-Otyeñ.*[1]
He fixed in the earth his finger which speaks of war.
30   He rose into the clouds, and the sound of his passage was
duk-duk-duk!
He came to the home of Akoma Mba.
To! He lay face down before Akoma Mba.
He told him, "By the tomb and all the dead, while we mourn
Ngema-Ekañ!
"I beg you to take captive the child named Mekui-Mengômo-
Ondo.
35   "Cut off his head, or send him into exile."

[Akoma Mba sends Abe-Mam-Ondo to fetch Mekui-Mengômo-Ondo. At
first Mekui-Mengômo-Ondo resists; there is fighting until his mother
intervenes and tells him to find out what Akoma Mba wants of him.
After Mekui-Mengômo-Ondo arrives, his father Ondo Mba asks Akoma
Mba to exile the son, and Akoma Mba summons the great men of the
clan for a council.]

Canto 7

In the morning,
Everyone came together: young and old, women and children.
They gathered before Akoma Mba at Fen.
Akoma said to Ondo Mba, "Now all the people of Ekañ are
gathered here.

---

1. "Sword-of-the-cruel-heart."

40 "You have asked me to exile Mekui-Mengômo-Ondo.

"Tell the people of Ekañ on what grounds you have asked for
 his exile."

Ondo answered, "Since the time when our ancestors of the Ekañ
 left, one after the other, the following lands,

"The ancient lands of Anyu-Ngom, of Biba, of Mfulu-Amvam,
 of Bivele-Vele,

"Of Ewa-Mekon, of Ebap-Yop, of Ekutu Mintum, of Aya-
 Minken . . . .

45 "Have we ever heard of a son asking his father when he would
 marry?

"That is why I say you are no man," he said to his son.

"A man would never ask his father, 'When shall I marry?'

"That is why I am banishing Mekui-Mengômo-Ondo,

"So that no longer will he resemble a woman here among us in
 Engoñ-Zok."

50 A heavy silence sat over the assembled Ekañ-Mebe'e.

Canto 8

Kpwo! Medañ lay face down before Akoma
And told him, "I have something to say.
"I address this request to Akoma.
"Let Ondo entrust Mekui-Mengômô to me, and I shall get him
 married,

55 "For Ondo seems to me a poor man."

Ondo answered, "That is out of the question!

"No other man shall arrange the marriage of my son."

Kpwo! Meye-Mengini in turn lay face down.

He said, "It shall not be Medañ.

60 "I shall be the one to marry him off, oh Akoma!"

Ondo answered, "I am not of that opinion."

Kpwo! Ebi-Zok, the son of Mba-Ndeme-Eyen, lay face down.

Otuna Mba!

He said, "Neither the one nor the other.

65 "I shall be the one to marry him off."

Ondo answered, "No one in Engoñ-Zok has the right to marry
 off my son."

Then all the Great Men of Engoñ-Zok became angry.

They told Akoma, "Exile Mekui-Mengômo-Ondo."

    Here we sing and dance!

70   Let us sing of the deeds and exploits of the Ekañ, ehee!

    He took pity on me! Ehee!

    And we hear on the other side of the mountain,

     My ears carry far, ooo!

    O, Mba! What a marvelous story!

     My ears carry far, ooo!

> A matter without equal, a matter of great interest,
> > My ears carry far, ooo!
> Do you hear me, people of Abaña? Ehee!
> > Ehee! Ehee!
> Ehee! Aya! The fine man!
> > Ah, the white lover has crossed Ayina!
> The lover has crossed Nkomo!
> Ahaye! It is true that Akoma will win again!
> Silence!

[Akoma Mba wonders to which land he will exile Mekui-Mengômo-Ondo, and he sends for Nnômô-Ngañ the diviner to seek out the answer.]

Canto 9
85 Nnômô-Ngañ placed his healer's bag on the ground.
He plunged his hand into the bag,
He withdrew a mirror and placed it on the ground.
He withdrew a horn and a leather cushion.
He took his magic eyeglasses and put them to his eyes.
90 He seized the horn and blew it, *ko-o-o!*
He spoke, he said, "I ask the spirits of the people of Ekañ,
"Of Ngema-Ekañ, of Oyono-Ekan, of Mintya-Ekan,
"I ask you,
"Are you willing to send Mekui Mengômo into exile over a
    question of marriage?
95 "Let your desires and your consent be known!"
His divining tools flamed up.
The oracle had said yes.

Canto 10
Nnômô-Ngañ said, "How shall I know into which land to exile
    him?"
He looked in his mirror,
100 He saw a road leading out of Engoñ-Zok.
The road ended at a great river.
The river split into three other rivers . . .
His gaze crossed the forest . . . and another forest. . . .
He saw a road which led to the land of Yeminsiñ.
105 The queen of that land is named Ntye-Ngon-Oye-Ndon.
She has a mysterious power
Which she uses to gain wives for her brother.
This is how her magic works:
She owns many, many pigs.
110 The pigs are neutered.
Any time she desires to get wives for her brother,
She first sends the pigs to the village she will visit

So they will eat all the foods of the village.
When they have finished eating the village's crops, they invade the village.
115   They go into the houses.
They eat the food in the kitchens,
They take the pots from the fire.
That is when all the villagers throw themselves on the pigs to kill them,
All the men and women.
120   When Ntye-Ngono knows that they are all gathered, then she sounds her horn.
Immediately, everyone is caught within an iron fence.
Ntye-Ngono appears in the middle of them.
She has a magic jewel on her breast,
And as though by magic, any man who moments before might have boasted he could marry five women, grows breasts on his chest, and on his head he has women's hair.
125   She tells her brother, "You may marry them all. There are no longer any men among them; the men have all become like women."
That is when Nnômô-Ngañ asked, "Could Ntye-Ngono keep Mekui-Mengômo in exile?"
He blew his horn, *ko-o-o!*
The shades remained silent, the oracle did not approve.

Canto 11

He stopped looking in that direction.
130   He saw a trail.
The trail led to Mvele-Mekomo, son of Mekomo-Obama, himself a descendant of the Yemiñyon.
He had announced that no longer would he tolerate meeting a smoker of tobacco, on the road or around himself,
Because tobacco disturbs the order of the world.
Any smoker he met immediately lost his head.
135   He hated tobacco for this reason.
In old times,
Only adults over thirty had the right to smoke.
But now, today,
Children of ten can smoke.
140   Women smoke.
They smoke tobacco wrapped in a leaf.
They smoke it in short-stemmed pipes.
They smoke it in ceremonial long-stemmed pipes.
People treasure tobacco.
145   Even toothless gums will chew tobacco.
Tobacco is always the medicine used for a purge.

That is why he had said to himself, "If that's the way it is,
    tobacco must disappear."
He came to limit the way in which the Ekañ consumed their
    tobacco, for there had been shocking excesses.
His encounter with the Ekañ is worth a mvet to itself alone.
150 Nnômô-Ngañ asked, "Could Mevele-Mekomo keep Mekui-
        Mengômo in prison?"
He blew his horn, *ko-o-o!*
The shades remained mute.

Canto 12

His gaze followed another path
Which led to Angono-Zok-Obama-Ndon, son of the Yemeñyiñ.
155 This was a man who had said that so long as he was alive,
He could not accept that anyone else bear the same name as he.
But he learned that another man answered to that name, a son
    of the Ekañ-Mebe'e.
He called him to a meeting at a place known as Mefan-Mevin:
"We will learn," he said, "which of us deserves to bear the
    name of Angono,
160 "And let no one else interfere in this business.
"When you come to meet me, bring also your wife Nda-
    Mengono.
"Then we shall learn which of us two deserves to be the hus-
    band of Nda-Mengono."
Only the mvet is worthy to tell what happened between the
    two men in the forest.
Then Nnômô-Ngañ asked, "Could Angono-Zok-Obama-Ndon
    hold
165 "Mekui-Mengômo-Ondo in exile?"
He blew his horn, *ko-o-o!* The shades remained silent.

[He continues to look down paths and through forests. The spirits continue to refuse the places.]

Canto 23

He looked to another side
And followed the third path
Which leads into the forest of the Yemenjañ.
170 If you go through that forest,
You come to Enye'e-Minsili, home of Ekañ-Dume-Mve, son of
    the Blue Men.
Looking to the other side of the mountain,
You see a village high up named Bengobo,
Home of Efeñ-Ndoñ, the Blue Man.
175 Then Nnômô-Ngañ asked, "Might I send Mekui-Mengômo-
    Ondo in exile to the land of the Blue Men?"

He questioned the spirits: *so-o-o!* The oracle approved.
Then Nnômô-Ngañ told Akoma,
"Send Mekui-Mengômo in exile to the land of the Blue Men, to
the house of Efeñ-Ndôñ."

[Mekui-Mengômo-Ondo and his escort travel to the land of the Blue
Men. They stop in several villages along the way, where the escort displays a ravenous appetite and wakes everyone up in the middle of the
night.]

Canto 30
180   Our young men were sleeping soundly when, in the middle of
           the night,
       Kpwañ-Ondo took his horn and blew, *ko-o-o!*
       Immediately, the animals that announce the morning greeted
           the new dawn.
       From the other side of the mountain, the master heard the first
           morning activities.
       First came the long call of the *daman*,[2] who said,
185   I went up, o!
               I came down, o!
               I went up, o!
               I came down, o!
       That was the *daman's* greeting the first glimmers of the dawn.
190   There was another call:
               I come, I move with little steps, here I am!
       That was the owl greeting the first glimmers of the dawn.
       There was another call:
               Tyorooot! bañ! bañ! bañ!
195   That was the bat greeting the first glimmers of the dawn.
       And there was another call: *Aïe! aïe! aïe!*
       Where did this call come from?
       It was the toucan, suffering from a violent toothache because he
           had eaten some *engo*.[3] He flew off to the mountaintop to be
           treated by the healer.
       His brother followed him, holding a bag of coins which he
           wasted in gambling.
200   As he pulled out the coins, one could hear him:
               Nep! Nep! Nep!
       That was the toucan greeting the first glimmers of the dawn in
           his way.
       One could hear another call:
               Vovolivo mewo! Was!
205   Those were the parrots, passing through the clouds, greeting
           the light of day.

---

2. A bird. 3. A tree.

One could hear another call:
> O, death! O, death!
> I am good hearted.
> Is that why I must eat raw mice?

210   The elegant white cat was greeting the dawn in her way.
One could hear another call:
> *Kpwraa! Ma'a!*
> Move on!

The ram was bleating while joined with the ewe in the early
    morning.
215   One could hear another call:
> *Ko! Ko! Ko!*
> See how he goes!
> O-o-o!

The rooster was greeting the dawn.
220   And one could hear also:
> *We, we, we,*
> We are together!

While the mother called:
> Hurry up, hurry up, hurry up!
225   The hen was calling her chicks while greeting the start of the
    day.

[The men continue on their way through other villages.]

Canto 32
    There is a meeting place of three roads.
    The first road leads to Akok, home of Tolo-Obama-Ngema,
    The man with a single eye set into his armpit;
    His face is blind and you see in it only the ears, the mouth, and
        the nose.
230   The second road leads to the land of the man named Nkum-
        Etye-Ndon, of the tribe of the Yemenjañ.
    The third road leads to the land of the Blue Men, to the land of
        the man named Ekañ-Dumu-Mve, of the people of the Blue
        Men and of Efeñ-Ndôñ.
    That was the land to which they were leading Mekui-
        Mengômo-Ondo for his exile.
    In those days, the masters would spend the night in Ngon-
        Esele-Mendim.
235   When morning came,
    They left Ngon-Esele-Mendim,
    And headed for the forest of the Yemenjañ.
    They stopped in the land called Nne-Zam, home of Ondo-Nkoo-
        Ela.
    Before them, they saw a country splendidly shining! The earth
        was blue, blue.

240   The dwellings were blue.
       To! They stopped at the threshold of the men's hut.
       They took out the writing they had brought from Engoñ-Zok,
          from Akoma Mba.
       They presented it to the man named Ekan-Dumu-Mve.
       When Ekan-Dumu-Mve saw what was in the message,
245   He returned the writing to Kpwañ-Ondo and said that he was
          not Efeñ-Ndôñ.
       "Go to that wide land you see over there, up on that mountain.
       "When you reach it, go to the foot of the iron tower,
       "So that the man named Efeñ-Ndôñ can see you through the
          clouds, from the sky lands where he lives.
       "And then he will send a vehicle to fetch you," he said.
250   The young men replaced the writing in the bag.
       Kpwo! They rose above the ground.
       Up there in the clouds, they made a noise like thunder.
       Inside his house, Efeñ-Ndôñ turned his ear.
       He asked, "What is making the air mass move that way?"
255   Efeñ-Ndôñ was on the threshold of his lofty home.
       He saw the young men spinning in the clouds.
       Suddenly, they stopped at the foot of the iron tower.
       "This is the place we were told of," they said.
       As soon as Efeñ-Ndôñ looked through his glasses,
260   He saw our three young men there at the bottom of the iron
          tower.
       The master took the cushion which sows the storm, and a great
          wind shook the sky.
       The wind came from the top of the sky.
       The great wind blew to the place where our young men were
          standing.
       All at once, *mek!* the wind carried them into the air.
265   And *To!* They found themselves at the threshold of the heaven-
          ly home of Efeñ-Ndôñ.
       Kpwo! Kpwo! Our young men lay face down before Efeñ-Ndôñ.
       Kpwan-Ondo took out the writing and handed it to the man
          they call Efeñ-Ndôñ.
       Efeñ-Ndôñ took the big paper and he read.
       Efeñ-Ndôñ then asked, "Which among you is named Mekui-
          Mengômo-Ondo?"
270   *Kpwo!* Mekui-Mengômo-Ondo himself lay face down and he
          said, "I am the one named Mekui-Mengômo-Ondo."
       He added, "And these two men are Kpwan-Ondo, son of the
          daughter of the Yemingel, and Njik-Zok-Ekum-Nge."

[Mekui-Mengômo-Ondo is sent to prison. The next day, Efeñ-Ndôñ
summons him to impose tasks upon him.]

Canto 33

> . . . Efeñ-Ndôñ told him, "I am not the one who put you in prison.
>
> "Akoma is the one who exiles you.
>
> "And so now I will show you the jobs you must do.

275
> "I will make you build roads,
>
> "And all the prisoners you find in the prison will work with you.
>
> "The first road you built will go from here to the land of the man named Nna-Beyeme.
>
> "When that road is built, you shall start building a second road leading to the man named Evo-Menumu.
>
> "When those roads are built, I will give you other jobs."

280
> Mekui-Mengômo asked, "How many prisoners are there in the prison?"
>
> Efeñ-Ndôñ answered, "I have three hundred prisoners."
>
> He said, "Listen. I will work with the prisoners,
>
> "But I don't want to see a single soldier watching over them. I will be with them myself.
>
> "Also, I ask you to make sure that I am properly fed.

285
> "Each day, I must have two sheep and three chickens.
>
> "And for the prisoners, you must provide a hundred chickens and fifty sheep.
>
> "And my stomach can certainly hold two bunches of pounded plantain.
>
> "So much for the meals.
>
> "Now, let me take possession of my tools, for tomorrow we start work."

[Mekui-Mengômo-Ondo lines up the prisoners and gives them their instructions. He collects tools. Efeñ-Ndôñ sends food to the prisoners, but Mekui-Mengômo-Ondo instructs the women that boiled vegetables are not acceptable.]

Canto 35

290
> When day came, Mekui-Mengômo rose.
>
> He dressed himself.
>
> He took his war belt and bound it around his waist.
>
> He took in his hand the flaming sword,
>
> Assembled all the prisoners.

295
> The master opened the storehouse.
>
> He told the prisoners: "Take these tools and let's get to work."
>
> The prisoners asked themselves, in low voices, "Who is this man who leads us to work? Will we come out of this venture with our lives? Are we rushing to our doom? Where does this man come from?"
>
> Mekui-Mengômo told the prisoners, "Let us go."

And they went.

300 When he and the prisoners had come before Efeñ-Ndôñ, he
prostrated himself and said, "Today we start a great job."

Efeñ-Ndôñ told him, "First, you shall build the road leading to
the land of the man named Nna-Beyeme."

He asked, "What distance separates us from that land?"

"That land is two months' march away."

He said, "I think it will take me two days to finish the road
which leads there."

305 When he and the prisoners came to the work site, he told them,
"Place yourselves here. This is where we shall work."

Mekui-Mengômo then asked the prisoners, "Do you know my
land?"

The prisoners answered, "We do not know where you come
from, or from what land."

Mekui-Mengômo told them, "I am a man of Mbayan Bikop,
where the dwellers of Ekan-Mebe'e are accustomed to dry
human skins in the sun, like pumpkin seeds and peanuts.

"That is why I tell you, truly, that until I blow my whistle to
stop the work, you will work without a moment's pause."

310 Mekui-Mengômo said this to the men: "Take your places on
either side of the road."

The prisoners took their places.

Mekui-Mengômo drew his flaming sword.

He swung the flaming sword to one side, and *fuuum*, all the
trees were cut down.

He swung the flaming sword to the other side, and all the trees
fell.

315 He struck his breast, and vomited a golden egg.

He dropped the golden egg and sword, "Oh, my fathers
Mebe'e-Me-Ekan, Ngema-Ekan, Oyono-Ekan-Nna, give me
the strength to build this road."

He hurled the golden egg into the air,

To! It fell to the ground, and *fuuum!* the road was built in an
instant.

That day, you could see the road stretch from the threshold of
Efeñ-Ndôñ's home out of sight.

320 Then he told the prisoners, "The only work you have to do is to
sweep any litter on the road. Let no one touch the other
tools. Put all this stuff on the ground, we have worked
enough for today."

He looked at a sundial and saw they were at midday.

He told the prisoners, "We must go home."

When they got back, he told the prisoners. "Go, wash yourselves. I can't stand to have dirty prisoners near me."

He took a large block of soap and gave it to the prisoners.

325 When the prisoners had come back from their bath,

Mekui-Mengômo dipped his hand into his bag and drew out
    the little cushion that sows the wind.
He threw the cushion in the air, and *tin!* a large trunk appeared
With a ring of keys as large as a hand.
The man took the keys and opened the trunk, and *kpwin!*

330   He lined up the prisoners.
To each he gave clothing to cover the top of the body, and cloth-
    ing to cover the lower part of the body.
To each prisoner he gave a pair of sandals
As well as a headdress to cover their head.
He said, "This is the right costume for prisoners.

335   "I don't like to see badly dressed prisoners."
He left the prisoners gathered in the courtyard.
He pressed into the ground the finger which announces war,
    and in the wave of a hand he was in front of Efeñ-Ndôñ.
He said, "Come see the prisoners dressed in their finest."
Efeñ-Ndôñ said, "I will come see the prisoners today, early in
    the afternoon."

340   Early in the afternoon, Efeñ-Ndôñ joined Mekui-Mengômo at
    the prison.
Mekui-Mengômo lined up all the prisoners.
Efeñ-Ndôñ saw that the prisoners were clean and well dressed.
Then Efeñ-Ndôñ congratulated Mekui-Mengômo-Ondo thus:
    "You are a good man to take such good care of my prison-
    ers."
"When shall we have food?" asked Mekui-Mengômo.

345   Efeñ-Ndôñ answered, "When I get back to my house, I shall
    send you food."
When Efeñ-Ndôñ got back, he told the bodyguard to collect
    food throughout the village and bring it to the prison.
An instant later, you could see a crowd coming from the
    village, taking food to Mekui-Mengômo-Ondo.
After the master had distributed the food to the prisoners, he
    chose two prisoners and told them,

350   "You shall stay with me and prepare all my meals."
He also said, "I say to all the prisoners that we shall only work
    once in a day.
"Prepare all this food that people have brought you, and eat it
    without leaving the prison."
The prisoners took the food.
Then four men prepared a meal for Mekui-Mengômo-Ondo.

355   When the meal was ready, they went to tell Mekui-Mengômo-
    Ondo.
The master arose to eat.
He took two sheeps' heads and offered them to the prisoners.
Then he ate everything prepared for him, leaving no scraps.

The prisoners exclaimed, "Is it true he ate all the food and left no scraps?"

360   Night came and the master lay down and slept.

[The next day they finished the work with the same division of labor as before. Mekui-Mengômo goes to tell Efeñ-Ndôñ that the job has been finished.]

Canto 36

Efeñ-Ndôñ clapped his hands, *tyoe!* and caught the fold of his mouth between his two hands.
Efeñ-Ndôñ rang a bell, *kangan!*
A young woman answered from inside the palace.
Kpwo! The young woman lay face down before her husband.
365   He said, "See, here I present you a strange man.
"I asked him to build me roads; he is in prison here.
"He has gone twice, and now he tells me the road is finished."
The young woman asked, "What country is this man from?"
He said, "Let him tell you his tribe himself."
370   "I am a man of the Ekan-Mebe'e. My father's name is Ondo-Mba.
"The king of the Ekan-Mebe'e is named Akoma Mba."
"And why are you in prison?"
"My father reproaches me with a lack of respect toward him, because I answered back to him while he spoke.
"So he brought me before the court and asked for my banishment,
375   "Without any further sort of process,
"And here I am in exile."
At that point, Efeñ-Ndôñ said, "Let's stop talking about that.
"Go back to your prison; I will go to the site to see your new road.
"You say the first road is built; you must begin work on the second."
380   Mekui-Mengômo admired the enchanting Nlem-Okele-Abum, wife of Efeñ-Ndôñ.
Mekui-Mengômo admired her beautiful hair, glittering with jewels bright as coins.
Mekui-Mengômo said farewell to Efeñ-Ndôñ and said, "I must go back to my prison."
Efeñ-Ndôñ and his wife said goodbye.
Mekui-Mengômo admired the young woman a last time, staring at her. He admired her face, shining like the full moon rising over the horizon.
385   Mekui-Mengômo said to himself, "When I have accomplished the tasks which Efeñ-Ndôñ has set me,

> I will get this young woman as my reward, or let me die and
>   see the dead whom we mourn, by Ngema!"
> And then Mekui-Mengômo went back to the place where he
>   spent his nights.

[Mekui-Mengômo builds the second road as quickly as he built the first.
Efeñ-Ndôñ leaves to summon his Great Men to see the work that has
been done; he leaves his wife in charge and tells her that Mekui-
Mengômo and his prisoners should sweep up the town while he is
gone. Mekui-Mengômo dresses up and goes to talk to the woman about
his work.]

> He spoke to her with these words. "I have come to ask you
>   what jobs I must do to serve Efeñ-Ndôñ and be useful?"
> She answered, "He wants you to keep order in the city, and to
>   keep it clean."
> He said, "That was the first point!
> 390   "Also, I must admit that I am madly in love with you.
> "How do you feel about it?"
> The young woman had trouble hiding her feelings, and she
>   answered,
> "What! If I tell you I love you, what should you do?
> "I am no longer a maiden; I am the wife of another man."
> 395   He answered, "What do you mean, the wife of another man?
> "Aren't I another man myself?"
> The young woman said, "If that is so,
> "Then I tell you I love you as much as you love me."
> He said, "I must go now, but I will come back later tonight."
> 400   The master went back to his prison.

[Mekui-Mengômo and the wife of Efeñ-Ndôñ carry on an affair while
Efeñ-Ndôñ is absent. Efeñ-Ndôñ returns with all the important men,
and they hold an assembly to discuss Mekui-Mengômo. They offer him
the kingship, but he refuses. He wants to be paid. Efeñ-Ndôñ says he
will not be paid.]

> Without any further ado, Mekui-Mengômo-Ondo went back to
>   his chosen home and took his war belt, which he fastened
>   about his waist.
> He also took a great haversack, tying the straps about his waist.

Canto 42
> Mekui-Mengômo fixed in the earth the finger that speaks of
>   war, while anger rose to his head.
> He raced off toward the palace of Efeñ-Ndôñ.
> 405   He was heard to say to Efeñ-Ndôñ, "Pay me my wages, for I
>   must leave."

Efeñ-Ndôñ told him, "I don't owe you anything."

When Mekui-Mengômo heard Efeñ-Ndôñ say he didn't owe
anything, he growled, *to!* and became angry with Efeñ-
Ndôñ.

After he growled, he reached out his right hand and seized
Nlem-Okele-Abum, the wife of Efeñ-Ndôñ, and carried her
off in his haversack, *to!*

And he said, "This woman is the price of my wages, for the
work I did for you.

410   "Because of that, she is mine, and I will take her to
Engoñ-Zok."

He swore by Mebe'e-Me-Ekan and Ngema-Ekan and raced off
toward the courtyard, carrying the young woman in the
sack;

He had tied the straps around his waist, he held the flaming
sword in his hand.

He meant to go back to Engoñ-Zok.

That is when Efeñ-Ndôñ growled.

415   As he growled, thick shadows invaded the courtyard.

At that moment, Mekui-Mengômo-Ondo in turn blew his horn,
ko-o-o!

The sun backed up on its steps and reappeared at the east, as
though at dawn.

One could see Mekui-Mengômo fixing in the earth the finger
that speaks of war

As anger rose to his head.

420   Immediately the young man carried the woman off above the
clouds.

Then Efeñ-Ndôñ struck his breast to vomit a charm; he struck
the earth with the charm, *to!* and a stone wall rose from the
earth to the sky to block any ways to Engoñ-Zok.

Then Mekui-Mengômo growled like thunder, *to!* and the iron
[sic] wall parted in its middle, *mek!*

The young man went through to the other side, he had the
young woman with him.

As soon as Efeñ-Ndôñ realized the young man had burst the
stone wall,

425   The master reached out his right hand, and with his hand as a
trap cut off the path of Mekui-Mengômo and his wife. *To!*
they were at the palace.

Wos! Efeñ-Ndôñ took back his wife.

Kpwo! Mekui-Mengômo again seized the young woman and put
her in his haversack.

You saw him place in the earth the finger that speaks of war,
and soon the master rose through the clouds.

You heard Efeñ-Ndôñ blow his horn, *ko-o-o!*

430   He took out a great iron net, he hurled it into the sky.

Mekui-Mengômo meant to head for the other side, and *vias!* the
iron net picked him up as well as the young woman.
And *to!* both of them were again before the palace of
Efeñ-Ndôñ.
Then Mekui-Mengômo spoke a prayer, "Oh, Fathers of the
Mebe'e-Me-Ekan, Ngema-Ekan, Oyono-Ekan, tell
Nnomo-Ngan that misfortune is striking me in the land of
the Blue Men, the land of Efeñ-Ndôñ."

[The spirits pass the word on to Nnomo-Ngan, who tells Akoma Mba.
Akoma Mba sends Mbot-Ekam to help Mekui-Mengômo; along the
way, Mbot-Ekam sells tobacco. When he arrives and tries to help
Mekui-Mengômo, he is propelled back to Engoñ-Zok. Akoma Mba
summons an assembly with a special drum, and a rescue party is
formed. Nlem-Okele is seized and brought to Engoñ-Zok. Medan Bot
wages war for two months, but eventually asks Akoma Mba for help.]

Canto 55
435   As soon as he received the message, Akoma sounded the gold-
en bell, *kangan!*
And then appeared Menye-Me-Akoma and Medja-Me-Akoma,
both sons of Akoma Mba and twin brothers.
To! They lay face down before their father.
Their body was covered with scales from head to foot.
They did not look like human beings.

[Akoma Mba sends them to help Mekui-Mengômo. On the way, they
ask the spirits where to find Efeñ-Ndôñ. Mebe'e-Me-Ekan comes with
them.]

440   They went to the man named Etam-Mot-Nkomo-Boto-Ovo-Boto-
Akuk-Boto.
There, they were working the bellows which gave Efeñ-Ndôñ
the strength to fight.
Then Mebe'e-Me-Ekan gave the young man the magical charm,
holding his hand.
He said, "Strike the earth with this object."
As soon as the young man struck the earth with that object, all
the bellows burst.
445   All the spirits which were working the bellows lost the light of
their eyes.
He said, "Strike the earth again with your charm."
As soon as the young man struck the earth, a great trunk came
out of the entrails of the earth.
He said, "Strike the trunk with your charm."
The trunk opened like a mouth.
450   Out came the statue of a man.

He said, "Here is Efeñ-Ndôñ."

He said again, "Strike him on the breast with your charm."

Then, all the magics which were in the belly of Efeñ-Ndôñ
    came out.

He said, "You can go and capture him now."

455   At that moment, Mebe'e-Me-Ekan struck the young man on the
    head with a cushion of bat skin, and immediately the
    young man was back with Medan and the others.

He said, "I am back. Now we must capture Efeñ-Ndôñ."

Medan called Otuna-Mba and told him, "Go block off the way
    in the home of the spirits.

"Meye-Mengini will go to the moon and keep watch.

"Angono-Zok will go to the sun. Let us close off every way
    out."

460   They called Okpwat, and said, "Now you may go and chal-
    lenge him."

No sooner had the words been spoken than Efeñ-Ndôñ
    appeared at the head of his army.

As soon as he charged down where the sons of Ekan-Mebe'e
    were assembled,

Medan made straight for him.

Then Medan vomited a golden egg.

465   With a sharp blow, he struck Efeñ-Ndôñ in the back, and *to!* his
    backbone broke.

And *lotototo!* They captured Efeñ-Ndôñ.

They captured Efeñ-Ndôñ and took him before Akoma.

Then Akoma Mba said to them,

"My son was exiled to your land,

470   "And you made him your slave and bound him to road build-
    ing.

"So I tell you that his reward shall be this woman he has
    seized."

He struck him with the magic cushion,

He took away all the charms which made him so formidable.

Then they put out one eye.

475   They cut off one ear.

They cut him on the back and gave him four scar marks.

They said, "By these signs, people will know that you have met
    the Ekan along your way."

At that time, they gave him a writing which raised him to the
    rank of Great Man.

Now he obeys the orders of Akoma.

480   They took the young woman and gave her to Mekui-Mengômo-
    Ondo.

He has already married her.

I have said all I know about this story of the mvet.

23. The Epic of Jéki la Njambè Inono
Narrated by Pierre Célestin Tiki a Koulle a Penda

Recorded in Dibombari, Cameroon, in 1972 by Lucien Endene Mbedy and Eric de Rosny. Transcribed and translated into French by Joseph-Marie Epée. Edited by Joseph-Marie Epée and François de Gastines and published as Les merveilleux exploits de Djéki la Njambè *by Pierre Célestin Tiki a Koulle a Penda in two volumes by Éditions Collège Libermann in Douala, Cameroon, 1987. This excerpt edited and translated into English by Ralph Austen.*

THE HEROIC NARRATIVE OF JÉKI LA NJAMBÈ IS PERFORMED among the Sawa-Bantu-speaking peoples of the Cameroon coast, including the community which has given its name to the port city of Douala. The epic appears to be very old, probably preceding the establishment of the long-distance trading networks which made the Douala people prominent in precolonial Cameroon history. In fact the epic contains no direct references to any historical developments and when first recorded in extensive form around 1910, its performers claimed, "Our fathers and forefathers often recited this epic but they could not discover its meaning or what it is supposed to teach us" (Ebding, 1938, 36-102).

There appears to be no immediate connection between *Jéki* and the occasions upon which it is most frequently performed, such as funeral wakes. Skilled performers are well known but they have no formal social or ritual status and the epic is also recited by various men and women in quite casual circumstances at family gatherings or fishing encampments. Recent published and televised performances (including the one from which the present excerpts are taken) have been accompanied by extensive efforts at interpretation by local intellectuals, but these seem to belong more to a contemporary discourse of ethnic, national and Pan-African identity than to any meaning the narrative may have had in earlier times. The name "Njambè Inono" can be translated in some Sawa-Bantu languages as the "Creator God, son of the Eternal," but there is little agreement as to whether such a sense is valid, still less what it might signify.

Jéki exists in many variant forms but the basic plot seems to be fairly standard: Njambè is a village chief whose first wife (here called Ngrijo) initially bears him a daughter who is soon kidnapped by the spirits of the dead. Ngrijo then becomes pregnant with Jéki but remains in this state for many years without giving birth. Njambè banishes Ngrijo to a peripheral dwelling and takes several new wives who all bear him children, male and female. Following Jéki's delayed and remarkable birth, described in the first section, he undertakes a number of dangerous quests on Njambè's behalf (see second excerpt), stakes his life on various athletic contests with his brothers or other local champions, and also in many versions, rescues his sister from the underworld. The story is consistently said to "have no end," but in some versions there is a resolution where Jéki either dies, kills his father, or takes over from him peacefully.

The source of the present version of *Jéki*, Tiki a Koulle (b. 1918),

is, like most of the few coastal bards who have been recorded, a man well educated in French who earned his living as a teacher and administrator in the local Catholic school system. He learned the epic from earlier well-established bards, although he admits some episodes (not included here) are his own. Tiki is presently the only public performer of *Jéki* and has developed, especially for the project of publication, a more structured version than is common but otherwise seems to be a valid representative of the regional tradition. The songs included in the excerpts here are all performed in variants of the Douala *ngoso* ("parrot") style closely associated with the rhythms of canoe paddling. Italicized exclamations in the right margin are audience or performer interjections.

Jéki's Birth

One day Dibengelé[1] came to Ngrijo and said to her: "Ngrijo, it has been a long time since I last saw you, many years since I came here. There is such a famine at the house! It is time for us to go fishing in the river; there are great quantities of shrimp in our stream just now. We must go fishing!" "I agree! I too am beset by famine."

On her way home Dibengelé met their husband. "Dibengelé, where have you been?" "I was telling my co-wife that we ought to go fishing tomorrow morning." "Hum! That co-wife of yours, it is sterility that she will die of, that worthless thing! Can she give birth? Each of you has eleven children by now; how many does she have? Can she bear a child and see it? That worthless thing, can she bear a child and see it?"

While he spoke in this manner, Ngrijo Epée Tungum approached and heard him. She spoke to Njambè, saying: "Yes, husband!"

"If you continue to call me your husband I will kill you on the spot! Am I your husband? Are you stupid? Who told you to call me your husband?"

"Yes, husband, I too want so much to give birth. I too, it would please me to hold a child in my arms! I too want the happiness of having a child! Do you think that it is I who holds back my womb so that I do not deliver? Why then do you mock me?"

[Song:]

> I, too, let me bear a child!
> Oh husband, let me bear one and let me see it!
> Oh husband, let me also bear a child!
> Let me bear one, I too!
> Let me bear one, oh husband!
> I too, let me bear one!

---

1. The senior of eight wives.

"I too, I want so much to give birth. I want to give birth! It would please me so much to hold a child in my arms! But I cannot get there!"

[Song:]

> The heart of a sterile woman
> Cannot really be happy!
> At least have pity on me!
> Let me also bear a child
> And let me see it!
> Let me give birth to one!
> And let him also make me happy!
> Let me give birth to one!
> And allow me also to walk with him in the village!
> Let me bear one, let me bear him!
> I also, let me bear him and let me see him!
> Let me bear one, let me bear him!
> I also, let me bear him and let me see him!
>   *Eh! Eh! Engingila ye! . . . Eyese e!*

At the break of day, the women thus went fishing. Once at the river, they were as far from Ngrijo as from here to Yaoundé,[2] because her stomach pushed them away. They began to fish at the river. They fished and the shrimp were so plentiful! As they continued to fish they finally moved out onto the water. Each of them had already filled a basket of shrimp.

The tide had gone out, completely gone out. Then the wind began to blow. As soon as the wind began to blow, the water rose. And as the water rose, the wind became terrible; the waves began to break. "Let's go back" said Dibengelé to the others. "If the tide cuts off our way out of the river we will be trapped!"

So they began to go back with the waves. It was then that a voice spoke from Ngrijo Epée Tungum's womb: "Ina! Sit down in the water and give birth to me!"

"Oh, what am I to do? Shall I give birth to you on the water with these waves which are breaking so powerfully?" "Hurry up, give birth to me!"

Njambè's wives were overcome with fear. The voice sounded to them like thunder. And it said: "Hurry up, give birth to me!"

Inambolo e!

"Here on the water with these waves which are breaking so violently? Gently, gently, I am going to give birth!" The voice repeated: "Have mercy, hurry up, give birth to me!"

---

2. Capital of Cameroon, 300 kilometers away.

[Song:]

       Wave, go gently, gently!
       I am going to give birth on the water!
       Wave, go gently, gently!
       I am going to give birth on the water!
    The other day
    I was going to look for firewood
    And I gave birth in the forest!
    Today I will see it in all its colors!
    I have to give birth on the water, my brothers!
    Gently, gently!
    Me, I am going to give birth on the water!
    The waves are breaking
    And covering everything, covering everything!

Ngrijo Epée Tungum was pushed against the water and she gave birth on the water, *"Poo!"* But when she wanted to touch the child it objected. "Do not touch me!"

The child began growing right away, all of a sudden. How large it became! Njambè's wives fled, they threw all their shrimp on the ground! Dibengelé ran without stopping and went to tell her husband: "Something frightening just happened! Ngrijo Epée Tungum gave birth on the water!" "Ngrijo Epée Tungum just gave birth on the water?" "Yes!"

Then Njambè went out and sat down in his courtyard. He sat down to see the child who was born on the water. His wives came running and encountered the child where he was standing on the beach. He said to them: "Where are you going? Go back to where you came from, quickly!" Njambè's wives then turned back. "Dip your baskets into the water," he said to them. As soon as they dipped their baskets into the water they filled up with shrimp. Njambè's wives completely filled their baskets.

Inambolo e!

The women who had dipped their baskets into the water filled each one of them with shrimp. Then the child said to his mother: "Ina, sit down on the water, I am going to enter your womb!" His mother sat down on the water and he returned to the womb. Njambè sat at home, in his courtyard, to see how the child was who was born on the water. Njambè's wives came, each with a basket full of shrimp. The first ones were in front, others followed, and others continued to pass by. . . .

Njambè, seated, saw the stomach arrive, passing, passing, passing. "That womb, hasn't a child come out of it at last?" The stomach passed, passed, passed. All at once he saw Ngrijo Epée and, clicking his tongue against his teeth, said to her: "What filth there is beneath the heavens! I said that this rotten woman has a sterile womb, she cannot give birth!"

"Dibengelé, didn't you tell me that Ngrijo Epée had a child on the water? Where is that child? This worthless thing, can she bear a child? That nasty piece of goods! That one, the witchcraft of her father, Epée Tungum Bokambo, has filled her entire womb! Can she give birth? How can she not give birth at all?!"

"Yes husband, should you kill me? Even if you go to the Whites you will find sterility; among the Grassfields[3] , likewise; among the Ewondo, likewise! Am I the most sterile of all? Must I kill myself? Tell me!"

[Song:]

> I, must I kill myself?
> Oh husband, must I kill myself?
> She said to him : "Must I kill myself?
> "Tell me now!
> "Must I kill myself?
> "Sterile women even among the Whites.
> "Must I kill myself violently?
> "O husband! Must I kill myself?
> "Should you go among the Whites
> "You would find sterile women!
> "Should you go among the Mulattos
> "You would find sterile women!
> "Should you go among the Ewondo
> "You would find sterile women!
> "O husband! Must I kill myself?
> "Tell me!
> "O husband! Must I kill myself?"

And she went on her way. Upon arriving at her house, she unloaded the shrimp and cleaned, cleaned, cleaned.

Inambolo e!

The next day, as Ngrijo Epée Tungum was seated, a voice spoke from her womb: "Ina! Ina!" She said: "Yes! Here we go again!" "Ina!" She answered: "Yes, my child, I hear you!"

He said to her: "Tomorrow morning, as soon as you awake, sit down somewhere; don't do anything. When noon comes, set out for that silk cotton tree down there; it is there you will give birth to me. Tomorrow, precisely at noon!" To make a long story short, here we are at noon; it is impossible to distinguish the sky from the land. At high noon a darkness falls, a darkness which you can feel with your hands. Thus Ina sets off to place herself under the silk cotton tree. Hardly has she come under the tree when she begins to give birth. Let everyone lend their ears and listen!

---

3. Region in western Cameroon.

At the moment of delivery—

She gave birth to fly whisks, fly whisks, and fly whisks, up to nine.[4]

She gave birth to white cloths, white cloths, and white cloths, up to eighteen.

She gave birth to velour cloths, velour cloths and velvet cloths, up to eighteen.

She gave birth to miseseko rattles, to miseseko rattles to accompany singing up to two times nine.

She gave birth to leg rattles, leg rattles, and leg rattles for singers, up to two times nine.

She gave birth to harps and harps and harps, up to two times nine.

She gave birth to ancestral cutlasses and ancestral cutlasses, up to two times nine.

She gave birth to ancestral axes, ancestral axes, axes to cut tree trunks, up to two times nine.

She gave birth again to the ancestral whetstone, for sharpening cutlasses and all sorts of tools.

Then she gave birth to the ancestral spears, the ancestral spears, up to two times nine.

She gave birth to the ancestral rifles and she also gave birth to the ancestral cannon.

Then she gave birth to the *ngalo*,[5] the *ngalo*, and the *ngalo*, up to ninety-nine.

Then she gave birth to Ebènguè Njonga,[6]

Then she gave birth to the elastic vine which freezes,

    Then she gave birth to the elastic vine which burns,

    Then she gave birth to *Tombise Dikonbinjok*,[7]

    Then she gave birth to Esidijiji,

    Then she gave birth to Esidingengesingesin,

    Then she gave birth to Esidingongong.

Then she gave birth to the canoe with the palm-leaf sail and the nine-pointed paddle.

Then a voice spoke from her womb: "Ina! Now arise from here, go and give birth to me on the broken bottle glass down there and the fragments of demi-johns;[8] it is there that you must give birth to me. Do not place dead leaves or cloth or anything on the ground or on the broken bottle glass!"

And Ngrijo went off; her womb was very much lightened. Then she gave birth to the son of Njambè Inono on the broken bottle glass and fragments of demi-johns. She said to the child, "Should I pick

---

4. Fly whisks are symbols of authority. Nine is considered the perfect number. 5. Amulets. 6. What follows is the list of Jéki's magical weapons. 7. "That-which-can-run-over-the-elephant." 8. Large glass containers.

you up?" The child replied: "Pick me up, cut the umbilical cord, pick me up! Today is the day of my birth!"

[Song:]

> I, the son of Njambè,
> I was born on the bottles!
> I come out of the bottles,
> And I will return to the bottles.
> I, the son of Njambè,
> I was born on the bottles!

Inambolo e!

[Jéki's birth does not reconcile his father and mother. On the contrary, Njambè develops a violent hatred for his son and orders him to undertake a series of dangerous quests which he hopes will cause Jéki's death.]

Ngando ["Crocodile"]

[Early on the following morning, just as dawn was breaking and light appeared on the horizon, Budubudu and Eboy[9] appeared at the house of Jéki and his mother.]

"Toc, toc, toc! Father wants you to come!" Jéki went out, started on his way a few steps, then stopped and sent this message to his mother: "Ina! Father wants me to come this very day. I am going!"

When he arrived at Njambè's house, his father said to him: "Now listen to me, my son! In two days I will have visitors here, but there is nothing in the house for them to eat. There are plenty of crocodiles in the river. If you kill one of them for me, even a small one, I will have what I need for my guests!" "Very well!" said Jéki.

When he returned home, Jéki said to his mother: "Ina! Father wants me to go down the river and kill a crocodile for him!" Jéki's mother rose up off her feet and then landed hard on the ground. "Haven't I told you that your father does not like you. He has placed an enormous crocodile in the river and he hopes that when you go down there, the crocodile will kill you. Haven't I told you that your father does not like you?"

Jéki replied: "Not me! The panther did not kill me[10] and the crocodile cannot kill me either. Don't worry about me!"

At the crack of dawn "our man" took his canoe, his palm-leaf sail and his nine-pointed paddle. As the canoe got under way he tried to move slowly, slowly, slowly out of the river mouth. He guided the canoe, gradually, gradually, gradually moving in a curved path. He came out into the open sea, set up his palm-leaf mast, looked up at the

---

9. Jéki's half brothers. 10. In a previous episode.

sky, took hold of the rudder, and watched where he was going. Then he called out, asking for the great sea wind, asking it to come and carry him along.

[Song:]

>Take me, me, I am on my way! Take me . . .
>Great wind, take me! Take me . . .
>Yes, I am on my way! I am dying [of joy]! Take me . . .
>Even if it is to the west of the ocean! I am dying! Take me . . .
>Yes, I am always on my way! Take me . . .
>Great wind, take me along! I am dying! Take me . . .
>Even if it is to the west of the ocean! I am dying! Take me . . .
>So take me! Take me. . . .

And the wind came in floods, in gusts, blowing hard, filling the leaves of the mast very full and moving Jéki along at a very rapid pace.

The canoe now cut hard through the water: "*Wai, wai, wai, wai, wai, wai, wai!*" And the waves broke and spread out: "*Wea, wea, wea, wea, wea!*" And the canoe moved along at a dizzying speed!

Jéki then stopped the great wind short and took hold of his nine-pointed paddle. Then he called to the *ngalo*[11] "Now bring me my paddle!"

[Song:]

>My paddle! Oh my paddle!
>Bring me my paddle! Oh my paddle!
>My paddle! Oh my paddle!
>Bring me my paddle! Oh my paddle!

He barely thrust it into the water and "*Vongom, vongom, vom, vom,*" the canoe flew off like from here to Yaoundé.

He paddled: "*Vongom, Vongom, vom, vom!*" and the canoe took off at full speed and the water split: "*Wai, wai, wai, wai, wai!*" and the waves rose: "*Wea, wea, wea, wea, wea!*"

Eh! Eh! Eh! Inambolo e!

Then he saw something standing up in the sea like a wall, a wall which thrust straight up into the sky. He could no longer see before him, the wall having cast the whole place into darkness; so he stopped paddling. He gave his *ngalo* a brisk shake to consult them, saying, "Tell me what kind of wall this is!"

The *ngalo* replied, "You really do ask questions! The crocodile you have come to find, the enormous crocodile, isn't that him? Dear boy, it is surely your father's crocodile."

"So then! Is that crocodile really so big?"

"And how! A crocodile who swallows entire boats! Do you

---

11. Amulets.

know what your father is like? Njambè is such a one that, when you go into the waters, you find him there; when you go into the forest, you find him there; when you go into the clouds, you find him there again. Do you know what your father is like?"

Jéki said to himself: "Let's see, how will I get done with the crocodile now? Can I approach this beast?"

He shook his amulets and they said to him: "Listen, lay your paddle down in the canoe and let yourself be drawn nice and gently by the current. The crocodile, on his own, will thunder very loudly at you. Do you understand?" "Yes," he answered.

As he was told, he laid his paddle down in the canoe, which began to sail along. Then the crocodile clacked his teeth: " *Kwako-kop-kop-kop-kop*!" A blinding lightning bolt appeared in the east and flashed. The crocodile thundered, "What is going on here?!"

Jéki said to him, "Cousin, I have come to look for you because there is to be a meeting at our uncles' place which requires your presence!" The crocodile laughed and said, "There you are! Didn't I say so? If I do not come to my uncles, what kind of meeting could they possibly hold there?" He asked further, "To the east, to the west, to the north, or to the south, where are we going now?" "To the east," answered Jéki.

And the crocodile began to turn. He turned very, very clumsily toward the east and said to Jéki: "Now take your canoe, you will lead me with slow strokes of your paddle, slow paddle strokes to pass the cape, slow paddle strokes to pass the cape. Do not make any rapid little strokes at all. Lead me with slow paddle strokes, calmly, gently; that is how I will travel through the water with you, do you understand?" "I understand," answered Jéki.

So Jéki thrust his paddle into the water: "*Vongom, Vongom, vom, vom*!" And the canoe set forth slowly with the crocodile.

[Song:]

> Slow paddle strokes to pass the cape!
> > Motor-power paddle!
> > Oh, motor-power paddle!
> > Motor-power paddle!
> Slow paddle strokes to pass the cape!
> > Motor-power paddle!
> > Oh, motor-power paddle!
> > Motor-power paddle!

The canoe moved forward lightly with the crocodile. You should have seen them coming from the west out of the great ocean!

[Song:]

> > Oh, motor-power paddle!
> > Motor-power paddle!

> Slow paddle strokes to pass the cape!
> Oh, motor-power paddle!

He traveled a long time with the crocodile, lightly, lightly, lightly; straight, straight, straight, and finally grounded on the sand!

Inambolo e!

When they were grounded on the sand, Jéki shook his *ngalo* to consult it. The *ngalo* told him: "Listen, this crocodile should not stop on the beach; send water right up to the village!"

Jéki called the water; the water came in great quantities; it began to enter the village in waves, great waves. The water came like a hurricane. When Njambè himself noticed this water, he fled and entered his house. He said to his children: "Everyone get into the house! Something terrible is on the way!" How the water did come into the village! It even flooded the houses.

The crocodile came in, very, very clumsily. He came in with the water. Then Jéki stopped the water and told it to return to its bed . It returned completely and the crocodile was grounded on the sand. The crocodile was grounded among these houses, preventing the people to his right from seeing those who were to his left, because his back stood right up to the sky. He was so furious that when he saw a duck, he ate it; if he saw a dog, he ate it; a goat, he ate it; even a child of Njambè or whatever else came beside him, he wanted to eat it.

Njambè said, "No, Budubudu and Eboy go through the forest,[12] only through the forest and go to tell him to take back the crocodile!"

Budubudu and Eboy now departed, walking only through the forest. When they saw him [Jéki] they said, "Brother this is going very badly; the crocodile wants to exterminate us. Take him back quickly!"

Jéki and his mother exploded with laughter and said, "Didn't we tell you so? You cannot do anything more with the crocodile?" He went then and called the water, asking it to come. The water came in great, great quantities and the crocodile began to float again. Then Jéki said to him, "Go back now!"

[Song:]

> Crocodile, go forever.
> Crocodile, go forever.
> Crocodile, go into the river.
> Crocodile, go forever·

The crocodile reentered the river easily, easily, and went off.

> Crocodile, go into the river!
> Crocodile, go forever!

---

12. To Jéki at his mother's house.

The crocodile went away and descended deep into the water down, down, down, until it disappeared.

Eh! eh! eh! Inambolo e!

Njambè's hatred for Jéki and his mother became greater and greater. In effect, Jéki had annihilated the crocodile, he had so stultified it that it would not do anything, that it had become like a corpse.

baNyanga Epics of Zaïre

THE BANYANGA ARE A BANTU-LANGUAGE PEOPLE of northeastern Zaïre, dwellers in the equatorial forests; their lifestyle remains based on a mix of hunting, fishing, foraging, and limited forms of agriculture. They did not develop states or kingdoms; local communities are governed by hereditary chiefs. They coexist with the Pygmies of the region, from whom they have acquired many of their forest-dwelling skills, and who appear in the epics as servants of the chiefs.

The performance tradition from which Mwindo and Kahindo spring is rooted in the hunting camps which lie outside the settled communities. In that venue, the occasion for performance is simply the need to pass the time away from one's home and family, although Biebuyck and Mateene do note that a performance may be commissioned for the town as well, as a conspicuous and lavish entertainment put on by a person of means and prestige. Performers are initiates in the *Karisi* spirit cult, but in other regards performances are entirely secular affairs. The epics published by Biebuyck and Mateene were collected in the 1950s, at which time the baNyanga numbered some 27,000; we have little information on modern conditions and performances.

In the 1950s, there were few expert epic performers left among the baNyanga; nevertheless, in contrast to the neighboring Mongo and Nkundo traditions of Lianja, the Mwindo epic tradition seems vital and fertile. Biebuyck has published four different versions, each quite distinct in its presentation of the story. We find few signs of the contraction of material, the standardization of episodes, and the repetitiveness which mark Lianja and the modern Jéki tradition of Douala. Mwindo is a far more polymorphous vehicle for a variety of artistic and social concerns, while still sharing certain identifiable regional traits of which the principal one may be his reliance upon an older female relative for assistance and support in his adventures.

Biebuyck and Mateene have published the texts as prose, rather than with line divisions as is the case for most of the other texts presented in this volume. The performance does, however, involve a rhythmic or musical accompaniment like the others presented in this book, and the texts themselves have been termed "epics" since their first publication. We present the texts in prose, then, with the reminder that these are textualized translations. We have also omitted Biebuyck's extensive annotation.

24. The Mwindo Epic
Narrated by Mr. Shekwabo

Recorded in Mera, Zaïre, in 1954 by Daniel Biebuyck. Transcribed and translated into English by Daniel Biebuyck. Edited by Daniel Biebuyck and published in Hero and Chief: Epic Literature from the Banyanga (Zaire Republic) *by the University of California Press in 1978. This excerpt edited by Stephen Belcher.*

THE HERO MWINDO, "LITTLE-ONE-JUST-BORN-HE-WALKS," is in some regards a culture hero for the baNyanga; his exploits define the limits of their world and the modes of their life style. He is an utterly exceptional being, from his mode of birth to his departure from the world. In many regards his story conforms to "universal" hero-models: after his exceptional birth, such a hero often encounters considerable hostility from his father; his exploits lead him to the underworld, following either his father or a lost sister; he also travels to the sky. Throughout, he is often assisted by his paternal aunt.

The following excerpt is taken from the second of the four texts published by Biebuyck and presents a recurrent episode in Mwindo's career: his encounter with the supernatural being Nyamurairi and his daughter Kahindo. In this case the encounter is complicated by the presence of Mwindo's father Sheburungu in the underworld.

[The story starts with the miraculous birth of Mwindo and his sister. His sister is then married to Lightning, who lives in the sky; she brings down the knowledge of cultivation. She and Mwindo then find an egg, which hatches into a huge and ravenous bird that devours the village. The sister destroys it from within. Mwindo then draws the enmity of other chiefs.]

After Mwindo had distributed buffalo tails[1] to his peers, the chiefs, these peers harbored hatred against him because he ruled in fame surpassing them. Where Itewa dwelled, he pondered in his heart, saying that because Mwindo surpassed them, because his fame surpassed theirs, he wanted to go and fight a war of spears with him. Having spoken to himself in this manner, Itewa said to his people: "You all, each man a spear! Let him take it up to fight war with Mwindo, for tomorrow we shall set out to fight with Mwindo!" When his (Itewa's) people heard this, they prepared themselves with the spears. Where Mwindo remained, when he heard this news of warfare with Itewa, he was deeply grieved, saying: "Truly this is rough! The bad thing is that Itewa summons war to fight with me, and I am the one who gave him the chieftainship that he now holds. Indeed, on earth there is no good. So, he shall come to know me; tomorrow he shall know how strong I am." He said to his people: "Tomorrow we shall be

---

1. Symbols of authority.

attacked by Itewa. So, then, prepare yourselves!" After he had spoken to his people in this manner, they remembered it; they prepared themselves with the spears, saying: "Indeed tomorrow we shall set out to fight." When sky had changed to dawn, Little-call-of-Itewa left his village with his people; as he went to fight with Mwindo Mboru, he was singing:

> Little-call-of-Itewa, Little-call-of-Itewa
> Is being trapped, Little-call-of-Itewa.
> His antelope,
> Little-call-of-Itewa.
> His warthog,
> Little-call-of-Itewa.
> His waterbuck,
> Little-call-of-Itewa.

Where Mwindo dwelled, when he saw Itewa marching against him with the war of spears, he said to his people: "Leave your spears; just go like that. I shall take my scepter; it will fight with Itewa." They went like that. They went to the place where Itewa made his appearance. As they confronted each other, the people of Itewa hurled their spears against the people of Mwindo. The people of Mwindo were annihilated; they died. After they had died, Itewa took all the things of Mwindo and climbed with them and his people to his village. He was calling loudly for Munkonde, the one who had forged the spears for him, saying that where he had gone to war he had won. And he was singing:

> E! Munkonde, forger of large spears,
> Forger of spears.
> Munkonde, forger of large spears,
> Forger of spears.
> Munkonde, forger of things that are feared,
> Forger of large spears.
> Forger of things that are feared.
> E! Munkonde, we are going to Roba-Land,
> But not we.

After Itewa returned home, he took one goat; he gave it to the blacksmiths of Munkonde, saying that they had forged for him the spears with which he had fought. After he had finished giving this goat to Munkonde, the people entertained him; they played the drums and the horns for him. Four days passed and they still kept on dancing without going to sleep, because of the joy of winning the war.

In the place where Mwindo had remained, after he had been overcome in the war, he returned to his village, he himself and his dogs, Ndorobiro and Ngonde, and his scepter; that is all. His people are

287

decimated. And his father Shemwindo still dwells in his village of Tubondo. Mwindo meditated by himself, saying that the one who overcomes a strong one, let him not say that he overcomes (someone else), (rather) that he is overcoming himself. Having had this kind of meditation, he said: "What now, a true man does not die on the ground. Act first! I, Mwindo, I am not rubbed twice with the sign of war!" He stood up in order to fight with Itewa. He went with his two dogs and his scepter; he went singing:

> I shall overcome the Snails.
> I shall fight over there, in the place of
>   Chunks-of-meat.
> I shall overcome the Snails.
> I shall fight over there in the place of
>   Chunks-of-meat.

Where Mwindo Mboru went, as he arrived at the entrance to the village of Itewa, he threw his scepter on the ground. As he arrived in the middle of the village place, he looked around here and there: all the people, together with their chief, Itewa, were dead; and all the chickens, the goats, and the flies—all these things had perished! Mwindo Mboru praised himself in the middle of the village, saying: "Itewa, wake up now. He who went to sleep wakes up again. You usurped power and force for yourself, thinking that you would be capable against me. Today, you here are the one whose fang is stuck in the ground. I had told you that a young man cannot be saved by playing with his elder brother. Lo! He is miserable, the one who tries to measure up to me; he climbs on a difficult tree." After he had thus praised himself in the middle of the corpses of the people of Itewa, he took all his goods; he cut off two of Itewa's fingers, and his tongue, and his penis. He returned home with all these goods, singing:

> Mburu passes through the hunting grounds with good things.
> Nyamasangwasangwa is not dead.
> *Muntindi* bird passes through the hunting grounds with good
>   things.
> Nyamasangwasangwa is not dead.
> Mburu passes through the hunting grounds with goodness.
> Nyamasangwasangwa is not dead.

After he had returned home, Mwindo said: "My dogs are dying of hunger; what shall I do now?" He spoke to his scepter, saying: "You, scepter, because I was born already possessing you, up to now you have overburdened me like a *murimba* stone and a *mutero* stone." He said: "Produce food for me now so that these dogs of mine may eat it." After he had spoken in this manner, he looked beside him: cooked

foods were already there! While giving this food he made a proclamation, saying: "You, Masters-of-the-subterranean-world, you who are on earth, and you who are in the sky, and you who are in the air, come to appear here to meet with me here where I am; give me heroism and much force and honor to surpass the other so-and-so chiefs who are next to me." Having finished speaking like that, he gave the food to his dogs. Having finished feeding the food to his dogs, he coughed, saying: "What now (about) my people? How now, you, my scepter?" He took his scepter; he threw it on the ground: all his people woke up; they were completely saved! When they had finished recovering, they went to bathe, and they were singing:

> We are like the ones throwing one another in the pools.
> We will throw Karunga in the pools.
> We are like the ones throwing one another in the pools.
> We will throw Karunga in the pools.

On leaving the river where they had bathed, they went, singing:

> E! Batondo,
> My kinsman, yoyo.
> My senior father,
> My kinsman, yoyo,
> Said that I shall not eat banana paste,
> Unless I eat the banana paste with meat.
> My kinsman, yoyo.

When they were now back in their village, all the houses were standing up again; they had finished building themselves! Mwindo Mboru was the one who had said to his scepter to erect the houses again. When Mwindo went to sleep he placed his scepter underneath his armpit.

When Mwindo's village was filled again like that—his children had been born, chickens were scurrying around like locusts—he said to himself that he, Mwindo, had not yet arrived at the place of God, being fully alive; that he was not himself, that it was befitting for him first to go and see God, so that he might meet with him. He said to his people: "Remain here, you all, together with those my dogs. When you will be met by difficult things arriving at the end of the village, those my dogs will fight against them; they will bring me the news in the place where I am. I am with you, however; I do not go far."

Having spoken like that, he grasped his scepter and a long billhook knife; he went with them. He arrived at a *kikoka* fern; he pulled it out; he entered at the place where he had pulled it out. Where he went, he appeared at a wading place. There he met with the daughter of Nyamurairi, called Kahindo. Mwindo was singing, saying:

E! Hawk, the termites destroy the trees.
Hawk, the termites destroy the trees.
E! Hawk, the termites destroy the trees.

After Mwindo Mboru had finished meeting at the river with Kahindo, daughter of Nyamurairi, (he noticed that) scabies covered her entire body: it begins at the big toe of the foot and arrives at the tussock of the hair. This Kahindo, daughter of Nyamurairi, when she saw Mwindo Mboru arriving for her, the heart burned her while she was scrutinizing him. She said: "Truly! A splendid young man, how beautiful he is, this one. Truly!" Having spoken like that, this Kahindo said to Mwindo: "You, young man, clean for me this scabies." Mwindo began cleaning her entire body, removing the scales very well. When Mwindo had finished cleaning her, Kahindo said to him: "May you be healed, you, Mwindo." She asked him inquisitively: "You, where are you going?" Mwindo answered her that he was going to Nyamurairi. Having finished bathing Kahindo, Mwindo fainted. (Mwindo) having fainted, Kahindo shook him, saying: "E! Mwindo, wake up! A hero does not die from one spear throw." Mwindo returned to life; he sneezed. While Mwindo was going to Nyamurairi, Kahindo shouted on the road, saying: "Go over there and when you arrive at Nyamurairi's, go close to the men's house where he is (seated). My father Nyamurairi will show you water that is in a jar, asking that you wash with it. You say to him: My father, the beer from which you drink, is that for me to wash with? You refuse firmly, even though he goes on pressing you, saying that you should wash with it. You go on refusing until he stops pressing you with it." Kahindo also said to him: "When you arrive at my father's place, then you sing for him this song:

"I am not with those who have killed Ringe,
"Ringe of the chief, Ringe."

After Mwindo had been briefed in this manner by Kahindo, he went and sang while climbing the mountain (road) to Nyamurairi:

Kabira, beat the drum for me.	Kabira, beat the drum for me.
This one here is Waterbuck.	This one here is Waterbuck.
Kabira, beat the drum for me.	Kabira, beat the drum for me.
This one here is Warthog.	This one here is Waterbuck.

After Mwindo had climbed up to Nyamurairi's village, he mounted the steps near the house of Nyamurairi. He arrived at the men's house. When Nyamurairi saw him, he said to Mwindo to bathe in the water that was in the jar. Mwindo replied to him, saying: "E! My father. I cannot wash myself in the beer that you drink." Having spoken to him in this fashion, he sang for him the song:

I am not with those who have killed Ringe,
Ringe of the chief, Ringe.

When he (Mwindo) had finished singing this song for him, Nyamurairi was full of joy, saying: "I rejoice, my father, because you have arrived here, but tomorrow morning I want you to go harvesting honey for me which is over there at the entrance to the village." After he had finished speaking to Mwindo like this, they cooked banana paste for him. When the banana paste was ready, it was brought to the men's house where Mwindo was. This banana paste was of the *kitehe* variety; it contained frogs that were cooked; they were the garnish of it. It arrived there; Nyamurairi told Mwindo to sample the paste. Mwindo refused it, saying: "You, my father, your followers say about you that you do not eat them (the frogs) with banana paste. This now is difficult!" After Mwindo had spoken to him like this, the frogs stood up; they clapped their hands (in astonishment), saying: "Yes, our Mwindo. We are saved. Lo! You also know things after they had spoken in this way." Nyamurairi said to Mwindo: "So now go into the house of Kahindo, my daughter, to sleep therein." Mwindo went into it (the house). When he arrived there, Kahindo stirred banana paste for him. This banana paste, Mwindo ate it. Having finished eating the banana paste, the sky turned dark; he slept with Kahindo in her house. When the sky had changed to dawn, in the early morning, Nyamurairi said to Mwindo: "You, my son, go to harvest the honey for me which is there on the tree." Mwindo went there. When he arrived at the foot of the tree, Bat gave him nails to stick fast to the *mpaki* tree; and Spider gave him cobwebs (to serve) as ropes to climb the *mpaki* tree. They gave him these things because Mwindo had made a blood pact with Spider and Bat. As he was going to climb the tree, Nyamurairi gave Mwindo his belt (stitched with cowries), saying that he should climb with it. And Mwindo left with Nyamurairi his billhook knife, saying that he should remain with it on the ground. On the belt of Nyamurairi there were cowries. Mwindo climbed up. When he had arrived near the honey, Nyamurairi sent a call to where he was, saying: "You, my belt, bend him." The belt smashed Mwindo; his mouth was smashed against the tree; Mwindo's breathing found no way to come out. The strands on which he had climbed were completely still.

As Mwindo was troubled to death there in the sky, he implored Lightning, saying: "E! My friend Lightning, bring me help and counsel." The scepter that was on his back turned itself toward the face of Mwindo; it removed his mouth from the trunk of the tree. While Mwindo was now dropping excrement because of the fear of being bent against the tree, where Mwindo had sent his call for help, he had called for Lightning. Lightning came down; he cleaved the *mpaki* tree twice; the honey fell to the ground. Mwindo made a call, saying: "You, my billhook knife, may you also smash Nyamurairi." Where Nyamurairi dwelt in his village, the billhook knife of Mwindo smashed him and

planted him with his mouth on the ground: excrement and urine, coming from where Nyamurairi was, dispersed everywhere. After Mwindo
had climbed down, he reached the ground; he collected the honey; he
arrived with it in the village. As he saw Nyamurairi (with) the mouth
planted on the ground, Mwindo snatched his scepter from the back; he
beat Nyamurairi with it on top of the head, saying: "E! Nyamurairi,
everyone who went to sleep wakes up again. Why have you imperiled
Mwindo? Why?" When he had finished beating Nyamurairi on the
head with his scepter, Nyamurairi came to life again; he recovered; he
stood up; he said: "Long life! Long life (to you), Mwindo!" All the
honey that Mwindo had brought went into the house of Nyamurairi;
and Mwindo on his side went into the house of Kahindo, daughter of
Nyamurairi, to sleep in it. When he arrived in the house of Kahindo,
Kahindo stirred banana paste for her lover. Mwindo ate it; he went to
sleep having placed it on his chest.

[This pattern of task and trap continues with two other attempts by Nyamurairi on Mwindo's life. Mwindo is sent to clear a banana grove and
again the belt crushes him against a tree; he is sent to a pond. In both
cases, he calls on Lightning and is released and then punishes Nyamurairi.]

   Nyamurairi said to Mwindo: "You here who have recovered
from this danger, tomorrow in the early morning you shall go to play
the dice with Sheburungu. When you have beaten Sheburungu in the
game of dice, then you may carry off your father." At night Kahindo
cooked five dishes of banana paste for Mwindo; she placed meat on
them; she said to Mwindo: "Go tomorrow with these banana pastes;
traveling on the road you will meet with newborn babies who are collecting the eleusine of Nyamurairi. You will give them these banana
pastes, together with the meat, and they will show you the way to go to
Sheburungu."
   When the sky had changed to dawn, Mwindo began the journey; he took the five banana pastes together with the meat. He first left
to Nyamurairi his billhook knife, and Nyamurairi gave Mwindo his
belt, saying to go with it. Where Mwindo went, as he arrived at the entrance to Sheburungu's village, he met two thousand children collecting
the eleusine of Nyamurairi. Nyamurairi had poured out that eleusine
there so that he (Mwindo) would not recognize the road leading to Sheburungu. When Mwindo met those children, he removed the banana
pastes from his shoulder bag; he distributed them together with the
meat to all the children. After the children had finished eating the banana pastes, they clapped their hands, saying: "May you be healed!
May you be healed, Mwindo!" Mwindo told the children to show him
the road to Sheburungu. They showed him the road, saying: "In that
cave dwells Sheburungu, but the men's house is located inside the
cave; that is the place where you will play dice." Mwindo Mboru went;

he arrived at the men's house of Sheburungu where his father Shemwindo was hidden. When Sheburungu saw Mwindo, he took a hide; he spread it on the ground; he poured the dice on it. When the dice were on top of the hide, Sheburungu said to Mwindo: "Take up the dice now." Mwindo took up the dice. In the place where Nymurairi remained in his village, he said: "You, my belt, see to it; bend him." Where Mwindo had gone, the belt of Nyamurairi bent Mwindo; all the dice threw themselves into his mouth; they made his cheeks swell. It (the belt) planted him with the mouth on the ground on the hide; excrement and urine could not find the one who could clean them; the breath failed to find a way to come out. As the belt was bending Mwindo in this way, his scepter turned around; it came before his eyes; it removed Mwindo's mouth from the ground: the breath was released. Mwindo shouted loudly to Lightning: "My friend, I am dying." Mwindo stood up; he removed the dice and the hide; he went to place them into the mouth of Sheburungu: excrement dropped down. His people said that Sheburungu was dead. Mwindo stood up; seeing Sheburungu, he said: "Now why does Sheburungu imperil Mwindo?" He (Mwindo) said to his (Sheburungu's) people: "Give Sheburungu water to drink." They answered him: "How shall it pass through? Look how the dice are stuck in his mouth; he does not know what to do, and excrement are stuck to his buttocks; they fail to find the one that can remove them!" Sky became dark without Sheburungu having sneezed. His people said: "Bring Shemwindo out from the place where you have hidden him in the cave, because this Sheburungu has no life left; he is close to expiring." Where Shemwindo remained they went to take him out; they arrived with him. They gave him to Mwindo, saying: "Your father here." Mwindo got hold of his father; he took his scepter; he beat it on top of the head of Sheburungu, saying: "Now, Sheburungu, everyone who went to sleep wakes up again. Wake up now. Now you have stuck Mwindo onto you; you have carried him on the back." As Sheburungu was being beaten by Mwindo with his scepter, Mwindo said: "Sparrow is Shebireo, and Katee is crackling of dried leaves."

After he had been beaten by Mwindo's scepter, Sheburungu recovered completely; he stood up. When Sheburungu had recovered, Mwindo returned with his father; he returned with the wives of Sheburungu and the goats of Sheburungu because he had beaten Sheburungu and taken all his goods from him. Returning with his father, he went to arrive at Nyamurairi's. Nyamurairi gave Mwindo his billhook knife, and Mwindo gave Nyamurairi his belt. Mwindo slept in the house of Kahindo. Among the spoils that had come from Sheburungu were two maidens. Mwindo took one maiden; he gave her to Kahindo, his lover, because she performed very many nice things for him.

[The story continues with a number of seemingly disconnected incidents involving a dragon-ogre and hunting adventures in the forest, and at the end Mwindo is made a chief.]

25. The Epic of Kahindo
Narrated by Muteresi Shempunge

Recorded in January 1952 in Mutakato, Zaïre, by Daniel Biebuyck. Transcribed and translated into French by Daniel Biebuyck and Kahombo C. Mateene. Edited by Daniel Biebuyck and Kahombo Mateene and published as "Anthologie de la littérature orale Nyanga," in Mémoires de l'Académie Royale des Sciences d'Outre-Mer *(1970). This excerpt edited and translated into English by Stephen Belcher.*

THIS TEXT WAS THE SHORTEST OF THE EPICS BIEBUYCK RECORDED among the baNyanga; it is also unusual in that the protagonist is female. Women are a constant presence in the epic traditions of central Africa but rarely move into center stage; more often they are content to guide, to motivate, and to assist the hero. Here, Kahindo and her supernatural namesake play a role in a mythical drama which reflects some notion of how the universe became organized and the human world defined. The name Kahindo occurs in the Mwindo texts; she is there the daughter of a supernatural being whom Mwindo must manage to defeat. (See the *Mwindo Epic* for an example.) It seems likely that despite the tale-like quality of the plot, we are here faced with deep cultural roots.

Because of its brevity, the text is presented in its entirety.

There was a chief named Muhuya. He lived well and quietly with his people in his village, and his subjects made him ecstatic, for his rulings improved their own lives. As he and his people did so well, he married many wives. One of the wives was the mother of a young girl. The girl's name was Kahindo, one who spreads joy, an only child. The other wives had no children; they were barren. The father made bells for his child, and a *sanza*;[1] he gathered bunches of hairs and tied them into an *ndorera* bracelet which he put on her. And that day, she was shut within a fence and she did not leave it.

When she grew up, her father named her Ngarya, and her mother called herself Nyangarya. Some days later, her father decreed that no one should ever take his daughter to the fields. Any one who did so would have to deal with him! And he told his daughter that she should never try to go into the fields; her only job was to stay within the fence.

When some seasons had passed, one day when her father and mother had gone off to the fields, some girls from her age group came by. They suggested she could come with them to bathe in the river. She agreed. They went off to bathe. When they came to the river, they all undressed. Ngarya piled up all her precious things apart from the others. They plunged into the river. When they finished bathing, they dressed again. Ngarya forgot her calabash and the *ndorera* bracelet. They went off; Ngarya had only her water jug and the *sanza*. And her age mates didn't remind her about the other things; they were running

---

1. A thumb piano.

to the village, afraid of being scolded for having taken someone else's child without permission.

Near the path to the river lived a little old woman, a *Mpaca* spirit who had killed off the men and who had a girl-child who was also named Ngarya. She wore large clothing, which dragged on the ground. As this little old woman of the forest was coming down the river looking, she came to the place where the girls had bathed and she saw the things that had been forgotten. She picked them up and wrapped them in her clothes that dragged on the ground, since she had just heard the noise of the young girls. So the little old woman waited for the owner of the objects.

On the way back, the girls had come half way. They had gone over two plateaus when the owner of the objects remembered them; she said to herself that she had left the things where they had bathed in the river. She asked her companions to go back with her to pick up the things; they refused to go with her and went back to the village. After they said no, Ngarya went back alone to pick up the things she had forgotten by the river.

When she reached the place where she had left the things, she found the little old woman sitting there. The old woman said to her, "What are you doing coming around here at this time? Always, when night falls, this place belongs to the others who live in the forest." The girl said to her, "It's you, old woman, who have taken my things." The little old woman said, "The things I have belong to my daughter." The girl came crying up to the old woman, and the old woman moved aside. She said, "Gently, gently! Is it my fault that at this time night is falling on you in the forest?" The little old woman slipped off, she ran away, and the girl followed her. They chased each other. The girl put sound in her voice and sang,

> The little old woman went off with Ngarya.
> I am pursuing them, ooo!

When they came to the halfway point (where are you coming from? where are you going?), still pursuing each other, they rested. They abused each other; the one said the other had stolen her things, the other answered that the things belonged to her daughter. After they had rested, the old woman took flight again, putting her legs 'around her shoulders,' and the girl raced after her, following. They chased each other. Chasing each other, they came to the village of the little old woman, where her daughter was.

They saw each other: one was named Ngarya, the other was named Ngarya. When the old woman's daughter saw that her counterpart's body was suffering, covered with scratches, and that her clothes had become rags because of the thorns, she made a gift of what she was wearing. She warned her friend, saying, "My friend, the mistress of this place is hard; she wants to eat you. Each time she calls us, we shall

have to answer together, and if she sends us on a task, we shall have to go together. Neither of us can be alone, or we will be eaten." This was their trick to escape death.

When the old woman saw her two children, she said to herself there must be a way to eat the girl who had just come. One day she sent the two to pick bananas. When together they came to the place, they cut down the bunch of bananas together, and together they peeled them, and they brought the bananas back to the village together. When they came to the village, together they cut the bananas lengthwise. So that was a trial they passed.

When the old woman saw them get through that trial, she made another trap with some roast boar; they got through that test also. She tested them with another trap: grilling the bananas. Again they escaped. When she saw that they had passed these tests, she asked them to sing for her. Just as they were about to sing, the daughter of the ogre told her companion, "While we are singing, if you complain that the old woman ran away with you, Ngarya, you will give yourself away." So that evening, the old woman danced while they sang for her. They sang:

> Something escapes me, eh, ree-ree.
> I don't recognize my Ngarya,
> I don't recognize the child, eh, ree-ree,
> I don't recognize my Ngarya.
> You have made me happy, oh, my mothers,
> I don't recognize my Ngarya.
> My mothers, think of me with nostalgia, eh, ree-ree,
> I don't recognize my Ngarya.
> Little old woman, close to God, eh, ree-ree,
> It's tight among children.
> Someone who has gone to God will never return, eh, ree-
>   ree,
> It's tight among children.
> Oh, my mothers, what shall I do? eh, ree-ree.
> It's tight among children.
> So there you are, small bladder,
> It's tight among children.
> Saliva falls out of the mouth, eh, ree-ree,
> I don't recognize the child.
> Nostalgia says, "I am surpassed," eh, ree-ree,
> I don't recognize the child.

Hearing how the voices sounded, the voices of the children singing, the old woman hopped here and there, saying, "My mothers, sing on, I am pleased with you." When she was tired of dancing, she sent them to the river to catch her a crab. They went together. When they went there, together they turned over the stone, together they put their hands under-

neath; they drew out a *mungai* crab; they brought it to her. She was pleased when she saw them and said, "Thank you, mothers who feed me, thank you. Thanks to you I shall bite on crabs' legs." So once again the children had succeeded in passing the trial.

During the night, she got her knife and sharpened it, saying, "The day that dawns shall not be one of defeat. And so today my little pot will shine." Her knife was as sharp as a razor. When they went to bed, the ogre's daughter said to her friend, "If you mention the sparks, you shall die."

They got their things and put them together; they exchanged things as they dressed. Each wore the clothes of her friend. Once again, the daughter said, "When we go to sleep, you sleep on the far side and I'll sleep near the hearth; also we'll have to twine our legs together. Even if she turns us over and over during the night, if we don't let go of each other so there is a space between us, she won't be able to kill either of us. And so you mustn't let yourself be startled during the night, or she will cut your throat."

In the middle of the night, when they were asleep, the little old woman lit the resin torch at the hearth; sparks and more sparks leaped out. The one warned the other in the night and said, "She is coming."

Then the little old woman burst into the house where they were; their spirits fled! They were really going to die! She turned them over and over. She wore herself out working like a chicken, turning them and turning them, thinking that one would let go of the other so that she could kill one of them.

When she was worn out, she left them there. They went back to sleep, their hearts calmed. They said, "Once again, we're safe for the moment."

When day came, she left them the task of pounding and grinding the bananas and went into the forest. When she was in the forest and they were in the village, the children said to each other, "When the wind rises it will be her about to come, and if we are talking we shall have to be quiet." All at once, there she came with lots and lots of meat. When she came, she asked the children who had stayed in the village for her pipe and some tobacco, 'to hold her breath.' They gave it to her. She told them to go butcher the animals. They went there. When they came to the butchering place, they cut up some and they left others as they were—those were the ones where she had put traps. When they finished the butchery, they went back to the village; they smoked the meat and cured it.

When night came and they were asleep again, she came once more. She touched them and touched them and said, "I am surprised! This is very hard! Which one is mine? Which one shall I slaughter?" The little old woman didn't know what to try, she didn't know which of the two she should slaughter.

The next morning, they beat the drum and sang for her while she danced up a storm. The night after that, she told the girls to put the

drum in her courtyard so she might bid them goodbye; she was off to find riches for them. When they heard that, the girls went all out on the drums and beat them hard. They sang,

> Oh, you children!
> Greetings, greetings,
> I'm going off today.
> Greetings, greetings.
> You stay here,
> Greetings, greetings.
> Keep this place,
> Greetings, greetings.
> Keep your hearts low,
> Greetings, greetings.
> Preserve this place,
> Greetings, greetings.
> Joyful one (whose joy) makes you grow,
> Greetings, greetings.
> Joyful one (whose joy) makes you grow,
> Greetings, greetings.

When she finished dancing, she headed out of the village after she had said goodbye to her children. Two days after her departure, as the daughters had heard nothing from the direction in which she went, the girls thought up a trick of their own. They brought red powder and an *nkuki* brush and they spread the powder all over the way she had gone, so that when she came back she wouldn't know which way they had gone. The third day they went to the whetting block and slipped in under it—those two girls! They came out at the place where Kahindo had left her clothes.

They went off and climbed up to the village, they reached it. The chief, at first, did not recognize his daughter. No one in the village went to work in the fields, and the whole village had become very quiet, thinking the chief's daughter was really dead. The father and mother had let their hair grow out unkempt, 'like this!' and they didn't eat anything anymore—they had become like the *kangerangera* bird because of their anguish. When the children came, the chief and everyone in the village were very happy. They put the two girls in a guest house.

Once she had rested, Kahindo told her daughter how she and her friends had gone to bathe and how she got lost and how she was saved by the young girl, Ngarya. When her father heard the story, tears ran down his face. He said his child had really been lost! He summoned the young girl who had saved his daughter and assigned her a number of servants and a strip of land. He told her, "We shall name you Nyamumbo, and you shall give birth to a chief who shall inherit my power."

298

After that, they told him the news, saying, "Chief, you must listen. When the little old woman comes back from wherever she went to find riches, if she comes to this village and you tell her we are here, we shall be slaughtered along with everything else." When the chief heard this he sent three young men off to spread the red powder with the *nkuki* brush in the direction the old woman had taken, so she wouldn't find out which way the children had gone. After they had done that, the young men went home.

A few days later, on her part, the old woman began to feel a longing and concern for her children, because they had stayed all alone in the village without anyone to watch them. She went home. When she came to the village where she had left the children and put down her loads (what a joke!), the bags of salt went one way and she another. Looking at the ground—what sadness, what pain in her eyes! The tears she shed right then gave birth to a small stream. She said, "The ones who gave me warmth have left, but whether they were taken by some eater- of-food or some other member of the clan of God, whoever it may be, I will make myself known to them." She threw herself on the ground, seven times and seven times more. Sky and earth met; rain and lightning and the hurricane came forth; trees fell; rivers everywhere filled up; in the forest the animals did not know where to go, they were caught by the night. Having accomplished this deed, she boasted and said, "The one who will knock me to the ground is not known."

In this state of worry, she feverishly sought her children here and there, at the river and among her traps, in her banana plantation—everywhere she had used to send them. She found not a trace of their passage. She said, "Did they go through heaven or by the earth?" While looking, she came to the whetting block, and she smelled something where they had gone. She threw herself on their trail.

And in the village where the girls were, they worried. They told the chief and his people, "She is coming! She has returned from her expedition. If she comes here, you will have to strengthen your hearts; tell her what we have told you. Even if she brings amazing things, refuse them. Eventually she will pass us by."

Following the track of the children, she appeared in the chief's village; she threw herself to the ground in the middle of the village so that houses almost fell over. She said,

> I return from my trip.
> I go in pursuit
> Of Sereka and Ngarya,
> I go in pursuit.

She came to the chief of the place, and she asked him to give her news about the passage of her children. The chief told her, "One day, when the sun was at its brightest, after all the men had gone into

the forest, I saw your children. They passed us by; one of them was carrying a *sanza* and the other had a strap over her shoulder with a calabash holding little bells and woven bracelets."

When she heard that, she did not delay; she headed out of the village and continued her hunt. She went to Lightning. When she tried to ask Lightning where her children had gone, Lightning, as though he had not heard, fell on her seven times. She fell on the ground, belly up. She got up. When she tried to sniff Lightning with her muzzle, once again, Lightning fell upon her once more. He raised her and threw her here and there. She said, "This time it's not him. He leaves nothing on me! Are we equals? Could we be servants of the same court? He has strength and he is tough."

She went back to Lightning, she boasted. "Here I am, and by your mother, Lightning, I shall not die on earth." She seized all Lightning's servants and killed them. They stopped marching by; they died. When Lightning looked backwards, there was no buzzing behind him. At the second blink of his eyes, his partner appeared in front of him and said, "Let's throw dice."

They threw them in the air. The dice of Lightning were of copper; the old woman's dice were shaped like knives. The *kangancu* bird caught Lightning's dice in the air; the old woman's dice fell loudly on Lightning's head. So Lightning became her servant. His partner picked him up and put him into her large game bag. She picked up her dice and went on.

Continuing her chase, she came to Murimba the Roc. When she and Murimba met, each threatened the other. Murimba got angry and dropped two huge white stones on her; the old woman stepped aside and they missed. Escaping this first danger, she collected herself and then she appeared in the middle of Murimba's village.

When they met, they threw their dice. Both sets, hers and Murimba's, stayed aloft for seven suns, twined together, and neither set could make the other come down. On the seventh day, the old woman's dice fell, while those of Murimba were held above and could not descend. Coming down, the old woman's dice fell on Murimba's head; Murimba's brain ran out and spread in all directions. She boasted, "Today, their challenges are turned back upon them, they are climbing a hard mountain." She grabbed and took away as booty all the possessions of Murimba. She went off with all his men.

Continuing her pursuit, she appeared at the home of Rundurundu (Fog). As she went up, the cloud ceiling was above and below. When they met, they challenged each other, and they threw their dice. Rundurundu's dice were held in the air, they disappeared; the old woman's dice fell back down and killed Rundurundu. She took Rundurundu's skull and set it 'just so.' She went off.

Continuing her pursuit, she came to Mutero (Hail). When they met, they insulted each other, and they threw up their dice. Mutero's dice were held above, the old woman's dice came back. And so he also

became her servant. As she was leaving Mutero's home, resuming her path, she heard the music of *sanzas* and the sound of singing voices. She was pleased, saying this must be her children. But when she came and saw, it was the clan of toads singing and the clan of bats beating the drums and the clan of the stars (fireflies) lighting the fire. When she came to the stars, she perished.

After the old woman died, back where the two girls had stayed, the chief sent out Pygmies as scouts. They came and found that the old woman was really dead. They came back. That is when men's hearts came down. And so the men and the chief and the two girls lived in prosperity.

> That is why:
> Spoiling a child is idiotic; you should not prevent a child
>   from playing, because this is how the child gains
>   knowledge;
> The world requires helping others; the person who helps
>   another will be helped in turn one day;
> The rashness of a single man will not fail to leave a mark; it
>   brings disaster.
> A brave being surpasses us: the all powerful.
> You have good fortune only if it is your fate.

Bibliography

I. General Works

Belcher, Stephen. *An Introduction to West African Epic*. Forthcoming, Indiana University Press.

Biebuyck, Daniel. "The African Heroic Epic." In Felix Oinas, ed., *Heroic Epic and Saga*, pp. 336-67. Bloomington: Indiana University Press, 1978.

Finnegan, Ruth. *Oral Literature in Africa*. London: Oxford at the Clarendon Press, 1970.

————. *Oral Poetry*. Cambridge: Cambridge University Press, 1977; 2nd ed. Bloomington: Indiana University Press, 1992.

Hale, Thomas A. "Griottes: Female Voices from West Africa." *Research in African Literatures* 25:3 (1994): 72-91.

————. *Griots and Griottes of West Africa*. Bloomington: Indiana University Press. [forthcoming].

Johnson, John Wm. "Historicity and the Oral Epic: The Case of Sun-Jata Keita." In Robert E. Walls and George H. Schoemaker, eds., *The Old Traditional Way of Life: Essays in Honor of Warren E. Roberts*, pp. 351-61. Bloomington: Trickster Press, Indiana University Folklore Institute, 1989.

————. "On the Heroic Age and Other Primitive Theses." In E. V. Zygas and Peter Voorheis, eds., *Folklorica: Festschrit for Felix J. Oinas*, pp. 121-38. Bloomington: Research Institute for Inner Asian Studies, 1982.

————. "Yes, Virginia, There Is an Epic in Africa." *Research in African Literatures* 11:3 (1980): 308-26.

Kesteloot, Lilyan. *L'épopée traditionelle*. Paris: Fernand Nathan, 1971.

————. "Myth, Epic, and African History." In V. Mudimbe, ed., *The Surreptitious Speech*, pp. 136-43. Chicago: University of Chicago Press, 1992.

————. "La problematique des épopées africaines." Université de Dakar: *Annales de la faculté des lettres et sciences humaines* 17 (1987): 43-53. [Reprinted in *Neohelikon* 16:2 (1989): 247-64; English translation in *African Languages and Cultures* 22 (1989): 203-14.]

Kesteloot, Lilyan and Bassirou Dieng, eds. *Épopées d'Afrique Noire*. Paris: Karthala [forthcoming].

Okpewho, Isidore. *African Oral Literature: Background, Character, and Continuity*. Bloomington: Indiana University Press, 1992.

Okpewho, Isidore. *The Epic in Africa: Toward a Poetics of the Oral Performance.* New York: Columbia University Press, 1979.

———, ed. *The Oral Performance in Africa.* Ibadan, Nigeria: Spectrum Books, 1990.

Panzacchi, Cornelia. "The Livelihood of Traditional Griots in Modern Senegal." *Africa* 64:2 (1994): 190-209.

Seydou, Christiane. "Comment définir le genre épique? Un exemple: L'épopée africaine." *Journal of the Anthropological Society of Oxford* 13:1 (1982): 84-98. [Reprinted as Veronika Görög-Karady, ed., *Genres, Forms, Meanings: Essays in African Oral Literature/Genres, formes, significations: essais sur la littérature orale africaine.* JASO Occasional Paper, 1982.]

Westley, David. "A Bibliography of African Epic." *Research in African Literatures* 22:4 (1991): 99-115.

II. SPECIFIC TRADITIONS

A. Soninké

Bathily, Abdoulaye. "A Discussion of the Traditions of Wagadu with Some Reference to Ancient Ghana." *Bulletin de l'Institut Fondamental d'Afrique Noire* 37:1 ser. B (1975): 1-94.

Dantioko, Oudiary Makan. *Soninkara Taarixinu: Récits historiques du pays Soninké.* Niamey: Centre d'Études Linguistiques et Historiques par Tradition Orale, 1985.

Delafosse, Maurice. *Traditions historiques et légendaires du Soudan Occidental. Publication du Comité de l'Afrique Française.* Paris, Comité de l'Afrique Française, 1913.

Diawara, Mamadou. *La graine de la parole.* Stuttgart: Franz Steiner Verlag, 1990.

Dieterlen, Germaine. *L'empire de Ghana.* Paris: Karthala, 1992.

Jablow, Alta. "Gassire's Lute: A Reconstruction of Soninké Bardic Art." *Research in African Literatures* 15 (1984): 519-29.

———. *Gassire's Lute.* New York: E. P. Dutton, 1971. [Republished in 1991 in Prospect Heights, Ill. by Waveland Press.]

Meillassoux, Claude, Lassana Doucouré, and Diaowa Simagha. *Légende de la dispersion des Kusa.* Dakar: Institut Fondamental d'Afrique Noire, 1967.

Monteil, Charles. "La légende de Ouagadou et l'origine des Soninké." *Mémoires de l'Institut Français d'Afrique Noire* 23 (1953): 358-409.

B. MANDE

i. The Sunjata Tradition

Cisse, Youssouf Tata, and Wa Kamissoko. *La grande geste du Mali: Des origines à la fondation de l'empire.* Paris: Karthala/Association pour la Recherche Scientifique d'Afrique Noire, 1988.

———. *Soundjata, la gloire du Mali: La grande geste du Mali, Tome 2.* Paris: Karthala/Association pour la Recherche Scientifique d'Afrique Noire, 1991.

Diabaté, Massa Makan. *L'aigle et l'épervier ou La geste de Sunjata.* Paris: Pierre Jean Oswald, 1975.

———. *Kala Jata.* Bamako: Éditions populaires, 1970.

———. *Le lion à l'arc.* Paris: Hatier, 1986.

Innes, Gordon, ed. and trans. *Sunjata: Three Mandinka Versions.* London: School of Oriental and African Studies, University of London, 1974.

Jabaté, Kanku Madi. [Collected, translated, and annotated by Madina Ly-Tall, Seydou Camara, and Bouna Diouara.] *L'histoire du Mandé.* Paris: Association Société Commerciale de l'Ouest Africaine, 1987.

Jansen, Jan, Esger Duintjer, and Boubacar Tamboura. *Het Sunjata-epos verteld door Lansine Diabate uit Kela.* Utrecht: Published by the authors; distributed by Drukkerij Organisatie Oude Muziek in Leiden, 1994. [Translated by the authors as *L'épopée de Sunjata, d'après Lansine Diabate de Kela.* Leiden: Center of Non-Western Studies, 1995.]

Johnson, John William, and Fa-Digi Sisòkò. *The Epic of Son-Jara: A West African Tradition.* Bloomington: Indiana University Press, 1986 [2nd ed. (text only), 1992].

Johnson, John William, and Magan Sisòkò. *The Epic of Sun-Jata According to Magan Sisòkò* (FPG Monograph Series, no. 5). Bloomington: Folklore Publications Group, 1979.

Koné, Tiémoko. [Ed. Lassana Doucouré and Mme. Martal.] *Soundiata.* Bamako: Institut des Sciences Humaines du Mali; Niamey: Centre Régional de Documentation pour la Tradition Orale, 1970.

Laye, Camara. *Le maître de la parole: kouma lafôlô kouma.* Paris: Plon, 1978. [Trans. by James Kirkup as *The Guardian of the Word.* London: William Collins Sons, 1980; New York: Fontana Books, 1980.]

Niane, Djbril Tamsir. *Soundiata, ou L'épopée mandingue*. Paris: Présence Africaine, 1960. [Translated by G. D. Pickett as *Sunjata: An Epic of Old Mali*. London: Longman, 1965.]

ii. *Other Mande Traditions*

Bird, Charles S. "Heroic Songs of the Mande Hunters." In *African Folklore*, ed. Richard Dorson, pp. 275-93. New York: Anchor Books, 1972. [Reprinted by Indiana University Press in 1979.]

———, ed. and trans. "Bambara Oral Prose and Verse Narratives." In *African Folklore*, op. cit., pp. 441-77.

Camara, Seydou. [Ed. and trans. Charles Bird with Mamadou Koita and Bourama Soumaoro.] *The Songs of Seydou Camara: Vol. I: Kambili*. Bloomington: Indiana University African Studies Program, 1974. [Original text published as *Seyidu Kamara ka Donkiliw: Kambili*. Ed. Bourama Soumaoro, Charles S. Bird, Gerald Cashion, and Mamadou Kanté. Bloomington: Indiana University African Studies Program, 1976.]

Conrad, David. *A State of Intrigue: The Epic of Bamana Segu According to Tayiru Banbera*. Oxford: Oxford University Press for the British Academy, 1990. [Union Académique Internationale: Fontes Historiae Africanae, Series Varia 6.]

Coulibaly, Dosseh Joseph, ed. and trans. *Récits des chasseurs du Mali: Dingo Kanbili de Bala Jinba Jakité*. Paris: Conseil International de la Langue Française/Edicef, n.d.

Dumestre, Gerard, ed. and trans. *La geste de Ségou*. Paris: Armand Colin, 1979. [Classiques Africains.] [Previously published at the University of Abidjan, Institut de Linguistique Appliquée, no. 48, 1974.]

Dumestre, Gerard, and Lilyan Kesteloot, eds. and trans. *La prise de Dionkoloni*. Paris: Armand Colin, 1975. [Classiques Africains.]

Frobenius, Leo. *Dichten und Denken im Sudan*. Atlantis V. Jena: Eugen Diederichs, 1925.

———. *Spielmannsgeschichten der Sahel*. Atlantis VI. Jena: Eugen Diederichs, 1921.

Geysbeek, Timothy, and Jobba Kamara. "'Two Hippos Cannot Live in One River.' Zo Musa, Foningama, and the Founding of Musadu." *Liberian Studies Journal* 16 (1991): 27-78.

Hayidara, Shekh Tijaan, ed. and trans. *La geste de Fanta Maa*. Niamey: Centre d'Études Linguistiques et Historiques par Tradition Orale, 1987.

Innes, Gordon. *Kaabu and Fuladu: Historical Narratives of the Gambian Mandinka*. London: School of Oriental and African Studies, University of London, 1976

———. *Kelefa Saane: His Career Recounted by Two Mandinka Bards*. London: School of Oriental and African Studies, University of London, 1978.

Innes, Gordon, and Bakari Sidibe. *Hunters and Crocodiles*. Sandgate: Paul Norbury/ U.N.E.S.C.O., 1990.

Kamissoko, Wâ. [Ed. Youssouf Tata Cissé (?).] *Les Peuls du Manding*. Niamey: Centre d'Études Linguistiques et Historiques par Tradition Orale, [1974].

Kesteloot, Lilyan. "Le mythe et l'histoire dans la formation de l'empire de Ségou." *Bulletin de l'Institut Fondamental d'Afrique Noire*, ser. B 40:3 (1978): 578-681.

Kesteloot, Lilyan, ed. and trans, with Amadou Traoré, Jean-Baptiste Traoré and Amadou Hampaté Bâ. *Da Monzon de Ségou: Épopée bambara*. 2 vols. Paris: L'Harmattan, 1993. [First published in 1974 in Paris by Fernand Nathan, 4 vols.]

Thoyer, Annik, ed. and trans. *Nyakhalen la forgeronne, par Seyidou Kamara*. N.p., 1986.

Thoyer-Rozat, Annik, ed. and trans. *Chants de chasseurs du Mali*. 3 vols. Vols. 1 and 2 by Mamadu Jara; vol. 3 by Ndugace Samake. Paris: n.p., 1978. [Reprinted in Paris by L'Harmattan, 1995.]

Wright, Donald. *Oral Traditions from The Gambia: Volume 1. Mandinka Griots*. Athens: Ohio University Center for International Studies, 1979.

———. *Oral Traditions from The Gambia: Volume 2. Family Elders*. Athens: Ohio University Center for International Studies, 1980.

iii. Background Materials

Ba, Adam Konaré. *L'épopée de Segu*. Paris: Pierre-Marcel Favre/Agence de Coopération Culturelle et Technique, 1987.

———. *Sunjata: le fondateur de l'empire du Mali*. Libreville: Lion, 1983.

Bird, Charles, and Martha B. Kendall. "The Mande Hero: Text and Context." In Ivan Karp and Charles S. Bird, eds., *Explorations in African Systems of Thought*, pp. 13-26. Bloomington: Indiana University Press, 1980.

Brett-Smith, Sarah. *The Making of Bamana Sculpture*. Cambridge: Cambridge University Press, 1994.

Camara, Sory. *Gens de la parole: Essai sur la condition et le rôle des griots dans la société Malinké*. Paris: Karthala, 1992. [First published in Paris by Mouton in 1976.]

Conrad, David, and Barbara Frank, eds. *Status and Identity in West Africa: Nyamakalaw of Mande*. Bloomington: Indiana University Press, 1995.

Cissé, Youssouf. "Notes sur les sociétés de chasseurs Malinké." *Journal de la Société des Africanistes* 34:1 (1964): 175-226.

Diabaté, Massa Makan. *Janjon et autres chants populaires du Mali*. Paris: Présence Africaine, 1970.

Durán, Lucy. "Jelimusow: The Superwomen of Malian Music." In Graham Furniss and Elizabeth Gunner, eds., *Power, Marginality, and African Oral Tradition*, pp. 197-207. Cambridge: Cambridge University Press, 1995.

Hodges, Carlton, ed. *Papers on the Manding*. Bloomington: Indiana University for the Research Center for the Language Sciences, 1971. [African Series 3.]

Levtzion, Nehemia. *Ancient Ghana and Mali*. London: Methuen, 1973. [Studies in African History, vol. 7.]

McNaughton, Patrick. *The Mande Blacksmiths: Knowledge, Power, and Art in West Africa*. Bloomington: Indiana University Press, 1988.

Monteil, Charles. [Notes by Jean Bazin.] *Les Bambara du Ségou et du Kaarta*. Paris: Maisonneuve et Larose, 1977. [First printed 1924.]

———. *Les empires du Mali: Étude d'histoire et de sociologie Soudanaises*. Paris: G.-P. Maisonneuve et Larose, 1968. [First published in *Bulletin du Comité d'Études historiques et scientifiques de l'Afrique Occidentale Française* 12:3/4 (1929).]

Niane, Djibril Tamsir. *Histoire des mandingues de l'ouest*. Paris: Karthala, n.d.

———. *Le Soudan occidental au temps des grands empires xie-xvie siècle*. Paris: Présence Africaine, 1975.

Person, Yves. *Samori, une révolution dyula*. 3 vols. Dakar: Institut Fondamental d'Afrique Noire, 1968.

Wright, Donald. "The Epic of Kelefa Sane as a Guide to the Nature of Precolonial Senegambian Society—and Vice Versa." *History in Africa* 14 (1987): 287-309.

C. SONGHAY

i. Primary Sources

Dupuis-Yakouba, A. *Les Gow, ou chasseurs du Niger*. Paris: Ernest Leroux, 1911. [Reprinted in 1974 by Kraus.]

Hale, Thomas A. *Scribe, Griot, and Novelist: Narrative Interpreters of the Songhay Empire*. Gainesville: University of Florida Press, 1990. [2nd ed. (text only) reprinted as *The Epic of Askia Mohammed*. Bloomington: Indiana University Press, 1996.]

Laya, Diouldé. *Texts Songhay-Zarma*. Niamey: Centre d'Études Linguistiques et Historiques par Tradition Orale, 1978.

Mounkaila, Fatimata. *Le mythe et l'histoire dans la Geste de Zabarkane*. Niamey: Centre d'Études Linguistiques et Historiques par Tradition Orale, 1989.

Tandina, Ousmane Maliamane. "Une épopée Zarma: Wangougna Issa Korombeïzé Modi ou Issa Koygolo, mère de la science de la guerre." Ph.D. diss., University of Dakar, 1984.

Watta, Oumarou. "The Human Thesis: A Quest for Meaning in African Epic." Ph.D. diss., State University of New York, Buffalo, 1985. [Ann Arbor, UMI 8528296.]

―――. *Rosary, Mat and Molo: A Study in the Spiritual Epic of Omar Seku Tal*. New York: Peter Lang, 1993. [American University Studies in Theology and Religion 135.]

Zouber, Mahmoud Abdou, ed. and trans. *Traditions historiques Songhoy*. Niamey: Centre d'Études Linguistiques et Historiques par Tradition Orale, 1983.

ii. Secondary Materials

Hama, Boubou. *Histoire traditionelle d'un peuple: Les Zarma-Songhay*. Paris: Présence Africaine, 1967.

Olivier de Sardan, Jean-Pierre. *Les sociétés Songhay-Zarma*. Paris: Karthala, 1984.

Rouch, Jean. "Contribution à l'histoire des Songhay." *Mémoires de L'Institut Français d'Afrique Noire* 29 (1953): 137-269.

————. *La religion et magie Songhay.* Paris: Presses Universitaires de France, 1950. [2nd ed., Éditions de l'Université de Bruxelles.]

Stoller, Paul. *Fusion of the Worlds: An Ethnography of Possession among the Songhay of Niger.* Chicago: University of Chicago Press, 1989.

Stoller, Paul, and Cheryl Olkes. *In Sorcery's Shadow.* Chicago: University of Chicago Press, 1987.

D. FULBE

i. Primary Materials

Allaye, Beidari. [Ed. and trans. by Bocar Cisse and Almamy Maliki Yattara.] *Poullo Djom Ere et le Touareg.* Niamey: Centre d'Études Linguistiques et Historiques par Tradition Orale, 1984.

Bâ, Amadou Hampaté , and Lilyan Kesteloot. "Une épopée peule—Silamaka." *L'Homme* 8 (1969): 1-36. [Reprinted in Lilyan Kesteloot. *L'épopée bambara de Ségou.* 2 vols. Paris: L'Harmattan, 1993. First published as *Da Monzon de Ségou: Épopée bambara.* Paris: Fernand Nathan, 1972.]

Equilbecq, François-Victor. *Essai sur la littérature merveilleuse des noirs, suivi de contes indigènes de l'ouest africain.* 3 vols. Paris: Maisonneuve et Larose, 1913-16.

————. *La légende de Samba Guéladio Diégui, Prince Fouta.* Dakar: Nouvelles Éditions Africaines, 1974.

Corera, Issagha. [Ed. Samba Guladio.] *L'épopée peule du Fuuta Tooro.* Dakar, Institut Fondamental d'Afrique Noire, 1992. [Initiations et Études Africaines 36.]

Ly, Amadou, trans. *L'épopée de Samba Gueladiegui.* Dakar: Institut Fondamental d'Afrique Noire/U.N.E.S.C.O., 1991. [Éditions Nouvelles du Sud.]

Meyer, Gerard, ed. and trans. *Récits épiques toucouleurs: la vache, le livre, la lance.* Paris: Karthala/Agence de Coopération Culturelle et Technique, 1991.

Ndongo, Sir Mamadou. *Le Fantang: Poèmes mythiques des bergers peuls.* Paris: Karthala; Dakar: Institut Fondamental d'Afrique Noire, 1986.

Ngaïde, Mamadou Lamine. *Le vent de la razzia.* Dakar: Institut Fondamental d'Afrique Noire, 1981.

Sare, Ougoumala. *La guerre entre Ndje Fara Ndje et Hambodedjo Hammadi.* Niamey: Centre d'Études Linguistiques et Historiques par Tradition Orale/Organisation de l'Unité Africaine, n.d. [1974?].

Seydou, Christiane, ed. and trans. *La geste de Hambodedio ou Hama le rouge.* Paris: Armand Colin, 1976. [Classiques Africains.]

———. *Silâmaka et Poullôri.* Paris: Armand Colin, 1972. [Classiques Africains.]

Sow, Alfa Ibrahim. *Chroniques et récits du Fouta Djallon.* Paris: Librairie Klincksieck, 1968.

Sy, Amadou Abel. *Seul contre tous.* Dakar: Nouvelles Éditions Africaines, 1978.

Vieillard, Gilbert. "Récits peuls du Macina et du Kounari." *Bulletin du Comité d'études historiques et scientifiques de l'Afrique occidentale française* 14:1 (1931): 137-56.

———. [Ed. Eldridge Mohammedou.] *Récits peuls du Macina, du Kounari, du Djilgodji.* Niamey: n.p., n.d.

ii. Secondary Materials

Robinson, David. *The Holy War of Umar Tal.* London: Oxford at the Clarendon Press, 1985.

Seydou, Christiane. *Bibliographie générale du monde peul.* Université de Niamey, Institut de Recherches en Sciences Humaines, 1977. Études Nigériennes No. 43.

———. *Contes et fables des veillées.* Paris: Nubia, 1976.

———. "La devise dans la culture peule: vocation et invocation de la personne." In Geneviève Calame-Griaule, ed., *Langage et cultures africaines,* pp. 187-264. Paris: Maspero, 1977.

———. "Panorama de la littérature peule." *Bulletin de l'Institut Fondamental d'Afrique Noire,* ser. B, 35:1 (1973): 176-218.

Sow, Abdoul Aziz. "Fulani Poetic Genres." *Research in African Litératures* 24:2 (1993): 61-77.

E. WOLOF

i. Primary Materials

Dieng, Bassirou. *L'épopée du Kajoor.* Dakar and Paris: Centre Africain d'Animation et d'Échanges Culturels/Khoudia, 1993.

Diop, Samba. "The Oral History and Literature of the Wolof People of Waalo." Ph.D. diss., University of California, Berkeley, 1993. [Ann Arbor, UMI 9407934.] [Republished under same title, Lewiston: Mellen Press, 1995.]

ii. Secondary Materials

Barry, Boubacar. *Le royaume du Waalo*. Paris: Karthala, 1985. [First printed in Paris by Maspero, 1972.]

————. *La Sénégambie du XVe au XIXe siècle*. Paris: L'Harmattan, 1988.

Boulègue, Jean. *Le grand Jolof*. Paris: Façades/Karthala, 1987.

Diop, Adboulaye-Bara. *La société Wolof*. Paris: Karthala, 1981.

Diouf, Mamadou. *Le Kajoor au XIXe siècle*. Paris: Karthala, 1990.

Kesteloot, Lilyan, and Bassirou Dieng. *Du tieddo au talibé: contes et mythes Wolof II*. Paris: Présence Africaine, 1989.

Makward, Edris. "Two Griots of Contemporary Senegambia." In Isidore Okpewho, ed. *The Oral Performance in Africa*, pp. 23-41. Ibadan: Spectrum Books, 1990.

F. ARABIC

Connelly, Bridget. *Arabic Folk Epic and Identity*. Berkeley: University of California Press, 1986.

Galley, Micheline, and Abderrahman Ayoub. *Histoire des Beni Hilal et de ce qui leur advint dans leur marche vers l'ouest*. Paris: Armand Colin, 1983. [Classiques Africains.]

Guignard, Michel. *Musique, honneur et plaisir au Sahara*. Paris: Geuthner, 1975.

Lyons, M. C. *The Arabian Epic*. 3 vols. Cambridge: Cambridge University Press, 1995. [University of Cambridge Oriental Publications no. 49.]

Norris, H. T. *Shinqiti Folk Literature and Song*. London: Oxford at the Clarendon Press, 1968.

Reynolds, Dwight Fletcher. *Heroic Poets, Poetic Heroes: The Ethnography of Performance in an Arabic Oral Epic Tradition*. Ithaca: Cornell University Press, 1995.

Slyomovics, Susan. "Arabic Folk Literature and Political Expression." *Arab Studies Quarterly* 8:2 (1986): 178-85.

Slyomovics, Susan. *The Merchant of Art: An Egyptian Hilali Oral Epic Poet in Performance*. Berkeley: University of California Press, 1988.

G. CENTRAL AFRICAN EPICS

Austen, Ralph. *The Elusive Epic: Performance, Text, and History in the Oral Narrative of Jeki la Njambè (Cameroon Coast)*. African Studies Association Press, 1995.

Awona, Stanislas. "La guerre de Akoma Mba contre Abo Mama (épopée du mvet)." *Abbia* 9/10 (1965): 180-213; 12/13 (1966): 109-209.

Biebuyck, Daniel. *Hero and Chief: Epic Literature from the Banyanga (Zaire Republic)*. Berkeley: University of California Press, 1978.

Biebuyck, Daniel, and Kahombo C. Mateene. "Anthologie de la littérature orale Nyanga." *Mémoires de l'Academie Royale des Sciences d'Outre-Mer* 36:1 (1970): 29-39.

Biebuyck, Daniel, and Kahombo C. Mateene, eds. and trans. *The Mwindo Epic from the baNyanga (Congo Republic)*. Berkeley: University of California Press, 1969.

Boelaert, E. *Nsong'a Lianja: L'épopée nationale des Nkundo*. De Sikkel: Anvers, 1949. [Reprinted by Kraus in Nendeln, Liechtenstein, in 1973.]

Boyer, Pascal. *Barricades mystérieuses et pièges à pensée*. Paris, Sociétés d'Ethnologie, 1988.

Clark , J. P. *The Ozidi Saga, Collected and Translated from the Ijọ of Ọkabou Ojobolo*. Ibadan: Ibadan University Press and Oxford University Press Nigeria, 1977. [Republished by J. P. Clark-Bekederemo, with a critical introduction by Isidore Okpewho, in 1991 by Howard University Press, Washington D.C.]

De Rop, A. "Lianja: L'épopée des Móngo." *Mémoires, Académie Royale des Sciences d'Outre-Mer. Classe des Sciences morales et politiques*, n.s. 30:1 (1964).

Eno-Belinga, Samuel Martin. *L'épopée camerounaise, mvet*. Yaoundé: n.p., 1978.

Pepper, Herbert. [Ed. P. and P. de Wolf.] *Un Mvet de Zwé Nguéma: Chant épique fang*. Paris: Armand Colin, 1972.

Priso, Manga Bekombo. *Défis et prodiges: la fantastique histoire de Djéki-la-Njambe*. Paris: Armand Colin for Classiques Africains, 1993.

Bibliography

Tiki a Koulle a Penda, Pierre Celestin. *Les merveilleux exploits de Djéki La Njambè*. 2 vols. Douala: Éditions Collège Libermann, 1987.

Towo-Atangana, Gaspard. "Le Mvet: Genre majeur de la littérature des populations Pahouines." *Abbia* 9/10 (1965): 163-79.

Index

Oral epics are catalogs of cultures because they contain such a variety of names, places, objects, plants, animals, customs, and references to events. Names are especially important because they reveal both the human panorama conveyed by the epic and the multiplicity of attributes for a particular hero. In the index below, the names of all the characters referred to in the epics are listed under the heading 'characters.' In some cases, different names for the same hero are grouped under a single heading, for example Askia Mohammed, Askia Mohammed Touré, and Mamar. But in other cases, the many different names for the same character have been listed separately. We have distinguished between names of characters, who are listed as they appear in the text, and names of narrators, accompanists, translators, researchers, and others, which, in most cases, appear last name first.

320

John William Johnson is Associate Professor of Folklore and African Studies at Indiana University. His numerous publications include an edited translation of *The Epic of Son-Jara*.

Thomas A. Hale is Professor of African, French, and Comparative Literature at The Pennsylvania State University. His publications include a translation of *The Epic of Askia Mohammed*.

Stephen Belcher is Assistant Professor of Comparative Literature at The Pennsylvania State University.

LaVergne, TN USA
23 August 2010
194281LV00001B/3/P